DI006439

THE
ONLY
THING
TO
FEAR

THE
ONLY
THING
TO
FEAR

A NOVEL BY

DAVID POYER

A Tom Doherty Associates Book

NEW YORK

This is a work of fiction. All characters and events portrayed
in this book are either fictitious or are used fictitiously.

THE ONLY THING TO FEAR

Copyright © 1995 by David Poyer

All rights reserved, including the right to reproduce this book,
or portions thereof, in any form.

This book is printed on acid-free paper.

"April Showers" by Buddy DeSylva and Louis Silvers. Copyright © 1921
by Warner Bros. Music, Inc. Copyright renewed; extended term of
copyright deriving from Louis Silvers assigned and effective
March 30, 1980 to Range Road Music, Inc. and Quartet Music, Inc.
Used by permission. All rights reserved.

A Forge Book
Published by Tom Doherty Associates, Inc.
175 Fifth Avenue
New York, N.Y. 10010

Forge® is a registered trademark of Tom Doherty Associates, Inc.

Design by Ann Gold

Library of Congress Cataloging-in-Publication Data

Poyer, David.

    The only thing to fear / David Poyer.
      p. cm.
    ISBN 0-312-85709-8 (hardcover)
    1. Kennedy, John F., (John Fitzgerald), —1917–1963—Fiction.
    2. Roosevelt, Franklin D., (Franklin Delano), —1882–1945—Fiction.
    I. Title.
    PS3566.0978055 1995
    813'.54—dc20

                      94-47226
                      CIP

First edition: April 1995

Printed in the United States of America

0 9 8 7 6 5 4 3 2 1

ACKNOWLEDGMENTS

Ex nihilo nihil fit. For this book I owe thanks to Peter Abresch, James Allen, Natalia Aponte, Charles Barnes, David Bell, Beverly Bullock, George Coleman, David D'Alessio, Nan Dennison, Tom Doherty, Gladys Dunlap, John Ferris, Roy Gainsburg, Noel and Doris Galen, Robert Gleason, Frank and Amy Green, Genie Gooch, John Hodges, Helen Johns, Milton Kellam, Elizabeth Knighton, Anna Magee, Mike McOwen, Alan Nicas, Creston Parker, Jo Black Pesaresi, Larry Pipes, Lenore Hart Poyer, Catherine and John Rice, Michael D. Shadix, Beth Storie, Kay Stough, George Tames, Ray Teichman, Lee and Gerrie Thompson, Mary Thrash, Don Toutant, Mary Hudson Veeder, Alycia J. Vivona, Giles Upshur, George Witte, and many others who gave generously of their time to contribute or criticize. Thanks for help, information, and use of their facilities to Pine Mountain Regional Library, the Roosevelt Warm Springs Institute for Rehabilitation, the Naval Historical Center, the Palm Beach Library, the Georgia Department of Natural Resources and the Little White House, the Franklin D. Roosevelt Library at Hyde Park, and the Virginia Beach and Eastern Shore Public Libraries. All errors and deficiencies are my own.

Nothing comes from nothing.
Imagine a screen. A blank, white, rectangular screen filled with light.
Then on it numbers, black and sere, dancing, grainy, but still clear, stabbing like cold.
1945.
On the screen now, faces. Like ours. Some are ours, but so young. So faithful, so fearless, so casual. Our parents, or our grandparents. They look like us. They were us.
A long time ago, yes. But today was there then, in embryo, in plan—or else causality means nothing.
1945.
The last year of the greatest war in history.
On the screen, flame and ruin, images those who see them will carry to their graves. Buildings fall in the slow silence of the past. The emaciated, tumbled bodies of Dachau. The shadows on the walls of Nagasaki. The beginning of a world won, or lost forever, depending on whose side you'd fought for.
1945.
Some of those we loved then went away.
Their decisions, courage, sacrifice, created the world we live in now. On the screen the soldiers trudge endlessly forward, forever liberating the world from darkness. The film will crackle, seared by the slow burning of time.
Gradually they will fade from sight, from memory.
This book is dedicated, not to those who died, for they are marked and remembered, but to those who returned, and were never the same again.
One was my father.
Never count the casualties on the day the war ends.
Nothing comes from nothing.
And nothing ever ends.

While much is too strange to be believed,
nothing is too strange to have happened.

—Thomas Hardy

THE
ONLY
THING
TO
FEAR

From the Diary of Dr. Joseph Goebbels, Berlin, Tuesday, 20 February 1945

Today our troops once again succeeded in halting the Anglo-Americans in an enormous defensive victory on the Rhine. In East Prussia the Soviets have also been unable to make progress. The general situation remains fluid. Our troops still believe in victory and in Hitler with mystical fanaticism. Yet war on two fronts is hammering us to pieces.

At midday a visit from General Vlasov, an extremely intelligent and energetic commander. It is fortunate that he renounced Bolshevik ideology for ours. A wide-ranging discussion of the situation.

This evening in the bunker I had a long conversation with the Führer. I am pleased to find him extraordinarily alert and resilient. Aside from the nervous spasm in the left hand, more noticeable since the July bomb incident. Accompanying us was the Japanese Ambassador, Baron Hiroshi Oshima.

The Führer takes a hopeful view of the political situation. England is war-weary and numerous strikes have broken out in the ports. The Americans are suffering mountains of dead in the West. In addition our Japanese allies have inflicted heavy casualties on the island of Iwo Jima. A serious quarrel between the Anglo-Americans and the Soviets is developing over Bolshevik atrocities in Poland. At the same time Stalin is suspicious of the other Allies over reported negotiations with us in Italy.

I mention my reading of Carlyle's *History of Frederick the Great*. There have been other periods in Prussian-German history when our fate has balanced on a knife-edge. Yet we were saved—in that instance by the death of the Czarina Elizabeth and the reversal of alliances when the enemy coalition was on the verge of victory. Why should we not hope for a similar turn of fortune!

The Führer agrees emphatically. The Anglo-Americans cannot accept the Bolshevik domination of Europe. Yet Washington's response is muted, since the Americans hope Stalin will enter the Pacific war. He must make his mind up by

13 April. That is the pivotal day. On April 13, the Soviet-Japanese nonagression pact either must be revoked or it will automatically be renewed for another five years.

I am struck by the coincidence of that date with the horoscopes cast for us in 1933. They clearly predict the turning point in the middle of April, 1945! We have used them as propaganda, but what if there should really be something to it?

The Führer is skeptical, but states that the enemy coalition will break up whatever happens; the only question is whether it will come in time to save us. If it does, National Socialism, reborn and purified, may still turn out to be the victorious ideology of our century.

And then it occurs to me. The most brilliant and ruthless idea of my career, perhaps.

I emphasize to him that there is no doubt in my mind regarding our victory. Nevertheless, we cannot wait passively for the verdict of history. Measures of a decisive nature must be taken. The moment has come to shake off the last bourgeois eggshells.

The Führer asks me what I have in mind. I explain the essence of the operation to him and Ambassador Oshima.

I have proposed to the Führer that we draw a bead on the crippled gentleman. Yet simple assassination is not the answer. We must strike in exactly the right way. Like a diamond, the enemy coalition will fracture along the seams that are more evident with each passing day.

The Führer was extraordinarily nice to me during this conversation. One can see he is pleased to talk to someone who does not give way at every crisis. He is Germany's bravest heart and our people's most glowing wish. And he agreed with me that although the hour was late, such a blow, if entrusted to the right people, might well result in success out of all proportion to the resources committed to it.

I take this as an order, although nothing exists in writing. Perhaps that is wiser, after all. Upon leaving the bunker, I call General Vlasov and Colonel Eichmann. We agree to meet tomorrow to prepare plans for the action.

At home Magda has one of her headaches. We discuss what will be our fate if Germany falls. If despite so many efforts, so many sacrifices, only the void remains . . . if the Reich crumbles, I tell her, then the whole nation will go under with us, so gloriously that even in a thousand years the heroic apocalypse of the Germans will have pride of place in the history of the world. Against such a backdrop, neither I, nor she, nor any of our children will survive the debacle.

I am tired as a dog but can manage only a few hours' sleep before the British night raid arrives. These raids are becoming heavier and more distressing day by day. . . .

PROLOGUE

Wednesday, March 21, 1945: Ten Miles off the Virginia Coast

When the one-armed man woke, a seaman in shorts was bending over him. In the dim blue light the youthful face looked frightened and skeletal. "We're here," the sailor murmured.

He swung his legs off the leather-covered bunk, wincing as his feet touched grit, shattered glass, and a stickiness he knew was blood. The close air smelled of diesel oil, rancid food, and crowded, frightened men. Moving gingerly, he knelt to unlash, then skid a bulky wooden crate out from its nesting place beneath the bunk.

Burned into the box were two thunderbolts below a stylized eagle, wings outstretched and head turned to the left. In its claws it clutched a swastika. He unlocked the crate, lifted the lid, and began pulling things out.

He dressed silently, listening to the sounds around him. A moaning from the bunk above, air whistling in and out of a throat wound. The muffled throb of the pumps. The drip and trickle of condensation. The rattle of a chain, followed by muted shouting. And past him, outside the curved metal walls, the endless hissing rush of the sea.

Sweating already, he pulled on wool socks, long underwear, and wool houndstooth suit trousers. The clothes were worn but well made. He unwrapped a starched shirt, folded the french cuffs, and inserted pewter cuff links with a square Art Deco design. Then, holding it clamped under his chin, working with his right hand only, he pinned the empty left sleeve back.

As he was forcing brown oxfords into galoshes another sailor opened a hatch leading forward. Through it he glimpsed a shadowy, clanking cave where long, dark shapes lay. The sailor, who looked exhausted, half-saluted as he wriggled past, though he was naked except for shorts and sandals.

The tall man unwrapped a suit jacket, pinned the left sleeve up, holding it under his chin as he had the shirt, and pulled it on too. The overcoat and black fedora he hung on a valve wheel.

Dressed, except for a tie, he bent again. This time a cheap-looking green suitcase popped open on the bunk. He paused, head cocked, listening again. The narrow corridor stretched away empty. A massive steel door at the aft end, between the tiers of bunks, stirred against its stops. Beyond it were more dim lights and the murmur of voices.

From the suitcase he took two more shirts, underwear, socks, ration books, and a billfold. Below them were a glasses case and a leather shaving kit. He laid these to one side. The socks began to slide as the bunk tilted, and he wedged them between the shirts.

Beneath them were twenty-five bundles wrapped and taped in brown paper. Each bundle was an inch thick. He counted these quickly and silently, ranging them in rows like a hand of solitaire.

Above him the wounded man shifted painfully, choked gasps fluttering through the edges of his throat. The tall man ignored him.

He was looking at the pistol.

It was a standard Army-issue Walther automatic. He touched it as it lay in the suitcase. Then looked down the corridor, which was rolling now about its long axis.

At the far end a red light came on.

He looked at the gun again, frowning, then picked it up. Pointing it at the overhead, he started to check it.

A shout from aft interrupted him. He dropped the gun into the pocket of the overcoat. Moving rapidly now, he repacked the suitcase. First the wrapped stacks, set in edge-to-edge till they covered the bottom. Then the clothing. Last, on top, the shaving kit, ration books, and billfold.

He bent again and felt deep into the crate. Coming up with a thin green sack of parachute fabric, he pulled this over the suitcase and lashed it shut, using his teeth in place of his missing hand. He kicked the empty crate back under the bunk.

He took the overcoat and hat from the valve and shrugged them on. Then carried the sack aft, carrying it by the lashings, turning sidewise as he pressed between the tilting, shadowy racks of bunks, like a man carrying luggage aboard a crowded bus. Past tiny staterooms, a radio room, green curtain half-drawn; then a control room. Red light illuminated dials, gauges, handwheels, and the lower supports of the periscope stand. As he crossed it, he looked up briefly into a vertical ladderway. A cold wind blew steadily down it, ruffling his graying hair. Bending again to pass through a second massive door, he reached the compartment beyond.

In the galley another man sat at the checkered tablecloth, drinking a steaming liquid from a heavy mug. Wordlessly, he shoved a plate toward the tall man as he slid in opposite. He picked up black bread and sliced sausage, dexterously building himself a sandwich with one hand. A sailor brought out another mug. It was a meat broth, very salty, but hot and good.

The man opposite was heavier but not so tall. His face was round and his hair blond, silky, about two inches long on top and cut to the tips of his ears. His eyes were blue, but his cheekbones were high and lips full; Slavic rather than Nordic. He looked chubby, friendly, ineffectual. His suit was black and rumpled. A dark scarf was wound around his neck, and a black felt hat with a plain band perched on the back of his head. He ate voraciously, with utter concentration, reaching out for more of the canned salami and cheese.

The tall man was lifting the mug to his lips again when suddenly the broth flooded toward him, running down his chin, scalding him. The surface of the table tilted alarmingly. From above came shouts, a short choked scream. Then a thud and clang of metal, followed by a cascade of water. It hit the floorplates, eddied this way and that, foaming, and drained away out of sight. It was followed down the ladder by a seaman in foul weather gear. He poked his head through the door.

"The captain says we're here."

The night was completely dark. The tall man felt slippery wet steel, greased metal, rough nonskid decking. He let hands guide him aft, groped about, found a handhold. He clung there, shivering in the icy wind, and looked slowly around.

A faint amber light came on a few feet away and contracted to a tight circle. Two figures bent over it. The wind ululated ominously in antennas and radar detectors. He gradually became aware of a continuous thunder from the darkness ahead. The stern—behind him—seemed to lift, and the craft coasted ahead for almost a minute, tilted nose-down, before subsiding again to roll and sway in the rigid darkness.

When he could see a little he staggered forward. One of the figures moved back. He couldn't see its face, but he recognized the tired hoarse voice. It said, *"Guten morgen."*

"Good morning, Captain. How much longer?"

"A while. But I wanted you on deck early."

"I agree, that's wise." The tall man leaned over the amber light. It was a waterproof torch, propped to illuminate a chart. Beside him he felt the Russian, looking too. A penciled line on wet paper led from offshore toward a blue gap in the land. "Mach-i-pon-go," he said slowly, feeling the word out. "Great Machipongo Inlet. Where are we now?"

"I'm not perfectly certain," said the captain. The icy wind blustered at his words. "We've been running dead reckoning for two days. My best estimate is that the mouth of the inlet is slightly to starboard."

"Tide?"

"We'll cross the bar three hours after dead low. That should give us enough water to get in if we hit the channel dead center. If we don't, the tide will be rising, so we should be able to free ourselves and try again."

"Once we're inside?"

"An hour to find a disembarking point, rig gear, and get you over."

The Russian listened silently. He put a stubby finger on the chart, then moved it inland. The names were in English. Man and Boy Marsh. L on Channel. Mink Island. At the bottom of the chart were the words *Coast and Geodetic Survey, March 1938.*

Out of the dark, a quiet voice. "Shadow bearing two eighty. Less than a kilometer."

The tall man, who was German, raised his eyes. In the interval clouds had unmasked a quarter moon, poised low and orange to port. Its ruddy, flickering light illuminated a black mass below it. The thunder of breaking surf came from both sides now.

The captain said, "Steady as she goes. Engines one-quarter ahead together. Blow remaining tanks."

The stern lifted again, and the tall man clung to a jagged piece of steel. In the moonlight he saw that the aft periscope stand was sheared off, ending in a stump. With a grinding roar the sea shouldered the boat upward, rolled past beneath them, and disappeared into the blackness ahead.

The captain said quietly, "It's possible to see perfectly clearly even with a new moon."

"Is that so?"

"I've done it many a time, attacking convoys."

"Why does it seem so dark tonight?"

"The sensitivity of the eye depends on diet. Fresh, raw vegetables. Leafy things. Not the sort we've been getting lately."

From the opposite side another voice said, just as quietly as the first, "Land to starboard, sir."

"Very good. Left ten degrees rudder, steady two-eight-zero. Slow to minimum revolutions."

"Have you been in these waters before?"

"No. Siegmann entered the Chesapeake south of here in U-230 two years ago. But the American defenses are much stronger now."

"You're sure there are none here?"

"I'm sure of nothing," said the captain. "But I assume the people who sent you reasoned it out too—no? No towns, no factories, therefore it's reasonable to assume, no defense installations. No population till you get inland. Just hundreds of square kilometers of nothing. Marsh. Estuary. Islands, shoals, and birds. Like the North Sea coast, around the Frisians."

No one said anything for a time. The boat lifted, higher this time, rushed forward through the blackness at frightening speed, and subsided, rocking violently.

The captain muttered into a voice tube, asking if all tanks were blown. Rubbing his face—his cheeks were already numb, frostbite damage made them sensitive to cold—the tall man stared toward the shadow to starboard. The thunder roared from all around them now. The boat rose, rushed forward wildly, subsided. From somewhere forward and below a voice called, "Depth: ten meters."

The captain raised his voice. "Lookouts! We're closing land rapidly. I need to know instantly, any light, any vertical shadow that might be a buoy or marker."

The boat lifted, shaking herself, and flew forward at a steep downward angle. Then dropped away, swaying, with a suddenness that left their stomachs floating. The captain tensed. Was that a scrape, the deadly whisper of sand brushing the keel? It didn't return. Instead U-630 trimmed out and floated forward, driven silently into the black heart of the land by the whirring of electric motors.

I hate this, he thought. Rather take on a convoy. Sweating, he bent to the chart again, glanced at his watch, and made a tentative mark between two inward-curving jaws of land. Shoals were the teeth. If only he knew where he was. The stink of marshy land was heavy and frightening on the roaring wind. Only occasionally, when cloud uncovered the moon, could he sense rather than see a blacker black to port and starboard. That to port seemed slightly closer. "Right rudder, steer course two-nine-zero," he said into the voice tube. He looked at the chart again. Another seven hundred meters and the channel would divide, one branch going southwest, the other north.

"Seven meters," the hushed voice floated back. Then, a few seconds later, "Six and a half. Shoaling fast, sir."

"Lay the rigging party on deck," the captain said through dry lips. He glanced at his watch again. An hour and a half to high tide.

"Five meters!"

"Steady ahead," said the captain, gripping the bent metal of the coaming. He remembered the raw horror of the last attack, the whine of aircraft engines out of the black night where he'd thought he was safe. Then explosions, screams, Engelmeyer disemboweled by machine-gun slugs, still lashed to his lookout station as they'd dogged the hatch and slid under.

Beside him the tall man felt the boat suddenly steady. For a moment he thought they had entered still water. Then the captain said, his voice taut, *"Scheisse.* Belay sounding, we're aground. Both engines full astern."

The boat shuddered but held fast. "No luck, Captain. We'll have to wait for the tide."

The tall man asked, "Can we disembark here?"

"This is not the shore. This is some sandbar, a shoal."

"How long?"

"Perhaps half an hour—maybe more."

"That leaves us how long?"

"You're right," said the captain. "If we lose too much time here, we won't make it out before the tide traps us. I don't want to be sitting out here at dawn. *Obersteuermann!* Make ready forward tubes. Flood forward tubes. Open doors."

"Forward tubes ready."

"Won't they explode?"

"There's marsh all around. They won't run far enough to arm. Fan shot, all tubes—fire."

The deck shuddered beneath them. Phosphorescent trails hissed out into the blackness. "Both engines back full, back emergency power," said the captain. For several seconds nothing happened. Then, relieved of tons of weight, the bow stirred, grated. The captain snapped orders. Then they were moving forward again. On deck men were dragging things out of hatches, another was shinnying up the periscope stand.

"Slow ahead now. Slow . . . slow . . ."

The boat grounded again, this time with a jolt. The captain muttered, "This should do it. *Oberleutnant,* take charge."

On the U-boat's blunt bow, two husky sailors in rubber suits swung themselves into the icy water. Trailing a line, they kicked toward where they guessed the shore should be. The cold struck through their hands and loins. Then their thrusting boots sank into soft bottom. They hauled themselves up a mucky, giving slope, into a crackling thicket of dry marsh grass. Looking back, they made out the boat as a black shadow against the racing clouds. They crept inland on hands and knees, swearing as the tussocky ground gave way unexpectedly. When the line came taught, they unlashed the grapnel and dug its points deep. Then stood and cupped their hands to shout: "Ready."

The Russian stood patiently on the conning tower, leaning back into a rope chair. His luggage was looped around his neck, a heavy brown leather valise.

"Ready," they heard faintly, borne on the wind.

"Up periscope," said the exec.

As the slender steel shaft hummed upward it lifted the line whose far end led to the shore. Lifted, too, the chair. The Russian rose, legs dangling.

"Lower away," said the exec.

As a knot of men on deck paid out line hand over hand, the blond man swayed out over the foredeck, over the dimly visible wire of the radio antenna. Then blackness yawned beneath him, and the plash of small waves. A blast of cold wind swayed the chair. He heard a brittle whicker of grass stalks. Then his dangling feet crashed into the ground.

"Next," the sailors shouted, holding him by the shoulders as they unsnapped the buckles. "You okay? Your *Kumpel* will be here in a minute. Just stand by."

The stocky man didn't answer. He shifted his weight, testing with his boots the soft, uncertain soil of America.

Back on the tower, the empty sling came to the German's upstretched hand. The captain helped him step into it. "Keep your fingers clear of that block, Colonel."

"All right."

"Good luck in Washington," the captain added softly.

"Shut up, you fool," snapped the tall man. "You never saw us. You never heard of us. We never existed."

Then he was aloft and sliding through the windy dark. Over the foredeck, over the black water. Ahead he sensed a vast, flat emptiness. Water? Land? He couldn't tell. His legs brushed winter-dry vegetation before he expected it, and he landed stumbling, almost falling before the sailors grabbed him and set him on his feet.

Then they were standing close together. The sailors slapped their backs, said, "Good luck" and "Good hunting," and were gone. Their footsteps squished and cracked away.

The tall man stood rigid, watching the shadow of the boat. For minutes it looked the same. Then it seemed to shrink.

When the moon fingered the waves again, it was gone.

When he turned the Russian was turning up the collar of his coat. He spoke, for the first time. "Cold," he said. In English.

"You have the compass?"

"West's that way." He pointed inland. "Ready to go?"

"Lead on," said the German. He reslung the suitcase more firmly around his neck, tugged his hat down against the wind, then slid his hand into his coat pocket. The gun was there, heavy, reassuring, familiar. He'd carried it since the war began in 1939.

The Russian turned away. The tall man looked to seaward again, listening. No sound came back but the roar of the surf. He swung back, caught the faint gleam of the other's hair a few paces ahead.

He took a few steps after him, stumbling over uneven ground. "Not so fast," he called.

The Russian slowed, half-turning in the dark.

The colonel's hand came out of his coat, holding the automatic. He stepped up behind the waiting shadow, put the muzzle to the back of its neck, and pulled the trigger.

The clack of the hammer falling on an empty chamber cut through the boom of the surf and the rattle of dead stalks.

When the other swung round, the colonel, taken by surprise, grunted as he took the first blow in the chest. He stumbled back, bringing the pistol down violently on something soft. The moon faded, and darkness cloaked them both. Clutching at each other's clothing, they struggled like drunken dancers across the treacherous ground. Finally the German broke free. Panting, he thrust the pistol under his armpit. With a sliding click the magazine fed a round. He held it out and waited for the crackle of reeds. The first flash lit a humped, dark figure. The second and third showed him only the swaying, wind-bent grass.

He lowered the gun, staring as green and yellow afterimages chased themselves across the clashing, shifting shadows.

From the right, frighteningly close, a shot tore the night apart. The bullet clattered away through the reeds. He swung and fired four more times, spacing the rounds out at waist level, bringing the Walther down again each time it kicked.

Silence succeeded. His thumb rubbed the slide. He had one round left. The other had five or six. He crouched there as minutes passed.

Footsteps crackled stealthily behind him. He pivoted slowly. Then began moving away, silently, creeping through the reeds.

They ended abruptly, without warning, and he fell down a short bank into black mud and water. Instinctively his right arm shot out, trying to break his fall. His weight drove it deep into the muck.

When he realized what had happened he groped frantically, but only cold slippery mud met his clawed fingers. The gun was gone.

The steps came closer, slow, deliberate. As they neared the German wriggled himself down into the mud. Realizing his face was lighter than the surrounding darkness, he turned it away from his pursuer.

Then he lay still.

"Where are you, Colonel?" said the quiet voice. The accent was American, flawless and idiomatic. "You know I'll find you. Then kill you. You turncoat son of a bitch."

He lowered his face to the icy mud, coating it, then lifted his head. In the faint ruddy light of the quarter moon he made out the other's outline above him, where the grass ended, looking out over the flat blackness of the slough. Waiting.

He lay motionless, hardly breathing, as his hand and then his feet turned slowly to ice. It felt familiar. He'd lain this way before, waiting. In the snow, halfway around the world, in a city called Stalingrad.

Where he'd left his arm.

Finally the shadow moved away. He waited for half an hour, then got to his knees, scooping sticky mud from his coat.

From his left came the chuckle of water. From the right, the ceaseless clatter of grass, dry, dead. He half-slid, half-crawled, dragging the suitcase, sweating in the cold mud that now and again ripped his fingers and clothes with unseen razors, some kind of barnacle or clam.

Much later he heard another shot, behind him, far off. Only then did he straighten and climb back onto firmer ground.

When dawn came two hours later, Hauptsturmführer-SS Hans Dieter Heudeber, muddy and exhausted, found himself on a little wooded knoll, two or three feet above the level of the marsh, from which he could look out across it from cover. The marsh stretched out for miles, yellow and flat under an open cold sky, waving and rippling as the wind swept over it. Far to the west, across snaking darknesses that might be more mud sloughs, was a low line of forest.

It reminded him of the Van Goghs he'd studied long ago, before the Party had branded the Dutch impressionist an artistic degenerate. *Green Corn*— and the *View of Arles,* yes, which he'd made a point of seeing in Prague in 1940—and *Spring Wheat at Sunrise.* The bending reeds had the same economy of brushwork, the same transcendent and mysterious rightness, as though one more stroke would spoil it all.

He watched for a long time, but no human figure was in sight.

He stood slumped, legs trembling with fatigue and cold. He'd let his quarry escape. Worse, he'd warned him. Clever, clever; he was sure he'd locked the box. Obviously the other had been suspicious.

Now he'd have to accomplish his objective in some other way. It would be more difficult. But it could be done.

A rustle moved through the withered leaves above him. He crouched, then remembered. It was only the wind.

Shrugging the suitcase back into place, he set off.

PART I

OUTSIDE

CHAPTER 1

Washington, D.C.

Congratulations, Lieutenant Kennedy," said the President as he stretched his hands up to drape the ribbon over my head. I bent from attention toward him, looking past his thinning hair as his fingers adjusted the gold and red and bronze of the Navy and Marine Corps Medal.

When I straightened it was a barely discernible weight on my blues. I smelled Camels and aftershave lotion and my own sweat. The air in the Blue Room was overheated in an already-warming March 1945. I lowered my eyes to find the President's big freckled hand extended.

"Thank you, Mr. President," I said. FDR grinned, pumped my hand—it felt like he could break it—and cocked his chin as the photographer's flashbulb went off.

When our palms parted a somber-looking aide rolled him back and spun him round. Moved him one pace to the right, and spun him again, to face the next hero. As the wheelchair moved deliberately down the ranks Abe Lincoln gazed sadly down at us from his frame, at boys in blue and olive drab and khaki, fresh from a war even greater than his. Boys missing arms, jaws, eyes, hands, pieces of their skulls. An Air Corps major and I were the only whole men there.

As the aide pushed him past the one without legs the President raised a hand. The chair stopped, and he leaned forward.

Roosevelt said a few words in a low voice, head bent confidentially. The boy chuckled. "Yassuh, Mr. President. I'll bear that in mind when I get home, sure enough will."

"Stand at ease, you men he's already talked to," muttered a husky admiral. He glanced at his watch, then at a civilian who lingered by the door.

I relaxed to a half-assed parade rest, surreptitiously grinding my fists into my back. The pain had begun again, a dull ache that told me that it, like so many things in this late winter of the war, had dug in for the duration. I tried to ignore it, looking across the room. Through the window the first green buds on the elms were visible.

When I looked back the President was making the last presentation, a posthumous Medal of Honor on top of a folded flag handed to a weeping man. He held the father's hand for almost a minute, not saying anything. Just holding it. When he finally motioned to the aide the father's reddened eyes stayed on the flag.

Franklin D. Roosevelt's hands trembled as he leaned back, screwed a Camel into an amber holder, scratched a match. Smoke rose slowly, separating into layers, then gradually coalescing into a motionless haze, like fog over the sea off Cape Cod.

We servicemen glanced at each other, then relaxed. A Marine lit up too, and then, digging a white pack of Luckies out of his sock, so did a second class gunner's mate wearing a brand-new Navy Cross.

The idea penetrated that the ceremony was over. The line of men broke, scattering across the glossy parquet floor to waiting relatives. FDR glanced around with a sigh. "Deacon, tell Maysie I imagine these brave men are as ready for a little drink as their commander in chief. You, Lieutenant—Joe Kennedy's younger boy, aren't you? John, that's it. Join me, John?"

"Uh, yes sir," I said. "I'd be . . . honored."

"Fine, that's just fine. Bill, make sure the lieutenant gets whatever he wants. And the same for these other brave fellahs."

He raised his voice on that last, cocking his head back over his shoulder, and tired excited faces turned toward us for a moment from the little crowd of parents, reporters, senior officers. Now that the President was out of camera range, flashbulbs rippled like outgoing 40 mm fire at night. I noticed two men against the wall, arms folded, watching everything silently. One kept his eyes clamped on me.

The bottles and fixings came in on a metal cart pushed by a middle-aged Negro in a white mess jacket. It tinkled as it rolled. FDR kept talking as the cart approached. "Put it over there, by the window. No, you serve, Maysie, I'm a little weary just now." A large black Scottie followed, sniffing at passing legs before it came over to us and flopped down, shoving its head under FDR's dangling hand. He scratched Fala's ears absently. "John, I hope you'll forgive me for sitting down. It makes it a lot easier, not having to drag around ten pounds of steel on my legs."

"That's fine, sir. I understand."

"Pull that chair over . . . you don't look so chipper, either."

"A little malaria, sir. That's why the yellow coloring, the docs say."

The colored man brought me a glass of whiskey on a tray. I swirled it, looking closely at the man who'd just awarded me the only medal I'd probably ever get.

I'd seen him before, with my father, but he was no longer the fleshy, robust Roosevelt of the thirties, before Pearl Harbor and the War. Now his gray suit hung off his shoulders and his cheeks were gaunt. His skin looked ashen and the graying hair, never very thick, crept toward baldness on top. But he still looked lively, and he still made you feel, when he talked to you, that you were the only person in the world whose opinion he really valued.

"Well, you're back in one piece, that's the important thing. We're proud of you, John. Proud of every man in here today—and every hero who's still out there."

"Actually I'm not a hero, sir."

"No false modesty, Kennedy. I read the article. How you saved your men after that Jap destroyer ran you down. PTs, eh? That's one rough-riding son of a bitch, Ernie King tells me."

"It is, sir. They'll slam your guts out in a five-foot sea."

"One-oh-nine. Higgins, or Elco?"

"She was an Elco boat, sir. One of the eighty-footers."

"Thirty-eight tons. Twelve men. Three Packard engines. Four torpedoes, Mark Eights."

"That's right, sir, and a couple of fifties." I knew enough not to sound surprised. The President had been assistant secretary of the Navy back during the first go-round with Germany, and he'd spent a lot of time at sea since December of 1942.

The murmured conversations, the clink of glasses was muting behind us. Turning my head carefully, I saw the civilian ushering the others out. His face was courteous but firm, making it clear it was time for the man who'd been reelected for an unprecedented fourth term to move on to the next event on a busy schedule.

He came back and looked at FDR. The President pursed his lips, then shook his head.

One of the men left the wall and closed the french doors gently from outside.

Suddenly we were alone together, lead crystal and straight Ballantine weighing down my hand. I straightened in my chair, trying to keep my back quiet. For some reason I felt apprehensive. I tried to shake it off, to look eager, or at least relaxed.

The President was still talking, hadn't ever really stopped. "Did you know I had to wrestle the Navy brass to get the PT? Back in '37, I forced them to take fifteen million dollars and develop something small, fast, and heavily armed. They wanted more cruisers."

"Is that right, sir? I didn't know that."

"But then these are the same people who used to boast to me they'd lick the Japanese before breakfast, in three weeks at the outside."

"That was before Pearl Harbor, sir."

"Would it have been any different? They still had more carriers than we did. They'd have sunk the battleships, in harbor or out.

"I remember back in the old Navy days, and William Jennings Bryan, the secretary of state, used to come tearing into the office, his back hair at right angles to his coattails, like Tom Powers used to draw him, and he'd shout: 'Roosevelt, can you give me a battleship? I must have a battleship to send to the capital of Haiti—the city with the funny name.' 'Port au Prince,' I said. 'Yes,' said the secretary of state. 'They have cut the president of the country into four parts and they're carrying the pieces in processions through the streets. The revolutionists will kill all the white people in the country. I must have a battleship there today.'

"Well, I explained to W. Jay B. that all the battleships of the Atlantic Fleet were on maneuvers off Narragansett Bay. 'But I must have a battleship there today,' he kept saying. I explained that Port au Prince was four days' steaming distance from Narragansett Bay, but that I had a gunboat in Guantánamo Bay, Cuba, a few hours away. And Bryan shouted, 'Roosevelt, don't be so technical about it all. When I say "battleship," I mean a boat with guns on it!' "

I chuckled; it seemed to be expected. FDR went on. "And then boys like you took the war to the Japs—not in battleships, but in a modern kind of gunboat. I don't know how much damage you did. Leahy says hardly any, but I quote Mahan at him. If the enemy has you cornered, and your force is inferior, you've got to attack. 'From such a position, there is no salvation except by action vigorous almost to desperation.' You fellahs were all we had, and you came through for us . . . Well, it's only what I'd expect of a Kennedy. I respect Joe. Although we've had our arguments. Which ain't exactly a secret to you, I imagine. What do you hear from your father?"

I remembered all the things my dad, once an admirer, had said about the President. Not just at the breakfast table in Hyannis Port, but in public. Things that had finally gotten him recalled as ambassador. Dad had angered the man before me so much he hadn't answered my father's telegram asking for a wartime assignment. But aloud I only said, "My mother writes. My father's not much for letters, Mr. President."

"Rose is a rare one, Joe's a lucky man. Eleanor's a wonderful woman, too, but it's not easy being the chief assistant to Joan of Arc." He went on, the cigarette holder familiar from a thousand newsreels trailing smoke across the closed-in air. I noticed a ring on the little finger of his right hand, a bloodstone or garnet. No question about it, the rumors I'd heard of his being a dying man were way off base. "She wanted to go out to Guadalcanal during the fighting. I didn't mind her visiting the boys in hospital, but she refused to go unless I cleared her for the battle zone too! Well, I finally had to give in. Then as soon as she left I sent Bull Halsey a cable. Told him not to let her get within a hundred miles of the place. God help me if they ever declassify that one."

Through the doors both Secret Service men were watching me now. One had a pencil-thin moustache like Ronald Colman's.

FDR's mobile face sobered. "I was sorry to hear about your brother. A Navy Cross won't make much difference, but it was all I could do."

I looked down at my hands. Joe Jr. had died flying B-24s in a mission they still hadn't declassified. I couldn't think of anything to say.

"I heard about him on the *Baltimore,* when we were on our way to the Aleutians. I remember it was the same day Missy . . . and the same day President Quezon died." Roosevelt rubbed a hand across his forehead. "That was the day I had to order the Army to run the Philadelphia transit system. The white motormen went on strike because somebody hired eight Negroes."

I was glad we weren't going to dwell on my brother. "Did they go back to work?"

"You bet. Told 'em if they didn't I'd arrest every one over thirty, and every man under that would be classified One-A and go to the front. They came around fast."

I raised my eyes to find him looking across the room. His murmur seemed to be directed not at me, but at the Lincoln portrait.

"General Marshall tells me things are just about over in Europe. Soon we'll close the chapter on Hitler, Mussolini, Tojo, the dictators who feed on hate and ignorance and fear.

"But there'll be more. There always are. We can't just shake hands all around and go home, like we did in 1919. Or we'll have to do it all over again in twenty years, and the next war will make this look like kids squabbling in a sandbox. We've got to put together an organization, a way to stop them before they get too powerful. Whatever Winston thinks. I thought he was rude the first time we met. But we've grown close over the past years. Without him, we'd be facing Hitler alone now. You've met Winston, I believe?"

"Yes sir. In thirty-nine, while I was writing the book."

"Why England Slept. And a damned good book it was."

"You read it?"

"Sure I did. I thought it was perfectly splendid, too. That goddamned Tugwell is always patronizing me about my reading. Hell, I read *Gone With the Wind* in one night! That's when you met Winston, eh? I remember when he was here in '44, and somebody—Hap Arnold, I think—asked him if he wanted water in his whiskey. 'Water! Do you know what happens in water?' he said. 'Fish fuck in it!' Broke us all up." He frowned at my glass. "Don't care for scotch?"

"I'd never say so in front of Fala, sir."

He threw back his head and guffawed. "I love it! Not in front of Fala! But where'd it come from? I never heard old Joe crack a joke in his life. Let me fix you a martini."

I sat half smiling, but feeling dead inside. Where did it come from? I could have told him. From growing up in a family that bored in mercilessly to ridicule every sign you cared, or could be hurt. That picked off any scab and dug till they hit bone. You learned to defuse tense situations with a laugh. And gradually you learned to paper over the emptiness in your gut with a joke, a woman, a prank, anything to throw between you and the hollowness. Because there were things down there you didn't want to know.

FDR was looking at me curiously, and I remembered: martini. I said, "Oh, I couldn't do justice to that either, sir. The malaria."

"Oh, sorry. . . . So, what's the next duty station? Or are you waiting for orders?"

"Neither, sir. I'm medically retired, effective next month."

"Is that right? How old are you, John? Wait a minute, I should remember. You were class of 1940."

"And you were . . . 1904?"

"Close, '03. Groton?"

"Choate."

"Crimson, right? Editor?"

"No sir. Played ball, and swam some."

"What position?"

"End, mostly, sir. Just the freshman team, though. I was too light."

"Class of '40. My God! Anyway, that'd make you—"

"Twenty-seven, sir."

"You know, at your age I was representing Duchess County in the New York State Senate, District Twenty-six."

"That's the kind of thing my father says." I stopped myself. But too late; FDR said, "Well, he's right. The war's not going to last forever. What do you plan to do with yourself?"

"I haven't decided yet, sir. I'd like to do another book sometime. I think . . . well, I think I might want to be a writer."

"No political ambitions?"

I glanced up to find him examining me with those shrewd, good-humored, deadly eyes. "I'd never run against you, sir."

He threw back his head again, and the hearty haw-haw echoed through the empty room. I wondered then where everyone else was. Mrs. Roosevelt. Byrnes. Hopkins. Daniels.

"Well, it's good to know I'm safe for a fifth term. But seriously, as soon as the war's over I'm through with politics. I'm going home to Hyde Park, finish the house on the hill. Might make that another first in my career—the first president to resign before the people throw him out.

"I'm tired, John. And the tragedy of it is, I've never been able to find anyone to follow up for me. The generals, Eisenhower, that son of a bitch MacArthur, they'll go straight to the Republicans."

"You don't think Tom Dewey will run again?"

"Dewey has glamor, but he's a dirty fighter. You read what he said this last campaign. First he accuses me of selling out to Communists, then he accuses me of being a monarch. Well, really, which is it—Communism or monarchy? After this war the people will want a military man. It's American history."

"How about General Marshall?"

"I respect George Marshall immensely, but just between the two of us and the lamppost, he's too goddamned honest to be a politician. Maybe secretary of state, or an ambassador. Not president."

FDR tapped ash; the wheelchair squeaked as he leaned back. "You see, Jack, we Democrats are still a minority party. Those big New Deal majorities have whittled themselves down every term. If the Republicans organized that strength into an intelligent opposition, they could render a real service to the country. But instead they'll go back to business as usual. Fill your pockets, tax cuts for the rich. They'll run MacArthur, I'm very much afraid. He'll present it as saving the two-party system, but it'll be selling the people down the river.

"But who do I pass off to? Wallace has screwed himself with the South, he's shot his mouth off too often. Garner's too old. I need Barkley where he is, in the

Senate. Jimmy Byrnes is an ex-Catholic, which is about the worst of all worlds politically, you might say. Truman's all right, but we'll need fresh blood not very far down the road. Why not a war hero, another Harvard man?"

I said, "I'm not my father, sir. Or my brother. Maybe I'll just try a novel."

"I love Mark Twain," said the President, swerving deftly aside. "I took the term 'New Deal' from *Connecticut Yankee,* did you know that? I learned a lot from old Sam Clemens. I wrote a movie script once. Nobody in Hollywood was interested. Did a few pages of a novel, too. Think I ought to try again?"

I smiled. "Maybe so, sir. Maybe we could collaborate."

"Good way to get your head shaved, I hear." He tossed off the last of his drink. As if on some signal, the colored man was whisking the glasses away, carrying the ashtray off. The President sighed, tapped the ash off the nearly finished Camel, and laid the holder across a fresh ashtray. His hand found a paper, brought it to his lap; I glimpsed the SECRET SEALED stamp. "Again, congratulations, Lieutenant. If you're in town for a few days, come to dinner. Thursdays are best. If you can stand sweetbreads, that is. My least favorite part of the cow, but Eleanor likes them. Do you?"

"Well, I—"

"I hate 'em. Once I sent her a note about it. I said, 'I am getting to the point where my stomach rebels, and this does not help my relations with foreign powers. I bit two of them today.'"

This time the laughter boomed out through the open windows to the lawn, causing heads to turn, smiles to appear. Taking that as dismissal, I got up, wincing as my back reminded me who was boss. "Thank you, Mr. President."

I didn't intend to, but I found myself saluting. I didn't like what he stood for, but somehow this gaunt, crippled man inspired respect.

"Oh, you damn reservists," FDR said. "You know the Navy don't salute indoors."

As the butler ushered me out I glanced back through the closing doors. For a moment the setting sun glowed around the man who sat there. He'd already lost the transient spark of gaiety, slumped forward in the wheeled chair, mouth sagging slightly open, cigarette smoldering. In the failing sunlight the smoke looked red. The paper dangled forgotten in a hanging hand. He was staring up at the portrait of the assassinated President.

Then the Secret Service opened the doors for me, and I went out, into the hall, into the suddenly chill air.

"What was that all about, Shafty?" said Captain "Bubba" Mackall, USMC. I knew him from my stint in Naval Intelligence, long before the PT thing. I'd run into him over at Bethesda, where they'd been looking at my back for about the fifteenth time, and asked him to come along to the White House. His face was red from the free booze. We picked up our coats and caps, skirted the bronze seal in the floor, and clattered down the steps of the North Portico.

"Just personal stuff."

"Personal stuff with the President?"

It seemed strange to me too. Why had he asked me that, about my future? The son of a man he hated? "Well," I said, "My dad used to work for him."

"He did, huh? Who's your dad, that he knows FDR?"

I stopped on Pennsylvania Avenue and stared at him. "You've never heard of Joe Kennedy? Head of the Securities and Exchange Commission? Chairman of the Maritime Commission? The ambassador to the Court of St. James?"

"Jeez, don't get sore, Shafty! What's the Court of Saint James?"

"The ambassador to Great Britain, you goddamn dummy!"

"Oh, *that* Kennedy. You related to him? I di'n't know. . . . You ready to do some steaming? Check out some of that good ole Home Front All-American pussy?"

I glanced back once across the lawn, through the fence. Across the winter-browned lawn the shining facade looked ageless and imposing. There was only one gate open, and a sentry stood stiffly at it, M-1 at ground arms. The barrels of antiaircraft guns poked skyward from the top of the Treasury Building. We had to cross the street; since the war started, they'd closed the sidewalk on the White House side. Fortunately there wasn't much traffic. I couldn't get his face out of my mind, though. The man who lived there. How tired he'd looked.

The son of a bitch.

"Well, whaddya say?"

Mackall was waiting. "You're right. Enough of this political shit," I said. I loosened my tie, cocked my cap back, and grinned that fair-haired smile that for some reason knocked every woman who saw it back on her heels. "Look, sorry I got steamed. Okay? Got any money on you?"

"Couple of bucks. Why?"

"Great. Let's go get laid."

CHAPTER 2

Birdsnest, Virginia

By late morning, when Krasov found the road, the bitter cold had eased a little. He stopped, still hidden by the scrub, and studied it for a long time. His full lips parted as he watched a hawk circle, balancing on the wind.

After he'd lost Heudeber in the darkness, he'd stood motionless and silent in the marsh, gripping his gun. He didn't like not knowing where the SS man was. He came close to freezing, but all through the night he'd stayed alert, listening to the wind rattle the dry stalks. He'd hoped to find the German when light came. Preferably dead, caught by a lucky shot during their brief firefight. Or, if he could find his tracks, he could follow them through mud and grass and liquidate him. But when the sun had reluctantly enlightened the gray horizon it had shown him only bland, flat marsh stretching away like an endless dirty tablecloth. Rising again, the tide had wiped out both their tracks as if they'd never existed.

With that he'd shrugged. Beaten himself with his arms to drive away the cold. Then picked up the cheap, scuffed, already muddy leather valise. Looked closely at the sun, then at a soggy map he took from inside his coat.

Then he set off.

Five hours later he was covered with mud, scratched, bleeding, and panting. The map didn't show miles of brambles and grass that cut like razors, or boggy ground that yielded suddenly just when it looked most solid. It didn't show winding mud sloughs, too gluey to wade, too shallow to swim, nor the one deep channel he'd had to sidestroke across, holding the grip above his head to keep it dry. That got most of the mud off, at least, but he'd twisted his knee clawing his way out.

When he'd seen the line of trees ahead he'd thought it was land at last. It was, but only for fifty meters. The roots of the water oaks and corkscrew-twisted marsh pines groped nakedly down into mushy putrescence, black, smelling of rot and mold in the chilly morning. Past it the flat open marsh resumed.

Resumed, but different now. A forlorn dotting of gray sticks zigzagged across it, tilting under the cloudy sky. When he reached out to lean on one it crumbled, frangible as biscuit. The vegetation changed too, no longer spartina but a coarse, chest-high bush that quivered in the wind. When he broke off a branch the heart was green and fibrous. He rubbed it between his fingers and held it to his nose. It smelled faintly of juniper or sage.

Now he limped, and his breath hissed through his teeth each time his weight came on his injured knee. Another line of trees drew slowly closer.

He set down the valise—it was heavy and tiring to carry—and wiped both hands back over his hair as he studied the road. One lane. Dirt surfaced. He peered along it cautiously, not stepping into view yet. At its edges lay weathered boards, trash, shattered bricks crusted with old mortar. A gleam at his feet drew his eye. Something once familiar, yet now strange. A curved bottle, thick emerald glass . . . the blue innocent eyes narrowed as he chased the memory. Something about a road, and Coca-Cola . . . but it didn't come.

He made his decision. He'd never liked the idea of their traveling as two clergymen. Now, with Heudeber's treachery, it would be doubly dangerous. Opening the grip, he pulled off the muck-smeared black suit, rolled it, and thrust it under a bush. The cold air bit his skin. He didn't shiver or flinch. Just bent again and pulled on gray twill work pants, a plaid shirt, and a thin, worn leather jacket, the kind mechanics wore. A work cap. He tucked the automatic, a 7.62 Tokarev, into his belt.

As he straightened his stomach knotted painfully. He was hungry again. His lips shaped Russian syllables. Then he stopped. Whispered it again, slowly, deliberately, this time in English. "Hell. Should of brought the rest of that sausage. It 'ud come in handy right now—"

He suddenly drew his lips back over his teeth, remembering Heudeber had the money. He pulled out his billfold and went through it rapidly. The 1940 Michigan drivers' license. Social Security card. Draft card, 4-F classification, with doctor's note explaining his eye condition. Folded-small letter from his girlfriend in Arlington. A, B, and C series ration books.

One five-dollar, one two-dollar, and three one-dollar bills.

He stood there for a few minutes, then realized he was wasting time. He had to keep moving.

The alternative was to find the traitor, kill him, and take the money himself.

Unfortunately, that didn't seem possible. He'd been lucky last night. If he hadn't suspected the SS man and taken precautions, picked the lock on his box, he'd be dead now. The flesh of his nape stirred, remembering the icy kiss of gunmetal. The German could be anywhere. Miles ahead, or right behind him.

But wherever Heudeber was, he, Krasov—he still had a goal. The plan was *kaputt.* So? He'd come up with another.

The target remained the same.

He shook himself, sucking in cold piney air. Was that a tang of woodsmoke, faint on the wind? Taking another deep breath, he picked up the grip, pushed through the bushes that fringed the road, and stepped out.

Ah, he thought. Firm ground. His trembling legs steadied as he swung into a marching pace. The sparse sunlight fell through the arching branches of old oaks in moving patterns of shadow. He moved with every sense alert, swinging along with one hand concealed on the butt of the gun. He frowned; once again something about the silent, twisting road, the call of the birds, the sense of waiting, made him feel he'd been here before.

Then, out of nowhere, déjà vu crystallized into memory.

———

He was standing on the hill, looking down the road toward the river, gripping his mother's hand. He remembered the sharp smell of the melting snow, the drip of it from the eaves of the wooden houses that perched, canted like holed and sinking boats, along the ankle-deep, strawy, horse-manured road that led down to the river. The river was green and white, tearing at its banks like a maddened horse at its traces. Men were rushing about, shouting and dragging things away from it. Trees swept by in the murky froth, and dead animals, and bushes and logs and torn-down walls. He'd looked on in awe and fear. It seemed the river would tear everything away, the town, the hills, everything.

He asked her what it was called. She told him it was the Ohio. Then she took him into the store, and bought him a whole bottle of Coca-Cola, because he cried for it and sat down and refused to walk until he got it. He drank it all, and it had made him sick, and he'd thrown up on the railroad tracks, walking home.

When he was six they moved from Cincinnati back to Brooklyn, where his father and mother had lived before he was born. He remembered parlors full of men, smoking and drinking and arguing in Russian and English. When someone asked him a question in one language, he'd answer in the other, to make them laugh. The women came out, listened, then disappeared again into the kitchen to make pans of pirozhki, sweet bread, pickled eggs, borscht, potato dumplings. Once his father presented him to a young man with sparkling glasses and an unruly mound of red spiky hair. My son, he'd said. Ivan Okulov. Johnny, remember today. *Ponemayetye?* Today you met Comrade Trotsky.

Trotsky had asked him what he thought of the Dodgers' chances.

When he was ten they went on the boat. He remembered a party, going down to the piers, then days in a cabin with another family with four daughters. He'd hated them, the girls. Then long days on overheated trains, the smells of coal smoke and hair oil when you put your nose to the horsehair seat covers. Strange languages, strange costumes, strange people sitting across from them as the carriage swayed and rattle-clacked across endless fields and forests and steppe. They were traveling, it seemed, past the end of the world. But then at last the smell like his mother's kitchen, the gay exuberant sound of Russian.

With them on the boat and train had been a new red Farmall tractor, crated up. His father had bought it with his savings from the mill. It was his contribution to building Socialism. Ivan remembered the first time they got it running. Snorting, huge, it rolled and bucked across the field in the hot bee-buzzing day. Smoke blasted from its stack, dancing the little lid on its pipe. Behind it lurched something with long metal arms that lifted and dropped, laying out the stalks behind it in long, uniform rows. He'd worked behind it, wearing the kerchief of a Red Pioneer. Then later it stopped running, and the peasants stood in a silent circle as his father cursed them, said they didn't deserve a tractor, didn't know how to take care of it.

He remembered the beginning of the fear. His father had dug a pit behind the house, bagged their share of the grain, and buried it. Then in the winter the soldiers came. "Give us the grain, vipers." "Hand over the surplus." "We know you've got gold here, salted meat, wheat. Where are you hiding it?" "Give it up, kulaks." His father had laughed, told them he'd been a Social Revolutionary when they were bowing down before ikons. The soldiers hadn't laughed. His father had cowered on the ground as the rifle butts rose and fell like peasants' flails. Ivan had cried out and run forward, pleading with them to stop, he knew, he would tell them. The soldiers had slapped his back, grinning down at him. "The boy knows. You're a real Soviet man, aren't you? Where is it, Comrade?"

When they left, taking the bags of grain in the family's cart, his father and mother were in it too, tied with wire. Ivan had run after the creaking wheels for miles, following the drops of blood in the snow.

He remembered winter. He and his grandmother huddled on the stove as outside the frozen white silence grew in the stark forest. To make him forget the cold she told him magical stories in a cracked whisper. She had spent her whole life in Koprovno, but her stories took him to palaces and strange lands of dwarves and fairies, where animals spoke and were wiser than human beings. No food. Bark tea. Dizziness, visions, darkness. He could have died then. Maybe, in a way, he had.

Gholod y cholod. Hunger and cold. He didn't remember what had happened to his grandmother. Lost and vanished like so many in that endless Russian winter . . .

One day the column had come out of the forest. Hundreds of people, dragging or carrying bags, suitcases, makeshift sleds, wading through the chest-deep snow in street shoes, the women bare legged. He'd watched in silence from the woods as they were lined up and counted, then set to work building first stockades, then guard towers, and last log shacks to live in. When they fell down the others moved them aside, stacked them, and the snow fell on them, and the piles grew higher.

He'd joined the cutting parties, and the clop, clop of axes and the snore of two-handed saws had echoed through the falling snow. And once in a while, shots. When the guards had asked his name he'd given them his grandmother's: Krasov. Something in his face or voice seemed to make them trust him. First they sent him on errands or to deliver messages. Then they let him hold their rifles while they went off with one of the women. Finally they asked him jocularly if he'd ever thought of joining the Cheka.

He didn't tell them about his parents, or that he'd lived in America. By then, somehow, he knew what lies to tell, and what truth to keep with the silence of the frozen birches.

He'd never seen Stalin or Beria, but he'd been assigned to Kaganovich's bodyguard in 1936. His unit had gone to the Ukraine with Iron Lazar to look into espionage and sabotage. He remembered "The Bootmaker" telling the members of the court, "Put them on trial, then shoot them, the wreckers, the spies, the bastards."

Ivan Krasov had worked hard and risen in the ranks of the NKVD. In those days it was easy to rise. You opened a copy of *Pravda,* and suddenly found one's senior officers were really traitors, White Guardists, rightist deviationists. During the day he studied German, English, dialectics. The English came back like the language of dreams. He hadn't spoken it for years. In the cellars at night he studied interrogation techniques.

In 1938 he marched with the others to demand the destruction of the bandits, of Kamenev and Zinoviev, Pyatakov and Bukharin. Trotskyites and deviationists had to be put down. He shouted, "Thanks and praise to the great leader of the party, who follows in the footsteps of Lenin!" He shouted, "Stalin is thinking about us!"

He remembered June of 1941, the shock and horror of the unexpected attack. Listening to Molotov on the radio: "Our cause is just. The enemy will be broken. The victory will be ours." He'd been reassigned to SMERSH, armed forces security and counterintelligence, in a border guard unit.

That autumn he'd faced the Germans himself, heard the roar of the Panzers across the smoky plain. They'd fought, but somehow the fascists had surrounded them, broken them, defeated the invincible Red Army. He'd barely managed to throw away his identifications before they were disarmed and marched west. The Nazis had special squads attached to their advancing armies. They shot Communist Party members out of hand.

In the nightmare of the German camps he'd met famine again. The Nazis had no interest in feeding Soviet prisoners. Neither did Russia. Red Cross packages went to the British, the French, but not to Russians. The Soviet Union had never signed the Geneva Convention. He was starving, not in the empty forests, but behind barbed wire with thousands of other desperate men. There was no heat, no clothing, and no news that winter of 1942. But there was something he'd never known before.

In the hell of the camps, deserted by their Motherland, men were free to say whatever they liked.

For night after night in holes they dug in the ground, men coughing to death around him, he'd listened. He never said very much. But gradually he'd grasped what Stalin had done to him, to his family, and to his country. Never once had he said no to the tyrant. Never once had he made a decision for himself.

Then one day the Soviet prisoners of war had been called to attention. Those starving, shambling skeletons who were left. The general had been wearing a strange uniform. Slowly Ivan Krasov had realized it was a Russian uniform, but with Wehrmacht insignia.

General Vlasov had asked for volunteers to join a new unit. A force that would fight against the Soviets. An army of Russians, but not Communists. Fighters for the future of a new Europe, free of Communist-Jewish-capitalist tyranny. Fighters for the future, under the Führer.

Ivan Ivanovich Krasov had been the first to step forward.

―――

The deserted road curved gently left and right, walled by woods. The oaks died away as he left the sea behind, succeeded by scraggly brush, then patches of ten-foot-high pines set close together in rows. The land was flat as the steppe. He passed an abandoned house. Gray weathered shutters, black gaps in its swaybacked roof. Behind it a shed was subsiding into boards around a sturdy-looking chimney of red brick. A harrow lay rusting in the weeds. The trees cut off the wind and he partially unzipped his jacket, his eyes always moving, sweeping the road in front of him, or looking back.

He unfolded the map again, to find that he was walking across the southern extremity of a peninsula that jutted down from Delaware and Maryland. Not counting the marsh he'd just crossed, it was eleven kilometers—no—seven miles wide at the point where they'd put him ashore. On the far side of it was the Chesapeake Bay. The map showed one road running up the backbone of the peninsula. He'd have to make his way north up it, then head west. The road he was on wasn't on the map. If he headed west, though, there was no way he could miss the main highway, or the railroad beside it. The sun, at zenith now, was where his fist would be in the left-handed Communist salute. So he was headed due west.

He looked at his watch, a parkerized Elgin his briefers had issued him in Berlin. Taken, probably, from a downed American flier. He shook it and pressed it to his ear. Nothing. Too much water, too much knocking around. Well, maybe he could sell it or have it fixed.

While he was thinking this he heard the far-off drone of a motor. He stopped, head cocked, then hitched up his pants and went on.

Now the road crunched under his boots, paved with oyster shell. It curved through another stand of pines, past a railing of bolted pipe. Within it worn stones nodded to each other in ancient courtesy. HIGBEE. LEADNER. ASLEEP IN JESUS. Behind it drowsed a white clapboard church.

He walked on, through birches and maples now, then all at once he was surrounded by fields, bare and sere. White shreds lay tangled in the stubble. He realized it was—groped for a moment for the English—cotton. Then, for the first time, he saw people. Tiny figures on the far side of a field, and the leaping red-orange of fire. Smoke stained the sky. Crows racketed up, clattering overhead in a black waver. Telegraph wires sang and buzzed in the wind.

Larger houses now, plain frame houses with steep pitched roofs. They were weatherworn, homely, but each had trees in front and a garden to the side or back. Washing flapped. A hound howled. Woodsmoke streamed blue from the chimneys, and the smell came to him plain on the chill breeze.

He took a deep breath and walked *crunch, crunch* down the center of the road, shifting his grip to his left hand. The gun was hard against his stomach. Ahead was the black-and-white cross and red ruby glass of a railroad crossing. US POST OFFICE, he read above a brick building with slate roof and fretted gables. BIRDSNEST, VIRGINIA. Then, a few feet along, GENERAL STORE.

He touched the gun again, a surreptitious nudge through the leather jacket, and went up the creaking, unpainted steps.

As the door jangled shut the air closed around him like a hot, stifling, doggy-smelling muffler. Three old men stared at him from stick chairs around a coal stove that occupied the center of the room. To the right a woman in shirtsleeves leaned on a counter. Behind her, plank shelves held rows of canned goods, cloth, combs, sundries. A poster showed a villainous Oriental in uniform, bowing. *This Is Join Honorable Ancestor Week,* it read. *Send them on their way with an extra War Bond.*

"Morning," he said through a suddenly dry mouth. "Can I get a sandwich here? Get somethin' to eat?"

"Got some ginger snaps. Or raisins, or—"

"Raisins sounds good. How much are they?"

He got a box for a dime and tore it open and pushed handfuls into his mouth. The sweetness melted on his tongue, and he swallowed hastily and pushed in more. The woman turned away and began sorting screws into pigeonholes. He turned his head to see the oldsters still examining him. Their eyes switched away as he returned their stares. One stretched out his feet, puffing on a short cigar. The smoke eddied around the stove, then disappeared, sucked inside by the draft. Another rattled the pages of a newspaper. The third reached down a hand to a charcoal-gray cat that slipped gracefully and silently out from beneath the curved legs of the stove. The air was very close and he unzipped the jacket a little more, cautiously, because of the gun.

If they suspected him, he'd have to kill them all. Find the cashbox. Then kerosene. They'd sell kerosene here. There'd be no evidence.

He went over to the stove and stood beside it, taking off his cap. The cat came over and sniffed his boots, very delicately and for a long time, working its way from toe to heel. He wolfed more raisins, looking down at it. Did it smell diesel oil, sea, gunpowder, miles of marsh, fear? It looked up at him with immense jade eyes, then turned away and disappeared under the stove.

"Want a look at the paper?"

"Sorry?" The speech was so soft and rapid it was hard for his ear to separate it into words.

"Said, you want a look at the paper?"

"Yeah, thanks." He took it, shook it out, and looked it over. Strange how every language looked different. Russian, with its close-locked rows of thin, graceful Cyrillic. The dense black-letter German. The English looked spaced, oddly convoluted. The headlines were war news. The British and Americans were negotiating through Switzerland for the exchange of 30,000 POWs. A Sir Archibald Sinclair had denied in the House of Commons that Britain was conducting terror bombing. The county Junior Womens Club was packing food, sugar, and soap for Russian War Relief. A shipyard in Newport News was hiring. The rest of the front page was news clips on local boys in uniform.

He turned the pages slowly. Sealtest's March special flavor was Velva-Fruit. Walter Wilson of Cape Charles had been found lying in a pool of blood. A man of means, Wilson had been in the habit of carrying large sums of cash. Lydia Pinkham's Vegetable Compound removed monthly female misery. Brand names stirred faint memories. Oxydol. Duz. Oakite. Ivory. The prices were much higher than he remembered them. Veal roast, 29 cents a pound. Asco Coffee, two pounds for 47 cents. Men's suits were $22.50 and dresses, $8.50 to $19.75. Runaway inflation, he thought.

The editorial page ridiculed a statement by a well-known columnist that the fall of the Reich and Japan would be the signal for immediate disarmament. The editor warned that Soviet actions in Poland made disarmament premature. He read it with a strange mixture of feelings.

The men were talking now, about whether to burn brush or mulch it up and plow it under. Two of them were burners and the other, in a red plaid shirt, said that was a waste.

"Here's your paper back," Krasov said, breaking into the argument. "Say, look. I need some help. I'm off my ship, tryin' to get up home. How can I get up to Washington from here?"

"Wondered where you were from," said the man with the cigar. "Where'd you say's home?"

"Up around Washington."

"You not from Washington."

"No. My girl's up there."

Now all three of them were examining him. He saw their eyes linger on his boots, his jacket. "What'd you come up this way for? Be more convenient, from Norfolk, just take the train up. Leaves right from downtown."

"Guess I made a mistake. Well, how do I—"

"Say you off a ship? What ship?"

He smiled slightly. "I can't tell you that, mister. We're under military contract."

They nodded slowly, approvingly, and he thought, That was the right thing to say. The one in the plaid shirt said, "Well, you want to get you up to Washington, there's a train goes through here twice a day. Pennsylvania Railroad. Then there's a bus—Eastern Shore Transit—that'll cost you a dollar seventy-five up to Salisbury, and you can catch Greyhound from there."

"Love Point Ferry'll take you across t'other side t'bay. Gets you in to Light Street. That's only fifty cent. You come across on the *Pocahontas?*"

He didn't know what that was, so he shrugged. "Can I hitch rides?"

"Can try," said the man with the paper. "Got to be careful, though. Old colored man, he got his self hit a couple weeks ago, walkin' along the road near Eastville."

"Don't Frank and Tom Pete got a truck, goes up to Washington? To the Fish Market there?"

"Say, that's right. Couple of fellas here, mister, they ga' an erster truck 'at goes up 'ere couple times a week. Pooled they gas ration, got them a old Studebaker. They mought could gi' you a lift. Where'd you say you 'er from?"

"I was born near Chicago. Grew up in New York, though."

"Chicago, eh? You one of them gangsters, must be."

He smiled. "That's right. Don't get me mad, I'll pull out a rod, shoot ya all."

The old men laughed, slapping their knees till dust came off. "You want us to check with Frank and 'em? About the truck?"

"When did you say they was going?"

"Think they planning to go up tomorrer, or maybe day after."

"I'll try my luck on the road first. If that don't work out, I'll be back." He hesitated, looking toward the counter. "Can I get a pack of—can I get a pack of cigs?"

"Give 'm a pack of your stoopies, 'Becca," said one of the men. The others laughed. The woman ignored them. "What kind?" she asked him.

"Uh—Pyrgos. Number Ones."

"I'm sorry?" she said, and he knew he'd said something wrong. Didn't know what yet. But she was frowning. He dropped his hand slowly toward his belt.

" 'Pyrgos Number Ones,' he said, 'Becca," said one of the old men, loudly. "I 'member those, but ain't seen them since Lindbergh flew over't th' Atlantic. Where you been getting those, mister?"

"My paw used to smoke 'em," he said. "I didn't know they quit makin' 'em. Well, what've you got?"

All she had was something called Old Bill and one pack of Fleetwoods. He pushed the quarter and his ration book across the counter, watching her closely. Were the books good? Instead she shoved them back. "You don't need those for cigarettes. But I can only let you have one pack."

When he left the old men were talking about plowing brush under. Two of them said it was good, riched up the soil. The other said he believed it was better to burn it.

He stood outside, by the highway. A truck went by, then after a time, another. They were both headed north.

Suddenly an immense eagerness expanded his chest. They'd accepted him. He was safe. Shaken free of the traitor, he could disappear into the teeming millions of the most diverse nation on earth. Indistinguishable. Anonymous. Just like all the rest.

Till it was time to step out of the crowd, and raise the gun.

Smiling faintly, his fair, slightly chubby face bland and innocuous, he stood by the side of the road, thumb extended. Waiting for a ride.

CHAPTER 3

Hollywood, California

The most glamorous woman in the world, sweating through powder makeup, sucked a quick puff off her cigarette, then almost flung it away as she swung her arm out. Flaming red hair glowed in the focused light as she took four quick strides, hit the tape, and wheeled. Her purse clicked open. Then she was holding a letter out, eyes narrowed.

"Oh, really? Just because I don't remember who I am, doesn't mean I'm a fool. What about this? It came this morning."

"The letter. . . . My dear, *look* at it. Read it. Then tell me I'm pulling the wool over your eyes."

She hesitated, then tore it open. The envelope fluttered away. Her eyes scanned down the page, then widened. Rose again, slowly.

"You—my husband?"

"Yes—darling." The dark-haired, handsome man with the perfect white dentures moved forward, made as if to take her in his arms.

"Oh—David. This is all so sudden."

"I don't know if you—I don't think you—" The actor hesitated, then made a wry face. Turned to the darkness. Called, "Sorry. Line, please."

"Cut," came the call from high above. Stepping immediately out of the man's arms, taking the cigarette from her mouth, Lauren Wolfe raised her eyes to the dim recesses above her. Past the staring lenses, the shadowy snarl of cables, lighting, mikes, overhead cranes.

"Incey, this dialogue stinks," she yelled. "Who *wrote* this crap? It's worse than *Bad Girl.*"

"Stand by for take five."

"Wait a goddamn minute. Unless you want to mop the stage, I need a pee break. *Now.*"

"Break," the English voice called reluctantly. "Break on the set. Five minutes."

She waited till he descended, then beckoned him off the set. The director said stonily, looking at her collarbone—she was taller than he was—"You can tell me here, Lauren."

"Okay, here. Look, Incey, we've got to fix this scene. This is not even B dialogue. It sounds like *The Thin Man* rewritten by third-graders. Can't we change it so that she knows what's going on? It would play better, it'd make more sense, deepen the character—"

"Now, Lauren. It's written, it's blocked, it's lit, we can't change everything at this point."

"None of that has to be changed, Incey. Just the *words*. Look, I can do better dialogue than this off the cuff."

"We'll shoot as written." The Englishman nodded icily to her and turned away, shouting, "I want more magenta on Wolfe, and fix her eyebrows, please." She stared after him, started to speak, but was distracted by a wave. It was her personal secretary. "Carla. We're about to resume shooting, what is it?"

"This came in. I figured you'd want me to rush it over."

As the makeup girl erased and re-etched her eyebrows she scanned the package with growing horror. It was a script and a preliminary shooting schedule, with a covering note. *Dear Lauren: Take a look and think about supporting casting, tell Morty if you want anyone special. We'll start two weeks after HEARTS AND HANDS is in the can. Affectionately, LKL.*

"I told that son of a bitch I wouldn't touch this piece of shit with elbow-length gloves!"

"That's why I brought it right over—"

The director pointed a finger. A distant buzzer shrieked in the cavernous space, echoed by shouts. A prop girl ran up, tore the letter from her hand, tucked a fresh, unopened one into her purse, thrust a lit cigarette into her fingers. "Places, please. . . . Scene thirteen, take three. Lighting . . . focus . . . hold it for a still. . . ." A flashbulb detonated, a signal light came on. "Camera." The buzzer cut off, the sound sync card clicked. "Action!"

Feeling sweat run down her ribs, she sucked another quick puff, then swung her arm out. She took four quick swinging steps, hit the tape, then whirled. Her purse clicked open.

"Oh, really? Just because I don't remember who I am, doesn't mean I'm a fool. What about this? It came this morning."

Gable looked her over lazily, insolently. He drawled, "The letter. . . . My dear, *look* at it. Read it. Then tell me I'm pulling the wool over your eyes."

She hesitated, then tore it open. The envelope fluttered away. Her eyes scanned down the page. Then rose again, slowly.

"You—my husband?"

"Yes—darling." He moved forward, reached out to take her in his arms. She could smell his breath. It was horrible.

But instead of falling into his embrace she was backing away. A different expression took her face, resolute, cold. "Hold it right there, Mister Wonderful. I've got something to tell you. Something you need to hear. About your sister, and—"

"Cut. *Cut!*" the English voice bawled angrily.

She spun, hands balled into fists. "Goddamnit, let me *try* it at least!"

"Red, darling, for the last time, you can't rewrite the dialogue while the camera's rolling!"

Gable shrugged and grinned ruefully at her. "Positions, everyone," the director yelled. "Now, if we can get everyone to agree not to try to improve this already very fine script—"

"Oh, bullshit," she shouted, and flicked the cigarette toward him in a fiery arch. Around her people gasped in the cupping darkness. She spun, slammed into a grip, and pushed past, cursing. Past startled technicians at the lighting banks and mixers and engineers at the sound consoles. Past the camera booth and into a long, low tunnel with zigzag concrete walls covered in black felt. She'd always thought that if the Japs did attack, a sound stage would be the safest place in Los Angeles. Three-foot-thick concrete walls. . . . She gestured impatiently and a guard leaped for a switch. Motors hummed, and the two-ton soundproof steel slab rose quietly, admitting the stunning heat and blinding light of a California afternoon. Waiting extras scattered from her path as she strode quickly across the lot, heading for the immense cream-colored office building that rose above Santa Monica Boulevard.

———

VOICE OVER, she thought, seeing it all in her mind, like a script.

LEO LEVINSOHN is a wizened, foreshortened man, like an image in a funhouse mirror. His immense yellow bald head is almost noble, but beneath that and the cigar his body dwindles away like the end of an exclamation point. He'd come to the U.S. before the first war and grown up in Massachusetts, then New York, drove a trolley bus, hustled pool, made a fortune in furs, then lost it; made another in drug stores, but sold out and went West, arriving in Hollywood on the very same day, as he liked to tell people, as Charlie Chaplin. Intending to open another pharmacy chain, but getting sidetracked into another, newer business. . . .

The OFFICE, she thought. Monumental. Twenty-foot ceilings, and the desk on a raised dias, framed by windows that look out and down on the shooting lots and the long warehouse-looking buildings of the sound stages. Marble FLOORS. The circular DESK, not walnut, but more marble. The only marble desk in town. She remembers that when she first joined the studio, a picture of Mussolini used to stand on it. Levinsohn looks up now, noticing her, and flaps his hand at the young WOMAN with him. WOLFE runs her eyes down her, evaluating her face and body professionally; not his secretary, Lisa is fifty and looks like the Wicked Witch of the West; this is what, a new starlet, a script girl, a researcher? She smiles shyly at WOLFE, and leaves, heels tapping across the perfect polished tesserae.

LEVINSOHN: (on telephone) Look, I gotta have this. What do I have to do to get the rights? Oh, you are thinking a trade? There would have to be something on the side. You know what I am talking, maybe forty, fifty? Ha, ha. That is very funny. No, you are paying me the fifty grand.

WOLFE: (shouting) Leo, I've had it.

LEVINSOHN: (waving at her to wait, intense blue eyes flicking up to dwell on her) No, I tell you, my biggest star just walked in and she looks wonderful.

She is working on the biggest picture of her career. She is working on her second
Academy Award. I tell you, Louis, this is not a—
    WOLFE: (*screaming*) Leo!

——

She blinked, controlled herself, pulled a cigarette from her purse and lit it with
quick nervous gestures. She paced quickly back and forth, wheeling at each
turn. This isn't a screenplay, she reminded herself. And no way in hell am I
going to make *House of Women*. This has got to stop.
    Levinsohn said, "Louis, listen, I call you back, all right? I think we might
have the deal, but we will have to straighten out the points. All right. All right.
So long."
    He hung up and smiled down at her. "All right, what is it, sweet? You are
looking simply fantastic today, do you know that?"
    "I look like I've been overworked, then insulted, Leo. I am not taking crap
anymore from that creep Craven."
    "Neville Craven is a very famous director."
    "In England, maybe. Over here he doesn't know his asshole from a
wide-angle lens. Didn't anybody but me read the play? *With Hearts and Hands*
is a serious story, it has a message about the People and how they endure while
everything else passes, and—and he's turning it into some second-rate drawing-
room comedy. This could be your answer to *Grapes of Wrath.* Instead it's going
to be another bomb."
    "I don't know about the People. We make the movies, let's let Western
Union deliver the messages, okay? I have been watching the dailies, and it's not
that bad. You know how I judge a picture—"
    "I know, if your ass starts to itch it's bad, if it doesn't it's good. You told me
before. Okay, it'll be so-so. Like a million other pictures. Great, you're happy
with that. How about this, then. He's a fucking sadist. We did twenty takes on
the scene where Clark gets thrown from the horse. He doesn't like horses
anyway, and he couldn't even walk the next day. He won't allow me a double in
the shots where the roof falls in."
    "No double? Oh, that is not a good idea. What if something happened to
you? That will be corrected." Levinsohn nodded, leaned back, lit his cigar. "You
know you're our most valuable player, Lauren. That's why we have you
co-starred above the title. You know, I kiss the feet of talent. That's why I am
going to call Mr. Craven in and have a heart-to-heart with him about his
treatment of you."
    "That's good, Leo."
    "But in return, I want two things. One, I want you to work with Mr. Craven.
You know, you always complain about your directors. Van Dyke, you called
"One-Take Van Dyke" because he didn't do enough takes, now, Mr. Craven
takes too many? So tell me, how many is enough? Also, I want you to stop the
carping about your scripts. You know what Will Rogers said to me, he said, 'You
know, Mr. Levinsohn, the more I learn about motion pictures, the less I know.'
So maybe you don't know everything yet either."
    "Not enough, Leo. I want to direct."

"Mr. Craven is already engaged."

"You know what I mean! Not this picture. I've been asking you for three years now."

His secretary put her head in, fixing Lauren with a steely glare. "Mr. Levinsohn? Your memo."

"Put it on the desk, Lisa, I'm speaking to Miss Wolfe. Lauren—I will have to think about that. I don't want to throw you away behind the camera just when you are getting such good box office. And it's not so simple to direct. First you have to assist on two, three pictures. I would want to find you the right vehicle, the right writers—"

"That's what you said three years ago! I want a directing package. And I want it now!"

Levinsohn shrugged. He got up and looked out the window. It couldn't be possible, she thought, that he's actually shorter when he gets down out of the chair.

"Listen, Craven, you don't like him, we'll replace him. How about Niblo? How about Cukor? You liked Cukor, didn't you? You see how much I want to make you happy."

She thought about that. The trouble was that as little as she cared for Craven, if RCA replaced him in mid-film it would be the end of his career. She said reluctantly, "No . . ."

"I will if you want me to."

"No."

"Good, so now we are cooling off a little. You have to realize, bubaleh, how much we've spent on making you a star. It takes ten years to make an overnight success. We've got a lot invested in you, you've got a lot invested in us. So you don't like this script, ish kabibble? Next time we'll get you better."

The secretary again. "Mr. Levinsohn, Mr. Cohn's secretary on the line."

"Tell her to hold, I'll be done in a moment—"

Now she was getting angry again. *Next time, we'll get you better.* "Leo—I've seen the next script. I told you, I won't do *House of Women.* I told you that when you sent it over. I don't like the way you keep casting me in these glamor roles—"

"What is the matter with that? You're glamorous. What else am I going to put you in? You can't dance; you're too modern for costumers; you won't do a dog drama. You hate the women's pictures—"

"That schmaltzy crap—"

"So what do you want me to do—"

"Try putting me in serious roles. Leo, the trouble with the glamor is, I won't be able to carry it off forever. You're setting me up for a fall."

"Lauren, dear. This studio, I have always tried to run it as a family. I build careers. We take care of our own, through thick or thin. Look at Marie. Sexy she is not, but she still eats. She still gets parts."

"Bit parts, character parts. Forget it! I don't like being taken care of, Leo. You know, there are more parts a woman can play than sex goddess. But you've got to give me the vehicles."

"House of Women, I spent fifteen thousand for the book, it's a fine book. A tremendous test for an actress. You'll see, it's going to be one of your greatest roles—"

She said in a flat tone, "You're not listening again. I won't do *House of Women,* Leo."

Levinsohn stared down at her from the dias, through the thickening screen of cigar smoke that bit at her always-sensitive eyes. And gradually the china-blue gaze went barricaded, narrow.

"So. Maybe you are right. You won't be keeping your looks forever, Lauren."

"What is *that* supposed to mean?"

"I mean that as friendly advice, like a father to a daughter. I never had a daughter. I always considered you my daughter—"

"Don't give me that father-daughter routine. Was that you being fatherly, when you tore my blouse? If you've got something to say, spit it out."

"All right. It's this way. Not every part is a star part. Not every film is an 'A' film. But Lauren Wolfe *is* under contract to Leo Levinsohn. For three more years. Lauren Wolfe is a property, like a book or a set. She belongs to the studio. That was the deal, a million and a half, three pictures a year. I keep my deals, now you should keep yours—Amy Weilbacher."

It had been so long since she'd used it, or heard it, that for a moment she didn't recognize her own name. It gave her a weird feeling, as if he was talking about someone else. "It's not the money, Leo. It's never been the money."

"Then why did you bring Myron Selznick into it?"

"What, I was supposed to take a thousand a week?"

"It's him, isn't it? Your agent's telling you you're not getting the right parts—"

"No, Leo. It's me. Believe it or not, I'm capable of having a thought of my own."

"You should be careful how you talk to me, Lauren."

"Why? You don't listen anyway—"

"Because one day, you're right, you won't be the glamorous goddess. Men won't look twice at you. One day even the best makeup man will not be able to make you beautiful. That is when we should think about becoming a director. You are far too young."

"I'm thirty-seven, Leo. Almost forty."

He swiveled. "Forty, that's not old."

"It is for a woman. In this business. You know that, Leo."

He didn't answer, and with an effort, she softened her tone. You're an actress, so act, she thought. "Can't you see, we're both talking exactly the same thing? Leo, right now, standing here, I'm a better director than half the conceited pricks you have on the lot. I'm smarter and I know more about pictures, dialogue, I can handle stars, all I need is a top cameraman to hold my hand on the technical end. Give me one picture. Just one! If it's not one of the top ten grossers of 1946, I'll go back to acting. I'll even renegotiate."

"I don't think you're ready, Lauren. And you know, he who eats my bread sings my song."

It was the same thing he'd said in 1942, in this same room. And she knew now that it was what he'd always say, until it was too late. She had to do something or she was doomed. She stood, seeing herself again separately, seeing it all like set directions.

———

ACTRESS: (*standing*) All right, Mr. Levinsohn. I understand what you're saying. I have to do whatever you say. I'm a slave.

STUDIO HEAD: You are too well paid to be a slave. Save the acting for the screen.

ACTRESS: But that's what you've just told me. So . . . you can take your bread and cram it you know where! I'm taking my vacation now.

STUDIO HEAD: What? *What?* In the middle of the picture?

ACTRESS: In the middle of the fucking picture.

STUDIO HEAD: You'd break your contract? Nobody breaks contracts with Leo Levinsohn.

ACTRESS: Watch this.

STUDIO HEAD: Come back here. Come back here right now! You pisher! You bitch! I'll drum you out of this industry! You're through, you'll never make another picture in this town!

CUT TO: DOOR, slamming.

STUDIO HEAD: (*faintly, through door*) You're not quitting. You're on suspension! As of right now, today! And you'll come back, you'll come back crawling, begging . . .

CUT TO: A bottle-green PACKARD convertible charging out the gate.

CUT TO: LAUREN WOLFE, red hair streaming as she turns onto Santa Monica Boulevard.

———

Blinking through angry tears, she pressed the accelerator till the wind rose to a scream in her ears. She went through one red light, then another. Fortunately traffic was light, with gas and tire rationing most people walked or took the bus now. Fortunately, too, no cops saw her. After the second red light she slowed to forty-five.

An unaccustomed sense of freedom warred with fear in her heart. No more Craven! But maybe, too, no more Levinsohn, no more RCA, no more Family. Could he really do that, blackball her? Could this be the end, the long road that had started when she'd stepped out on stage at the Imperial, and everyone had laughed at the tall, gawky redhead with the long skirt, they'd laughed before she ever said her line . . . and after that, Broadway, then thirty-nine feature films, *eighteen years* in movies, Christ. . . . No, she didn't really think it was the end. At the very worst she could go back to Broadway. But he could hurt her, refuse to loan anyone to co-star with her if she went to Paramount or Columbia or Warner Brothers. It had happened before.

But where was she going now? The car was headed east. Good choice, there wasn't anything west of here but the ocean and the War. But where was she going?

A good question, she thought, turning onto Route 66. A damned good question.

Maybe it was time she tried to come up with an answer.

CHAPTER 4

Washington, D.C.

I turned right and headed east on New York, Bubba keeping step. At six o'clock Eastern War Time the sidewalk was crowded with workers pouring out of the government buildings. Buses grumbled past, dirty windows pasted over with the colorless blank faces of typists and yeomen and staff sergeants from the Munitions Building and the shabby War Department temporaries lining the Mall. Past us came clerks, stenographers, secretaries, limping little 4-F civil servants, Negro workers carrying lunch pails. The Transit Authority streetcars, headlights taped over, pivoted past with an earsplitting squeal and a smell of ozone and scorched rubber. A group of whites clustered around a furtive-looking colored boy. "Well, what was the number today?" somebody was asking him as we shoved past. Sailors saluted us, their faces crimped with impersonal resentment.

"What you want to do tonight, Jack?"

"I don't have any plans. Be here, be there, see what happens."

As I said it two girls, swinging along the pavement, smiled at us. Brunettes, with snoods and cloth coats and cotton stockings with sensible shoes. Mackall said, "Evening," but I elbowed him; we could do better. They swayed by, looking disappointed.

"Want to hit a bar?"

"No bars in this town, Bubba."

"What you mean, no bars?"

"It's the law. Got to be sitting down when you drink."

"Christ, who made that one up?"

"FDR."

"How about in there? I see guys drinking in there."

He was looking in the windows of the Willard. "You got a nickel?" I said. Bubba forked over, and the newsboy slipped me the afternoon *Daily News.* War news filled the front page of the thin wartime edition. Mopping up on Iwo Jima. Patton was driving hell for leather into Germany. The Dow Jones industrials had closed at 156.37, down one and a half in moderate trading.

We went into the Willard. The line was out the door, but I caught Dickel's eye. The maitre d' unhooked the red velvet rope and waved us in past the others.

Drew Pearson and Bob Allen were there, two or three senators, and some other newspaper people. Earl Godwin was there, and Daniel Bell, from the Treasury. Loads of admirals and baby-faced Air Corps generals in tailored pinks. Behind us one of the men in line raised his voice; Dickel's was low, soothing. We ordered Pinch, one of my dad's brands.

Mackall said, "So, you never said: What you been doing with yourself, since you got back from the Pacific?"

I looked out the window, at the rainy dark falling on a city that now looked forward to victory, and thought about the last time I'd been there, and everything that had happened since. About the end we could all see coming, and a future that once had been nearly unimaginable. "It seems like, mostly in and out of hospitals, Bubba."

"When'd you get back from the Solomons?"

"January of last year. Stayed in L.A. for a while, saw some people I knew. Stopped by the Mayo Clinic on the way across on the train. Pulled some leave, then went to Melville to teach."

Mackall nodded, tossing back liquor as his eyes searched the room. I didn't go on. I was thinking again—thinking about where '44 had gone.

The PT instructing job had fizzled. I'd finally had to throw in the towel and put in for medical leave. Charlie Houghton, my roommate at Harvard, was PT/DE detailer at BUPERS, so there was no flak about that. But then it was like, when I took the uniform off, there was no John F. Kennedy, Civilian, any-more. Or maybe the old one had gone, and there wasn't any new one there yet.

So in between the medical stuff I'd knocked around. Palm Beach, Hyannis Port, Boston, New York. That was where I ran into John Hersey, at the Stork Club. I was telling him about the 109 incident, and it was him, not me, who brought up the idea of doing a story. I told him to talk to my crew, they were still up at the base. Telling it myself would be too much like something Dad would do. Then I went into the hospital at Boston to have my back looked at.

Finally I called Houghton back and said I was feeling better. At least they'd got me to the point I could walk. He got me orders to Miami, a shakedown unit for deploying PT squadrons. The staff partied a lot. I dated a couple of girls. Nothing heavy. Then my back went out again.

That decided things. In May I'd gone in for the operation, the one they weren't sure would work. Dad set me up at New England Baptist, the best back place in the country. But the damn doc should have read another book before he picked up the saw. They had to strap me down in bed, I had another attack, and my weight went down to 126, 125. Gradually it got better, but I had a hell of a time even walking for about two months after that.

Then in August we got word about Joe. It was a Sunday afternoon at Hyannis Port. Mom was reading the paper; Dad was upstairs taking a nap. We kids were shooting the bull in the living room when a couple of priests knocked at the door. That wasn't so strange, there were always nuns and priests coming by to see Mom or Dad, put the touch on them. So we didn't think much of it till Dad came out on the porch and told us. Missing in action. Presumed dead. And the way they told it, there didn't seem to be much chance of a mistake.

It knocked us all back pretty hard. I guess out of nine kids somebody's got to go first, but we never thought it would be Joe. I remember thinking how it should have been me. Then a month later Billy died, Kick's husband, and she left for England.

I was an outpatient at Chelsea Naval all this time. This fucking back trouble—and there's something else wrong, too. I feel fagged out all the time. I can't drink like I used to. It's not malaria. I can take quinine and atabrine till I'm Jap-yellow but it doesn't dent it. Anyway I was just at loose ends. Did an article for *Life* on the fall storm that wrecked Cape Cod. Worked on a book about Joe, but didn't finish it. Once in a while I'd report in to the base, go down to the pier and watch the new guys slam the boats around.

I guess I just don't know what's going to happen next.

Christmas was miserable. The Bulge scared everybody, the Nazis weren't as close to the end of the string as we thought. We were all sad about Joe, but it hit Dad harder than anyone else. You couldn't laugh around him anymore. He'd turn icy cold and say, "Haven't you got any respect for your dead brother?"

After the holidays I went before the medical board. There wasn't anything else they could say. Shit, if I hadn't lied my ass off they'd never have let me in the service in the first place. I'd be retired on medical disability on March 26.

Next week, in fact. Getting this medal from FDR was in all likelihood my last official act in the Navy. Correction: in the Navy Reserve, as the fucking regulars were always pointing out to us. Then I'd have to decide what to do next.

Which was something everybody around me seemed to know, more than I did myself.

Mackall poked me. "Deep in thought, huh? Hey, you know any of these people?"

"They're just like anybody else, Bubba. No reason to be impressed."

"If you say so. You gonna take that medal off? People are looking at you."

"Let 'em look, fuck 'em."

"Where you want to go tonight?"

I took a deep breath, shaking myself back to 1945. "Oh . . . we can go to the Press Club, or one of the hotels. There's usually something going on at the Hay-Adams. That's a poker-ass crowd, though. Good booze, but if you want to score, forget it. The Statler, or the Shoreham, always something happening there. Later on we can go to some joint, if you're still holding out by then, I mean."

"Whatever you think, Jack. You sure you feel all right?"

"I'm fine," I snapped, and snagged the waiter as he went by. "I can sign for this, right? Okay, let's roll."

As we came out into the dusk something must have disturbed the starlings. All at once they took flight, thousands of them, from the trees along the avenue, a sound like a low explosion. I fought the impulse to duck, and felt Mackall flinch beside me, too. "Damn, it's getting cold out here," he said, sounding angry.

We took a taxi to the Shoreham. I told the girl to take the long way, through Rock Creek Park. We got there at seven-thirty, party-starting time. The elevator operator, a dwarf with a hunchback, told me the best one was in 301. He held his hand out, grinning up at me; I said "Thanks" and shoved past him.

At 301 a very drunk man in black tie opened the door. "Sorry we're late," I said. "Jack Kennedy."

"C'mon in, jus' in time. Jack Kenney, eh? Bar's over there, cigars, help yourself."

The suite reminded me of a powder magazine, it was that full of alcohol fumes. All the oxygen had been sucked out of the air and replaced with cigar smoke and perfume. Lobster salad and smoked salmon paté, cucumber sandwiches on the sideboard. There was no whiskey drought here, no potato liquor or industrial-grade torpedo juice. Three waiters in white tie were mixing and pouring Old Granddad and Dewar's at top speed. A combo was playing swing. The civilians were in tuxes, with little colored pennants in their buttonholes. But there were a lot of uniforms, too. There wasn't a woman there over thirty, and they were all gorgeous. I had the feeling none of them was married, either, at least not to the men in this room. A redhead with a USO button and eyes like Rita Hayworth gave me the once-over. I grinned back, but the man beside her grabbed her elbow and swung her around. Poppa wanted what he was paying for.

Mackall had disappeared for a head call. As I was getting a Pinch and water, no ice, I spotted a gloomy-looking lieutenant commander and drifted over. His medals looked familiar, but he didn't. Dark hair, Bob Hope nose, an air of not belonging here. "How's it going?" I said. "Jack Kennedy, PTs."

"Nick Nixon. I'm in contracts."

"Those are Pacific ribbons."

"Noumea and Bougainville. Supply Corps, no action."

Something about his dour modesty appealed to me. "When were you in Bougainville?"

"January of last year. Then we moved to Green Island. Got back to the States in June. How about you?"

"I was out there in '43, fighting the Tokyo Express in the Slot and Blackett."

Now he was focused in on my medal. It was still around my neck, dangling on the ribbon they presented it with. "Wait a minute. PT boats. You're not—what's his name—"

"That's me," I said. "Glad to meet you. Who's giving this party?"

The two-and-a-half-striper lowered his voice. "It's rubber."

"You crashing too, huh?"

He looked suspicious again. "I don't know what you mean."

"I mean, you don't have any more business here than we do."

"I used to work for OPA, in tire rationing. And I'm doing contract work with them now."

"Who's the colored fella?"

"Name's Bunche, one of Frankfurter's boys. Nelson Rockefeller brought him."

"The Navy's landed, eh?" said a fat man with a red flag pin in his lapel. "Blanchard and Davis made you look sick this year, didn't they?"

"Who's that, sir?"

"West Point, boys, West Point. Don't you—"

Nixon said coldly, "Sorry, sir, we're not Annapolis. Strictly for the duration."

I punched his arm and drifted off, stopping here and there to catch a few sentences and check out the dishes, then moving on. One group was deep in something called SICs and PROs. In the next somebody was telling a rubber joke, a long story about how the War Production Board proposed making condoms only half as long.

"There's not one tire for a B-24 in inventory, not one tire for a medium bomber."

"I don't know, I just can't go for Davis or Stanwyck. For a pure bitch, give me Wolfe."

"And then the farmer says, 'Yeah, sure, but what have you done for me lately?' "

"BUNA-S. Our production in '44 was 92,000 tons. If I can get the alcohol I'll make it 112,000 in 1945."

"The man wanted rubber for diaper liners. Said the ersatz stuff leaks. Nelson gave him two hundred tons on a Schedule 112."

"The postwar period will be unlimited. Nobody's had a new car since '41. Or a new corset—right, Margie?"

"Margie don't need a corset. All she needs around her's my arms."

"Langley sent us a request for bid. It's solid, it's got a fantastic specific impulse, and best of all, the ingredients are natural rubber, aluminum powder, and an oxidant."

Gradually from halfway okay I started to feel uncomfortable. My father said all businessmen are sons of bitches, and these guys looked like the nuts de la nuts. The guys in the dark suits and shoeshines were contractors, lawyers, dollar-a-year-men overseeing war contracts to the same companies they managed in peacetime. The staff officers in their carefully tailored Thomas Saltz uniforms had never seen anything bloodier than a paper cut. One of the tuxes was telling his pals about his hemorrhoid operation.

"The doc wanted an X-ray before he started. So there I was lying on the table, and I said, 'Make it a good likeness, Nurse, so I can send it to that goddamned fool in the White House.' "

They all roared. I moved on, getting mad. We heard jokes about FDR and Eleanor in the front lines. They were funny, but with an undertone of respect. These people sounded like they hated them.

Eddying and moving, touching the drink to my lips, I bumped into the guy who'd asked about West Point. He looked malevolent now, fat and evil. Up close, I saw that the little pennant in his lapel was not a Red flag, but some kind of production award. "Navy again," he said. "But not Annapolis. So what the hell are you?"

"Reserve, Mr.—?"

"Stibner. Goodyear, vice president of sales. What are you doing here, Lieutenant?"

"Isn't this the RKO party?"

"No, it isn't. I know your type. Whenever there's a free drink to be had." He caught my shoulder as I turned away. "Hey! Not through talkin' to you. Going to say, I was the same when I was in the Army. And far as Dick Stibner's concerned, anybody wearing the uniform of the U.S.A.'s welcome here. Drink up, goddamn it!"

He waved some of the others in. One was Hemorrhoid Story, still talking. "Tell you what I heard, she's been sleeping around on him. You know that Youth Congress of hers? It's riddled with Commies, and—well, there's ladies present, right, Margie? Anyway there's a lot of young men ought to be in the front lines, instead they're doing the Eleanor Glide."

"I thought the Russians were our friends," said a petite girl, prettily confused.

"They're our buddies now, doll, but soon as Hitler's down for the count we're gonna be bayonet to bayonet with Uncle Joe." His bloodshot eyes lit on me. "Ain't that right, young fella? What they think about that out in the Fighting Fleet?"

"I'll tell you one thing we don't do in the Fleet, mister, and that's spread disaffecting gossip." The conversation went dead as they swung on me. Suddenly I felt the old shyness. But I plunged on. "And another thing: if I was a spy, I could have picked up anything I wanted tonight. If there was less partying here in Washington, we'd get this war done sooner. And a lot fewer guys would die."

Hemorrhoid turned white. Then, to my surprise, he came back at me. "You know, when I was in France in '18, if some gold-braided son of a bitch told me that, I'd have pissed my pants. But I'm fifty-five, and I'm not in uniform, and I'll tell you something, you smart-aleck jackass, you're full of shit! That Man isn't winning this war. It's American productive capacity, and these are the people" —he waved his glass, almost hitting my face—"the people right here in this room. The ones who produce! The ones who meet goddamn payrolls!"

"You've got an awful short fuse, mister," I said.

" 'Yewve got an awful shaht fewze,' " he mimicked. "Where the hell'd you get an accent like that? Who the hell *are* you, anyway?"

Just then Mackall slid between Hemorrhoid and me. "Jesus, Jack, these people friends of yours?" he muttered. "Don't they know guys are dying on Iwo right now? All they care about's their goddamn rubber."

"Yeah, let's get out of here."

The hallway, away from the noise and smoke, was clear. I wiped my eyes with the back of my hand. The asthma was acting up again. "Shit," I muttered. "That fat prick."

What the hell, I was remembering Joe, too. How he used to referee at the touch games at home. How he used to—well, he was my brother. Of course I loved him.

Now he was dead, drilled into some unnamed field in France, burned so bad

nobody could recognize him. Whose fault was it? My dad said it was FDR's. If
he'd agreed to see Ribbentrop there'd never have been a Blitz. If we'd have
guaranteed their conquests in the East, there'd never have been a war in the
West. Pearl Harbor? From what I'd heard there'd been plenty of warning.
Warnings George Marshall had left sitting on his desk, while he went for his
daily canter on the morning of Sunday, December 7.

"You okay, Jack?" Mackall, big and drunk, bouncing off the walls. Someone
shouted from inside one of the rooms. I grabbed him and hustled him into the
elevator, told the dwarf, "Lobby, Grumpy, and make it snappy."

"Thought we were goin' to that party on six."

"Forget that, we'll go someplace live."

The dwarf still didn't have the gate closed. "I told you to hurry it up," I told
him.

"Up your ass, you cheap son of a bitch." He slammed it.

Outside it was full dark now, and when you looked down the park was
nothing but shadow. Like looking down from the bridge into black ocean, and
you know nothing's there, nothing could be there, but suddenly something is. I
buttoned up my bridge coat. A Diamond pulled in, a junky-looking '38 Ford,
but the only hack in sight. We piled in. "Press Club," I said.

On the thirteenth floor we could hear the bar from halfway down the hall. It got
louder as we got nearer, and it was dim and smoky with two or three hundred
people all having a good time. "This's more like it," Mackall said. "But
goddamnit, I'm out of cash. Can't you get the taxi once in a while?"

"I got the drinks, didn't I? Have you paid for a goddamn drink since you
ran into me?"

"Yeah, but they were free, Jack."

Suddenly I was mad. Without me he'd have been sitting in some dingy
officer's club, knocking back quarter shots of GI booze and listening to "Mairzy
Doats" on the juke box. "Take care of yourself then, you asshole." I broke off
and headed over to where somebody was waving at me.

The Press Club's the kind of crowd where you don't know faces but once
they say their names you know them: radio people, columnists, writers. I like
press people. Arthur Krock had helped me polish up *England.* I knew Bill White
and Henry Luce at *Time,* and Gertrude Algase, my agent, got me work there
before I went into uniform. My sister Kathleen had worked on the *Times-
Herald* for Frank Waldrop. Dad always made a point of introducing us kids to
the reporters when he was at Maritime, and later as ambassador. And people
talk about each other, in journalism there's the incestuous thing, that's how you
get news. A guy gives you a black sheet—a carbon of his story—you take it and
do your own, and the next week you pass him one back. There's an energy. Most
of these guys are educated, not well off, but smart and on the ball.

The pack was out tonight. I saw a glitter of blonde hair and diamonds, a
daring black dress, blue eyes: Clare Luce at a table, slim and glossy, talking with
quick animation to a heavyset beard I didn't recognize. I remembered her
wonderfully cutting remark that every politician had his characteristic gesture:

Hitler, the stiff-armed salute; Churchill, the V sign; Mussolini, the outthrust jaw. Asked what FDR's was, she wet her finger and rotated it in the wind. . . . I saw I. F. Stone, hearing aid clipped to his coat pocket. Then somebody blocked my view. Somebody in a black silk dress and a chest that gave me shooting pains.

"Why, if it isn't Jack! Is it? It is! We've been reading about you!"

"Allie," I said, getting up and taking her hand. "It's good to see a familiar face."

"Dear old Stanford, and dear old Dr. Barclay! We've come a long way from Political Science 201."

The card file in my head, under brunettes, brainy, Protestant, knockouts, West Coast: Alice Fents. We were both rapporteurs for the 1940 sessions of the Institute for World Affairs. In our case it had been not a world-class affair, but a hell of a nice time. We stayed at the old Del Monte Lodge once. She was twenty then, a slightly chubby but attractive kid. Now the baby fat was gone and she was a beauty. "I'm sorry we lost track," I said. "I always hoped I'd run into you again. I'm kind of at loose ends these days—"

"It's the same old grin, isn't it?" Alice said, patting my arm and giving me a knowing smile. "I'm not. At loose ends, that is. I'll always fondly remember, but you can turn off the come-hither wattage. I'm Mrs. Jan Sobelski now."

"The economist? The emigre?"

"He's in the exile government now. And we're very much in love. So—let's just remember a beautiful friendship."

"How's your dad?" I said, recalling now how weird she'd been about her father, an explosives manufacturer. The Nye Committee had raked him over the coals for war profiteering, bribery, and supplying the Army with gas masks that didn't work.

But the jab went right past her. She smiled radiantly and put her arm through mine. "Haven't heard from him in years. I'm independent now, Jack. I make my own way. I'm a working girl now."

"Oh yeah? Who for?"

"For the International News Service. By the way, there's someone I want you to meet."

"Lead on," I said. "As long as my heart's broken, let's offer it some divertissement." Then I stopped laughing.

The massive man with the smooth face and the rumpled gray hair was surrounded by what looked rather like a court. To his right sat a heavy but still striking blonde. To his left a dark-haired, slim, fortyish woman in sable tilted a diamond-studded cigarette holder. Several men shared the table, but they seemed of less account than the three white poodles. As Alice brought me up something moved in the big man's lap. It was a dachshund, whining and growling restlessly. One hand moved continually, stroking it. He looked up at me with chill unwavering blue-gray eyes. "The young Mr. Kennedy," he said softly. His voice was high, almost falsetto. "Please sit down. Alice, where did you find him?"

"He just drifted in, Mr. Hearst. I thought you might like to have a little talk."

"I would indeed, I would indeed."

I said, "Good evening, Mr. Hearst. Mrs. Patterson. Miss Davies."

"Good evening, Mr. Kennedy," Cissy said. She sipped smoke from the holder and stared at me.

I folded myself into a chair. The blonde was Marion Davies. The big man had spent seven million dollars to make her America's Darling, and failed. The dark-haired woman was Cissy Patterson, multimillionaire heiress and editor of his Washington paper, the *Times-Herald.*

"W. R., remember what you were talking about before, with Mr. Hunter?"

"Yes, I remember," said Hearst. He was still studying me.

I didn't know what the attitude was here. I knew Hearst, of course. One out of every four Americans read a Hearst paper every day. He'd been dabbling in Hollywood at about the same time Dad had.

But mostly I was remembering the politics. Hearst was a Democrat, at least considered himself one. Once he'd had presidential ambitions, but he hated Al Smith so much that in 1928 he'd thrown his papers behind Hoover. Hearst had boomed Garner in '32, and achieved the near-miracle of winning California, divided between Smith and Roosevelt, for Garner, a Texan and almost an unknown. But Smith was still strong in '32, and when Garner lagged during the convention, Dad had called Hearst and asked for his support. The old man had chosen the next president with one phone call, swinging Texas and California to FDR. But he'd turned against what he called the Raw Deal. What I didn't know was his attitude toward the Kennedy family. I decided to break the ice. "I often think of that weekend at Wyntoon, sir. Thanks for the invitation."

"I was glad to meet you, Jack. What did you think of the place? You never said, as I remember."

"It's absolutely fantastic, Mr. Hearst. Virgin forest, and in the middle of it—castles."

He smiled, but Patterson kept her hooded glance on me. Hearst said, "I'm glad your father called, let me know you were up at Stanford. What are you doing now?"

I explained about the back injury and my limited duty status. He interrupted to ask about the medal. When I mentioned the President a shadow passed over his face. "You saw him? This morning? Just between us, what do you think of his health?"

"I can't say, sir. He's lost a lot of weight." I tried to joke him up a little. "Actually, I can't throw any stones. I'm down about thirty pounds myself."

Mrs. Patterson said, "I'd like to have the son of a bitch's head on a bloody pike. He's a filthy, plotting, lying traitor. Do you know, he doesn't even have polio?"

"He doesn't?" I said.

"No. It's actually the last stages of syphilitic paresis. The worst part of it is, down in that place in Georgia, he swims with innocent little children, exposing them to his loathsome disease."

"Down, Cissy," said Hearst, patting her wrist with his free hand. The other stroked the dog, over and over. "It's true, he lied us into the war; but we're in it now, and we must win. It's afterward we must plan for. You know we came out for the GOP last year, Jack."

"Yes sir."

"I hated to, but there comes a time in every man's life when he must place principle above loyalty. *That man* abandoned me long before I renounced him. What about you? You're not a Roosevelt man anymore, are you?"

"No sir. Not after what he did to my father."

"He's a shallow, tricky charlatan, and it's only a few people, like myself, who've prevented him from becoming a dictator. If he doesn't finish out this term, we'll have Truman. A small-time chiseler with his own wife on the Senate payroll. We don't need a guttersnipe like that in the White House."

"All I can say, sir, is he seemed to be in control up there this afternoon."

Hearst petted the dog thoughtfully. "Jack, I'm glad Alice brought you over. I've been doing some thinking. The Japs may hold out into '46, '47. But newsprint restrictions are going to let up as soon as Hitler throws in the towel. The Organization will be expanding again. I'm going to need some bright young people."

"Are you thinking the *Times-Herald,* sir?" I said, glancing at Cissy. Her smile was edged, like broken glass.

"No. I'll let you in on a little secret. The Hearst Organization is going to publish the first worldwide newspaper. I'm not sure yet what I'll call it. I'll need editors who can travel, study a country, get inside the situation as it affects us here at home. The kind of thing you did with your book. You've got the education and the social connections. You've got the GI touch too. But if you'd prefer the publishing end, rather than the writing . . ."

I thought about it. Hearst had money. He had clout. Almost single-handedly, the aging man in front of me had taken the country into war with Spain in '98. His papers paid the best salaries in the business. On the other hand, they were shrill and sensationalist, and there were those who said they were pro-German. "It sounds good," I said at last.

"You don't need to decide now. But I'd hate to see a man of your ability get sucked into Luce's little empire, for example. If you have an offer from them, I hope you'll give me a chance to match it. Will you promise me that?"

"I'm not in a position to make any promises right now, Mr. Hearst. I'm still in the Navy."

"For how much longer?"

I grinned the boyish grin and just sat there. After a moment he smiled too, and made a little gesture with his hand. I stood, bowed to the ladies—and caught my breath. "Are you all right?" said Miss Davies, looking concerned.

"Just a little twinge," I said, but I could hear my back teeth grinding together.

Somehow I got vertical again and staggered off. God, it was going out again. Sweat prickled on my face. I had my hands to my back, looking desperately across the sea of faces. Looking for Alice, but she must have slipped off while I was talking to Hearst. Hell with her, I had to lie down. "Christ," I muttered, to keep from screaming. Back into the little attached kitchen. A butcher-block work table, fortunately scrubbed clean. I crawled up on it. The twisting knives stabbed again as I pressed my spine into the hard wood.

When I went out again, half an hour later, Mackall was talking earnestly to a honey blonde in a tight sweater. She looked skeptical but interested. He grabbed me as I edged by. "Hey, Shafty, want you to meet somebody. Joan Fair. She's press relations at OPM."

"Hi," I said. "Jack Kennedy."

"Is this drooling wolf really in the Marines, Jack?"

"Believe it or not," I said. "Bubba, come over here."

"Funny as hell," said Mackall when I got him a few feet away. "Man, don't she just fill that sweater?"

"A regular Lana Turner. Look, I'm going to move on, Bubba. You game?"

He glanced back. She lifted her eyebrows, cocking her cigarette. "Uh, I don't think so. I'm feelin' lucky—"

"Say no more."

"She's probably got a friend—"

"Forget it," I said. "Catch you around, Bubba. Have a good war."

——

It was almost midnight now, and cold as a brass baboon's balls. No taxis, either. I walked east, snugging up the coat and wishing I had a sweater too, or a watch cap. The Navy combination cap doesn't do a thing to keep your ears warm. There were four or five cold, dark blocks, the naked trees getting fewer and then vanishing, the street getting more littered. Then light and sound grew again, and I was in Northeast.

The last shows were letting out. I stopped in front of the Gayety and checked out the posters. Margie Hart, Hinda Wassau, Ann Corio were the strippers, and some comics I didn't recognize. Enlisted men were streaming out, a shutter falling across their eyes as they saw me.

On the curb a boy was crying the last edition of the *Star*. I stuck a copy under my arm and strolled. Past greasy spoons, tattoo parlors, juke joints. A haze floated above the asphalt, a murk of cigarette smoke, exhaled breath, exhaust, dust, gunsmoke, unspent lust. The flat crack of .22s pumped from shooting galleries. The dance joints were going strong, jitterbug blasting out into the street and echoing off snorting late-night buses disgorging soldiers from nearby bases. MPs and Shore Patrol stood on the corner of Ninth and H, swinging their nightsticks, then straightening as they registered my approach.

At Twelfth and H a neon sign buzzed the outline of a running horse and a martini glass. I climbed a narrow stairway and said to a very large black man, "Any seats left? I don't want to stand up."

He said to go on up and find my own seat. I climbed slowly up another floor, into a noisy, smoky, delirious crowd of sailors and girls, soldiers, marines, and mingled with them, though not at the same tables, the colored, whose club the Pimlico had been before the war and would be after it. I shoved my cap back and looked for a table. The only open one was too close to the band. It was littered with half-killed drinks and smoking ashtrays.

"Ladeez and gentlemens—it's the king of swing, the duke of blues, jazz, and jumpin' jive, back in Washington, Dee Cee—the incomparable Louis 'Satchmo' Armstrong." A rotund Negro with dark glasses lifted a trumpet and started firing riffs at the ceiling, invisible through the smoke and glare of the spots. The rest of the band straggled in, picked up sax, drums, and bass, and launched into "The Muskrat Ramble." I took one hit of "scotch" and set it back down. It tasted like rainwater.

"Hey, Admiral, that's our table." Three soldiers came out of the smoke on canes and crutches. I bullshitted them, but they wanted their chairs back. I spotted some folding ones behind the band. When I started carrying one away the dogfaces waved me back, shoving theirs around to make room.

They were out of the same hospital, taking liberty together—weekend pass, they called it. "Where you fellas from?" I asked them. When men in uniform asked each other that it didn't mean their home state. One of the boys had got it in New Guinea, the other in Leyte. The one on crutches had lost his toes in the Aleutians. They were at a VA hospital in northern Maryland.

"They treat you okay there?"

They shrugged. "What you doing back, Admiral? Or ain't you been out yet?"

"Two bars is a lieutenant in the Navy. I'm in the same boat you guys are."

"What, you wounded?"

"Yeah. My back."

They hitched their chairs closer. The one without the crutches, a long lean guy who kept the left side of his face to me, said, "That's right, you got the Heart. Where'd you cop that?"

I told them Guadalcanal, and told them about 109. "You might have seen it in *Reader's Digest,*" I said.

"Naw, we don't get to read much on the ward. They got pigs and drawing classes and shit. We cut out model airplanes for recognition kits. It's pretty okay, all the milk you can drink. How was it in the Canal?"

"Shitty. Malaria, blackwater. No water half the time."

"Sounds like the Kokoda Trail. This Nip destroyer, he ran you down, huh? What, you were slower than him?"

"Not exactly. He came out of the dark on me."

"Then what? You shoot at him?"

"Tried to, but he was inside my torpedo range before I could get the bow around."

The long lean guy said, "I got mine from a sniper at the Nadzab drop. The bullet went in here." He put his finger just below his cheekbone, on the puckered area I noticed now just below his eye.

"That doesn't look too bad."

"—And it come out here."

The others watched me as he turned his head. The other side of his face was a blank, corrugated mass of pinkish-red scar tissue from forehead to the twisted cut of mouth. It didn't look human.

"The bone's gone. That's why it's lumpy. By the time they got me packed out the gas gangrene was going strong. I wouldn't have made it except for penicillin. You know what I was thinkin', they were carrying me back? X-ray specs."

"What?"

"The kind in the back of the Superman comics. See through walls. See through clothes. I never had nineteen cents to order a pair. That's what I was thinking, they were carrying me back on the litter. That I never got to look through a pair of those X-ray specs."

"You were lucky."

"It ain't luck, brother. I'll tell you one goddamn thing it taught me. They already got us written for dead. Me, you, the fucking Nip bastard that shot me—" He waved his bottle and I realized he was drunker than I'd thought. "Talk about the Forgotten Man, that's me, cousin. My pop died in the mines. I grew up in the fucking CCC. Then infantry, a dollar eighty-seven a day. I just hope after it's all over they fix it up so us poor fucking bastards don't have to fight no more. That's all I want out of it."

I asked them to save my chair and went looking for the head.

When I came out a group of Army were standing in the entrance looking around. Tailored, crisp, summer-weight uniforms. To my surprise, I recognized Alan Ladd and Ron Reagan, but I didn't know the short guy with the silver leaves of a lieutenant colonel.

Suddenly I was glad Alice had given me the brush. Standing with them, holding her coat demurely, was a woman in WAVE blues. She had a little tilted nose, pale blonde hair in a french braid, deep-set blue eyes and a bee-stung mouth whose corners slowly curved as she looked me over. She made me think of the starlets my dad was always "having dinner" with when we visited him in L.A.

"God," I said. It never hurts to let them know they impress you.

"Hi, sailor. New in town?"

I said hi to Ladd and Reagan. Alan said, "Jack, the lady's with me, but I'm going to take a risk and introduce you anyway. This is Taney Royce, official heartthrob of the U.S. Navy. Taney, Jack Kennedy; his dad used to own FBO, KAO, Pathe, RKO, United Artists?"

"He made a few pictures out there, before talkies. Hi."

"And this is Colonel Jack Warner, Jack Kennedy; Ron Reagan, Jack Kennedy."

Warner looked me up and down without friendliness, but didn't say anything. "I'm sorry, gentlemens," said the small colored man appearing at his elbow. "We just are full up. If you want to wait here a few minutes, I'll find you a place."

I said, "I've got a table, over by the band. Come on, we'll all wedge in somehow."

Ladd and Reagan waved to the troops as I led them over. But when I got there the little Negro was ahead of us, motioning the dogfaces up with his hand. "This table's reserved, gentlemens."

The boy without the toes leaned back and put his palms flat on his own chest. "Hell it is, boy. We been sittin' here since eight."

The Negro glanced around, eyes white in the glare of the spots. Sweat spitshined his skin. "Come on, Mr. Soldier. Just askin' you nice to move your ass out of them chairs."

"Just move over, fellas," I said. "Look who I brought you—"

But they weren't listening. "What'd you say, nigger?"

"Said to get your ass out, before I—"

The crutch caught him with a crack that whipped every head in the room around. It sounded good, but the next thing that happened was that the big boy, the bouncer, was jerking Aleutians out of his chair and breaking the other crutch over his knee. Then he went for Arkansas, and the two other boys were on him, and guys in olive drab were standing up, and then the guys in blues too. I hung back, content to let the able-bodied have at it, but then I noticed an ominous silence in the rest of the club. I turned my head, and saw the dark tide a second before it hit.

It was real confused for a couple of minutes there. I got a couple punches in, not sure who they hit. Then I caught a glimpse of blonde. I dove for it, found her hand, and pulled her toward the door.

We were almost there when the lights went off, plunging us into blackness. But only for a moment. Then they came on again, spotlighting a huge American flag. I saw the blades of a fan begin to turn. The flag began to ripple, and then over the clatter and shouts came the superamplified opening bars of the national anthem. The battling men hesitated, then turned, dropping their fists. Their arms came up in unwilling salute.

———

"What are we doing out here?" she said. We were walking fast north on Twelfth, I was pulling her by the hand. Her hair waved around her face, and her lipstick was smeared. She looked great.

"In five minutes the MPs are going to be hauling butt around that corner."

"So what?"

"So in case you didn't notice, both of us are in uniform. Some marine from Camp LeJeune, he doesn't care who we are. I don't want to spend the night in the brig."

"I see your point," she said. She had a funny, slightly goo-goo smile that reminded me of Lucille Ball. "What about Alan, and the others?"

"I can't rescue everybody."

"So you picked me."

"You looked like you needed it most."

"What was your name again?"

I told her. We got around the corner and found a cafe, and did a Hopper imitation sitting by the window.

Turned out she was from Hartford and had gone to Radcliffe. Graduated from nurses' school in 1943 and volunteered for the Nurse Corps. She was attached to the War Department, doing physicals for overaged retreads. "It's a contribution," she said. "I keep putting in for the Pacific. Maybe I'll get there in time."

"So you work at Main Navy, you live—?"

She shared an apartment with another girl near Logan Circle. Bingo, I thought. I kept asking her about herself, boring in. It was late enough that when we left there, we were either going to her place or we weren't going anywhere.

We were on our second cup of coffee when I noticed two men in overcoats across the street. I didn't pay much attention till two more joined them. They all looked alike, in dark wool coats, gray felt hats. White smoke drifted from their mouths, but they weren't smoking. A black limo with curtained windows stood at the curb.

"What are you looking at?"

"That Chrysler," I said. As I said it two more cars pulled up, plain four-door sedans with dimmed lights.

Sirens began to wail on the next street over. The doors of all the cars slammed open suddenly and lots more men spilled out, taking positions at the doors of what I now saw was the back of a building that fronted on H.

"Let's go out and watch," I said. "It's some kind of raid. Spies, maybe."

"Now this is worth staying up for," she said.

We stood on the mist-slicked pavement, leaning against the window of the United Cigar Store, and watched five squad cars roll up, one after the other. The men in overcoats backed away from the doors, still facing them. Lights came on, focused on the doors in the alley.

They sprang open suddenly, and men began spilling out. Some were in suits and ties, others in shirtsleeves, hastily pulling on jackets. There were uniforms, too. One sailor was still carrying a bottle. His white, frightened face stared into the sudden brightness, and the bottle dropped and burst. The cops moved in, and for a moment they were hidden from sight. Shouts and a single thin scream rose above the scuffle of leather on concrete and the murmur of idling engines.

One of the D.C. cops came our way, shielding a flame as he lit a short cigar. He had a sour look, as if he'd just stepped in dogshit. "Gambling?" I asked him.

"Vice."

"Cat house?"

"We thought," he said, glancing at my uniform. "But Detective Sergeant Blick looks like to be wrong."

Passersby were gathering. "So what is it?" I said, but he didn't answer. Just puffed his cigar and cut his eyes to where the lights lit everything like a movie set. I saw men being handcuffed, shoved along, half pushed, half hoisted into the Black Marias. Still there were no women. Suddenly I understood. One guy was struggling against the cuffs, shouting something; the cops were shoving him up, their faces disgusted. He had a pencil-thin moustache, like Ronald Colman.

"I know one of those guys," I said.

"Maybe not as well as you thought," the copper said.

"There's some important people being shoved into that van," I said to Taney. "I wonder if—"

"Oh, look over there. Isn't that Hoover?"

On our side of the street, a short, stocky man in a long black coat and light colored hat watched the roundup in silence, hands in his pockets. A taller man stood with him, dressed to match. The head G-man was scowling.

I shook off Taney's arm and crossed the street. As I got in reaching range of

Hoover the other stepped forward, blocking me. I knew this jut-jawed, long-faced guy. "What do you want?" Clyde Tolson grated.

"I need to tell Mr. Hoover something."

"Tell me."

"I don't know what's going on over there," I said, speaking not to him but to Hoover, behind him, who was scowling at me now. "But you've just arrested one of the President's Secret Service men."

Tolson glanced back at his boss, but Hoover's face didn't change. Tolson growled to me, "Then he'll have to take his medicine. We don't want queers that close to the President, anyway."

"Is that what they are?"

"That's right, swabbie, it's a fag raid."

"You better go back to your dame, Lieutenant," said Hoover, behind him.

"You've got a prominent congressman there too. I just wanted to let you know—"

Tolson snarled, "Shut your trap, you Mick pansy-lover, or we'll take you in too."

I stepped back as another truck snorted up, men dropping off the running boards. Two ran over to Hoover. One carried a shotgun, the other a big black Speed Graphic. Hoover took the shotgun and he and Tolson began walking toward the van. The photog trailed them, fitting a bulb into his flash.

When I got back to her Taney was looking anxious, rubbing her hands together. "Is that him?" she said. "I've only seen him in the papers. Did you tell him?"

"It didn't make much of an impression."

"I'm cold. Aren't you cold? Maybe we ought to think about calling it a night."

She was right. It was starting to rain. The water glittered in her hair. Around us the spectators muttered as more men stumbled and swayed and limped from the alley, hats shielding their faces, eyes downcast. Some of them clung to each other.

Suddenly one broke free. A middle-aged man, desperate-eyed, lunged unexpectedly between two inattentive blue-suits and was in the open, like a tailback who to his surprise has just caught a long bomb. He ran clumsily, shoes clattering. A pair of G-men sprinted after him. They gained quickly, then one stretched his body in a flying tackle.

The runner slammed down, face hitting the curb at our feet. I heard the snap of breaking tooth and bone, and a toupee flew off, rolling to rest in the gutter like a run-over squirrel. The other agent threw himself on the man's back, pulled back unresisting wrists, snapped on steel bracelets. His face was a mask of blood as they pulled him upright. His shoes dragged as they hauled him toward the vans.

"Fuckin' queers," a man said, loud, behind us. "Lookit Hoover over there, putting the cuffs on 'em himself. He's got the right idea. Ought to put 'em all in camps, like Hitler does."

"I'd better take you home," I said to Taney, and she nodded. Thoughtfully, we watched the Black Marias pull away.

CHAPTER 5

Virginia

The one-armed man stood at the end of the road, head thrown back, eyelids drooping nearly closed. Between the unfocused haze of his lashes the bay sparkled in the setting sun. Lingering in his ear was the liquid plash of waves, the wind's exhaling sigh. As it passed the grass swayed and bent, whispering stem against stem like a hushed crowd before a speech. A hawk rose from the far side of the creek.

Hans Dieter Heudeber blinked out at it through tired eyes. Nature unadorned, unchanged, unconcerned with Man and his bloody doings.

Unconcerned with war . . .

For a moment he stopped breathing. In that moment the moving shimmer became the glitter of a thousand polished bayonets passing in review, jostling and blazing above undulating waves of goose-stepping young men.

Became the flashes of machine-gun fire in the freezing, snow-shrouded darkness of a night on the steppe.

Became the white, pale flutter of hands. They tried to cover nakedness; reached out, as if palms could ward off bullets; lifted to the sky in supplication. Before this tongue, this mobile flap of flesh that lived in his own mouth, had told the sergeant to fire.

Became, in his mind, the blaze of a hundred parachute flares falling over the black ruin that had once been Berlin.

He blinked, and his mind emptied of memory. The dancing light became again merely a shimmer of sun on the wind-rippled green water of a narrow, mud-bordered tidal creek; and far off, beneath the dropping bloody ball, the broad, dark charcoal-line of the open Chesapeake.

Heudeber, staying in cover and moving more cautiously than the man he'd struggled with in the night, had taken till that afternoon to leave the marsh. He was older, too, and had to stop occasionally. Battling the desire to sleep, he'd trudged up onto firm ground at last in the midst of a patch of woods. He heard dogs barking far off, but angled away from them. Dogs meant farms, homes, people. They also meant something existed to be guarded against. He had never been in America before, but he'd read Karl May's Indian tales and Fenimore Cooper. . . . Were there mountain lions in these woods? Wolves? Wishing he still had his pistol, he passed through a broad belt of silent forest, pines and maples and oaks, before coming out at last on a paved two-lane road.

He waited in the shadows till the hum of motors faded. Then crossed the road hastily, when no cars were in sight.

He'd thought it all over during the night. Pondered it during his rest breaks, when his weakened body sagged to the mucky ground. And come to some conclusions.

First: he'd made a serious mistake, one no military man should make. He'd underestimated his enemy. The Slavs were a suspicious race. That suspicion had served Goebbel's tame Russian well.

I failed, Heudeber thought, rubbing his mouth slowly. But perhaps not beyond repair. He hoped it was not beyond repair. Krasov had to be stopped.

Heudeber thought, I've got to stop him.

The problem was that now he was at a disadvantage. It wasn't just that he was forty years old, handicapped, and tired of war. This was an objective problem.

In the overt plan—the one his SS superior, Adolf Eichmann, had presented to Reichsminister Goebbels in their midnight meeting in the Reichskanzlerei— Heudeber and Krasov were a balanced team. The English-speaking German and the American-born Russian. The Hauptsturmführer-SS, with the money and the ideological trustworthiness that went with the double lightning-flashes. Krasov, with the technical skills, the ability to speak the language like a native, and the resourcefulness and determination the last part of their mission would demand.

The veteran of the SD—the intelligence arm of the SS—and the willing collaborator provided by General Vlasov at the request of the clubfooted little Minister of Propaganda.

The trouble was, now that Krasov had evaded the bullet that would have ended his mission, Heudeber had to stop him on his own. And on his own, he was vulnerable. His English was schoolbook, with a British intonation. At Stalag 10B, the camp he'd commanded after losing his arm, he'd honed it with hours of conversation with captured American pilots. But to an American ear it would still carry European overtones. He might get by with a few muttered words in passing. But in any extended conversation, sooner or later he'd give himself away.

Balanced against that, of course, was what lined the bottom of his suitcase. The Americans were a mongrelized, Jew-dominated race. They had no principles. Anything could be bought. Their own films made that abundantly plain.

Maybe, Heudeber thought, we're still evenly matched after all. But our strategies must be different. The Russian will seek to submerge himself, to become part of the mass. While I must isolate myself. Avoid contact if possible.

How then to make his way to the target? How to intercept and frustrate, and if possible, destroy Krasov—or whatever name he would take on return to what was in effect his native land? He'd pondered this as he trudged through the sandy, needled silence of the forest.

And after a while, he had his answer.

On the far side of the road he turned north and paralleled it, moving through the trees, maintaining cover. The maples and oaks reminded him of Hungary. A mile farther on he came to what he wanted: a marl road, leading west. This might lead to what he hoped for. Or he might have to try the next one. Sooner or later, though, he'd find what he needed.

Now he stood where the road ended, in a wheel-rutted trail in the midst of sunlight and the cries of wheeling gulls. He lowered his eyes and ran them along the length of the boat.

It rolled slowly in the groundswell, rubbing against the splintered wood of a rickety-looking pier with faint poignant squeals. It was ten or twelve meters long, built of curved planks, low and beamy. The counter was lettered ELLA EYRE, ONANCOCK. Beneath the name the white paint was dirty and flaking. Four-fifths of it was open deck, a shallow well with a wood-enclosed box on the centerline. An engine; the sooty pipe sticking straight up told him that. A small deckhouse was crowded into the bow, with a low door from the open deck. He strolled forward a few feet, looking down. No antennas; good. Then he saw something else.

A shotgun was wedged in against the wheelhouse, propped in the corner by the door.

He leaned, catching a stench of bleach, fuel, and rotting clams. The water moved between hull and pier, and he saw tiny fish milling and roiling, sparkling as each turned its belly to the sun. He glanced up the road, toward where mounds of blanched shells were heaped higher than his head.

"He'p you there, mister?"

He snapped his head around.

The man must have come out of the wheelhouse, but Heudeber hadn't seen him in there. He stood now dumping dirty water over the side from an enameled basin. His white hair spun in a thinning cyclone from under a black wool cap. From under turned-back cuffs emerged wrists as thick and solid as Heudeber's ankles, circled with tattooed chains. A star was tattooed on the web of each thumb. His hands were like padded, sea-worn grappling irons. Deep blue, age-bruised eyes peered up around an immense hooked nose.

"He'p you, there?" the American said again. Heudeber lifted his head suddenly. "Oh. Sorry, I mean—Reverend."

"It is a fine boat you have," he said.

The fisherman lifted his head, eyes going intent on Heudeber's face. For an instant he thought the old man knew. Then the gaze dulled. "Thanks, Reverend. Gettin' hard to keep 'er running. No parts since the war started. No nails, no copper, no glue, no gaskets."

"May I look?"

The old man cast a dubious eye along the deck. "Well—sure, if you want.

Step down there." Just then Heudeber saw him notice the missing arm. He was used to that. You could see people register it, see them trying to decide how to act now. "Step down careful," was what this man added.

He jumped down cautiously, aiming his boots for a worn coil of rope, breaking his drop with his good arm. He left the suitcase on the pier. When he straightened he found himself towering over the old man. He looked along the deck. Worn oil-soaked boards, bent iron hooks and tongs, rubber boots and oilcans and engine parts were jumbled together under the gunwales.

"What sort of fish is it you catch?"

"Fish? Don't do much fishing. Oysterin' when I can, and crabbing when I can't. Shoot a duck, oncet in a while get me a goose for dinner."

"The oystering, it is good?"

"Can't complain. Just offloaded twenty boxes. Found a bed of three-inchers, deep-dish, just like a cup." The old man spat over the side, then peered up again, eyes slitted against the sky-glare. Then he was holding out his hand. "M'name's Davitt Austin."

"My name's Gunther. Hank Gunther."

"Rever'nd Gunther. You one of them weekend artists?"

"An artist?"

"Can't think what else you're doing down here."

He half-smiled, envisioning the colors Van Gogh would have found to etch this muddy verge, the ramshackle, zigzag pier, this workaday craft. The Paris-period style of *Sand-Boat Unloading.* He lowered his voice, speaking into a weathered ear. "I wish I were here to draw, Mr. Austin. But I need to go across the bay. I can pay. Will you take me?"

The old man didn't answer. Heudeber waited, then touched his arm.

Austin started, turned to face him. "D'you say somethin'? Sorry, I'm mostly deaf. Can understand if I'm looking at you, at your mouth. I can read yours good, not like those that chews their words up. But if I ain't, you can shout your head off and I'll go right along, I guess. . . . What was it you wanted?"

"I said, how far can you—can you travel in this boat?"

"What, this'n? About anywheres I like. Full tanks, I can go over't the James, or up to Kent Island. Down to Portsmouth, or—well, like I say, most anywheres I want to go."

Heudeber didn't know where those places were, or how far away. "Can you go to Washington?"

"Washin'ton? I guess I could get there, if it didn't kick up too much."

He didn't understand what that meant, but it sounded right. By his map, directly across the bay and up the Potomac to the capital was less than two hundred kilometers. A boat like this wouldn't go very fast, but even at ten or fifteen kilometers an hour, he'd be there in a day or two. Most likely, well ahead of a man traveling by land. Without money, the Russian's progress would be slow—riding boxcars, begging for lifts.

Best of all, traveling by water he'd have to deal with only one man.

"Say, where do you preach, Reverend? Don't believe I've heard of you, unless you're that new fella they've got up to Nassawadox."

Heudeber looked back up the road, then out over the water. The only witness was a blue heron, dipping low over the wind-roiled surface of the creek. It disappeared into a stand of trees, and a moment later a harsh screech echoed around the inlet, eerily unlocatable. He strolled casually toward the deckhouse. The old man lingered by the stern, frowning now. Fingering a bar of iron that stuck up from the engine.

Heudeber laid the packet of bills on the engine cowling. Then waited till the old man's eyes moved from it to his face.

"I want you to take me to Washington."

"What's that? To Washington? Who are you, mister?"

"That doesn't matter. You can take me there. Not so? You have enough fuel?"

"Should be near enough, but, look, I don't know nothin' about you. Who the—hell, you ain't no minister!" The old man started to his feet. "Who the hell are you, anyway?"

Then he stopped, looking at his own shotgun. Heudeber took a step back, thumbing the hammer on the single barrel back to cock. He motioned with it to the engine. "You would not do it for money. That is too bad. Now you will do it as an order."

"Grampaw?"

The little boy stood in the wheelhouse door, knuckling sleep out of his eyes. He saw Heudeber, and his mouth opened comically and his eyes grew wide. "Grampaw!"

"Come, quickly, start the engine," Heudeber said, jerking his eyes back to the old man. He put more anger into his voice. "Quickly!"

Austin recollected himself. Keeping an eye on Heudeber, he edged forward and flipped a line off the pier. Coming back along the side, turning to slide by, he muttered, "Let me put the boy ashore. Then I'll take you wherever you want. All right?"

For a moment he was tempted. The boy looked like a German child, with his blue eyes and sandy hair. Like his brother, the one who'd died in 1919 when, weakened by starvation and cold, so many fell from influenza. Then he steeled himself. Mercy was weakness. Whatever his racial stock, the child was an enemy, and old enough to tell what he'd seen.

Children, in tumbled rows, and the line of men standing over them. It had to be done. To assure the future of the Reich, the future of Germany.

There are those who do not choose to say only, "I believe." There are also those who also say, "I will fight."

Once he'd believed those words. Obeyed orders. How many children had he killed already? Too many. He was tired. . . . He could not let himself think of this. Not now. Lifting his chin, he motioned again with the barrel. "No. He stays. To ensure your cooperation. Now start the engine."

"God damn you," said Austin.

When the motor caught the stack blatted soot and sound into the quiet creek, a shattering racket that drove Heudeber back a step. No wonder the waterman was deaf. There was no muffler on the metal pipe. Glancing at him, the old man cast off the last line, shoved the stern away from the pier, and shuffled forward to a wooden post. He grasped an iron bar, eased it in, and the boat began moving forward, toward the open bay.

Heudeber motioned the little boy back beside Austin. He went slowly, his eyes wide.

He went into the deckhouse and looked around, keeping an eye on the old sailor through the open door. He pulled out drawers, checking for guns or knives, but found nothing threatening. He made sure there was no radio. There weren't any charts either. Austin must know these waters well. But an antique compass was bolted to the low overhead. So, he could keep the old man on a proper course. All he had to do was stay awake till they got there.

"Does it faster go?" he shouted, stepping back into full view. Across the oil-stained, tilting deck, through the roar of the unmuffled engine, Austin understood him. His eyes full of hate, he shook his head slowly.

Heudeber glanced ahead to where the declining sun balanced ahead of the nodding prow. To the opening horizon of the Chesapeake. He smiled sadly and found a comfortable place on the gunwale. Propped the shotgun on his lap, and settled in.

CHAPTER 6

Thursday, March 22: Washington, D.C.

It doesn't happen every night, that I have the dreams. But when it does, I don't sleep well early on, then go deep toward morning. So I don't know how long the phone was ringing before it woke me up. Probably a while. I rolled over, grunting, and collided gently with soft perfumed flesh and tangled hair.

For a couple seconds I was confused. I'd been back in the Pacific all night long, slipping back to the same dream every time I dropped back into the depths. Then I remembered. The Pimlico Club. The fight. Taney, what was it . . . Taney Royce. She was lying with her back to me. I ran my hand over the curve of her hip, admiring it against the dawn light that came through the curtains. Then slid it into the damp tangled nest that opened to a sweet warm cave. She shifted a little, accommodating me with sleepy murmurs. The phone kept ringing.

"That for you?"

"One of the other girls. I'm off today."

I remembered she shared the apartment. I felt under the weather, thirsty, and a headache was dug in deep in the back of my skull. She found me a bathrobe from her closet—a man's bathrobe—and we went out to the kitchen. I looked over a three-day-old *Star* while she fixed Postum and coffee. Taney said she didn't know where the other girls were; possibly on morning shift. In the daylight she looked older than she had the night before. Her hair looked like straw. First thing after breakfast she lit a Chesterfield.

The bathroom was littered with girl stuff: drying hose, hairbrushes, douche bags, jars of grease. No shower, but she had one of those telephone attachments in the tub. I was hosing down when she knocked at the door. "Yeah?" I yelled.

"Somebody here for you."

"What?"

"There's somebody here who wants to see you."

I understood her that time, but the problem was, nobody knew I was here.

"Whoever it is, tell 'em to get in bed and put their legs in the air," I yelled through the door.

"Jack, he wants to see you now. It's a marine."

I toweled off and did a Dorothy Lamour sarong with the towel. Then padded out in my bare feet.

The jarhead was about seven three, standing like a WPA poured concrete abutment in the middle of the sitting room. Blues, holstered .45, the works. And a look that said he'd heard my remark about the bed and didn't think it was funny. "Lieutenant John Fitzgerald Kennedy?"

"That's me."

"The Admiral's compliments, sir, and he wants to see you on the goddamn double."

"Watch that language to an officer, Sergeant."

"Them's the Admiral's words, sir. 'On the goddamn double' is exactly what he said. I got a jeep in the street." Taney came out of the kitchen in her bathrobe, and he got a slow eyeful and added grudgingly, "Sorry, sir."

"Yeah, but—How the hell did you—?"

"It took me some time, sir. But I finally ran into somebody who said, check with Miss Royce."

"I'll be right out," I said. But he didn't leave, just stood there looking grim and envious at the same time. I went back into Taney's room and started collecting parts of my uniform. As I was buttoning the shirt she came in. "What is it, Jack? What's he want?"

"Some admiral wants to see me."

"Admiral? Do you know any admirals?"

"A couple." I threw my already-knotted tie over my head, two-blocked it, and checked myself in her mirror. "Where's my hat?"

"In the living room. Wait a minute." She came close, plucked a hair off my lapel. "Blonde. You're safe."

"It was terrific."

"Will I see you again?"

"I'll call. Gotta run." I gave her a quick kiss, pushed her hand off my neck, and went out. "Ready to get under way, Sarge."

This early there wasn't much traffic. The jeep, driven by a colored corporal, turned right onto Rhode Island and built up speed, bucking as it went over the old trolley lines. The wind was icy. "Who'd you say wanted me?" I twisted to ask the jarhead, who was riding in the jump seat in the rear.

"Admiral Leahy."

"Admiral *Leahy?*"

"That's right."

Fleet Admiral William D. Leahy wasn't one of the admirals I knew. They had one or two stars. He had five. In fact, he was the highest-ranking officer in the Armed Services. He was the Chief of Staff to the President and the Chairman of the Joint Chiefs.

The Willys' little engine was howling. But when I caught a street sign I saw we were passing Twenty-second already and still headed south. "Aren't we going to the Munitions Building?" I shouted over the engine.

"No. The new building. The one they call the Pentagon."

The Potomac looked sullen and green, with little whirlpools dimpling its surface. We crossed the Roosevelt Bridge—Theodore, not FDR—then came over a rise. "My God," I said.

The colored corporal chuckled. "That's what they all says, first time they sees it, sir. Sure is something, ain't she?"

"Hell, I been stationed on islands smaller than that, Corporal."

The New War Department Building was across the Potomac, on the patch of flat land below Arlington Cemetery. I figured we were headed for the Navy Annex, on Arlington Heights. Instead we bored steadily toward the huge mass that grew larger and larger as we approached. We threaded barbed-wire barricades into a wilderness of mud, concrete mixers, steam shovels, ditches, and unpaved parking lots. As the corporal downshifted we jolted from side to side through huge mud holes, slamming up sheets of brown water. It wasn't doing my back any good. The sheer granite faces loomed slowly up as we crept in, till it towered over us, filling the sky. Just then we hit the biggest hole of all.

The corporal braked suddenly at a muddy stair, and the sergeant swung himself out. "Up this way, Lieutenant. Have your ID card ready."

I was still rigid. "Agh. *God,*" I gasped.

"You all right, sir?"

"No. It's my fucking back." I bent over, panting, and sort of rolled slowly out the passenger side. I limped up the steps. When I got to the top I put my back to the stone facade, and straightened, trying to feel each disc back into place. Sometimes that helped. The sergeant watched.

When it backed off a little we headed in past grim-faced Army guards with Thompsons. The marine flashed a pass and said I was okay. We went up ramps, through corridors, up more steps. The sergeant kept a fast pace, leggings flashing ahead of me through dim corridors where women in coveralls were installing wiring and phone lines. I had to tell him to slow down. Finally he turned into a brightly lit transverse passageway. Under a quarter-mile of harsh fluorescent lights hundreds of people in uniform were standing in line. "What the hell's this?" I said.

"First shift for lunch . . . through here, sir." We turned again, down a corridor so narrow we had to walk single file. The smell of new paint was choking. Two Army sentries checked our IDs again and nodded us into a receptionist's office. Two colonels and a four-stripe captain, all standing, looked at me. When I nodded to them they looked away.

"Kennedy," the marine said to a very plain WAC with bangs, pointing at me with his thumb. Without a glance she pressed a key on an intercom and relayed the information somewhere else. When I looked around he was gone. The WAC didn't ask me to sit down, maybe because there were no chairs other than the one she occupied. Which she promptly swiveled to face the wall, and began typing at about a hundred words a second. "Back the attack, be a WAC," I tried, but the clatter of the keys never faltered.

"Colonel Benson," said the intercom, and one of the Army guys flinched, straightened, and marched into the inner office.

There were some photos of old ships on the wall. I checked them out while I fingered my back. *Dolphin. Oregon. Oglala. New Mexico. West Virginia. California.* There was a clock, too. Its electrically controlled minute hand jerked forward thirty-nine times before the intercom barked out, "Lieutenant Kennedy."

I checked my ribbons, stuck my cap under my arm, jerked the door open and went in.

A lanky, balding old man in blues looked up from a stack of message folders. His eyes were piercing under heavy black eyebrows. "You wanted to see me, sir?" I said. But the minute I did, I knew I'd screwed up already.

"Stand at attention, Lieutenant. Report in the regulation manner."

"Sir, Lieutenant Kennedy—"

"I know who you are, *Mister* Kennedy. Get your eyes in the boat!"

The cold voice had a Midwestern twang. The old man unfolded, and kept unfolding, as if there were more of him feeding up hydraulically from somewhere under the desk. His service dress blue had five rows of ribbons. His arms were solid gold from cuff to elbow. His gaunt, long face supported a wattle of loose flesh beneath a prominent chin. When he finished getting up he came around the desk and stood peering down at me through rimless pince-nez, as if I were something he'd just stepped in on the parade field.

"The war hero from Guadalcanal. What are you doing in Washington, Lieutenant?"

"Getting an award, sir, I was at the White House—"

"I saw you. That was yesterday. What are you doing here now?"

I felt annoyed. And, yeah, intimidated. So I let him have the unvarnished truth. "Getting laid, sir. In honor of all the guys in the Pacific who can't."

"And your plans?"

"To get laid some more."

I was getting a look now like a roach on a wedding cake. "You're a funny little shit, aren't you, Kennedy?"

"There are those who think so, sir."

"Don't count me among them." Leahy turned away abruptly and stalked the room like a flamingo. He wheeled back to catch me relaxing. "You're at attention, Lieutenant. Or did anyone ever instruct you on that position?"

"Yessir." I straightened again, but I couldn't do the brace he obviously wanted. There was something out of place in my back. The pain was less stabbing now, more a throbbing presence. Well, I could stand it. Still I felt sweat beading my forehead.

"Yes, you're just amusing as hell," Leahy went on, his voice cold as an Arctic sea. "A funny little Harvard smartass, whose stock-promoter daddy bought him a Navy commission. I met your father, you know. He called on me in '39. I never met a more defeatist, no-win, yellow appeaser."

"Sir, I don't—"

"I am still speaking, Kennedy. I wasn't impressed with him and I'm not impressed with you. In my book you're a shallow, overprivileged playboy. After I noticed you yesterday, I called a few of the men you've served under. It doesn't seem the Navy's changed you much. Frankly, you insult me by wearing that uniform." He sat down, and I looked around for a chair before I caught his glare and stiffened again.

"Let's review the record." Leahy turned over a few carboned flimsies. "Direct commission from civilian life. Fired from the Office of Naval Intelligence because of sexual involvement with a German sympathizer. Saved from cashiering by his father. Sent to public relations work in South Carolina. Fired from there for failure to perform. Can I believe all this?"

"Sir, Inga Arvad isn't a sympathizer. She's a—"

"Oh, not a sympathizer. Just a personal friend of Göring, and one hell of a hot lay, is that right? Very interesting, this FBI transcript of your bedtime conversation."

This time I knew enough to keep quiet. Leahy snorted and went on. "Well, all right, cunt can make a man look awfully silly at times. But then your father steps in again. You're sent to sea. Your last chance to make a man of yourself. What happens? You lose your boat and two men because you decide to ignore recommended tactics. Is that right, Lieutenant? Please correct me if any of this is in error."

"If that's the MTB Flotilla One after-action report, sir, it specifically says that I was turning toward the Jap tin can when it hit me."

"I should hope so," said Leahy coldly. "But that's not what interests me about this action. Do you mind if I try to reconstruct what happened? Let's see. We had word the Express was coming down the Strait, four destroyers making a night run to land troops at Guadalcanal. Ted Wilkinson put Arleigh Burke and his Little Beavers out there to ambush them, with a backstop of fifteen PTs in four divisions in Blackett Strait. You were in Division B, with three other boats. When the Jap destroyers evaded Burke the other boats in your division engaged them. But not you. Why not?"

"That's not exactly right, sir. My boat and another were in a separate element. We were not at the scene of that action, sir."

"Then where were you? Blackett Strait is quite a narrow passage, as I recall."

"I saw no Japanese destroyers, sir."

"This report says there was firing, searchlights."

"We saw some lights, yes sir." I fidgeted, trying to ease the ache in my back. "I thought they were shore batteries."

Leahy said coldly, "So you did not understand that this was the enemy, which the other boats were engaging less than two miles from you?"

"That is correct, sir."

"Was there no radio traffic during this engagement? I understand the small craft use tactical radio very freely."

"Our radio wasn't working that night, sir."

"So the Japs head on south and carry out their landing, reinforcing their men and bombarding our troops."

"I don't know where they went, sir."

"But you knew they had to come back through the Strait again that night, did you not? This report says: 'When Lieutenant Kennedy thought he had reached the original patrol station, he started to patrol on one engine ahead at idling speed.' Why were you at idle speed in a battle zone, with only one engine out of three engaged?"

"There were float planes out that night, sir. With three engines they could see my wake."

"Why were you sent to Blackett Strait, Lieutenant? Were you out there to avoid attack, or to stop the Tokyo Express? Which you knew was headed back in your direction?"

Sweat was slipping down the crack in my ass. I said, "Sir, those planes were out after us every night. One of them bombed us ten days before and wounded two of my men. If I kept my wake down, and engines muffled, I could concentrate on looking for the enemy ships, instead of watching out for planes."

"I see. How about this: 'Suddenly a dark shape loomed up on PT 109's starboard bow 200–300 yards distance. At first this shape was believed to be other PTs. However, it was soon seen to be a destroyer identified as the Ribiki Group of the Fubuki Class bearing down on PT 109 at high speed. The 109 had started to turn to starboard preparatory to firing torpedoes. However, when PT 109 had scarcely turned thirty degrees, the destroyer rammed the PT, striking it forward of the forward starboard tube and shearing off the starboard side of the boat aft, including the starboard engine. The destroyer traveling at an estimated speed of forty knots neither slowed nor fired as she split the PT, leaving part of the PT on one side and the other on the other. Scarcely ten seconds elapsed between time of sighting and the crash.'" The admiral glanced over the paper at me. His twang was incredulous. "Is that how it was, Kennedy? Is that *really* how it happened?"

"Well, sir—essentially."

"But you knew they were coming through your area. How in God's name did you allow a destroyer traveling at forty knots to get within three hundred yards on a clear night? I know what a bow wave looks like at night in the Pacific. Did you have anyone on lookout duty at all? Were any of you *awake?*"

Leahy was leaning forward over his desk. He wasn't shouting, but his voice had a kind of steely gravel to it. I didn't answer. I couldn't.

At last the admiral said softly, "Let's be honest with each other. You *fucked up,* didn't you, Mr. Kennedy?"

"I . . . guess so, sir."

Leahy went over to a chalkboard and studied it for a moment, his back to me. I dragged my sleeve over my face. When he turned back I was at attention again.

"You made an error. And two men died, and you lost your ship."

"Yes sir," I said, short and angry. "Thanks for reminding me."

"We're trying to win a war, Mister Kennedy. We can't do it by political preferment, or assigning men on the basis of personal charm."

"Yes sir."

"We do it by putting ordnance on target. Not by losing our own ships and boys through thinking we don't have to keep a lookout, or don't have to obey orders like everyone else in the Navy."

There was something blocking my throat. I remembered the men I'd lost, Marney and Kirksey. There wasn't a day went by I didn't remember them.

He was talking to the blackboard again. "Not that you were in a major action. PTs are toys. There are a lot of people who think this little project or that little pet weapon will win the war. Well, I don't think so. It's the heavy units, the capital ships Hoover and Coolidge wanted to trade away, that are winning this one for us. As we knew they would."

I took a deep shuddering breath and got myself under control. When Leahy turned again he looked at me for a long time. He glanced at the report, weighed it for a moment, then dropped it into a burn bag. When he spoke again his voice was reflective.

"This may come as a surprise to you, Kennedy, but I'm not bringing this up to humiliate you. Or put you on the tree. There are very few men completely *sans peur et sans reproche*. You're not the first officer who's had something like this happen. It was your first contact with a skilled, battle-hardened enemy. But it is the duty of every soldier to forget his own troubles and to fight on with what remains. That, in the end, is the essence of courage, and of honor. What I am trying to ascertain is whether you have learned from your mistakes." He shoved his glasses up on his nose. "Have you?"

"I hope so, sir."

"Then let us say no more about the matter. What is your current duty status, Lieutenant?"

"Limited duty, sir, due to injuries sustained in action. I'm looking at medical retirement, effective next week."

"Is that what you want?"

"I don't think I have a choice, sir."

"Is your back really that bad?"

"It gives out unexpectedly, sir. And there's something else wrong with me. Some of the docs think it's malaria, but others don't."

"Stand at ease, Lieutenant." Leahy gave the faintest nod, and I relaxed warily. He eased himself back into the chair like a torpedo being loaded into a firing tube. I eyed the empty chair beside his desk, but didn't dare move. He steepled his fingers and looked at me from under those snarly eyebrows.

"How would you like to stay in for another few months? Till the war is over. Not overseas. Right here in the continental United States."

This was unexpected. "I'm not sure what you're driving at, sir."

"I mean a staff assignment. Limited duty. No running up and down ladders or riding small boats. Would you be willing to consider it?"

"It seems to me, sir, that whatever it is, you could find somebody better qualified than a Harvard playboy."

"Perhaps I was harsh," said Leahy quietly. For just a moment I saw past the icy martinet into some immense private sadness. Then he withdrew again into the steely shell of a battleship captain at punishment mast. "And perhaps you need to consider that we're at war, Mr. Kennedy, and that you have taken an oath to do your duty."

"I have always done that, sir, to the best of my ability." Whatever he thought about me, that, at least, was true.

"Very well then; I am glad to hear it. Your record says that right after you joined, you worked for Al Kirk."

That was Rear Admiral Alan Kirk, formerly head of the Office of Naval Intelligence. "Yes sir."

"What were your duties in his unit?"

"Well, I was in Captain Hunter's section. We had an office over at OP-16. We collected data from various sources and put together the daily briefing."

"Whom did you brief?"

"Well, mainly the CNO, Betty Stark—I mean, Admiral Stark, at that time, sir. Prior to Pearl Harbor, and just after."

"Where did your information come from?"

"We attended the daily State Department briefing, and attache reports, newspapers, and—special information."

Leahy said, "Special information?"

"Yessir. Special information."

Leahy said, looking away, "Mr. Kennedy, just what does the word 'Magic' mean to you?"

I tensed. "It's . . . highly classified, sir."

"That is quite correct. But what is it?"

I hesitated, reviewing where I was, and who he was, and whether anyone could overhear us. I finally decided that if anyone was eavesdropping on us here, in the heart of the Pentagon, it sure wasn't my fault, and that if the Chief of the Joint Chiefs wasn't cleared for it, nobody was. I said, not very loud, "That's the code name for our ability to read encrypted Japanese radio traffic, sir."

Leahy studied me over his glasses for several seconds. At last he said, in a low voice, "Mister Kennedy, I am considering attaching you to the President's naval staff."

"The President's? Why is that, sir?"

"I see from your record that your secret clearance is still current, Lieutenant. I will warn you, therefore, that what I am about to impart to you is highly classified and that you will treat it as such. If I learn you have communicated even a hint of it to any other person whatsoever, you will face a wartime court-martial. Do you understand?"

"Yes, sir," was all I could say. He put it so . . . clearly.

"Very well then. It is possible that someone close to the President is planning an attempt on his life."

I was so surprised I sat down. "On *FDR's* life, sir?"

"That is correct. By someone who would in the normal course of events have personal access to him—within his inner circle."

I shook my head. "That's hard to believe, sir."

"It is? Why?"

"I mean, I can see if it was right after Pearl Harbor, it would confuse everything, but what difference would it make now, this late in the war?"

The admiral looked surprised, as if a lump of shit on his shoe had asked an intelligent question. He lifted his head, appearing to marshal his thoughts.

"Victories bring stresses in coalitions, Lieutenant. The rivets are working out of this one right now. Stalin mistrusts us and the British. We're suspicious, and I think rightly so, of Soviet intentions in Poland. Above it all hangs the question of Russian participation against the Japanese.

"If there is a spy in place, events are moving rapidly to erode his usefulness. This may be the other side's last chance to use him. Granted, it's a desperate hope, but it may be all they have left."

I still couldn't get my mind around it. "But assassination—sir, that seems so—"

"You've worked in Intelligence, Kennedy. You know such things happen. More often than we like to reveal. There were several attempts to kill me when I was governor of Puerto Rico. Remember the Darlan affair, in 1942? He was the only man with enough authority to command the French army and navy in Africa. His assassination made our campaign there much more difficult. I believe de Gaulle was behind it. Certainly he was the only one who benefited.

"Next case in point: Teheran, year before last. The Soviet secret police uncovered a plot to assassinate FDR there, in Iran. For that reason, we moved the President to the Soviet compound for the duration of the conference. On the other side, there have been three attempts on Hitler's life. The Czechs assassinated Heydrich. And most recently, there was an attempt to assassinate General Giraud, in Algiers.

"Believe me, Lieutenant: as gentlemen, Americans, and Christians, you and I may not like murder as an instrument of policy. But the fact remains that there are those who do."

"I can accept that, sir. But what makes you think FDR's the target now?"

Leahy considered this. Finally he said, "I will answer that question, but only partially. We discussed your duties in OP-16. Did you have access to Magic in your position there?"

"No sir. Not directly. That came out of OP-20. Captain Kirk and Commander Kramer hand-carried it. But I knew about it."

"Then perhaps you already know that sometimes the meaning of a given message is less than crystal clear."

I did. I remembered December 7, 1941, coming back from playing touch football on the Mall when the news came over the car radio. How dark the mood had been at ONI, knowing we'd be blamed—intelligence always was—wondering whose head would roll for the failure to generate clear predictions from inchoate, contradictory information. "Yes sir," I said. "Like at Pearl—Admiral Kimmel didn't think attack was imminent. Neither did MacArthur, in the Philippines. But Admiral Hart had the Asiatic Fleet on alert on the first of December, and they were dispersed when the attack came. He made the right interpretation. Nobody else did."

"Then you'll understand that what I'm going to tell you next could be anywhere from the horse's mouth aft."

I smiled grimly. "Yes sir."

"You already know that for some time we have been reading Japanese traffic in PURPLE, their highest diplomatic code. What has happened is that, quite unexpectedly, this has given us an entry into the highest circles of the German command."

"The *German* command?"

"That is correct. The Japanese ambassador in Berlin, a Baron Oshima, has instructions to make periodic reports to his country on their ally's progress in the war. He sees Hitler and the other top leadership often—and reports to Tokyo via shortwave radio and PURPLE. Since Stalingrad he's sounded rather gloomy. Recently, though, they've taken a more optimistic turn. He seems to expect something to take place soon that will alter the political complexion of the war. We even have a date and a code name."

"A date for whatever it is that will happen?"

"Not exactly; it's more that whatever has to happen, has to occur before the end of April, and preferably before April 13. I have no idea why."

"How do you link it to a threat to the President, sir?"

"That is from an even more sensitive source," said Leahy, and I understood that there was no point in asking more questions about that.

It was fascinating, but there was one part of it that didn't make sense. "Granted that your interpretation is correct, sir, I don't understand why you're asking me to take on this duty."

"You're suited for it, that's why. It came to me yesterday, watching you chat with him. You have charm and intelligence. You have the social contacts to move smoothly in any circle. The President knows you. You're a war hero—in print, at any rate. You can fit naturally into a staff job. And you have an intelligence background." Leahy hesitated, seemed about to add something, but shut his mouth firmly. For a moment I could hear the faraway "count, cadence, count" of a lunchtime drill unit somewhere outside.

"Would I be reattached to ONI for this, sir?"

"No. Domestic surveillance is not legally within ONI's purview."

"Then how would I—"

Leahy said, "On paper, you would be simply a naval aide. But as regards the confidential aspect of your assignment, you will report directly to me."

"But what would I do?"

"Your orders will attach you to the Map Room as a briefing officer. The same type of duties you performed at OP-16. You will carry those duties out punctiliously. But at the same time, you will become a member of the President's social circle. You will make it your business to meet each person who has access to him. You will investigate to the best of your ability the people around the Commander in Chief, and will report any suspicious circumstance immediately to me."

"Isn't this really Secret Service business, sir? Protecting the President?"

"I have already consulted with the head of the Secret Service detachment." Leahy shot his cuffs. "Mr. Reilly agrees that FDR tends to neglect personal security. At the same time, I can't take even Reilly fully into confidence. Why? Because it's perfectly possible that the putative assassin may *be* a member of the Protective Detachment. That's why I want someone who is totally outside the current setup over there."

I thought about that for a minute. Then I asked the obvious question. "Sir, if you really think there's a threat to the President, why would you assign *me* to protect him? If you think so little of me?"

Leahy tilted his head up, fixing me with that blue glare like sun off water.

"The answer is that I seem to be the only one who feels there may be something to it. Internal counterintelligence is an FBI function. If there is a threat against the President's life, that falls within their purview. But when I consulted Mr. Hoover as to my suspicions, he all but laughed at me. Implied that I was"—the admiral looked especially grim—"becoming prone to see danger where none existed. Well, I may be, I may be. But you are at least a gesture toward reassuring me. Any other questions?"

"No sir, I don't think so."

"Then I do. So far, Lieutenant, your war has been against the Japs. But you're Catholic, Mr. Kennedy. Irish. Your father was anti-British right up till we got into the war. I want to hear from you where you stand."

For a moment I was so angry I couldn't speak. Then I got up. "Admiral, your question is not that of one officer, or even one gentleman, to another. I may be Catholic, and I may be Irish, but I love my country as much as you do."

"Very good," said Leahy, rising too. "I will accept that. You will receive orders tomorrow and report to the White House as soon as possible. You will report to me weekly, or whenever you develop information of interest."

"Just a moment, sir."

"Yes, Lieutenant?" He stood waiting, tall and grim and gaunt.

I took a deep breath. "I'm not volunteering, Admiral." Then anger grabbed me and shook my voice. "I don't like being called incompetent. I don't like having my loyalty questioned. And if it's not treason to say so, my family and I are no longer particularly partial to Franklin D. Roosevelt."

"You're in uniform, Mr. Kennedy, and you'll do as you're told!"

"That's exactly right, sir. I have my detachment orders, and I intend to carry them out."

I got two seconds' more glare, then a barked "Dismissed." As I about-faced Leahy grabbed the door from my hand. "Yeoman Marshack: Show the lieutenant out," he growled. The door slammed behind me.

Outside, in the transverse corridor, the marine sergeant who'd brought me over was nowhere in sight. I headed into the maze, but in seconds I was lost. Each turning looked the same. I didn't remember where I was, and didn't know where I was going.

Which was pretty much the way I felt, too.

I was wandering down one of the broad, light-filled inner corridors, looking for the ramps I vaguely remembered, when the press of hurrying uniforms seemed to freeze. Through the gazing men and women strode two men, trailing a retinue of staff. Admiral Ernest King, expression bleak and fixed and severe, in the gray uniform he'd designed himself. General George Marshall, six feet tall, straight, graying, sandy hair and direct blue eyes, so impressive you didn't notice the unremarkable features. I watched them go by. The men who directed the war.

Suddenly the charge I'd got out of talking back to Leahy seemed cheap. Who was I to tell him off? A failure as an intelligence officer. A green, panicky reservist who'd lost his ship and killed his men. While past me marched the professionals who had turned a peacetime nation into the greatest military power on earth. They'd retrieved disaster in Europe and Asia, run a war, were winning total victory against the odds. Those hard faces held no doubt, no hesitancy, no self-questioning.

I turned away, found the stairway down at last, and limped slowly out into the open. My breath drifted away on the cold wind, over the torn-open earth, and disappeared as it rose into the air.

CHAPTER 7

Pocomoke City, Maryland

His round face bland and innocuous, Krasov stood outside the diner, lighting a Fleetwood. He shook out the match and flicked it away, snugged the worn, soft leather jacket up around his neck, and stuck his hands back in his pockets.

He looked back at the diner. It had obviously been a dining car once, from a train, and through the windows he could see people sitting comfortably at the counter. He wished already he was back in the pie-smelling, gravy-rich warmth. The heavy country food was hot in his belly. He couldn't believe the size of the portions, the butter, the soft white bread and real meat. He'd lingered over real coffee, remembering the acid bite of the ersatz Berlin brew, hoping one of the customers would offer him a ride. But they looked as if they'd be there a while.

He bent to pick up the valise. Stood a moment more, watching the diner. Then gave up. Turning on his heel, he started walking, gravel crackling under his heavy brogans.

I got to get moving, he thought. This is taking too long. I don't want to spend another night out here on the road.

But for a long while no cars went by, and the wind cut into his face as he hiked along, throwing an occasional glance over his shoulder. The town petered out fast into farmland again, like that he'd walked and hitched through for the past two days. Dead leaves and trash rustled across it, driven endlessly by the wind. He walked through the noon light, his mind empty of memory, thought, emotion. Empty of everything.

He shivered.

He'd worked his way up through Virginia, walking and in a series of short lifts. Picked up by trucks carrying produce or plows or scrap metal. Rolling along at thirty-five or forty through Exmore and Accomac and Oak Hall he looked out at the shotgun shacks where frozen laundry hung stiffly on swaying lines, at the privies that fronted on the railroad right-of-way. At farmhouses back in the woods, their white frame or red brick topped, each one, by a distinctive doghouse-shaped attic window. Then mile after mile of woods and fields again.

Beside the road a pile of brush was crackling in fierce heat and a high, wavering flame. The smoke burned his eyes, whipped into them by the wind. The smell brought back the days of retreat, burning villages, the terror of a defeated army being swept up in the Nazi net. He nudged the pistol surreptitiously. Solid and small under his belt. He'd thought about carrying it in the valise, but he felt safer knowing he could get to it fast.

The distant rattle of an engine. He took his hand out of his jacket as a Model T truck rounded the curve, clattering toward him. When it was a hundred yards away he threw the cigarette to the ground, stepped to the pavement, and extended his thumb. A glimpse of a worn-faced old black man, three fingers lifted from the wheel in sardonic acknowledgment. A blast of sound, dust, wind, and it was past him, a swaying, shrinking speck slowly clattering away.

He bent for the still-smoking butt, picked up his burden again, and hunched his shoulders once more into the walk.

Two cars later a big yellow sedan slowed, honked, pulled over, and rocked to a stop. He ran after it, the grip bumping against his leg, and yanked open the back door and threw it in and got in the front.

"Passed a couple soldiers a few miles back," the driver said. He was smoking a pipe, and the interior reeked sweetly of cavendish. He wore a bright yellow tie and a gray overcoat and a gray hat tilted back. He nudged the shift lever with the back of his hand and the car began to roll, gravel snapping under its tires, then bumped back up to the asphalt. "You may ask: Why'd I pass 'em? Well, I figure they'll get a ride easy. Fella like you, a young guy in civvies, you could be out here a while. And it's a cold day."

"Sure is. You didn't see another fella hitching, did you, a tall guy in preacher's clothes?"

"Can't say I have. Friend of yours?"

"No. Just saw him on the road."

Where had Heudeber gone? What had happened to the SS man? No sign of him since the landing. Could he have hit him, wounded him during their scuffle in the darkness?

"No, haven't seen anybody by that description."

"This is a nice car," Krasov said, looking at the dash, then the upholstery. He touched the fabric, awed. Stalin himself probably didn't have a car like this. It even had a radio. Things had changed since he'd been away.

"Yeah, used to drive a Lincoln, but I could see this war coming. Know what did it? Franklin Doublecrossing Roosevelt tellin' everybody he'd never send the boys overseas. Whenever he says something, friend, I figure just the opposite, and I've never been far wrong. June of '41 I got me one of these Hudson Sixes. Not as much power, but she'll do twenty miles on a gallon and two thousand on a quart of oil. I've got eight good used tires back in my garage. Hey, I'm set."

"You travel a lot."

"That's my living, buddy. Used to be a grocer. Believe that? OPA put me out of business. Best thing ever happened to me, losin' that store. Aside from getting a perforated eardrum. Like Frank Sinatra, I told the Army docs. They didn't like it, but not everybody can go."

"You a salesman?"

"Customer's rep." He kept talking, an easy flow about the line of home canning goods he represented. He didn't ask about his passenger or bring up sports. He just kept talking about himself, his car, his company, his clients, his new suit. Krasov was first relieved, then bored, and at last irritated. National Socialist or Communist, no one had any use for soft men like this.

"How's the radio in this crate?" he said at last.

"Oh yeah, great radio." Just as he'd hoped, Gray Hat leaned forward and snapped it on. It warmed up with the familiar frying bacon sound and then voices came through the hiss. Voices, and suddenly he was a child again, and they were sitting in the apartment in Brooklyn. He felt a sudden dizziness, as if he were several people, and he couldn't tell, really, which one was himself.

Two Negro voices, exaggerated, one slow, the other sharp and conniving. He recognized them at once, like old friends. He'd listened to this when he was a boy. Now, suddenly, he remembered the radio. The movies. And the comics, the big color pages that folded out of the paper. The Katzenjammers, Blondie and Dagwood, Maggie and Jiggs, Little Nemo in Slumberland. He felt strange. He'd missed fourteen years of the comics.

"Darn, look at that, getting low. Say, you got any gas points?"

"Any what?"

"You a little hard of hearing, aren't you? I said, have you got any gas points?"

Krasov guessed he was referring to rationing. He took the booklets out of their cloth pocket and fumbled through them. The guy thought he was stupid. Okay, he had no trouble with that. "I don't know," he said in a slow voice. "I can't read so good, mister."

"Jesus, let me look." Gray Hat reached over, thumbed through them with one hand, and tore off several stamps skillfully. "Get those out of sight now."

A Sinclair station came up on the right and he leaned on the horn. A young woman came out, washed their windshield, pumped the gas, and checked the oil. Gray Hat joked with her, called her "Auntie," pretending she was old. She smiled back tiredly and went inside to break his five-dollar bill. "How you go for that stuff?"

"A little young."

"Old enough for Errol Flynn, right?"

That must be a joke, Krasov thought, so he smiled. The girl came out with the change, dollar bills and shiny quarters and pennies. She gave them to Krasov. When he handed them to Gray Hat the man's wallet opened for a moment and he saw a thick vein of green. That decided him. With this car, he'd be in Washington in a few hours.

Gray Hat put the car in gear and they swung back onto Route 13. As the speedometer needle crept toward 40, Krasov looked ahead. He wanted a deserted, forested strip. Force the driver off at gunpoint. Take him into the underbrush. He went through it once in his mind. He had to be sure to get everything useful: clothes, ID, cash, papers. With a salesman's papers he could go anywhere. And the key, had to be sure to get the keys. He slid his hand into his jacket and gripped the Tokarev.

"You see *National Velvet* yet?"

He didn't know what that was. "No, I ain't. I been at sea."

"Yeah? What you think about the news from Europe? Looks like we've got those Jerries licked."

"I sure hope so." That stretch ahead? No, there were shacks, too close.

"Patton's really kicking tail. Well, I'm as loyal as the next guy, but you got to wonder if we're fighting the right people."

"How you mean that, mister?"

"You got to admit Hitler's had some right ideas. Like kicking the Jews out of the banks, stop them running the country. We could do with a little of that here at home, if you ask me."

"You might of got something there," said Krasov, looking out the window.

"The Russians are doing okay too. But what I wonder is, what's going to happen when we meet up."

Krasov became suddenly alert to the political undercurrent. "What do you mean?" he said, still gripping the gun.

"I mean, when we run into the Russkis. What's gonna happen then? Maybe it's time to clean house, now that we're geared up. Knock out Stalin the same way we kayoed Hitler and Benito. Now the Krauts have chewed them up some."

"You think we ought to declare war on the Soviet Union?"

"Well, we're going to sooner or later, aren't we? Those Reds are going to come over here as soon as they've got Europe sewed up. You know? If our own don't take over first. Hell, we got to clear everything with Sidney and John L. Lewis anyway." Gray Hat seemed to recollect himself; gave him a quick glance. "Course, there's a lot of union guys are loyal, as good Americans as the next guy. You union?"

"Naw," said Krasov. "I don't go for that stuff."

"That's the ticket."

"You think we could take the Communists? They're tough," he said, unable to resist probing again, though he ought to concentrate. A place to turn off, the first one that came up. If it didn't look right once they were stopped he'd say he had to take a leak, would the guy mind waiting.

"Hey, it'd be a knockout in one round. America's got the best planes, the best tanks—and more of everything. Their whole economy's based on slave labor. Once they get a whiff of freedom, it'll come apart right down the middle."

Krasov smiled faintly at his comfortable vehemence. In a way he felt sorry for this overweight, pampered man. But there was no room in war for pity. Not when you were the messenger of History. The man in the gray hat was only a footnote. The first casualty of the war that would succeed this one. The war that would end Stalinist tyranny forever.

He bent forward suddenly, looking at a wood-lined road ahead. Gray Hat glanced at him. "What's wrong?"

He felt tension wind his stomach and had to keep his voice steady. He never had to worry about his face. But sometimes his voice wasn't totally under his control. He said, "Can you let me off? Up ahead? Just turn down that little road."

"Here? I thought you were going all the way to—"

"Changed my mind. We're stopping here, buddy. Right *now.*"

He was actually pulling out the gun, his finger was on the trigger when the sedan breasted a rise and he saw the police car parked behind the billboard.

"That so? Well, pardon me, fellah." The Hudson hammered along the berm, braked, then the engine muttered again and the brake came off and they coasted another hundred yards. They stopped within stone-tossing range of the squad car. "That's as far as you want to go, be my guest. Hey, you want my advice, you ought to watch giving orders to people who're doing you a favor."

He got out, not answering, in a cold, detached rage, almost forgetting to get his grip out of the back seat. The police car wasn't fifty feet away. The wind was keen after the overheated, smoky interior. He waved as if in thanks as the yellow car dwindled, cursing himself. It had happened too quickly. He'd guessed wrong, then been too slow to retrieve his chance.

When he lowered his arm and glanced over they were watching him. He felt his heart freeze, and before he could control it his hand had gone to his belt. Was hitchhiking illegal? Would they stop him, as Soviet or Nazi police would, ask for *papieren?* But the eyes slid away. One cop lifted a wax-paper-wrapped sandwich. The other yawned. Krasov nodded to them. He brought his hand out casually and felt in his pocket for a cigarette. He picked up the valise and sauntered up the road.

He marched under the slanting light of afternoon, cursing himself.

Outside Fruitland three black men in an antique Chevy hearse stopped for him. A drawn curtain closed off the back. Krasov didn't ask what was behind it, or what the chemical smell was. He didn't feel confident taking on three men. They took him through Salisbury and asked him if he wanted 13 or 50. He guessed 50. They dropped him at a farm hamlet called Sharptown.

At Sharptown traffic dried up altogether. He walked for over an hour, carrying the heavy valise, till his feet were numb and his hands were numb and his face felt like cast lead left outside overnight. Then a White Horse dairy truck driven by a veteran with a wooden leg pulled over for him. He watched the amputee switch his leg from clutch to brake and occasionally hit both at once. He didn't even think about trying to steal the truck. It was so small the wind blew it from side to side and he held tight, afraid it might turn over.

The vet dropped him at a beer joint in another small town. "This here's the best place to catch a lift, it's easy to stop and people are looking for somebody to talk to, and if nothing works out you can get warm, at least. Well, inka dinka doo."

"Inka dinka doo," said Krasov, showing his teeth as the truck drove away. He pulled his jacket down and smoothed back his hair and lit another cigarette, looking at the flashing red neon in the window. Only ten butts left. He'd better take it easy.

If only he'd acted a little sooner, in the Hudson . . .

He was pondering a beer when a truck came around the bend. He shoved his cap back and once again, wearily, lifted his arm in the dusk. As the big Dodge two-and-a-half drew nearer he made out a woman eyeing him through the flat plate glass.

He grinned as the brakes screeched and loped the last few yards, swung the door open and hauled himself up while the truck was still coasting forward. She put it back in gear and they moved back onto the road, swing blaring from a portable radio at his feet.

"Hey, slugger. That's not the first time you done that, is it?"

"That's right, lady. Thanks for stopping."

"Where you headed?"

"North, I guess, then over toward D.C. Going that way?"

"Taking this load of parts up to Baltimore. I can take you far as Annapolis. You can get a ride or a bus from there easy."

They lapsed into silence. He leaned back, sucking the smoke deep. Then he remembered her and held the pack out. She took one and he lit it for her, holding the match over the steering wheel. In the yellow flicker she wasn't bad looking. Weathered face under a kerchief. Gloved hands on the worn ebonite wheel.

"So, how's your day been?" she said, leaning back, puffing out smoke, talking around the cigarette.

"Okay."

"Where'd you start out?"

He'd learned from the store not to say Norfolk. People didn't go this way from Norfolk to Washington. He said, "I'm a driver at the air base down at Cape Charles, and my mom's sick."

"They made you hitchhike? That's coldhearted."

"Had a crate, but it gave out on me."

"You see a lot of people on the roads. I try to give them a lift. Especially the service boys." Her eyes flicked to his chest. "How come you ain't in? A husky, good-looking boy like you?"

"Perforated eardrum. Same as Frank Sinatra."

"That's too bad. You got a girl there, in Washington?"

"No." He looked out the window.

"Got a girl in Cape Charles?"

"Not really. They keep us busy down there."

They were looking at each other now, she pulling her eyes away to keep the truck on the road. He smiled. "What's your name?"

"Marina Lee. What's yours?"

"John. John Kondratowicz," Krasov told her. That was the name on his driver's license and draft card.

"Funny name. Polish?"

"My folks, yeah. They come over from the old country in ought-nine, ought-ten."

"Well, glad to meet you, John."

"Same here, Marina."

"Like I was saying. Way I was raised, lovin' is something you put some time in thinkin' about. Looking forward to. But it's tough for a woman these days, let me tell you that."

"I can imagine."

"You got to work like a man 'cause the only men around is too old or too young. Like the song says. Or those 4-F guys. I tell you, sometimes you look at one of them with a limp, or blind, and they look pretty good. A woman, alone, you get man-hungry. It don't necessarily have to mean nothing. I'm no angel. I done a few things I'd hate to admit to my mom. You know what I'm sayin'?"

"You got men in the service?"

"Sure, who don't? My brother's in the Coast Guard out in the Pacific. Boatswain's mate. And cousins and such. My sister, she's a riveter for Fairchild, in Hagerstown. But her name ain't Rosie." She laughed.

"Where's your husband?"

"He's dead."

"Sorry."

"We had us a good life while it lasted. He joined up right after Pearl Harbor. Air Corps, he was a mechanic. A jeep turned over in England and he was in it. Never got to see D-Day, none of it."

"I'm sorry," he said again. He reached out and took her hand. Through her glove he felt it grip his, quickly, shyly.

"I don't want to cause you no trouble," she said. "Just that back home, with his mom there in the house and all—small towns, you know how it is—but you sound like you're on the square—"

"You ain't telling me nothing new," he said. "Tell me, they expecting you in Baltimore any special time?"

"Any time I get there," she said. "Why?"

"'Cause, you know, I do think you're an awful pretty girl to go to waste."

They held hands for a few miles, then she pulled the truck off the road. They bounced down a dirt track and came to a stop in the woods. Then they were kissing, and the worn leather jacket fell behind the back seat and lay in a crumpled heap.

A few minutes later he lifted his head from her lips. What was that song, on the radio? He'd heard that honey-smooth voice before somewhere.

> *Though April showers*
> *May come your way,*
> *They bring the flowers*
> *That bloom in May;*
> *So if it's raining,*
> *Have no regrets*
> *Because it isn't raining rain, you know,*
> *It's raining violets . . .*

He slowly realized she was watching his face in the light from the dial. "You like that song, don't you?"

"Yeah."

"I like it too. That's Al Jolson." He could hear her breathing in the cab.

"Oh, yeah. I saw him in the Winter Garden when I was a kid. He was in *The Jazz Singer,* wasn't he?"

"That's him."

And once again, just like before, on the road, he felt that strange sense of being split apart. He was becoming more than one person. Resolving into component selves. Am I an American? he thought then, startled at the thought. What am I?

"Oh, Johnny, oh," she said. "Kiss me some more."

When her hands got close to the pistol he disentangled himself. "What's the matter," she said, throwing her hair back with one hand. Her voice shook a little.

"Got a blanket?"

"Sure, in back."

"Let's find a place we can lie down."

"Okay," she said, and he heard the smile in her voice, though he couldn't see it, it was so dim. "You like the music? We'll take the music too."

———

It was full dark when he returned to the truck, carrying the radio and a heavy iron rod. He wiped the tire iron with a handful of dead grass and tossed it into the bed. He went around to the driver's side, climbed up, fitted the key in. He knew how to drive these. Soviet trucks were copies of U.S. models, and he'd driven trucks full of prisoners many times in the NKVD.

The motor caught with a roar. Half a tank, the gauge said. Sixty-two bucks in her purse. She must have just gotten paid.

He turned the radio on and found a station that was playing swing. His fair hair rumpled, round face pale but impassive, he backed till he sat foursquare on the empty highway. Pulling out the knob that turned on the lights, he headed north.

CHAPTER 8

The Chesapeake Bay

Heudeber's fingernails dug grooves in the wooden gunwale as he stared into the whistling, heaving dark. Was that a light, far out in the night? A glimmer on the sea?

Then his guts spasmed, and he lunged forward. Nausea wrenched his jaw open and he kicked his boots in agony on the salt-wet, slimy deckboards. Nothing emerged from his empty gut but drool and acid. As he lifted his face, gagging, a wave took the place of the sky. It glowed faintly, towering above the heeling boat, which lay bow lower than her stern, as if kowtowing in submission before the enraged and sovereign sea.

The wave fell like a dropped block of black glass, smashing itself apart into boiling foam and dark water across the deckhouse, the deck, the engine box. The exhaust blew spray aloft in a long streamer. The engine clattered and blared without cease, its hollow, deafening roar loud even against the howl of the squall. The ruddy stack-flare lighted a hellish circle: the engine itself; forward, the empty wheelhouse; to starboard, a separate, congealed tableau—the old man, Austin, and the boy, Paulie. One of the waterman's massive hands was wrapped around the steering post, as it had been all night long. The other arm was around the boy, who had fallen asleep.

To port, slumped against the gunwale, hand frozen around the shotgun, Heudeber seemed to see himself. A hollow, sick, driven skeleton of a man, emptied of everything but obedience. Hans Heudeber, the art student, the sensitive, rather shy youngster who had yearned above all to create beauty.

For a moment, exhausted, he asked the empty sky: How did I come to this?

———

The evening before, when he'd ordered Austin to get under way at the point of the old man's own shotgun, *Ella Eyre* had chugged peacefully enough out of the creek that was, apparently, her usual port. When they passed rocking over the bar the old man tossed a loop of line over the tiller post and stumped forward.

Heudeber halted him, suspecting some trick, but when the waterman explained he motioned him brusquely on. Austin had dragged out the gasoline lamp from some hidey-hole inside the cabin, filled it from a metal can, and scratched a match. He hung it on a bent nail inside the deckhouse, where it gleamed out crazily oscillating beams through the windows into the gathering night. Then the old man went back to his post.

As they hammered onward, leaving the land behind, the wind grew colder. The shore faded, merging with the growing darkness to the east. Off the bow the sun seemed to quiver as it approached the far-off line of horizon. It struck sparks off the sheet-steel sea like a red-hot grinding wheel. Heudeber watched it hesitate, assume an hourglass shape, then suddenly collapse, a pricked bright bubble, and run down suddenly into the bay. It left a salmon sky-glow that faded so imperceptibly its final vanishing was a matter of imagination.

Before that full night, he'd noted where the old man stood—across the deck, on the far side of the engine box—and broke the shotgun and checked the breech, holding it up to catch the last remnant of reddish light.

The green brass base of a long-carried shell. A chance it might not fire, then. But obviously Austin believed it would. That, Heudeber thought, should be adequate to ensure obedience. So long as he remained alert. He snapped it shut again, then leaned to peer into the deckhouse. Above the untenanted wheel, which moved slightly as *Ella Eyre* rolled, the hissing Coleman threw shadows and glares across the incremented face of the compass.

It showed almost due north. He straightened, penetrated by alarm, and swung toward the old man.

"Why aren't we headed west?"

No answer. Heudeber remembered then, and moved aft, till the glare of the lamp fell across his face.

"Why aren't we headed west?"

Austin shifted his eyes scornfully. "We got a lot o' northing to do before we turn west," he shouted over the racketing engine.

"Why? My map shows islands up there."

"You makin' me take you, mister, how about lettin' me get us there?"

Heudeber reined anger back; he had to maintain control of himself. This was his third night without sleep. The air attack, when U-630 was running surfaced; then the night of the landing, the long nightmare flight through the marshes. Now every cell in his body yearned to sag to the deck and give up consciousness.

"What if we compromise, Captain? Go right up the middle?"

"In the shipping lanes? Like as not to get us run over by one of them Liberty ships. They run down out of Baltimore at top speed, blacked out, no lights. And they keep lousy lookout, mister, believe you me."

"But my map shows islands where you want to go."

"That's right, it should, Tangier an' Goose Island and Smith. And right now they're cuttin' off the seas from us. Northeast wind, strong as this, there be white horses kicking their heels out over the Cabbage Patch. I want to give this wind a chance to blow itself out."

Heudeber shrugged and sat back down. He didn't know what all that meant, but it sounded as if the old man knew what he was doing.

The hours wore on, and he nodded off and jerked his head back up; paced across the deck till his legs ached; pulled himself again and again back from the brink of sleep; and the wind didn't drop. It blew stronger and colder, and a black hatch slid shut over the stars like the heavy bombproof door of a bunker. The boat dug deep, then rose sickeningly, again and again, till his rump was sore from sliding forward and back.

But he could take that. Had taken worse than that on the way across. Unable to go deep after the near-miss bombing, the U-boat had driven through storms that seemed as if God had decided He'd failed and decided to dissolve the world again.

Sitting there, he thought of what he'd wondered before. How he'd come to this. He lay back against the gunwale, glanced aft to make sure Austin was still at the wheel.

And remembered.

———

He'd gotten the call-up to active duty in September of 1939. His first set of orders assigned him as the administrative and personnel officer of Einsatzgruppe 23, a special task group of the SD. Formed by Himmler just before Case White, the invasion of Poland, its mission was to carry out political operations the Army found too distasteful to undertake—though they had no objection to the SS doing it. Working from lists prepared by the SD and Gestapo, the "Action Groups" rounded up lawyers, doctors, priests, businessmen, nobility, politicians; anyone around whom opposition might crystallize. Heudeber had not killed anyone personally in Poland, but he had written the outgoing reports and read the incoming ones. Including the final after-action report, twenty-seven days after the war began, reporting that ninety-seven percent of the Polish upper classes had been liquidated and the rest had fled abroad.

A little over a year later, with Operation Barbarossa in the final planning stages, Heudeber, promoted to Hauptsturmführer, had been assigned to command Einsatzgruppe E. He reviewed the troops, five hundred men. He signed papers. He attended and gave briefings, approved reports, answered questions from higher-ups, administered personnel. The usual things any unit commanding officer had to do in wartime.

Then the invasion began.

Over fifteen hundred miles of front, three million Germans moved forward. Armored spearpoints penetrated the lines of the unprepared Russians, encircling and smashing whole Soviet armies. Special Mobile Task Force E followed closely behind Army Group South's advance. Their orders were to "take executive measures affecting the civilian population." They rounded up the chaff left behind by the threshing machine of mechanized war: displaced persons, defeated and disarmed troops, lost children, deserters. They checked papers, conducted short interviews, and used their own judgment to sort out such personnel into categories. Surrendered troops went to POW camps. Soviet deserters and disaffected elements, skilled laborers, and other able-bodied but racially sound men were sent west, to the factories of Krupp and I. G. Farben. Women were released, unless they fell into a suspect category. Aryan-looking, healthy children were sent west to be raised as Germans.

Jews of all ages and both sexes, Gypsies, criminal elements, the mentally ill and physically incompetent, inferior Asiatic types, politicals, homosexuals, and Communist Party members were shot on the spot.

___

At two in the morning the old man straightened suddenly, peering off to starboard. Heudeber turned too, searching the darkness, but saw nothing.

"Tangier," the old man bawled.

"What's that?"

"One of them islands you don't like."

Looking away from Heudeber, Austin bent to the steering post. As the bow swung to the new heading the motion gentled a bit. About time, Heudeber thought. The endless pitching was making him dizzy. He let go the gunwale and staggered up, balancing precariously on wobbly legs.

Suddenly the boat hit a wall of water. Spray flew up, dashing across his face. He staggered back, taken by surprise. At the same moment the deck rolled, so deep and hard and sudden his leather soles lost their grip. He shot backward, arm flailing, across the slimy work-polished boards, and slammed into the davit. Only long discipline kept his grip on the weapon, but the barrel clanged into hanging, swaying cables. Rusty steel grated skin from his face and hand. He ignored it, wrenching himself back around, bringing the barrel up and the hammer back to full cock with his thumb.

Austin stopped, halfway around the engine compartment, a heavy socket wrench in his glove. They eyed each other across the hammering engine. For one unmasked moment Heudeber saw the flinty hatred. Then the old man looked back at the boy, who was huddled, eyes wide, under the stern.

"Get back," Heudeber shouted, but Austin was already turning, seaboots planted wide in a gait that rode the bucking boat as if he knew her every thought.

Suddenly he felt unutterably weak. He tottered, then sank to his knees, collapsing against the splintered gunwale. But still he kept his head up, eyes locked on the baleful, waiting glare of the deaf old man.

"Where are you going now?"

"West, mister, west. Right where you wanted to go. Right across the bay."

Heudeber licked spray from his lips. He searched the dark again, but still made out nothing. A sudden clatter from the deckhouse jerked his head around. It was the lantern, gyrating crazily, smashing against the roof at the extremes of its swing. With every slam the gas flame flared white as lightning. Austin shouted, "An' we better put that light out."

"You said there'd be freighters out here."

"An' there are. But if that gas spills they be hell to pay."

The gun was still cocked. He fumbled at it with numb fingers, eased the hammer back down. Then he shoved himself up, using it as a crutch, and hobbled forward grimly, driving himself by will.

He remembered, as if from some previous life, a lecture back when he'd joined the SS. The strong, the victors, the winners: what did they have in common, all of them? Not all Aryans were supermen to the eye. Not all were wellborn, well nurtured. What counted was within. It was inborn, stronger than steel, rustless and hard as diamond.

As he took down the lantern, closed the valve—Austin had been wise to send him for it, gas was already dripping out, the deck was wet with it—Heudeber's mouth twisted into a cynical, bitter smile. Eighty million Germans had believed that. Believing, they'd conquered all Europe and half of Asia, ruled from the Channel to the Urals, from Norway to the Sahara. Because one man had insisted on his unquenchable will.

But then they'd lost it. Lost everything. Till even their own country was no longer theirs.

What did that say about will?

He settled back again and yawned. His thoughts milled aimlessly. But they were images, not thoughts. Aristotle, he remembered: man thinks only in images.

Feels, in images.

And dreams, only in images.

Leaning back, still not entirely asleep, Heudeber dreamed.

———

A day in the late summer of 1941. He'd long ago forgotten the name of the place, if he'd ever been sure. Opochka, or Orochka, or some such mouthful of unpronounceable Slavic. The troops of one of his subordinate detachments had assembled a collection of seven or eight hundred people from the surrounding villages. Perhaps three-quarters were Jews. They were loaded into Army trucks and brought to Einsatzgruppe E's temporary encampment in the woods east of the town.

Heudeber had stood tapping his thigh with a riding crop as the junior officers conducted what interrogations remained. Most of these prisoners had already been classified. They were useless mouths. Unable to contribute to the Reich in any way, they had no role in the New Europe.

The retreating Soviets had dug an antitank ditch outside Opochka, abandoning it when the Panzers threatened to encircle them. This ditch Gerhard Buchner, a former lawyer from Thuringia and one of Heudeber's company commanders, had selected for the operation.

Heudeber strode back and forth before his command car, watching. He caught a glimpse of himself reflected in the Mercedes' windshield. He looked competent and determined. In active service the SS wore field gray, like the Army; only the death's-head cap badge and lightning-strike collar patch distinguished him from a regular officer.

He did not feel as determined as he looked. This was not the first such operation he had witnessed. They were never pleasant to observe. However, Buchner had laid things out efficiently. The trucks parked on the far side of a stand of trees. Flanked by guards, the material to be processed walked along a winding path for perhaps two hundred meters before they reached the first pile.

As they wove among the heaps, noncoms shouted orders at them. Eagerly, fearfully, they complied. Their shoes went first, laces tied together and thrown onto a massive pile. Clothing next; Germany needed cloth for machine tending, for making shoddy, insulation, packing material, paper. Underclothing went on the last mound.

Shivering and naked, hugging themselves, yet still carrying their lashed-together suitcases, their shabby bundles, the people—mostly men, but a few women, and children down to the age of eight—turned the last corner to confront the ditch and the waiting soldiers.

When they were told to abandon their luggage, they began to understand.

Shouting, flailing with truncheons, the troops got them into position in a ragged line at the lip of the trench. Heudeber paced back and forth, forcing himself to watch.

Buchner appeared and saluated snappily. He was a small, precise man with glasses, reminding Heudeber of Heinrich Himmler, except that he wore no mustache. "Heil Hitler, Hauptsturmführer," he barked.

"Heil Hitler."

"Will the Hauptsturmführer condescend to give us the order to prepare?"

"Yes, go ahead." Buchner's rigid, popinjay manner irritated Heudeber. It was a dirty business; all right, to clean anything, someone must dirty his hands. But there was no point to this Prussian pomp, this parade-ground punctiliousness. On the other hand, Buchner permitted no irregularities. Under his fastidious gaze occurred no unnecessary brutality, no theft, no rapes, hardly any escapes. There was even something like mercy, in that not till the very end were the victims faced squarely with what was happening to them. If Buchner irritated his superior occasionally, that could be lived with. The Einsatztruppen had a high rate of personnel turnover. Men broke down and had to be replaced. Several had committed suicide. Others became dependent on alcohol, morphine, or veronal, or committed unspeakable crimes. They sank to the level of beasts. This disgusted Heudeber. On second thought, he wished he had a dozen more Buchners.

"Coffee, Hauptsturmführer?"

He was accepting the steaming mug from the aide when an order rang out. He made himself turn and watch.

At Buchner's command, two trucks had started their engines and driven off. Parked blocking the prisoners' line of sight, their departure revealed two machine-gun squads. Facing them, the queue of naked human beings wavered. Some screamed and hid their faces. Others dropped to their knees. A few turned their backs. Heudeber took a deep breath. The hot schnapps and coffee on an empty stomach made him feel nauseated. Get it over with, he thought.

Buchner again at his elbow, arm shooting out. "Heil Hitler!"

"What now, Untersturmführer?"

"Sir! Will the Hauptsturmführer give the order to fire personally?"

Heudeber stood riveted to the ground. He steadied the cup with his left hand. "What are you talking about? What is it that you want?"

"Give us the order, sir. The men will feel inspired, hearing it from you."

"*Scheisse,*" Heudeber muttered. He threw the mug aside angrily and strode forward, pushing Buchner aside. His boots scuffed up dust that whirled toward the prisoners. Already the line was wavering. They were realizing there was nothing now to lose by running. From the corner of his eye he saw the machine gunners staring his way. He made a jerking gesture at them, pulling his closed right fist back toward his hip.

The clearing echoed with the rattle of breechblocks, as the gunners charged the heavy Czech machine guns.

He took another two paces, halted beside a whitewashed stake—Buchner always marked his fields of fire neatly—and stopped, propping fists on hips, gazing at the ribbon of shocked pale flesh fifty meters away.

Men, men, women, men. Dark-haired, for the most part. A few blonds. The women covered themselves instinctively as his look swept the line.

Then the sound began. He couldn't tell if it was prayers, curses, or begging. Maybe all three. There were so many. Open mouths, distorted faces, reaching arms, fists. A man spun around crazily, then sank sobbing to sit on the banked earth. The chorus grew from whimpering to thin despairing shouts that rose in the chilling autumn air into the pale, empty sky.

Heudeber stared at the condemned of the earth and could not open his mouth.

These were not numbers, not neat tabulations in typed reports. They had faces. His gaze slowed, focusing on them one by one instead of on the mass. The white-bearded old man with ruddy cheeks, as if he'd just pinched them. Another, wild-haired, lips pleading, tears running down his face as he held out his hands . . . a hunchback, scowling, glancing sideways at the others as if fearful of their rejection now that his deformity lay naked to the sun . . . a middle-aged woman, still wearing glasses, shaking her fist at him; no—it was the Communist salute.

At the far end one man stood loosely at the end of the line. At the lip of the trench. His eyes met Heudeber's. He was thin and wolfish-looking. High, Mongoloid cheekbones, thick, bitterly downturned lips, but the bony outthrust nose of an Aryan. A reddish fringe of eyebrow on heavy shelf of bone. A scrubby reddish beard spiked his cheeks. His left ear was mutilated, the lower half missing, as if hacked off. The man was mad. The eyes said that plainly.

Suddenly they riveted Heudeber's sight, those eyes. Deep-lidded and slanted, blue as the sky, they glittered with deep orange fire that swirled in the sunken sockets. Above in the night the stars burned with yellow-white whirlpools of fire.

Why is it night, he thought deep in the dream. Why is it night in the middle of day?

Buchner, beside him. "Hauptsturmführer! The gunners await your order. We have many more to process today. Sir—"

Heudeber turned away. "Who are these people, Buchner?"

"These people, sir? Who are *these people?"*

"That is what I asked you, Untersturmbannführer. Please respond."

"Yes sir. These—these are the ones to be liquidated, sir."

"You are certain of this? They look so—"

"This is how they all look, sir." Buchner's voice hardened. "They all look like this. *Wo gehobelt wird, da fallen Späne.* Are you going to give the order, sir? Or shall I?"

Heudeber looked back at them. He'd heard it before. "Where there is planing, shavings fall." The man at the end of the line was looking upward now, fingering his penis. For some obscure reason Heudeber was glad he was no longer looking at him.

He shouted suddenly, before he could think any more. *"Los,"* he shouted. "Fire! Fire now!"

The clatter started instantly, both guns at once. They began at both ends of the line and proceeded toward the center; thus no one could escape. Bodies doubled over or flew apart at the impact of the heavy bullets. Chunks of meat and blood spraying out over the dirt, they bounced backward into the trench like billiard balls skillfully sunk. Right to left, left to right, the steady hammering went on, breechblocks chattering like typewriters. Shell casings flew like gold coins from a sack. Blue smoke blew toward the trench. The bodies leapt and whirled, dancing briefly on the edge of eternity, then fell from sight behind the heaped rusty mounds, into the trench, into the open mouth of the earth.

Heudeber stood watching, hands pressed to his stomach under the thick gray uniform cloth.

The clatter ceased suddenly, leaving an echoing silence and a ringing in his ears. Instantly the troops were among the bodies, flinging those that remained on the berm into the trench and kicking dirt over the larger pools of blood. Then they fell back, and Buchner shouted orders, and from behind the piles of clothing and shoes and baggage came answering shouts.

Heudeber stood motionless, slightly bent. He dimly understood that something irretrievable had happened. A guillotine blade had fallen from the sky, slicing off everything he had believed justified this. His belief that these people were subhuman. His faith in Hitler. Exposing, within himself, emptiness where his soul had been.

He was not a surgeon, cutting off diseased flesh in order that a better humanity might live. He was not a scientist, culling out the unfit.

It was the "unfit" who had created art, science, literature, religion.

He stood shivering under an apocalyptic sky. The last mask had fallen away, and he stared face to face at what he had become.

The squads remained in place until the antitank ditch was three-quarters filled with the dead and dying. Then that section was covered. They moved two hundred meters to the left, and began again.

That day Einsatzgruppe E executed four thousand five hundred people.

Heudeber had his evening meal in his tent that night. He knew what had happened. He'd seen it happen to others. He'd broken. Now, though, he understood it differently. It was not like breaking. It was like waking up.

When Stellen, his adjutant, left, he took out his pistol, checked it, put it to his head, and closed his eyes. A vision of crows, wheeling above a cornfield.

He sat like that for a quarter hour, alone in the tent. He discovered that he could no longer shoot anyone. Even himself.

He no longer wanted to live.

But he was not yet ready to die.

———

At 3:00 A.M. the storm burst over them. Out of the roaring black came a sudden, intense blast of freezing-cold rain. Heudeber couldn't see. In the black howl he couldn't tell where the old man was. He hesitated, then retreated into the deckhouse and slammed the door. The wheel moved against his back in short jerks, left, hard right, left again, and he knew Austin was still out there.

The rain and spray lashed the windows. The old boat groaned as she flexed, and beneath his feet iron things clattered and rolled. The jolting hammer of the engine was a muffled drumbeat here. The air smelled of fish and paint and gasoline. He glanced at the compass: west by northwest; the right course, as far as he could tell. It wouldn't be too far across the bay here.

Wondering *how* far, he pulled his map out of his overcoat pocket. It was soaked and falling to pieces, but he measured with forked fingers, the way he'd measured in 1941 how far the Panzers rolled in a day. How long ago that seemed . . . he shoved the bitterness away. No more than thirty kilometers, then they'd be in the Potomac, and the seas should let up.

Staring into darkness, his wide-open eyes returned him to the past.

———

The day after the massacre at Opochka, Heudeber had called his superior and requested transfer to a fighting unit facing the Soviet Army. He was relieved within four hours. When a man said he could no longer serve in the Special Action Detachments, Adolf Eichmann detached him instantly.

In 1942, after tactical and divisional operation training in Germany, Heudeber was assigned to a Waffen SS division. He fought through the summer as part of Von Paulus's Sixth Army. In the Battle of Kharkov, despite head injuries from Soviet strafing, he led a successful infantry counterattack, recovering a strategically placed hill and winning his Iron Cross.

That June, the second summer in the USSR, the Red Army seemed to suddenly disintegrate in front of Army Group B. The Sixth Army drove eastward like a steel fist, punching through, then scooping in chopped-up, confused Soviet units. Heudeber first saw Stalingrad in September, saw it as a towering pillar of smoke by day and a column of fire by night.

When his unit moved into the city he found his brothers there ahead of him. Erich, the youngest, was attached to the repair elements of the 14th Panzer Division. Sepp, a year older than Hans, was a liaison officer with the Rumanians holding the line to the north and south of the Sixth. The three had a little reunion one day, sharing their field rations in Sepp's mess.

Then came winter and the Russian counterattack.

Heudeber was lucky. He was wounded badly, and early.

Oddly enough he could not remember how, though he'd heard similar stories from others in the various hospitals and treatment centers. Usually this partial amnesia was a shock effect, the result of a high-explosive near miss. He remembered being operated on, though. It was in the cellar of what had been a workers' dormitory near the tractor factory. The walls were concrete, sweating with moisture. As the stretcher carriers slid him onto a plank table he caught sight of a pail filled with meat. On top was a lower jaw, the teeth plainly visible; two had silver-colored fillings. He turned his head to see the surgeon's silhouette, a bending head against a light so blinding hot he had to close his eyes.

When he recovered consciousness he was in a truck and he no longer had a left arm. His head wound had been sewn up with hasty, large stitches. The shell fragments had been left in his legs. The medical service troops unloaded him at Pitomnik airport. He lay in the open all night, tagged for embarkation, with only an overcoat over him. He was lucky: the temperature was only a little below freezing then. In a few weeks it would fall to eighteen and twenty below zero.

Nor did his luck end there. A shot-up Heinkel 111 overshot the runway trying to land and skidded through a line of waiting wounded. He moved up seventy-two places on the evacuation roster. He was not left to freeze and starve in the surrounded, twice-conquered city. He was flown out in a JU-52.

Later he heard on the radio, on Kurt Dittmar's program, that in the last days before surrender the Rumanian division to which Sepp was attached had mutinied, killed all its German officers, and gone over with its weapons to the Soviets. His efforts to find out about Erich were rebuffed by the Army at first. Finally they'd told him his brother had been shot during the siege. By an SS detachment. The charge was stealing food.

———

He realized what woke him even as he came back to himself in 1945, huddled in a locked little deckhouse in the dark. It was not a sound. It was the absence of one. Around him the sea still swayed and boomed. Spray still rattled against the windows. But the hammer that pulsed through *Ella Eyre*'s timbers like a stuttering heartbeat had suddenly stopped. Only fitful gleams accentuated the darkness, and the howl and whistle of the wind was deafening.

He dragged himself up and checked the compass. The phosphorescent needle danced a tarantelle between SE and S. He groped for the shotgun, found it on the floorboards. He got up and the deckhouse rolled and he blundered painfully into a bulkhead. The door rattled. Someone was outside, trying to get in. Heudeber flipped the latch off with the end of the barrel.

Austin lurched in, water streaming off a yellow oilskin reefer and a floppy red canvas hat. "What is wrong with the engine?" Heudeber asked him. "Are we out of petrol?"

"What? Oh, gas. No. Not yet. But gettin' mighty low, by my guess."

"Guess? Don't you know?"

"Never been a gauge on *Ella Eyre,* mister. This ain't no yacht."

"You said we had enough to get across the bay."

"Heavy seas, they eat up fuel fast. Could turn out I was wrong."

Heudeber aimed the flash behind him. The deck was empty except for the silver mist of dancing rain and the sliding veneers of water. He flicked it back to his own lips, so the old man could hear. "Where's your boy?"

"He's safe where he is. Look, mister, whoever you are—you ever been out in a boat this size?"

"I've been to sea."

"But in ships, 'm I right? I don't know that you understand we got no business in hell being out here in a storm like this. Something goes wrong, it blows any harder—or if it just stays like this, and we spring a seam or the pump quits or the engine seizes up— Another thing. This here boat ain't got no deep keel keeping her top upright. She's shallow. If I miss a trick, a heavier'n usual sea hits us when we're hove over—we're goin' down. I'm scared, mister. I'm talking level with you."

"What do you want to do?"

"Turn tail. Put her stern to the wind and run. Duck into the Wicomico, an' hole up in Fair Port or Reedville till she blows over."

"How long will that take?"

"I can't tell you what this wind's going to do, mister. I been on the water forty-six years now, and anybody'll tell you he can read a northeaster, he's lyin' to ye. It'd be a day, maybe three before I'd guarantee to put you up into the Potomac."

"How close are we now? There will be shelter there, will there not?"

"Oh, not too far in miles," said the old man. The flashlight caught his hand, hanging onto a beam. Traced the blue chain of the tattoo. "No more'n ten or twelve, near's I can guess. Hour's run in smooth water. But it's like climbing a cliff, now. Sea's coming in off t' starboard beam. Wants to blow us onto Smith Point. Tellin' you, mister, that engine stops, we all be a portion for the crabs before morning."

The problem was that he didn't know if the old man was lying or telling the truth. He didn't know boats. He didn't know this coast. Austin could be giving him fair warning. There was no way to tell.

"Keep going," he said.

The old man's mouth hung open. "What are you, anyway?" he all but whispered. "What are you fixing to do, when you get to Washington?"

"You don't need to know."

The old oyster boat rolled madly, almost on her beam ends, as the sea whined and roared and battered at glass and old juniper. Austin held himself vertical by pushing against the cabin ceiling. Heudeber, with only one hand, had wedged himself into a corner and wrapped his arm around a stanchion. He kept the shotgun pointed at the old man.

"You know what I figure, mister? I thunk it all out. Out there on deck. Figured at first you was some kind of refugee. Off one of them ships come into Norfolk. But there's folks help them kind of people. They don't go alone. No, I figure you're a German. Some kind of spy."

Heudeber didn't answer.

"Like the ones they caught in New England, and down in Florida, comin' ashore from those soob-marines. That's what I figured out you are. And I'm damned if David Austin is going to carry any spies across the bay."

"You'll do as you're told," Heudeber told him icily. In a way he admired the old man; but he had to obey. "And you'll do it now. Get back out there. Get back on course."

"Better I steer from in here. The boy's cold. He'll get sick—"

The deck staggered back as the old boat came partially upright. Heudeber felt his temper going. He lunged forward and rammed the muzzle under Austin's throat, slamming his head back against the hatch. "Get outside!" he shouted. "Or I'll kill you now, and steer myself!"

The door swung empty, the wind battering it against the frame. With each swing spray spattered in. For a moment Heudeber relaxed. Then suddenly sickness shook him, and he bent, drooling into the bilges while his eyes strained outward like squeezed grape-seeds, staring into the clanging darkness.

When his fit was over the old boat was lying on her side and the sea was hammering on her bottom like, he thought blindly, the bass drums at Bayreuth banging out the *Götterdämmerung*. "Wagner," he muttered. "How appropriate."

He thrust the shotgun under the stump of his left arm, stock forward. Grasping the jamb with his right, he pulled himself up and through it, out of the deckhouse, into the storm.

The booming was not just the sea. Through the blowing spray and pouring rain flickered a white hellish glare. An instantaneous sheet of blazing fire showed him driving clouds, and below them a frozen tableau of the old man and the boy in the stern. Halted by the flash, rain and spray glittered in the air around them like elongated diamonds.

"Austin!" he screamed into the storm. The old man didn't turn. Then it was utter dark again. He fumbled for the flashlight. Its pale beam lanced a silver shaft through the rain and ended on the boy's face. So small, Heudeber thought.

The old oyster boat was being hammered by each successive wave. Austin was hunched over the steering post, staring out to starboard from under his hat. The wind pressed Heudeber against the gunwale, and he had to bend to make his way aft. As he got to the stern the old man straightened, as if to see over the oncoming seas, then reached down by his boot. The motor coughed, then roared, and the bow twisted right and rose with terrifying swiftness, everything around them the roaring, singing black. Heudeber clung to the scarred wood. It looked inevitable to him that they were going to capsize.

But they didn't. *Ella Eyre* nosed over the crest and dropped, hard, slamming down into the hollow trough behind it. At the same time she rolled, trying to shake them off. The motor hammered at top speed. Flame percolated from the stack. Heudeber felt his gorge rise. This time he only turned his head as his cramping belly buckled him over. He had nothing in his stomach to lose.

—

He'd taken a long time to recover, back in Germany. Infection had set in the untreated wounds in his legs. For weeks he'd slipped in and out of consciousness. Not until 1944 was he able to return to limited duty as the commander of a POW camp. He had amused himself by polishing his English and painting a little. But he also spent a great deal of time alone, thinking about what had happened in Poland, and in Russia, and in Germany.

Inside him now, instead of belief in victory, was emptiness. Instead of a desire to live, a barren desert. He'd picked up a Bible once, curious what it said about forgiveness, but it seemed distant and fictional and irrelevant. Why hadn't he died in Stalingrad with his brothers? Occasionally, late at night and full of alcohol, he had an almost mystical feeling that his story was not yet complete. That the design sketched of his life had not yet been filled in.

On 20 February 1945, he was suddenly ordered to report in person to the head of the Reich Department of the Interior, Commander of the SS, head of the Abwehr, SD, and Gestapo: Heinrich Himmler, Reichsführer-SS.

——

He didn't know how much later it was when he came back to the rolling boat. The engine was faltering now. Running for a few seconds, then choking. It stopped; a starter ground; it started; faltered again.

The wind blew a spatter of rain past his head as he scrambled out of the shelter of the gunwale. His feet skidding, he ran aft, along the canting, wildly bucking deck, and slammed into Austin. He recoiled instantly. Too close to those muscular arms and he'd be fighting for his life, old as the man was.

Austin was already talking. "That's it, she's dry. We ought to be four, five miles off Smith Point. Can't tell, though. Land's low there."

"That's it? No more fuel?"

Heudeber couldn't tell if Austin heard him or not. The engine went b-r-r-r-u-p, b-r-r-r-u-p. Through the darkness he felt the old man examining him.

"Been thinking, though."

"What?"

"Got that Coleman fuel. What we used in the lantern. That's white gas. Might run her another twenty, thirty minutes. Maybe far enough to get under Point Lookout."

"Then what?"

"Heave the anchor over. Might hold, once we get into shelter. Here, you steer. Keep her nose north. Motor stops, give her a second or two, then start her again."

He moved off into the darkness. Heudeber hesitated, looking after him, then stepped into his place. A compass glowed faintly just in front of him. He tucked the gun under his stump and seized the post. The wood was smooth under his hand. Due north—that would be nearly into the wind and sea. The compass began to swing. He corrected, then glanced around the deck, trying to interpret shadows.

Where was Austin? He stirred, suddenly apprehensive. Just then a humped shape on the far side of the engine told him the waterman was at a safe distance. A clatter told him he was looking for the gas can.

He looked down to find the needle off, too far to the west. He cursed himself. Pulled on the post, sweating, trying to follow it, to match it. No use. It moved faster and faster, left, left—maybe he was turning the rudder the wrong way—

Something huge and heavy and icy cold closed around his neck and face. Heudeber staggered back in horror, trying to jerk free. It had teeth, rough sharp points that dug into his neck and cheek. It stank of oil and seaweed and fish. When he tried to wrench himself free its jaws scraped along his collarbone, heavy, biting in. He brought the shotgun around, clubbing with it. Instead of the thud of metal on meat it sounded hollow, like wood.

A lightning flash showed him Austin on the far side of the engine, holding the handles of an immense pair of tongs. Heudeber staggered back, trying to wrench his head loose. The iron jaws only bit the more cruelly, stabbing deep into his flesh. The old man was strong, and the levers gave him mechanical advantage.

Heudeber realized he was unable to breathe. The lower part of the oyster tongs met across his throat. He remembered the gun then and brought it up with his good arm, aligning it where he figured the old man to be. Then waited for the next flash. Christ, when would it—

A terrifying crashing dazzle directly above the boat showed him Austin's face, contorted in effort and hatred. He was working his way in along the oak handles. The flash showed him the windows of the deckhouse forward of the waterman. He pressed the trigger. Was surprised, through his growing pain, that nothing happened; then remembered, and thumbed back the big old-fashioned hammer. Dimly through the roar of the storm he heard Austin shouting then. "No—don't, it's a *flare*—"

The shotgun bucked in his hand, but its boom was a puny crack in the conflagration of the heavens. The flare left the muzzle in a straight line of red fire, passing over Austin's hunched head, and smashed through the rear window of the deckhouse. It hit a centerpost and ricocheted out of sight downward. A second later the deckhouse blew up.

Austin's head snapped round toward the thud and glare. Simultaneously, Heudeber made his final, desperate effort to free his head. The tongs clicked together and slammed to the deck. He had the gun by the barrel now, and brought it around with all his strength into the old man's forehead. Austin staggered. He took a step forward; then his knees buckled and he went down.

Heudeber dropped the now-useless gun and ran forward.

The interior of the deckhouse was a white hell of crackling flame building rapidly to a roar. The wheel, outlined in fire, jerked to and fro before something snapped and it spun hard right, throwing sparks like a catherine wheel. Heat radiated through the shattered window. He looked around for an extinguisher, a hose. Nothing. It wouldn't do much good against that, anyway.

Staring into the fire, he'd forgotten the sea. The next wave hit from astern. The boat jerked upward violently. Suddenly his feet shot out from under him on the slick wet boards. Kicking, screaming, he slid downhill, toward the open doorway and the fiery oven within.

The next wave rolled the boat hard left, and he curved that way and crashed into the gunwale instead. He grabbed it and hauled himself upright with desperate strength. His bag. He had to find his suitcase! It was somewhere here, in the mass of clamrakes and spare shafts and rat-wire stuffed and lashed along the port side.

Suddenly everything around him took on a ruddier, more brilliant immediacy. The fire had burned through the thin overhead of the deckhouse and was soaring upward now, in a huge hollowly roaring pyre that hurt his eyes and seared his face.

He was staring at it when Austin bulled into him from behind, grabbed him around the waist and slammed him down. Heudeber saw a red flash as his head struck a fairlead. He shook it off and rolled, lashing out into the old man's face, but it was like trying to stop a bear with one fist. "You squareheaded son of a bitch," the waterman was snarling. "Burn my boat—not going to—"

Heudeber got his thumb in the old man's eye socket. He felt the orb shift, dug deeper, and tore it loose. Austin gave a horrible low scream. His weight lifted, then doubled as the boat rolled viciously, throwing the old man back on top of him.

Heudeber suddenly went rigid, almost forgetting his opponent. Something dark and bitter cold was rubbing itself against his back. Something so cold it felt more solid than liquid. He knew what it was, though. It was the sea.

Ella Eyre was going down under them.

Austin scrabbled away across the deck, holding his face, and hauled himself up on the far gunwale. When he dropped his hand his torn-out socket ran blood and fluid as he searched with his good eye aft. "Paulie!" he screamed.

"G'ampaw!"

"Stay there! Hear me? Stay there!"

Heudeber staggered up, clinging to the gunwale. The burning deckhouse roared like a furnace. Every stanchion, every board inside it was limned in flame. Flame sparkled on the glass teeth in the shattered windows. Flame curled out of them and clawed upward at the rushing clouds. He stared across ten feet of deck at Austin.

The old man let go, and grew rapidly larger. Before he could evade them Heudeber felt two huge hard hands close around his throat. He groped for the other's crotch, but the old man didn't react. The big worn hands just closed tighter. The roar of the fire grew in his ears, merging with the roar of his heart.

Suddenly the deck came up, and over, and blackness closed over them both. The shock of the cold sea stopped his heart. It burned his skin like liquid fire. Yet still the hands stayed locked on his throat. Heudeber felt himself sinking, Austin still above him. Pressure leaned on his ears. He hammered at the softness, again and again, till he lost consciousness.

When he came to he was floating on the black sea, held up by air in his clothing. A few feet away flame was guttering out in the blackness. He didn't see or hear the old man. He gagged, but nothing came up.

He slowly became aware of thin high cries from the direction of the flames. Taking deep breaths when the sea let him, he side-stroked slowly toward them.

The boy fought at first, screaming and flailing at him, and Heudeber had to put his weight on his head and duck him under. That quieted him. He shouted, "Swim! Can you swim? Hold yourself up in the water!"

The boy choked and coughed. When he had his breath again he screamed frantically, "G'anpaw! G'anpaw!"

"Shut up!" Heudeber looked around desperately. With only one arm, he couldn't both swim and hold the boy up. In the dancing dying flame-light, debris littered the waves. Timbers. Floats. Then a familiar shape. He lunged and grabbed the suitcase. It should float for a while. He pushed it toward the boy and fastened his small hands around it.

But staying afloat wasn't going to be the problem. The Chesapeake was bitter, winter cold. Already his legs were numb. The boy's eyes looked fixed. His smaller body would freeze first. Heudeber tried to think of something to do. At last he swam closer to the floating, tossing torch that was the remnants of the boat. It was useless. As close as he dared to get, it heated their faces, but their bodies remained under water.

Then the last flames sank and died, and they were alone in the dark. The sea tumbled them like laundry, drove salty cold down their gasping mouths. Heudeber tried to hold the boy up. But each time he pushed, his own face sank below the sea. He was tiring fast. It was all he could do to keep himself up. He thought of letting the child go. No, he wouldn't. He struggled back to the surface and boosted him back onto his perch on the suitcase again.

Out in the darkness a pale disk of light winked on. It moved erratically across the water. At last it gleamed brightly, swung around, and fixed itself on them.

The boat came from behind the light. It loomed terrifying over him, then crashed down. The hull almost crushed them. Then men were leaning down with poles. One of the boat hooks snagged the boy's jacket. It lifted him up, up, water streaming from his clothes. Heudeber blinked into the dazzle. The hull surged and rolled beside him, frighteningly huge. Caught under that, he'd never come up. A line spun down and splashed across him. He threw the loop over his head, clumsily fitting it under the stump. He couldn't feel his hand. A few more minutes in this water and they'd have both slipped numbly beneath the surface.

Then he too was rising, to the accompaniment of shouts and clanking. A steel arm wheeled above him, then swung inward. When his dangling legs brushed the deck, hands seized him. A flask pushed between his icy lips. He sucked, coughed, swallowed. A light came on and played over him.

"Take it easy, mister. Coast Guard. What ship? What happened?"

"Ella Eyre," he gasped out. He caught a glimpse of the boy, naked for a moment, then disappearing into an immense towel.

The voice behind the light said, "Saw the fire from upriver, over't Piney Point. Turnt around and got over here soon's we could. Anybody else in the water, you figure?"

"No. Just us, and—and the captain. He—the boat's gone. Caught fire, then capsized. He must have—must have died as it went down."

"Take it easy. Have another belt. Just the two of you, out there with him?"

"That's right."

"This your boy?"

"No. His name's Paulie. Lives in Nassawadox, I think."

The little boy was crying, keening and sobbing. Heudeber could make out words. "Bad man," he was saying, "Hurt G'ampaw." One of the sailors was soothing him. But none of them seemed to be listening to what he said. He was too small to take seriously.

"Whereabout's that?"

"Across the bay."

"How about you? You're not crew, are you? An' in this bag you got—" The light came closer. It touched his collar. Hesitated there, then went out. "Sorry—Reverend."

"He was taking me across the bay. I have a—funeral service to do up in Washington."

"We'll be dockin' at Indian Head tomorrow. The ordnance station. Not far to D.C. from there."

Heudeber heard how shaky his voice was. He took a deep breath, trying to steady it as someone draped a blanket around him. "Can you put me ashore then? I'll make my way from there."

"Sure, Reverend."

"And take care of the boy."

"We'll sure do that." The shadow behind the voice turned away. Shouted, "Get them below. Rubdown, dry clothes on 'em. Flynn! Kilhoffer! Bear a hand!"

Sitting alone, his shuddering hand resting on his luggage, Heudeber's expression did not change at all.

CHAPTER 9

Friday, March 23: Palm Beach, Florida

P alm Beach, Palm Beach." The conductor's singsong rose and fell as he made his way through the coach, waking me from a doze I'd nursed since Jacksonville. A porter followed, reaching down to shake those who still slept. I got up to stretch, then pulled my tropical khaki jacket out of the overhead rack and unrolled it carefully. No luck, it still looked like I'd spent the night in it. Past the streaky windows the sun struck so bright off asphalt and stone you couldn't look outside for long. "Ten minutes stopover. Thanks for riding the Florida East Coast Railway. Stand clear of the wheels. Signal you a redcap, Cap'n?"

I shook my head and pulled my overnighter down from the rack. A fast trip for wartime, twenty-six hours from Washington. There was DC-3 service from National to Morrison Field, and as a wounded vet I could have flown standby. But I'd wanted time to think. For that, give me a train. In Vero Beach, a fifteen-minute stop, I'd found a pay phone and called the house. Teddy had answered. "Kennedy residence."

"Howzit going, Fatstuff?"

"Johnny! Are you home?"

"Almost. Pulling in around eleven, the downtown station. Tell Dad, okay?"

"Gee, this is great! Are we going out in the boat?"

"Maybe," I said. "See you soon. Remember to tell Dad, okay? Have somebody there to pick me up. I don't want to have to walk."

"Okay, Johnny. Wow! It'll be great to see you."

I made a kissing noise and hung up, grinning. Edward was everybody's favorite. A puppylike kid, chubby but good-natured. He was crazy about his three older brothers. No, that wasn't exactly accurate. We had a way of fathering each other, in our family. Joe Jr. had been my dad when I was growing up, day to day. I'd done that for Bobby, and Bobby, who was nineteen now, had done it for the kid. It made for closeness. But it only partly made up for a dad who wasn't around much, who spent more time in New York or Hollywood or London than at home.

And that made it all the tougher when the brother you loved was gone. My eyes blurred, looking out into the glare. It was impossible to think of that hard body dissipated to floating atoms in a cloud of smoke. They'd never found any part of him, any part even of the plane, the explosion had been so violent. It must have been fast. There was that to be grateful for. But he'd always seemed so fucking *alive*—

"Wait till the train stops, lads. Palm Beach! Ten-minute stop."

We slid into the station past another train standing at the platform. Gray steam curtained the windows as we squealed to a halt. The conductor slid the door open and swung down, grunting as if solid ground hurt his feet. I set my cap, stepped down behind him, bag in hand. Glanced around me, and froze to the pavement. I was surrounded by Japs.

By scores, no, hundreds of Japs. They leaned down from the windows of the other train, showing their teeth and waving. Crowded past me in a khaki stream. My throat closed in horror. I couldn't make sense of what was going on. A band was striking up "Dixie" over in front of the station. Redcaps and civilians stood watching with broad grins. Some held flags. A banner ahead read "American Legion Post 12 Welcomes the 442nd." Under it middle-aged men in aprons handed out hot dogs and limeade. I recognized Stan Peeler, the mayor. The smell of popcorn blew over the crowd from a Moose booth. Smiling young women handed out apple turnovers, peaches, homemade cookies, pints of milk, iced tea, orange juice, Coca-Colas. The dark-faced, small men in U.S. Army uniforms ignored the sweets and pastries and milk. They went for the Coke and juice and fruit.

Suddenly it snapped into focus. I'd read about these guys. Nisei, first-generation Japanese-Americans, they'd bloodied the Germans' noses in Italy. A unit of white soldiers was detraining behind them. I shook myself and moved toward the gate. My guts still felt loose, though. One caught my eye and nodded. "Where you fellas from?" I asked him.

"Hey, Lieutenant. Italy. The Krauts have had enough, now they're shifting us west."

"West? Where?" I said, surprised, then remembered security. "Sorry, I don't need to know that."

"No problem, sir, we haven't been told yet anyway. My gosh, what a lot of people turn out to see us, eh?"

"Yeah. They do it right here." I found a paper cup of orange juice in my hand and looked after the girl, trying to give it back. The corporal I'd been talking to took it from me. It was gone in one long swallow. Juice must have been scarce in Italy.

Outside the station the lot was full of people and cars and bicycles. Palm Beach had made it a point to cheer the troop trains all through the war. It had started small, somebody's idea of a nice thing to do, but what does Jimmy Durante say? "Everybody wants ta get inta da act." The white and yellow soldiers mixed cheerfully enough, but my heart was still whanging away like a pair of fifties.

I remembered one day at Tulagi we went to pick up a Jap pilot who had hit the silk after being shot down. We pulled alongside him, about twenty yards away. He was a young guy, well built, powerful looking—short black hair. He suddenly threw aside the life belt he was wearing, pulled a pistol and started firing. We let go with everything we had but couldn't seem to get him, till one old soldier took the top of his skull off with a Springfield.

I shaded my eyes and stared around. They'd probably send the red Plymouth, the convertible. Behind me a whistle shrieked; conductors shouted; the stop was almost over, the khaki tide was streaming back aboard.

There it was, parked facing Railroad Avenue. The driver was sitting in it, reading a paper. I could see the back of his hat. Keyed up as I was, I felt a flash of annoyance. Why hadn't he met me on the platform? I might have had luggage, or needed help. I had a sharp word ready as I came up. It stuck in my mouth as the hat turned.

It was Dad, face ruddy from a recent dose of sun, wearing a pair of round-lensed sunglasses I hadn't seen before. He looked at me blankly for a moment over the close-printed pages of the stock reports. Then his face came to life. "Jack! Hi, boy! Jesus, you look good. Jump in."

"Dad. I figured you'd send the Gator, I—"

"He's gone."

"Gone?"

"That's what I said. I had him working down on the seawall, patching it where the sand washed away. He complained the work was too hard. He wanted a raise. So I sent him back to Boston."

"You're a tough guy to work for, Dad."

It was funny, the sunglasses made me realize he didn't use his eyes to smile with at all. "Teddy said you called. Could have sent Eunice, but I decided to get you myself. That all you got? Throw it in back."

I did, and got in, moving gingerly, but he didn't remark on it. The engine snarled and caught, and he craned around, backing out fast between a station wagon and a Rolls. "What're all the Chinese doing on your train?"

"Those are Japs, Dad. A unit of Japanese-American boys back from Italy."

"That so. How was the trip down?"

"Okay. Fast."

"He give you the medal himself?"

"Yes, Dad. He asked about you. And he—"

"I don't give a goddamn if he asked about me. The son of a bitch."

He meant Roosevelt. I thought about the rest of it, what the President had asked me, what he'd said about Joe Jr. But there was no point telling Dad, though FDR probably intended me to. The rift between them went too deep for words to bridge.

I took my hat off and leaned back, enjoying the hot kiss of the South Florida sun. The passenger station was on the far side of Lake Worth from the island itself. Henry Flagler had laid out the town of West Palm Beach to house the workers and servants necessary to the paradise he planned. Not so long ago, the trains had backed across the bridge to bring the Vanderbilts and Astors and Stotesburys and Goulds to his private island, till the engine noise bothered his new bride; then he relocated the station. The hood of the convertible tilted up, and the engine purred deeper, and we arched up over the broad blue of the Intracoastal Waterway. To the left I could see boat yards; way down there was the inlet and the ship channel, the West India Company docks, and the green mass of Peanut Island, the Coast Guard base.

And ahead, Palm Beach, one of the strangest towns in America.

Dad played a lot of golf. That was what had brought him here back in the thirties. It was warm and dry, and you could play all winter. He stayed at the Royal Poinciana then, but in '33 he bought one of the Mizner houses on North Ocean Boulevard, where the beach ends and then there's just the road. In the most exclusive enclave in America.

Sometimes I wondered why he bothered. I think he knew, deep down, that they'd never accept him, no matter how much money he had. He had the wrong ancestors and the wrong religion. But he couldn't give up trying. He'd wanted it so long the hunger had become part of him.

I can't say I understood my father. I knew him, but I didn't understand him. One thing I was sure had affected him. He'd been passed by for the Porc at Harvard. As he saw it, because he was Catholic. After that rejection, he'd never felt loyalty to any institution, and not really to any person, outside of his family.

The funny thing was that FDR, Episcopalian, old school, old money, had been passed by too. Maybe that was what they'd seen in each other once.

A roar shattered the sultry breeze. I lifted my eyes to a C-54 droning in from seaward, laying brown trails of exhaust across pale blue. Wounded men from Europe. I knew the war had come to Palm Beach in other ways too. The luxurious Breakers Hotel was now Ream Army Hospital, packed with amputees and the badly wounded. Morrison Field had become the headquarters of the Army Air Transport Command. The ground Army had a camp set up to guard the inlet, and Boca Raton had a supersecret base where they did radar training for the Air Corps.

The tires came off the bridge with a thump and we were on Royal Palm Way. Four lines of the great trees strained the scattered clouds between their fronds. I could hear the ocean now. To the left a many-gabled wooden structure rambled behind a stuccoed wall. Gambling was illegal in Florida, but it was tolerated at the Beach Club because the owner, "Colonel" Ed Bradley, supposedly barred it to any full-time resident (though I'd seen plenty there). Heavy contributions to local churches, charities, and political campaigns didn't hurt either. Away to the right, glowing in the sun, rose the twin Italian Renaissance towers of the Breakers.

"Been to the Beach Club?"

"Last week," said Dad. "Old Ed hasn't been looking too good. The old bastard."

I looked toward the Royal Poinciana so he wouldn't see my face. Bradley had sold Dad his majority interest in Hialeah in '42. Later that same day, FDR had closed all racetracks for the duration to save gasoline. One of the few times Dad had been outsmarted.

"When he kicks off, the old zipperoo will go out of this place for sure. You'll have to go to Havana for any action."

"What's the news at the Beach?"

"The Breakers is open again, and the Cocoanut Grove. Grimes is still the maitre d'. The Germans are on strike."

"Sorry?"

"The prisoners they brought in at Belle Glade, to pick fruit. They went on strike because they're not getting enough cigarettes. Imagine what'd happen to our boys if they tried that in Germany," said Dad. "Those bastards are lucky we don't shoot them all, and they want more smokes."

He fell silent abruptly, and I knew he was thinking about the people the war had taken away from us. I thought about Cy and Peter and Orv and Gil, and Kirksey and Marney, too. And most of all, about Joe. I looked away, at the familiar buildings as we waited for the light, then headed north on County Road.

We passed the Paramount, where before the war we kids used to go for matinees. Past St. Edward's, where Mom went every morning for Mass. The road narrowed and wound through Australian pines that looked like clipped poodles, and lipstick-colored hibiscus and fig trees and more palms. Past the Stotesbury estate and, set back in greenery and walls, Los Incas, and Casa Bedita, Memaw, Amado, Louwana. The Towers, where the Duke and Duchess of Windsor stayed when they visited.

Past the Club the road turned toward the ocean again. Another few blocks and we'd be home. I shaded my eyes and glanced at my dad. He looked grim, but there was sadness under there too.

"Seriously, Dad, are you doing all right?"

"No."

"What's wrong?"

"I'm damn well fed up with sitting on my fanny here instead of doing something, that's what's wrong."

"But you're keeping busy."

"Yeah. The trust bought a couple blocks on Lexington Avenue, Fifty-first and Fifty-ninth."

"Coca-Cola working out?" He'd bought some kind of franchise in Latin America.

"Still negotiating."

"You really think the Brazilians will like it?"

"I'll goddamn well make them like it."

Same old Dad. "How about Howard Johnson?"

"I think he's got something. There'll be a lot of travel after the war, if we don't get the Depression back. Might be a good idea, a restaurant chain. Got to study it some more, though."

Just as we got to the house he pulled the wheel left. I tensed, waiting for someone to come around the curve into us, but he hauled right again and we rolled into the bush-screened lot of number 1095.

━━━

Bobby was at Harvard, in the V-12 program. Rosemary, who had gotten worse after we left England, had been at St. Coletta's, an institution in Wisconsin, since I went into the Navy. Kathleen was still in England with the Devonshires. Though with Billy's death, she no longer had any claim to their houses or holdings, the family had accepted her as a member. She still wrote, but in some mysterious way seemed to belong more to them now than to us. As if she'd made her escape. . . . Pat and Jean were at school. So it was just Mom, Dad, Teddy, Eunice, and me.

Mom was in the living room as we came in, listening to the radio. I went up behind her and put my hands over her eyes.

"Hello, John."

"Darn, Mom, how'd you know?"

"Irish mothers have second sight. Come give me a hug."

She smelled of lavender and looked great in a blue-and-white print frock and white wedgies. Slim-hipped, dark curly hair and blue blue eyes, my quiet mother didn't look fifty-two. She'd worked hard in England to get her weight down and she'd always taken care of her face. The Brits couldn't believe she had all us kids. She was a little weird. What can you say about a woman who pins notes to herself so she won't forget things? But still she's my mom. "What a great dress. Where are you headed?"

"Mrs. Pierrepont's having a luncheon for the St. Mary's Advisory Committee. Princess Pignatelli will be there. Then we have to tour the hospital and meet the new director."

"And after that?"

"The Four Arts, for a recital; then the tea dance, I suppose. Want to come? They'd love to see my young hero."

"My mom, the social butterfly." It was a jab, but I was glad. I remembered how depressed and isolated she'd been when we were small, when Dad spent all his time on the West Coast. London had lit something bright in her, some gaiety from her girlhood she'd almost lost. Her faith was a rock; it let her accept everything and go on in confidence that God and the Pope knew what was right. Sometimes I admired that. Sometimes it frustrated the heck out of me. I caught Dad's frown and slight shake of the head. "Thanks, but I think Dad's got something planned. Maybe you can show me off to your friends tomorrow. Which room have I got, Mom?"

Eunice came in in tennis clothes, all in a glow. She squealed and crimped my hand, and we wrestled for a second. There was a Spanish-looking guy with her, Rodrigo or Ridrico. I didn't bother to remember his name since she said she'd just met him. As she went off upstairs to change I fell into one of the stuffed chairs and looked around.

The house looked the same. Aside from new furniture, we'd never bothered to redecorate. It had a musty smell, and the wooden floors were worn and the tile was chipped. Sometimes Mizner aged things himself; he chipped his marble staircases to look like spurs had nicked them, he whipped furniture with chains to make it look old; but these were real scars, from a few years of Kennedy kids and a few million guests. "Where's Teddy?"

"Edward is out on the beach."

Mom left, giving me a kiss. I returned it dutifully, then wandered back to the kitchen to check on lunch. I didn't know the cook, but that didn't surprise me. Servants didn't last too long in our household. She was making chicken salad and fruit and stuff.

I let myself out the back. Over the beautifully kept-up lawn, to the edge of the seawall, and stood there, looking down. The sea had eaten a few feet into the property. But the palms still clashed whisperingly above me and the blue Atlantic still hissed and boomed right in our backyard.

No Teddy, though. I took another step forward, till I was on the very teetering end of the wall. Looking down.

He was under it, playing in the sand. A sort of sand fort . . . no . . . humps of sand with bits of sticks and trash stuck into them. He sat alone among them, a chunky ungainly kid, sandy-haired, surprisingly pale. Suddenly I felt sorry for him. He'd been a baby when we sold the house in Massachusetts. He must have been to ten different schools since then, shuttling around from New York to England to Hyannis Port and Florida. Then I heard what he was saying, a rapid low muttering to himself.

"The Jap battleship's closing in . . . but here comes the 109. It's attacking again. Fire one! Whoosh. It's running fast. The Japs see it. They're trying to turn. They're trying to run. It's too late. *Banzai!*"

He dug his hand under one of the clumps and flung it skyward. The wind showered me with damp sand. "Hey!" I said.

An upturned face, wide eyes; then the sand-ships were trampled as he flung himself toward me. I caught his head and held him off. "Take it easy on the uniform, Skeezicks. Just shake hands, all right? How you been doing?"

"Jeez, I wanted to go to the station with Dad, but he wouldn't let me. Then you took so long—"

"Well, here I am."

I let him talk me into a walk up the beach, and he pestered me with questions about torpedoes and engines the whole way up to the Cabana Club and back. When we climbed back up to the lawn, my shoes caked with sand and salt, lunch was ready on the patio. I wasn't too hungry, but I drank three glasses of lemonade. Teddy really chowed down, though.

"You want to play this afternoon?" Dad said.

"I guess."

"You're not too tired?"

"If we don't play all afternoon. The PB?"

That was the Palm Beach, the mainly Jewish club my dad had joined when he didn't get invited to the Everglades. He played there a lot, but this time he shook his head. "I'm burned out on that course. Let's go up to the Seminole."

"That's a long drive."

"We'll take the boat. I haven't used it for a while, let's see if they're taking care of it."

"Can I steer?" I said. It was a running joke. He always had to steer when we were kids.

"Sure. Till you fuck up."

"Can I come, Dad? Hey, Jack, can I come?"

"Some other time, Teddy," Dad said, and the kid looked up at him for a couple of seconds, his mouth open, then looked down at the floor.

"What about clubs?"

"You can play with mine. I'll spot you two strokes."

"Five."

"Three."

"Four?"

"Three," said Dad. "Final offer."

"All right," I said. "Just let me change."

━━━

I still had some clothes around the house. I washed up and shaved, then picked out a pair of tan slacks and saddle shoes, a short-sleeve shirt, and a sweater vest—Seminole could get windy. I gave the maid my uniform to iron.

We drove over to the Sailfish, a marina and clubhouse up on the north end, where the inlet cut a path in from the sea. Dad had called ahead and the runabout was fueled and warmed up at the pier. It was kind of strange, after being used to eighty-foot monsters with enough power practically to take off and fly, to step down into the little boat and remember how huge and powerful it had seemed when I was sixteen.

It still moved out, though. When I shoved the throttle forward we leapt out of the slip. It carried us like a song out into the lake in a long curve. I aimed for the left cut of Peanut Island. A freighter was coming in from seaward and I kept the throttle open, trying to get across its bow before it made the turning basin. Dad shifted beside me. "You don't want to slow down, let him by?"

"Hell with that, Dad."

"You're right. Hell with that." The dark glasses gleamed sun at me.

Up at the north end of the lake the Intracoastal took a left and headed up toward Jupiter Inlet. We took a right and then things got narrow. At the very end of Little Lake Worth is a shallow spot you can pull your boat up on, and there you are, practically at the gates of the Seminole Club. I coasted in, careful of the prop, and ran her up on the beach. We got off over the bow and slogged up the bank, Dad carrying his clubs.

━━━

The Seminole's about the best course in the country. They have fairways as smooth as the greens most other places. The clubhouse looks down from a promontory out over the ocean. We walked up toward it along a stretch of gravel path, past the Packards and Chryslers, under the big sundial above the entrance into a coolly shadowed hall. After we signed in I followed Dad up onto a flagstoned terrace shaded by cocoanut palms and sea-grape trees. Beyond that was the big saltwater pool, empty at the moment, tennis courts, and the vivid green of the course. From up here we could see the lagoons sparkling in the distance. The fairway looked smooth, and it was. Except for the hazards, which were intentionally nasty.

My old shoes were in Dad's locker downstairs. My feet must have gotten bigger in the Navy; I could hardly get them on. I worked them on looking up at the mounted heads. A hum of conversation came from the bar.

On the greens a group of older men stood talking. One gestured toward a distant line of palms. Then they noticed us. "Hello, Latham, Howell, Elmer," Dad said. "You remember Johnny."

They gave out with some sentiments about the returning hero, and I grinned and shrugged. A line of Negro caddies waited in the shade. Dad jerked his thumb to one. The next in line looked at me. I shook my head and pointed to the one bag. He stepped out anyway. Dad lifted his eyebrows at me above the blank-disced sunglasses. "You got a hat?" he said. "You ought to have a hat, Jack."

"Don't care for 'em, Dad. I'll just play like this."

"Without a hat? You'll burn."

One of the men offered me his. I thanked him but said no, I needed some sun.

We headed out for the first hole, the caddies trailing us and fighting in subdued whispers over the single bag. When I looked back one was carrying it and the other had about half the clubs over his shoulder. "You know that guy, offered you the hat?" said Dad.

"Yeah?"

"Before the Depression, he used to be worth forty or fifty million dollars. Now he'd be lucky if he could scrape together two or three million. But he still hangs around here, just like he still had it. . . . There's a real shortage of balls these days."

"What?"

He groped in his pocket, then held out a closed fist. "Here. Take it, take it, goddamnit." I slipped my hand under his and found a pack of premium Spauldings, wrapping still unbroken. "You have to turn in your old ones, and even then, all you get are old cores with new covers. Retreads. Been saving these for you. Take it easy on the water holes, okay?"

The Seminole course is a par seventy-two, designed by Donald Ross just before the Crash of '29. The richest men in America told him to build the finest course money could buy, something that would challenge the best golfers in the world. So he did. Especially when the sea wind comes twisting over the dunes. It's beautiful, but Seminole has the reputation of being a manicured bitch.

Out on the first tee, we looked northwest at three hundred eighty-four yards of velvety but slick Bermuda grass. We tossed the tee for honors. Dad bent, then straightened. "It's yours."

I took a few slow practice swings to loosen up. I felt stiff, but okay. As I teed up Dad said, "How about a bet?"

"Sure. What kind?"

"How about this. A block of Manhattan versus your going into politics."

The dark glasses studied me. I just laughed. If only it could be that easy, just laugh Dad off. But it was going to be a long afternoon on the links.

I got into position and, aiming toward the middle of the fairway, got off a nice smooth swing. I tried for solid contact, that was all I wanted on this first tee. It paid off with a near-two-hundred-yard drive down the right side.

I handed Dad the driver. He went through his routine and finished slightly ahead of me in the middle of the fairway. We strolled down side by side, enjoying the warm breeze and looking around at the rolling dunes.

I went first again, being farther from the hole. A four wood dropped me short and left of the green. My father hit short too, but straighter. Hell, I thought.

When I called for the wedge my caddy moved up beside me. "That's a chip shot, sir. I'd recommend a seven iron."

"Oh yeah?" I said. Maybe it would be, considering how long it'd been since I'd played.

I hit fat and found myself laying three and still off the green. "Fuck," I muttered. My fourth shot ended up about fifteen feet from the cup.

Dad chipped well to the green, stopping about ten feet away. We managed two putts, with him carrying a five and me a six.

The second hole was longer and with water. I wasn't enjoying the day as much now. We both bogeyed, a respectable score for a long par four. "You're still one stroke down," said the Old Man.

So far we'd concentrated on the game. These were long holes, though, and as we were walking up on the third, a par-five four hundred sixty-five yards, Dad said, "Now, look, the bet was a joke. But we got to talk about what you're going to do."

"I don't know, Dad. There's still a war on. I kind of still belong to the Navy."

"You'll be out in, what? Two weeks? With a good record."

"Yeah, I guess you're right," I said. Sometimes that worked, just agreeing, then changing the subject. "What do you hear from Washington?"

"From Washington?" He looked down the fairway. "I don't hear shit from Washington, Jack. Just the telegrams he sends, when we—lose somebody."

"Dad—" I hesitated. The rule was, there were some things you didn't ask Joe Kennedy. Things you either figured out, or guessed, or other people told you; but you didn't ask. Still, sometimes you had to. "What do you think of him?"

"You know what I think of him. He's the President."

"I mean personally."

"Personally? Personally? I think he's a war-mongering, lying, cheating, left-wing son of a bitch."

"Jesus," I said.

"Well." His tone relented, but not much. "I guess I—I still have some affection for him. But I can't abide that crowd around him. They're not only incompetent, they're opening the way for the Communist line. Rosenman, Morgenthau, Frankfurter—Christ, just listen to the names. He's not the man I knew. He's lost all his pep. They can put anything over on him they want, and he hasn't the mental energy to resist."

"I saw something in the *Star* about you possibly taking over for Jesse Jones in lending."

"That was a feeler I put out. I asked Drew to spread it around. I'm thinking of going up in a couple of weeks, talk to Hank Wallace personally. Trouble is, that son of a bitch Ickes will blackball me. If Byrnes doesn't first."

"What about the new veep? Truman? I thought you liked him."

"He's an American, kind of a hick when you get right down to it, but I don't think he swings much weight. I saw him with Bob Hannegan when he was campaigning in Massachusetts, saw him with Hannegan and Gallagher."

"Which one?"

"Which what?"

"Which Gallagher."

"Ed Gallagher. What other Gallagher . . . oh. No."

"Did you give them anything?"

"He got five grand out of me for the campaign. But that's it, Jack. Absolutely it." He turned away and started lining up, since he kept honors on the third tee. Using the driver again, his ball came to rest in play just over two hundred yards out.

I felt good now, looser. I put more force behind the swing and pulled the ball into the left rough about a hundred eighty yards out. It was down, not leaving me much chance for a long club and distance. The caddie nodded when I asked for the eight iron. I got the ball back onto the fairway, but I was still a long way from home.

Joe had taken the three wood after my shot. I could follow his figuring. Four hundred fifty-six yards would take two woods and an iron. He caught the rough too, but close enough to the green to make it with a third shot.

He came over to my ball as I was setting up for my third shot. I knew I couldn't make the par five in regulation, but I figured to get close and avoid the numerous sand traps between me and the green.

"Good shot," said the caddie as we watched it fly. But it turned out a little too good, and trickled down into a trap I'd thought was out of range.

Dad hit onto the green with his nine iron while I left my fourth shot in the trap. Then I blasted out, landing about twenty-five feet from the pin. I putted up to "gimme" distance and Joe tapped in for the first par of the day.

"You're three down now," he told me. "And even, with the spot."

I didn't say anything. I knew the damn score.

There's a rise above the fourth green, and you can look down at the whole course spread around you. It was like looking down on the world. The sun glinting off the water hazards; the surf beyond the line of windbreak trees that protected the club beach; palmettos and sea grape; the dozens of traps and bunkers; and the green, endless rolling acres of it like God's own lawn. We stood there together for a while, resting and just looking. The wind was cool up there, tearing in off the tops of those waves, but the sun was good and I was glad I hadn't worn a hat.

Number four's a tough hole for anyone, with a huge trap coming into play, and it's long for a par four, four hundred and forty-some yards. I struggled to my second double bogey. Dad kept his rhythm with a bogey five.

Heading toward a distant clump of palmettos, he said, "No, I got to face it . . . my political career's over. It was that Lyons interview that did it. When that son of a bitch printed that stuff about how democracy was finished, stuff I told him plainly was off the record . . . always be careful with the press, Jack. You need the fuckers, but don't ever turn your back on them or the knife will slide in right up to the hilt."

"That was years ago, Dad."

"Well, the way the war's gone, I know what they call me. Defeatist. God-damn them! That's what they call you when you try to keep hundreds of thousands of American boys from coming home feet first! Thank God I never had anything to do with getting us into it. But the way things have turned out, maybe the best thing I can do is keep my mouth shut." He raised his eyes from the putt. "I'm more interested in what you're going to do."

Damn, there it was again. I frowned and fidgeted with my driver.

The fifth hole was the biggest challenge yet. There were nasty crosswinds, a tropical jungle to the right, and a well-trapped plateau green. The par three was playing all of its one hundred ninety-five yards that day, and I knew club selection on the tee would be critical. Joe still had the honors. He looked it over for a while, then said, "Three wood to the green."

"Show me how, Dad."

He took extra time with the shot, and I stood back. If he screwed up here I'd be up with him. The wood met the ball flush and Joe grinned at me as he came off the backswing, knowing he'd hit it sweet. The lofting ball drifted as the wind hit it, fell out of the sky and bounced off the back right side of the green out of sight. The grin turned sour. "Fuck me," Dad said, and kicked the dirt.

"Do you think a four wood's right? What's the yardage on this thing?" I asked the Negro. He told me a hundred and ninety-five yards, and that a four wood was a good choice.

Time to get back some of those lost strokes. I kept my head as steady as I could. My swing cracked the ball down the left side. I leaned sideways, giving it some body English as the crosswind funneled it toward the green. "Be there! Be there!" It hit the green, held the putting surface, and I was on in regulation on one of the toughest holes on the course. Not so bad! I thought. Dad looked grim as we strolled toward the pin.

He said, "Don't tell me you haven't figured I was going to ask you this."

"Yeah. I did."

"Good. So what did you plan to tell me?"

"Well, I uh, I think I might want to—write. I've had offers from several papers—"

"For Christ's sake, Jack! Is that what you plan to do with your life? Scribble crap for Hearst or Luce?"

"No, I thought—books, maybe."

"Because of *Why England Slept.* That it?"

"It did all right," I said. "Didn't it? And you said it was pretty good. I've got ideas for others."

Dad looked out over the fairway. His mouth had twisted bitter. "But you didn't write it by yourself, Jack. Krock worked his ass off knocking it into shape. *I* helped you. You think it was your beautiful prose that got it published? They wouldn't have looked at it twice if you hadn't been my son."

I couldn't meet his eyes, so I looked at the ball. He could be raw when he wanted something. I told myself there was no point arguing with him.

He was still going, though. "I've set up the trust for you. There's no point in your making more money. Is there?"

"I guess not."

"Stop guessing, Jack. Is there or isn't there?"

I felt thirteen again. Glanced around; the caddies were hanging back, out of earshot. I mumbled, "No, sir."

"So what are you going to do?"

"What do you want me to do?"

"You're a smart kid. You don't have a real outgoing temperament, but Christ, look at Coolidge. Anyway you can fake that. Women love the hell out of you. You've got the goods in the brains department. And now you've got the war record. I think you ought to look at public service."

"My war record's not that great, Dad. Anyway, what do you mean? Be on some board or something?"

"There's a couple possibilities. I still have some chips I can call in with Forrestal. I can get you a spot in the Navy Department. Maybe assistant secretary. That's how Teddy and Franklin started. That would fit in with your experience."

I mumbled something. He kept on, talking half to himself, half to me. "But that kind of short-circuits the process. You'd still have to go to the electorate at some point, show the boys in the back room you can draw the votes. The alternative's to start off running you in Massachusetts. Maybe for lieutenant governor, or if the Eleventh District opens up in '46—"

"We don't live in Massachusetts anymore, Dad," I reminded him. "And anyway, Jim Curley's got the Eleventh District."

"I know that, Goddamn it! But we've got name recognition there. John—*Fitzgerald*—Kennedy. Your granddad'll be half the draw. Dave Walsh will help us—"

"You haven't talked to him already—"

"Just what-ifs, Jack—"

"Dad—"

Joe had his troubles on the backside of the green too. Once on in three, he two-putted for a double bogey. I always feel more confident putting. I got it down in two for my first par.

"Gained two strokes on you that time," I said, trying to inject some humor.

"Fuck you."

I looked at the caddies. Their faces were careful blanks, as if they didn't speak English.

"I asked Joe Kane about you. How he thought you'd run up there."

"That ward heeler?"

"He's not a ward heeler, and you'd better expunge that particular expression from your vocabulary. He's smart and he's savvy, and your granddad wouldn't have got three votes in '42 without him. He liked that speech you gave at Honey Fitz's dinner."

"He talked to me about it once," I said.

"And you said?"

"I said Joe Jr. had priority."

Dad didn't say anything for a while. He looked at the next shot. "And now?" he said.

"I'm not in very good shape yet, Dad."

"Arizona didn't help? The docs at the Mayo didn't help? The operation?"

"Sure, everything helps, but it isn't just the back, Dad. Some of them think it's malaria. But they're not sure."

"How does it feel?"

"I feel punk. Dizzy. You see how yellow my skin looks. And I feel—weak, Dad. Real weak."

"Christ, I never heard you whine before, Jack. No problems in the women department?"

"No, sir, no complaints there."

"You'd better pull yourself together. It sounds to me like you're worrying too much. Not getting laid enough. And not eating near enough." He poked my ribs so hard it hurt. "How about the Patio tonight?"

"Dad, you don't have to take me out. We can eat with the family."

"We'll all go. It's an occasion."

"What occasion?"

"That you've picked up the banner."

"But I haven't, Dad. God! I feel like I'm being drafted!"

"It's not like that," he said, sounding hurt.

I got the honors for the first time of the day on the fifth hole, so I teed up first on number six. A three-hundred-eighty-eight-yard par four, considered by some the best par four in golf. With sand traps to the left off the tee and a sloping fairway to the right, placement was critical again. But I couldn't have done better if I'd been Bobby Jones. The drive went down the left side with the ball kicking right and stopped in the fairway better than halfway out. Joe hit a shorter tee shot but he cleared the hazards too. We both got to the green in regulation and came out with pars. Walking toward the seventh tee, I took stock. I felt good after two straight pars, but I was getting tired.

This was another long par four at four hundred thirty-three yards. Dad kept cooking with a bogey five, but I got into trouble. The wind screwed me and I hit rough and sand and carded my worst score yet, a triple bogey seven.

"Yeah," he said. "The Eleventh District. Now, as you so kindly pointed out to me, Jim Curley's got the seat now. But it so happens that he's under federal indictment for mail fraud. He just had to pay forty-two thousand back, he lost the last one, and I think he'll lose this one too. I had Timilty talk to him, and we have a deal. We pay off his debt and support him for mayor of Boston again, and Curley vacates his congressional seat."

"Holy shit, Dad—"

"The whole family will help. You know, we've got a lot of horsepower, if we all pull together."

It was time. I took a deep breath, but my voice still came out shaky as I said, "I guess the truth is, I just don't want to be a politician."

He looked at me, and I tried to keep my eyes up, but they wouldn't do it. I kicked at a bit of turf. "Don't divot the goddamn green," he told me.

"Sorry."

"Jack, let me tell you something about America. The first generation makes the money. Doesn't matter how. These bastards that built this club: Nobody asks how their fathers made their money. The second serves the public. That's what makes the country great."

"I don't think that's exactly what you've got in mind, Dad."

"What's that mean?"

"I mean, there's something almost—" I wanted to say "sick," but the word wouldn't come out. "I mean, first you wanted to be president. Then you wanted Joe to. Now he's dead, so I'm the next in line. Is it that important?"

"Don't talk that way about your brother."

"It's something about being Irish and Catholic, isn't it? About not belonging, and not making it in the right club at Harvard, and—"

I was afraid he'd start shouting, but instead he just shook his head. "No. It's not about that, Jack. What kind of psychological bullshit is that? It's about shouldering our goddamn responsibilities. Paying back some of what this country has done for us. Joe was ready to make that payback. Now he's gone you owe it to him, to the family, and to your country." He moved in, and reached out and gripped my hand suddenly so hard I winced.

"Jack, look at you. Your great-grandfather Fitzgerald was a peddler on Ferry Street. Your other great-grandfather sailed from New Ross with nothing. Now we're playing golf with the Fords and Rockefellers. I know you can do it. And you will, or you'll kick yourself the rest of your life. Because, damn it, you know you can. You can be President of the fucking United States."

"But *why*, Dad, if I don't *want* to? I don't have that drive, like you and Joe. Politics, to me—"

"I told you, Jack. 'Politics' is Tammany Hall, Irish glad-handers, patronage and graft, your grandfather singing "Sweet Adeline" at wakes in Ward Six. You're going to be a *public servant."*

"And if I don't?"

"Then you're not a Kennedy, Jack. At least, not my kind of Kennedy. It's that simple."

"Jesus, Dad."

"That's how it is. So what do you say?"

I didn't answer.

"Jack," he said.

I swallowed. "I've got something to tell you, Dad. I've been . . . asked to volunteer for some special duty."

"What?"

"I can't tell you. It's sensitive."

"Something for ONI?"

"It's intelligence-related."

"You can't do it."

"Dad, I—"

"It's out of the question. It would kill your mother, losing another of you."

"Oh. It's not that kind of thing, Dad. This'd be desk work, that's all. I wouldn't even be out of the country."

He looked relieved but still suspicious. "Then I don't understand. What kind of desk work would be so—"

"I can't tell you, Dad. Security."

I felt him evaluating my face, trying to read me. I kept looking out to sea. It was the truth, wasn't it? Not that I'd taken it, but that Leahy had asked?

And now it looked like I didn't really have a choice.

The eighth hole's a two-hundred-thirty-three-yard par three, with all of them over water. Tough as hell. Since I lost on the last hole, I could see Dad reaching for everything in his bag. He swung deliberately and carried the hazards, but he came down off-line and missed the green.

I took the same driver, still warm from his hands, and bit my lip. I was feeling weak, God, why now. Dizzy. But I had to play. I forced the swing and sliced into the water.

"Sorry," I said.

"They're your balls, goddamn it," my father said angrily.

I felt lucky to card a five, but I still managed to tie him. Eight holes, and he was only up by one stroke, if you counted the spot. I was glad to see the ninth tee. I could still win this. Neither of us spoke as we climbed up to the tee.

A par five at five hundred nineteen yards, with open fairway on both sides. We both drove into the fairway and played three wood second shots. I caught a trap, blasted out, and was lying three in a second trap short of the green. Joe was hitting three with a seven iron. He pulled the ball to the left. As we got up to the green I could see the need to win tugging the corners of his mouth down. Hell, I felt it too. I felt shitty, but I wanted to beat him. Just this once.

I blasted out of the sand trap, catching the ball thin and winding up over the green lying four. But then I snubbed the chop. My wrist turned; the ball dribbled a few feet and stopped. It took me six strokes to get to the putting surface.

Dad chipped onto the green in four, landing inside my ball. Well, that was the game. I felt empty, but lined up anyway for the final putt. About a fifteen-footer, with left to right break. My head felt clearer now, and I tapped it and the ball died into the cup on its last turn.

Dad finished with a bogey six and a forty-five on the front nine. I scored fifty, losing by two with the three-stroke spot.

"Nice putt," said Dad. "How about a break before the second nine? Buy you a drink."

"You mind if we just play nine today, Dad? I don't feel up to eighteen."

He looked surprised, then shrugged. Handed his putter to the caddy. "Okay," he said, his voice cold, like when he'd told Teddy he couldn't come with us. "Tired? No problem. Just quit."

I felt something snap inside me, like a breaking icicle. "My goddamn back hurts, all right, Dad? Does that make me a fucking quitter?"

He was turned away, tipping his caddy. Mine looked expectant. I pointed at Joe. Dad gave me a glare and handed him a quarter. The Negro stared at it on his palm.

"How long are you in town for, then?"

"I don't know. Probably not long."

"Well, you think about what I said."

"I will, Dad."

"And we'll talk later. Let's go."

I nodded. He never gave up. He never would.

———

I called the number Leahy gave me when we got back to the house. A woman answered. The WAC, probably. She took my message without comment, that I'd thought it over and decided to answer the call of duty.

The Western Union man knocked at three that morning. Mom, sleepy and tousled in her nightdress and robe, brought me up the telegram. She sat by my bed as I opened it, and I knew she was thinking of the other telegram, the one Father O'Leary had brought.

ORDERS ICO LT J F KENNEDY USNR TO NAVHOSP CHELSEA MASS HEREBY TERMI- NATED STOP SNM REPORT FORACDU LIMDU STATUS TO RADM BROWN USN WHSTFMANO WASHINGTON DC CLT 0700 26 MAR 1945 STOP TRAVEL ARRANGE- MENTS REPORT COL CORTLANDT JOHNSON, CO HQ CARIBBEAN DIVISION, AIR TRANSPORT COMMAND, WEST PALM BEACH FLA FOR TRANSPORT PM 25 MAR STOP

"What is it, Jack? Not one of your friends?"

"No, Mom, just a change of orders. The good old USN jerking me around again."

"You're not going back to the Pacific?"

"No. Washington."

"Thank God. When are you leaving?"

"Monday. Tomorrow. Sounds like they have a flight set up for me tomorrow afternoon."

"Good. We can go to mass together in the morning. You'll write, won't you? When you get there?"

"I always do, don't I?"

"And you'll be careful."

"It won't be anything dangerous."

"Crossing the street can be dangerous, son. Remember your grandfather was run over by a truck when he was just sitting there, watching a baseball game in Nantasket. I know there are things you have to do. But I want you back, after you do them. Now that your brother's gone on ahead, you children are even more precious to me."

I couldn't believe she felt that way. Through my own puzzlement and anger I felt a perverse need to hurt her, to strike through that serenity into what I was sure lay beneath.

"Come on, Mom," I said. "Do you really believe that? Or are you just as broken up as Dad is?"

"God never gives us a cross we can't bear, John. And those crosses are the way we grow. They're our chance to show we love and serve Him." She put her hand on my forehead; it rested there, soft and warm. "I miss Joe. I grieve for him every night. But I know he's happy now, with God and all the saints, and that I'll hold him again in Heaven. That's the miracle of our faith. It sustains us in times of doubt and trouble. That's why I hope you keep yours real and living, all your life long."

My flippancy and anger died away. I turned over in bed, facing away from her. "Sure, Mom," I said. "I'll be careful, crossing the street."

CHAPTER 10

Saturday, March 24: Washington, D.C.

Heudeber flinched at the sudden racket as the fleeing shadows fell across his face. Gray birds whirled through the gray sky. The gray and white walls stood up against it, heavy neoclassical buildings of concrete and marble, towering above the stark bare trees in their bronze gratings.

He stood on the corner of New York Avenue and H Street, where the bus from Indian Head had let him off with two Coast Guard sailors in flat pancake hats. At 7:00 A.M. the city was still waking. Buses rumbled heavily to curbs, disgorging crowds of stoop-shouldered men and mousy women. Trolley bells clanged as the long red cars maneuvered around corners. He couldn't believe how many blacks and Jews there were.

He realized that his sight had gradually readjusted itself during the years of war. He had become used to seeing only Aryans in good cloth coats and stockings and business suits and ties. Become used to seeing people like these, the ones walking rapidly with briefcases and buying sandwiches and papers at little stands, only at the point of a gun, or as apathetic shaven-skulled *sklaven* in German factories and camps.

He stood suspended, poised, on a street lined with liquor stores, movie houses, shoe stores, barber shops. He knew where he had to go. Men had died to put him on this corner. But something in him was reluctant to go on. Too much depended now on luck. On what he said and whom he met in the next few minutes, and how they reacted.

He turned west and started walking. Past department stores with Jewish names. He waited for a trolley to pass, clanking and sparking, carrying a line of incurious eyes past him without contact or interest. When the street was clear he crossed and stood in front of a window, hand in pocket, staring in at a USO display. Whatever USO was.

His back, turned to the street, felt exposed. He shivered, but didn't turn, examining the passing faces in the dark mirror of the window.

Where was the Russian? He could be dead. The other possibility was that he was still alive, and still continuing his mission. Knowing the ex-NKVD man's record, the latter was the more likely. He'd had the sense, ever since he got to solid land, that the other wasn't far behind and might well be ahead of him.

Now, again, stalking forward through these awakening streets, some hunter's intuition speeded his heart and sharpened his senses. Krasov could be around the next corner. Heudeber's hand itched for the pistol. He'd carried it through Poland, Russia, even brought it back from the hell of Stalingrad. But now it was gone, buried in the black mud of Virginia. He stopped in front of another storefront, staring in without looking inside, using the glass to scan the people behind him.

"Whatcha lookin' at, bub?"

Some sort of official, middle-aged, his gut sagging over a uniform belt. Heudeber suddenly realized that the storefront he was examining so minutely was empty behind the dusty glass. The man was staring at him. Heudeber didn't recognize the uniform. He wasn't armed, but he had a whistle.

"Was this once a tobacco store, sir?"

"Don't know, bub. Looking for one, one over on McPherson Square. You from out of town?"

"Chicago." Heudeber lowered the suitcase to the pavement, felt for his identification. But the other was still talking.

"Yeah, you might look over in McPherson, think I saw one open over there. One block thattaway, then hang a left." He pointed, then started away. Heudeber raised his hand. "Yeah?" he said, coming back.

"Pardon me. I'm not far from the White House, am I?"

"Three more blocks down New York, bub. Sightseein'?"

"That's right."

"Have a nice time." He saluted, sloppy but quick, and Heudeber's arm jumped a little, involuntarily. He froze in horror, looking after the retreating back. He'd almost thrust his arm out, rigid in the *Hitlergruss.*

Three blocks. It wasn't long before he glimpsed, past a large Corinthian-pillared facade, the building he wanted. He paused again at a cross street, waited with dozens of other men with briefcases. A pepper of uniforms, U.S. Army and Navy mainly, but a few British, Dutch, Free French with the Cross of Lorraine on their shoulders. He stood in their midst, then followed them across the street with the light.

A peanut cart stood on the sidewalk opposite, in front of the Treasury. The smell enriched the cold air. He halted. A mustached oldster shoveled him a heavy bag for a nickel, twist-folded it closed with a quick flip, handed it over. He threw his head back, trying to hold the sack and pick it open with his fingernails. Like so many things, it was difficult one-handed.

"Here, let me open that for you, Colonel."

Heudeber tensed, staring at him over the heaps of roasted nuts.

"So, am I right? How I know you a colonel? Something, the age, the way a man carries his self. Hey, I see you here before? I'm Steve Vasilikos, everybody knows me."

"How do you do," said Heudeber, keeping his tone casual. This would be a good place to put a sentry. If this were Germany, this "Vasilikos" would be an

SS informer. More likely, there'd be an armored car standing here, instead of a peanut wagon. So far American security did not impress him. Nor did Washington. The narrow streets looked shabby and bereft next to Berlin.

Next to the Berlin that once was, he reminded himself, with a feeling like physical pain. That city of broad streets and solid architecture existed only in memory now. Now the capital of Germany was nothing more than miles of shattered bricks, twisted pipes and mains, cratered roads, laid-out rows of bomb victims like bundles of discarded clothes.

"You thoughtful today, Colonel."

He roused himself to the windswept street, the snort of buses, the racketing clatter of pigeons. The Greek handed him back the opened bag. Heudeber threw a few into his mouth. "Have you seen a man by here today? Or yesterday, standing about here? He would be shorter than I, fair hair, a round face."

"Seen a thousand guys like that every day. You looking for somebody in particular, you wanta check over with Link at the guard post." Vasilikos pointed. "Right over there."

Heudeber nodded. Still chewing—he'd forgotten how good fresh-roasted peanuts tasted—he tucked the bag into his coat, picked up the suitcase, and headed toward the gate. Before he got there, though, he stopped, looking in through the fence.

He looked past half-inch-thick iron bars at the white house with the tall carriage entrance and the massive, suspended lamp. A black closed car stood off to the right, under a great tree. Ah, there *was* security, quite a deal of it actually, though unobtrusively located. The finned barrels of two Oerlikon guns poked out at the left corner of the roof. He could see men in American-style helmets moving about near them. A massive-linked steel chain locked the entrance gates. What looked like concealed machine-gun emplacements dotted the lawn between him and the house, though the guns, if that was what they were, were covered by green canvas tarpaulin.

And the most immediate barrier: a guard shack with three men in it. One civilian, talking into an old-fashioned telephone; one soldier; one blue-uniformed cop. He knew the American police uniform. Everyone in Europe did, from Hollywood's endless stream of gangster movies.

He put down the suitcase and slowly rubbed his hand on his thigh. The air was chill this early in the morning. Not nearly as cold as it had been out on the bay, though.

He shuddered again as he remembered the boat capsizing under him. Recalled the old man's hands at his throat, then the freezing curtain of the sea.

Odd, how a man who didn't want to live could still fight so hard not to die.

The cop in the booth was looking at him. Before he could think any longer he bent, picked up the suitcase, and walked up to the gate.

"Excuse me. Is the President in?"

The civilian, in a gray suit under an unbuttoned gray overcoat, spun round, still holding the phone to his ear. He had a tough Irish face under a gray felt hat. He took Heudeber in with one glance, from toes to hat, dismissed him, and turned away again.

The cop said, politely enough, "Do you have an appointment, sir?"

"No, but he'll be interested in what I have to say."

"You don't have an appointment?"

"That is right."

"He's not here."

"Not here?"

"That's right, he's not here. Now move along, please."

The soldier came over to them. "What's he want?"

"The President. No appointment."

"Nut case?"

"You a nut, mister?"

"A nut?" Heudeber glanced over his shoulder at the stand, puzzled.

"Funny," said the soldier. "Real funny. Now get out of here, Jack Benny. Beat it. Skedaddle. Shake a leg. Scram!"

Heudeber took a step forward, toward the open gate. The soldier's eyes widened and he fumbled the rifle around in front of him. The cop, though, just put his hand flat on Heudeber's chest and shoved him back, not urgently, not angrily, just very firmly.

"I tell you, I have a message for the President. It is important."

"Look, mister. Nobody gets through here without a pass. No pass, no gettum in, no seeum big white father. Kapeesh?"

"How can I get a pass?"

"How can he get a pass? Mike?" the soldier asked. The cop stared at Heudeber.

The civilian said, "Shit," and slammed the earpiece back on its hook. He glanced out at the street, pulled out a pack of cigarettes, lit one, then glanced expressionlessly at Heudeber. "What's he want?" he said in a low, grating voice.

"Wants to see the Chief. Says he has a message for him."

"What's it about, chum?"

Heudeber took a deep breath. He'd hoped to save this till he was with the President. The Reichsführer had assured him this was the most sensitive secret the Allies possessed. But if these fools wouldn't let him in. . . . He looked behind him, making sure no passersby were within earshot. He saw the peanut man watching them, chewing his mustache thoughtfully. He faced the gate again and lifted his chin. "It's about . . . Tube Alloys."

"Tuba loys?" said the soldier. He popped his gum blankly. For a moment all three of them looked at Heudeber. "Mean anything to you, Mike?" said the cop.

"Not a fuckin' thing."

"Look, if you will take me to someone who knows something—"

"We don't know nothin', huh?"

"Get out of here," said the cop. "Go on, get moving, or I'll have the wagon here for you. Hear me? Vamoose."

"Where can I get a pass?"

"You want a pass, jerk, go to the FBI. Go pester J. Edgar, you want a pass."

"That sounds like a good idea," said Heudeber, although the mention of the dreaded U.S. counterintelligence agency made his heart sink. "To the FBI. And where is that?"

Drawling, his lip curled, the cop told him where to go.

———

From across the street, from a seat under the elms and magnolias of Lafayette Park, Ivan Krasov watched the one-armed man in the dark coat turn away from the gate house, anger in the set of his shoulders. He sat on the green park bench like a bag of laundry, bundled in the heavy men's jacket he'd found behind the seat of the truck. His blond hair was hidden by a blue stocking cap, the kind merchant seamen wore. He looked somnolent, but the muscles along his arms had gone tense. Deep in the capacious pockets, he gripped the pistol.

He'd been waiting here, strolling away occasionally on side streets, for almost two days.

Sitting here, waiting for the contact to be made, he'd thought from time to time of what fortune might drop into his lap. Sooner or later the big black car had to stir. Sooner or later those chains would release the iron gates, the bars would swing open, and it would roll out into the street. Bulletproof? He knew, from his service with Kagonovich's bodyguard, at least three reasonably dependable ways to kill a man in a bulletproof, sealed car. The simplest, of course, was to make the occupants open it themselves, usually by throwing yourself in front of it and feigning injury. He could also stop it with the truck, which he had parked two blocks away, with his satchel in it. Close enough, if he saw signs of activity at the portico, to sprint to before the limousine emerged. Coolness was the key to a successful attack. The self-possession to simply place more than one bullet in the same place. No glass light enough for a car could resist multiple impacts. The first bullet would dent and weaken the laminate. The second or third would penetrate.

The trouble was, any of these meant that the target's bodyguard would be on the assassin in seconds. He'd be executed on the spot. Or if not then, not much later.

Four ten-year-old girls plopped themselves down on a bench twenty feet away from his along the curving asphalt path. He ignored them, thinking: So that's not how we're gonna play this ball game. He shifted on the hard wooden seat as Heudeber, across the street, walked slowly away. We got till the thirteenth of April. I'll take my time, plan it, find a way to do it without being caught.

It wasn't as if he'd be doing it alone.

He took a honey roll from his pockets and began gnawing at it, relishing the sticky sweetness. The girls hopped off their bench and began skipping rope. His ears registered what they sang without really listening.

> *"He'll never die of hunger*
> *He'll never die of thirst,*
> *He's got one son with DuPont*
> *And another one with Hearst.*

Oh, the president is getting bald
Toupee, toupee,
The president is getting bald
A dollar down and two months to pay.
The president is getting bald
Kreml, Vitalis, das ist alles."

His eyes followed the German's departing figure. Noted the suitcase. Everything would be easier with money. Even when Fence made contact, it would help. He could set things up for his disappearance afterward. He could change his clothes, his appearance.

He stood up suddenly, brushed the crumbs from his lap, and began walking swiftly, paralleling Heudeber, but on the north side of the avenue. Mingling with the growing flow of pedestrians and clerks, he kept the German in sight while concealing himself. As Heudeber turned right on Fifteenth Krasov crossed the street. He found himself a hundred yards behind the man he followed, but tall as the German was, he was still plainly visible ahead as he turned east and left the Treasury behind, heading toward the Washington Hotel.

Krasov hurried forward. He wondered for a moment whether he should have left the park. The message he'd left at the drop said he'd be there. But Fence was an experienced agent. He'd know, if no one was at the rendezvous, to return in an hour or two. Whereas the SS man was dangerous. Heudeber knew what was going on, could describe him, could ruin everything.

Heudeber, the traitor.

He hurried forward, through the crowds that were more numerous now. Eight-thirty, the clock said at the corner of Fourteenth and Pennsylvania. The German's head bobbed fifty yards ahead. Krasov raised his gaze from it to the huge white pile in the distance. Heudeber was headed toward the Capitol. Was that his goal? He'd been rebuffed at the White House. Where then would he go next?

Another block, almost running, dodging through the pedestrians; and now the German's head bobbed only a few yards ahead of him.

With a sudden, fierce exultation Krasov realized he had the other exactly where he'd been himself. In the marsh, covered by night and the trust he'd placed in him, Heudeber had tried to kill him from behind. He liked to plan things. But sometimes you were given opportunities. The other man didn't even know he was here. If he did it, it should be done quickly. Speed itself concealed, in a crowd. One shot, fired through the overcoat pocket. It would look like a chance jostle from a passerby. A cloth-muted pop like a backfiring taxi . . . one bullet, directly into the lower spine . . . as the German fell he'd snatch the bag and keep walking, screened by other anonymous bodies as they stopped to gather round the body sprawled on the dirty pavement.

Crossing Twelfth Street, still catching up, and now Heudeber was only three paces ahead. Krasov speeded up, wove between two heavyset black women, and fell into step on the German's left shoulder. Exactly so. In his pocket his thumb found the hammer of the Tokarev. Beyond the German a bus was angling in to a stop. Its engine snorted. Exhaust blew toward them on a cold wind. Ten more feet, at the next corner, a knot of pedestrians had gathered, waiting to cross. He'd be directly behind him. He'd wait for the crossing light, fire, then snatch the bag and keep walking as Heudeber fell.

He had just cocked the gun when the German's head turned, looking up at the building they were passing. A tall stone facade. Sloped red-tiled roof.

Heudeber stopped so suddenly that Krasov, taken by surprise, collided with him. He hunched off-balance, groping for the trigger. Now. *Now!* But just as his finger found the half-moon of smooth steel the German turned right and stepped away. Not looking back, he went up a short flight of steps between two aluminum torchieres, shoved through a heavy pair of brass and oak doors, and vanished.

Krasov stared after him, halted on the pavement, looking up at the immense limestone walls. The black women slammed into him. He shoved them away roughly. One screamed in dismay as she dropped a bag. Potatoes rolled across the sidewalk between dozens of legs. The women muttered, but stopped when he looked at them and bent to try to retrieve the rolling vegetables. He stared at the massive metal doors, decorated with lions and heads of wheat, through which Heudeber had disappeared. JUSTICE DEPARTMENT, a cast aluminum plaque read. And below that, FEDERAL BUREAU OF INVESTIGATION.

——

"I would like to see Mr. Hoover."

"Who are you?"

He sucked air down to his gut, looking across the counter to a seated man in a double-breasted gray suit. "I am Colonel Hans Dieter Heudeber, of the Sichersheitsdienst."

There. It was said.

"You're who, of the what?"

"I said: I am an officer in the German secret police."

"Oh yeah?" The man looked away, out at the street. "Yesterday Napoleon walked in. Today it's a Nazi spy. Give us both a break, okay? Get the hell out of here."

Heudeber leaned forward, over the counter. He fixed his eyes on the slouched, rumpled man. In the icy Prussian tone of a field-grade officer, he said, "You are on duty. I have just informed you that I have important information relating to enemy agents in your country. Do you understand? Announce me to the proper departmental official. Now!"

"Oh." Something changed behind the eyes. He straightened; his hands hunted nervously for something to do. They adjusted his tie, slid over his hair, then opened a book, ran a finger down a column. "Let's see . . . you said, enemy agents . . . Domestic Intelligence. That's what you're talking about?"

"That's right."

"That'll be Mickey Russell. Wait a moment, sir, I'll ring his office."

The interior corridors were blue walls and terrazzo floors, with indirect lighting from cast aluminum fixtures. Russell was on the second floor, a small man in a small office. He looked tired. He shook Heudeber's hand briefly and pointed at a worn leather sofa. "So, say you saw some Nazis landing?" he said.

"Not exactly."

"What is it, then? In twenty-five words or less."

"I'm an emissary from the German government. I have information to transmit to the President."

"Well, that's not so remarkable," said Russell. "There's a few things I'd like to tell him myself. But it ain't gonna happen, and I'll tell you why.

"You see, friend, we have a lot of guys come walking in off the street like you. They come from all over the country. I don't know what you people want. We don't pay for information. It's just to get your name in the papers, I guess. Or it's something those voices in your head tell you to do. Do you get those? The voices in your head, the radio-control guys, the Martians?"

"I don't know what you mean."

"Yeah, well." Russell sighed and stood up. He took Heudeber by the elbow, not ungently, and began walking him toward the door. "Now, you go home and keep a sharp lookout. That's what would help us most. If you see any more of these Nazis you sit right down and write us a letter about it, all right? We like to get letters. Some of them, we have a bulletin board downstairs we put them up on, the best ones, that is."

"I assure you, this is not a joke—"

"No, no joke." Russell opened the door. "Once again, thanks for coming by—"

Heudeber shook himself loose. He took two quick steps to the desk, threw the suitcase up on it, and unlocked it. When he flipped it upside down eighty-seven thousand dollars cascaded out and poured over the sides of the too-narrow desk, onto the worn green carpet.

"Holy smoke," Russell whispered. He bent and picked up one of the damp packets. Riffled through it, stopped to look at the inside bills. Dropped it on the desk.

He looked up at Heudeber as if seeing him for the first time. "Is this stuff real?"

"I would like to see Mr. Hoover."

"You just might get to." Russell reached for a phone. He didn't dial it, just picked it up and spoke. His voice was muffled. Still Heudeber could hear: "Clyde? Mickey Russell. Just got a very interesting walk-in, you might like to see his bona fides."

He listened, then hung up. "Let's go see the assistant director," he said. "And after that, I think, you just might get to see the big guy himself."

———

The Office of the Director, Room 5633, was carpeted in cherry red, and it was huge. The ceiling, Heudeber thought, had to be five meters high. A rubber runner led from the door across the room to the desk at the far end. Behind it were two American flags on polished brass standards crowned by spread eagles.

Heudeber blinked in the cold air, the chill breeze from two slowly oscillating fans. He could still see the grim display in the anteroom: a glass case containing guns, broken glasses, and a death mask made of some white material. It glowed faintly in focused spotlights, like the Mask of Agamemnon in the Museum für Vor- und Frühgeschichte in Berlin. The empty eyes stared at the ceiling. It was flanked by photographs of a man Heudeber didn't recognize.

He recognized the man behind the desk, though. Before the war the *Illustrierter Beobachter* had published his picture many times, following the Bruno Hauptmann–Charles Lindbergh case. Hoover was shorter than he expected, jowly, overweight. But fastidiously dressed, fastidiously groomed and manicured. A hint of perfume in the air. Something about the way he looked at the man behind him, the little fluttering movements of his fingers. . . . Heudeber understood suddenly what kind of man this was.

Then he frowned. That didn't matter. Not for his purposes. What mattered was that he listened.

"This him?" said Hoover, placing his hands carefully in the pockets of his suit jacket and leaning over the desk. Heudeber saw his suitcase beside it on the carpet. One snap was open, the other locked. Behind him the small man, Russell, said respectfully, "That's right, Chief. Walked right in off the street. With the cash."

"Have you searched him?"

"Just before I brought him in, sir. He's unarmed. Except for a bag of peanuts."

Hoover fixed him with a stare that was meant to be baleful, Heudeber supposed. The cold little eyes in their pouchy sockets noted his shoes, his overcoat, his pinned-up, empty left sleeve.

"Your name," he snapped.

Heudeber said, slowly and clearly, "I am Hauptsturmführer-SS Hans Dieter Heudeber. The equivalent American Army rank is colonel. My Party number is 134045. I am a personal emissary bearing a message from Reichsführer-SS Heinrich Himmler to the President of the United States."

"Mr. Russell here says you mentioned 'Tube Alloys' to him. What is that?"

"This is the joint U.S.-British code name for the Allied research program into the possibility of a uranium bomb."

Hoover stared at him for a few seconds, then sat down. Sitting, he looked taller. Heudeber suspected a built-up chair. He looked behind him—he was feeling tired—but saw no convenient seat. "May I sit?"

"Get him a chair. Colonel—Heudeber?"

"That is correct."

"How do we know you are who you say you are? How did you reach our coast? How did you get to Washington?"

"That's of no real importance. What is important is the reason that I came. I have been sent by the Reichsführer to warn President Roosevelt of an attempt on his life. I have details. I can describe the assassin and his equipment. I also

have an idea of his personality and methods. With this information, you should
be able to find the man, or at least, to so protect the President that the danger is
past. There is a period of maximum danger, by the way. After the end of April, if
he does not succeed by then, his orders will—"

"Will what?"

"Will—lapse, that's the word, I believe."

"Slow down, friend. Where did this—" Hoover nudged the luggage with a
polished toe "—this cache of money come from?"

"I brought it with me from Germany."

"How did you get here from Germany?"

"By submarine. Since then, by boat and bus." Heudeber unbuttoned his
coat and saw Hoover's eyes narrow as he took in the clerical collar. "Yes," he
said. "Part of the disguise. Now. The letter."

Hoover looked at Russell. The assistant stepped over beside him, opened
the envelope with a snap, and laid it out on the director's desk. Hoover bent
forward in his chair, staring down at it. Then he frowned, and bent closer.

"This is from Heinrich Himmler," he said.

"That's correct."

"It says—let me see: 'The attempt was to depend on the assistance of a
person close to the president.' Then it gives a name."

"That is correct," said Heudeber.

"Get Tolson in here," said Hoover. Russell all but saluted, and brushed by
Heudeber on his way out. At the door he seemed to recall something; he turned
back. "Chief, he could be dangerous—"

"I'll be careful," said Hoover dryly. Then sat there, staring steadily at
Heudeber.

Two minutes later the door opened again. A large athletic-looking man
came in silently, nodded to Hoover, and took a position behind him. "Clyde,"
said Hoover, "This gentleman presents himself as a German SS colonel, bearing
a letter from Himmler himself. Take a look at it."

"I saw it, Boss. Looks genuine. But we'll need to have Documents check it
out."

Heudeber said, "Let's return to the point: the attempt to be made on
Franklin Roosevelt's life. Whether you believe me to be genuine or not, it is your
duty to forward this document to the President, and to warn those whose task it
is to guard him."

"Yes, let's return to that," said Hoover. His fingers splayed across the letter.
"Because according to this, by the time the President should be reading it, the
conspiracy should already have been 'terminated.' If that's the right reading."

Heudeber unbuttoned his coat the rest of the way. Despite the fans he felt
warm. "That is the right reading. Unfortunately things didn't go as planned,
after we landed."

"How were they supposed to go?"

He said, wearily, "I was assigned to kill the assassin."

"Why?" said Tolson.

"To prevent his succeeding, obviously. Actually it was left to me, whether to kill him or to turn him over to you. But he is younger and stronger. I judged it best to follow the former course."

"But you didn't succeed."

Heudeber shook his head. He told them in flat short sentences about the night on the marshes, his error, how Krasov had escaped. Hoover's face was unreadable. He was either making notes or doodling, Heudeber couldn't see which from his seat. When he had finished the director grunted, "And then?"

"Then I made my way here."

"Why? You could have turned yourself in at any police station."

"It was difficult enough to make myself believed here. I also hoped I might encounter him en route and be able to correct my mistake."

"But you didn't."

"No. Therefore I must warn you of his target, his timetable, and his—" Heudeber searched his mind. "The German word is *fähigkeit—*"

"Weapons? Methods?"

"Not exactly . . . but it is close. He is armed and has a limited amount of explosive. But also, a very dangerous and wholly new compound developed by our chemical industry. I will brief you in full. Your military intelligence will be interested. It is hundreds of times more toxic than previous poison gases—"

"Let's go back to this letter." Tolson nodded toward the paper. "What's Himmler's game? Why did he want to louse up the assassination? Seems like somebody went to a lot of trouble to set this up, get people trained, get you over here."

"The Reichsführer is a realistic man. He realizes Germany has lost the war. Unlike others. He is seeking to open negotiations leading to recognition of himself as an alternative to the Hitler government. Of course, this is a dangerous position for anyone in Germany to take. . . . Thus, when the Abwehr proposed this mission, on orders from the highest levels, he quickly arranged that the assassin be accompanied by an experienced SD man, one of his own. That man was myself. My assignment was to prevent the plot succeeding and to convey the Reichsführer's personal message to the President."

"Without Hitler's knowledge."

"Exactly. As a bona fide." Heudeber smiled.

"What about this other—this 'Fence'? What does that mean?"

"I have not read the letter. I have heard 'Fence' referred to by my superiors. I assume that is the operational or cover name for an agent in place who works in close proximity to the President."

"An agent in close proximity to President Roosevelt," repeated Hoover heavily. "You're quite certain of this?"

"That is correct."

"A German agent."

"No. 'Fence' is actually a Communist."

"A Communist!" said Hoover, lifting his chin.

"Yes; originally an ideological convert, now a deeply buried agent of the NKVD. As you know, the Communist Party operates in isolated cells, controlled from above."

Tolson said, "The Director is well known as America's foremost expert on Communism."

"Then you can follow how he was taken over. Abwehr agents first captured the contact to whom Fence reported. Over several weeks they persuaded him to explain the recognition and reporting procedures. Finally, he was replaced by a double agent of our own. Therefore, unknown to him, this very important and well-placed agent has since 1940 been controlled, not by Moscow, but through a diversionary cutout, by Berlin. Without his knowledge, he has been working for us."

"A Soviet agent, but actually working for the Nazis?" said Tolson.

"That is correct." Heudeber permitted himself a small smile. "The reality of his situation is the opposite of his understanding."

"And you're certain he doesn't suspect?"

"No. It is a clever operation and has resulted in much useful intelligence . . . I understand that the letter gives his actual identity."

"So it does," said Tolson, studying not the letter, but Heudeber. No one spoke for a while.

"Interesting," said Hoover, breaking the silence. He glanced at Tolson. "Clyde?"

"You're right, Boss. Very interesting."

Hoover stood, and was short again. "Excuse us," he said. Heudeber nodded.

When they were gone he relaxed back into the chair and closed his eyes, flooded with relief. It was over. It was done. It would have been better to kill Krasov. But this would stop him just as effectively. His own war was over. He could look forward now, if a man without a soul left could look forward to anything. Internment—possibly a POW camp. But he'd heard that even that, run by the British or Americans, wasn't so bad.

Hoover again, Tolson behind him. They stood close together by the door. "Colonel."

"Yes?" He looked up.

"Come with us, please."

Tolson took his coat from him and picked up the briefcase. He went first. Then Heudeber, swaying with fatigue, then Hoover. They got into a small, apparently private, automatic elevator. Hoover pressed the down button.

They emerged in an uncarpeted, damp-smelling basement area. The walls were of painted concrete. Incandescent bulbs in wire cages were spaced too far apart. A half-familiar smell hung in the air. Tolson led the way past a row of lockers, past a line of booths and tables, into an open area. Thin cables of braided steel ran above their heads. The far end disappeared in shadow. Heudeber recognized the smell now. He heard the rattle of a locker behind him. Heard a shout: "Clear the range."

As he turned he felt rather than saw Tolson break into a run. Shoe leather scraped rough concrete.

A bank of lights came on above the booths. Dozens of them, focused on him.

It was the same smell he'd inhaled in remote forest clearings in Poland, in Russia. The pulse-speeding, doom-laden reek of burnt gunpowder and gun oil and hot metal. He staggered a few paces, lost his balance, and fell to the gritty, damp concrete. He saw that it was littered with tiny pieces of cheap paper, like chewed-up newsprint. He saw flakes of unburned powder and scattered coppery glints, scraps of shattered metal.

He looked up into the lights, to see J. Edgar Hoover aiming the famous Tommy gun.

PART II

INSIDE

CHAPTER 11

Monday, March 26: Washington, D.C.

Lieutenant Kennedy, reporting for duty." I shoved my orders and ID card at the cop at the Pennsylvania Avenue gate. While he and a marine were examining them I asked, "Where would I find this Admiral Brown? Navy type, blue suit, big gold stripe?"

"Could be anywhere in there," said the cop. He looked colder than the temperature called for. The crisp air felt good after Palm Beach, and the morning sun was peeling long shadows off the black iron fence and pasting them across the sidewalk. "We don't keep track of the military. Did that, wouldn't be able to do anything else."

"You know him?" I asked the marine.

"No sir, I've only been here a week. See your bag a minute, sir?"

When they gave my papers back I shouldered my duffel and headed up the walk between two dug-in, tarped-over machine guns. My watch read 0700. The plane had been delayed in South Carolina, and then I'd wasted an hour at National Airport trying to persuade the routing officer I rated an official car. I should have just called the taxi. No way to sleep on the plane, a war-weary passenger-converted B-17 with stamped-steel seats, no insulation, and no heat. I felt like shit and looked it too, judging from the looks I got as the dress-blued marines presented arms on the portico. They made it plain without a word that they were used to saluting more important people than reserve lieutenants.

I wasn't sure where to report, but I knew who'd know. Chief Usher Howell G. Crim was perched at his desk in his cubbyhole office, a balding, fussy little man in a black suit. He heard me out, blinking. "That will be the Map Room, Lieutenant. Follow me, please."

I remembered the layout of the White House from when I'd visited with Dad. The first floor was the rooms everybody knew from pictures, the East Room, the State Dining Room, the Blue Room. The second floor was the Roosevelts' personal quarters. I'd expected the military communications center to be in the West Wing, a Teddy Roosevelt-era addition. or the new East Wing office space that had been added during the war. Instead Crim led me down a set of service stairs to a ground floor I hadn't known existed. Low ceilings; old brick floors; a damp smell; storage rooms and furnaces. The rattle of pans and loud Negro voices through an open door told me the kitchen was down here too.

A steel-reinforced door read NO ADMITTANCE. Another marine leaned against it, a .45 on his hip. He eyed me as I came up. "New man for your people," said Crim shortly, and turned and went away, or walked through a wall, or faded into thin air; it was hard to tell which; he had a butler's genius for instantaneous evaporation.

"Pass, sir?"

"Don't have one yet. I'm reporting for duty."

He jammed down a button without taking his eye off me. A second later the door buzzed and unlocked and an Army major peered out. I fed my orders through the crack. He glanced over them, then called to someone inside.

The admiral filled the door. He had to be six-four, at least two-fifty, real Notre Dame lineman material. His eyes drilled me like rotating icicles. I came to attention. "John Kennedy, reporting for duty, sir."

"He's expected," said Brown to the jarhead, who took his hand off his gun. To me he said, "What's in the bag? Don't bring personal gear here again. Our JOs bunk in a TDU over on the Mall."

"TDU, sir?"

"Temporary Dwelling Unit. Those your orders?"

"Yes sir." Brown didn't seem to understand who I was, but I didn't say anything. It was easier when that happened just to agree with people, then make my own arrangements. As he scribbled the date and time on my orders I looked around curiously.

The room was larger than I expected. Two windowless walls were papered with large-scale Army maps and Hydrographic Office charts of the Pacific. The windows were obliterated by closed blackout curtains. Two gray safes squatted under a map of Eastern Europe. Beside them a bank of teletypewriters hammered under soundproofed hoods. Cables snaked to a dozen black and red phones and three of the new electric coding machines. Cords dangled from twenty-four-hour wall clocks labeled LONDON, BERLIN, MOSCOW, CHUNGKING, TOKYO, HONOLULU. A half-open door showed a washbasin and tile deck. To the right was a coffee mess, a baize-covered table, and a mismatched collection of file cabinets and glass-fronted bookshelves loaded with blue and green binders. I nodded to a Navy senior chief, a first-class yeoman, another Army officer, and a couple of sergeants.

Admiral Brown informed me, looking pointedly at my khakis, that Navy wore blues or grays on duty at the White House. Then he said he had to meet with King that afternoon and turned me over to the same major who'd opened the door. His name tag said Abrams.

He must have been the senior watch officer, because the first thing he did after Brown left was pencil my name on a list on the wall. "I'll put you on the midnight-to-six first. That'll let you get up to flying speed, read yourself into the pubs. By the way, the name's Ed, at least when the skipper's not around."

"Jack." I shook a rather cold hand, looking into tired blue-gray eyes. I didn't know Air Corps medals, but I could see he'd flown a few missions. Air Medal, Purple Heart, Flying Cross, Silver Star.

"Where'd you serve, Ed?"

"Eighth Air Force, B-24s, Africa and Germany. You?"

"PTs, Guadalcanal."

"Sounds rough."

"So does Germany."

"Well, that's all over now. Welcome to the Wounded Heroes' Rest Home. Only there's not much rest." He introduced me to Captain Pete Hollins, USA, Chief Tavelstead, Sergeants Rose and Santorini, Yeoman First Branch. "There's a couple more officers, they'll be back pretty soon. How you fixed for smokes? Santorini's got a few cartons stashed."

"Don't use 'em, sir, thanks."

"Then you don't mind if he draws your ration for you?"

"No sir. What's the working schedule? Is that it for me, midnight to six?"

"You wish. That's just the guard. Regular working hours start at seven. We stay available from then to 1700, later if there's a conference scheduled, or a battle on, or the Boss wants a late briefing. When we're not actually briefing, answering his questions, or helping the Chief of Staff draft messages, we read incoming traffic. Tinsel and Flash keep the maps current. Important thing: everything comes off the wire, the watch officer looks at. If it's something the Boss ought to see, send a runner up with it pronto."

I looked at the map of Western Europe, where the red pins of the Soviets and the white and blue pins that were Montgomery and Patton were only a few inches apart. They pinched the invaded Reich into an hourglass shape, with almost all the sand run out. "When are the morning briefs?"

"We brief at the President's pleasure. He comes in once or twice a day for the full brief, and sticks in his head now and then when he's going by. So you'll get to meet him pretty soon."

"We've met."

Abrams gave me a glance over steel-rimmed specs. "Sorry, I'm kind of altitude limited today. Been up since—Saturday? Say you already know him?"

"That's right. My dad—"

"Oh, you're one of those Kennedys. I'm in the picture now. Okay, good; we can skip the usual lecture, how not to be nervous, all that. The Boss is pretty casual about us lower-level guys. It's Brown you've got to watch out for. Fumble a fact in front of FDR, he'll just correct you calmly and you'll think Oh, what a nice guy. But as soon as the President's out of the room the admiral'll tear you a new asshole."

"Thanks for the warning. Is there any kind of logic to the way they've got the charts up?"

Abrams glanced at his watch, but took me around. He explained how the message files on clipboards beneath each map related to that theater, that the briefer had to know general officers down to the corps level, how he could refer on the fly to lists of division commanders and equipment and logistic data. The safes and a vault held the sensitive shit: the Magic books, containing the latest cryptanalysis and translations of enemy traffic; action reports; secret technical references on Allied and Axis aircraft and weapons; records of important joint conferences; copies of the President's communications with Stalin, Churchill, Chiang Kai-Shek. "This is the only complete collection," he said, handing me a red badge and swinging the vault door shut. The tumblers clanked as it locked. "The Boss sends his outgoing messages through the Army comm channels. Incoming stuff comes in through the Navy. So he ends up with the only full set. Marshall runs the war, but even General Marshall doesn't have the big picture politically."

"Savvy."

"Wear that badge whenever you're on duty, it gets you in the front gate too. Yeah, he's kind of devious. The more I see of him the less I understand, you know? He never approaches anything from the front. Always thinking, but you never know what."

I stared at one of the pubs by the coffee mess. The cover said it was a progress report on something called a Lockheed YP-80A jet fighter. On a chart behind it little symbols showed the current location, name, and call sign of every U.S. submarine on patrol against Japan. Christ, I thought; a spy would give his left nut to get half an hour with stuff like this.

"Who gets to see this, Ed?" I asked him.

"Gets in here, you mean? FDR, Leahy, Marshall, Arnold, King. Harry Hopkins when he's here, but he's been sick; I don't know if we're going to see him around any more . . . Grace Tully. Brown, and the watch officers and enlisted. And that's it."

"How about Congress? Secretary of War? Stettinius and Forrestal?"

"Not even the Secret Service, Lieutenant. When the President comes in, be prepared to wheel him around yourself."

"Jesus. Truman?"

"Who? Oh, the new veep. If he's with the President, I guess. Otherwise . . . I don't think so. Anyway, he's never been here."

"What about travel, shit like that?"

"Good question." He put his hands in his pockets and looked at the map of China, flipping change. "This is all written in sand, but the Boss plans to be here through the end of the month. You probably read in the papers about him getting back from Yalta, talking to Congress."

"I heard him on the radio."

"Well, since then he's been resting up. He'll probably stay here for a while. Maybe go up to Hyde Park for the weekend."

"Do we go with him?"

"Some of us. He's got his own Army signals team. So do the Secret Service types. There's map room setups at Hyde Park and Shangri-La. The admiral goes. But if it's just for like a weekend, he might just take two guys to help and brief the Boss himself. The big conferences, like Teheran, Yalta, the flagship handles traffic. En route, anyway; then they set up a message center wherever the conference is. That's all classified, by the way," the major added as he sauntered toward the table. "Anything having to do with where he is, or where he's going. What you see here stays here, understood?"

"I get you."

"Coffee?"

"Thanks. Black." I looked toward the head. "Okay if I grab a shave?"

"Help yourself. Towels 'n' stuff in there."

Abrams followed me into the head and leaned against the bulkhead while I patted on the Burma-Shave. "Just get into town?"

"Yeah."

"Got a place to stay yet?"

"Brown said the JOs bunked over at the—"

"Some of 'em. Joe Grabb and I share a place in Alexandria. He's Navy, lieutenant commander. You're welcome to make a third."

I had no intention of rooming with him, but I said I'd think about it and asked what time he wanted me there that night. He said 2330 would be all right. "Leave my bag here?" I asked him.

The marine outside came to attention this time, his eye locking on the badge. I nodded to him and went out into the main corridor.

Preceded by a rapid clatter of heels, a tall woman trotted into sight around the corner. Blue skirt and white ruffled blouse. Wisps of gray hair straying from under a pillbox hat. Mrs. Roosevelt. Her voice was high-pitched, shrill, and so rapid it was hard to make out what she was saying to the dumpy woman who hurried along, flushed and grim, a step or two behind her, taking dictation even as they rushed. The First Lady's toothy smile swept over and past me; she didn't remember me, obviously, but she was used to strangers in her house. I caught a word. "What about Mr. Carusi? There are unused quotas; can't he accept refugees out of the quotas that are filled?—Good morning, Mike! How are you? How is Roby doing?"

I turned. "Mike" must be the slabsided, dark-haired guy in blazer and slacks who had stopped behind me. He stayed when Mrs. Roosevelt swept on, checking out my badge first, then me. His face looked strangely blank, as if only his eyes were alive. When I started to step around him he put out an arm in front of me. I caught the bulge under his armpit. I stopped.

"You're Kennedy?" he said. "Got a sec?" When I nodded to both he jerked his head toward the elevator.

We bypassed the first and second floor and got off at a third. The rooms were tiny up here, the plaster cracked under exposed wiring. The doors looked as if they'd been taken off an old steamship. A child's crib perched atop a stack of miscellaneous furniture. The guy pointed me into one of the rooms. It must have been his office, because he slammed himself into a chair behind a worm-gnawed desk that looked like a holdover from the Van Buren administration. He pointed to a chair. I sat, taking it slow; the glue was loose and the rear legs were getting ready to go.

"They call this 'the Deck.' You oughta feel at home here. Looks like a ship, don't it? I'm Reilly."

"Secret Service?"

"That's right."

"Did Admiral Leahy—"

"He told me you were coming. Didn't say why." Reilly swiveled, staring at me. "Suppose you supply me that lack."

"I'm sorry. Military secret."

"I'm cleared."

"Not for this."

Reilly examined the cracked ceiling patiently. "Kennedy, my full title is Supervising Agent, Presidential Protective Detail. That means I'm completely and ultimately responsible for the safety of Franklin Delano Roosevelt, the highest priority-A target on the planet for Nazis, Japs, Italians, and Republicans. And not just enemy. A nut case with a bomb, busted switch when he's on the train, Fala gets rabies—anything threatens him is my business. That makes me privy to anything I think is suspicious, see? And when I get suspicious, I don't sit around and wonder. I ask. I snoop. I apply my Irish charm. I find out."

"I'm suspicious? That it? Maybe you ought to frisk me."

"Cut the crap, Lieutenant. In the first place, we already frisked you electronically coming in the front door. We heard every word you said to the guards. Fluoroscoped your bag. You even got a Geiger counter check. In terms of weapons you're harmless. But motives? Son of formerly prominent politico, now very definitely persona non grata around Washington. One day you're a has-been boat jockey, then bang, you're chums with the Chief of Staff, you're installed in the White House. How? Why? Give out with it, pal."

Maybe it was his job to be suspicious, but the way Reilly did it made him easy to dislike. "If you need an explanation, get it from the Chief of Staff."

"You're here. He ain't. I'd rather you fill me in."

"I've got other plans. I spent last night on a plane and I've got watch starting at midnight."

"Tell it to Mr. Whosis on the 'Goodwill Hour.' You know how many threatening letters we get here a month? Five thousand. I check out every one of them. I keep a running file on forty thousand nuts."

Reilly lit an Old Gold, waved out the match carefully, and dropped it into a mayo jar filled with several inches of butts. He blew smoke toward the ceiling and said, "Let me acquaint you with some facts. See, I'm kind of nutty on this assassination thing. I made a study. Americans like to kill their elected leaders. Ever hear of Richard Lawrence?"

"No."

"He was the first guy to try it. He went after Andy Jackson, but his pistol jammed. Lincoln got it. Garfield. McKinley. Teddy Roosevelt got it after he left here. Zangara came within two feet of cooling FDR in '33, in Miami. That's why the Boss sleeps with a .357 under his pillow. But you know what really worries me, a lot more than a nut with a gun?"

"Poison?"

"Bombs. Bombs sweat my butt, Lieutenant. We do bomb drill here almost every day. X-ray the mail. Once we got a package in the diplomatic pouch. They lost the documentation, nobody knew what it was. I put it under the machine.

Something dense. We called the bomb truck, took it to Virginia, hoisted it on a rope, dropped it into a hole, smashed it to bits. Know what it was?"

"No idea."

"Turned out to be a bunch of records Churchill had sent over. A collection of his speeches. The Boss resigned himself to the loss. Then we got all the brilliant GIs out there, want to send FDR a souvenir. I've got a better collection of live shells and hand grenades than the Ordnance Museum."

"So you earn your pay, that the point?"

"No. The point is, I don't take anything for granted. Not the mail, not the guy who fixes the engines in the *Sacred Cow,* not a single face in a crowd. When somebody pops out of noplace, like you—there's only two kinds of people around here, the Boss's people and Eleanor's people. You one of Eleanor's boys? You friends with Mrs. R's protégés?"

"Not particularly."

"Or else it's some kind of political insider type stuff. You a Democrat?"

"Of course I'm a Democrat. My father's a Democrat. My grandfather's a Democrat. But there's nothing political about it. I told you, this is an official Navy assignment. You want to see my orders?"

"All in good time, my pretty. Navy Personnel's supposed to notify me when a new guy's assigned here. I got nothing on you."

"I told you, I got clearance."

"And I told you, I don't give a gilded shit about your clearance! I want to know what you're here for!"

"I don't work for you. In the immortal words of the military, you're not in my chain of command."

"That how you want it? Fine. Then I'll react the way I'm supposed to to unexplained people close to the President." The head bodyguard grinned, as if nothing would give him greater pleasure. "You get two of your own personal guards every time you're within fifty feet of him. I strip search you every time you come in the gate. I fluoroscope you every time you come out of the Map Room. I ask the FBI for a background check, then tell the papers you're under investigation for reasons pertaining to national security." Reilly stopped, his face red; it had lost that blank look, anyway, I thought. "That how you want it? Or do you want to rethink your attitude about cooperating with Michael F. Reilly?"

I hesitated. Maybe he had a point, about being responsible for FDR's safety. Then I thought of what Leahy had said. *Someone close to him. In his inner circle—someone with daily access to him, personal access. Someone who would in the normal course of events have his complete trust.*

That meant Reilly, too.

But then I thought, wise up, Jack. If this guy wanted to ice FDR, he'd have done it long ago. Anyway, who cared? I was only here because two old bastards were squeezing me too tight for me to be anywhere else. I wasn't going to start taking this goose chase seriously.

"All right." I went to the door and closed it. "I'll level. You play hard ball, though."

"You forced my hand. But that's better. Smoke?"

"No. I don't like your attitude, Reilly. Here it is, words of one syllable. Admiral Leahy thinks there's someone trying to kill the President."

"Like I said, five thousand—"

"Someone on the inside. Somebody he knows."

Reilly went silent, the big rocklike head tilted slightly. My respect for him went up a notch. Forget the dumb-Irish act. People who listened like that could usually think. I gave him a *Reader's Digest* version of what Leahy had given me. I didn't tell him about Magic, though, or about the Jap ambassador to Berlin. Only that intelligence said there was a threat, that it had been confirmed from two sources, and that it was from the inside.

"Any suspects?" he said when I was done.

"No names. No hints. Just that."

The phone on his desk rang. He picked it up, snapped, "Reilly." Then: "Yeah. He's here sitting in front of me. Okay, I'll give him the word," and dropped it back onto its cradle. To me he said, "That's not much to go on."

"Have *you* got any suspects? Anyone you've ever been not sure of?"

"If I was, they'd be gone." Reilly swiveled his chair, like one of those electric fans that goes back and forth while you keep getting hotter and hotter. "I guess it's possible, that there's some kind of sleeper in his organization. But if there is, he's good, 'cause nobody comes to mind. Maybe the Heinies are just trying to shake us up. Make us distrust each other."

"Admiral Leahy thinks the source is trustworthy."

"What's the rationale behind the date? This April 13 thing?"

"I don't know. Just that if we can get him past there, the danger should be over."

"Huh." He thought about that a while. "And your plan is, whoever it is, you're gonna ferret them out?"

"I'm going to try."

"Why you?"

"Like you said. Political connections."

"But your dad and the Boss are on the outs."

"FDR said he'd help my . . . elder brother in politics. He owes my dad. I know people. And I've got some of that Irish charm myself." I waved away the smoke. There didn't seem to be any ventilation up here. "You wanted to know, now you know. You're responsible for his safety? Fine. I've just informed you of a threat to it."

"Well, I'm still skeptical," Reilly said. He swung forward and stubbed out the cigarette, very thoroughly, and added it to the top layer in the jar and capped it. "Both that there's anybody here, anybody working against us from the inside; and of your ability to find him if he exists."

"But you'll help us?"

"Who's 'us'? Oh—you and Leahy. Let's get one thing straight, Kennedy. I don't work for you or your admiral. I don't even work for FDR. Protective Detail gets its marching orders direct from Congress. But I'll go along with you—for now. Revocable at any time. And provided that if you get anything solid, Uncle Mike's the first to know."

I was standing up when something else occurred to me. "What about FDR? Should he know?"

"No."

"No?"

"It won't do any good. He hasn't got any fear. Or at least none I've ever seen. There's no point telling him. He'll just laugh and tell me security's my job."

I nodded and picked up my hat. "Anything else?"

"Not a thing," said Reilly. He stretched. "Except Mrs. Helm wants to see you."

"Who?"

"Eleanor's social secretary. You're on for lunch."

———

The private dining room on the first floor, adjoining the larger and more ornate state dining room, was set for twelve. Hand-lettered cards were already propped at our places. Mrs. Roosevelt's was set not at the head, but at the center of the table. I didn't see any for the President. Two women were standing by the door as I came in. We exchanged "good mornings." One was the heavy-set, mannish woman I'd seen in the hall with Mrs. R. She introduced herself as Miss Thompson. She didn't seem happy to see me, but I got the impression it wasn't personal. The other was Mrs. Helm, Eleanor's social secretary. We stood around for a few minutes while a tall Negro in black tie and tails directed several servants, of mixed colors, setting the table and rolling in serving carts. I noticed that the chandelier was dirty and there were cobwebs in the corners. The drapes were faded and mismatched. The carpets could have done with a good cleaning too. Then I forgot about the housekeeping and thought about my conversations with Abrams and Reilly.

In one sense, I was lucky. FDR's handicap kept his personal staff small. Everyone knew he'd had polio, but most people thought of his "victory" over it as a recovery; they didn't realize he was still crippled. Having seen him with Dad, I did. His fireside chats gave the illusion of presence, as did photographs and carefully managed newsreels. But he was rarely seen in public. Eleanor was his eyes and ears, his substitute presence at ceremonial functions, ribbon cuttings, dedications. The newspaper coverage of her travels to coal-mining towns, WPA projects, resettlement villages obscured his absence. And since the war began, his movements had been shrouded in secrecy.

Outside, inside. Reilly seemed to be on the ball as far as protecting him from the outside. What about domestic help? I'd have to look into that. The White House servants. Then his political staff. I had to meet everyone who had personal access to him.

If the Navy had taught me anything, it was to write it down. I took out my notebook, flipped to the back, and began noting the name of each person who had access to the President, worked in the Map Room or offices, or lived in the White House.

I had sixteen names already, and I knew I hadn't really begun.

Excited voices in the corridor, and the butler took his place by the door. I got up, noticing as I tucked the notebook into my service dress blouse that I was starting to smell pretty ripe.

Eleanor came in, still in white shirtwaist but without her hat, followed by a considerable but subdued-looking group. I was the only uniform, and the only man under middle age, too. "Good morning, everyone. Isn't this a fine gathering. Find your place card, please, and make yourself comfortable." Her eye snagged on me. "Mr. Kennedy, I understand you're joining our naval staff."

"That's right, Mrs. Roosevelt. I—"

"That's fine, it will be so nice to have you. How are your father and mother?"

"They're fine. They—"

But she had turned away, was pointing out something to a small fellow in a sober suit. I smiled into the air, as politely as I could manage, and moved my fingers around for a while till I found I could stick them in my back pockets. The trouble with service dress khaki, it looks like it has pockets, but they're fake.

Gradually we got ourselves sorted out and sat down. I was looking forward to the food, having had nothing since a Red Cross doughnut and tepid coffee at 0500, when a petite girl slid into the seat next to me. Things were looking up. "Hi," I said. "Jack Kennedy. What agency do you head?"

"I'm Margaret Truman."

Aha, I thought. Who'd have thought the new vice president had a daughter like this. She turned out to be a junior, majoring in music. I tried a couple of subjects, and struck gold on movies. She loved Robert Montgomery and Joan Crawford and Katharine Hepburn. She'd seen *The Scarlet Pimpernel* a dozen times. So I told her about Gloria Swanson visiting us at Hyannis Port, and Claudette Colbert, and the other stars us kids had met visiting Dad in Hollywood. She stopped eating to listen. I was working the conversation around to myself when a Midwestern voice cut in. At first I thought the matronly woman was smiling. Then I caught the glint of steel in her eye.

"And what do you do, Mr.—"

"Kennedy. I'm Ambassador Kennedy's son."

"Is that so. How old are you, Mister Kennedy?"

"Twenty-seven, ma'am."

"And my daughter is twenty. Don't you think that's a little young for you to be mashing her?"

"Don't mind Mama," Margaret said. "She's wearing two guns this morning." But something had changed in her voice. The contact was broken, the current died away.

I tried the guy next to me, but he was some New Deal bureaucrat; he droned on about conditions in West Virginia as we dug into the sparse, ration-coupon lunch. I was glad when it was over and Mrs. R stood at the door, talking to four people at once in her shrill voice. She gave me a curt smile for a tenth of a second as I slid past.

———

Outside, on Pennsylvania Avenue, I stood still for a moment. It was a lot warmer. A peanut vendor was doing land-office business on the corner. Where the hell was I going? I headed for a phone booth, digging out the little book again. This time I went for the front, where the good stuff was logged.

My nurse of last week, at the Pimlico Club—Taney Royce—wasn't in. Her roommate was, though. Said her name was Adrienne. English accents turn me on. After the Court of St. James I can do a pretty fair Oxbridge myself. I wavered, then said I'd call back.

I knew what I was going to do then. Knew by the way my heart speeded up and my hands got wet. Knew I shouldn't even as the nickel dropped and the gongs sounded in my ear. My finger spun in the familiar digits. BInford 5-2378. The receiver clicked in my ear as the line buzzed, as I waited, waited, feeling a little dizzy.

"Hello?" Her voice.

"Surprised to hear from me?"

A pause, then her laugh. "A little maybe. What took you so long?"

"I've been busy. Navy stuff . . . and my back's been bothering me. Well, how about it? Want to get together?"

"I don't think we should. I'm not trying to be stubborn. I'm only trying to help you. You know that."

"Give me a break. Just for an afternoon."

"What about Palm Beach? What will he think?"

"I don't care what he thinks, Inga."

"You know that's not true, Jack. You will always do what he says. You might not right away, you fight a little, but you will always do it. You are a little puppet that he makes shadows with in the light . . . you know, I never understood what he didn't like about me. What's so wrong about being in love?"

"Well . . . you're older, and married, and . . . there's the religion. But mainly it's those people in Europe you used to know."

"Jack, that was ages ago."

"But it's wartime now. That changes things."

"So you know the reasons why not. But still you call Inga Binga up. What if I get the divorce? Will that change anything?"

I closed my eyes. "That's up to you, whether you get it. I told you before, I don't want to influence you in any way in getting it."

"This whole talk is childish. You call me after months and months. Nothing changes. You want me because I'm safe for you, because if it goes too far your father will step in. This is not fair to me, Jack. We decided not to see each other anymore, didn't we. Have you any doubts?"

"I really want to see you," I said.

"I don't think things are at all like you think. You know somebody is always listening in on this phone."

"On your phone? How do you know?"

"Don't you notice when we talk there is some cut in it, we are always cut off for a fraction of a second. And the same thing happened when I just talked to New York."

"Well, what are you afraid of? That they'll catch Hitler giving you assignments?"

"Yes, and he's so cheap, he always calls collect."

"Inga!"

"I am just kidding, Jack. Though God knows it is not funny."

"I just wanted to be sure this is what you want to do. From what you said, I didn't have anything to do with you getting the divorce."

"You pushed the last stone under my foot, but that doesn't hold you responsible for anything. Meeting you was the chief thing that made up my mind. But as far as I am concerned now, you don't exist. It is too hard, with your father. He hates me, but he tries to get into bed with me. I still love you as much as always and always will. But you don't figure in my plans anymore."

I couldn't say anything. Finally I managed, "I'll call you again next week."

"Don't, Jack. It is all over. That is how you wanted it."

Nothing else is as final and as sad as the sound of a phone hanging up. The people passing by looked in at me curiously. A Navy lieutenant in uniform, sobbing in a phone booth. Even then, miserable as I was, some shadowy someone inside me enjoyed being watched.

CHAPTER 12

Lafayette Park

For two days after the German had turned away from his gun into the office of the FBI, Krasov had warily examined every pedestrian who passed his bench, suspected every shadow, tensed each time a military truck went by. He was waiting for security forces to arrive, barricade off the area, and begin combing out the park. He had an escape route planned in case they did.

But to his astonishment, nothing had happened. No one even asked him what he was doing here, other than the cop on the beat. And he'd bought the story about him waiting for his brother, he was coming up from Norfolk on leave from the Navy and they'd agreed to meet in Lafayette Park.

At first he couldn't believe American security was so ineffective. It had to be a trick, he *had* to be under surveillance. He was fifty meters from the wrought-iron fence, a hundred and fifty from the White House itself. If he'd had a Panzerfaust, a grenade launcher, he could have fired it through a window! But gradually he'd relaxed, still wary, yet resuming his vigil beneath the budding elms in the shadow of Andy Jackson on a rearing horse. He found a stub of a pencil in a trash can and made notes in the margins of a copy of *The Good Earth* someone had left after an open-air lunch, watching everything that went on opposite him. And gradually he noted patterns and rhythms, when the guards changed, when employees came and went. Humming to himself.

> *Though April showers*
> *May come your way . . .*

Among other things, he noticed that three times a day a dark-brown-and-cream panel truck swung in from the east, was waved through the gate after a short search, and rolled out from the grounds again about twenty minutes later.

Always the same man driving. He had strolled across from Lafayette at last to check out the discreet gold-leaf lettering on its side.

It read *Hahn & Hurja, Fine Laundry and Specialty Cleaner.*

———

That night he was squatting on the sidewalk outside an old brick building on a back street south of Garfield Park when a door came open and a slow trickle of men and women ebbed out. From the open door came a glare of light, the hiss and thump of manual presses, the rumble of extractors, a hot steamy breath of steam and solvent. The outgoing shift lit cigarettes with quick starving gestures as soon as they were in the open air. The yellow flare of matches lit faces drawn with fatigue. They were mostly black, with a sprinkling of whites.

Krasov got to his feet, pulling the leather jacket down at his waist. He touched his cap to a meek-looking woman, scanning the other faces swiftly as they scattered. There, that was his man, just turning the corner.

He caught up as the Capital Transit trolley screeched to a halt at one of the raised boarding platforms. The man flicked a butt away in a glowing arc and reached up to haul himself aboard. Krasov ran up the steps and boarded behind him, dropped a dime in the glass box, and pushed after him through a limp, exhausted-looking crowd toward the rear. There were no empty seats. He grasped a strap and leaned against a window as the streetcar jerked and storefronts started moving past. It was dark inside the trolley and dark faces surrounded him, workmen, cleaning women, exhausted and closed, oblivious to him and everything else. No one spoke. The leather strap was slippery-smooth in his palm. For a moment he wondered if he could become one of them. Darken his hair, his skin somehow . . . in this city they were invisible, they could go anywhere with a broom or bucket in their hands . . . then he realized his eyes would always give him away.

"Hey," he said. "Ain't you the guy delivers for that cleaning company over on Canal Street?"

The man glanced up, a startled, long-faced, coffee-freckled fellow of forty-five or fifty with hunched shoulders and a bony neck coming out of the sweat-stained shirt. The streetcar jolted and swayed, and Krasov caught a whiff of tobacco and what smelled like paint thinner.

"That's me, mister. Route man for Hahn and Hurja."

"Your name Jason?"

"Jason? Jason? No. I'm Francis Smalls. Who's Jason?"

"Nobody—I thought that was your name. Look, Mr. Smalls—I followed you on this trolley. Truth is, I'm trying to find a job in this here town. I need some advice. Thought I'd buy you a drink, you could maybe help me out."

"A job? You askin' me about a *job?*" His eyes narrowed. "How you know about me, anyway?"

"Maybe I asked somebody. Let me buy you a drink," Krasov said again. "Come on, how about it?"

Smalls was suspicious but finally said he knew a place they could go. Krasov remembered then that they could not go into just any bar together, a white man and a colored. Not in Washington, D. C.

Several stops later Smalls jerked his head. Krasov followed him off the trolley and down a side street. Down an alley behind nineteenth-century row houses. Up a landing.

Smalls knocked tentatively on a door, waited, knocked again.

When the heavy white man in suspenders and shirtsleeves and tilted-back gray fedora opened it, Krasov saw the revolver tucked inside his waistband. The white man grunted, "Frank. Who's the guy?"

"Friend of mine, Mister P."

The goon ran his eyes up and down Krasov, then gestured him to raise his arms. He did, glad he'd left the Tokarev in his rented room. The big hands ran up and down his ribs, then he gestured them in. He followed the black driver down a short entrance foyer.

In the rooms beyond dice clicked and a ball skittered around the pink blur of a roulette wheel. Cigar smoke hung choking-thick above tables where men sat over cards, their bodies contracted like closed fists. Soldiers, sailors, civilians, black and white, smoking, holding glasses, calling out bets to a thin, sweating, shirtsleeved Jew at a chalkboard. Through a side door he saw silver, bills, and poker chips stacked on a table, a black man sitting with a shotgun propped behind him against chipped wainscoting.

At the bar faces turned briefly to survey them, incurious and blurred, then forgot they existed. Smalls ordered a jill of whiskey. Krasov ordered beer. "Nice place," he said, counting out change for the drinks. His heart sank as he saw how little he had left. The sixty-two dollars he'd taken from the woman in Virginia was nearly gone. It was astonishing how much things cost . . . pint of milk a nickel, doughnut a dime, the narrow, dirty room he flopped in ten dollars a week . . . and he was always hungry. A man went by carrying a tray of sandwiches, and he got halfway to his feet and reached himself two, tore his teeth into the first before he sank back opposite Smalls. He held out a dime but the man just shook his head and kept going.

"They're free," said Smalls. "Long as you're drinking."

"Yeah? Nice place here."

"Yeh, Jimmy owns it."

"Jimmy?"

"Jimmy La Fontaine." The driver slid his eyes to a corner, where Krasov, turning his head slowly, saw a shockingly obese man in an untied bow tie and suspenders sitting by a telephone. "They feed the action over to his place in Prince George's County. You play the horses?"

"Sometimes. Not too often."

"Say you from out of town?"

"Yeah. Pittsburgh."

"So, what you want, mister?" Smalls said, setting down his empty glass and licking his lips.

"Understand you're in charge of the delivery."

"I'm not in charge of nothing, but I been on the route for Missus Hahn for fifteen years. Why you ask? Got somethin to sell me?" Smalls grinned past him, not meeting his eyes.

"I need a job," Krasov said. He unfolded his last five-dollar bill and laid it alongside Smalls's drink. "Any chance of getting me in there?"

"Army needs men, I hear."

Krasov showed him his draft card. Smalls looked at it blankly and Ivan realized he couldn't read. "Got a deferment," he said. "Blind in one eye. How about you?"

"They don't take no old niggers in the Army. Plus I got four kids. Plus I got the sugar. No, they don't want no part of Francis Smalls." He giggled.

"Ticket, mister?"

A small boy by his elbow, big ears, red hair. "What?" Krasov said.

"Want a ticket? You can get in for a nickel. Pick three numbers."

"Go on, buy you a number," said Smalls, smiling tightly at him. "Don't worry, Tonio pays off. He remembers faces."

He picked two, four, seven. The kid took his nickel and handed him a ticket. Krasov tucked it away and said to the black man, "The what?"

"What's that?"

"You said you had 'the sugar.' What's that?"

"Oh. The sugar. It make you sick, make you swell up."

"Uh huh. Well, I done some driving in my time. How much time you spend on the road?"

Smalls said he worked from six to eight, with an hour off for lunch. He ran down a list of places he had to go each day. Hotels, hospitals, Union Station, officer's quarters.

"You do the White House too, don't you?"

"Oh yeah, we got some of the best trade in the city. I goes by there three times a day, the pickup and delivery. I seen Missus Roosevelt once, down in the basement. A real nice lady. She said hello and shook my hand."

Krasov sat back in the chair. "Want a cigarette?" Smalls shook his head and he tore open the fresh pack of Fleetwoods, lit one slowly, sucked in smoke, exhaled.

"That pays pretty good, don't it? Route man."

"It ain't too bad, depends on how hard you want to work, that's all. I don't get no regular pay, y'see. Route man gets twenty-five percent of what he collects. That way they sure you out picking up and delivering, not parked someplace taking a long lunch." Smalls winked. "Route man, it's not like working in the plant all day. You get out and about, meet the people, meet a lot 'a lonely women. Sometimes you take what you can get in trade, know what I'm saying?"

"I hear you, that don't sound bad. Well look, you think you could get me in there? I could help you out, maybe—"

The Negro cupped his drink instinctively. "Get you in? Don't hardly think so. Me and Roscoe and Tenny, we the route men. We got all the drivers and spotters and pressers and baggers and such we need. People stays around there till they gets old. Don't hardly nobody leave. No, ain't no place for hiring, sorry."

"I wouldn't want much, Mr. Smalls. I'm hungry."

Smalls didn't look at all compassionate, he looked even more suspicious. "What you doing down here, anyway? Say you from Pittsburgh, huh? Ain't they making steel up there no more?"

Krasov lowered his voice. "I got in trouble. Union trouble. You know what I'm talking about."

"Maybe," said Smalls, his voice flat and uninterested. "Maybe not. So what?"

"So I had to move on."

"You check the hotels? I hear the Statler's hiring again, now they got that fire cleaned up. They always needs busboys, waiters."

"Maybe I'll try there. Thanks for the tip. One more drink?"

"Okay, sure."

Krasov gave him time to drink it. He felt sorry for the man. It couldn't be easy, being a Negro in America. And waiting, he hummed to himself.

> *When the sun gives way to April showers,*
> *Here's the point that you should never miss. . . .*

"Man, I got to piss," Krasov announced later, shoving himself back from the table. "Where do you go around here—"

"I'll show you," said Smalls.

It was just an alley. That was all. At the bottom of a flight of slippery, creaking wooden steps. Unlighted except for a distant window. Stinking of urine and worse. Krasov waited politely for Smalls to go first. He looked into the shadows as the black man faced away from him, confronting a brick wall. Water rattled, and a sigh of relief echoed and ebbed.

"That sure feels good . . . say. You never did answer, mister, I asked how you knew about me."

Krasov did not answer now either. Instead he considered the angle of Smalls's downbent head, turned away from him, unsuspecting, unresisting.

> *So if it's raining,*
> *Have no regrets . . .*

CHAPTER 13

West Texas

Because it isn't raining rain, you know,
It's raining violets . . .

Lauren Wolfe in sunglasses, telltale red hair shielded from dust and recognition by a silk scarf, hummed along with Jolson as the bottle-green 110 convertible coupé ba-*dump*ed across a railroad crossing. Thank God she'd kept the Packard. Five days of rutted roads, boiling-hot desert noons, hour after hour climbing mountains. She'd fed it black-market gas, alcohol, even kerosene. And still the engine purred like a cat. May they never stop building 'em, she thought.

Five days out of Los Angeles, and it seemed like a million miles away now . . . after stopping at the house for clothes, she'd left town by Route 66, then changed to 60 at San Bernardino. Three, sometimes even four lanes, a broad magnificent highway east. The first day out the country was familiar. Citrus groves, truck gardens, and mile after mile of bungalows. Then more orchards, solid trees for miles, grapefruit, orange, lemon, walnuts just starting to burst into waxed white blossom; then horse farms and the San Jose hills rising ahead in the crystalline air. Later the long climb to the San Gorgonio Pass, the narrow descent; then, suddenly, cactus, deerhead, beavertail. Desert.

She spent the first night at Palm Springs, but was packed, dressed, and on the road again before full light, feeling whatever she was fleeing too close behind. Was it Levinsohn, Craven, or Hollywood itself, the stagefront never-never land where the only thing the cinematographers and special-effects men could not diffuse or erase or fake was the deep-within-her knowledge that time was always passing. Now that the place lay behind she realized how deeply it had imbued even the way she saw; that it startled her to look at a palm tree and know that it wasn't a pole covered with burlap and composition plaster, or see a stone wall she couldn't put her fist through. She took a side trip to look out over the flat, sluggish waves of the Salton Sea, then pursued the shimmering lanes of 60 and 70 east into the desert. When mountains rose before her like a Ben Carré backdrop she angled south, 89 to Phoenix, spending an afternoon on foot searching for pueblo ruins her WPA guidebook promised, never finding them, but thrilled anyway at the spectacular views and an encounter with an enormous rattlesnake. At Globe she had to choose again, north or south. She chose south, taking a break from the dry wind and glare with beer and tamales at a sunparched saloon in the middle of planed-flat nothingness.

She didn't try to make mileage, or even drive with any goal in mind from day to day. She wasn't going anywhere, after all. It was escape, hooky, she was Eve on the lam from the Garden, a fugitive from the Promised Land. Funny, she thought dryly; they say that's why people go to movies. She'd always wanted to drive across the country, and now she sometimes sent the car hurtling down the long, straight, empty roads at 110, 120, till she remembered to conserve gas and reluctantly lifted her foot from the accelerator. Fleeing, *free,* not a soul on earth knew where she was. The mountains gave way to sunblasted sand and rock so flat she could sense the earth's curvature under the unrelenting sky. She shouted Shakespeare aloud into the empty wind. She gaped at buttes and cactus, marveled at the thousand shifting colors. So beautiful and so empty that one evening she'd pulled off under a sunset like a dome of rose petals to spend the night in the car—and came as close as she'd ever come in her life to freezing to death.

In the emptiness of New Mexico she switched the radio on, waited as it warmed, then fiddled with the Bakelite knob and listened to Woody Herman, Cab Calloway, Tommy Dorsey, June Hutton with the Paul Weston Orchestra, Ella Fitzgerald, Coleman Hawkins. West of Alamogordo, in the middle of nowhere, she was caught behind a convoy of military trucks; when she tried to pull out and pass, MPs in jeeps tore after her with sirens until she pulled off and let it go by. Strange, that the trucks were filled not only with soldiers, but with pale middle-aged men in ties and glasses who looked like university professors.

She took a side trip to Carlsbad Caverns and sent everyone she knew penny postcards. Then got back on 70 through Las Cruces and then Roswell, and stopped to wade in the calf-deep Pecos. Cattle country now, flatland, small towns that hadn't changed since 1880, the weathered general stores and clapboard churches and hitching rails familiar, familiar from a hundred Westerns. The marquees in the larger towns jarred her, as if trying to pull her back, spoil her fun; Philip Dorn and Mary Astor in *Blonde Fever,* with a Li'l Abner cartoon. Pat O'Brien and Carol Landis in *Secret Command,* with late news and shorts. A double feature of *Maisie Goes to Reno* and *Sonora Stagecoach.* Sometimes, her own name, her own eyes staring out at her from sunbleached posters for *Morocco* and *The Forsaken Hills* and *Beyond Midnight.*

Now evening was coming on blue across the hills, and she'd passed a sign a few miles back, Welcome to Texas. Apparently in earnest. She saw that she was just about out of gas. Again . . . she'd started with a full tank of studio gas, but ran out of ration stamps in New Mexico. She'd begged five gallons here, a tankful there, traded a signed War Bond poster for white gas at a grocery store, but now she was almost out of cash too. One grizzled, leering geezer at a crossroads store had sold her what she strongly suspected was kerosene. She'd had to keep the engine racing, and black smoke had unrolled behind her, but the Packard had kept going.

And now, Lauren dear, are you ready for . . . Bovina, Texas. Population 640. Another main street, cracked dusty asphalt. She saw a woman walking and pulled over to ask if there was anyplace to stay. The cracked, dusty face with voice to match gave directions to a hotel two miles up the road. She checked in with sunglasses and scarf on, signed the register "Mrs. Violet Simpson," and asked when dinner would be served. The man behind the desk stared, but said only, "Anytime you like, I guess, ma'am. Hope you like pan-fried steak."

"Hello, operator? Long distance, please . . . give me Los Angeles. Yes, this will be a person-to-person collect call for Carla Matthews. TAlladega 4-3678."

She examined her chipped fingernails while she waited, hearing the local operator talking to Los Angeles, then L.A. talking to Pasadena. And at the same time, the clatter of plates from the kitchen. The phone was in the parlor, and she perched uneasily on a horsehair sofa that smelled like old face powder. She studied the flyspecked faces of pioneers in heavy, flaking gilt frames.

"Hello?"

"Carla? It's Lauren."

"This is the operator, will you accept the charges?"

"Yes. *Yes!* Miss Wolfe. It's Miss Wolfe! Oh, my God. We thought you were kidnapped, or . . . or dead!"

"I'm not dead, I just walked off the set."

"God, I mean, Miss Wolfe, where *are* you? They've been driving me crazy. They just won't believe I don't know where you are. Everyone's been calling."

"Does 'everyone' include Leo Levinsohn?"

"Four times a day. More."

"Good. Look, I need you to wire me some money. I've checked and there's a Western Union office in Amarillo. Wire it there in care of Violet Simpson. Got that? Violet Simpson. Five hundred should be enough."

"I understand, Miss Wolfe. But, Lauren, where are you? Mr. Selznick wants to talk to you. Two men called from the Los Angeles Police Department. Your lawyer, Mr. Holcomb. Mr. Levinsohn, Mr. Craven, Louella Parsons called, Mr. Cukor called, your ex-husband—"

"Which one?"

"Eddie."

"How nice, he never cared when we were man and wife. Carla, listen. I'll give you the number, but you have to promise not to give it out to *anyone* but Myron and Mr. Holcomb. Understand?"

"Yes, but—"

"You have to promise."

"I promise, Miss Wolfe."

She read it off the hotel receipt. When she had it, her secretary asked, "Why did you leave, Lauren? Where are you going?"

"I'm not really sure. But I'm enjoying the trip. Remember about the money now, all right? I'll call again in a day or two. *Good*-bye!"

━━

She was in the tub when the tap came at the door. The old guy from the desk. "Miz Simpson? There's a call for you."

"Can you bring the phone in?"

"Told you, onliest phone we got's in the parlor. Gotta go down there, you want to talk."

"Shit, damn," she muttered. Into her bathrobe, a towel over her hair, she went downstairs.

"Hello?"

"Lauren? It's Myron."

"Myron, how nice of you to call."

"Are you in good health? There are all kinds of rumors flying around."

"I'm fine, I just couldn't take working for that prick Craven one more minute. He was always lighting me from below. Plus Leo and I had a set-to about my next script. He told me I had to do it, and I told him. I haven't worked my ass off for twenty-two years to turn out saccharine poop like that."

"That might not have been wise, Lauren. He sent over your suspension notice. You're not only off salary, it stops the clock running on your contract. But . . . since it's already done, let's see how we can work with it."

"What have the papers been saying? I can't get the *L.A. Times* or *Variety* here, and the radio hasn't—"

"Nothing. Absolutely nothing. No one told them you were gone. Hell, for all we knew, you drove off a cliff. Did you know the police are trying to find you?"

"You can call off the cops, but I want to keep the pressure on Leo. Have you talked to him yet?"

"He called, and I've never heard him hotter under the collar. They're still shooting, scenes you don't appear in, but they don't have much more cover. I told him I had no idea where you were."

"I told him, I'm on vacation. My contract says ten weeks a year, and I haven't taken a day for two years."

"But where *are* you?"

"Somewhere in west Texas. Look, the idea here is to get him to give me what *I* want. Then I'll come back and be sweet and cooperative as Shirley Temple."

"What do you want? Your contract runs for three more years. Do you want to renegotiate?"

"Not necessarily. I've had time to think about it, driving. Here's what I want: no more than three pictures a year, and the freedom to choose what I make."

"Script approval."

"Exactly. And an ironclad agreement that I'll get to direct one film a year, starting the year after the war ends—that'll avoid any conflict with the bond tours."

"Lauren, why do you want that? You're a great star. You're the biggest money-maker in the business. You're at the peak of your fame."

"Which is exactly why I've got to make the change now. I don't want what happened to Garbo to happen to me."

Her agent made equivocal noises, how one woman couldn't change the studio system, that Levinsohn was hurting, maybe they should deal. She cut through. "Look, concentrate on winning this one and getting me back into production. I'm gone until Leo buckles, so you better start thinking about how to persuade him. Can we use the newspapers to pry him out?"

"We could, but it might bounce back and hurt you. A lot of people aren't going to see you as Eliza on the ice, Lauren. They're working at defense plants, sweating out their kids being overseas. They'll say, hell, what is *she* whining about?"

"I'm not afraid of that. I think my public will be with me, once they understand what I'm fighting for."

"Maybe," said Selznick, but he didn't sound convinced. "Will you call me tomorrow?" She said she would.

The phone rang as soon as she hung up. Faces showed at the doorway, peering in, but she glared and they disappeared. She picked it up. "Hello."

"Lauren."

She almost hung up, but didn't. Curiosity made her say, "Why, Leo. How nice of you to call. But how ever did you get my number?"

"Never mind that. Where the fuck are you?"

"A quaint little town in Texas. Something to do with cows, I think."

"You're in violation of contract."

"Leo, have you thought about what we discussed?"

"You're in violation of contract. Even your fucking lawyer agrees. You'd better get back here, right now—"

"Leo, I keep telling you, I didn't scratch and claw my way to the top just to fade away into some overaged glamor girl. And gradually I've realized it's not just for me. This is for every actor, every actress, and every starry-eyed wannabe who ever dreams of being discovered at the corner of Hollywood and Vine."

"I've talked to Myron. Offered the son of a bitch another fifty thousand a film. That applies to *Hearts and Hands,* too. And I've taken your name off *House of Women."* She could hear his enraged breathing over the line. "Satisfied? Now find out if there's an airport there. I'll send my plane. Where's the nearest fucking cow pasture?"

"We're getting close, Leo. But do I have script approval?"

"Red, have a heart. So I do it for you, then what do all the other stars want? If actors only do properties they like, the studio, what's a studio? We can kiss the industry good-bye—"

"I told you before, Leo, it wasn't the money. So offering me more cash is not going to solve your problem. Do you even remember what I wanted?" She waited, but heard only his erratic heavy breathing. "No? Well, here are the rushes. I want roles that take talent, that challenge me. I want scripts and films that don't insult the intelligence of everyone who watches them. Is that really so much to—"

Even over nine hundred miles of wire, his interrupting roar made the receiver vibrate in her hand. "I'll sue you for every penny we're losing on this production. All the other contracts are running. That's eighty thousand a day you're costing me!"

"Starting to pinch, isn't it, Leo?"

"You *paskudnyak.* You come back right now, or you'll never work in pictures again. I own you! You're thinking Broadway, I know you. But you'll never appear as Lauren Wolfe, I'll close the production down, no one will touch you. Where are you? I'm flying out. Are you near Amarillo?"

"Don't bother. I won't be here tomorrow." She slammed the phone down, said to the hovering faces, "Don't answer it. Yes, it's true. I'm Lauren Wolfe. But I'm not here. Understand?" They nodded slowly, awestruck.

———

Lying that night in the lumpy swaybacked bed, thinking about the cowboys and whores who had probably made these ancient springs squeal, she had a few minutes of pure terror. What if Leo didn't fold? There were such things as understudies. With sharpened knives all ready for her back. Beyond a certain point it would be cheaper to scrap all her scenes, put in another actress, start shooting *Hearts and Hands* over again with Dolores Moran or Irene Dunne.

Then she thought, if I can't refuse to act in utter trash, maybe a career isn't even worth having.

After several minutes of rigid staring into the darkness she fought it back down. She couldn't quit. She had to keep squeezing his nuts till he said uncle. She knew Leo Levinsohn. Once he won, once he knew she was weaker, there'd be nothing but bit roles in total drivel from here on in. She *had* to win. Her hero, FDR, was right. Unconditional surrender; there was no way back but victory.

Okay, she wasn't going back yet . . . but where *was* she going? New York in March didn't appeal after fifteen years in Southern California. She didn't know anyone in Massachusetts anymore. Anyone she cared to visit. In fact, on the whole eastern seaboard, she—

Just then, with a delicious little shiver, she remembered. How could she have forgotten . . . Jim? The thought of his arms around her made her skin feel warm, electric. They'd only had four weeks together before he got orders east, but it had been one month she'd never forget. He wasn't anybody, just a soldier, a sergeant from some town in Arkansas no one had ever heard of. She'd met him at a bond rally, one of the most handsome men she'd ever seen. And in bed, *oy vay,* as Leo would say. . . . For a month she'd taken him around town, to the Beverly-Wilshire, to Solly's for the show and the Tick-Tock for dessert, taken him on the set, to parties . . . even to Victorville when he wanted to see a rodeo. Then just before the Army sent him east he'd said it, said he wanted to get married. Silly boy! Well, that wasn't in the cards, but a few long hot nights might be.

She decided to get out the map in the morning and find a short cut to Georgia.

CHAPTER 14

Tuesday, March 27: Washington, D.C.

I had no dreams that night, thank God. Instead I was stuffed into a black hole of unconsciousness so deep it seemed to last only for a split second.

I was brusquely jerked out of it by the clanging of a windup alarm clock. "Jesus, what's that," Taney mumbled. I groped over her, trying to remember why in Christ's name I'd set it for 2300.

Then it came back. My first watch in the Map Room, midnight to six.

I groped around for shorts and shoes, found what I hoped was my tie, and stumbled out into the darkened living room. The half-parted curtains showed me someone else on the couch. Through the window wartime Washington stretched off to the black horizon, some long-abandoned city whose last departing inhabitants had dimmed the lights. It was so cold I could see my breath. It'd be worse outside, but I didn't have anything like an overcoat or reefer. Since the Solomons I'd tried to stick to warm climates and agreeable places. California, Palm Beach, the Stork Club.

So how the hell had I ended up in Washington, D.C.? Last on everybody's list of fun places. Well, it was either take orders from Leahy, or face Dad with a decision I didn't want to make.

Shit, I thought, fumbling myself out the street door, not sure how it locked, but it didn't much matter. Taney didn't bother to lock her apartment either.

Christ, it was cold. What had happened to yesterday's promise of spring? The varnished pavements were empty. I flipped up my collar, stuck my hands in my pockets, and leaned into a black breeze windtunneled to gale strength by the three-story fronts of row houses. By the time I got to McPherson wind-tears were streaming so fast I could hardly see.

The White House gate. A beam of light perused my ID, then my face. "Pass, sir," a voice said. I ran up the walk, shivering uncontrollably.

Halfway to the shadowy bulk of the building, in a pool of darkness between the gate house and the portico, I stopped suddenly. Looked at the fence, at the darker lines of the bushes, at the faint square blacknesses that were the windows, five or six feet above the ground.

I hesitated, then stepped off the path. Grass crackled faintly beneath my soles as I slid toward a patch of shadow, closer to the house. From there a concealed man could see into the—

"Halt! Who goes there?"

I froze as forms rose out of the earth at my feet, from my right, behind me. Lights came on, fixing me like a bug. I raised my hands as someone frisked me roughly from behind, then swung me around.

"Who the hell are you? What're you doing here?"

"Lieutenant Kennedy. On my way to the Map Room. Here's my pass, I—"

"Stay on the goddamn walk, Lieutenant. You gotta take a whiz, do it before you get here."

They escorted me to the portico. That wasn't too smart, I thought. But I'd proved one thing to my satisfaction: Nobody was going to sneak in and bump off FDR in the middle of the night. Not without wading through half the Army first.

"Look like you crawled out of a snowbank, sir," said Tavelstead. "Just cooked a pot of fresh joe. You like any coffee in your sugar?"

"Thanks, Chief. Hold the sugar, but make it a long hot one." I beat myself with my arms, looking around.

The basement corridor had been dark and cold, but here the egg-crate fluorescents were on full behind the blackout drapes and the radiators were glowing like toaster elements and the Teletypes were hammering like Pappy Boyington's machine guns on a dawn strike. The close air smelled of steam heat and ration cigs. Santorini and Rose were arguing over a pub change. Tavelstead thrust a heavy white mug into my hand. I inhaled about a quart of it and breathed out, blinking, as it ran down inside over all the frozen parts.

All at once I was plugged in again and the tubes were warming up. I took another long slug and went behind the rolling curtain that reminded me of the things they put around your bed when you're sick. Abrams was sitting there asleep, eyes wide open, over an open codebook. Two marines stood flanking him. One had a leather briefcase chained to his wrist. The other, a Thompson slung over his back.

"Ready to relieve, Major. Who're these guys?"

Abrams blinked and flinched. "Damn it . . . sit down over there till I get this broke. Read the incoming boards."

"Gotcha." I started near the door and began reading myself in.

The flimsy yellow sheets on the message boards made me forget everything else. Deep in what had been Nazi Europe last summer, the Allies were maneuvering like meat slicers through bologna. I concentrated on the map, reading each message with an eye on the pin that represented that army's HQ. Pretty soon, maybe today, it would be my turn to brief the President.

Germany first, western front, north to south. The Canadian First and British Second Armies were advancing fast north of Essen after smashing across the Rhine on a twenty-five-mile front. The U.S. Ninth was in Duisberg, deep in the industrial Ruhr. Montgomery commanded these three armies; he was off the dime at last and racing for Berlin. South of him the U.S. First, General Courtney Hodges, had burst out of its bridgehead on the 25th and gained thirty-five miles in the last twenty-four hours to take Limberg and Hechkholzhausen. The Third Army had lunged forward too; its vicious-looking salient was one hundred thirty-six miles inside Germany, cleaning out Frankfurt am Main. The German communique reported Patton's Fourth Armored near Fulda, but comm breakdowns had left us in the dark since his secret crossing of the Rhine three days ago. Patton, too, looked like he might cut Germany in two, and in the south Patch's Seventh was at the gates of Karlsruhe.

On the eastern front details were sketchy. The Soviets didn't report to us or to Eisenhower's SHAEF. The only data we got from them was the official communique, and since Hitler could read that as easy as we could, it wasn't too specific. Still, the Map Room watch officer had to be ready to brief on all the Allies, and on German movements too. The Third White Russian Front had "liquidated" a pocket southwest of Koenigsberg, capturing over twenty-one thousand officers and men. The Second Ukrainian Front was advancing rapidly in the Carpathians. The Third Ukrainian Front had captured Papa and Devecser, rail junctions covering the approaches to the Austrian frontier.

On the Berlin front, though, the Soviets seemed to have stopped fifty miles east of the city. They said they were being held up by spring floods on the Oder, but Zhukov was reinforcing and expected to resume the offensive at any time.

In the air, the British had bombed a German convoy in the Skagerrak, believed to be rushing troops from Norway to the western front. They'd apologized to the Dutch for hitting The Hague in error early this month, killing eight hundred people and making twenty thousand homeless. U.S. Eighth Air Force B-17s had attacked a tank factory at Plauen and a synthetic oil plant at Zeitz. The Fifteenth Army Air Force had bombed industrial targets in Berlin. Other U.S. bombers out of Italy were bombing in front of the advancing Reds in Hungary, Austria, and Czechoslovakia. The Russians said they had bombed German military objectives in encircled Danzig.

In the Pacific, the Fifth Fleet carriers and resurrected battleships from Pearl Harbor were pounding airfields and bases on Okinawa. MacArthur's headquarters reported that the Americal Division, which had landed in the Philippines yesterday morning, was within sight of Cebu City. A Twentieth Air Force B-29 raid had destroyed the Mitsubishi engine plant at Nagoya and the British and Chinese were making progress in Burma. I reviewed the weather, then the international stuff. The only interesting news there was that Argentina had declared war at last.

No question about it in my mind. The end of the war, I mean. Hanson Baldwin was saying in the *Times* that it could all be over as early as April, but that the moderate guess was June or July. Unless Adolf had something up his sleeve.

"Up to flying speed?" said Abrams. The marines were leaving, the devil dog with the Thompson following the one with the briefcase. Tavelstead shot a deadbolt behind them, and for the first time I noticed the door itself. "Hell," I said, "Is that armor plate?"

"Inch thick, sir. That's cruiser hull plate, that is."

"I'd have loved to have some of that on the old 59."

"Fifty-nine?" said Abrams, in his drugged voice.

"Gunboat Number One, we called it. The boat I commanded after 109." I valved myself more coffee. "We were doing a lot of barge hunting, Jap barges they used to stage out of Vella Lavella, run supplies to their guys on the Canal at night." I went over to the southwest Pacific map and found Vella for Abrams, and the Slot. "We took three old seventy-footers and stripped the torpedo tubes and depth charges off, and loaded them up with forty-millimeters and fifty-cals. Made them PT gunboats. We had a full auto forty on the bow and another one on the stern, and three Browning aircooled fifties port, three more starboard."

"Those are great guns, Brownings. We carried those on 24s."

"I put two more twins up behind the cockpit, and two twin thirties flanking it. Shit, we had twelve mounts! Trouble was, we didn't have any weight allowance left over for armor. There was a little tinplate around the mounts, but we set up a sheet of it and fired the fifties at it. It didn't even twitch when the bullets went through."

"Not much more than that in a Liberator."

"Yeah, but all we had around the gas tanks was a half-inch of plywood. I'd have killed for that door. I'd have put chains on it, hung it over the engaged side like a sandwich board."

"D'you get any barges?"

"Oh, a couple," I said, although we hadn't; 59 had never fired at anything that could shoot back, except a float plane one night, as it was headed away from bombing us. We'd spent most of our time nursing her tired old engines in and out of repair sheds. The war had moved on and Choiseul was a backwater. Finally I'd had enough, I couldn't see wasting my time in a rear area, and arranged a transfer back to the States.

"When was this, sir?" the chief asked me. I told him, July, August of '43.

Out of nowhere—maybe it was just the hour, being dog tired—Abrams started talking all at once. "Forty-three," he said. "July. That'd be just about the time we were finishing up Sicily and getting ready to hit Ploesti."

I looked at him. Everybody in America knew that city in Rumania. The biggest refinery in Occupied Europe, the one target Hitler couldn't keep fighting without. "You were in on that?"

"That's right."

"I read the papers when it happened. Was it as fucked up as they say?"

"It wasn't fucked up," he said, and I could see I'd hit a nerve. "It could have been done. The plan was just too complicated. Perfect timing, perfect navigation, perfect bombing, perfect luck—if we'd had all that it could have worked."

"So what went wrong?"

"They planned it low level, where we'd always trained for high. We thought it'd surprise them. It didn't. Plus we thought the flak was Rumanian. It wasn't. It was Luftwaffe, with radar, a shitload of ME 109s, and Krupp 88s on flak towers. Ad Baker's group hit the oil tanks too early, and visibility went to shit.

"Nothing but black smoke and us flying through it, sticking our hands out the cockpit windows feeling for smokestacks and barrage balloons. We couldn't find our target. But our section leader spotted a cracking tower north of town and we put three dozen five-hundred-pounders down on it."

The thousand-yard stare, I thought; so fliers got it too. "That was the easy part. Then we had to get out. Flying low, you burn a lotta gas. We started throwing shit overboard, seats, radios, guns, first-aid kits. I'll never forget looking back and seeing that gauze unrolling in the air. The Messerschmitts steered clear of it. I don't know what kind of secret weapon they thought it was. But we were so low, coming back that when they dove in on us they couldn't pull out. After two of them plowed into the ground the rest let us alone."

"How low were you?"

"Wait. I'll show you." He slowly extracted his wallet. In one of the glassine pockets was a flat yellow mass. "Sunflowers. Off the lower antennas. We lost fifty-four planes out of a hundred and seventy-eight."

"So you earned that Air Medal," I said.

"I could fly once."

"You'll be back flying again."

"I don't think so."

"How about after the war? Civilian airlines are going to be a boom industry. I could help you get a job with one."

"Yeah, I read the article in *Yank* about that," said Abrams. "But like I said, I don't think so."

This time I noticed he'd pulled his pants leg up. And that some kind of black plastic gleamed in the harsh, cool mercury light.

I said, maybe too casually, because Rose looked up from his cutting and pasting: "Pete, on that mission over Ploesti, tell me something. Were you, uh, were you afraid?"

"My mouth got dry," said Abrams. "But I was too busy flying that sucker to have any time to be scared. That how you felt on those PT boats during an attack?"

"Yeah," I said. "That's just how I felt."

———

Luckily, I was still awake when Brown came in at 0600. He asked a lot of questions, most with no answers I knew of. I asked if I could get some breakfast. He glanced at his watch and nodded silently. Meaning: okay, but don't take long.

The kitchen staff was chattering when I swung the two-way door open. The next second silence had fallen like at the movies when the sound goes dead, black faces and white turning to look at me. Back here the floors were linoleum, not parquet or carpet, and the ceiling was black with grease. A row of gas masks hung over the table like sagging rubber skulls. I took a chipped chair next to a white woman who was stitching bedclothes. "What's it take to get a plate of eggs around here?" I said, flashing them all my hungry, shy, boyish smile.

"Don't give him any, Bluette. You'll have to explain it to the President, why we're using so many eggs."

"He's just a boy, Mrs. Nesbitt, he needs 'em."

"And there's a war on, and we have to eat same as everyone else."

I eventually got what everybody else seemed to be having, one egg and one slice of bacon. I could have as much toast as I wanted, though.

I kept smiling and complimented the food, and gradually they got used to me. I told them I worked in the Map Room, my name was Jack, that I expected to be there a while so I thought I'd better introduce myself. That seemed to work, and they went back to what they were doing, polishing silver, brushing clothes, shining shoes, loading things into a big GE dishwasher. A buzzer sounded, and a big Negro said something I didn't catch. The maids laughed, and he left.

I made friends with a woman with crutches propped beside her chair. She said she was Lillian Rogers Parks, "Little Lillian," everyone called her. She'd had polio as a child; her mother had been the First Lady's seamstress before her, had served Mrs. Taft, the two Mrs. Wilsons, Florence Harding, the Coolidges and Hoovers. Now Lillian was Mrs. R's seamstress. What was she working on? Oh, it was one of Mrs. R's coats, alterations, a black-and-gold silk Chinese jacket that Madame Chiang Kai-Shek had presented her when she visited the White House. I listened to a couple of her stories, then asked her about the others.

The big butler, Alonzo Fields, had been hired by Mrs. Hoover in 1931. The little guy in the corner was Harold Thompson, head engineer. The woman who hadn't wanted to feed me was Henrietta Nesbitt, the housekeeper. She'd been with the Roosevelts since he was governor of New York. The two maids, Wilma and Bluette, had been there since Coolidge. The pantry girl was Wilma Collins. Most of the women were in black uniforms, except for Mrs. Parks and Mrs. Nesbitt.

"Gosh," I said. "How many people work here, anyway?"

"Oh, there's twenty staff, and then there's Arthur Prettyman, and Grace Tully, and Mabel, Mrs. Roosevelt's maid—then there's the Usher—"

"I know Mr. Crim."

"And the three boys who work for him, Mr. Searles, and Mr. Claunch, and Mr. West. Then there's the doctors, and Mr. Fox, who does the massage—"

"About forty people," said Mrs. Nesbitt. "If you count the housemen. There used to be more, but since the war started they've cut way down on the florists and gardeners."

"Are there any new staff members? Since the war started?"

"Oh. Well, there's a new gardener—Richard Tracy. We call him Dick." I chuckled with her. "But that's all. The three housemen, the cleaning men, they've been here forever and probably their grandfathers before them. We were going to get some young ones but they got drafted. Like you, I suppose."

"I volunteered."

"Good for you. My husband's in the Army, but I don't hear from him very much." A shadow crossed her face, but she batted it away and lifted her needle to catch the light. "I hear the President's thinking of going to Warm Springs."

"Is that right?"

"I hope he does," said one of the maids, Bluette. "He looks bad, he's lost so much weight, and he won't get new shirts."

"Why not?"

"He doesn't want to waste, he says . . . a man with his money! I hope he does go to Georgia, he always looks so much better when he comes back."

"Then you could do some housecleaning," said a large black woman. She was getting herself more coffee. "Lil, some of your sugar?"

"One spoon, Lizzie. You have to bring in your own. This is Lizzie McDuffie, of Atlanta, Georgia. Do you know Mammy, in *Gone With the Wind?* We all thought it was going to be Lizzie, for a while. She had the screen test and everything."

I twisted in my chair, looking the room over. A pantry or scullery back of it. Everything looked old and not terribly clean. "So this is where the food comes from."

"Well, most of it. There's another little kitchen on the third floor."

"That's for—"

"For the President." Parks lowered her voice, glancing to where Mrs. Nesbitt was lecturing one of the maids. "He hates Mrs. Nesbitt's cooking. But Mrs. R insists she stays. So he has his own cook. She used to work at Hyde Park, for his mother."

"But he don't seem to care any more what he eats, even if Mrs. Campbell, she lay herself out making it for him," McDuffie said.

"Is that all the staff?" I said. "Are there any more people live here? Or work here full-time?"

"Oh, lots more. There's Admiral McIntire, and that nice Dr. Bruenn, and Captain Brown that's an admiral now too, and Major Abrams and the Chief and, oh, you know them already. Anna Roosevelt, Mrs. Boettiger I mean, and little Johnny. Then there's the boys on the roof—the antiaircraft people. Then the switchboard operators, and all the clerks and such in the West Wing—"

I nibbled toast, fighting a sinking feeling. I knew FDR had his secretaries and assistants, Grace Tully and Harry Hopkins and Steve Early and Bill Hassett, and Eleanor had her own staff. I knew about the ushers and the butlers, the men in the public eye. But I hadn't realized there were all these people backstage. Dozens of them, and a lot Negroes. Fortunately most of the staff proper, those who were physically closest to the President, had been there so long it seemed remote that they could be plants or spies. And if Reilly was as good as he looked, he'd checked them out long ago.

"What about this Tracy?" I said. "You said, he's the only new one on the staff?"

I guess I overplayed it with that, because suddenly her eyes narrowed. "My, you're just full of questions," she said, putting down her cup. "You might better ask Mr. Reilly about things like that. He investigates all the new staff people. Very thoroughly, I understand . . . and now I'd better be getting upstairs, see if Mrs. R's going to need anything this morning. Nice meeting you, Mr. Kennedy. But from now on, you really better ought to eat with the other boys in uniform."

―――

When I got back to the Map Room, Branch, the yeoman, had his shoes propped on the sill. One of the Teletypes sat silent, its cover off and tools and parts scattered across the floor. A second class I didn't know had his head inside it and his ass in the air. I took a quick look around for Brown, but he wasn't in sight. "What's going on, Branch?"

"You missed the morning brief, Lieutenant. Admiral wanted to know where the fuck you were."

"Getting breakfast, like he said I could."

"Well, the President's been here and gone, sir."

"Shit," I said. I'd wanted to see the briefing. "Who's got the watch now?"

"Mr. Grabb."

I reported to Grabb, a nearly bald lieutenant-commander who'd taught at some jerkwater college in New Hampshire, then done escort work in the North Atlantic. He'd been torpedoed, then sent home with some battle-fatigue type diagnosis. He didn't have anything for me to do, but thought I'd better stick around just in case. When was Brown due back, I asked. He didn't know. The hell with that, I told him. I'd been on since midnight and I was going to go take a shower, see if I could get some clean underwear.

━━━

Taney's apartment was still an icebox. I put my hand on the radiators. Heatless. I decided to have a talk with the landlord. Then I smelled something funny. I went through the little hall and through the living room, following my nose. The bathroom door was open and without thinking I went in, brushing hanging stockings aside like a man guarding his face from spiderwebs in a cave. The next second I stopped.

"Who the hell are you?"

"Kennedy."

"Who?"

"Jack Kennedy, Taney's friend. She gave me a key."

"She gave you a *key?*"

"She said I could stay here for a few days. Till I found a place."

So this was the lonely-sounding roommate with the Brit accent. Wavy brown hair, and nice legs under the short bathrobe. Hazel eyes and pouting lips. The smell was gin. She caught where my eyes went and pulled the robe closed. "So, you're the Irish Catholic boy whose father's rich as Daddy Warbucks."

"Not that rich," I said, "But the rest is right. You're—?"

"Adrienne. Adrienne Sloane."

She reminded me of another brunette, one I'd dated at Stanford. But Nancy never drank—it was something to see her order milk at the Mark Hopkins at one in the morning—and she never came across either. Gorgeous but prim. This Adrienne didn't look prim. I was suddenly aware of the empty apartment, the steamy, woman-fragrant air. That glimpse of her tits had started the old yen for romance. There was no mistaking the look I was getting, the way she let the lapels fall open. A challenge.

She turned back to the mirror and started brushing her hair. I leaned against the jamb. Great ankles, great feet, great everything. I smelled soap and lotion and shampoo. Her hair was wet, clinging to the flushed skin of her chest in little tight ringlets. The radio was on, out in the living room. Art Mooney. "I don't know enough about you," I said.

"What?"

"That tune. 'I Don't Know Enough About You.'"

She glanced me a sideways glance. "All you have to do is ask."

"Where are you from?"

"Ensenada."

"You know, that's funny, I thought of California when I saw you. You look like a girl I used to know at Stanford. But, hey, what's with the accent then?"

"My parents are English."

"Is that right. You married?"

"No."

"Steady beau?"

"I date around. Doctors. People I meet."

"No special man?"

"A boy from my hometown. He's in the service, Coast Guard, someplace in Africa. We write."

"Lucky guy."

"Maybe someday. It's not a good time yet, not for him, not for me. Maybe we'll settle down after the war."

"A little house, a little family?"

"Maybe." She gave me another glance. "Right now, I'm enjoying myself."

I grinned. "So, where's Taney?"

"At the hospital. They called her in."

"Know when she'll be back?"

"Not for a while." Adrienne put the brush away and looked at me. "Want a drink?"

"Thanks, you go ahead."

"You don't drink?"

"Got to go back on duty this afternoon. Course, there's one thing they can't smell on your breath."

"Yeah?" She came closer. Daring me. "What?"

"A little of this," I said, and slid my hand under the bathrobe. No knickers, no garter belt, just girl. She let me explore for a second, then slapped me casually. "You fresh bahstid. What do you think you're doing?"

"Anyone ever tell you you look fabulous naked?"

"Only in your dreams. You're not going to see me naked."

"I already did. Last night, when you were asleep. You had the covers off. I had a nice long look while I was getting dressed."

"You son of a bitch," she said, and started to slide past me. I caught her hand and a moment later she was pressed against the tiles, the bathrobe was coming apart.

"I thought good Catholic boys didn't do this," she whispered into my ear.

"We can *do* it, as long as we feel guilty afterward."

"Do you feel guilty?"

"It's not afterward yet."

"But you're Taney's boyfriend. And here we are, oh, doing it in her bathroom."

"Not officially a boyfriend. Just a guy she met."

"A guy she gave a key to."

"Well, it's your key, too, right?"

Her nails raked my back as we left the tile wall and, locked together, reeled into the living room. The bathrobe fell away. "Pick me up," she whispered. Without thinking I hoisted her, and her legs locked behind my back, and then without any warning at all something went CRACK inside my head and a white hot steel shaft ripped right up through the bottom of my skull to the top.

I screamed and let go as my back locked, and we both went over onto the table. I saw it all happening in slow motion but couldn't stop it or do anything but hang on through the white blaze. The lamp swayed and the gin bottle toppled. Glass burst soddenly across the carpet. The lamp followed, the bulb bursting with a fizzing pop as it hit the floor.

All at once blue flames were running across the gin-dripping table, and Adrienne Sloane was screaming, and Taney Royce was standing in the door, hands to her mouth as she looked down on us naked on the burning carpet. It all seemed to stop there, a long count while some cosmic umpire waited for me to get up again. But I couldn't. Then the fire singed me and I was rolling aside, hands to my back, while the girls beat at the flames with blankets, screaming at each other.

Then I was outside in the hall. An old woman in a shower cap and flowered housedress was shaking her head down at me. Taney appeared at the door, blonde hair flying, and threw the rest of my things out after me. I leaned against the wall, still unable to straighten up or speak. Toothbrush and Burma-Shave tube, AWOL bag, cap. Last she pitched out a gilt cardboard Thalheimers box. Tears were running down her face. The cover flew off and I saw a man's scarf. Not my color, though. The corridor stank of hot alcohol and burnt wool. I had never known so quick a succession of lust, agony, and shame.

"Shit, shit, fuck," I said to the old lady. Looking inexpressibly shocked, she pulled her head back out of sight, like a maliciously entertained, gloating, gleeful old tortoise.

The look I got from Brown as I limped into the Map Room told me what was coming. I started to leave, but he grated, "Kennedy. In the Code Room." Reluctantly, I followed.

The "Code Room" was the vault; it had pretty obviously been a walk-in closet before the war. Now it had a reinforced door and a combination lock, and the clothes racks had been replaced with shelves. The admiral pulled a chain, and the naked fifty-watt bulb illuminated a full wall of cheesecake. I panned slowly across movie stills, grainy black-and-white pinups from *Yank* and *Life,* posters for *Morocco* and *The Dying of the Light,* and the famous Cecil Beaton full-color shot on the beach, the one that had put a certain red-haired actress on the cover of *Vogue* and in the fantasies of every male in America.

"Jesus. Somebody's a Lauren Wolfe fan."

"Santorini. He got to talk to her for about six seconds down in Warm Springs, when she visited FDR."

"She visits FDR?"

That did it. He exploded. "Jesus Christ, will you *stop talking?* Where the *hell* have you been, Lieutenant? Anyone told you about duty hours?"

"Yessir, I was just having lunch. A friend of mine was in town—"

"We mess in the Executive Wing. You know that! I don't know what kind of habits you Pac Fleet people pick up out there, but around here when we're on duty we're on duty."

"Sir, I—"

Brown's eyes widened suddenly. He leaned toward me. "And *drinking!* I don't care if you're Leahy's long-lost bastard son, I could court-martial you for this!"

It was too complicated to explain, so I just said yes, I'd had one drink at lunch. The reference to Admiral Leahy told me something, too. Otherwise it was a pretty standard Navy chewing-out, intense, but a couple notches below Dad's best. I pretended contrition and looked scared at the appropriate places, meanwhile thinking how much I'd like to cut Brown's throat. And maybe, given a little luck, I could do just that.

"Now get the hell back to your post. You leave without checking out with me again, and I'll have your commission. You'll walk out of here a slick-sleeve seaman recruit, under guard. Got that?"

"Yes sir," I said, though I knew he couldn't slap my wrist without procedure, hearings, plenty of time for Dad to ring up his friend the Secretary of the Navy. While he was shouting I thought I heard something, but Brown was still monopolizing my attention when someone began hammering at the door. He cracked it and the Chief said, "Air raid drill, sir."

"Christ! Why now? Leave Branch here with the pubs," he snapped, and bolted out into the corridor.

"Don't follow him! He's going to check on the President. We go this way, sir," shouted Tavelstead. "And grab your gas mask."

I didn't feel like running, but everybody around me seemed to. Groaning, I tried to keep up as the klaxon grew louder, as the wail of fire sirens rose outside the building.

Funny, I didn't see the President or Mrs. R, or Reilly either, during that sprint down the arcade. The shelter was under the East Wing, down three flights of stairs in a forty-by-forty concrete-walled room. Once there, I found myself in a mass of people, all smoking, all talking, and all packed close together under the ceiling, sitting on boxes of canned goods or on the bare springs of the bunks. I fought my way toward the bunks. If I could lie down, this goddamn pain might ease off. There were people sitting on them, but I guess I looked pretty bad as I staggered up, because they gave me startled glances. "Hey, can I lie down, please?" I gasped.

"Sure, Lieutenant. Say, buddy, you okay?"

I knew the press room was in the West Wing, but this was the first time I'd seen the reporters. They never came in the Map Room, of course, and I hadn't seen them in the corridors either. Anyway here they were, and some of them I recognized: Merriman Smith of United Press, a little guy with a Dewey mustache; Harold Oliver, the soft-spoken AP correspondent; young George Tames, the president's photographer. Two other guys I didn't know turned out to be radio people. Once they heard my name they wanted to know what was wrong with me. "Wrenched my back coming down the stairs," I muttered. "You know, old PT injury."

"What you doing here, Kennedy?" Oliver asked me. "Thought you were in the Pacific."

"Just got assigned to the Map Room staff."

"That okayed for release?"

"Have to ask Brown that."

"Brown never gives us a goddamn thing."

"Well, you'll have to ask him, I work for him. He chewed my butt once today already because I came back a few minutes late from lunch."

Something nudged me, and when I looked down I saw it was a hand. With a flask in it. "Thanks, but no thanks," I said.

"Kennedy, Kennedy," mused Smith. "I read your book, back when it came out."

"What'd you think?"

"It was okay. Kind of vague, though."

"Too political," said another voice.

"But that's what's important," said a woman's. It was familiar, but I couldn't see her. Actually I kind of tuned out of everything then, my back hurt so fucking much. To distract myself I tried to remember feeding it to Adrienne. She'd be number 39. Or wait, did it really count, since we hadn't finished? I decided it did. "Penetration, however slight, is sufficient to consummate the offense"—I remembered that from some military justice lecture.

"Is he all right?"

I opened my eyes to an upside-down pair of long legs, and struggled to sit up. Anna Boettiger. The reporters were asking her about her dad, did FDR feel all right, why had the conference been postponed. She just shook her head and smiled. It was his smile, all right. She even tilted her head up a little, the way he did. But she was sexier.

"Turn over," she said.

Rolling over, I listened to the springs creak as she rubbed my back.

CHAPTER 15

The White House

Behind the basement window the blue innocent eyes turned from the street outside back to the woman who spoke on and on in a droning monotone. Two hot-water heaters hissed steadily, gas flames visible through ports. A huge black-iron mangle crouched in a corner. He wondered how many fingers its nicked rollers had crushed over the years. The heat pressed down on him in the low-ceilinged room, walled with raw, unfinished stone on two sides and rough brick on the others. Paper-sheathed suits and dresses on wheeled racks stood against them. The floor was burnt tile the color of clay, with a square drain set in the middle. He nodded, to show he was listening, and shifted from foot to foot, easing the binding at the crotch of his pants. The worn deliveryman's uniform was too small for him. But he didn't look eager.

It wouldn't do to look too good at this job, Krasov reminded himself.

"Working at the Executive Mansion is an honor and a privilege. We are entrusted with the safety and comfort of the First Family and many important guests. You are part of that family now, in a way. Hahn and Hurja has been serving us for many years.

"If there's anything I need to know about you, please tell me now. You look like quite a strong young man—"

"I'm strong enough, but I'm blind in one eye, ma'am."

"Where is your eye patch?"

He stopped, mouth open. The question was so unexpected he had no answer ready. They stared at each other.

"Well?" she snapped.

"You don't . . . you only need dark glasses or a patch if your bad eye looks bad. If it's missing or something. Mine looks okay, just don't work."

To his relief she nodded. "I suppose that makes sense . . . I wondered why you were not in Service. But working here is a contribution to Victory too. Your eye shouldn't affect your pickup work. We will have everything hung and tagged here three times a day. I daresay you'll do. . . . Though it is certainly terrible about Francis. I knew he drank, but to have such a thing happen to him . . . it's too bad."

Krasov nodded, keeping his face vacant and agreeable and a little dull, a little slow, as he remembered what had happened to Francis Smalls.

The woman gave him a sharp glance, as if he smelled bad. And it was true, he hadn't been able to bathe for days. That did not matter, though, it didn't matter at all. "Smalls . . . yeah. I din't know him, but they said he must of fallen off the stairs and landed wrong. Busted his neck clean. Tough luck for him. But, well, I was glad to get the job, ma'am."

"How *did* you get the job?"

"Just luck, I guess. I happened to stop in an' ask the same day they found they needed a man."

"They wanted references, of course—"

"Oh, sure," he lied. All they'd actually asked to see was his driver's license and draft card. "I used to work over at the Statler, but then they had the fire. They checked to see if I had a criminal record too. I come out all right, I guess."

"I see. Well, I think that is about all you need to know about our procedures here. The gate guard will search your truck each time you enter. Bring your finished clothing here and we will distribute it.

"Now, on sorting and so forth: If you find lace or silk clothing in the bins, turn it over to the maids for hand laundering. You may observe at times that the laundry you pick up is worn or torn. We practice economy at the White House. We don't throw out old pillow cases, for example. Instead we restitch them inside the new ones, so that the ticking of the pillow does not show through and the pillow actually looks whiter. Draperies are cut down and reused in shorter windows, then the interlining is used to make silent cloths to go under the tablecloths. If you think a piece is beyond its useful life, please bring it to my attention.

"If you should see money, jewelry, or anything else of value left around, do not touch it. I recall Mrs. Hoover used to leave her diamond ring lying around, all over the house. She would take it off, then walk away and leave it. We were always searching for it, but it always turned up." She fixed him with a stare. "I do not wish to indicate any suspicion of you. I am sure you are quite honest. Should it turn out otherwise, however, we will not hesitate to advise your employer."

"I'll bear that in mind, ma'am, I sure will."

"Have you any questions, Mr.—?"

"Kondratowicz. What about tips?"

"Mrs. Roosevelt often tips the staff, as do our guests, but I don't believe laundry pickup is a tipping position. If you're asked to do anything special, you might receive a gratuity on that occasion, but I shouldn't expect it as a matter of course."

"How about if we see them? The President, or Missus Roosevelt—"

"You won't, not often. We stay out of their way. But if it happens, just act natural. Don't speak to them, but don't hide either. You work here and so do they, that's what Mrs. R told me once, so just act natural."

"I get you," Krasov said.

"One other thing—if you are making a delivery and the President should come by, keep your hands out of your pockets and don't make sudden movements. His Secret Service people won't like it."

"Okay, I guess I better get going. These for today?"

"Those go out today, that is correct."

He tugged down his cap, set his shoulder to the rack, and steered the cart out into the basement. Whistling under his breath, as he swept his eyes across the corridor, the stairs going up, the elevator doors.

> *Because it isn't raining rain, you know,*
> *It's raining violets . . .*

CHAPTER 16

The mess hall in the West Wing wasn't much to brag about. Nor was dinner, swiss steaks and desiccated strawberry shortcake. I could see why FDR kept a separate kitchen.

Back in the Map Room, I found Captain Hollins on duty. Lieutenant-Commander Grabb came in at six, bridge coat sodden with rain. After he relieved Hollins I drifted over. "Is there going to be an evening brief?" I asked him. He said he didn't think so, the President had been in right after the air raid drill; but that he'd be in early tomorrow, a press conference was scheduled and he'd want to be up-to-date on the military situation. I asked if he had anything to go up. He looked at me funny and said if there was, Tinsel would take it up.

Okay, great. I put in some time getting smart on the coding machines. These were the new electric models, not the manual type we'd used at ONI. They looked like big black electric typewriters. Paper tape, typewriter keyboard, five-letter groups. The sensitive part was the coding wheels. They had to be inventoried and signed for by each watch and kept in the safe when you weren't using them. Finally I figured I had it doped out. I went back into the vault and looked at the spines. Took a couple out at random.

Yeah, Tojo would give his eyeteeth for this stuff. One book, the spine weighted with lead bolt-on strips, showed the location of every armored deck on our carriers, including the new *Essex* class. Get that to the Nip pilots at Midway and they could have blown away our whole air arm. Something called "S-1" occupied a shelf of its own, but when I opened a page at random it was nothing but physics.

I slotted it back as another set of documents caught my eye just below the pinups. In the hot, close air of the old closet I took one down. I was reading an intercepted, decoded, and translated conversation between Göring and a Luftwaffe general named Kammhuber, the chief of air defense over Holland. Another volume, and a message from the Kriegsmarine to the *Bismarck*.

This was the most closely guarded secret of the war. Cities and convoys had been sacrificed to protect the fact that we were reading Axis communications in real time. What I held were British intercepts. The product of their code breaking was called Ultra. Ours was called Magic. Shortly after Pearl Harbor, Op-20-G, the Comms Security Section of the Office of Naval Communications, had succeeded in breaking JN25, the Imperial Japanese Navy's operational code, and we'd been reading it and most of their other high-level codes ever since.

Somewhere in this room was the message that had made Leahy suspect an assassin close to the President. I wanted to keep looking, find it, but this wasn't what I was here for now. I needed to get up to speed on current events.

FDR sent a lot of stuff, of course, but what I wanted to read was the highest level, his correspondence with Churchill and Stalin. Abrams had briefed me on the routine. Leahy saw FDR every morning. They went over the incoming messages, talked them out, and the Chief of Staff went away to draft the responses. Sometimes FDR signed off on them, sometimes he sent them back for rework. Since they went out through us, it behooved me, as one of the communications watch officers, to know where to find back copies in case the President sent down for references.

What I finally found were not only the originals of those outgoing messages, but, in separate binders, the answers. The headers, cover sheets, and route sheets were still attached to most of the outgoing stuff, on Army forms, along with Leahy's and FDR's releasing signatures. Stamped on them were the transmission dates and times and Chief Tavelstead's or one of the sergeants' initials. The incoming file was all in clear text, on standard Navy NCR-18 message blanks with a big red SEALED SECRET stamp at the bottom.

I turned through several folders before I found the one for March 1945. There was a proposal for warning the Germans against harming our POWs before their camps were liberated. There was friction between Wedemeyer and Mountbatten in Indochina and a discussion of a pending aviation treaty with Ireland.

By far the majority of the telegrams were from Churchill, though—long ones. The last two were dated yesterday. The Prime Minister was upset about Stalin's interpretations of the Yalta decisions. Molotov was refusing to admit Western observers into Poland, and Churchill was warning Roosevelt that his goal was to install a Communist government.

This was dynamite. I'd been reading the papers, and no one had any idea this was going on. Everyone thought Yalta guaranteed a democratic Poland. If we were going to knock the Germans out of Eastern Europe only to turn it over to the Russians, what had we fought the war for? If somebody like Hearst got wind of this, papers all over the country would be screaming for impeachment.

I stood there thinking. If FDR was covering up something like this . . . wasn't it my duty to make sure certain people knew about it?

"Kennedy, you in there?"

I put the file back hastily. "Yeah."

"Ed called to check in. He wanted to make sure you got some sleep. Remember, you got the midwatch."

"Yeah, I know that, sir."

The vault door swung open and Grabb leaned in. "Hey, you from Michigan or Wisconsin?"

"Neither. Why?"

"Nemmind, we got absentee ballots for state elections next month." He looked at the shelf of Magic intercepts. The one I'd been looking at stuck out from the others. "What are you doing?"

"Seeing what we've got back here, like Brown said to."

I expected another question, but he only said, "Ed said you had a place to stay."

"I thought so. But it doesn't seem to be working out."

"Misunderstanding?"

"Jealous roommate. Understand you and him, you got a snake ranch out in town."

"I don't know if it's a 'snake ranch.' We're both married. Anyway, it's late. By the time you got out there you'd have to turn around and come back again. You might as well stay here tonight."

"Here?"

"There's bunks back in the clinic. Bruenn lets us use 'em if we get caught late. There'll be a corpsman on duty, but you might have to knock pretty loud, wake him up. Hey! Tinsel! Show Mr. Kennedy how to operate the emergency bunking system."

Branch, the yeoman, was getting dressed to leave as I came out. "Where's my watch cap?" he said plaintively, pulling out the pockets of his reefer. No one answered him. Santorini, the tech sergeant, stubbed out a butt. He heaved himself to his feet and rapped on the outer door. A clank from outside, then he unlatched his side. "I didn't realize we were locked in here," I said. "What if there's a fire?"

"We die peeing on the secret files, Lieutenant."

"I see," I said. "Say, why do they call you Tinsel? That an inside joke?"

"Oh, those bums—I got a little lit at the Christmas party. Fell into the tree an' knocked it down. Since then that's what they call me. This way, Loo-tenant. Follow me."

———

The clinic was around the corner, first room to the left. The corpsman stumbled back to his bunk after he let me in. I dossed down on one of the hospital cots.

Only I knew from the second I lay down I wasn't going to sleep. I wished I could, I was tired as hell. But the old noodle was still buzzing along. The last bangs and shouts from the kitchen faded, till all I could hear was the patter of rain outside. A scratching sound came through the thick sandstone walls. A bush, its branches moving in the wind, scraping the outer wall. Or mice; Branch had said something about mice.

When I went to Choate, which is in Connecticut, where the winters are cold, we had the same fag system they have in the British public schools. Nothing a fellow can't take, but there's some humiliation involved, initiation-type stuff. My senior was a fresh-air fiend, but he hated to put his feet on a cold floor. So, one of the things he made me do was close his window during the winter months, early, so that the room would warm up before he got up. So every morning I'd get up in practically total darkness and sneak into his room and close the windows without waking him up. You learn how to do that after a while. Then there's a couple of tricks they showed us at Melville, when we were in training for PT skippers. They had Butch Smith teaching us dirty fighting, but what I was trying to remember right now was what a marine officer had showed us once about how to scout and move at night.

At last I got up, shifting my weight so evenly and slowly the cot didn't creak. I pulled my blues trousers on and my issue sweater.

I pulled the wool watch cap out of my pocket, shook it open, and cut a hole in it with a pair of blunt scissors I found in a desk. Just a slit, in the crown. I pulled it on and adjusted the slit till I could see. Last, I slipped on the black leather gloves that were Navy winter uniform issue. Shoes? I decided stocking feet would be better.

I eased the door open. Checked that it wouldn't lock behind me, and slid out.

There were a few lights on in the corridor, enough to see and be seen. But no one was in sight but the Map Room sentry. He was pacing back and forth, keeping himself awake. Listening to the muffled roar of the Teletypes through armor plate, I waited till he turned away and ran lightly across the passageway. I ducked into the service stairwell just as he started to pivot back.

Two flights up the stairwell exited beside the Lincoln Bedroom. I peered around the elevator cage before stepping out of its shadow. I remembered the marine officer's advice. *Stay close to rocks and trees. Blend your shadow with theirs. Don't get caught vertical in the middle of a clearing.* I halted two steps into the hallway, blended with a bookcase, and looked the situation over.

The center hall was huge and shadowy. Oriental rugs covered a polished hardwood floor. Good, that would muffle my footsteps. At the far end, through an arched, open double doorway, the shadows of armchairs reached out toward me from a single bulb burning in a floorlamp. Square darknesses on the walls were portraits of former presidents.

I stood there for a long time, listening to my heart. At last it fell back to a halfway normal speed. *Use your ears,* the marine had said. *Use every sense, not just sight.* Maybe it was my imagination, but I thought I could hear someone breathing not far away. I eased my head slowly around the bookcase.

A Secret Service man sat to my right, slumped in one of the armchairs. His head was bent and his hat tipped forward over his eyes. A twisting ribbon of smoke curled up at his elbow. A frying sound came from the cigarette as it burned. It seemed I could hear the smoke, unreeling itself like spider silk upward through the cool air. I froze, my heart speeding up again. I didn't dare breathe. If he glanced up he'd see me.

When he didn't move I turned my head slowly. Left, then right. Looking for a way to escape. Back up? Yeah, that was the best bet. I might even make it. With infinite caution, I extended one foot behind me, preparing to ease my weight back.

To the right, past the motionless man, a doorway led to the President's oval study. Not the Oval Office—that was in the Executive Wing. This was private. The man in the armchair was between it and another door, closer to me. I'd been up here with Dad. I knew the layout, though I hadn't been in all the rooms, of course.

For example, I knew the President slept next to the study. So this closest door, twenty feet from me across the hall, should be the door to his bedroom.

The guard started snoring, lightly, but plenty loud enough for me. The cigarette burned fast, with little popping crackles. I was so close I could see the red ember eating the paper, turning the white cylinder to a gray sagging fuze of ash.

He wouldn't be asleep long, not when that creeping ember got to the nicotine-stained fingers. Still I took another fifteen seconds to judge my next step. It didn't look possible, to get the bedroom door open, or even get to it, without waking him.

That left one other way in. I took a breath, bent, and took five or six steps, short and slow, along the wall opposite him. The damn floorboards creaked. For once I was glad I was light. My toe knuckles cracked and my lips drew back in a rictus of effort. Another step, easing my weight from board to board, quiet as the molecules of air that hissed upward with the smoke.

Suddenly I froze. I'd just gotten a clear look at the sleeping man. I knew him. Or at least, I'd seen him before.

A natty-looking fellow, with a Ronald Colman moustache.

Whom I'd last seen on an icy night, being loaded into a Black Maria while passersby jeered.

I blinked and forced myself into motion again. It wouldn't be so hot to get caught out here. I could grin my way out of some things, and others Dad could get me off the hook for, but this might not fall into either category. Something scurried inside the wall just then and the guard stirred. I froze again, then took two quick gliding steps and fitted myself behind another bookcase as he cleared his throat and sat up, taking a last drag before he ground out the butt.

I stood motionless, hardly daring to breathe. I heard the crackle of a wrapper as he shook out another smoke. The click-scratch as he lit it, with a Zippo, it sounded like. Yellow flame wavered in the glass of a portrait opposite us. Yeah, there was the click as he flipped the lighter closed.

I stood there for ten or fifteen minutes, not moving. Finally I leaned forward. An eighth of an inch at a time, I edged my eye around the corner.

He was nodding again. This time the cigarette lay smoking itself to death in the tray.

I turned my attention to my right, to dark oak double doors. There was the doorknob, dull, the brass unpolished. I reached out slowly. The click as bolts detached themselves from the striker plates sounded like a rifle being cocked.

I took a slow breath, eased it inward, praying it had been oiled sometime since World War One, and slid inside.

No sound from the hall.

I eased it shut behind me, careful not to lock it again, and looked around the big oval room.

There were no lights on in here. Only a disappearingly feeble radiance bleeding in through the three windows that faced south, looking down over the lawn and the trees toward the ellipse, the tidal basin, the Potomac. I averted my eyes, looking toward the darker areas to my right and behind me. A clock ticked. At the same time I noticed the smells. Cigarette smoke, first. Years of it, like a poolroom. The tang of wood ash—the fireplace, probably—and beneath that, old leather and a dry mustiness that reminded me of the stacks at Widener, where I'd done the research for my thesis.

Gradually many small black rectangles emerged from the gloom. I could see them plainer if I wasn't looking right at them, a trick I'd learned on night patrol in the Solomons. You never looked right at what you wanted to see. You looked to the side, and somehow your eye picked it up. More of his naval prints, probably.

To my left a white marble fireplace shone eerily. I made out a cluttered desk centered between the windows. Behind it were irregular blurs, heaps and piles, like paper ready for a scrap drive.

I pivoted slowly. So far I'd known where I was going. I'd been in these halls and rooms before, though not at night.

Now I was going somewhere I'd never been. I had to do so with infinite caution. Just catching my sweater on a projecting edge could bring things clattering down.

The knob turned easily under my hand. The bolt snapped, and I halted, not breathing for nearly a minute, then inhaling slowly through an open mouth.

A distant creak. Steps? They said Lincoln's ghost walked the White House at night. I didn't think so. This was an old building. Old buildings settle. But still a shiver explored my back.

I swung the door ajar, a fraction of an inch at a time, and slid through it. I halted just inside.

This room was smaller than I expected, but small as it was it still looked almost unfurnished. As my pupils dilated I made out a wardrobe against the far wall. A window to my left, with blackout drapes drawn back to admit what little light the rainy night held. Another marble fireplace. Above it a mirror gave me a shimmering reflection of the window. The walls were covered with more prints and photos. Almost all were of ships, there was enough light to see that. White sails swollen above dark billows of sea. In the far corner I could just make out a round table heaped with books. A spindly shadow sat beside it. At first I couldn't figure it out. Then I realized it was his wheelchair.

Closer, in fact right beside me, was a bedside table, not just littered, but stacked two feet high with books and letters. The merest brush would bring the whole thing down. Round dials of what looked like a barometer-hygrometer combination. It could have been a clock, but I couldn't hear any ticking. A telephone. A brass reading lamp.

Beside it, a hospital bed, with a long humped shape under the blanket.

I stood there for quite a while, in the faint light coming through the sheers. Thinking of what lay there in front of me. The Hundred Days, the fireside chats, the New Deal, the March of Dimes, Social Security. The Fair Labor Standards

Act, the forty-hour week. Then the Day of Infamy and the Grand Alliance. The Presidency, the war, the Allied cause. They were all Roosevelt. Twelve million guys in uniform. He was their Commander in Chief. Right there, with the light shining on his sparse gray hair.

Reaching out, I touched his bed.

Then I backed away, very slowly. He grunted and moved a bit but he didn't wake. Only then did I remember what Reilly had said, about him sleeping with a .357 under his pillow.

This wasn't something I'd planned to do, believe it or not. Enter his bedroom. I'd only wanted to see how good the nighttime security was. But it was nonexistent. There was something going on. Nobody should be able to get in here as easily as I just had.

I decided to leave and let Reilly figure it out. I backed away, one step at a time. The snoring resumed. I got to the door leading to the study, eased it wide enough to pass, then stopped again. My fingers explored the lock. It was the old button type. Well, the place was what, a hundred and fifty years old. I pushed the button in, hoping it was the right one. Then I backed through, very quietly, and eased the door shut. Held the bolt as I closed it, so that as it eased in the last half inch the bolt slid in without any noise at all. Just the way I'd done it those winter mornings at Choate.

I heard a noise just then, a faint grinding squeal from the outer door.

Backing away from the bedroom, I faded back into the office. The door creaked again, almost inaudibly, but there was no question, somebody was opening it. I looked around, then crouched below the windows. *Blend with your surroundings. Check their outlines and conform with them.* I passed my gloves over each other, then glanced down to make sure no patch of skin showed.

It was getting hard to breathe, and I felt hot under the watch cap.

This wasn't good. If this was the Secret Service, and they caught me here, I was cooked. A dishonorable discharge would be about the best I could hope for. On the other hand, if it wasn't the guard, then I'd have to stop him somehow before he got to the President. But the only possible weapon I had was my belt. That can work in a bar fight, but it wasn't much of a kicker. Especially if the other guy had a knife, or a gun.

I eased over behind the desk. Reaching up, I felt around with my fingertips. Ashtray. Book. Lamp. My hand closed on something bumpy that fit my palm. I lifted it and it was heavy, lead or brass or iron.

The other was inside now, standing just inside the door. I could see a thread of yellow light where the jamb was, and a slice of President Jackson's portrait behind it. I didn't look right at it. The only advantage I had was that I was thoroughly dark-adapted.

The floor creaked again, and the sliver of light disappeared. I heard breathing. The faint brush of footsteps.

The rattle of a hand trying a doorknob. I rose slowly from behind the desk. If the door opened, I'd let him have it. Two long steps, and I'd bring the little statue or whatever it was down on this guy's head.

A silence. I felt my arm trembling. My heart was beating so loud I couldn't imagine how the other couldn't hear it. I felt like I was smothering, wanted to pant, but couldn't. Had to breathe through my open mouth, quiet, quiet.

Another rattle. Then a hiss, as if someone sucking his breath through his teeth in frustration.

Suddenly, before I could react, the one thing I hadn't figured on happened. I heard a click, and a brilliant beam swung round and fixed me. The son of a bitch had a flashlight! I blinked, caught full in the glare, so surprised and dismayed I couldn't move.

But the beam did, roving on, lighting the top of the big desk, a jumble of little donkey statuettes—that must be what I had, one of those—ashtrays, books, telephones. It flicked around the oval room as if searching for corners. As it left me I dropped, crouching swiftly behind the desk. I couldn't believe it, but apparently it had happened. I'd been standing, not in front of, but between the windows, and he'd missed me. God, if I hadn't dressed all in black . . .

The light went out as suddenly as it had come on. Dazzling as it was, I hadn't been able to see who stood behind it. All I had was an impression of shadow.

I was so relieved when the door closed that I groped behind me, found a chair, sat down. It took me a couple of minutes to realize I was sitting in FDR's armchair, which had been pushed back, apparently, the last time he'd left it. From where I sat I could see luminescent hands now, on a clock on the desk. It seemed like I'd been creeping around for a couple of hours, but it was only twelve-fifteen.

Suddenly I remembered I was supposed to relieve Grabb at midnight. I got up, put the statuette back, and opened the double door to the center hall.

Only it didn't open. The knob moved, I could hear a latch jump, but the door itself didn't budge. It was locked from outside.

Great, I thought. Now what? Out the window? I didn't like that idea. It was a sheer drop to the lawn. But I couldn't stay here.

Suddenly I needed light. Stripping off a glove, I fumbled around the desk till I found the lamp. Switched on, the bulb glowing to life behind a plush fringe, then quickly off, it showed me an unobtrusive door on the west side, to the right of the fireplace. I gave my eyes a couple of seconds to shake off the dazzle, then tried it. Sweat slid down my back under the hot wool.

Then I breathed out. I slipped through into a large square room. The Monroe Room, Cabinet Room, something like that—I wasn't sure, but I didn't care. I went quietly through and found the door to the center hall unlocked. Now when I peered out I was at the far end from the President's bedroom, and not only that, a divider wall with an arched doorway screened me from him. All I had to do was scoot across without being seen and I could go down the grand staircase. I dropped to my knees and peered around the corner.

The armchair was empty. A haze drifted above it, and the same cigarette, or maybe another one, was feeding it through a slowly dancing umbilical of smoke. But there was no sign of the Secret Service man.

It didn't make sense, but it was time for me to decamp. I ran softly across the landing and padded down the staircase. My stocking feet slipped on marble and I almost went down, but recovered at the expense of a reminding stab from my spine. I peeped into the entrance hall. Two of the White House cops were talking quietly just inside the portico. I ducked back and descended to the basement. In less than a minute I was back in the clinic, stripping off the sweater and watch cap, pulling on my tie and service dress blue blouse.

"Where the fuck have you been, Lieutenant? I sent the chief looking for you. He said you weren't in the clinic."

"I was looking for a head, sir. Guess I got lost."

"There's one right there in the medical spaces. I wouldn't go wandering around here after lights out, Kennedy. Might get yourself in trouble. And don't show up late to relieve me again. I'll let it go this time, but don't make it a habit."

"Aye aye, sir," I said, and steadied my voice and sat down. "This the latest poop? What's happening in Poland?"

CHAPTER 17

Outside, in the rain, Krasov stood close against the wall. He didn't move. Only stood, fist still clenched around the pistol in his pocket.

When he'd stepped out of the stairwell, the gun hard against his ribs, and seen the empty chair, the motionless layers of smoke, he'd thought it was as good as done. He didn't understand why there was no guard. He'd expected one, accepted that he'd probably have to kill him. But nothing, now, stood between him and the man he sought.

It had been relatively easy getting into the building, now that the men on the gate were used to his face and uniform. The big problem had been what to do with the truck. He'd solved that by showing up just before the guard was due to change, on foot, with a bag of cleaned suits over his shoulder, and explained that the truck had broken down and was being repaired; he was making only emergency deliveries, by taxi. He'd been waved through; the guard changed; and he'd concealed himself behind the antique mangle, in the little laundry room, until the activity in the corridor faded and finally the lights went off.

But after that, it hadn't gone as it was supposed to. As Fence had said it would. He'd found the right door, the door whose location he'd memorized. But then, to his horror, it had been locked.

He'd stood there, sweating, as the darkness around him reeled. He could try to pick or break it, but he knew modern locks, not this ancient thing. He could try to break down the door, but it was oak. He could tell by pressing gently against it how very heavy it was. No, that didn't sound like a good idea.

He'd drawn out the flashlight then, and swept it around the room, looking for a key, or another way in.

And seen the other.

A black figure, standing motionless between the desk and the windows. His hand had almost stopped. But his training had held. He'd swept the light on, as if noticing nothing, while he coldly evaluated the suddenly changed situation. The other would be armed, of course. Trained to kill. He hadn't expected this, a silent shadow inside the outer shell of security. The Americans were better than he'd thought.

He could attack, but that would destroy everything. Make noise, bring others, lose the advantage of surprise, without which he couldn't escape. He was no martyr, he wanted to escape. But why didn't the other attack *him?* It stood so still, holding something in its hand . . . a gun? . . . Perhaps he too was . . . arranged for? But Fence had told him the outer guard was all there was.

At the end of those racing seconds he was left with too many imponderables. He decided to withdraw while he still could. He'd make another plan. He was inside now, almost as close to *him* as Fence was. He'd seen no sign of Heudeber, seen no evidence anyone suspected his presence. He'd expected to find security impenetrable. Expected sketches of his face plastered all over the White House. But . . . it was as if the SS man had never existed. Yet Krasov had seen him with his own eyes, seen him turn away from his death and go up the steps into the building where they said the FBI had its headquarters.

The SS man had gone to the police, but nothing had happened. Obviously, the police hadn't believed him.

So he was still safe. He had time. He had Fence to help him. He would retreat, and regroup, and think everything out carefully in advance so that it was done right. That was the important thing. Doing it right. Killing *him* was not the point. Any fool with a gun could do that. He had nothing against *him, he* was not the real target at all. Though Fence still thought he was. Killing him the right way, leaving the right signs, then melting forever back into the teeming masses of America . . . *that* was the point. Only then would his mission be fulfilled.

Standing there, knowing that the other was watching, he'd clicked off the light. Waited, pointing the gun in his direction; and then, very slowly, withdrawn.

And now he stood in the rain, just outside the east-side entrance the servants and staff used, under the little overhang that didn't really shelter him. With a kind of detached amusement he felt his legs trembling. Hell, he thought. You ain't no Superman, are you? Shit, no. He was scared sometimes. If they caught him here, found out who he was, they'd hang him.

He let a little of the fear show itself. Yes, he said patiently to it. Thinking in Russian now. Come out. What is it you wish to say?

That I should perhaps step aside, abandon my plans?

Yes, and then what?

Then I could simply leave. Go to some far corner of America or Canada, become plain Johnny Okulov again. Drive a truck. Work in a factory. Or a restaurant. Get married, raise a family, let the years of nightmare pass away and bury themselves.

He let himself dream it, let himself see it; then smiled bitterly in the dark. And then, he thought. And then?

Then in ten years, or fifteen years, or twenty, the Communists would come.

He was getting wet, but he didn't care. It wasn't that cold. Not for him.

He lit a Fleetwood, cupping the flame in his hands, and turned his collar up. He looked out across the dripping shrubbery.

Out of nowhere, he remembered another rainy night.

A few years before the war, the Party had sent him to one of the outlying cities. The mass liquidation of all remaining enemies of the regime was under way. The NKVD arrested hundreds every night as the Terror built. The local branch assigned him a room in the older section of the city, in one of the brick apartment buildings that before the Revolution had belonged to lawyers, doctors, rich merchants. He went down the fire escape one day, taking his trash down, and the woman in the flat below was out tending the flowers she grew on her landing. They struck up a conversation on the cast-iron steps, and she invited him in for tea.

For a few weeks he thought he was in love.

Until one day when he was drunk he told her who he worked for, thinking to impress her. Instead her face went white. She told him that they were destroying Russia's future, they were no better than the Fascists. If he was one of them, she never wanted to see him again.

He hit her and told her she'd regret saying that.

That night, still drunk and angry at work, he was looking over the lists of those to be arrested the next morning. On impulse, he crossed out a name at random and wrote in hers. When he sobered up he was sorry, but it was too late to get the list back. He'd have been suspect himself if he had.

It was raining when he got back to his flat. The door to hers was open. The neighbors had already been in to take whatever they wanted. He'd gone in too, and found the note she'd been writing when the knock came on the door. She didn't use his name, but he knew it was to him.

After he read it he'd gone out on the landing and stood there for quite a long time, watching the leaves of her plants nod in the rain.

She was charged under Article 58/10, Anti-Soviet Agitation, and sentenced to fifteen years. He never saw her again.

It had taken him years to understand. He was guilty, yes. But beyond his personal guilt was the system of repression, terror, and illegality that was the Soviet state. He couldn't escape by changing his name. No matter how far he ran, one day it would knock on *his* door.

So he didn't have a choice. He could dream of the West, California, a family, but a red specter stood between him and the future. The regime of nightmare had to be destroyed. If war with the West would destroy it, then war had to come. And if he could start that war, then he had no right even to think of a life of his own.

Tonight he'd failed. Well, not all plans succeeded. Not the first time at any rate. Perhaps it was time to try the other, the one Fence had proposed—

"Hey . . . you!"

He stiffened as a soldier materialized from the night. A rifle. A shielded light, flicking across his chest. "Who the hell are you, Mac? What are you doin' here?"

The soldiers and the staff, he knew, hardly talked to each other. So he felt the confidence he put into his voice as he said, "Who am I? I work here, bub. In the laundry."

"Yeah? See your pass."

He didn't have a pass.

He stared at the rifle. Thinking: if he searches me it is all over. He will find the flashlight. The gun. Then it will be torture, then the rope, and it will all be in vain, everything I hoped for and tried to do.

The only thing he could do was kill him. Fast. Quietly. And run. It would wreck everything. But there was no other choice.

He picked out the point where he would strike. The throat. Instant paralysis, then soundless death. This close, he just might succeed.

But the soldier didn't search him. Just grunted, "What's the matter? You forget it or something?"

"Yeah. Shit, I forgot it. Left it home."

"What the hell you doing here so late? Standin' here in the fuckin' rain, for Chrissake?"

"We work late, bub. Not so easy, keeping this joint running. I'm standing here waiting for it to slack off. You got a problem with that?"

"Yeah, I got a problem you standin' here, I got to guard this area. I remember you now, I seen you going in and out in the truck. Beat it, Mac. Make sure you bring that pass next time, or I'll have to turn you in."

"All right, bub. Thanks."

Krasov flicked the cigarette butt into the dripping bushes. With steady, firm paces of his heavy brogans, he loped down the wet-glistening flagstones, back into the night.

CHAPTER 18

Wednesday, March 28: The Situation Room

Y ou look like shit, Kennedy. What's wrong with your tie? Those ribbons aren't in the proper order. You'd better get squared away."

"Yes sir," I said.

"I'll lead off with the situation in Germany, then you can brief the situation in the Pacific. You'll know how to pronounce the names, at any rate. Understand? Now, we usually have the junior man handle his chair. But Hollins will get it this time."

"I can do that, sir." My stomach was starting to hurt.

"No you can't. It's not as easy as it looks. We had one ensign dump him out on the floor. We'll borrow a chair and let you practice this afternoon."

"Yes sir," I said again. Brown half smiled, and I half smiled too. I don't know what his meant, but mine broke to read that I was going to pay this son of a bitch off some day.

I'd meant to see Mike Reilly first thing today. He needed to know about the prowler, and the Secret Service man—I still didn't know his name, the mustache—whom I'd seen arrested during the fag raid. And who'd been so glaringly absent when whoever it was had tried to get into the President's bedroom. But after the midwatch I'd gone back to the clinic and looked at my bunk, and the next thing I knew Tavelstead was telling me I'd better shake a leg. I shrugged inwardly and tried to concentrate on the daily reports from Nimitz's and MacArthur's HQs at Honolulu and Manila.

It was a little after 10:30 A.M. when the three buzzes that meant the President was on the move sounded out in the corridor. Brown and Abrams took their stations by the door. Tavelstead brushed lint from his blues. The sergeants went to parade rest beside their respective maps. I heard a clang and the grating rattle as the gate on the elevator was drawn back.

Then he was in the doorway. No Secret Service, just like Abrams had said. FDR's head swayed as the wheels bumped over the threshold. The chief stepped forward with a steaming cup of coffee, complete with gold-rimmed saucer.

FDR's head came up. To my surprise his color was better than when he'd given me the medal. His eyes were sharp as they swung around the room. "Brownie, Abe, Chief—how are you this fine morning?"

"Great, sir. Hunky-dory." Tavelstead edged the set-down cup away from FDR's elbow as Abrams steered the chair to face the maps. Roosevelt glanced back, making sure the door was closed, then reached inside his jacket. His collar gaped as he pulled out a pack of Camels. "You're looking good this morning too, sir."

FDR looked at him for a second. "Chief, that reminds me of the story about the drunk who was at a bah, and the bartender refused to give him another drink. 'Why, I'm as sober as a judge,' the drunk said. 'Do you see that cat coming in the door? He has got two eyes, and two is all I see. If I was drunk, I would see four, wouldn't I?' 'Hell, man,' the bartender replied, 'you're drunker than I thought. That cat isn't coming in the door, it is going out!'"

He relaxed back into the chair as we laughed, and lit up. His hands shook so that the flame wavered, but he sucked the smoke in with audible relish. "Proceed, gentlemen," he said, waving out the match.

Admiral Brown stood ramrod-straight in front of the small-scale chart of Western Germany, pointing out the six Allied armies engaged on the western front. The British Second Army had broken through on the Westphalian plain and was near Muenster. The U.S. Ninth helped in the capture of Dorsten and took Hamborn, site of the Thyssen steel works. The First and Patton's Third were tearing toward Leipzig and the Fulda Gap in the greatest concentration of armor in history. In the south, the Seventh Army was thirty-three miles east of the Rhine.

There were reports of rebellion against the Nazis in Frankfurt, but a more ominous note came from occupied Aachen, where the Allied-appointed mayor had just been assassinated. Brown related this to the "Werewolf" resistance movement we'd heard about on German radio. The Air Corps reported four-hundred-bomber raids on Berlin and another five-hundred-plane raid on Hanover.

On the eastern front, news was scarce again, Brown said dryly. The Russians were not keeping us well informed. Most of what we knew came from Wehrmacht communiqués. Gdynia had been captured and there was fighting in Danzig. The Red Army had crossed the Raba south of Budapest and was within ten miles of the Austrian border.

The overall situation was encouraging, but both Patton and Eisenhower were worried by reports that the Nazi high command were planning to continue the war from redoubts in southern Germany.

When he was done we looked expectantly at FDR. The President sat still, then spoke quietly. For a second what he was saying didn't make sense. Then I realized he wasn't talking about today's events, but from a vantage point far above them.

"The trouble's Europe. Every twenty years they have a war, and they drag the rest of the world in. This time we've got to make sure we get to the root of the problem. The Italians, Hungarians, and so forth, they're not our enemies in the same sense the Germans are. We can deal with them the way Lincoln wanted to treat the South. But the German only understands one kind of language.

"We've got to be tough with them. No marching. No uniforms. And we've got to do something about the German people, not just the Nazis. Either castrate them, or—or treat them in such a manner that they can't just go on reproducing. There are too many of them, that's all."

He nodded, his head giving the impression it was coming loose from the rest of his body, which had shrunk under it in the chair. "The second problem is the colonial empires. They take and take, and the native peoples stay in destitution. I've worried about Indochina for two years, what to do after the Japanese leave. If the French try to take it back, there'll be war. I brought up the idea of a UN trusteeship at Cairo, pending self-determination. Chiang liked it. So did Stalin. Winston didn't, of course.

"After the war the Four Policemen have got to keep the peace. Russia, Britain, the United States and China. If the UN can prevent a major war for two generations, it'll be a success."

I couldn't listen to any more of this. I said, "What about the Russians?"

Heads whipped around, and the admiral went white. But the President didn't seem surprised. He just said, "Stalin and I can deal."

"Like the deal you made in Poland, sir?"

"Lieutenant—"

"Take it easy, Brownie. Yes, we made a deal in Poland, and it wasn't a bad one. Winston and I didn't give Stalin anything he didn't have already. It's tough to argue with—how many divisions, Pete?"

"Over two hundred equivalent, Mr. President. Though theirs are smaller than ours."

Roosevelt turned his head to me, though his body stayed immobile and his hands lay limply in his lap. "You see, Johnny, the news today's almost all good. Isn't it, Brownie?"

"Sounds like it, sir. I'd feel better if the Ninth Army were moving faster out of their bridgehead, but it's good news."

"And in a way we owe it to the Russians. As long as we held the Atlantic, and as long as they held out, I always felt we were going to win it, once we got mobilized. I'd have given Australia or New Zealand or anything else, rather than have the Russians collapse.

"But I've got to ask myself, what can go wrong now? The only way the Axis can stave off utter defeat is if the Alliance splits up. The weak point's always been between us and the Soviets. That bastard Hitler knows it. That's why I'm suspicious of these 'feelers' Dulles keeps talking about from Switzerland. We have—we have just got to speak with one voice." He looked around at us. "I think we all realize that, here."

"You don't think the Russians would make a separate peace now, do you, sir?"

"I don't pretend to guess what they're capable of doing, Pete. I think I understand Uncle Joe, but I'm not sure to what extent he's in control of his military men."

I was looking at him then when I suddenly understood what Leahy had been driving at. If anything happened to FDR, it was true: the alliance could come apart. He was the human glue that had held Churchill and Stalin together.

While I was thinking this he was continuing, waving his cigarette as if he were drawing on the air. "Once we get Hitler knocked down, we'll redeploy against the Japanese. Now, the way they've fought on Peleliu and, what's the other place, the one the Marines just took—"

"Iwo Jima," said Hollins. "Sir."

"—tells me that's not going to be easy. We'll probably have to invade."

"There's another possibility, sir," said Brown.

"There is," said FDR. "If it works, it will save many American lives. But it may not. If we have to invade, I want the Russians with us."

I didn't understand this "other possibility," but I knew what he meant about invasions. At Guadalcanal we'd gone in with inadequate force and almost got our asses kicked back into the sea. "Their blood instead of ours, right, sir?"

"No, Johnny." He didn't look amused. "A Russian mother feels the same about her boy as yours does. What I'm hoping is, once the Jap emperor realizes he's got the whole world lined up against him, he'll overrule his generals and sue for peace. Thus saving a lot of boys—on both sides."

He took another drag and looked at me, waiting, but I didn't have anything else to say. I could feel Brown staring at me too. FDR exhaled and looked back at the maps. "Okay, what next?"

"Lieutenant Kennedy will brief on the situation in the Pacific, Mr. President."

I didn't know how they'd done it before, but I decided to start with a theater overview before I got into details. The biggest news was from Fifth Fleet. Nimitz reported damaging or sinking fifteen ships and shooting down thirty-eight Jap planes. MacArthur's advance continued, taking Cebu, the second largest city in the Philippines, and eleven other towns. The news from China wasn't as good. Jap armored columns had closed to within twenty-five miles of our B-29 base at Laohokow. Mopping up still going on on Iwo Jima.

"The Pacific Fleet is under way for the Okinawa invasion, one thousand four hundred fifty-seven ships en route from Ulithi to Okinawa. General Buckner will land four divisions on L-Day, April 1, leaving him three divisions for the follow-up and one in reserve. The first objective will be the Yontan and Kadena airfields.

"General MacArthur reports that the Philippines campaign is continuing, with the Sixth Army carrying out a three-directional offensive. I Corps toward the Cagayan Valley and Baguio; XI Corps to clear out the Sierra Madres northeast of Manila; XIV Corps moving southeast toward Batangas, Laguna, and Tayabas provinces. Yamashita is resisting hard but he's cut off from supply and weakening. Fighting is fierce in the jungles."

FDR was sunk in thought, chin propped on his fist. I stopped, wondering if he was listening. As I did he glanced up. "Please go on, Johnny. I was just wondering if I did the right thing, going along with Mac on that one. Nimitz wanted to bypass the Philippines, but MacArthur made it plain he'd feed me to the papers for lunch. He assured me he could do it without heavy losses. Do you have the figures?"

"The latest we have is twenty-five thousand, Mr. President."

"Dead?"

"No sir, that's overall casualties. Two-thirds are wounded and should recover."

The President stared grimly at the map, as though he could see through it to the Pacific. I didn't have much more, a couple more items about the Japs in China. They had a lot of divisions still there. I stepped back. "Any questions, sir?"

Roosevelt jerked his head up. He looked around. Tavelstead held out an ashtray. "Anything from Winston?"

"Not since yesterday, sir."

"The Chief of Staff's drafting a reply to that."

"We'll be ready, sir." Brown waited, then when the President said nothing more, nodded to Hollins. The captain pulled the wheelchair smoothly backward, spun it, and pushed it out the door as Rose swung it open. A slap and stamp came from the corridor as the marine came to attention, and FDR was gone, his head sagging to the left as Hollins turned him toward the elevator.

"All right, Kennedy," said Brown, the instant he was out of earshot.

"The vault again, sir?" I said, but when I did he spun around, and for a second I thought he was going to knock me down. Not that it'd have been hard, he outweighed me by a hundred pounds.

"You smartassed sonofabitch, you're relieved. Get your gear together. Five minutes, and I want you out the front door. Sergeant Santorini, help him pack."

"Just a second, sir. I don't think you understand."

"No, Kennedy. *You* don't understand. The Commander in Chief of the Armed Forces of the United States is not subjected to cross-examination by a briefing officer. And I'll tell you another thing." He glanced at the door. "I've seen that man on days when he had the whole thing in his head. The enemy. The alliance. History. Economics. The whole ball of wax. I've seen King and Marshall look at him like they were looking at—" He stopped suddenly. "What am I telling you this for? You're out." He turned on his heel. "Sergeant!"

"I don't think you can make that stick, Admiral," I said to his back. Hollins and Abrams winced; the enlisted men suddenly found interesting things to study on their respective maps. Brown's body went rigid, as if he'd grabbed a starter coil.

Just then the door buzzed. Tavelstead took two steps and cracked it. The guard's face showed in the gap, and beyond it, a woman's. I'd seen her before. The marine was saying, "No, ma'am, not under any circumstances. Yes, he's here. Yes, I'll give it to him."

"Who do they want, Senior Chief?"

"There's a note, sir."

"Hell," muttered Brown. He stormed by me, jerked it from the guard, and stared down at it. "Can you read this, Sergeant?"

"I can't read a word. Except—is that 'Kennedy'?"

Abrams leaned to look. "That's Mrs. R's handwriting, sir."

"Lieutenant! Go see what she wants."

"Do you know where she is, sir?"

Brown didn't bother to answer, just turned away.

———

I stopped in at the Usher's office and asked where I could find Mrs. Roosevelt. Crim suggested I try her office in the East Wing. She dictated "My Day" there in the morning. I started off, then turned back. "I don't have anyplace to stay yet, don't have—anyway, I like to change my shirts, and I like to stay clean. I need to send out some laundry—"

"Do you know Mrs. Parks?"

"The one on crutches?"

"That's right. She's in charge of the linen room."

When I found Mrs. Roosevelt's office the door was open. The woman I'd seen at lunch, Malvina Thompson, glanced up from a typewriter as I came in. I held out the note; she flicked her eyes to it. "Go on in, Mr. Kennedy."

Mrs. R was in her Red Cross uniform, open-collared, baggy, with a skirt and heavy scuffed brown shoes. A WAC-style cap lay on her desk, and she was writing, looking at a large leather-bound notebook propped in front of her. I stood waiting as she signed it, addressed an envelope, and put it in a wire basket with about twenty others. Then she looked up, at the same time reaching for another sheet of White House notepaper. "Yes?" she said, with an abstracted expression.

"Lieutenant Kennedy, ma'am. You sent for me."

"Oh, Mr. Kennedy. I'm sorry, did I interrupt you? Thank you for coming."

She looked tense, and her hair was coming unpinned. No doubt about it, Eleanor was homely, with buck teeth and not much of a chin. Her fluting nasal voice sounded artificial, and at the same time shy. I noticed she kept writing even as she said, "We had so little time to talk at the luncheon Monday. How are you settling in?"

"Aside from butting heads with the skipper, I'm coping, ma'am."

"The 'skipper'?"

"Admiral Brown."

"I'm sure you can work things out."

"Well, we have a regulation, ma'am. Naval Regulations, article number 252."

"And what is that?"

"Captains are seldom wrong, and admirals never."

She chuckled, not looking up. "How amusing. But you have everything you need, do you not?"

"Things are working out, ma'am."

I still didn't know what this was all about. I didn't think she just wanted to check on my well-being. So I decided to find out. "Was that all you needed from me, ma'am? I'm on duty right now—"

"Close the door for a moment. Sit down."

Okay, I thought. I followed orders and waited.

"Mr. Kennedy, do you mind telling me exactly what you are doing here with us?"

That was blunt enough. "I was ordered here, ma'am," I told her.

"Navy orders?"

"That's right."

"How odd. That it was you, I mean."

I waited her out. I knew that trick, where they don't say anything, and wait for you to spill it because you're getting nervous. But I wasn't going to spill anything. If I wasn't sure about Reilly, I *really* wasn't sure about Mrs. Roosevelt. Or more accurately, the people around her. Like that glowering hag of a secretary. I could see her putting a letter opener in FDR's back without a second's hesitation.

Finally she had enough, I guess. "Mr. Kennedy. You probably have a rather negative impression of me."

"Of you, ma'am?"

"You know what I mean. That I'm surrounded by radicals and Socialists. That I'm a Communist—"

"No ma'am," I lied.

"But they say that about anyone who has any interest in the better treatment of his fellow human beings. And there are more sordid stories. That I have Negro . . . friends. I hear them, you know. If I don't, then all I have to do is read my mail."

I thought about this. I'd heard Eleanor jokes, sure. Heard the rumors. "There are always people like that," I said. "There's a lot of dirt going around about my dad, too."

"Touché," she said. "And does he get the poison pen letters? The ones that start, 'I hope all your boys get killed'?"

"I don't think he reads those. I hope you don't either."

She gave me a real look now, as if she'd just realized there was somebody in the room with her. "John—may I call you John?"

"That's my name," I said, and bit my tongue. Sometimes I sounded like a smartass even when I didn't mean to.

"John, your father and I have not been the best of friends. But whatever you may think, I have never disliked him personally; and I think the world of your mother. Joe is a very intelligent man, and he can be charming. It was simply unfortunate that as time went on, his ideas . . . diverged from those of the President."

"I don't think Dad was treated very well," I said. "Considering everything he did for FDR early on."

"You may have a point. Franklin does have rather a tendency to . . . drop people once their usefulness to him ends. But you have to understand, there's still rather a lot of bad feeling about him. This is not related to his being a Catholic, or Irish. Not at all. Even being wrong about Britain could have been forgiven. But he has made rather a lot of enemies among Franklin's people. He has made threats, even to the President. Those remarks of his about Jews and Communists . . . people take these things personally. They just don't feel he belongs here with us, that it's best he stay in private life. Then he can express himself with less embarrassment all around."

I couldn't answer that. Dad could be abrasive. It seemed like everybody he worked with either turned into an employee or an enemy. But before I had a comeback Eleanor had moved on. "At any rate, I'm glad you have been *ordered* here. And I wanted to bring something to your attention. Perhaps make a suggestion."

"Yes ma'am."

"My husband doesn't have a large circle of friends. Acquaintances, yes, but intimates—only a few. I don't mean your Admiral Brown—the 'skipper', is it? That is amusing—or General Marshall, or Mr. McCormack. They bring the necessity for harsh decisions. What he needs is people he can relax with. He is very tired. He loves to talk, and it's very important to him to just be able to sit occasionally and have his martini and have someone to tell stories to."

"That seems little enough to ask."

"One would think so. He likes to have people around him, interesting, clever people. I suppose the children could do more, but they have their own lives; and of course the boys are in the service. It seems he eventually loses everyone close to him. Louis Howe. Missy LeHand. Cordell Hull is gone. General Watson, who just died; he loved Pa. Jim Byrnes is retiring, and now we're losing Harry Hopkins."

"Mr. Hopkins is retiring?"

"I hope he recovers, but I am afraid that he is dying. And that grieves me, not only for Harry, but . . . you see, in the past, when that happened, Franklin would find someone else. But over the years that has become harder and harder for him, I think. So that now he really doesn't try any more.

"You see, Mr. Kennedy, I can't be what Franklin needs. I know people think I influence him. Sometimes it seems that there is a concerted effort to make it appear that I dictate to him. When actually I do not see him often enough to do anything of the sort, and all I ever have done is pass along requests or suggestions that people have made to me." She stopped writing for a moment, then bent doggedly again to her notes. "I have tried, and I gave up long ago. I'm too much of a hair shirt."

"I'm sure he needs you," I said.

"I'm a spur, Mr. Kennedy, and eventually one tires of being spurred. He needs someone—well, it's almost like worship. An undemanding acceptance. There are so many other things that he cannot do, it does seem hard that he cannot have ——. Can you understand what I'm trying to say?"

"I guess maybe," I said.

"I understand he thinks highly of you."

I was startled. "I don't know that he—"

"Or so I am told. What I am wondering is, whether you have it in you to serve another person in that way. It takes a certain amount of self-abnegation. It's not really like being a friend. Franklin has no friends. Not one. I don't think he's capable of forming a personal attachment to anyone."

"You make him sound very cold," I said.

"No, that's only the way he is. It's unfortunate, you know, because he is so lonely. And he realizes it, I think. Do you remember when he said, in his speech, 'the only way to make a friend is to be one'? I felt rather queer when I heard him say that. No, what he needs is more like a—more like a disciple. Or a traditional sort of wife, supportive and uncritical."

I didn't say anything, just sat there, and she kept going, speaking rapidly and turning over sheet after sheet of notepaper. I'd figured out by now that she was writing notes to the parents of guys she'd met on her inspection tours. "At any rate, you seem to have a sense of humor, you're bright and attractive, you're a war hero. I may be wrong, but I don't gain the impression that you're at all out for anything for yourself. Do you think you might be interested in doing something for Franklin? Perhaps acting as an aide?"

"Well, I don't know, ma'am," I said. "I really just am here because the Navy sent me. I'd rather be out in the Pacific, finishing the job out there."

"Have you applied to go back?"

"There are medical problems."

"You do look rather thin. Have you seen a doctor?"

"Several."

"How about Dr. Bruenn? Or Admiral McIntire? As long as you are here."

"Maybe I'll do that," I said, but it was just to be polite. If the Mayo Clinic couldn't figure out what I had, I didn't think they could.

A tap on the door; Mrs. Roosevelt raised her eyes. "Yes, Tommy?"

"This is the letter to the Farm Security Administration you wanted as soon as I was done with it. About the sharecroppers. And you have two people waiting, Mr. Ross and Mrs. Bethune. Rabbi Steinberg called and would like to come in this afternoon."

"Do we have time for the Rabbi?"

"You have five minutes free after Mr. Szilard."

"All right. Thank you. Here are this morning's notes."

Thompson reached over me and picked up the wire basket. I noticed that while we were talking Eleanor had filled it. Then she was writing again, fast, as if there were too many things to do and people to help for her to spend much more time on me, or, I supposed, on her husband—if that was what this was really all about. I stood up. "Well, thank you for asking me up."

"Think about it, John. If you like, I will bring your name up."

"It's an interesting idea," I said. She nodded at that and looked past me to the door.

I sort of backed out into the outer office, where a large colored woman in a red hat sailed past without noticing me. I looked at Thompson. "Uh, is that all?"

"That's all, Mr. Kennedy."

I looked at my watch, wondering about lunch. I was hungry, but my gut was giving me hell again. I hoped it wasn't another attack. Finally I went down to the ground floor. The doors were open and a lot of noise was coming out of the kitchen. The marine sentry watched me hesitate. I didn't feel like resuming my conversation with Brown. Hell, maybe Eleanor was right. On impulse I told him, "I'm feeling kind of punk, Sergeant. Tell them I'm going to stop in to sick bay."

—

The corpsman, whose name was Chagall, was awake this time when I knocked and let myself in. "Hi," I said. "I'm Kennedy, Map Room staff. Any chance of seeing Dr. McIntire?"

"What's the problem, Lieutenant?"

"I don't know."

"I mean, is it sinus? Or something else?"

"Sinus? No. Stomach or bowels, I think."

"Dr. McIntire's nose and throat. Anyway, he's not here. Want to see Dr. Bruenn?"

That was him. The doctor with the German name. One of the guys I wanted to check out. "Okay," I said. "Whatever. Can you set me up to see him?"

"You can do it now, you got a minute, sir."

Bruenn was in the side office, reading a medical magazine. He was younger than I expected, not much older than me, though he wore two and a half stripes, lieutenant commander. He was in khakis, which meant he didn't take orders from Brown. He looked at me with an eager half-smile while the corpsman explained what was going on, then stuck out his hand. "Howard Bruenn," he said, pronouncing it like Bruin.

"Jack Kennedy." I made him as a fellow reservist; the regular Navy docs, and I'd seen a lot in the last four years, never told you their first names, any more than God did. He nodded to a chair. I sat down and he looked at my face for a while.

"So you're the new lieutenant. What seems to be the problem?"

"Are we confidential?" I asked him.

"I'm sorry?"

"Doctor-patient. Are we confidential?"

"If you like," he said, frowning. He closed his magazine and put it aside, pulled a yellow pad toward him. "Do you have your medical records with you?"

"No. They're trying to catch up, I think."

"All right. What's the problem?"

"Stomachache. No appetite. Dizzy." I went through the rest of it, while he just kept looking at me.

"How long have you had these symptoms?"

"A long time."

"Months?"

"Since I was fifteen or sixteen. On and off. Seems to be getting worse, though."

"Are you in pain now?"

"A little."

"Are you usually in pain?"

I shrugged, then told him the truth; there was no way he could help me unless I did. "Most of the time. Yeah."

He made a note. "Tell me about your childhood diseases."

"The usual stuff. Scarlet fever, mumps, measles, whooping cough."

"Chicken pox?"

"I think so."

"German measles?"

"Yeah."

"Were you healthy as a child?"

"My mother says I was sickly. My brother Bobby used to say he felt sorry for the mosquito that bit me—it would probably die."

"Did you receive medical care?"

"I've seen every kind of doctor they make." I ticked off the various diagnoses on my fingers. "Flu, noninfectious parotitis, leukemia, blood condition, hepatitis, poor immunity, agranulocytosis, if I'm pronouncing that right—"

"That's the correct pronunciation, go on," said Bruenn.

"And a lot of other stuff. Oh, and I had a dose of the clap at school."

"Was your gonorrhea treated?"

"They gave me sulfa. But it still hurts when I piss."

"Hm." Another note. "Do you still have your tonsils?"

"They took those out. Appendix too."

"Have you been seen by Navy doctors?"

"A bunch of them. They called it as a hernia at first."

"Who did? When?"

"Heintzelmann at Chelsea Naval. But after they did the tests, last November, they ruled out hernia, and ulcers too. Finally they went for chronic colitis, which lets them off the hook, since there's nothing they can do about that. Then I went to the board over at the Annex. Admiral Dorsey was the chairman, you might know him."

"I know Dr. Dorsey," said Bruenn. He seemed fascinated by my nose. "What was the board's conclusion?"

"They went with chronic colitis and recommended a medical discharge."

"Why are you still in, then?"

I decided to keep it simple. "Needs of the service. Voluntary extension."

"Well, there you have it," said Bruenn. "You decide, Lieutenant. Either you're okay, in which case you're perfectly fine in uniform. Or you're ill, in which case you should be retired."

"I didn't come in asking for a disability determination, Doc. I'd just like to have somebody tell me what's wrong with me. The pain doesn't bother me. But every once in a while everything just seems to give out. A couple of times they thought I was dying. Then I do a Lazarus act and pick up my bed and walk."

"Uh huh," said Bruenn. He got up and stretched. "Well, it sounds like you've had competent attention. I don't know that I can do anything more for you, but. . . . Take your shirt off. Let's have a look."

He did all the usual doctor stuff, blood pressure and listening to my chest.

Looked at my eyes with a little light. Then he went into the other room while I got dressed again. He was out there a while. When he came back he was carrying a couple of books.

"Tell me about your skin, this color change. I thought it was a tan at first, but it's not, is it?"

"No. Actually I'm darker than this sometimes."

"When did you first notice it? After overseas duty?"

"No, before I got to college. '35?"

Bruenn showed his teeth, like a second-former confronted by a calculus problem. "Are you sure? Because that rules out the weird tropical stuff."

"Yeah. The Army tried to draft me in 1940, before I got in the Navy. They offered me a commission in a Negro regiment." I grinned.

"Did the doctors there check it out?"

"Where?"

"College. Where did you go to school?"

"Oh, yeah, I went to Princeton first, then Harvard. That was the leukemia diagnosis. Only I guess that was wrong."

"No, you don't have leukemia. But how on earth did you pass a Navy physical?"

"Well, it's not all the time I feel this way. I'll go along for months feeling okay, and then suddenly I get a fever and start shaking and turn brown. Then I wake up flat on my back in the hospital. I guess the Medical Corps caught me at the top of the bounce."

"And you didn't mention these problems."

"Hell! I didn't want to miss the war." But he didn't smile, just looked at me.

"How about during your active duty? Your time in PTs?"

"How did you know I was in Peter Tares?"

"Come on. When you get written up in *Life* magazine you have to figure someone's going to read it."

"It was *The New Yorker*," I said. "Not *Life*. Anyway, I didn't feel too bad out there. Lost weight, but we all did—it was hot as hell and the food wasn't too great."

"Atabrine?"

"Every day."

"Any adverse reactions?"

"I had an upset stomach a lot. I don't know if it was the atabrine or what."

"And this back problem. It dated from there?"

I didn't see why he had to know that, so I just said, "From the collision, yeah. A Jap destroyer cut us in two. You know."

"What was it like?"

"What was it like?" I said. "What was it *like?* Well—you know those scenes in the old silent movies, where the train comes toward you, then rolls right over you? It felt like that. Then there was a hell of a big explosion and we were all in the water."

"I see you've been operated on."

"Yeah, last year. Twice."

"Twice? I see scars at the fourth and fifth vertebrae—"

"Once on the back at New England Baptist. Once on the asshole at Chelsea Naval."

"How's your back now?"

"It hurts."

"Does it give out?"

"At the most embarrassing times," I said, thinking of the brunette and the gin and the fire.

"Are you on narcotics, Lieutenant?"

"Not now. They were giving me codeine after the back job, but they tapered that off pretty quick."

"What else were they giving you?"

"I guess everything they had."

"What about the rectal operation you mentioned? Did that relieve your pain at all?"

"No, just gave me another one."

"Tell me about the last time you had an attack."

"I guess the last bad one was a couple years ago. First the stomachache. Then fever, nausea, hives. Then I crashed. Couldn't eat. Couldn't move. Went down to a hundred and twenty-five. I bounced back after a couple weeks in bed." I rubbed my face. "You wouldn't believe what the ugly nurses will do to you when you can't fight back."

"This stomach problem. Let me ask you something, off the record. Have you got any, you might say, psychological conflicts in your life? Something you're not happy with, or something somebody's trying to make you do that you can't quite . . . swallow?"

"You think I'm a nut case? That's a new one."

"There's often a psychological component to stomach and back problems," said Bruenn. "And combat strain has been known to exacerbate things like that. The pigmentation, though—that's a real anomaly."

"Yeah," I said. "Same with everybody. The scurvy and bedsores they can take care of, but that kind of has them all stumped."

Bruenn kept ignoring my cracks. "There's a lot we don't know about the immune system. But basically, it's what keeps us well. It sounds to me like there's something off-key with yours. A Fifth Column type of thing. Then when you get a disease, whether it be flu or malaria or whatever, your body takes a long time to fight it off. But whatever it is, you don't belong on active duty. You need rest and sunlight."

"There are lots of people holding down important jobs who should be resting, Doc," I told him. It was time to slip the needle in. "Like your principal patient."

"I'm sorry?" He went stiff and tilted his head back.

"The President. He's in a lot worse shape than I am."

"I'm happy to help you if I can, on your problem," said Bruenn, "But we will not discuss the President's health. At all. As far as you're concerned, he's a little fatigued, touch of bronchitis, but in satisfactory health and full fitness to perform his duties. Is that clear, Lieutenant?"

"Like crystal, Commander," I told him.

"Let me look at one other thing," said Bruenn, getting up again, as if something had just occurred to him.

When he came back this time he had another book, an even bigger one. "You mentioned weight loss," he said. "And abdominal pain, and occasional dizziness. Nausea?"

"Yeah."

"And you have the pigmentation. Fatigue?"

"Almost always. What have you got there?" I asked him, trying to get a look at the cover.

"I'd like to call a couple of people, get some opinions," Bruenn said. "I'm not a specialist in this area, you see. Meanwhile I'm going to give you a little elixir of pepsin. That should help your digestion."

He wouldn't let me see the cover, but I knew that routine. Doctors are the biggest shits there are. I buttoned my blouse and got up. Then I remembered I was going to find out about Bruenn. "What kind of specialist are you, exactly, Doc?" I asked him.

He didn't want to answer that one. "Don't you guys all specialize?" I asked him again. "An internist? Urologist? Surgeon?"

"My specialty is cardiology."

I nodded. A heart specialist. That was interesting. "Where are you from, Doc?"

"Bethesda. I was a resident there till last year."

That wasn't what I'd meant, but it told me something, too. "Are you a regular, Doc? Or one of us?"

"I'm a reservist, if that's what you mean. I was in private practice when the war started."

"Republican, huh?"

"I'm not sure that's any of your concern," said Bruenn. "Though as it happens, I voted for the President in November. And if as I suspect your next question is going to be, is my name German? The answer is, yes it is, third generation. I've been through this with Dr. McIntire and again with Mr. Reilly. Any other questions?"

"I guess not. Thanks for looking at me, Doc."

——

Brown wasn't in the Map Room when I went back. The Teletypes were chattering as the evening traffic came in from Europe, five hours ahead of Eastern War Time. Santorini and Rose were dashing around, bells were ringing. Ed and Pete were hammering away at the decoding machines. Abrams put me to work punching out decodes too. I parked my butt and turned to, not reading what I was typing. I was thinking over everything I'd seen that day, from FDR, to Eleanor, to Bruenn. I had the definite feeling that not one of the people I'd talked to had told me the whole truth.

Sometime later the door clanged. I didn't look around till I heard Admiral Brown, behind me, say "Kennedy." I finished typing the line, made a pencil mark where I'd stopped, and swiveled my chair. Brown was standing there with a strange guy in Marine Corps green. "Yes, sir?" I said.

"This is your relief. Brief him and turn over any classified material you have."

Brown wasn't very good at concealing his triumph. I said, through a sinking feeling, "Where do I go, sir?"

That wiped the half-smile off his face. He turned for the vault, tossing over his shoulder, "You're moved to personal staff. I don't know what you'll be doing there. See Hassett."

Bill Hassett was the President's secretary. I'd met him with Dad, a taciturn Vermonter who reminded me of Cal Coolidge. Jesus, I thought, that was fast. I wondered where the order had come from—Leahy? Eleanor? Or somewhere else? "Do you know what I'll be doing, sir?" I asked him, rubbing it in.

"Whatever Hassett tells you to do. But my advice to you, Kennedy, is to keep your fucking mouth shut around the President."

I was standing out in the corridor, holding my B-4 and wondering whether to crap or go blind, when the three soft buzzes sounded through the building. There was a clatter of heels above me and several Secret Service appeared in the stairwell. One was Reilly. "Mike," I said.

"What?"

"I gotta talk to you. About one of your guys."

"One of my guys? Who?"

"I don't know his name. He's got a mustache. Last night—"

"Can this wait till after the press conference? We're running late."

"Well, it's important, but—I guess so."

"Understand you got promoted."

"I don't know if promoted's the right word, but—"

"Good. When he comes down, take his chair."

"Now?"

"Yeah. Now. You're his aide now, right? Any problem with that?" Reilly jerked his chin at one of his men, who came over and ran his hands over me. He stepped back and nodded as above us an electric motor hummed and the cables began to turn.

Bruenn came out of the clinic and leaned against the wall.

The car appeared, slowly descending. Then the gates clashed open, and a large black man—Prettyman—eased the President's chair out onto the landing. Roosevelt sat silently in it, face gray as his suit. An unlit Camel in a maroon plastic holder sagged almost to his lapel. He was wearing a red bow tie and the rimless pince-nez that made him look like Woodrow Wilson. As Bruenn hovered over him with nosedrops the Negro ran his eyes around among us, and I stepped forward.

This was a different wheelchair from the one at the awards ceremony. This was light steel. It was tricky to maneuver, but not as tough as Brown made out. You just had to think ahead, like conning a boat in a narrow channel. The Press Room was in the West Wing. We rolled out the ground-floor corridor past the pool and the Rose Garden, which we could see out the windows of the colonnade. The wheels bumped over laid-out fire hoses, which were leaking water. No one said anything. The President sagged slightly sideways as we turned the corner into the executive offices.

An officious-looking guy with a big nose and a lot of black hair joined us as we got to the West Wing. He raised his eyebrows at me. "Mr. Kennedy, Mr. Daniels," said Reilly. "The press secretary. The lieutenant is joining us as an aide, sir."

"All right, bring on the wolves," cracked FDR.

"Somebody light his cigarette," said Daniels.

Reilly bent with a lighter as Jonathan Daniels went ahead of us, through a couple of corridors, down a ramp, then held a door for us. I got it dead center and we were in the Press Room.

"The President of the United States," said Daniels, but the reporters were already on their feet, surging and jostling. The air was solid with blue smoke and whiskey fumes. "All in," one of them said.

Then a weird thing happened. I'd seen FDR drawn, yawning, barely listening to what we said. He'd sagged like a sack of laundry when I took the corner. But now, facing the press, he suddenly seemed to glow, like a dying fire when a wind hits it. His head came up, he puffed on the cigarette as he grinned around and waved to various people he knew. I steered the President to the point Daniels indicated, swung him around, and stepped back to stand beside Reilly.

FDR faced about fifty men and women, every one with pencil and pad poised. There were photogs, chewing gum, but their cameras dangled; none was aimed at the President. He jutted his chin and searched the room, then lowered his eyes to a sheaf of papers Daniels handed him. His voice was strong and resonant.

"I think the most important thing I have today is setting up an inquiry into the question of guaranteed wage plans. As some of you know, I have been talking about this for ten years. In other words, what might be called the annual—annual take-home a person makes under our wage system. And it is only recently that the trade unions have become interested in the question. I wrote, last December, to Justice Byrnes, and he took it up with the War Labor Board, and suggested that a study should be conducted examining the experience industry and labor have thus far had with these plans. I will give you a copy of this when you go out.

"Several of the facts have been studied before by the Department of Labor—quite a bit to go on. An annual—annual wage is relatively simple in some industries, and exceeding difficult in others. We will know more about it when this commission reports."

He looked around again, and his voice was softer as he said, "I think that is about all the news I have got for you right now."

The first reporter shot up. "Mr. President, does the government have any plans for preventing stoppage of work in the coal mines, should the operators and the unions not reach agreement by March 31st?"

"I am sorry to have to say that that really is an 'iffy' question."

"The word 'if' wasn't in there, Mr. President."

"It *was* cleverly phrased, I'll say that," said Roosevelt, and they laughed. I did too; his delivery was perfect.

"How are you feeling now, sir?" another man asked.

"I'm feeling fine, Merry-man, fine. Just a little tired."

"Any trace of your bronchitis?"

"I think it is all gone, but Admiral McIntire is going to put me through the usual checkups, to make sure it is all fixed up. Regular thing, you know."

I waited for them to pursue it, but to my surprise they just went on with, "Could you discuss the food situation, Mr. President?"

"The food situation? Oh, I read an awful lot of—awful lot of stuff on that. I don't think I am ready to answer that yet. I think the country ought to know, though. I will try to have something by Friday on it. It's worth analyzing."

"Will that—your plan for Friday, sir? Is that a statement you plan, or a message to Congress?"

"No, I don't think so. I thought I would just talk."

"Can't hear you back here," someone said from the rear. Roosevelt repeated the answer, taking his cigarette holder out of his mouth. He was the most relaxed guy in the room as he straightened in the chair, smiled, tapped ash to the floor, and nodded to another hand.

"Do you think, sir, that a congressional investigation would be advisable?"

"That's a trick question." Just the way he said it was funny.

"It's a what?"

"A trick question. I know, you didn't mean it, right? Well, I don't like to criticize Congress. I feel a little bit—you had better put this off the record—"

They groaned, but he went on as if he didn't hear them. "—Off the record, but what can we find out that we don't know already? What is a legislative body going to do? Resolve that hereafter, in America, all the food in the country is going to be just twice what it is right now?"

A woman's voice, and I straightened; I recognized it. Hell, yes, it was Alice, Allie from Stanford, now Mrs. Sobelski. In a knockout black dress in the Press Club a couple weeks back. Today in a green suit-dress with padded shoulders and a little Robin Hood hat. She was asking, "Mr. President, INS News Service. Can you give us anything that might be helpful in respect to the questions you expect to arise at San Francisco?"

"No—I don't really have anything on that. Even for Mr. Hearst."

They laughed, he was a regular Bob Hope, but Alice kept boring in. "How about the American voting procedure? Will it be a unit rule, or—"

"I don't honestly know. I don't think the question has come up. Stettinius hasn't said anything about it to me."

A tall guy in front. "Mr. President, have you decided when you are going to San Francisco? Are you going to open the conference? Or go at the—"

"I will either go at the beginning or the end. I see that one paper says the beginning, and another one the end. One of them is right."

He was playing them like a stand-up comic. Someone yelled, "Which one, Mr. President?" but he ignored it, pointing his cigarette at another reporter.

"Mr. President, do you think the recent developments in Rumania square with the Yalta declaration on liberated areas?"

"Oh my God," said Roosevelt, rolling his eyes. "Ask the State Department."

"We have, sir. They refer us to the War Department, and they tell us to ask the White House."

"What?" said FDR, as if he couldn't believe it.

"Mr. President, is it true that under the Yalta agreement on voting procedure that two of the Big Powers can overrule discussions on any proposal that might be brought up? Not only the use of force, but anything else?"

Roosevelt propped his chin, and now his mobile face was thought personified. "As I remember the thing—the simplest way of putting it—on everything that is procedural, not the actual use of force, you have to have seven out of eleven, or maybe six out of eleven. Don't say it's seven. It's a majority."

"Whose plan was that? And there's no veto power, say, by the Soviets?"

"That—that's the problem with answering that question at all. Whatever the voting arrangement is, people, certain papers, they will line up and say it was a victory for Mr. Stalin, or Mr. Churchill, or for me. I should say it was a common agreement. That means it wasn't a victory for anybody. In—what shall we say?—history, the question of who proposed it first is the—is the smallest end of it. If any of you have a better idea, we would be glad to consider it at San Francisco. And the conference will be open to the press and the radio—movie and still pictures. It will be all right."

I watched them look at each other and shrug. One reporter said, "Mr. President, would you care to commit yourself on the subject of night baseball?"

Roosevelt made it even funnier by taking it seriously, and talked about how he'd helped start night baseball, and how it was a good thing to take people's minds off the war. But they didn't leave the scent, and the next question was about the postwar status of Austria and Italy. FDR wove some vague response involving postwar commissions and Allied councils.

"Mr. President, yesterday you saw General Bill Donovan. Is there anything you can tell us about your talk with him?"

"Nothing, Jim. Just clearing up some routine matters. Nothing of importance."

"You didn't take up this proposed superspy agency—"

"No. He never even mentioned it."

"Can you tell us anything about your plans there? For the postwar intelligence setup? I remember in '36—"

"The Smith-McKellar-Robinson deal. That didn't pass."

"And Mr. Hoover's still in charge of the FBI."

"This is off the record," said FDR, and they all groaned again. He raised his eyebrows, and said, "All right, it's not off the record—I just won't say it! Next question, please."

"Mr. President, there have been rumors of peace feelers from Germany. One of them was supposed to have come via Sweden."

"I saw that this morning. In the papers."

"Well, can you give us any illumination as to—"

"We have nothing here at all."

"Is there anything on the zone American troops are to occupy?"

"I'm glad you mentioned that, because it is something I need to bring up with General Marshall."

"Mr. President, have you made a decision yet on the new command setup for the Pacific?"

"No." Roosevelt looked back at Daniels, then half-turned his head, seeming to search behind him for someone. I caught a glimpse of his face. His jaw was sagging slightly, the holder drooping perilously close to his chest.

"Do you expect to soon, sir—"

"No, no," said Roosevelt, and there must have been some signal I didn't see, because an older man stood up and said, "Thank you, Mr. President," and the other reporters all stood up too and echoed him. Daniels nodded to me, and as FDR waved a gay farewell I turned him around and wheeled him up the ramp. Behind me I heard a stir and murmur.

"Where to, sir?" I asked the gray head below me. FDR didn't respond, and I said again, louder, "Where to, Mr. President?"

"The Oval Office, please, Billy."

I didn't know who he thought I was, but I didn't bother to correct him. I still couldn't believe how well he'd carried off the press conference. The Secret Service men followed me through the office area. The hallway was empty, the green carpet worn. A clock told me it was five-twenty-five.

A wood fire crackled cheerfully as I pushed the silent President through the oak doors of the Oval Office. Crim bowed wordlessly. Prettyman and Maysie stood behind a drink cart. Beyond the windows trees laced a darkening sky, and the vertical shaft of the Washington Monument cut a black slice. Without a word Reilly opened them and leaned out, looking left and right. He waved to someone I couldn't see.

The chair moved, and I let go. FDR gripped the wheels, and shakily pivoted himself toward the cart. Then he lifted his hands. I took over again, rolled him to it and put the brakes on and stepped back.

Voices grew in the corridor. The other two bodyguards took positions on either side of the doors, one reaching into his coat to adjust a shoulder holster. Neither had a mustache, I noticed. I was thinking of trying to finish my discussion with Reilly, when Daniels led five or six reporters in. They fell silent as they passed the threshold, and those who still had hats on took them off.

"Jim! Merry-Man! Who else is around?" said Roosevelt, picking up one of the shakers and giving it a sort of trial shake. "Crimmie, how about stepping out and seeing who's home? See if Hacky and the Duchess are around."

"They're probably eating, Mr. President."

"Well, see who would like a little drinkie . . . anyone see the Doc? Good, then I can have one too."

Hassett came in, tall and silent, and Grace Tully and Dorothy Brady from next door. The reporters took over a leather settee and lit up. It was all very relaxed. One of the reporters asked who I was, and we batted the breeze for a couple of minutes. I glanced at the President. He seemed to be enjoying himself, joking with two of the reporters. I tuned in.

"I was asking you that about General Donovan for a reason, Mr. President."

"I figured you had one, Jim."

"There's talk going around that even if you don't merge the OSS, FBI, and Navy and Army intelligence—after the war, I mean—that Bill Donovan's a logical successor to Edgar Hoover."

"There's always talk, Jim. If there wasn't, what would you fellows have to write about?"

"Wouldn't it help if I floated a trial balloon? You could get some public reaction—"

"I said it's off the record, and maybe that's where it had better stay for now. Ready for another little dividend on that drink?"

Daniels came in then, and Jim Wright tried him next. "How's the schedule for tomorrow, Jonathan?"

Daniels looked sour. "I write 'em up, I mimeograph 'em, and you still don't read 'em."

"We would if we could," said Merriman Smith. "But you said anybody credited to the White House had to be illiterate."

"Byrnes will be in at ten. Then the President will meet with the U.S. delegation to the United Nations. The British ambassador at noon; Senator Barkley at twelve-thirty; then a special presentation to a valued member of the President's press staff just before lunch." Daniels looked smug, waited for them to ask. Wright said, "What's the President having for lunch?"

I wasn't really in the mood to listen to them trade wisecracks. Reilly was leaning against the window. I drifted over, trying to not attract any press attention.

"Lieutenant? Oh, yeah, you had something to tell me." Reilly turned his back to the rapidly falling night. Over his shoulder I saw troops spaced along the iron fence facing Pennsylvania Avenue. "Okay, shoot."

I told him about the guy with the mustache; first, about him being picked up by the FBI during the fag raid. His eyebrows lifted, and he glanced at the other men by the door. The biggest one left his post and came over. By the time he reached us I was telling Reilly about my night patrol. "And when I came out, he wasn't on duty," I finished. "I figure the guy with the flashlight I saw was either him trying to get in the bedroom, or else he left his post to give somebody else the opportunity to get to the President."

"But you locked FDR's door, that what you're telling me? So he couldn't get in?"

"That's right."

The doors opened again and Anna Boettiger came in. None of the reporters stood. Behind her were uniforms—Admiral Brown, Ed Abrams.

"How do I know this is on the level, Kennedy? You ain't exactly—"

"What?"

"Nothing. How do I know this is all on the level?"

I shrugged, as if to say, If you don't believe me, what can I say? "Where's Rivers?" Mike asked the other agent, who had listened to the last of this with a bored expression I truly admired. If I had a poker face like that I could have retired from the Navy with more boodle than my old man. "He shown yet?"

"Huh-uh."

"Is Rivers the guy with the mustache?" I asked them. Reilly nodded shortly. "D'you call his house?" he asked the big guy, who bent and cupped his hand to his ear. It was getting noisy around the drink cart. Reilly repeated himself.

"Yeah. His wife answered. She ain't seen him since Tuesday morning, when he came to work, but she figured he's been working late a lot, she didn't think nothing of it."

The rattle of ice interrupted us, and a burst of laughter from the corner. Roosevelt's voice boomed out, "So then I said, 'Mud! You dumped me in the mud, you chumps! What if you'd done that to Napoleon?' Who wants an old-fashioned?" A dog was barking outside: Fala burst through the door and trotted around, found his master, parked himself by the chair.

"Okay, Kennedy," Reilly said. "Apparently the guy's disappeared. And our guys don't disappear. Not if they're kosher. You might have caught something just in—"

A sudden crash and clatter interrupted him. A woman screamed. Instantly Reilly and the big guy were running, guns coming out from under their blazers. The reporters scattered, and as they cleared to the right and left I saw a pair of legs kicking, down on the floor. A choking howl made the hair rise on the back of my neck.

CHAPTER 19

Suddenly every reporter had a 35 mm camera in his hands. Then Reilly was among them. "Clear off," he shouted. "Give him room!" FDR was staring down at the body on the carpet. "Abe," he said softly. "Why, what's the—"

"Secure the area," Reilly snarled, holding up two fingers like a quarterback calling a much-practiced play. The third agent was already slamming and locking the doors as the second bulled his way to a blocking position between the President's wheelchair and the crowd. I heard Grace Tully, quietly efficient, already on the telephone. "He's not there? Then come yourself, please. No, not the President. One of the military staff. No, we don't know. Some sort of seizure, I think."

I guess most of us had seen men die before. I had, in the Pacific. So it didn't hit me quite as hard this time: that numbing compound of terror, disgust, and rage you feel the first time a buddy goes down. I got past the clicking cameras and knelt above the body.

But Abrams wasn't dead. At least, not yet. But he was rigid and shuddering. His arms quivered like a dying bird's wings. Drool ran down his cheek into the worn carpet, and his pupils had shrunk to intense black periods, marking the end. His breath came in gasps, as if his lungs were petrifying. I got his tie down and his collar open. When I unbuttoned his blouse the Air Corps wings caught and I had to tear his shirt to get them free.

"Brushed it," he muttered. "Half open."

"What? What's he trying to say?"

He vomited suddenly, and I turned his head to keep his airway clear. "No one touches anything," Reilly shouted. "Nobody leaves! Grace! Get some labels. I want a label on each man's drink. What it was, who mixed it, whose it was."

That made sense. I saw Prettyman and Maysie, looking about as pale as Negroes could get, backed up against the wall. They probably figured they were going to be the prime suspects.

A rap on the door: Bruenn, with the corpsman. I got up and they took over. The heavy breathing filled the room, each breath longer and more agonizing. Then Bruenn hesitated, smoothing his hair back with an uncertain hand.

"What is it, Doc?" said FDR, rolling his chair forward, forcing the Secret Service man aside, though he followed, revolver held down by his thigh.

"Not sure yet, sir. It looks like a grand mal seizure, but he doesn't have a history of epilepsy. Chagall, get the oxygen cylinder. Get an anticonvulsant, too. Pentothal or paraldehyde, whatever you see first. Stat!" The corpsman left on the run.

"It's not epilepsy, Doc. It's poison," said Reilly. He looked around, examining the pale but professionally intent faces, the focused cameras. They were still clicking, Leicas and Kodaks. "And my guess is, somebody here gave it to him."

Ed Abrams seemed to be struggling to speak, or to breathe, I couldn't tell which. He was staring up at us. It was pretty horrible. He knew he was dying. Roosevelt bent forward, reaching down, but the outstretched fingers couldn't quite reach him. "Take it easy, Abe," he said. "Keep quiet. It won't hurt if you keep quiet."

Ed stopped breathing. A last shudder hit him, then eased off. His eyes stayed open.

Bruenn was filling a horse syringe from a vial. I winced as he leaned on it, driving the needle deep into the major's chest. Chagall came back with the medical gear. Other faces showed behind him, but the agent at the door closed it on them. Bruenn broke out a mask and got it on the motionless officer. Oxygen hissed. "Help me turn him over," he told me, and I got Abrams's ankles, flinching at the hardness before remembering one was artificial, and got him on his stomach for artificial respiration. But he didn't move at all, not after that last shudder, and the gas hissed past motionless cheeks, open eyes, staring now at whatever follows life.

"That's all I can do," said Bruenn at last. He took a deep breath and rocked back on his heels. "He's gone."

Reilly asked him, "What was it?"

"Offhand I'd say you're right—poison—but."

"But what?"

"But it was only two or three minutes, right? You called me as soon as he went down. There aren't many poisons that act that fast. And they don't produce symptoms like this."

"What was he drinking? Maysie, anybody remember what he had to drink?"

"I think a whiskey sour, sah."

Several faces turned even paler, examining the glasses they still held. Tully came back from her office and went around the circle, passing out gummed labels and pencils. Reilly stooped, searched around, and pulled Abrams's highball glass out from where it had rolled under the settee. He sniffed it, frowned, and passed it to Bruenn, who sniffed too, much more cautiously, waving air toward his nose with a cupped hand.

"Prussic acid? Cyanide?"

"You'd smell those. I don't smell anything but whiskey."

"Any chance it was what you thought at first? A seizure?"

"I just can't tell at this point," said Bruenn, looking at the body. "We'll have to do an autopsy. Blood tests."

Knocking again. Reilly jerked his head at Number 2. Three more Secret Service men entered, and the security chief started snapping orders. Then interrupted himself, turned quickly, and knelt by the President's wheelchair. I couldn't hear what they said, but when Reilly stood he looked enraged. "Jerry," he said, "Take two men and escort the President to his quarters."

"Can we go?" said one of the reporters, and they all began jostling each other in an accelerating drift for the doors and, I was sure, the phones in the Press Room.

"Hold your horses," said Reilly, waiting till the doors closed behind FDR's chair. "Miss Tully, are all the glasses labeled?"

"Yes, Mr. Reilly."

"Okay, listen close, boys. Here's what we're going to do. This is a matter of national security—"

"This is news, Mike!"

"Hell! This's got nothing to do with the war!"

"Shut up!" Reilly roared. "If an assassination attempt isn't national security, what is? Anyway, that wasn't an order. I'm asking for your voluntary cooperation. As soon as we know something, I'll have Mr. Daniels brief you—" he looked to the press secretary, who nodded "—and you can file then. So quit your beefing and clear out, or you can kiss your accreditation good-bye!"

One by one, not looking happy about it, they nodded, glancing at one another.

"Okay. You're free too leave. *One by one.* As you exit, I want you to submit to a voluntary search. The cameras will stay here, too."

Once again a babble of protest rose, and again Reilly roared, "Shut *up!* Didn't you hear me? This is a *voluntary* search. The Secret Service has no police powers." He waited a beat, then added, "Of course, if anybody wants to be a sap, turns down the search . . ."

"Me first," I said, playing Good Example. Reilly looked at me funny, but just said, "Okay, Kennedy leads off. Check him out good, McMullin, down to his socks. Long, write down everything he's got on him. Anything looks like a needle or drops, anything suspicious, take it off him and label it . . . Grace, how about you help Mr. Hunley search the ladies?"

"Ed Kelly on the line, Mike."

"Tell him I got a situation here. Keep it under his hat, but send over five uniformed cops and the homicide dicks. Have 'em come in the south gate. And no goddamn sirens this time."

I held up my arms and let them go through my pockets. They went through my wallet (empty except for my Navy ID) and even checked my shoes, prying at the heels with a pocketknife. Finally they let me leave.

We didn't go far, though. The reporters, of course, didn't want to leave the grounds in case something else broke. I didn't have anyplace else to go except back to the clinic. And I still felt sick, after watching Abrams check out. So we all adjourned to the Press Room. Flasks were broken out and coffee put on and the UP phoned out for hamburgers. Shortly we were all relatively jovial, in a subdued way. I guess we were all thinking, what if we'd got that particular highball instead of Abrams. I met the rest of the reporters, and it turned out we had friends in common, in England if not in the States. They all knew who I was, of course, and if they didn't Alice soon enlightened them.

At a little after ten we heard several cars draw up outside. "Quiet," called a guy from one of the West Coast papers, in a hoarse whisper. We turned, and saw him listening on the phone at Daniels's desk. He lowered it silently after a moment, still holding his hand over the mouthpiece, and winked at us. "The G-men are here."

"Hoover's boys?"

"The fingerprint squad."

"Reilly's gonna love that," said Wright.

"He doesn't like the FBI?" I asked, using my naive voice. Sometimes it got me stuff I had no business knowing. The newsmen, though, just looked at me scornfully; they knew that trick.

Daniels came in around eleven-thirty, but he didn't have any news. Allie asked him if the schedule for tomorrow would be scrubbed. He said he didn't think so, everybody the President had to see he had to see; they'd go as planned unless FDR decided otherwise. Jim Wright offered him a drink. Daniels thought about it, then shook his head. "I'd better keep my head clear," he said, and left.

I got up and walked around a little, knowing I ought to go back to the clinic and bunk down, or at least find an empty couch; but I couldn't, I was still on edge. Everybody was smoking and drinking Irish coffee. Finally I sat down again next to Alice.

She was looking very good indeed tonight, long dark hair swaying forward as she lit a Pall Mall, then tumbling backward as she lifted her chin to exhale. There were blondish highlights in it I didn't remember from before. She offered me one, and I said, "Thanks, but I still don't smoke. When did you start?"

"After Stanford."

"What happened after that, Allie?" That was what I'd used to call her. I just didn't like the sound of 'Alice', although she said it never bothered her.

"I told you. I got married."

"Where'd you meet him? This, this emigré? And how did you get so chummy with Citizen Kane?"

"It's a long story."

"We've got all night." I looked earnest. "I'd like to know, because I thought about you a lot. Out there in the Pacific, running up the Slot on dark nights, the guys would talk about the girls they used to know back in the States. And I'd tell them about you."

"Oh, that's so touching, Jack. Considering you never wrote."

"I had no idea where to reach you. I wasn't writing much from Guadalcanal anyway, nobody was. Anyway, wait, I did write you once. Care of Stanford. But I never got an answer."

"Be honest. Did you really write to me care of Stanford?"

"Cross my . . . heart," I said, making a cross, but lower down.

"I thought so," she said. At least I was making her laugh. "Well, after the Institute for World Affairs thing I went back to dull old Poli Sci. Graduated in '41 and went to New York. That's where I met Jan. I was undecided about postgraduate work. My family wanted me back on the West Coast. Not my father—we haven't spoken in years—but my sisters; so I went back for a visit, not really sure where I wanted to call home—just in time for Pearl Harbor.

"Then one day I saw a Japanese family being moved out of their house. I wrote about it to *Esquire,* how unfair it was, how un-American, really. And they ran it as part of a series.

"I got a letter from Kate Mitchell, she was the editor of a magazine called *Amerasia.* We corresponded, and she asked for samples of my writing. I sent her some of the things I'd done—and a copy of our report, the one we worked on together, remember?"

"Sure I do."

"Well, eventually they asked me to come back to New York and work for them. So I said yes, thinking I might see Jan again. I did, and met other interesting people too. We had a lot of fun. But the pay wasn't so great. And it didn't always come on time . . . so later on when the Hearst Organization made me an offer I decided to try it. I was delighted when they assigned me here. I guess because all the male reporters are either in uniform or covering the front."

"It knocked me for a loop, seeing you with Hearst and Cissy in the Press Club. I never thought you'd end up with that bunch."

"They're a little to the right of Adolf Hitler, but the pay's good. Speaking of W.R., did you read Aldous Huxley's novel about him?"

"Swan? Yeah. I don't think it was about him, though. Huxley just used the castle."

Hunley, the big agent, put his head in the door. "Oliver," he said. Harold Oliver got up and went out.

"Uh huh. So, what's Mr. Sobelski doing now?"

"Something hush-hush. I'm not really sure what it's about. I suspect he's overseas a lot."

"Sounds like you don't see him very often."

"Often enough not to get ideas about other men. Even attractive young Navy heroes."

"Aw, Allie—

"Wright," said Hunley, sticking his head in again. Jim Wright looked around, got up, and went out. "What's going on?" I said.

"I don't know . . . and don't 'Aw, Allie' me. I remember that night at the Del Monte, Jack. I gave you something I'd never given a man before. And I expected to be . . . I don't know . . . I didn't expect marriage. I don't think I'd have been interested even if you had asked. But a girl likes to feel appreciated afterward. And I didn't."

"Kennedy," said the big guy, and I told Alice, "Excuse me a minute."

The assistant supervising Secret Service agent towed me back down the hall to the Oval Office. All the lights were on, though it was now past midnight. The blackout drapes shut us in. Four or five guys in dark coats stood around, and a photog in shirtsleeves was taking closeups of the drink trays. Every time a bulb went off it made a sound like frying ham and left me blinking at green afterimages. Ed's body was gone. A geezer in a smock was kneeling over the vomit stain, and a hair dryer was whining. Drying it to powder so it could be analyzed, I figured.

Reilly crooked a finger and I walked over to an ink-and-pad setup. "Hey, they got these when I joined the Navy," I said, but the pastyface just took my bronzed and godlike hand and started messing it up with dirty black ink.

Reilly introduced me to a guy I'd recognized already as Clyde Tolson, the square-jawed laddie I'd seen with Hoover at the fag raid, and to another flatfoot named Kelly, the Washington, D.C., police chief. The third overcoat was named Mansfield, apparently the lead District homicide detective. Tolson didn't seem to recognize me, which I thought was unimpressive for a cop. Or maybe he was playing dumb, waiting for me to make a slip. Mansfield asked me some questions about what happened, where I was standing, did I see anything. I glanced sideways at Reilly. "You mean, at the—the cocktail hour here, or before?"

"He means, at the cocktail hour itself," said Reilly, giving me the gimlet eye.

"No. I was just standing by, waiting to take the President out when he got tired."

"What are you? His aide?" Kelly grunted.

"That's right, Chief."

"How come you don't got one of those gold rope things on your shoulder? Thought aides all had those. I was in the Army myself, last war."

"I was just assigned. Haven't had time to get an aiguillette yet."

"Assigned from where?"

"I was in the Map Room, downstairs. They decided I'd do better as an aide."

The dick who'd taken my fingerprints spoke up suddenly. He sounded excited. "It's a match!"

"What's a match?" said Tolson. He'd taken off his hat, and I saw he wore his hair slicked back like John Barrymore.

"This guy. His fingerprints match the prints on Abrams's glass. They also match the ones on the neck of the bourbon bottle. That must be where he held it to dump in the poison."

"Horseshit," I said. "I was nowhere near the bottle, or Ed either."

"How'd you know his first name?"

"He told me his first name. And I told him mine. It's called introducing yourself."

"You little mick smartass. You'll see if it's horseshit, when we strap you into the chair."

"You're way off the beam," Reilly said. "Nobody's going to fall for that routine."

"You'd be surprised what people will fall for." Tolson gave me a nasty look. "Like, some joes will take a dive for a dame nobody else would touch. A squarehead tramp whose love letters go straight to Berlin."

"What are you talking about?" said Reilly.

"Nothing. Anyway, we're not going to crack it tonight. We'll send over a team first thing. Get to work on it in earnest."

"Like hell you will. This is Secret Service business. I don't need Einstein to tumble to what you G-men want."

"Someday we'll get it, too. We'll clean house over here and in State, and I'll bet we find a lot of dirt under the carpet, too."

"Tell your fucking . . . *boss* we can handle our own investigations. We don't need the Gestapo." They glared at each other; then Tolson sneered and turned away. Reilly said to Hunley, "Okay, Jerry, send in the next victim."

"Can I go?" I asked them. Tolson didn't bother to look at me. Reilly nodded, then, as I left the office, sauntered after.

The first thing he said when we were out of earshot from inside was, "We haven't found Rivers yet. And somehow I don't think we're gonna."

"I don't think it was him, if that's what you mean."

"Then who was it? You got something else you haven't told me?"

"No, no. I mean, I think we've got to look for somebody who's still here."

"Yeah, I agree, but who? That's the problem. We gave Maysie and Lizzie the third degree about the drink cart. It's not as secure as I thought. It's stored in a locked cupboard, all right, but when they're setting up to serve it just sits out in plain sight while they're cracking the ice and cleaning glasses. There are probably thirty people who could have gotten to it. If it *was* poison."

"You don't go for that?"

"I did at first." His mouth twisted in frustration. "Kelly's gonna have his lab boys check everything out. The residues in the bottles. The . . . vomitus, I guess is the word. But when we collated who had what, we found four other people who drank drinks mixed from the exact same bottle Abrams did. And who mixed the drink? FDR. So I don't think we're going to find poison. And if that's true, I'm back to wondering if the Major had some kind of fit or seizure, and it was a natural death."

"That didn't look natural to me. Or to Bruenn."

"He wasn't that sure. He's a specialist, anyway."

"A cardiologist."

Reilly examined me. "Yeah. A cardiologist. How'd you know that?"

"I asked him. Did you know he's German? He said you did, but did you check him out?"

"There's a lot of guys, German names. Eisenhower. Wedemeyer. Patton. We did the whole background check, family, hometown, colleagues, back in '44 when McIntire brought him over. He came up roses." Reilly studied me, sucking a tooth. "Seems to me you're getting mixed pretty deep into this, Kennedy."

"It passes the time."

"How'd you get to be FDR's aide?"

"I was going to ask you the same thing. I got the word from Hassett. Who'd you get it from?"

"Hassett, but I got the idea he wasn't too hot on it. So it must have come from somewhere else. Who you got an in with?"

"Nobody I know of," I told him. "Not around here, anyway."

"What was that Tolson was talking about, about a dame? And Berlin?"

"I don't know," I said, but I did. It was Inga. But I'd already paid for that. That was why I'd gotten fired from ONI. I wasn't going to let them plaster me with that again.

"Well, tell me this, then, Kennedy. Tolson's little tricks aside—tell me again why I should trust you. How do I know you didn't kill Abrams, trying to get the President?"

"I told you about what's-his-name. Rivers."

"Who we still haven't found. Who could be laying out drunk. Or you could have iced him and dumped him in the Potomac. His not being here don't clear you."

"Okay, how about this: If I'd have been aiming for FDR, I wouldn't have got Ed. Hell, I liked Ed."

"Can the cute stuff, Kennedy. I'm this far from tossing you out of the White House. Just to be safe."

That was the last straw. I told the big Irishman that, One, I hadn't volunteered for this job, or the Map Room either for that matter, and Two, that if I'd gone by the letter of the law I'd be medically retired, sitting at the bar of the Palm Beach Club sipping rum punches and chasing bobby-soxer tail. So if he wanted me to shag ass, nobody would be happier. Three, he had a major security problem, and the more eyes he had around FDR the better the chance of intercepting the next try. And Four, what time did the President wake up, because until Reilly made up his mind, I was going to find a cot and hammer a pillow till then. I left him looking like a steamed lobster and headed back for the clinic.

It took a long time before I could get to sleep, though. I kept seeing Abrams's dead face. I kept thinking, just like, I guess, everybody who'd been there probably was too:

Me. It could have been *me*.

C H A P T E R   2 0

Southeast Washington, D.C.

The clerk was a little man who looked, Krasov thought, rather like Heinrich Himmler. Yes, he'd seen Himmler, and not just in the *German Weekly Newsreel.* They'd been face-to-face once, when the head of the SS had inspected the "Russian Army of Liberation." A little, unimpressive man with a pince-nez and a twitch, who never looked anyone in the eye and seemed embarrassed as he minced between the rows of Soviet POWs in German uniform. Just as he'd come abreast of Krasov, one of the PK-men, Wehrmacht combat photographers, had lifted his Leica. And later Krasov had seen the photograph in *Signal.* Somehow they had made Himmler look bigger, colder, more ruthless. Whereas in reality he looked just like a hardware clerk. . . .

"Was about to close up for the night when I saw you standing out there. Help you, mister?"

Krasov cleared his throat, looking around at the nearly bare shelves. "Yeah. Thanks. I need some gloves."

"Gloves? What kind?"

"I'm working for the government, doing some spraying. Keep the bugs down, you know? But that Flit gives me a rash if it gets on my skin."

"You want rubber gloves, sounds like to me. But we only got one pair left, ain't seen those come in in a long time."

He got the last pair, the clerk telling him four times they were the last real rubber he'd see till after the war. Then he asked for a small jar of axle grease and a length of chain. It came to a dollar even. He paid with his last bill.

Outside he walked rapidly toward the corner, the paper poke dangling in his hand. Under the leather jacket the hard smoothness of the loaded Tokarev pressed against his belly. In the left pocket, the spare magazine. In the right, the small hard cylinder of the grenade.

When he reached his destination, ten blocks farther on through the falling night, he was sweating despite the cool darkness.

He stood in the open air for almost two hours, watching the pattern of traffic in and out of the townhouse. A little blue star banner hung in the lower window, but he was pretty sure that was only camouflage. He was remembering how it had been the night he went there with Smalls. The big man at the door, revolver tucked into his waistband, checking each visitor out. The crowded rooms of men drinking highballs and whiskey and smoking and playing poker, craps, blackjack, roulette.

And the bare, small wainscoted room in back.

He'd thought about this for a long time, lying on his back in the little basement room where he spent his nights. Thought about where to get some money. And going over everywhere he'd been since he came to Washington, he suddenly remembered where he'd seen it. Stacks of it. Green bills, and silver, and stacks of poker chips.

The back-room bank, at Jimmy LaFontaine's.

At about ten he went around the corner and had coffee and three doughnuts in a People's Quick Lunch. He eased his belt open a notch as he sat, realizing he was gaining weight. So much food, food was everywhere. . . . Then he sauntered back, resuming his vigil.

A little after midnight there was a general exodus, sailors and soldiers coming down the stairs and out the door and weaving their noisy way down the street. He knew that the last buses for Fort Belvoir left at 1:00 A.M., and the streetcars stopped running at two. True to his expectations, the civilians left not long after the men in uniform. He smiled coldly in the shadows opposite. Predators and prey.

It was time.

But the men up there were armed. And alert.

This would not be as easy as killing an old man in an alley.

He groped in his trousers pocket, found the case, and slid the needle out. Steel gleamed for a moment before he jabbed it into his arm and pressed the plunger down.

When he finished the injection he dropped the empty needle and pushed away from the brick wall and crossed the street. Walked slowly and as silently as he could down the alley toward the back of the townhouse. Into darkness and the stink of man-piss and rotting fish. A cat fled, hissing. He took his time. Ten minutes, that was how long they'd told him to wait after the injection. It needed that long to take effect.

He felt his heart speed up . . . and blinked into the darkness that suddenly seemed even darker, more impenetrable.

There it was, the flight of tilted wooden steps. Unlighted except for a gleam from a distant window. There was the brick wall where Smalls had died, holding his penis in his hand.

Above him a door opened suddenly, spilling light out onto the landing. "So, g'night," a rough voice said. The stairs creaked as an enormous shadow eased itself down them. It was LaFontaine, obese and awkward. Krasov froze in the shadows as the gambler passed not five feet from him. He smelled of sweat and whiskey and talcum powder.

When the alley was empty again Krasov drew the automatic and went up the steps quietly. But when he reached the top he hesitated, thinking, No. This was wrong. He wasn't ready yet.

He slipped the hammer off and shoved the pistol back into his belt. He took out the two-foot length of chain snipped from the roll at the hardware store. His other hand slid into his right pocket, closed around the heavy cold cylinder.

Of a Soviet-made RTD-1942 economy grenade.

The RTD-1942 was the Soviet version of the infantry grenade that the British called Mills bombs, the Americans "pineapples." This one looked like the standard 1942. The tin canister with the round pin and the light metal "spoon" that flipped off on throwing, igniting the delay fuse.

But inside, it was quite different.

He suddenly recalled that he had not yet taken his other precautions. Cursing himself—at any moment someone else could come out onto the landing—he laid the chain and the grenade on the rail and took the jar from his pocket. He pulled his jacket off and dropped it over the rail. Beneath it he had on a long-sleeved shirt, cuffs and collar buttoned tight. The cap tinkled on the bricks below as he quickly scooped and smeared a thick coating of grease over his face, his neck, his wrists.

Voices came through the door and he hurried, slapping the last handful of cold grease across his forehead and dropping the jar. He picked up the Tokarev again, got the grenade ready in his left hand, and hooked his little finger awkwardly in the ring. It made a faint click as he pulled it out. Live.

Sucking in as deep a breath as he could hold, he jerked the door open.

He looked in for less than a second, but the image imprinted itself in that short span so distinctly that afterward he could recall every detail. Four men were frozen in surprise, eyes startled. The suspendered goon from the front door stood holding a glass of beer, other hand thrust into a pocket, fedora tilted back. The Jew from the chalkboard stood with two black men. The shotgun lay propped against the chipped wainscoting. For one suspended instant, they all stared at him.

Krasov swung his arm in and released the grenade.

The lever popped free as it flew in a shallow arc toward them, striking the bare wood floor at their feet. Just as it hit, and as the hatted man's hand darted for his waistband, he slammed the door. Grabbing for the chain, he took three quick turns abound the handle, lashing it tightly to the handrail of the fire escape.

He barely had it in place when he heard the pop of the igniter. Followed, not by an explosion, but by a shot that tore through the wood not a foot from his head. He heard shouting, then the door shook under his hands. He held the chain twisted tight, shoulder to the jamb, hoping they didn't fire through it again. Someone hammered on the far side. There was another shot, sounding muffled.

Then silence.

He waited for thirty more seconds, counting under his breath as he kept sucking in cold air. But he heard nothing else but the warbling coo of nesting pigeons somewhere above his head.

Releasing the chain, he pulled the folded bag from his trouser pocket.

He'd cut it from one of the paper sleeves that dry-cleaned suits came in. Moving quickly, panting as his heart speeded up from the drug he'd just injected, he popped the bag open and slipped it over his head and tucked it into his collar. He looked out now through a narrow cut slit taped over with celluloid tape. Finally, satisfied it was as airtight as it would get, he pulled two more bags out and stepped into them, tied the strings around his legs. Then, last, drew the stiff rubber fingers of the gloves over his own.

He was ready. Sealing his grease-covered lips firmly together, he pulled the door open.

▬

Holding his breath, he crossed the room quickly, stepping over the writhing, vomiting bodies, and picked up a chair. He threw it through a window, smashing the glass. A second chair followed through another window. The cool night wind began blowing in.

He didn't pause, but kept going. Skirting a convulsing and gagging black man, he entered the small room off the hallway. And stopped dead.

When he'd been here with Smalls its surface had been covered with cash, coins, and poker chips. The chips were still there, arranged in neat stacks of red and white and blue and green. But there was no money at all. He spun, looking around the room for a safe, a container, a money pouch. Nothing.

He needed a breath now. The bag crackled around his ears as he eased out the locked-in air and took the first inhalation from within it.

Touching nothing, he walked quickly out into the hallway again. He looked down at the sprawled bodies. One was motionless, already dead. The others were preoccupied with dying, bodies rigid, breathing in gurgling asthmatic sobs between retches.

He knew it would sound strange, if the Americans ever captured him, but it was true: he had no idea what was in the grenade. The spectacled chemist from I. G. Farben had carefully explained the defensive measures he had to use. Never let the slightest droplet contact his bare skin. Inject himself with the counteragent no more than half an hour and no less than ten minutes before possible exposure. He knew that the slightest contact or breath would cause incapacitation within seconds and death within minutes; that ordinary gas masks were useless; that the agent, though unimaginably deadly, would quickly evaporate and disperse.

But they'd never told him what it was. Even the SS instructors had referred to it as "Trilon," which sounded dangerous in English but was actually the name of a German household detergent, like Ivory Flakes or Boraxo in the U.S.

He'd asked the chemist how they knew it was so deadly. He'd smiled frostily and told him they'd tested it in Bavaria, in a place called Dachau.

Now, looking at the pinpoint, staring pupils of the men on the floor, the mucus streaming from their nostrils, the froth bubbling at their open, straining mouths, he understood all too well how right the little man had been. It was colorless, odorless, and tasteless. But even the slightest touch, and it killed.

Sprayed with it by the grenade's detonating primer, these men had probably never realized what was happening to them.

The last body gave a gasping writhe and went rigid, its trousers darkened with urine and diarrhea. He suddenly remembered that he too was moving through a deadly atmosphere. He was stifling in the makeshift protective gear, breathing and rebreathing the same trapped air. He had only a few more seconds before he'd black out. He looked around again, trembling with rage. Where was the money? Where could it all have gone? Could the fat gambler, LaFontaine, could he have really taken all the winnings from the night with him?

Then he saw the safe. He crossed the hall quickly, hesitated, then reached out to twist the knob. Sweat squished in the rubber gloves. It was locked. Locked, and he had nothing with him that could open it. He had explosives, but they were back in the valise, back in his room.

Cursing silently, he sucked the heating air inside the bag through dry lips. He felt himself staggering. Was his vision dimming? They said that was the first sign—

He bent to the fallen men and turned their pockets out, fingered the wallets open with awkward rubber fingers. He stuffed the bills and change into the paper sack that had carried the grease and chain and gloves.

Then blinked, suddenly conscious that his nose was beginning to run, that his chest felt tight.

He had to leave. He had to leave *now*.

He kicked one of the bodies in impotent rage, stepped over it, and jerked the door open. A moment later he'd torn the bag off his head and was sucking and panting the fresh night air in and out, in and out. He scraped the grease off—careful, careful, the gloves must be discarded last—then the shirt. He snapped the strings and kicked the paper off his shoes and down into the alley.

Then stood clinging in helpless terror to the rail as the tightness in his chest increased and increased and his mouth suddenly and inexplicably filled with water. His eyes began to burn. He felt his hands start to shake.

Despite all his precautions it had reached him, a tiny droplet or whiff had penetrated his makeshift gear. He waited, trembling, hoping the antidote could counteract it.

Finally it did. The tightness slowly eased off, leaving him with a throbbing headache. Weak with reaction and relief, he let himself down the stairs step by step until he stood once again in the stinking alley.

He didn't know exactly how much money he had. He'd have to decontaminate it somehow before it would be safe even to count. But he knew it wasn't enough.

He found his jacket and pulled it on over his sweat-soaked undershirt. Disappointed, raging, he left the alley behind, and a door hanging open on four motionless and staring corpses.

———

Just before dawn he stood in the park again. Across the square and street the unlit White House rose behind its screen of ancient trees like a massive, faintly shining mausoleum. No cars or trolleys passed under the black sky. His vision was still darkened, as if by a sheet of black glass through which he peered. He stood motionless, waiting for enough light to see.

When it came he strolled slowly past the green metal trash container. He was exhausted, still shaky from aftereffects and tension, but now he forced all his senses back to alert. He scanned the rooftops for men with binoculars, checked the corners for suspicious loiterers or detectives. But in the early light he was the only man in Lafayette Park, as if no one else existed on a depopulated earth. Only on the far side of the black iron fence could he see activity, trucks and men, around the executive mansion, around the East Wing. Lights were on. Clearly something had happened. Could Fence have succeeded, could *he* be dead? He shook off the eerie feeling and turned and went back past the trash container. As he neared it his steps slowed. Then he knelt. Put his hands on his shoe, as if tying the laces.

His shoulder nudged the metal container up slightly, and his hand slid beneath its base.

He pushed the envelope unobtrusively into his pocket as he rose. He didn't look at it, just kept walking. He turned corners randomly, then doubled back. He encountered only one early riser, a middle-aged woman walking a small dog. Finally he slid open the door of a phone booth on G Street, propped the phone against his ear, and tore the note open behind his back.

A moment later the full lips tightened.

The attempt had failed. A man named Abrams had died, but not the President. Now Roosevelt's staff was planning to leave by train soon for Hyde Park. Security had been doubled.

The last sentence directed him to leave a weapon at their drop point, to be used in another attempt.

He sat motionless in the wooden booth, thinking.

Security had been doubled, Fence said. That meant he wouldn't be able to slip around at night as he had before. Even with access to the White House, it would be far more difficult to get close enough to kill the President.

But Fence, whoever he was, wanted to try again.

Krasov decided that whoever Fence was, he didn't trust him. And for a good reason. His shadowy and unknown accomplice didn't understand that killing Franklin Roosevelt was only half the plan. The other, most important half, was to have it blamed on the Soviets. Without that the murder was senseless, nothing more than vengeance for the Nazi hierarchy. Ivan Krasov had no objection to that, but it wasn't his goal.

But he couldn't tell Fence that, because Fence thought they were both working for the Communists.

He sat thinking for a long time, tapping a coin against the side of the phone booth, before he had his answer.

C H A P T E R 2 1

Thursday, March 29: The White House

T hought I'd find you here," Chief Tavelstead said. I blinked at him, searched for my wrist, then my watch. I'd obviously slept at last, because daylight bled grayly through the low ground-floor windows.

"I don't stand duty with you guys anymore, Chief."

"I know. But Mr. Hassett called down. Thought we might know where you were. He wants you."

"Hassett? Where?"

"Topside. I mean, upstairs."

I picked my grimy-collared shirt off the pile of dirty clothes around my bunk. Then stopped, eyeing the chief's.

When I got to the second floor I felt a little better, shaved and brushed, with a shower and a fresh, borrowed shirt. I noticed that the guard outside the President's quarters had been doubled. One of them was Hunley. I held my arms out from my sides as I went by him, inviting a search; he scowled.

The doors to the oval study were open. The secretary to the President was standing in the middle of the room, studying the floor. FDR was nowhere in sight. I cleared my throat. "Kennedy, sir."

The tall Vermonter glanced up. "Good morning, Lieutenant. I thought I'd best meet you before the President woke, and outline your duties."

I looked around. The room looked as littered in the daylight as it had night before last, in the dark, and smelled just as stale. Now I could see what I'd guessed at then. A large portrait of an imposing old lady—FDR's mother?—faced a studio print of a young Eleanor. Along with the naval prints I now saw a pull-down sheaf of roll maps, like they have in high school civics classrooms. On the desk—it was messy, all right—were paperweights, letters, newspapers, a wooden statue of Winston Churchill smoking a large cigar, and books. A guide to the U.S. Army, a dictionary of international slurs, *How to Win at Stud Poker* and a couple of mystery novels. Near the edge was the donkey statuette I'd picked up for a bludgeon the other night. The stacks under the windows were loose filing folders and letters, tied with string. The whole room looked as if a junior clerk had started to pack, been interrupted, and had never gotten back to it.

Hassett stood thin and stooped in a rusty-looking old gray suit and blue bow tie, looking toward the windows with his hands in his pockets. "If I may have your attention," he said patiently.

"Yes sir. Sorry, sir."

"Have you acted as an aide before, Lieutenant?"

"No, but I've done staff work."

"I was about to say, you'll find that working for the President is not like working for a senior military officer. It's more like being part of a family. The Boss will treat you as an individual. If you have problems, and he asks, don't feel shy about telling him. He's the best boss I've ever had, and the best friend.

"One thing that will be the same as the other job is security. Nothing that happens here should be mentioned on the outside. Are you married?"

"No," I said, surprised, but then, Hassett didn't know me that well. "I'm not married."

"That's good. We may need you after hours. Now, another thing. He may occasionally ask your opinion on certain matters. If that should happen, needless to say, you're not here to advance any personal or political platform. Give him your opinion, if you have one, but don't let him draw you into an argument."

"Aye aye, sir."

"He likes things casual. Hates formality and protocol. Even when there's royalty staying. By the way, may have some arriving tonight. Aides are expected to be available to make up a party. But don't forget, you're here to work. Don't get familiar. You'll pick up a nickname. But never forget, he is the President; and that's how you'll always address him—as 'Mr. President'."

Hassett looked at me. "How much do you weigh, Lieutenant?"

"I'm down a little."

"Well, he doesn't use his braces anymore. You may have to assist him in getting from his wheelchair to his armchair and so forth."

I thought of my back. "As long as I don't have to lift him."

"You shouldn't. All right, let's go on. The President doesn't like to be alone. He'll be dependent on you for simple things. If he drops a cigarette, pick it up instantly, and feel the rug—he's concerned about fire. Makes sense to me, it could be difficult getting him out. But you'll notice he'll never complain. So you'll have to figure out what he needs and try to help without being asked."

A high-pitched coughing came from next door, muffled by the walls. Hassett glanced toward it as I asked him, "Sir, can you give me some idea of the daily routine?"

"It's changed a bit lately. Doctor's orders, to build him up, get him some rest. He gets up around eight-thirty or nine. Has breakfast in bed. Prettyman dresses and shaves him."

"Will I be here that early?"

"No. You probably won't see him till around eleven. But be here in the study around ten in case he's early. He'll work for two hours in the morning, either in the study or the Oval Office. You'll be with him then, when he goes through his correspondence and his appointments. Lunch will be at one. No business, usually just a tray in his office."

"What about meals? Does he need help with those?"

Hassett frowned. "No. He's perfectly capable of feeding himself. You'll have to sense whether he wants you around then or not.

"We try to get him to take a one-hour nap after lunch. Sometimes that works, sometimes not. He just ignores us when we tell him it's time, and . . . there's a limit to what you can press him to do. He should stop work around three, but sometimes he goes until five. He'll have one drink then, then Commander Fox will do his massage and he'll have some ultraviolet light.

"Dinner is at eight, but usually he'll have a tray in bed. He'll read a detective story or work on his stamp collection, then turn in. He's got to conserve his strength.

"All right, Lieutenant. You'll have to feel your way from here. Any questions?"

I hesitated, then decided: If I was ever going to ask, this was the time. "Sir, I've seen the President before. He doesn't look very good to me. What do you think about his condition?"

Hassett thought. At last he said, in a low voice, "He is slipping away from us, and there will come a point when no earthly power can keep him here."

The next moment he sent me a guilty glance. "I'm sorry . . . I know some think he looks better without the extra weight, but . . . I still fear for him. The weaker he gets, the harder he works. As if he's racing time. He knows he's got to sell the United Nations to Congress, and that's not going to be easy." He gave a classic Vermont shrug. "But I'm the White House worrywort."

"Dr. Bruenn says he's in good shape?"

"Bruenn? Bruenn doesn't talk. I meant Admiral McIntire. He says that aside from his sinuses, the President's in better shape than most men his age."

"Yes sir," I said.

"Now, you're a Catholic, aren't you?"

I said I was, and Hassett nodded. "So am I, and Grace Tully is, and Dorothy Brady. So you're not alone."

"Does he have a problem with Catholics?" I asked him.

"The Boss? Actually, he hardly ever talks about religion." Hassett considered. "But occasionally you'll get a little self-righteousness, a hint that, oh, 'this is a Protestant country, the pioneers were Protestant, and the Jews and Catholics are here on sufferance.' Then the next minute he's talking about his friend Archbishop Spellman. But I think he's got a relationship with God—a perfect trust and acceptance. Do you?"

"Oh, sure," I said.

"It's too bad he's not a member of Holy Mother Church. Though he'd never have been elected. I doubt we'll ever have a Catholic president in this country. Al Smith—"

Hassett stopped, halting at the verge of loquaciousness. "Don't argue religion with him. I know I'm repeating myself, but we have got to keep things low-key and pleasant. He's got to get some rest."

The clock on the desk chimed, and Hassett started. "All right, he'll be out soon. Oh, and one other thing: We're thinking about going to Hyde Park."

Interesting, I thought. Hyde Park, New York, was FDR's boyhood home. Major Abrams's death had shaken things up. Well, that was fine with me. If we could cut down on the number of people around FDR, that had to decrease the chance the assassin was one of them.

A click of an opening lock, and the door to FDR's bedroom swung open. I turned, as did Hassett, but could see only the empty hospital bed, sheets thrown back. The head had been cranked up higher than the foot. The morning papers lay scattered over it, except for one front page which lay slowly uncrumpling itself on the rug.

"Who's that out there? Deacon? Come on in, come in."

"Good morning, Mr. President," said Hassett.

I followed Hassett toward the attached bath. Roosevelt was sitting in his wheelchair, head back. Prettyman scraped the last bit of foam off, holding the loose skin under his jaw taut with one hand, and turned away to prepare a hot towel. I heard a harsh panting, and looked down. From beside the railed bathtub Fala eyed us through black, shaggy bangs.

FDR opened his eyes and pointed to the toilet. "Have a seat on the can, Deacon, but remember your pants are up. We're on shave number six, on this blade. How are you? Giving our new lieutenant a grammar lesson?" To me: "He's my Bartlett, my Buckle, and my Roget. To know him, as Ben Jonson said, is a liberal education."

I leaned against the jamb as Hassett said gravely, "You mean Steele, sir. Speaking of Lady Elizabeth Hastings. 'Though her mein carries much more invitation than command, to behold her is an immediate check to loose behavior; to love her is a liberal education.'"

"I rather think that proves my point. Ready to assume your duties, Johnny-Kay?"

Hassett lifted an eyebrow at me. "Yes sir," I said. "You're in a gay mood today."

Prettyman dropped the towel and the tenor voice came muffled from beneath steaming cotton. "This morning, when I woke, the first thing I smelled was the wisteria. It's right below me, you know, on the South Portico. What a way to wake up! Perhaps we should take a drive, Deacon, and see whether the cherry blossoms are on our side or the Emperor's today."

"A drive would be good for you, Mr. President. Shall I set it up for after lunch?"

Prettyman whipped the towel off. A shadow flitted across Roosevelt's eyes, making him look like a schoolboy reminded his day is not his own. "Perhaps when it gets a bit warmer," he muttered. "I can't wait for it to warm up . . . Bill, I want to see Ed Stettinius and his boys today. First thing after Byrnes."

"Yes sir."

"I wish we could go sailing," Roosevelt said wistfully, still looking toward the window. "It seems like forever since I've held a tiller in my hands. Do you sail, Johnny?"

"Yes sir," I said. "Racing out of Hyannis Port, Wiannos mostly."

"One-designs. Gaff rigs."

"Yes, sir. I was in the Intercollegiate Regatta my sophomore year. My brother Joe had one of Harvard's boats and I had the other. We kept hauled out to leeward and did pretty good. Joe took a second and I took third, and the Crimson took first over Dartmouth by seven-and-a-half points."

FDR swung his chair left, then right. Even talking about the sea seemed to perk him up. "I recall one incident when a schoolmate and I, one Lathrop Brown, were out cruising in a knockabout off the coast of Maine. We put into Camden, and I boarded a craft commanded by an old Yankee skipper. I asked him what cargo he carried, and he gave me a look like the Deacon just gave you. 'Potatoes,' the skipper said. I opined that it was strange to be importing potatoes into Maine, whereupon the old man grew suspicious. I meanwhile had looked around a bit and remarked that my family had had long experience in the Chinese trade, and I added, 'It smells like you are carrying Chinese potatoes.'

" 'Young man,' said the skipper, waving a fist under my nose, 'you are too goddamned nosy.' He didn't dare kill me because Brown was watching from our boat, but he was smuggling Chinamen, all right. In those days it was a hundred dollars a head, smuggled into the country. Yes, when I retire, I think I shall write a history of American piracy. All our great fortunes were founded on it in one form or another. I admit to some opium trading in the Delano family. Old General Vanderbilt—did he ever say that, I wonder, about 'The public be damned?'—I shall have to tell you a story about my father and the Vanderbilts. It's just so difficult to tell without making him out to be a snob. And my father was no snob."

Suddenly I wondered if FDR was really talking about my father, and me. But instead of going down that track he veered into a story about scooping the Yale paper on the Harvard-Yale game when he was editor of the *Crimson*. I traded him one about the Mucker's Club I'd put together at Choate. He said I must have a lot of stories from being out in the Pacific.

"Yes sir," I said. "You heard the Mae West one? Mae West was walking down the street and bumped into President Roosevelt. He said, 'Hello, who are you?' She said, 'Mae West—who are you?' He said, 'Franklin Roosevelt.' She said, 'Well, Franklin, I've heard some interesting things about you. If you can give me half the screwing you gave the people of the United States, come up and see me sometime.' "

Hassett looked horrified, but FDR guffawed. "This young fellah has promise, Deacon, but you're going to have to teach him diplomacy. He can't talk like that to the President! Or can he?"

Suddenly he was out the door, rolling the chair along with lunging strokes of his powerful arms. Fala trotted after him, barking twice, as if announcing his movement. "What a grand morning," Roosevelt boomed, but I saw that though his tone was still light his mouth had taken on a grim set.

I stepped in and took the back of his chair. As soon as I touched it he released the wheels and leaned back, content to direct. The buzzer sounded out in the hall, telling everyone in the Executive Mansion that the President was on the move. "Take it easy through the door . . . there you go. . . . We'll see everybody in the Oval Office today," he called back to Hassett as we rolled into the corridor.

—

There was just enough room in the little elevator for him, the rear wheels, and me. Fala had halted as we got in, and looked down at us through the grillwork as we hummed and creaked downward. On the way FDR pointed out the woodwork, which came from the Old South Meeting House, where the Tea Party had been plotted.

Bruenn, Reilly, and Admiral Brown stood waiting as we rolled out into the ground floor corridor. And three more agents. I knew names now, Hunley and Long and McMullin. FDR waved gaily and said to me, "Hold it a sec." I braked the chair as the surgeon general of the United States, holding a napkin under the presidential chin, dripped three nose drops into each nostril as FDR sniffed. Roosevelt kept up a steady string of jokes and comments.

There were three other guys farther down the corridor, one unloading a laundry cart, the others pulling cases of food off a hand truck. I looked at FDR and McIntire, nodded to Reilly, and went over. I said to the laundry guy, "Hey, pal."

"Yeah, Mac?" he said, not stopping as he stacked sack after sack on his cart, checking each tag with a practiced flip of his wrist, not even looking toward the President. A marine stood not five feet from him, watching every move, one arm draped over a holstered .45. "Whatcha want?"

"I turned in some shirts a couple days ago. Gave them to Lillian. How long's it take to turn those around?"

He straightened and dragged his arm across his forehead. He had a round, innocent-looking face and slightly protuberant, clear blue eyes. "What, you talkin' white shirts? A couple days."

"Can you check on them? My initials are on them, JFK, and my serial number. You find them, I'm in the clinic over there." I pointed across the corridor.

"No sweat, buddy. I'll take care of it." He went back to work, straw-colored hair stuck to his forehead. I nodded and went back to FDR.

A sneeze, a wave of direction, and on we rolled, toward the West Wing. "A little faster, Johnny-Kay," the swaying head muttered, and I stepped up the pace.

When we bumped over the threshold into the Oval Office the windows were open slightly and the air smelled fresh and cold. I looked where Abrams had fallen, but saw no sign of anything untoward. The floor had been freshly vacuumed, and all the furniture gleamed—freshly polished, I assumed, to remove the traces of fingerprint powder. A lighter spot showed where the carpet had been scrubbed.

Grace Tully stood waiting, giving me a questioning look. I said nothing, just wheeled the President to his desk. It took a couple of tries to get the wheelchair situated, but when it was in position he reached over to the heavy armchair, lifted his body with his arms, and swung himself over without any assistance from me. Meanwhile Reilly stood by the windows, checking out the fence detail. He bulked big as ever, but slumped shoulders and five o'clock shadow told me he hadn't slept since Ed checked out.

I recollected the President and bent, but he was already lifting his legs, one at a time, with his hands. He placed glossy black shoes on a wooden support under the desk, leaned back, and said, "Reach me a cigarette, Lieutenant. And one for yourself."

"Thanks, Mr. President. I don't smoke."

"Do you want me to keep track of those today, Mr. President?"

"Oh, Duchess, let an old dog have his treats. A ciggy and a drink never hurt a man." The match flared and he inhaled, coughed, coughed harder, exhaled. "What have we got red-tagged today? Tell Hacky to get Daniels and Ed Stettinius on the line. Did you see that article in the *Herald-Tribune?*"

Tully saw me hesitating, and looked toward a chair in a side office, which also held a desk and typing stand. The door was open, and I could see everything, which was probably the idea; then I could come in and get him anything he wanted.

FDR and Tully went over the morning's mail, bills to be signed, correspondence. Then she came out and turned on the radio and went to work, leaving him at his desk. The phone rang eight times in the hour I sat there. Tully forwarded two to FDR. The others she rerouted. On the calls he took, I listened as his voice sank, then rose. He wasn't joking now. I wondered what it was all about, but couldn't hear.

At eleven I heard footsteps, then Crim's voice, orotund and solemn. "Mr. President: The Honorable James Byrnes."

Tully closed the door and started rattling away at her Royal. Harry James was on the radio. I belatedly remembered I hadn't had any breakfast. I glanced at her, decided not to interrupt, and got up and went out.

The next room was decorated with stuffed fish and photos of the President hauling them in. McMullin glanced up sharply from a couch, then went back to his monitor state, arms folded, lower lip thrust out as he guarded the back entrance to the Oval Office. Long must have been outside the main doors, in the corridor. No sign or scent of food. I checked the closed door again, then tried down the hall. Secretaries, noise, coffee. I got two doughnuts and went back to my post.

At eleven-twenty-five Tully's buzzer went off, playing a little shave-and-a-haircut-two-bits tune. The door stayed open this time. A minute or two later another Navy lieutenant came in. We looked at each other, then he introduced himself: Will Rigdon, one of the official stenographers. His eyes ate my combat ribbons.

At eleven-thirty it was Crim again. "Mr. President: The Secretary of State; The Undersecretary of State; Assistant Secretary MacLeish; Assistant Secretary Dunn; Assistant Secretary Clayton; Mr. Charles Bohlen."

Rigdon, a pencil stuck behind his ear, went in. I was ready to eavesdrop, but the door was too thick. I could hear raised voices, but I couldn't make out the words over the swing music and the typewriter, or whose they were.

Reilly came in. He and Tully shot the bull a while, then he looked at me. "How's the kid working out?"

"He's a pleasant face." Tully smiled at me. Fiftyish, with crimped hair and pearls, she had an easy, slightly sad smile.

"Got a sec, Jack?"

So it was first names now. "Yeah—Mike," I said, and followed him out into the Fish Room. McMullin glanced up, then went back to studying a stuffed marlin.

"Autopsy report on Abrams." The big agent tapped the pocket of his blazer.

"What's it say?"

"Same thing Bruenn did last night. 'Cause of death: Undetermined.'"

I said something to indicate surprise. Reilly nodded glumly. "Yeah. And, given that, I've got to assume it's poison. Even though we don't know how, who, or what."

"What did the Untouchables say?"

"You were there. I don't expect any breakthroughs from that quarter."

"You don't like Hoover's boys."

"They don't cooperate. ONI, OSS, they trade information. FBI, you've got to drag everything out of them. Like pulling a cat's molars. And there's something screwy in the political department. J. Edgar smells Reds under every mattress. Don't get me started on that. The last thing we need is him in our shorts."

"I see you doubled the guards."

"Yeah."

"But that's not going to help if the threat's from inside. We ought to move him."

"Of course we've got to move him! The question is, where?"

"Hassett said Hyde Park."

"Great, but I can't pull up stakes on his say-so. I wanted to get moving tonight, but it's too late for that. We could do it tomorrow, but that might not happen either. It takes time to pack and set up the railroad timetables."

"What's the problem? Just pack up and go."

"*He* doesn't want to go to Hyde Park."

"Well, then, how about that place in Georgia, where he went for his polio?"

"Too far. He's only been there once since the war started. Shangri-La would be better."

"Where?"

"It's in the Maryland mountains. We set it up in case D.C. got bombed. But he doesn't want to leave the White House." Reilly got up and paced from the marlin to the sailfish. "I can order him to go, but damn it, I don't feel right doing that. Shit, he's the President, after all."

"I think it's a good idea," I said, "For what my opinion's worth."

"Why?" Reilly asked me.

I told him my angle, that the fewer people he had around him, the lower the chances one of them was the assassin. "I'm thinking about household help, domestic staff," I finished up. "The personal staff's been close to him from way before the war; a lot of them from when he was governor of New York. I can't see a sleeper planted that far back."

"They could be blackmailed. Family reasons. Vices."

"That could happen to anybody. You guys too," I couldn't help adding. "Did you ever find Rivers?"

"No."

"He just what, disappeared? That's funny."

"Yeah, funny as a crutch."

"You had no idea he was queer?"

"It's not always easy to tell," said McMullin, looking at me too pointedly, I thought.

The door opened, and Tully and Rigdon came out of the Oval Office. Through it I saw Stettinius, Archy MacLeish, Chip Bohlen, and a couple other State types standing silently as FDR lashed them with a last few words. "Get it back to me by two o'clock. Let's get this out in the open, right now." Stettinius nodded quickly.

When they left I went in to see if FDR needed anything. He was leaning back in his armchair and his face looked cadaverous. I couldn't believe how quickly it had changed. I stood in front of him for a second or two. Then, when he didn't move, felt alarmed. "Mr. President," I said.

His eyes opened. They looked empty. He looked not at me but through me, and his mouth opened slowly, sagging down.

"Miss Tully," I said, scared now.

But the next second his mouth closed and his chin came back up. Only now I saw the strain that went into it. Then the effort too was concealed and he looked relaxed again, but very tired. His hand lifted, gestured toward a side table. Instead of handing him the cigarette, I lit it myself. The raw smoke made my eyes water as I passed it to him.

"Don't smoke, eh, Johnny-Kay?"

"Stunts your growth, my dad says, sir."

"Old Joe," FDR said and seemed about to start a story, but instead he seemed again to lose a thread; he muttered, "Can't get along with him, just can't get along." Behind me Grace Tully said brightly, covering his hesitation, "Mr. Daniels on the line again. He says the reporters are pressing him for the story on the voting situation. They also want to know about Major Abrams, whether they can release the story."

"Mike?" Roosevelt shouted. "Mike!"

Reilly leaned in. "Sir, I recommend against it. For now."

"Tell him to keep their lips buttoned. We'll talk about it when we get back from Hyde Park, all right?"

I turned to see if Reilly'd heard that. He had, and gave me a wink as he gestured McMullin in. He whispered to him, then pointed him out the door.

"The Ambassador of Great Britain; Mr. Oliver Lyttleton; Colonel J. J. Llewellyn," Crim boomed. I checked again that the President had all he needed, and left the room.

CHAPTER 22

At noon Krasov was driving back to the central city in the delivery truck, taking a break after doing the hotel route. He felt ragged, fatigued, but he could put up with that. He'd put up with a lot to get here. A sleepless night wasn't that bad.

He'd already been to the White House on the morning delivery. Just as he'd feared, security was airtight now. An armed serviceman had escorted him into and out of the laundry room, and marines and White House police lined the corridors. He'd caught a glimpse of FDR getting nose drops, surrounded by his staffers. But there'd been no chance of a shot, even if he'd dared bring in a gun. Not if he expected any possibility of getting out afterward.

A hundred and ten dollars sat tucked in his billfold, still damp, cleaned into harmlessness at the laundry with live steam and a bleach solution. Not the haul he'd expected. There'd been thousands on the table, the bank for a whole gambling and numbers house. He still felt enraged when he thought about it. But at least he had enough to live on for a while. Enough to pay for his room, to get around. He was still waiting for his first pay as a deliveryman.

On the other hand, he was still alive. After quite a few people had tried to kill him.

And maybe that meant something, Krasov thought, pouting in concentration as he passed Mount Vernon Square and started looking for a parking place. He spent most of his time thinking about how to get to his target. Visualizing problems and challenges, and his tactics and responses. And that was as it should be.

But he was still determined to escape afterward. Occasionally his mind moved on to wonder what would happen then.

He figured he'd stay in the U.S. after the war. Even if Communism was defeated, he saw no reason to go back to Russia. And Germany would be laid waste for generations; it would be a hundred years before they even had running water again. No, the good old U.S. of A. was where his future lay. But what could he do? Neither his NKVD nor his SS training were exactly designed to fit him for a civilian job. On the other hand, surely there were things he knew how to do that would come in handy in America.

Cooking, for example. He'd often whipped up bitki or shashlik for Kaganovich; "Iron Lazar" had been careful about who prepared his food, with good reason. It was always easy to find a place as a dishwasher or cook's assistant. But where? Maybe out West, on the frontier, Nevada or Montana, one of those wide square states with Indians. If only he had his share of the operations money! Not only would all this be so much easier, he could have bought a restaurant afterward with what was left. But without money he'd have to start small. Work his way up to chef, and sooner or later have his own place. He'd need clean ID. So he'd have to find someone who resembled him— someone, preferably, without family—and kill him.

As he mused, his hand went out from time to time to steady the leather valise that rode on the seat beside him.

In the note, Fence had told him to leave the weapon, if he could come up with one, near their prearranged drop point at one. He parked the truck on Franklin Park and lugged the valise two blocks to Lafayette Park. He rested on the bench for a while, reading a copy of that morning's *Post.* Looking for any mention of LaFontaine's, but there was nothing. Probably too soon. He'd pick up a copy of the *Star;* it would probably make the evening edition. He shook the paper out and folded it over, and found himself looking at heavy black brogans scuffed brown at the toes. His eyes rose slowly to striped pants, a blue suit, and a badge.

"You know, he's from here?" the cop said.

"What?"

"Al Jolson. Isn't that what you were humming? He's from here. Son of a rabbi here in town, old Morris Yoelson."

"Oh. Yeah, is that so? I didn't know that."

"Found your brother yet?"

Krasov cleared his throat. "Uh—yeah, matter of fact."

"He showed up from Norfolk?"

"That's right."

"Then what you still doing here? And what's with the uniform?"

Krasov saw him looking at his shoes, then at his hands, then at the Hahn & Hurja trousers and tunic. He had heavy jowls and an Irish nose, a paunch; just a beat cop, probably retired but for the war; but a .38 rode his hip, and a nickeled whistle dangled on a chain. He cleared his throat again, forcing his voice to stay casual. "I got a job driving for the cleaners."

"Just like that?"

He shrugged. "I saw an ad, I thought, hey, this is a nice town. So I went down and they hired me."

"A deliveryman, huh? Where's your truck?"

"Over on Fourteenth. But this is a good place to take a break, eat lunch," he said easily. "Say, what you think of these Japs? You been reading this, about Okinawa? Now they're diving their airplanes into our ships. Suicide planes. Can you believe it?"

"They should gas 'em," said the cop.

Krasov couldn't stop the newspaper trembling in his hands. Was the policeman goading him? Were they about to move in? With the valise right beside him there'd be no chance of talking his way out. Not with what it contained. He lowered the paper deliberately to his lap. "Ya think so?"

"Shit, yeah. What are we going to do with them after the war? I say it's open season; we're smart, we'll get rid of as many of those yellow monkeys right now as we can."

"You might have a point there," said Krasov.

But the cop didn't pursue the subject of Japs. Instead he put his scuffed heavy shoe up on the bench, right beside Krasov's valise. Krasov looked at it.

"How about I see some ID, bud," the cop suggested.

He got out his wallet and held it out. The patrolman knitted gray brows over the draft card, then perused the driver's license. Finally he handed them back. "Okay," he grunted. "Just checking."

"No sweat," said Krasov. "There's a war on, right?"

He looked back at the paper, and after a long moment, the cop swung his leg down and moved on, heavily, as if his feet hurt, swinging his nightstick idly at the pigeons. Krasov stayed still, though, just as if sweat wasn't running down the middle of his back.

Finally he got up and strolled off, casual, leaving the valise with its cargo sitting under the bench.

He walked to the corner of New York and Jackson, then hesitated, struck by a thought. He could still see the bench. Fence couldn't leave it out in plain sight for long. He'd have to be watching, would have to claim it within a few minutes. He could see the so-far-shadowy figure he was working with. And who, if everything went right, would end up kicking at the end of a rope.

Because if he got FDR, the authorities would have to come up with an assassin. Have to have somebody to pin it on. And a Red—that would put the cap on it, all right.

He struggled with the desire to wait. But instead yielded reluctantly to professionalism, turned and walked toward a newsstand. He bought a copy of *Liberty* and three Hershey bars and started wolfing them, one after the other. A moment later he was lost in the crowd.

CHAPTER 23

Friday, March 30: The White House

I stuck with FDR till he turned in, then went down to the West Wing to help pack.

Grace told me over the boxes of files about the President's travels since the war began. He'd been to Newfoundland, Quebec, Cairo, Mexico, Honolulu, Alaska, Teheran, and Yalta, made scores of inspection tours of war plants, camps, and bases, and on top of that conducted a full-scale campaign in 1944. Even when people thought he was at the White House he was often at Hyde Park or Shangri-La. His security and communications followed him wherever he went.

"Yeah, Ed Abrams told me that," I said.

They were still packing when I begged off at eleven and went back to the clinic. I was out on my feet. But the door was locked, and nobody answered. Fuck, I thought. Then I noticed an envelope taped to the jamb. LT KENNEDY, it read.

A key was inside. Yay, Chagall. I used the shower, pulled out some fresh sheets, and was about to toss myself on the cot when a thought struck me. It was the first time I'd been alone in the clinic.

Snooper time. But when I turned the light on in Bruenn's office I could see right away I wasn't going to get much. Everything was locked, even the files. The padlocks looked flimsy, but I didn't see any way to explain it if I broke them. I tried to read the labels of the drugs in the glass-fronted cabinet, but that got me nowhere. Most of them had droppers, like sinus medications.

Next stop: Chagall's desk. Unlocked, so I went through it without much hope of finding anything. Mostly it was just personal gear, web belts and shoeshine kit and stuff.

Suddenly a thought hit me. I went back to Bruenn's office and looked again, very carefully this time, at a wall chart I'd noticed. It was on graph paper with numbers along the edge. Small Xs had been marked on it, with dates. A pencil line connected them.

There was no label, but it didn't take a Ph.D. to figure that this was a blood pressure chart, and that the pressure was rising very fast indeed.

I looked at the bottles again. This time I took down some of the names. Spelling was never my forte, but I made sure I got these right.

I turned the light off, and turned in.

When I opened my eyes I could hear Bruenn talking in the next room. The hiss and clink of a sterilizer. I stretched, then swung my arm up to check my watch. I sat bolt upright and squinted at the bulkhead. Yes, God damn it, that clock said ten-oh-nine too. I threw my blues on and tore out.

The bedroom door was open. Prettyman's round face looked up surprised from stripping the bed. "He done gone down already to work, Lieutenant," he boomed. "Mister Hassett, he took him down. He kind of hot about you not being here, too."

I got to the Oval Office to find the doors closed and two MPs outside them, holding carbines at port arms. I ducked into Tully's office. The Andrews Sisters were crooning away today. She was at the typewriter, going a mile a minute and occasionally glancing at a steno pad. When she saw me she slid a file folder over it.

"Who's in there?" I asked her.

"It's off the record."

"You can tell me."

"I guess I can. It's the gold braid. Arnold and King and Marshall."

"What's in the letter?"

"You don't need to know."

"Hot stuff, huh?"

"There are things I have to type in this job I'll never be able to forget, Lieutenant."

That sounded so depressing I muttered, "I'll be right back, if he needs me," and turned to go to the head. Instead Hassett appeared in the doorway. His eyes widened as he caught sight of me. I sighed. The next couple of minutes went very slowly.

"One more time, Kennedy. You're late just once more, and that's it. And." Hassett looked me up and down. "I'm not in the Navy, but I believe your tie is on backwards. Was Admiral Brown right about you? He said you drank." He leaned closer.

"No, sir." Christ, at least I was clear on that count.

"Now, Bill, he's just a boy. It's only his second day on the job."

"He's not a boy, he's twenty-seven. He's got to be punctual and neat, Grace. He's the President's aide, for Chr—for Heaven's sake."

They sounded like George and Gracie. While he was diverted by her flank attack, I slipped out to the head, fixed my tie, and buttoned my blouse right.

When I went back, Hassett was slumped in my chair. Tully was typing again and at the same time telling him to be sure to check with Mrs. Nesbitt and Mrs. Helm about the dinner for Princess Juliana, and to make sure the place cards were right. I was looking at the still-closed doors when the phone rang. Grace snatched it, listened, said, "Yes, he's here," and held it out. "For you."

Shoot, who knew I was here? I said, "Uh—hello?"

"Jack?"

It was my father. "Oh. Hi, Dad," I said.

"How are you doing? You're right there in his office, aren't you?"

"Yeah. Right here."

"The son of a bitch. How are things going?"

I glanced at Hassett. "Okay."

"I hear there's eighteen women in Washington for every man. How are you making out sex-wise?"

"We need to keep that line clear," said Tully.

"I don't have too much time for it right now, Dad. Look, there's a conference about to break, we got to keep this short. Oh—wait—there is one thing you could have somebody from your office do for me—"

"Hold on a minute, it wasn't easy to get through long distance. Have you talked to him? What's the situation?"

"Uh, we've talked a couple of times." I remembered FDR's complaint: "Can't get along with him, can't get along." "He hasn't said anything about you," I lied.

"Well, how about you? Have you thought about what we talked about?"

"Dad, I've got to get off the line."

"What is it you want me to do? You said you wanted—"

"Yeah. Two things, actually. Do you remember the name of the guy you were talking to up at the Lahey Clinic when I was in there? Not Poppen, the other guy—Dr. Kenmore? Thanks. Have you got a number?"

"I'll have one of the boys call you back with it. Jack, it's not too soon to start building an organization—"

"Look, Dad, I'm really sorry, but they're going to cut us off." My fingers hovered above the cradle.

"You said two things. What else?"

"Yeah—where are you calling from? New York or—"

"I'm still in Palm Beach."

"Good. I gave Bobby some of my gear to keep before I went out to the Pacific. He's probably got it stuffed in a closet. A canvas musette bag, got a padlock on it. Can you have somebody throw that on the train? Don't put my name on it, though. Send it to me care of—care of Ed Abrams, 1343 Braddock Road, Alexandria."

He read it back, but didn't sound happy about it. I said fast, before he could object, "Tell you what, I'll write a letter as soon as I have a minute. What do you hear from Kick? How's Mom and the Tedster—" I hit the button, cutting myself off in midsentence, and exhaled and gave the handset back to Grace. She shot me a razor glance and hung up. Hassett looked at me strangely too.

The meeting broke up, and through the open doors I saw Marshall and Arnold. A map was up on an easel. I stared at it, my breath just about stopping, for one long second before a bird colonel stepped in front and flipped it closed.

Lettered across the bottom was OLYMPIC—DOWNFALL. I recognized the southern coast of Kyushu, the southernmost home island of Japan. The chart had been taped to show transit lanes, amphibious operating areas, and the main assault lanes for a massive invasion.

When I went in Hap Arnold, ears sticking out below his crew cut, was talking in low tones with Marshall at the door. Their faces were somber. King was already gone, but a familiar figure stood beside the President. Admiral Leahy's bushy eyebrows knitted into a gray squall line as he gave me the once-over.

"Thanks, Bill. Continue—continue the planning process," FDR said, but it was little more than a whisper. The President seemed to have shrunk in his chair. Leahy slid a folder from FDR's desk, nodded curtly to me, and left.

"Can I get you something, sir?"

"Glass of water," he muttered. "A million."

"Sorry, Mr. President?"

"Nothing, Johnny." He forced a terrible smile and bent his head to help the glass to his lips, the way I'd seen alcoholics with the shakes drink. Water ran down his chin and made a dark patch on his pants, on his immobile, shrunken legs, concealed from the generals by the heavy walnut desk.

"You know, I remembered another story they told in the Solomons," I said. "It was about a guy in my unit, a cook. He wanted to get to the front lines and shoot a Jap. He kept bitching and moaning about it. So finally we gave him an old Reising gun and pointed him toward the lines. A couple days later he came back. 'You get your Jap?' we asked him. He said no. We asked him why not. He said, 'Well, they were out there shouting. One of them yelled, 'To hell with Babe Ruth.' I shouted back, 'To hell with Hirohito.' He shouted, 'To hell with Woody Guthrie.' I shouted, 'To hell with Tojo.' I saw the top of his helmet coming up and I drew a bead. Then he popped up and shouted, 'To hell with Franklin and Eleanor.'

" 'So did you get him?' we asked.

" 'Hell, no,' he said. 'I didn't shoot. I'm a Republican too.' "

FDR smiled. I got him a cigarette and let him light it. I felt like going on. I felt like saying, If you're worried about casualties in Japan, sir, remember North Africa came off light. D-Day came off okay. The boys know their stuff. But I didn't.

Tully in the doorway. "Your congressional delegation."

FDR took a deep breath and pushed himself up in the chair. "Send them in, Gracie." He looked at the window and muttered to me: "Stick around. You might enjoy this."

"Mr. President: The Vice President; the Speaker of the House; Senator Alben W. Barkley; Senator Arthur Vandenberg; Congressman John W. McCormack; Congressman Joseph Martin; Congressman Lyndon Johnson."

I helped move seats into a semicircle around the President's desk as he leaned forward, shaking hands, greeting each man by his first name. Harry Truman was a natty shrimp with Coke-bottle glasses and a lavender bow tie. I nodded to McCormack, whom I knew from Massachusetts, and Barkley. They nodded gravely back, but didn't seem to recognize me. Crim closed the doors.

"How about a little tonic, boys?" said FDR, and I saw why he wanted me there. "I think most of you see Dr. Bourbon, don't you?"

When they all had their glasses—except Martin, who refused with a curt shake of his head—I went back and stood beside Reilly, out of sight.

FDR led off, leaning back and telling them how glad he was to see them again. At last Barkley said, breaking in, "Mr. President, we hoped we could talk about the Polish situation, and the Russian question. There are some points about it we needed to bring up with you."

"Alben, I know there are questions, and of course I stand ready to satisfy you at any time. But let me say a few things first."

"Of course, Mr. President," said Vandenberg.

"Some people want the U.S. to win this war, as long as England loses. Some people want us to win as long as Russia loses. And some people don't care who wins as long as Roosevelt loses. But I want all the Allies to win, and the rest of the world too.

"Speaking in all frankness, gentlemen, that will be in your hands. The decision of the Senate will determine the fate of the world for generations to come. Unless the halls of Congress concur in and support the decisions reached by the executive branch, this war will not lead to the peace we fought for. I'm not saying whatever plan we adopt at San Francisco will be perfect. It will have to be amended, as we had to amend the Constitution. Sometimes we even have to amend the amendments."

The split was on party lines on that one; the Democrats laughed, the Republicans didn't. Roosevelt went on. "The United Nations should spell the end of alliances, secret treaties, spheres of influence, balance of power—all those expedients that have been tried for centuries, and failed. We have to substitute a universal organization, with the power to keep the peace."

Vandenberg said, "Uh, as Alben said, Mr. President, we're concerned about Poland. Could you explain about the commission? There's confusion among the members as to exactly how—"

"The commission will oversee the broadening of the provisional Warsaw government. Then, as soon as possible, elections will be held."

"What's Churchill think?"

Roosevelt said blandly, "We're in communication."

McCormack said: "Mr. President, on paper the Polish deal looks fine. But is it accurate to say that we may get less than full implementation, simply because the Russians are in possession on the ground?"

"That's pure speculation," said FDR. "I believe Uncle Joe will live up to his agreements. By the way—do you know, he speaks a little English? Or he thinks he does. He has exactly four phrases. They are, 'So what,' 'You said it,' 'The toilet is over there,' and 'What the hell goes on here.'" The congressmen smiled but no one laughed. "There are . . . details we may quibble about. But I don't believe they're worth endangering the alliance over."

Martin said, "There's anger on the Hill about this three-vote situation for the Russians, Mr. President."

"That's going to be a tall order to sell in Texas, Mr. President," said the lanky fellow in the rear. Lyndon Johnson. He sounded like a hick cowboy.

"Boys, I still think I can argue him out of that when we get down to brass tacks. But you know, I just don't see that as a stumbling block. Stalin won't live forever. Over time, if we treat them firmly but fairly, I think we can turn them away from dictatorship toward a free society."

The Republican kept boring in. "What about this UN organization? It sounds like a surrender of sovereignty to me."

"Really, Joe, would you say that a policeman could be very effective if, when he saw someone breaking into a house, he had to go call a town meeting before he could arrest the felon? We have to endow this body with authority to act."

Truman said, "I read a good deal of history, Mr. President. I think if we and the Russians had joined the League of Nations after the Great War, there might never have been a second one."

"Harry, I can't exactly disagree; but that's crystal-ball type of stuff, you might want to check with Henry Wallace on it."

"And what you're saying about the Russians, I guess, is that you'd rather have them on the inside of the tent pissing out, than on the outside of the tent pissing in."

"Really. *Re*-ah-ly. I think you've just put it in a nutshell, Harry."

Martin sat forward, but Roosevelt went on. "Joe, Arthur, I invited you here to convince you that the UN must not be a party issue, any more than this has been a party war. I've tried to accommodate you gentlemen since Pearl Harbor. The New Deal went on hold. Stimson and Knox are Republicans. And Art, you and Harold Stassen are going to represent us at San Francisco. Fear is a luxury we cannot allow ourselves. We can't repeat the betrayal of 1920." He swung suddenly in my direction. "What about it, Lieutenant? You're fresh back from combat. What would the boys out there say we ought to do?"

They turned in their seats to look at me. I stalled for a second, then said, "Mr. President, they'd go for just about anything they were convinced meant they'd never have to pick up a rifle, or fire a torpedo, or drop another bomb again."

FDR waved his cigarette holder. "There you go, my friends. Multiply that by twelve million men. Who will be out of uniform sometime in 1946. And each one will have a wife soon. That's a hell of a lot of votes, boys. Sam, a little more flavoring in your branch water? Anyone else care for a little dividend?"

I slowly became aware that I was watching a political master at work. He met direct attacks with a soft answer, or else by a subtle turning away from the point at issue into an area where his attacker would agree with him. He never met attack with attack. When pressed too closely he slipped away behind a smoke screen of vagueness or a joke. The congressmen were by turns wary, half-convinced, amused, or subtly reminded that their reelection depended on him. It was a masterly performance, but somehow I thought a president should be less slippery, less clever. FDR enjoyed it too much.

The meeting ended. As they filed out I followed, pushing the drink cart. Hunley was outside; I pointed to it, then turned to go back in. Jerry said, "Hey."

"Hey yourself."

"Leahy left this for you, when he went out."

I took it. The chief of staff wanted me to call him at the first opportunity, and gave a number.

"Thanks, Jerry," I told Hunley, and went back in. I'd get to him later. I wondered if Leahy knew about Abrams. Probably he did.

The last appointments of the morning were short ones, fifteen minutes each with Nelson Rockefeller, Generals Hurley and Kenney together, and the ambassador of Panama. Then it was lunchtime. Claude Pepper and Lyndon Johnson, representing the new crop of congressmen, were eating with him, a tray at his desk brought down by Prettyman for FDR, sandwiches from brown paper bags for theirs. I decided the time was ripe for a little break for the Honorable John F. Kennedy. I checked out with Grace. She had a note for me, just "Dr Kenmore: Boston 2-4564." I pocketed it and went down to the clinic.

"Guy was here for you," Chagall said.

"What guy?"

"On your bunk."

The laundry guy had come through. On my bunk were four freshly washed and starched shirts, a clean set of blues in a crisp paper wrapper, and my net bag full of clean skivvies and socks. "He says you owe him, they lost the tag and were gonna toss 'em."

"Okay."

The corpsman gave my bunk a prod. He looked sour. "You ought to get a place over at the TDU, Lieutenant. You ought to keep things policed up better, too. Not throw your clothes all over. This is a medical space—"

I couldn't believe a second-class was giving me this. "Listen, can the crap, Chagall. You want shit picked up, pick it up yourself. Now I'm gonna get some sleep. Get me up in half an hour."

I didn't actually fall asleep, though. In fact, things were going through my head real fast. After ten minutes I got up, put on a clean shirt and tie and the fresh blues, and went down the arcade to the West Wing.

I was hoping to pick up the thread of our last conversation with Allie, but Merriman Smith and Harry Oliver were the only ones in the press office. I said Hi, slow day huh, and they said Yeah, slugger. I asked if they had an outside line I could use, one that didn't go through Hacky at the switchboard. They looked at each other. I said it was personal, and winked. Oliver pointed to his phone and disappeared in the direction of the secretarial pool.

I dialed the number Leahy had left first. A female voice answered, and I remembered the WAC. "Lieutenant Kennedy, returning the Admiral's call."

"Kennedy?" Leahy's voice.

"Yes sir."

"What were you doing in *his* office? I assigned you in the Map Room."

"I got reassigned, sir. I'm an aide now. Oh, and I need a fourragère. Do you know where I can get one, Admiral?"

Silence. I could just about see Leahy turning this over in his mind. Weighing how much trust he had in me. Finally he grunted, "You mean an aiguillette, not a fourragère. Any progress on your major assignment?"

"A couple possibilities, sir."

"If there's anything that looks dangerous, call me at once. I'll pass it to Reilly without letting him know the source."

I didn't tell him Reilly had tumbled to me real fast and that we were sharing information. Or at least that I was sharing information. "Aye aye, sir," I said in my most breathless ninety-day-wonder voice.

"I'll send you over an aiguillette. Another thing. Get a haircut. Today."

"Aye aye, sir," I said again. Leahy grunted and hung up.

I got long distance next, the number Dad's assistant had called back with. "Lahey Clinic," a receptionist said. I only then noticed the admiral and the clinic had the same name. Or almost the same.

"Dr. Kenmore, please."

"Whom shall I say is calling?"

"Admiral J.J. McGee. From Washington. Matter of national security."

A pause, then a male voice. "Admiral?"

"Doctor, you don't know me, but a friend of mine gave me your name. I mean Ambassador Joe Kennedy."

"Yes sir; I don't know the ambassador well, but I do know—you're calling from Washington?"

"That's right." I checked to see if anyone was in earshot. The AP Teletype sounded a bell just then and started up, making it sound, I guess, like I was right there in the Pentagon. "This is classified, Doctor, but I need some quick advice. A sixty-three-year-old man, paralyzed from the waist down, has a blood pressure of 186 over 108 and a pulse of 72 in March. One year later he has a blood pressure of 240 over 130 and a pulse of 90."

"Are you a medical doctor, Admiral?"

"No."

"I see. Well . . . I assume with those pressures . . . is he on Mersalyl? Ammonium chloride?"

I checked my notebook. "Yes."

"Digitalis?"

"Yes."

"Is he a smoker?"

"Yes."

"He is under a great deal of stress."

"That's right."

"Is he . . . heavy?"

"No. Pronounced weight loss, in fact."

"And the pressure's still up? That's not good. He seems fatigued? Has aphasic spells?"

"Say again?"

"Garbled speech, or inability to speak?"

"Maybe. Yeah. What would his condition be, Doc? Can you tell?"

"This is most irregular."

"You won't be quoted."

"Well, if you insist . . . it sounds to me very much like arteriosclerosis.

What's called 'hardened arteries.' The arteries are becoming clogged, in layman's terms. The heart must work harder to pump blood. The muscle enlarges, then begins to fail. Meanwhile blood supply to the brain becomes sporadic. That causes the aphasia."

"What's the prognosis?"

"Well, stroke, coronary failure . . . death, eventually."

I checked my list again. "What about heparin? Would that help?"

The far voice sharpened. "What? Heparin? That would be very dangerous. It could cause cerebral hemorrhage."

"Thank you, Doctor. Don't mention this conversation to anyone. Under any circumstances. If you do, we'll know."

"I won't," said the doctor. "But you realize that I know who your patient is, Admiral."

"No, you don't," I said. "I hope we understand each other."

He assured me that we did, and I hung up. And let my hand rest on the phone. I was remembering General Watson. "Pa" had died from a stroke on the way back from Yalta. And Abrams—could that have been a stroke? I should have asked Kenmore that while I had him on the line, but I'd forgotten.

Oliver came back. "You done?" he asked me.

"Yeah, thanks, Harry. I better get back, thanks."

The cabinet arrived at two. Stettinius, Morgenthau, Wallace, Stimson, Knox, Ickes, Perkins. While I was cooling my heels in Tully's office she told me about Winston Churchill's visits to the White House. I asked her if we were still scheduled to leave for Hyde Park that night. She said yes, as far as she knew. And the dinner for Princess Juliana? Yes, that was still on, and I'd be going.

"No, I won't," I told her.

"Oh, yes, you will. That's part of your job."

The afternoon wore on and I felt more and more worn out. Well, we could all sleep on the train. When the President was done working I took him by the clinic, stood by as he got what I now knew was digitalis, and took him up to his quarters and turned him over to Prettyman.

———

If you've never been to a state dinner you might think people enjoy themselves. This one was in the State Dining Room, and Crim had us all seated promptly at seven. The glass eyes of the first Roosevelt's immense mooseheads gleamed reproachfully in the candlelight. Eleanor was off traveling again, so Anna had the hostess's place across from FDR. I kept smiling, but I was counting the minutes till we got on the train.

Finally it was over. I did the quick change to traveling khakis, threw everything else into my B-4, and dragged it down the east arcade to the porte cochere where Reilly had said the staff would be picked up. But nobody else was there.

"Oh, you didn't get the word, Lieutenant?" said Claunch, at the Usher's office. "The President told Reilly to call off the train around five."

"Is it canceled? Or postponed?"

"You'll have to ask Mr. Hassett or Mr. Reilly about that. I really can't say."

Fucking great, I thought. I dragged my luggage back to the clinic, threw my clothes off and crawled in. As I drifted off I heard someone at the door. I didn't answer it. But the tapping kept on.

Then it creaked open, and my eyelids snapped up. "Who is it?" I said, groping for something I could belt him with.

"Jack?"

"Yeah. Over here."

The overhead fluorescents flickered on. "I thought you were going to come back," she said. "I hung around the Press Room all day. But you didn't show."

Allie Sobelski had on a perky double-breasted suit jacket, another little hat, a green scarf, and a cute, very tight tweed skirt. You don't see silk stockings much now, because of the war. Silk goes to parachutes, and so does nylon. She had 'em, though, with long long legs inside. The works.

"I was kind of busy," I said, sitting up.

She came over and sat down on the bunk. "Oh, don't get up. I didn't mean to disturb you. I just wanted to say, I was thinking about what you said."

"Oh yeah? About what?"

"You remember. About Guadalcanal. Did you really write to me?"

"I told you I did."

She looked around the clinic, then drew something on my skin with a long fingernail. Little shivers radiated outward from it. "You've grown hair on your chest," she said, sounding surprised.

"You like it?"

"It's all right. But you're a lot thinner." She smoothed my chest, then scratched it, like it was a cat's back. I felt like purring. "I always thought you were a very attractive guy. At Stanford we used to talk about you after lights out."

"Who's we?"

"The girls at Pi Phi. Remember the night you got drafted? And what we did to celebrate?"

"I wasn't drafted. They just pulled my name out to be classified. Anyway, stop flipping your lip. Ever done it on an operating table?" I invited.

"I'm tempted, really. But, you know, Jack, I'm a married woman now."

I remembered Tallulah Bankhead's line in *Lifeboat:* "Some of my best friends are married men." Or something like that. "Some of my best friends are married women," I said.

"That's nasty, Jack."

"I'm a nasty guy."

"No, you're not. You try to act like it, but you're not."

My hand slipped under her skirt, and got to her garter belt before hers closed on it. "I don't think so," she said.

"Then what are you doing here?"

"I just wanted to talk. I don't see old friends that often."

"What do you want to talk about?"

"I don't care. Your life. What it was like in combat."

"John Hersey beat you to it."

"I read the article," she said. She picked up the edge of the olive-drab wool blanket and peeped under it.

"Jesus, Allie. Have a heart. You can't just come in here and play with my chest hair."

"Why not?" She bent and, so help me, blew on my dick, but didn't touch it. "What did you do in the Pacific? There weren't any women there."

"This isn't the Pacific," I said, and made a grab for her. She let my arm go by, then pulled the blanket down to my knees.

"It really is too bad. Thinking of me when you were fighting the Japs. I feel like I ought to do *something*. And I can't afford any more War Bonds."

"I'll just lie back, then. See if you can figure out some reward I'll like."

"On the other hand," she said, running her fingers lightly up and down till I was about to come out of the bed straight up, "On the other hand, I don't want you to get the idea I'm easy."

"How about a kiss," I said.

She leaned forward and I tasted cigarettes and lipstick. I gave it all I had, a real Technicolor smoocheroo, and when our lips parted she said, "Well . . ." in a breathy voice. When I looked again she was hiking her skirt up.

But heaven only lasted for a second. "Hey. *Hey!*" I said, struggling to sit up.

"I'm sorry. I just can't. I'd better say good night." She swung off the table, a little tousled, but with her little hat still on. She turned at the door and gave me a half-smile. "You can dream about me, Jack."

"Shit! Come back here. You cock-teasing bitch!"

CHAPTER 24

Saturday, March 31: The White House

Standing in the President's study the next morning, I could smell the wisteria, just as he'd said. The sky was a clear hard blue, and birds were singing their hearts out from the massive old elms and magnolias below in the South Garden.

The brightness outside made the room seem gloomy. Behind me Tully and Roosevelt were going over the morning's work. Fala lay by his wheelchair, eyes following each piece of paper as if it were rare filet mignon. Reilly leaned against the door with his arms folded, his movie-star-hero face expressionless.

For some reason I was remembering London in the spring. The fleets of black Austin taxis. The Horse Guards. Herstmonceux, where Lem Billings and I had gone grouse shooting in '37. We'd gotten two, and I wanted to take them home. So we kept the birds in the ship's refrigerator, and turned them over to Kathleen to hold while we went through customs in New York. But they smelled so bad the first thing she did was throw them off the pier. I missed Kick. Maybe I should give her a call, if I could get through to her over there.

I felt closed in. I couldn't help thinking that if we'd taken the train last night we'd be at Hyde Park this afternoon.

Glancing over my shoulder, I saw Tully's look cross mine. She shook her head, then went back to the piece of paper FDR was querulously perusing.

I leaned on the sill and watched the soldiers on top of the Treasury Building go through loading drill on the forty-millimeter. Down on the lawn, the tripled guard stood along the perimeter, a soldier every ten feet now, almost within reach of each other.

I was still sore about Allie. Rubbing herself against me, letting me barely wet it . . . then walking out. She'd come around, though. When she did . . . I stared out, imagining it. Then sneezed, and cursed; I was probably going to be here all day, locked in with FDR and Fala.

The familiar tenor interrupted my thoughts. "You know, Johnny-Kay, from that same window Lincoln used to watch the Confederate campfires twinkling across the Potomac."

"Is that right, sir?" I looked at the old wavy glass, tapped it thoughtfully with a finger.

It was echoed by a tap at the door, and Reilly moved aside as Daniels and MacLeish let themselves in. "The statement on the voting arrangements at San Francisco, sir," the press secretary said.

FDR peered at it through his pince-nez. He motioned absently with his fingers and I got him a pen. He scratched his ear with the end, sucked it, then uncapped it and made a change in the first paragraph. Then scanned down the rest, nodding occasionally. He scribbled initials and handed it back. "Grand," he said. "Just the right note. Send it out right away, please."

"Thank you, Mr. President. Sorry to trouble you."

"No trouble at all, boys." From behind him I watched his shoulders slump as he turned back to the pile of mail and congressional bills.

At last Tully said, "Mr. President."

"Yes, Gracious?" he drawled, frowning over another letter.

"I wanted to say, you don't need to do all this. There is nothing urgent here today except the top bill. Mr. Latta said it should be signed today. All the rest can wait till we're on the train."

"All right, child." He sounded quietly grateful.

"Oh, but—maybe you'd like to sign this. It's the D-Day prayer you wrote. You promised your grandson Johnny a signed copy of it, and it's his birthday, and he's been so sick with the strep throat—"

Roosevelt signed it, then leaned back and groped inside his jacket. I knew by now this meant for me to get a match going. He had a Camel fired up and was blinking up at the smoke when there was another tap at the door.

Daniels and MacLeish, again, with the same piece of paper. I saw Tully's angry look, the press secretary's apologetic one. "Sir, that change you made in paragraph one. Would you like to reconsider it?"

"Reconsider it? Why?"

"Well, Mr. President, it—it doesn't make sense. Doesn't jibe with the rest of the statement. I wouldn't bother you, but I don't think we should release it this way."

The room was silent, except for the exuberant chirp of robins outside. Roosevelt held out his hand; silently, crossed out the correction he'd just made. Daniels and MacLeish looked relieved. They said, together, "Thank you, sir," and left.

"I need a rest," said FDR. "You're right, child, I *do* need a rest. But we have some things to do first. Can you get Bill on the line, please? Or just tell him I need to see him this morning about the note to Stalin. And Chip Bohlen, too."

━━━

All that morning he was closeted with Bohlen and Leahy, working on the message. Later he had Bob Dunn called in from the State Department. Still later Stettinius himself came over. FDR sent me down to the Map Room for the cables Churchill had been sending him on Poland, and had Hollins and

Santorini bring up the map of eastern Germany. Between errands I cooled my dogs in the center hall with Hunley and Long, trying to figure out the aiguillette Leahy had sent over. Reilly stayed inside, never more than ten feet from the man he called "the Boss."

I asked Hunley if he'd heard when we were leaving for Hyde Park. He said he had, but that it was classified. I asked where we met the train, and he said that was secret. "Great," I said. "So how do we know if we're going, or how to get there?"

"You'll be told. Till then, just keep cool, Lieutenant."

At one Prettyman brought over the President's tray. Hunley took off the cover, inspected it, then unfolded a pocket knife and cut a bladeful of the hash. He stared at the ceiling as we watched him chew. Finally he jerked his head at Prettyman. "Go ahead," he said.

A little later Grace opened the door and asked me to come in. I slipped in to find them all seated around FDR's desk. A few inches of varnished wood had been cleared, and Leahy and Bohlen were arguing in low voices about the closing and signature of the draft message that lay on it. FDR was picking listlessly at the tray, but set the fork aside as I came in. I followed his eyes to a map that hung draped over the fireplace, held up by little toy dogs and pigs ranged along the top of the mantel.

Leahy stood gradually and tucked the draft into a folder. He cleared his throat. "Mr. President, that about does it, I think."

"Thanks, Bill." Roosevelt waved his cigarette holder with weary but still elegant dismissal. "Please get that cleaned up and sent today. Thanks for coming by."

"It's nice that you are leaving for a vacation. It is nice for us too, because when you are away, we have much more leisure than when you are here."

FDR laughed and patted his arm. "That's all right, Bill. Have a good time while I'm gone. Because when I come back, I'm going to unload a lot of stuff on you, and then you'll have to work very hard."

Leahy nodded to me, and I followed him out. Then he pointed down the hall. I followed his tall, stiff figure, conscious as I did so of a sinking feeling. If you screwed up in front of Roosevelt, he'd shake his head sadly or laugh. But Leahy would snip the last shred of self-respect off you with cold Annapolis sarcasm.

In the east sitting room he folded himself down into an armchair. "Sit down, Lieutenant," he said. Then, "Oh, no. *That's* not how you attach an aiguillette. Come over here."

I bent forward as the highest ranking officer in the U.S. armed services adjusted my uniform.

"That will have to do . . . Sit *down*, Lieutenant. Are you packed? POTUS gets under way this afternoon."

"POTUS, sir?"

"The presidential train." The bald old admiral fixed me with a shaggy-eyebrowed stare. "Lieutenant, did I or did I not direct you, when you took this assignment, to report to me weekly, or when you developed information of interest?"

"You did, sir. Sorry."

" 'Sorry' . . . but you know, Kennedy, aside from that, you've done well so far. Better than I expected. How did you manage to move from the Map Room to personal aide so fast?"

"I guess I was in the right place, sir."

"Well, I believe in giving credit where credit is due. You seem to be taking hold of this assignment."

I don't know where it came from, but suddenly I had to ask, "What comes after it, sir?"

"After it?" Leahy frowned.

"Yes sir. My medical retirement is on hold. But it's still imminent, as I understand it."

"Oh, I see . . . well, like all reservists, Kennedy, you're only in uniform for the duration. As soon as the war ends, you'll be free to return to civilian life and do as you please." He thought about that. "If what you're asking is, is there a chance for you to transfer to a Regular commission after the war . . . well. Let's just say, I don't think either you or the Service would be the better for such a decision."

"I see."

"Don't take it negatively. You have talents. Charm. And the right connections. Most of us simple sailors are not quite up to the mark on such things. In fact, we tend to react disapprovingly, though I'm not sure that's fair. I remember we were in Hyde Park the night before the '44 election, and I made some asinine comment or other. And the President looked at me and said, 'Bill, you don't know a goddamned thing about politics, do you?' And I said, 'That, Mr. President, is the highest compliment you have ever paid me.' "

"Thanks a lot, Admiral," I said.

"Let's go back to FDR. If we can keep him safe till the end of April, we should be out of the woods. And we will all have the satisfaction of knowing we have done our duty. Where do you stand now?"

I started from Monday, the day I'd arrived. I went over my penetration of FDR's personal quarters, Rivers' absence, then disappearance, and what I thought about it. I told him how I'd checked out the household staff and the Map Room staff—

"You know about Major Abrams," Leahy interrupted.

"I was there when he died, sir."

"The consensus seems to be natural causes. But we can't be sure." He tapped the folder, then straightened. "Well, I have to get this typed and coded. Have you developed any suspicions? In case we're wrong about Abrams—and you're next?"

"Me, sir?" I sat up in the armchair. The soft cushions made my back ache.

"You're standing next to the bull's-eye. People in that position run the risk of catching a stray round."

"I'm suspicious of only one person, sir. Lieutenant-Commander Bruenn."

"The young doctor. Why?"

I gave him a summary of my suspicions about FDR's health, and about the medications. Then I told him what Dr. Kenmore had diagnosed, sight unseen.

"I think he's in worse shape physically than they're giving out to the press, sir. I can understand that, I guess. But it worries me that we've had two people go down from sudden seizures or brain hemorrhages since Bruenn joined the staff."

"That *is* interesting." Leahy studied my face, then abruptly got up. "About his health, first . . . McIntire insists he's fit."

"Does he look fit to you, sir?"

"You're right, I've worried about his appearance too. On the other hand, I'm not sure a difference of medical opinion necessarily indicates something out of line. The doctors at the Naval Hospital gave Secretary Knox a clean bill of health, and two weeks later he was dead. Do you think McIntire's to be suspected too?"

"That I can't say, sir. All I ever see Admiral McIntire do is pack FDR's sinuses. I don't know if he'd even know if there was anything wrong with his heart."

"I see. How serious is this, Kennedy? Bruenn's well respected over at Bethesda, I know that—"

"I can't tell you that, Admiral. You wanted me to report any suspicious circumstances to you. I'm doing that. But I can't tell you whether they're serious enough to replace people. I'm afraid that's a matter for the Regular Navy."

Leahy said coldly, "I see. I will take steps to check out Commander Bruenn. Who else? One of Reilly's men was apparently . . . unsound. Sodomy, you say? Unfortunate. What about the others? Reilly himself?"

"I think he's trustworthy, sir. In spite of being Irish."

That got me a withering glare. "That has nothing to do with it, Kennedy. I am of Irish descent myself, as you know well. It is simply that the fewer people that know, the better. That's an elementary principle of security.

"Very well." He cleared his throat. "Stay alert. Call me instantly if you develop more information. If I'm not at my office, leave a message with Chief Ringquist. She'll get it to me pronto."

"Aye aye, sir. How does the Soviet situation look, sir?"

"Not encouraging. They seem determined to control whatever government is set up in Poland. That is contrary to what they agreed to at Yalta." Leahy fingered the message jacket. "I've tried and tried to have him force them to acknowledge their obligation. Face them squarely—either they will mend their ways, or we will know once and for all they can't be trusted. Now finally he's done it."

That sounded ominous, but the way he shut his lips warned me off pursuing it. Instead I asked him, "Will you be going to Hyde Park, sir?"

"I haven't been told yet." Leahy looked at the folder again, scowled, then nodded abruptly at me and strode away toward the stairwell.

I sat back down, a few feet away from the door, close enough that Grace could call me, but far enough away from Hunley and Long's fags. I was starting to get a real asthma condition from the ever-present smoke and dog hair.

The atmosphere around the White House was tense, and it wasn't just the increased security. I could see why FDR was in a jam. He'd made the agreements at Yalta, then come home and sold them to Congress. Now the Russians were backtracking. He had to defend Yalta, or he'd be accused of selling out to Stalin. But he couldn't let the Soviets take Poland quietly, either; the war had begun over Poland; there were too many voters of Polish extraction, most of them in the Democratic fold.

That said, why didn't he stand up to Stalin? Two reasons I could see. FDR was worried sick about Japan. When he'd muttered "a million" yesterday, after the conference with Marshall and King, I knew what he meant. He meant casualties. He had to have Stalin hold down the Kwantung Army, on the mainland, while we invaded, and perhaps help by striking from the north at the same time we hit Kyushu.

The second reason, and the most obdurate, was that the Red Army was occupying Poland already. If reasoning didn't work, then FDR's only recourse was to threaten war.

And from what Leahy had said, that was more or less what that last message was doing.

Which meant World War Three was looming before World War Two was even over.

Reilly stuck his head out of the study. "Hunley. Kennedy." We both got up.

"Jerry, get on the phone to the station. Tell the railroad people there's a change."

"Shit, Mike, we already changed everything twice—"

"Well, the Boss wants to get a couple things done before he leaves. Kennedy, take this note to Hassett, will you? We've got to change the schedule. Get moving! The Boss wants to leave at eight. We've got a lot to do to get everything ready to roll by then."

CHAPTER 25

Fifth Floor, the Justice Department Building

The black-eyed, pudgy man in the inner office sat frowning, rubbing his heavy cheeks as he read through the immense stack of reports, memoranda, and transcripts. He studied each with his head cradled in his hand, then rapidly scribbled a few words in blue pencil, directing action to be taken, filing procedures, fresh investigations. Then, with a slight nod, laid each aside in the slowly growing stack of finished work. He had been reading all afternoon, occasionally picking up the telephone to question a point or issue an order; and now the lights were coming on in the blue-and-silver corridors. Behind the desk he seemed shrunken, overwhelmed. As if the lofty ceilings and lengthy vistas, the luxurious appointments did not magnify, but diminished him.

As the windows turned dark, he was interrupted at last by the intercom. "Mr. Hoover, will you need me late today?"

He glanced at the wall clock. "No, thank you, Helen. Good night."

But he himself did not pick up the phone, did not call for his chauffeur and his escort and his bulletproof limousine. Instead he worked on as night deepened, losing himself in the details of investigations in South America, of a tapped conversation at the Spanish Embassy, a departmental memo regarding rules for sharing FBI-generated information, a report that the daughter of a prominent labor leader was a secret Communist, a report by Special Agent Rex Ellis that Ronald Reagan, the actor, had reported to him certain remarks by Thomas Dewey that could be construed as a threat to the director of the FBI.

He sighed and shook his head. Scribbled a note on the report and set it aside. Picked up the next memo. Studied it, his frown slowly contracting into a scowl.

Massaging his neck, he got up and moved to a floor-to-ceiling window. Then opened it and stepped out onto a balcony.

The late March air was cool and fresh, and a slow breeze brought the scent of flowers to him. He looked down on the Hancock statue and on the tops of the elms that lined Pennsylvania Avenue. Then raised his eyes slowly, looking out across the city of his birth and his early struggle.

From here he had watched inauguration after inauguration. To the right, high on its hill, rose the shadowy bulk of the Capitol. In this fourth year of war it was still blacked out, more to save power than in any serious expectation of air attack; but he remembered it as shining with light. In his mind it always would shine; the symbol of government, of order and of law. That was what he was pledged to defend, against every enemy. That, and the bureau he had built up from nothing into a bulwark of the Republic.

Holding it up to the light that filtered through the open doorway behind him, he read the last memo again.

Washington Special Agent in Charge James W. McAffee to FBI Director J. Edgar Hoover, March 29, 1945:

There is set out below certain material developed during investigation of a multiple murder case in Washington, D.C. in which you may be interested.

In reference to your memo of Sept 6, 1939, to all law enforcement officials requesting them to relay to us any information obtained by them possibly relating to espionage, counterespionage, sabotage, and subversive activities, the Washington Field Office was notified today by the District of Columbia Police Force of the results of their investigation of a multiple murder perpetuated on the night of 28 March 1945.

Four men, two white, two black, were found dead on the second floor of a Southeast DC townhouse after reports of shots fired. The premises were determined to be used in illegal gambling activities. The victims were identified as petty criminals and ex-bootleggers, members of the LaFontaine organization. No money was found on the premises. The presumption is that the four men were in charge of activities at the gambling house, and were killed by person or persons unknown to facilitate purposes of robbery.

Particularly disturbing, however, was the manner in which the murders were carried out. No gunshot or other wounds were found on any of the victims, although firearms, one of which had been discharged, were found on two of the men.

The murder was apparently carried out by means of a grenade. However, the grenade case, which was recovered intact, was empty. One of the investigating officers picked it up and sniffed it. Within minutes he reported respiratory problems, shortness of breath, and had to be hospitalized. He is now partially recovered but has not yet returned to duty. No liquid or solid residues were recovered and the active agent is still unknown. Its effects are not consistent with any known poison.

The grenade has been identified by military experts as made in the Soviet Union.

Found outside in the alley back of the premises were the following items of interest in connection with the robbery and murder:

1. 24″ length of 3/8″ galvanized chain
2. Empty jar of grease
3. Three empty garment bags with the imprint of the Hahn & Hurja Laundry and Specialty Cleaner Company.

Fingerprints were developed from items 1 and 2. No match was obtained by the Identification Division.

A numbers runner aged ten, a minor, stated that he observed a man exiting the alley back of the premises around two AM on the night in question. His face was not clear but he had seen the man at LaFontaine's once before and was emphatic as to his identification. He described him as of medium height, muscular, blond, blue eyes, with a round face, thick lips, and a quiet manner. His accent was not local, possibly Midwest. The informant stated that he had been brought to the premises by one Francis Smalls, with whom he seemed to be acquainted.

Following up on this, I learned that Francis Smalls had been found dead on the same premises the week before. Smalls was an employee of Hahn and Hurja Laundry and Specialty Cleaner Company of Washington, DC.

At the request of the local police force, I am assigning agents to determine the identity of the assailant and the means of death.

The director of the FBI lowered the paper, staring out over the city.

He stood for several minutes in the cool wind, not feeling it nor seeing the city below him. He was working everything out in his mind. First the technical means, then the motive, and last, the ramifications.

The grenade was Soviet. He had long known that an immense and shadowy network was operating, not only in America, not only in Washington, but within the highest levels of the federal government itself. So that when he asked himself, Could a murderous Communist conspiracy exist, even as the Soviets were an ostensible ally? the answer was that it could. The State and Treasury

Departments—yes, Treasury, which ran the Secret Service—were riddled with communists and fellow travelers. He had three investigations going on right now within State. He was certain that when it came time to move in he would identify at least two major networks, both controlled from the Soviet Embassy. Even the presiding secretary general of the new United Nations Organization was a crypto-Communist, a man named Hiss. (Interesting how even their names sounded treacherous and disloyal.) And there were others. Thousands of them, both actual members and fellow travelers. He already knew one ring was headed by an economist in the Farm Security Administration.

A Jew, he thought. Naturally. Interesting, how almost all the Communist spies and sympathizers turned out to be of the Hebrew nationality. Fortunately the President had listened when he'd argued against admitting more of them into the country, after the start of the European war.

But the menace of a subversive organization could not be measured by its numbers. It had to be judged by the fanaticism and intensity of its members. They were dedicated to boring from within, by getting into important positions, carrying on propaganda, funneling important information to their masters abroad.

And this administration aided and abetted them by turning a blind eye to it all. One by one the defenses against a communistic state had fallen. The Supreme Court was no longer a barrier to the encroachment on American liberty. Labor unions were free to organize and strike, to destroy everything Americans had built, at the first word of command from abroad.

What did it mean now, this turn to violence? The death of Abrams and the mysterious raid at an obscure gambling den?

Or was this Communist-inspired? What if the SS colonel's fantastic story were true . . . that somewhere out there was an American boy who had become a Communist, then a Nazi?

What mysterious poison was he using?

Was it the same device or compound that had killed this White House staffer, Abrams?

Why was the Secret Service stonewalling FBI assistance?

He stared out for a long time, turning it all over. Interlocking each possible fact or explanation with a thousand other details, personalities, possibilities. His mind prowled among them as through the shadows of night, retentive, alert, relentless, subtle, and cunning.

At last he turned from the darkened rooftops, closing and locking the doors behind him. Crossing to his desk, he drew another file from a drawer, opened it, and compared the two. The second was headed RECORD OF INTERROGATION OF SS COLONEL H D HEUDEBER. He ran his finger down it till he came to the place he recalled.

No. The descriptions matched too well.

There was really no question as to who the mysterious assailant at the gambling hall was.

Only who he was really working for.

The Nazis? Or the Communists?

And did it really matter, after all? From the Department's point of view?

The short man leaned back, seeing now, like feral eyes glaring from the dark around him, the ring of enemies that waited for him to falter, to relax his vigilance. Enemies of America, and enemies of the Bureau. The enemy of one was the enemy of the other. For the Bureau defended America, and if it could be emasculated or destroyed, the last shield between Democracy and Communism would fall uselessly to the ground.

One of those enemies was Colonel William J. Donovan.

Donovan's agency, the OSS, had done some cloak-and-dagger stuff in Europe. But it had gone beyond operations against the Nazis. The seated man knew he was not supposed to know certain things. But he did. He knew that Donovan had set up a liaison office in Moscow. That he had supplied the NKVD with microdot equipment, cameras, projectors, transmitters, all the paraphernalia of modern spycraft. The Director of the FBI had protested, but Donovan had gone ahead. As he always did.

And now the colonel was hammering on FDR with his proposal for a super intelligence agency . . . headed by himself. The short man's eyes narrowed. One man would control all the intelligence assets of the country, Office of Naval Intelligence, Army G-2, the Secret Service, the State Department, the FBI.

It sounded efficient. But what it meant was that one man would decide what the President saw. He would control the foreign policy of the country. It was totally undemocratic.

It looked as if the President was going to approve it, too.

He sat in the darkness for a long time, thinking. At last he reached out and turned on a desk lamp. In the shaded light he reached for his blue pencil.

This is a matter for the local police. Recall agents you assigned. No further Department action. Do Not File. Personal and Confidential.

The bulldog head nodded twice, its expression unreadable. With slow deliberation, J. Edgar Hoover laid the memo atop the pile of finished work.

CHAPTER 26

The White House

B ut as it turned out, we didn't go at eight, either. Not till after eleven was the office staff told to report to the east entrance with their hand baggage.

Four unmarked sedans drove us slowly through a darkened city, past the unlighted loom of the Washington Monument, to a side entrance of a long, dark building near the Tidal Basin. I helped the women get their luggage out, then followed the others down echoing corridors that suddenly opened out into a shadowy cavern.

I put down my bags and stretched, easing my back. Eight passenger and baggage cars stretched away under the concrete roof. The shades were drawn on the green-and-gold passenger coaches, and the walls echoed with the slow hissing pant of powerful locomotives. A wooden ramp stood a few feet down the platform.

I was wondering where to board when a short figure came out of the tunnel behind me, weighted down with an overnight bag, sample case, and portable typewriter. A Leica dangled from his neck. Only when the light of the platform lamps hit him did I recognize Merriman Smith. "What's up?" I asked him.

"The usual shit."

"Going with us? So you knew all along."

The United Press reporter said in his fast, raspy voice, "Like hell I did. My wife said somebody called. Said they'd pick me up at ten at the southwest corner of Fourteenth and New York. Thirty minutes! That's all the warning they give the goddamn press." Smith spat. "I understand secrecy, but this war's damn near over. Seems to me you people ought to be easing up a little."

I told him I had nothing to do with it, but he just snorted. So I asked him, "You've been on his train before, haven't you? Where the hell are we, anyway?"

"This is where they ship the currency out of Engraving and Printing. Remember that rumble as you came down the tunnel? Those are the presses. Any more dumb questions?"

I said I guessed not, and he snorted again and climbed aboard. After walking up the platform to check out the locomotives—two big ones with steam up, radiating heat, their driving wheels as tall as I was—I hoisted myself aboard too.

The interior of the Pullman smelled musty. The lights were on, but most of the seats were empty. I remembered the packed overnighter to Florida. POTUS had that eerie feeling you get in places that are meant to be full of people but aren't. I parked my shit in the aftermost car, a lounge car, and went forward.

The tables were bare in the dining car, but two Negroes in Southern Railway uniforms glanced at me from the pantry. Forward of that was a sleeping car. Several berths had their curtains drawn already, and snores came from behind them. I went through it into another, more luxurious club car.

Civilization at last, and the press. The bar was already thronged. Cards, newspapers, and portable typewriters covered the tables. I got offered several drinks as I slid through. I waved thanks, said I'd be back in a couple of minutes, wanted to check the train out.

When I slid open the next door a startled sergeant straightened, barking his head against an opened equipment panel. Beyond him was what looked like the radio room on the *Queen Elizabeth.* "Who are you?" I shouted over the pounding of a diesel generator.

"Signal Corps. Who're *you?"*

"President's aide."

"I don't think you can come in here, sir."

"There are three more forward of you, right? Then the engines?"

"That's right, sir. There's a sleeping car for the crew. Then baggage, then a special car for the President's automobiles."

I said thanks and drifted back, hearing a lock snap shut behind me.

The tobacco haze in the club car was so thick I could barely see the far end. It occurred to me that it might be a good idea to know exactly who was aboard, so I took mental notes as I headed aft again. Past the newsies was a knot of staff. "How's the back, Kennedy?" Dr. Bruenn asked me.

"About the same, sir. Who's this?"

The man in civilian clothes sitting with him turned out to be George Fox, the president's long-time masseur. I said, "Hi, sir," then asked Bruenn, "Is Dr. McIntire aboard yet?"

"The surgeon general is testifying before Congress. I believe he plans to meet us when we come back."

I said oh, and moved on. Interesting, I thought. I could feel Bruenn's eyes following me.

"Lieutenant Kennedy."

A big guy in a trench coat draped loosely over a double-breasted gray suit, Pete Hollins beside him. He had a hard but familiar face. It took me a second to recognize him. When I did I was glad I'd left my blouse on and my tie tied. "Admiral Brown. Never saw you in mufti before. Hi, Pete. Are the rest of the Map Room guys coming?"

"No," Brown said. "Just us. Have you heard anything else about Major Abrams?"

"No sir."

"I had to write to his parents."

"Yes sir."

"How's the aide job working out?"

"Good, sir."

"That fourragère doesn't go on that way."

"It's a aiguillette, sir, not a fourragère. And that's how Admiral Leahy pinned it on me, sir."

Brown scowled. "By the way, we got something for you," said Hollins.

"What?"

Dad had come through. It was my old musette bag, with my gear from ONI. The lock was rusty but intact. "Joe Grabb says it showed up at his apartment, marked to you care of Ed."

"Personal stuff. From home," I said, and tossed the strap over my shoulder. "Thanks."

"Give FDR a kiss for us."

"Funny," I told Hollins.

In the lounge car two tables of girls were chattering over coffee from Thermos flasks. At least "girls" was how Grace Tully introduced them. Dorothy Brady, her assistant, I'd seen going in and out of her office. "Toi" Bachelder, another assistant, in a wheelchair in the aisle. She had polio, like FDR. Louise Hackmeister, the famous "Hacky," the switchboard operator.

A porter struggled aboard, carrying an immense cloth bag. A large black woman followed him. The cook, Lizzie McDuffie. She was followed by Hassett, carrying a suitcase and a heavy-looking leather briefcase. His gray fedora had its brim turned down reporter-style.

Iron wheels rumbled as a baggage cart passed under our window. I cracked the blind to see Reilly talking to McMullin, Hunley, and Long. Then the huddle broke, and the agents trotted off. He looked after them, then glanced at his watch. A moment later he wheeled and walked rapidly toward the engine.

Suddenly the floor rocked as a jolt dominoed down the train. Something heavy had coupled on from behind. The noise level in the club car dropped, then rose again.

We eased into motion a little before midnight, clicking over switches, rocking from side to side. The concrete roof drifted back. Signal lights glowed green, then red under their dimout hoods. The whistle gave a hoot and we began a gradual acceleration.

I stared up into the darkness, picking up the Dipper and the North Star from habit. I felt a little nervous, but I knew why. At night in the Strait we'd strain our eyes all night long trying to pick up the Jap float planes. They hunted PTs. You'd think they gave them a geisha bonus or an extra ration of sake or something for every one of us they got. But you just couldn't see them till suddenly there was the whine of their engines, the red flare of the exhaust as they pulled out, and then a second later the crash of a bomb in your wake or off your side, or if you were unlucky, right on your fucking deck. Yeah, I was glad I wasn't back in Blackett Strait.

Looking up at that sky, I was glad I wasn't in Berlin or Tokyo tonight, either. From what the papers said there wasn't going to be much left of either by the time hostilities closed. I'd never been to Tokyo, but I'd spent a couple of days in Berlin before the war. I wondered if the Hotel Excelsior was still standing.

"Close that shade, Slugger. This train's blacked out."

"Sorry, pal."

"There's sandwiches and coffee up in the dining car, sir."

"Thanks, George," I told the porter.

It occurred to me then that before it got too late I ought to check in with the President, see who was in his car, see if he needed anything. I got up, shrugged my blouse back on, two-blocked my tie, and headed aft.

———

The steel door to the rear coach, Number One, looked familiar. It had a dogging wheel just like a watertight door on a destroyer. I tapped on it. Waited. Then tapped again, harder, as I realized how thick it was. A second later I saw Jerry Hunley's eyes through the thick glass viewport. The wheel clanked and turned.

When he hauled the door closed again and dogged it behind me it felt like I was back aboard ship, a tight enclosed little space lit by one shielded bulb. The swaying motion was like a ship in a seaway. The rumble of the wheels sounded like the rumble of a screw. Suitcases and trunks were stacked against the wall, lashed with a crisscross of line.

"What you need?" Hunley asked me.

"He asleep yet?"

"Don't think so. Mind if I—"

I held my arms up for a quick pat-down. The Secret Service man jerked his head. "Go on in."

A suite of rooms opened past the vestibule. A kitchen-pantry, then an observation room stretching the width of the coach. The blinds were pulled down on large windows on either side. As I came in two women glanced up at me from a divan. "Yes, young man?" said one imperiously, and Bill Hassett looked up from a magazine.

"Margaret, Laura, this is Lieutenant John Kennedy, the President's new aide. John, this is Miss Margaret Suckley, the president's cousin, and a member of the library staff at Hyde Park. And Miss Laura Delano, another cousin of the President."

They were older ladies, maiden-aunt types. I said I was pleased to meet them, and asked if the President was still up. "He's awake, yes," Hassett said guardedly. "Mike was in a little while ago. Do you need to disturb him?"

"No sir," I said. "Just wanted to check."

"Look in if you like, but I think he's all right."

In the bedroom the masseur was working over a naked body stretched on the bed. Wintergreen tanged the air. Prettyman was shaking out pajamas. A black mass in the corner resolved itself at a second glance into Fala, head on his paws, his eyes flicking to me, then going back to the bed.

It took a shocked second before I recognized the flaccid body on it as the

President's. The wasted, sticklike legs were no thicker than my wrists. He had no thighs or buttocks to speak of; the muscles were gone. His skin was unhealthily pale, freckled and loose, and he did not move or make a sound as the masseur's hands struck his flesh. I hesitated, then turned and went out.

I lingered for some small talk with the ladies, but they were yawning politely and the lights were low. I excused myself. We'd be on the train for a while, en route to upstate New York. There'd be time to talk tomorrow.

I went back to the lounge car and reclaimed my seat. Tilted it back, and closed my eyes.

Gradually I relaxed. The last conversations around me dwindled to whispers and snores. The last lights went out. The train settled into its stride, a slow hum-click-hum that set my head nodding.

At last, I had what I'd wanted. Time to think. I had to think about the situation around FDR. I ought to consider what I was going to do, too. Once the President was past the danger date, Jack "Shafty" Kennedy would be out of uniform for good. I'd either have to break with Dad, or join him in trying to parlay a bad back and a lost PT boat into a political advantage.

An hour later the porter came by with thin wartime pillows. I tucked one under my head and spread out, my stocking feet sticking out into the aisle. Wartime travel. I couldn't sleep, though. I sat up again and eyed the blinds. Finally I eased them up again.

We were rolling now, so fast the phone poles and the embankment were a flickering blur. Beyond that stretched the American night, low rolling hills, woods, the occasional river a flat, dark ribbon beneath the trestles. Narrow roads led off into a heavy, tangible, invading dark punctuated by the orange flare of caution lights, the hollow staccato clatter of country crossings, the lonesome, long-drawn-out shriek of the whistle.

A crossing coming up. The ringing of the bell grew louder. As we rumbled and jingled past a single bulb dangling on the platform, I just made out the faded station sign. We were making pretty good time. We were in Pennsylvania already.

———

I must have drowsed. I don't know for how long. Strange half-dreams went through my head. In one, a library was on fire, and I was trying to save the books from what seemed to be a genealogical section. None of the heavy volumes seemed to have any Irish names in them. Then I was back at Harvard, trying to get ready for lectures, but I couldn't find any clothes to wear.

When I woke again my back hurt, and I knew I wouldn't get back to sleep. I cracked the blind again and stared out at the monotonous black. Then I realized what had woke me. We were standing still, and from outside came the high shriek of escaping steam.

I frowned, threw the blanket back, and felt around for my shoes.

The reporters had thinned out in the club car, but Oliver was still there. I was surprised to see Reilly too, a short scotch in front of him. "What's going on?" I asked the Secret Service chief.

"What do you mean?"

"I mean, we're stopped, that's what I mean."

"We're coaling." Reilly stretched and yawned. "Two locomotives burn a lot of coal, hauling the weight we're hauling. And the Informer's doing his duty out on the roadbed, under the close supervision of Dewey Long."

" 'The Informer'?"

"Fala. Don't sweat it. Everything's under control."

"How long will we be at Hyde Park?" said the AP man in his soft high voice.

"Can't tell you, Harry. You know that. Why ask?"

"They pay me to ask. I like to earn my money. Boosts my fragile ego. How about after that, then? I heard a rumor he might go to London and Paris once the European war's over. Might even keep on going, visit Berlin—"

"Idle speculation, Harold," said Reilly. "Don't indulge in it myself. Nobody's mentioned another working trip to me."

"Well, shoot," said Oliver. "It really is just Hyde Park, eh?"

I asked Reilly, "That's quite a setup, that—what do they call it? Number One?"

Reilly gave me the rundown on the presidential Pullman. The windows were bulletproof glass three inches thick. The walls were case-hardened armor plate that would stop anything up to a major-caliber shell. The interior doors were battleship bulkheads, and on the roof were three submarine escape hatches, in case it went off a trestle into a river. "That's why we've got two engines, we need 'em to pull that weight. There's a pilot train a couple of miles ahead checking the roadbed. And two cars on parallel roads, in case the track is cut."

"Sounds like you've got everything covered," I said. "Unless there's somebody already on the train."

"What kind of somebody?" said Oliver.

"Nobody, Harry," said Reilly. "The lieutenant's just amusing himself."

"You think there's a threat of some kind?"

"I always think there's a threat," said Reilly. "That's what they pay *me* for."

Oliver asked him, soft and courteous, "When are they going to let us break the story on Abrams? How about this: We're stopped to coal, right? I've got a release already written. How about I hand it to the stationmaster, along with a fin, and ask him to wake up the telegraph operator and file by wire from here?"

"Nice try, Harry. No dice."

"It's all voluntary. I could just go ahead and file. Not check it with anybody."

"Sure, you could do that. Be a hell of a scoop, wouldn't it? But you'd never drink whiskey on this train again."

I asked Oliver, "Where's the other reporters?"

"I guess asleep."

"What do you guys do at Hyde Park?"

"Not much happens on these side trips. Press conference, if anything breaks. We went down with him to Hobcaw Barony last summer, Bernie Baruch's place, just about died of boredom." He eyed me. "You play golf?"

"Used to. Before the war."

He and Reilly went back I guess to the conversation they were having before I came in, about who was the best infielder who ever lived, whether it was Pie Traynor or Travis Jackson or Charlie Gehringer. I went back to my seat and pulled my tie down. Before I knew it I was out.

——

Around five I woke again. The false dawn was a gray glow around the edge of the blackout blinds. Everyone else was asleep. Long was snoring, head back, mouth open, revolver showing under his jacket.

Gradually I realized it wasn't my back that had woke me. It was a sense of danger. I puzzled about it for a while. Till it occurred to me that this would be an ideal time for an attempt on the President. If there was anyone aboard to try it.

I decided to get up and find the head, and maybe look around too. Thought about opening the musette bag. But I'd lost the key in the Pacific and didn't have pliers or anything to break the lock with.

The head was a swaying vertical coffin in the rear of the sleeper. As I aimed into the toilet I could dimly see the roadbed flashing by beneath us. We were moving at forty-five or fifty, I guessed. I buttoned up and went out again into the darkened aisle.

This time a corporal was on duty in the comm car. He didn't look up from his paperback copy of *The Skylark of Space*. So I went on past him.

The crew car was dark except for a couple of off-duty firemen telling yarns around a cold stove. When they saw me one spat; the other rooted around and held up a pint of Don Q. I told him thanks, but no thanks, and went on forward.

Into regions of swaying darkness. The baggage car was untenanted. Just an aisle with padlocked doors on either side. The car coach wasn't any more enlightening. There was nothing forward of that except the tender and engines. I couldn't figure much I could do up there.

Going aft again, I couldn't help thinking of the train as a ship, pounding through the night. Only the engines were at the bow, and the captain's quarters—the President's coach—was at the stern.

The club car was empty now. The glasses over the bar tinkled faintly as the car swayed. I kept going, through the sleeper again, the dining car, lounge car. Snoring, dim lights, the slack, white ovals of unconscious faces. I opened the door and stepped onto the platform between the lounge car and Number One.

It was cooler here, where the night air leaked in around the streamlined sheathing. Noisier, with the thunder and clack of wheels, the occasional jolt of a misaligned rail, the sway of the roadbed. And darker, since the platforms were unlighted.

Only it wasn't completely dark. The door to Number One was open, cracked about an inch and a half. Yellow light leaked from inside. I hesitated, wondering if it was supposed to be that way. I couldn't see anything through the viewport. I knew FDR didn't like being sealed in, and that Reilly liked to leave escape routes clear in case of fire. The heavy door swung slowly, tapped against the jamb, then crept open again. That looked wrong. I pulled it open—which took some beef, it was heavy—and stepped through.

I was in the vestibule, where Hunley had searched me. But he wasn't here. For a second I had a sense of déjà vu. The White House, the night Rivers disappeared. Then I noticed the luggage. Neatly stacked and roped down before, now it lay in a tumbled, scattered heap across the floor, bags sliding as we went around a curve.

I was still looking down when I noticed that it was darker than before. At first I thought the light was failing, but when I glanced up it was still on. Incandescent bulbs either burn out or keep shining; I'd never seen one just fade, the way this one seemed to be doing. The shadows were getting darker. And I was getting a headache.

Suddenly I realized that the pounding in my head and the ache in my kidneys meant I felt very frightened. But I didn't know why. I was sweating like a horse, and it was getting hard to breathe. What the hell was going on? My mouth was bone dry. My lips felt numb. But it was funny. As soon as I thought it I realized that I wasn't scared. I *felt* scared, real scared, but *I wasn't scared.* There was nothing to be scared of. As far as I knew.

This is weird, I thought.

When I lunged over the tumbled luggage I saw a shoe. It lay on its side, rapidly dissolving in the spreading darkness. Now my legs were going. I reeled across the compartment and ended up with both hands against the wall, my head hanging between them. The headache was bad now, splitting, and my chest was getting tight.

Then I saw a leg, the foot wearing a sock but no shoe.

A hand, outstretched toward the door.

And one of the suitcases, the lid sprung open by the avalanche of luggage. A used-looking leather valise. But one glance told me that wasn't shirts and shoes inside it.

I kicked the other bags aside, careful not to touch or bump the open one. In the rapidly dimming light I saw that the guy on the floor was Hunley. He looked dead.

I stumbled back, groping for the hatch out, but I couldn't find it. I couldn't see. Worse, my chest seemed to be paralyzed. My hands were shaking and I couldn't stop them. I remembered Abrams all of a sudden. How he couldn't breathe. How his hands had quivered, then spasmed, and at last relaxed in death.

Shit, I thought. Now I *was* scared. I didn't know what was going on, but I wanted out. But where was the door? My hands scrabbled over cold painted steel but found nothing. Nothing but a thin useless cord between my fingers as everything inside my head turned black as the rushing, clattering night outside.

PART III

WARM
SPRINGS

CHAPTER 27

Tuesday, April 3: Warm Springs, Georgia

The train shed speed slowly, hundreds of tons of locomotives and coaches coasting through miles of pine-forested hills. Along the roadbed the bare dirt was the color of a fresh scar. Rails clacked and groaned as steel wheels passed over them. Brake shoes squealed, and black smoke rose straight up into a hard bright sky.

Far ahead, the whistle shrieked twice. Standing on the rear deck of Number One, the big man glanced at his watch.

Right on schedule, Mike Reilly thought. But it didn't make him feel any less exposed, or any less angry.

He unbuttoned his overcoat—the wind the train made was a hot damp breath—and leaned out from the observation platform, looking ahead. Steam and smoke mingled above the green articulated length of POTUS as it glided sinuously into the last curve. They were down to 15 miles an hour, so slow he could have jumped off. Or someone could have jumped on. If the doors hadn't been all locked from the inside. But he still couldn't see the town. Just woods and dirt roads, here and there a sagging shack along a dusty lane, colored kids playing in the red dust, and back of them the hills.

The last couple days hadn't been fun. Losing Jerry Hunley, and almost losing Kennedy. Wish I'd lost him instead of Jerry, Reilly thought. He didn't trust Kennedy. He'd tried to get Brown and Leahy to fire him, and thought he'd succeeded. Instead he'd bobbed up as FDR's personal aide.

But worst of all had been the bomb.

The first he'd known about it was when the air brakes slammed on, waking everybody on the train as they shot off their seats. Kennedy had grabbed the signal line as he went down. The engineers, seeing the brake signal from Number One, had of course slammed on every ounce of air pressure they had. He'd gotten to the President's car to find Hunley dead and Kennedy unconscious. He'd gotten the train on a siding and called a nearby Army base for help while they figured out what happened.

Whoever was after FDR, they'd almost done it this time. The bomb in the suitcase had been big enough to gut half the car and blow the rest off the track. What sweated his balls was the other stuff in there with it. Intended to work along with the explosive. Some kind of poison gas, but nothing anyone had ever heard of, not even the Army chemical warfare people.

That wasn't all that was worrying him, either. He didn't like the way the Boss acted. He was okay from about nine to one every day, but after that his mind was somewhere else. He was losing ground physically too. Usually moving him was easy. Get him in position and he'd reach over to the chair or the car and lift himself with one surge of those powerful shoulders. He did it with such speed and grace that thousands of people who'd seen it at baseball games and rallies never suspected he couldn't walk. Now, though, FDR was just dead weight. Had he gotten a whiff of the stuff? He'd discussed it with Bruenn. The doctor didn't think so. But now, thanks to Kennedy, he wasn't so sure he trusted Bruenn, either.

A hell of a way to make a living, Reilly thought.

Anyway, after that he'd decided to hell with Hyde Park, persuaded Hassett and FDR he was right, and ordered the railroad to reroute them. That took a fun-filled eighteen hours, sitting on a siding in Pennsylvania till they got the green light to head south. He'd put everybody off the train except the bare minimum of staff, and what had hurt most, put Dewey Long and Russ McMullin off too. After Rivers, and now Hunley, he had to assume the Service had been penetrated. He'd replaced them with Army MPs from the base, for the moment. The bomb itself, carefully disassembled by the ordnance specialists, had gone back to Washington for study.

And now they were pulling into Warm Springs, and it was early afternoon, and the station and the town were appearing out of the woods ahead.

"Shit," he muttered. Somebody had leaked.

Because there they were, standing at a respectful distance along the tracks by the little white gabled station house: four or five hundred people, practically the whole population of Warm Springs, Georgia. The big man's eyes examined them even as his mind moved forward. The crossing gates were down and old C. A. Pless was out there swinging his lantern. And there was the sedan, doors already open, driver standing ready, and two jeeps with marines. He felt better seeing them, but his eyes still kept roving the crowd.

When the train squealed to a stop he gestured angrily to the faces leaning out ahead. Men in olive drab uniforms and MP brassards jumped down and started pressing the crowd back, rifles at port arms, clearing a space between it and the waiting cars. Reilly waited on the platform. There was no wind now. Under his wool suit, in the close heat, sweat was basting him. The townspeople moved back slowly, smiling, waiting for the President to appear.

They're not going to get him, Reilly thought. Whoever they are. Wherever they're hiding. They may think they are. But I'm going to get them first.

━━━

I stood surrounded by the crowd, gripping the .38 in the pocket of my khakis. I'd had to break the lock on the musette bag, but I figured now I needed it. Hot, God, it was hot. The people pressed so close against me I could smell them. Small-town businessmen in suits and hats: sweat and after-shave. Women in cotton print dresses and hats and gloves: perfume and damp cloth. Farmers in bib overalls and scuffed boots: manure and field dust. Southern voices, so slow I could hardly make out what they said. But there were others, too, on crutches and leaning on canes. I stared at withered arms, hunched backs. A teenaged boy's legs were warped as if the bones had melted and run together. The shrunken limbs were wrapped with gleaming steel and leather straps. I looked from face to face for the one that didn't belong.

I'd come to with Reilly and Bruenn hovering over me. The train was stopped and it was just getting light. They had me outside, on the grass. When I turned my head I saw another guy lying next to me. Only he had a blanket over his head.

Hunley. And if I hadn't snagged the brake cord on my way down I'd have been dead too.

Reilly had taken the bomb off the train himself. Cleared everyone out, had FDR wheeled down the tracks, then picked it up and very carefully carried it down the steps and out to the armored-car-towed trailer the Army had sent over. The bomb disposal guys had found a little bottle in there with it, uncorked and set to tip if anyone opened the suitcase. It was empty. Whatever was in it had evaporated so completely they couldn't get even a trace.

It was so close. If that stack of luggage had been tied just a little more securely it wouldn't have fallen over and burst the suitcase open, so that when Jerry tried to restack it he noticed the bomb. It would have gotten FDR and everybody else in the last car. As it was, the stuff in the bottle had killed Jerry, and got me so bad even in the few seconds I was in there, I still had tremors in my legs.

And I was very, very browned off. I remembered Jerry Hunley telling how when they were campaigning cross-country in '44 FDR put his hat on him and gave him his cigarette holder, and put him in the window of the train so Roosevelt could get some sleep. He'd been so proud of that . . . goddamn it, a nice guy. And I'd liked Ed Abrams, too. I knew it was wartime. But they hadn't deserved to die the way they did, like poisoned coyotes. Without even a chance to shoot back.

Somebody was going to pay for all this. Whoever he was, he was on my list now. At the very top.

Anyway, Reilly and Hassett had scrubbed the trip to Hyde Park. They'd taken the train into an Army camp and searched everybody while the itinerary was being rerouted. When they were done they'd thrown everybody off but the basic staff, then got under way again.

They didn't announce where we were going. Only from watching the station signs as we went through Virginia, North Carolina, coaled at Greenville, and then Atlanta, had I figured out where we were headed.

"There he is," one of the farmers said. I pressed forward with them, gripping the gun.

The rear-platform elevator descended slowly, giving them all a long look at the man in the too-large blue suit, hands in his lap. An old gray hat covered his face. He didn't move.

"He didn't wave," a guy near me said. "He always waves."

"I swan, he don't look good."

An old man in a railroad cap pushed his way past us. "Just like setting up a dead man," he muttered.

"Couple weeks with us and he'll be fine again. Always is," someone else said, and voices chimed in, agreeing. I caught a glimpse of Merriman Smith, jotting notes; our eyes met; he smiled sardonically.

I flashed my pass to the MPs and reached the car, a big dark-blue Ford convertible, as Reilly and Prettyman were moving him from the chair. Reilly looked alarmed as he tried the first hoist. Roosevelt didn't move, didn't try to help with his arms. Prettyman had to step in and help. The crowd hushed as they carried FDR in locked arms to the sedan. When he was in the crowd parted and a couple of the locals called, "Mike! Mike Reilly!" The Secret Service chief hesitated, then gestured them through. I kept my hand in my pocket and turned to face the crowd. I caught a frown from Reilly, but then it swung away as people surged forward again, and the soldiers braced themselves, shoving back.

"Welcome home, Mr. President," said a chubby fellow in a suit.

At his voice FDR lifted his head. "Why, his honor the mayor." His hand moved, as if to adjust his hat, but it missed and knocked his glasses off. Prettyman groped on the floorboards. FDR snapped them on his nose, looking annoyed. The mayor stepped back, and a woman took his place. She didn't speak, just held FDR's hand. As she turned away her eyes were full of tears.

The police car started up and moved off. Dust rose as the Secret Service car and the President's car—FDR 1, the plate read—and a yellow roadster and finally the jeeps started off one by one. They went past the station house, and the crowd started drifting off now that the show was over. The little parade turned onto a dirt road and headed away, disappearing into a fog of scarlet dust.

I toted my luggage up Main Street, looking around as the locals slowly dispersed to wherever they spent their day. This was about the smallest town I'd ever seen. Just the station and one short street leading up the hill. Feed store, drug store, general store, a five and dime. I started to feel shaky after only a few minutes on my feet. So when I came to a barber shop I went in. It was getting long. As Leahy had helpfully pointed out.

Since I was in uniform, the haircut was free, but I had to listen to a lot of advice. The geezer on the other end of the scissors had to tell me about the Spanish-American War, and the fish hatchery, and the mayoral election in December, and the day FDR came to town in '24. I played along, putting in an oar now and then to steer things my way. By the time I pulled my blouse back on I had a pretty good idea of what was what around Meriwether County, Georgia.

Things were laid out in a triangle, the old guy said. The upper right corner was the town, the station where I'd just got off. The springs themselves, and the polio foundation FDR had built around them, were a mile to the west. The third point of the triangle was to the south, the house FDR had built in '33 on Pine Mountain. Everything was in walking distance, if you didn't mind hilly dirt roads.

The reason I saw so many people on crutches and canes and in wheelchairs was the Foundation. "Polios," that was what they called themselves, came from all over the country for therapy. It sounded like quite a setup. Private cottages for the rich folks. Hospital buildings for the rest. Surrounding it all, the old guy said, were a few thousand square miles of piney woods.

I asked him where people stayed when they came to town. He said that the President, of course, lived in the Little White House. Some of the staff lived in guest cottages there. If I had polio, I could get a bed at the Foundation. I said I'd been told I had just about everything but. In that case, he said, there was the Hotel Warm Springs, the squared-off pile of whitewashed brick across from the station. Frank Allcorn owned it, the guy I'd seen welcome FDR, and a Ruth Stevens ran it.

Looking doubtfully at my trop khaki, he said "Maybe they can find you a bed there, young fella."

———

The hotel had a big tiled lobby and potted ferns and a sixteen-foot ceiling with fans. It felt cool and empty after the glare outside. A rugged-looking, middle-aged blonde with strong teeth was wiping off the switchboard. She had an apron on and a wilted rose pinned in her hair. I told her I was with the President's party and needed a room.

"I'm sorry, I don't have a thing. We have two salesmen, a judge, the doctor, and the reporters who just arrived. That's really all we have room for."

For a second I thought of telling her who I was. Then I thought, if I was really cutting loose from Dad, I ought not to be using his name whenever I wanted something. So instead I said, "You're Ruth Stevens, aren't you?"

"Yes, but I . . ."

"Pleased to meet you. I'm John Kennedy, the President's aide. FDR said you could take care of me."

"Well, I really . . . let me see what I can do."

She left me reading the *Meriwether Vindicator* in the lobby while she went upstairs. The big news was about a local waitress killed by a jealous husband. There were also a lot of dogs being poisoned. A porky-looking Kate Smith was saving her used cooking grease to make explosives for Victory. There was an article on planting something called kudzu to halt soil erosion, and another on the Better Home Towns Program, which aimed to keep returning servicemen in Georgia by offering jobs suited to their new skills. Which were mostly maiming and killing, I thought. *Thirty Seconds over Tokyo* was playing in Greenville, with Spencer Tracy and Van Johnson, and John Wayne in *Tall in the Saddle* in Manchester. I had a feeling things would be slower around here than in D.C.

"Mr. Kennedy? I've set you up in room 22. I hope that will be all right till we have a vacancy."

"You mean there's somebody already in there?"

"Mr. Oliver, the newsman."

"Oh, Harold." He must have run straight over from the train. "Is it ready? I'm pretty beat—"

"You can go right up. Bathroom's at the end of the hall. Here's your key. That will be two dollars a day."

I told her I'd settle up when I left, and went upstairs.

It looked like Harold had come in, left his bags, and gone out again. I pulled the shades and turned the fan on. Slung my bags in the closet and hung my uniforms. Had to find a laundry, get some shirts done . . . I stripped and slid under the sheets. Then after a minute or two got up, got the revolver out of my pants, and put it under the pillow.

"What are you doing in my bed?"

I relaxed my grip on the .38. Fortunately Oliver couldn't see it under the pillow. "Hi, Harry. Goldilocks put me here. Stevens, I mean."

"In my *bed*? That's not yours, the bunk over there?"

"I got a bad back, Harry. Give me a break." I yawned. "What time is it? What's happening?"

"It's five o'clock. They're getting settled in. Unpacking. FDR wanted to go right to bed."

"How's he look to you?"

"Not too good, Jack. I don't think it helped, being on the train so long."

"Is Reilly there? Hassett? Brown?"

"Hassett wanted to know if I'd seen you. I said no."

"I'd better go check in. Hey, where does everybody eat, anyway?"

"They have dinner at Georgia Hall," said Oliver. "Down at the Foundation. Now how about getting the hell out of my bed?"

I was talking to Stevens, trying to find out how to get up to FDR's cottage, when heels tapped on the tile and I looked up to see Allie Sobelski. I stared. She looked almost Southern in a light loose skirt and blouse and a straw hat.

"Hello, Jack. Not still mad at me, are you?"

"Alice. What are you doing here?"

"They put everyone off but the wire service reps. INS is a wire service. So here I am."

"Oh. Have you been down to the—the polio setup?"

"The Foundation. I need to go there now, want to come? Miss Stevens, how are you? Can you help us get some transportation?"

Ruth said she'd try, and busied herself at the switchboard while Allie and I avoided each other's eyes. I wasn't mad at her anymore. She'd been a tease at Stanford too, it was my own fault I'd forgotten. But I didn't feel like more games. A while later a horn tooted from out front. We went out to find a black man waiting in a feed truck. Allie got in with him, and that used up the seating.

So I climbed in back. From the smell, the last riders back there had been chickens on laxatives. Yeah, I thought, grabbing the stake siderails as the Model T lurched into the street, things moved slower in Warm Springs.

Sure enough, we didn't go right to Pine Mountain. The truck turned off the macadam at a sign for the Warm Springs Foundation and clattered up a clay road between two piers of cut stone. We passed a white building with colonnades. People in wheelchairs were sitting out, soaking up the sun. We stopped to let some of them cross the road. I didn't see any springs or pools, though. Then we went uphill, past a chapel. The road wound around past cottages, then through woods. I glimpsed a flagpole above the trees.

We came out onto a circular drive and marines were running across the road, deploying in a firing line, aiming. At us. "Hold it!" I shouted, banging on the cab. The brakes locked and we skidded sidewise.

A Major Dickinson was in charge of the detachment, one of those spectacled bastards. The truck clattered away, and he watched carefully as his boys patted me down. I'd figured on this and left my .38 at the hotel. After examining my ID and checking by phone from the guard shack, he let me walk down through the gates and past the circular flower bed. Past that was the flagpole, then outbuildings—garages or servants' quarters—before I got to the house itself.

It was smaller than I'd expected. One story, not much bigger than our garage at Palm Beach. Just a white clapboard cottage with a little portico, four columns, green shutters, and white-painted brick chimneys. Elms and magnolias shadowed it, and the pine woods crowded close on either side and fell away behind. Looking past it I could see the treetops in a deep ravine. The gravel drive swept around, paused at the portico, then went out again. There weren't any steps. Everything was at ground level, so you could stroll, or roll, right in. The sun was low but it was still hot, and everything was very quiet, except for the rustling of squirrels back in the woods.

I was hesitating, wondering whether to knock, when Prettyman cracked the door and peered out.

"Mr. Hassett around, Chief?"

"Yes, he here, Lieutenant. Come on in. But be quiet, everybody asleep."

He let me into a pine-paneled foyer, simple, almost shabby, the walls covered with engravings of sailing ships. An engraving of the Old City Hall, New York. A photo of FDR with a shark. The two dentitions looked much the same. I followed Prettyman into a living room with a stone fireplace and built-in bookcases and low, comfortable-looking furniture. An MP was perched on one of the armchairs. He got up as I came in; I motioned him to carry on. I didn't see FDR anywhere.

"Mr. Hassett's out on the sun deck," the valet whispered hoarsely.

The semicircular terrace behind the house looked down into the ravine. The declining sun was still bright out here, focused by the white walls. Hassett glanced up from a lounge chair. "Lieutenant Kennedy," he said. His Vermont twang sounded doubly strange after the Georgia accents in town.

"Reporting for duty, sir. Sorry, I had to get my head down a little first."

"I should imagine. You'd better sit down, you look pale. Where are you staying?"

"At the hotel, in town." I unfolded a chair and sank into it gratefully. It was hot, hot, hot.

"I'm at the Carver Cottage, down the hill, with Grace and Dorothy. We have an agreement. I get the bathroom till eight, and after that the girls have it." He looked out over the woods. "See the finches?"

"Uh, sir, what's the plan? I heard, dinner at Georgia Hall, but I don't know where—"

"That's the Foundation. I'll take you over when it gets dark."

"Thanks. I'm still getting the layout straight. Okay if I snoop around?"

"Don't go in the bedroom, he's napping. That's to the left. The Duchess's bedroom's on the right, don't go in there either." Hassett pointed, then tilted his hat over his face again.

I wondered where Reilly was, but didn't ask. Since I couldn't go into the bedrooms, I looked in at the kitchen. It was spare and bare, a naked bulb dangling over a table and an electric range. I saw an icebox out on the service porch. Boxes of groceries were being unpacked by a tall spare Negro woman. She gave me a stare sharp as an ice pick. "Help you, mister?"

"I'm one of the aides. You must be—the cook?"

"I'm Daisy Bonner."

"Been with the President long?"

She looked at me as if I'd grown another eye. "You new around here, mister. I cooked the first meal he ever eat in this house. Country captain, French beans, baked grapefruit, chocolate souffle and coffee."

I gave her the grin. "I'm sorry. Sure, I've heard of you. They say you make the best food in Meriwether County."

"Don't know much, but I know how to cook."

Another black woman came in, and stopped short, seeing me. "This here is Lizzie McDuffie."

"Lizzie. Remember in the kitchen, at the White House?"

"Oh, you done met?" Bonner glanced at the boxes, and added, "Want a cup of coffee? I got some fresh made."

I sat for a while and gradually got the unvarnished truth about everything and everyone. Mrs. Roosevelt, for example. Daisy said, "No, Miz Roosevelt she hardly never stays in dat bedroom. Hardly ever come here exceptin' at Thanksgiving a couple of times. I don't think she like it here."

"Why not?"

"It's too country for her, I reckon. And I think they gets along better when they in different places."

"Why do you think that is?"

"She don't listen at him, you know, like a woman had ought. Got her own 'pinions, yes, ma'am. You know, I don't think there is a thing wrong with dat man, but that he is blue. Whole country dependin' on him, and he ain't got nobody just to talk to. I tries to feed him. I make that good country ham, pie, eggs, fried pork, everything a man's stomach cry for. But them fool doctors won't let him eat nothing good. You see how much weight he lost, Lizzie? Mm-mn, to where he just shrinking away to a pencil. But you watch, I get him fed up." She moved about the kitchen as she talked, lifting lids, and rich scents billowed up. "Daisy goin' to give him the things he like to eat, and to bomination with doctors. Fried chicken. Turnip greens. Hush puppies. Got a new waffle iron, cook him some waffles."

"He doesn't seem to have much of an appetite."

"Well, I'll do like always, tell Lizzie what to say to him."

"What do you tell him?" I asked McDuffie.

"I'll tell him we all having so-and-so for dinner, and Daisy says for him be sure not to eat any. Then we'll sneak him what we want him to eat."

"Where did it come from?" I asked her.

"What?"

"The waffle iron. You said you had a new waffle iron."

"Oh, that, Mr. Morgenthau give it to us. Yeah, I see what you mean. We done made waffles wid it two-three times already. We all ate them. They was good."

"Daisy! You in there?"

"In here, Ho-say. Put that ice in under the cream. This here is José Esperancilla, the houseboy. He's in the Navy, just like you, Mr. Kennedy."

I said hi to the houseboy, then finished my coffee and left them to getting the kitchen in order.

I went outside and walked around the house on the path. There were more guards below the terrace, at the edge of the woods. Marines with M-1s came to attention, then presented arms as I came within the regulation ten paces. I saluted back. Tall steel poles held floodlights. There seemed to be two layers of security. The inner was the white guardhouses, usually manned by Secret Service, but with Army MPs in them now. The outer was the green guardhouses, blending with the woods; the Marine Corps. They added up to a lot of eyes. Plus, the very sleepiness around here was reassuring. In rural Georgia any newcomer would stand out like a lighthouse on fire.

Night was almost on us. The air was cooler, and the shadows of the pines lay dark and soft across the path. When I lifted my eyes I saw yellow light in the windows. A strange, loud, drawn-out cry startled me before I realized what it was. A whippoorwill. When I lifted my eyes to the lacy darkness of the treetops the first stars were glittering.

Standing there on the path, I felt something knotted inside me slowly relax. I didn't see the attraction myself. The red clay South didn't appeal to me. But I felt that FDR had, in some way, come home.

"Kennedy."

Someone was standing in the darkness under the terrace. I hesitated, then walked toward them. Women's voices came from above us, then the President's hearty guffaw.

Brown and Reilly were standing against the terrace wall. "Good evening, Admiral," I said. "Hi, Mike."

Brown said, "I was just telling Mike, I think you've done all right here."

"Is that right, sir?"

"Take that chip off your shoulder, Lieutenant. Why don't we declare peace? We just got off on the wrong foot, in the Map Room."

The red coals of their cigarettes glowed, then faded. I said, "That's all right, sir. Anybody can make a mistake."

"I've got a jeep and a driver. Want to go over to the Hall, get some dinner?"

From above us came a clack, then a buzz. The floodlights glowed slowly into life, so bright they blotted out the night sky. And just as suddenly, all my suspicions flared back into life. Why was Brown lurking out here with Reilly? Why was he soliciting my friendship? And while I was at it, what about Reilly? So far he hadn't done shit to protect FDR, as far as I could see, till a fresh corpse forced him to put on a show.

From now on, I made up my mind, everyone was suspect. I had to protect the man above me, laughing on the terrace. If only to protect my own life. I'd spend every hour I could here with him. And I'd be armed.

"Aye aye, sir," I said. "I'd appreciate that very much."

CHAPTER 28

Red Oaks Mill, New York

T hat same night the blond man with the round face was sitting in a roadhouse in upstate New York. A copy of the *Herald* was open in front of him. He was reading the comics and drinking beer, glancing occasionally at his watch. The steel Elgin they'd issued him in Berlin. He'd had it fixed in Washington while he was making the rounds for the cleaning plant. Actually he'd done all right, just done as the old Negro had said. What had his name been? Smalls. He'd liked the old scoundrel, with his tales of horny housewives and underground gambling.

Krasov looked at his hands, remembering. You wouldn't think a man's spine breaking would make that much noise.

Then he went back to the comics, to Mutt and Jeff, Buzz Sawyer, Oaky Doaks, Moon Mullins. Occasionally he chuckled to himself.

At eight sharp the pay phone rang. He got up, glanced around casually, and entered the booth. He closed the folding door, but didn't answer right away. At the fifth ring he took it off the hook. "Hello," he said into the buzzing silence. "It's nice in the park today, isn't it?"

And the voice said, the voice that he'd never heard before: "Yes. It's very pleasant in the park."

Ivan Krasov nodded slowly to himself. Yes, he thought. Oh, yes.

Fence was a woman.

"Where the hell are you? I've been here waiting for two days."

"Plans have changed."

"Uh huh. Did it work?"

"No."

He shifted on the hard wooden bench, torn between regret and triumph. "I told you it wouldn't."

"Well, I thought it would."

"Okay, forget it. We don't have much time left. We'll do things my way now." He felt the map in his pocket, felt, beneath it, the hard angularity of the pistol butt. "Look, I'm just a couple miles south of Poughkeepsie. I've got a car. I can drive up and see you tonight—"

"No. You can't."

"Why not?"

"We're not at Hyde Park."

"What?"

"That's what I meant when I said things have changed. After they found the . . . suitcase, we were rerouted. The train. We didn't go north after all."

"Rerouted? Where?"

"We're in Warm Springs, Georgia."

"Christ! *Georgia?*" he almost shouted, then remembered and lowered his voice again. "Where the *hell* is that?"

"South of South Carolina."

"I know that, I mean—where is this town? Hot Springs?"

"Warm Springs. It's south of Atlanta. Did you say you had a car? Can you get gas? Listen, I'll give you directions from Atlanta."

Reining in his anger, he copied the directions on the back of the newspaper. Atlanta, *Atlanta,* Jesus, he thought.

"Okay, I've got it. I'll get down there as soon as I can."

"What do you want me to do?"

"I don't want you to do anything for the moment except try to figure some way for me to get close to him, when I get there. Can you do that?"

"I'll try. What else?"

"Nothin' else. Don't do anything to queer it, goddamn it, okay? Just sit tight. You got a number there?"

When the other hung up he slammed the doors to the booth open and went back to the bar. Swung himself up on a stool. Shook his head in disgust. Georgia!

Then he got out his wallet and counted his money.

There wasn't much. The money from the robbery at LaFontaine's had netted him only a hundred and ten dollars. To get here, he'd had to eke it out with a day's receipts from Hahn and Hurja. The last day, he'd made all his collections, then dumped the day's pickups in an alley and headed north in the truck. Which was parked outside now. He didn't know how efficient the American police were at tracking stolen vehicles, but he shouldn't keep it much longer. He'd planned to get rid of it tonight, find a bluff road and drive it over into the Hudson.

But now, they weren't in Hyde Park! They weren't in New York State at all. They were in Georgia! *Kapusta!* The whole thing was so screwed up. And all because the idiotic Germans had given all the money to the SS colonel to carry. Because he was more trustworthy! What a laugh! But Heudeber had vanished, and here he was trying to carry out the fucking mission with nickels and dimes. Part of the cash in that green suitcase was his, not just operating funds but his reward, his pay. Now he'd never be paid; that one-armed bastard had probably walked right through the lobby of the FBI office and out another entrance. He was in Cuba or Argentina by now, with enough to live fat and happy for the rest of his life.

"You want anything, buddy, or are you just gonna sit there and stew?"

Krasov looked up at the bartender. "Beer," he muttered. "Hey, and you got anything to eat?"

"Kipper sandwiches, chips, hard-boiled eggs."

As he gnawed bread and oily fish he wondered again whether he should give it up. Forget about the mission, as Heudeber apparently had. Just disappear, head west, look for that restaurant in Arizona.

But no matter where he started, he came to the same conclusion. He hadn't volunteered to fight for the Germans for money. He'd done it because the Nazis were the only ones around who looked like they could lick the Reds. And now that it looked like they couldn't, here he was in America, same deal. Maybe it was for his mother and father. Maybe for the woman he'd turned in. Maybe to make up somehow for everything he'd done himself. Whatever, it wasn't for pay.

He was doing this out of conviction. Because someone had to. He saw that clearly.

The bartender put a plate of sliced pickled eggs in front of him. Krasov snapped a dime down on the counter. "Hey, what's the quickest way to get down South these days, Mac? If you ain't got a lot of scratch?"

"Whereabouts south?"

"Deep South. Alabama, Georgia."

"Hope you got a priority, bub. You ain't, it ain't gonna be easy."

Krasov felt the automatic slipping down inside his pants. He started to reach for it, then felt the bartender's eyes drop to his hands. Instead he put them to his back, stretching, as if his spine hurt him, and adjusted the gun's weight unobtrusively. The bland lips curved in a smile. Not easy? No, it wasn't turning out to be easy. A less stubborn man might have been discouraged. But he'd always been determined. That was all that had kept him alive, that endless winter after they took his parents. And after that, in the POW camps; only that had kept him alive when so many others died.

It wasn't easy. But always, just when he wondered if he should keep on, he glimpsed a way ahead. Some mysterious destiny seemed to propel him onward. He was the agent of Fate. He was the angel of vengeance.

"Oh, I'll get there somehow," Ivan Krasov said.

CHAPTER 29

Thursday, April 5: Warm Springs

We didn't see much of FDR for the first couple of days in Georgia. Instead of wheeling furiously around for briefings and conferences, he kept to his room, resting. The rest of us stayed inside the tight ring of security Reilly had clamped around us.

When I got up Thursday morning I felt better, almost okay again. Even the trundle bed Oliver had relegated me to didn't keep me from a deep sleep once the room cooled off. I had breakfast with the other hotel residents in the mezzanine. Eggs and ham and grits, homemade biscuits and gravy. I ate more than usual, but my stomach didn't object. Then I put on a pair of combat boots I'd talked DeWitt Greer, the officer in charge of the Little White House's Signal Corps detachment, out of. Put my uniform shoes in a "poke" Ruth Stevens gave me, and started out.

The roads were dusty, but this early the temperatures were bearable. Instead of heading for the Foundation entrance I turned left at the railroad station and hiked down State 163. From there it was only half a mile downhill, then uphill again, to a dirt road that led up into the woods. It was hot by the time I reached it and I was glad for the shade. I started whistling as I went up the rutted track, a back entrance to the southern cottages, and the marines were alert when I got to the first sentry booth.

When I let myself in the front door a radio was playing in the kitchen and Fala was barking his ass off. I went through the living room and the open french windows out onto the terrace.

FDR was sitting in a lounge chair listening to Brown. A tray stood at his elbow. While the admiral briefed him, the President was feeding his breakfast to his dog. He was wearing a rather tatty bathrobe over pajamas, but he was shaved and his hair was combed back. He still looked gaunt, but better than when they took him off the train. Hassett, wearing his hat, sat listening from a perch on the balustrade.

When I glanced at the maps even less was left of Germany now. It didn't look like long before Hitler would be doing a jig at the end of a rope.

We sat around on the terrace after Brown left. The silence stretched out. The President broke it at last. "How about that one?"

"I'm sorry, sir?"

"Bill—there. Hear that? He just did it again."

They were talking about birds again. I tuned out as Fala flopped down at my feet, muzzle specked with muffin crumbs. His eyes rolled up to study me. I resisted the impulse to kick him.

"You like dogs, Johnny-Kay?" FDR asked me.

"Not a lot, sir. They give me hives."

"I think the papers pay more attention to Pup here than they do to me. A politician without a dog is almost as hard to sell as one without a wife."

"That leaves me out on both counts, sir."

"I remember he was so popular, this mutt, on the *Baltimore* last summer— we thought he was shedding. Then Sam Rosenman realized what was going on. He was going down to the mess decks, and the sailors would feed him, and of course they had to have a souvenir. I had to get the captain to order them to stop snipping hair off Fala, or he'd have been bald when we got to Hawaii."

We chuckled. "Old Pup," Roosevelt went on fondly. "I've told Margaret, if anything happens to me, I want her to have him. I'm sure Eleanor will be too busy to look after him, and he's devoted to Margaret."

Hassett and I glanced at each other. It was the first time I'd ever heard FDR refer to the possibility he might someday die.

Roosevelt looked at his watch, sighed, and looked around. "Do you mind—my cigarettes—"

I went in and got them off his night table, and stopped in the kitchen for a day's supply of kitchen matches from Daisy. FDR had it lit before I realized I'd forgotten the holder. I said, "Wait a minute, sir—"

"That's all right, don't bother." He inhaled with his eyes closed, and leaned back in the sun. "Have you gotten out into the town at all, John?"

"I'm staying at the hotel, sir."

"Isn't Ruth a grand cook? Her Brunswick stew is extraordinary. And that nut cake—Deacon, remember that cake she sent over last time we were here? We need to figure out how to get another one. How do you like the place, Johnny? A little different from Boston?"

"The people are friendly, sir. What's funny is they seem to accept us."

"They're more accustomed to visitors here than in most small towns. But that's not to say they're any different in Manchester, or Odessadale. You know, so much of what we're told about the South just isn't true on close examination. Did you know that no America First rally was ever held in the state of Georgia?"

"No sir, I didn't."

"I once visited a town near here, and I was the guest of the local Chamber of Commerce. They sat me next to an Italian on one side and a Jew on the other. I asked the president of the Chamber whether these two men were members of the KKK. He said yes, they were, but that they were considered to be all right otherwise, since everyone in the town knew them. I think that's a good illustration of how—of how difficult it is to really have any prejudices, racial, religious, or otherwise, if you really know people."

I asked him, "Did you know Senator Truman had been in the Klan when you asked for him as vice president, sir?"

"In the first place, I didn't *ask* for anybody. Truman was the bona fide choice of an unfettered convention." Over his shoulder I caught Hassett's rolled eyes. "And in the second, why, considering where he came from and when, you really couldn't hold that against him. Of course it was a club for the Republicans to beat him with, but . . . it was long ago and I think he's proven his liberal credentials pretty thoroughly since then. He's certainly been a great help in the Senate during this war."

We sat on the terrace and talked, or rather listened to FDR talk, about Truman's investigations, and the convention, and the election, and how low that son of a bitch Dewey was. He slid from that somehow into my grandfather's political career. To my surprise he knew more about ward politics in Boston than I did. It was like a card file, only most of the men he mentioned had been dead for years. "Politics runs in your family, Johnny, doesn't it?"

"Dad calls it public service."

"Why? Is there something wrong with the other word?"

"He thinks so."

"I have to disagree. Of course, in general terms, most of the public is far more interested in government than politics, as we understand it. And yet, a government without politics is by definition a tyranny.

"As to the word itself, there may be scurrilous politicians, as easily as scurrilous pastors. But the one reason a gentleman might be a politician, in my view, is that the faint possibility exists that he might leave the world in a better state than he found it. Unless you're a great scientist, or a truly great artist, I can think of no better way to benefit one's fellow man on a grand scale."

"If you make the right decisions. But what if you don't? You have these tremendous responsibilities—"

"Well, the way I feel about that—you see, public life takes a lot of sweat; but it doesn't need to worry you. You won't always be right, but you must not suffer from being wrong."

"But if it's a major decision, like Lincoln had to make—or the New Deal—"

"Granted, but you can't lose sleep over it. You know, if they made a truck driver president, just took him from his truck and installed him in this office, fifty percent of his decisions would be right, on average. They'd have to be. But we're not truck drivers. You, for example, have had a fairly good education. You've commanded men in battle. Your percentage is bound to be higher. So long as you keep it over fifty percent, and tell the people honestly what you are about, they won't get rid of you and send for a truck driver."

"I'm not sure everybody's got that understanding of it, sir. Or your appetite for it."

"Johnny, everybody seems to think I enjoy what I do. I admit, the first two terms we had a whale of a time. But if it hadn't been for the war I'd have been back at Hyde Park. Or down here, acting as medical director. Doctor Roosevelt, they used to call me. I was the first physiotherapist to work with polio victims in water. But I'm . . . getting off the trail again. I meant to say, I just want to end the war and fashion a peace that can last. There are times when a man has to set his own comforts aside and do what the times ask of him."

" 'This generation of Americans has a rendezvous with destiny,' " I quoted him.

"That still sounds rather well," he said. "It turned out to be even truer than I thought in '36."

"It reminds me of Rousseau, sir. 'As soon as any man says of the affairs of the state, What does it matter to me? The state may be given up as lost.' "

"My God, he quotes Rousseau. Deacon, we have a challenger for you here."

"It's nothing remarkable, sir," I said. "I keep a little notebook, and sometimes I jot things like that down."

"Our assistant secretary of state can sling the words. Archy MacLeish. Have you read his stuff? 'There with vast wings across the canceled skies,/There in the sudden blackness the black pall/Of nothing, nothing, nothing—nothing at all.' "

The passage seemed to sadden him. He sat nodding after the last line. "Nothing at all," he repeated, took a last drag on his cigarette, and stubbed it out. "Ah well. . . . When are the girls coming over?"

Hassett said, "I think they had some shopping to do, Mr. President. And Miss Delano said something about a hairdresser."

"I wonder what shade of purple it will turn out this time," said FDR. "I don't know why Aunt Polly thinks she has to color her hair like an Easter egg. It would look so good just silver gray, like M'ma's was." His hand moved to his breast, then paused; he seemed surprised to find he didn't have a jacket on. He fumbled another cigarette out of the bathrobe. "Johnny-Kay, would you mind—"

"Yes sir." I went in and this time found a well-chewed holder beside his bed.

Dr. Bruenn came out at nine, with his bag. He frowned when he saw the cigarette. FDR said expansively, "Ah, the medicine man."

"Good morning, Mr. President. How did you sleep?"

"I kept waking up. I hope you brought something for my sinuses. They're like sponges today." Fala whined, looking up at the tray. "Oh, look at those pleading brown eyes," said FDR, leaning forward to drop him the last bit of bacon.

"I can give you some drops, sir," said Bruenn. FDR signaled to me. I got up and wheeled him into the bedroom. Paneled in pine like the rest of the house, it contained a low desk and a bed. I noticed the head was propped up, as his bed at the White House had been. Bruenn bent over him as Prettyman watched from the shadows. I went out into the living area; the room was too small for four.

I was looking into the driveway when a jeep drove up and braked in a smoke of dust and a rattle of gravel. I figured it for the mail, which came in from Washington by air, landing at the Meriwether County airfield. But I was surprised to see who was carrying the leather dispatch bag: Dewey Long. "Hey, Dewey," I said. "What are you doing here? I thought we got rid of you."

"Can the wiseguy act. I'm the communications officer."

"I thought the Army took care of that."

"The military side comes in on the Signal Corps land lines. This is governmental . . . where's Mr. Hassett?"

"Here I am," said Hassett, coming in off the terrace. While the secretary to the President was signing for the pouch I drifted over to the bedroom door. It was open, but I couldn't see FDR. Probably Prettyman had him on the can. I wondered briefly how they got him on and off, then turned my attention back to Hassett. He was unpacking the bag, muttering to himself as he quickly scanned each letter or document. Most had red tags attached and these he looked at first, setting the others aside on a card table.

"You need me, sir?"

"Why? Got someplace to go?"

"No."

"Just stand by," muttered Hassett, intent on the mail. "He'll be out in a little while."

I wandered out onto the terrace again and looked over the balcony. There was a man in civilian clothes in the white guard shack now. The MPs must have been relieved. The marines were still on duty, though, in the outer ring. Hassett was right, the birds were going nuts today. Fala lay watching them through the spaces in the balcony. I wondered which were the finches.

Prettyman wheeled the President out again, now dressed in loose gray pants and a white shirt and blue bow tie. The effect was casual, at least for FDR.

"Why, hello there, Dewey. How was the flight?"

"Hello, Mr. President. Flight was okay," said Long.

"Got the scandal sheets?"

"Here you are, sir. *The Times, Herald Tribune, Sun, Post.*" He passed them over; FDR glanced at the headlines, then tossed them onto the sofa to be devoured later.

"How's the laundry today, Deacon?"

"About average, Mr. President. Just give me a minute to check it over."

"Have you been into town yet?" FDR asked me. I hesitated; hadn't we just had this conversation? "Yes sir, I have."

"How'd you like it?"

"It's restful."

"Uh oh," said Hassett.

"A croak of ill omen," remarked FDR. Hassett passed him the piece of paper. He studied it, head cocked doubtfully.

"Do you want to see him, sir?"

"Hold it," said FDR. "What's that?"

"Lincoln's sparrow," said Hassett, peering into the woods. "We need binoculars. Can't see him."

"You won't. That's a Bachman's. 'Seeee, slip slip slip'," said FDR, with an air of judicious self-satisfaction. "*Aimophila aestivalis.* You won't find a Lincoln's around here this time of year. Unless it's very cold. When we used to go riding they'd just pop right up all around us, this time of year."

"We'll just have the staff send him a form thank-you, that's all," said Hassett. FDR looked regretful, but didn't contradict him.

"What about our other visitor? From Aiken?"

"That's being set up, sir."

"Anything else on the schedule?"

"President Osmeña."

"Oh Lord. When is he due? What does he want?"

"He's flying in to Fort Benning day after tomorrow. I'll take your car, if I may, and pick him up early. I believe he wants to talk about independence."

"Good, good," the President said. "But I don't want him around all day. He's like De Gaulle, he always wants more time. Though it's a good deal more pleasant than a session with *Le Grand Charles* . . . Schedule us two hours, then set up a press conference. Do you ride, Johnny?"

It took a second to respond to the zag in the conversation. "I used to at the Jay Six, sir. Till a mule got me where I love. Stretched me out for a few blissful minutes."

"Jay Six. Out west?"

"Benson, Arizona, sir. Spent summers there when I was a kid. It's pretty f—pretty damned uncomfortable. Lice all over everything."

"They still have the stables over at the Foundation, don't they, Bill? Maybe we could call Frank. Or go over there."

"You're in no condition to ride a horse, sir."

"Doc?"

"I don't think horses are a good idea, Mr. President."

"I seem to be outvoted . . . will you be around this afternoon, Johnny?"

"Yessir, I'll be here."

"Deacon, we've got to get some work in on the Jefferson Day speech, too. Have you got somebody on it? Because otherwise I'm just going to have to get up early some morning and write it myself."

"Don't do that, sir. I'll check today and let you know when we'll have a draft."

We spent the morning sitting around. Vegetating. FDR kidded us unmercifully. I didn't blame him, I'd go nuts if I was cooped up here. I'd planned to stay all day, but my resolution was getting weaker.

At eleven Grace Tully came over and they went over some letters. Then FDR had lunch with her, from trays on the terrace.

After lunch he was supposed to take a long nap. When he disappeared into his bedroom I checked with Hassett to see if he needed me. He said he supposed not. I went out and asked Reilly if he had any objection to my using the roadster. He said no. "We've got enough cars around, with the jeeps and the sedans. Gas it up. There's ration coupons in the glove compartment."

"The President needs ration stamps?"

"Everybody does," said Reilly, bending me an unreadable look. "Don't you? Doesn't your dad?"

I said sure, not wanting to argue myself out of a car.

"And there's something I want you to do for me."

"Old Golds, right?"

"No, not Old Golds. Business. I've got more agents driving in from Florida and Texas, but I've just got enough right now to hold the perimeter. I don't have anybody to send out. Could you check a couple things out?"

"Sure, Mike."

"I was looking at the local paper. There's been a lot of dogs being poisoned—"

"I noticed that," I said. "Must be a serious dog-hater in town. Or a really smart cat."

"Yeah, well, that's the kind of stuff I make it my business to check out. How about going over to the paper and see if you can get a handle on it. See what they got."

It felt good to have a car key in my hand. The Willys was cute, a little yellow two-seater, and somebody had kept it oiled and polished. It had some kind of weird hand-operated gearshift, though, and I drove it around the fountain a couple of times before I felt confident enough to head off down the hill.

———

They didn't have too much to add at the newspaper office. The reports had come in from the sheriff. So I asked who he was.

I found C. H. Collier sitting in front of a black Hunter desk fan. It searched back and forth, ruffling his hair and fluttering the wanted fliers on the wall of his office. Collier looked like Winston Churchill, only with gray hair instead of bald. He locked his fingers in his lap and looked away from me and when I was finished said softly, "An' you say Mike Reilly would like to know what we have on it."

"That's right, Sheriff."

"You look right warm, Lieutenant."

"Don't you think it's hot?"

"Ain't too bad, this here. Cooler up here in the hills than most places. Well, I sure would like to cooperate with Mike. But I ain't got much more than what all it said in the paper. We don't see much crime in this county. When Jim Smiley shot his girlfriend that was about the biggest in years. But back to the dogs. Has been funny. Six or eight of them up to now. A man will wake up in the morning and it's quiet, and he'll go out and there's his dog just a-lying there. Nothing ever stolen. No signs of forcible entry. Just the dead dogs."

"Where was this?"

"It's been near about where you are. Woodbury, Sulphur Springs, Manchester, such as that. Don't think there's been any right there in Warm Springs, though."

"We're interested in protecting the President."

"Sure you are. We are too. You tell Mike if I get any idea who's doin' it, or if I figure any way it could be a threat to FDR, I'll be on the phone to him that very minute."

I was standing up when he said, still looking away from me, "You know, there is one thing I maybe ought to mention. Mike knows about it. He tell you about our local Klan?"

"No," I said.

"Like I say, they ain't much. It's the lowlifes been active in it. But a couple years ago, there was some talk when Mrs. R was here to—christen, that the right word?—that school for colored girls. Some folks said it was going to stir up trouble. Get them dissatisfied with their places. Now, we treat our colored right down here. They work hard and they're good people. But like I say, there was some didn't like what she was doing."

"They made threats?"

"Nothing like that, just fool talk. I made it my business to have a word with a couple of the boys. Told them we didn't need their kind of troublemaking around town. 'Thout FDR, a lot of people in this county wouldn't have jobs. They promised me they'd put the quietus on it, and so far they have—unless this dog business is something new I haven't figured out yet."

"One last question."

"Shoot."

"Is this a dry county?"

"Legally," said Collier. "There's probably a still or two up in the hills we ain't caught up to yet, but it don't amount to much. Ever taste Georgia moon, Lieutenant?"

"No, I haven't. Thanks for the information, Sheriff."

"My pleasure, Lieutenant. Give my best to Mike."

━━

The sun was at its height as I drove back to Warm Springs. I left my cap off and let the wind comb my hair. The road rolled up and down. Farm country. Mules on the clay road. It looked like something out of Faulkner.

The Foundation grounds were empty. Maybe the patients were all at siesta. I parked in front of Georgia Hall, near a fountain, and walked up and under the colonnade.

And there they were. Lunch must have just been over. They came crutching and rolling out, and I felt a sudden aversion. The happy faces and talk seemed not to belong with the twisted bodies beneath them. Three girls, kids, really, saw me and stopped chattering. I looked away, and they rolled by silently before bursting into laughter as they turned the corner.

I caught a clink of glasses and the hiss of soda. Yes! A soda fountain, right off the lobby. I ordered an egg cream and got a funny look. "Just make it a vanilla fudge sundae, then," I said.

Merriman Smith was sitting at one of the tables, stroking his mustache and talking to a fellow in glasses and golf duds. "Jack. Over here," Smith said as I sauntered past, spooning up ice cream. "Basil, this is John Kennedy, Joe's son, back from the Pacific as the President's personal aide. Jack, Basil O'Connor, director of the Foundation."

"Pleased to meet you, sir. I know you and the President go way back."

"About as far back as anybody could. As his lawyer, I advised him not to buy this place. What do you think of our facilities, Mr. Kennedy?"

"I haven't really seen them," I said, hoping he'd get the message, that I wasn't interested, either. But O'Connor had to tell me all about the Indians and their spring, and the Meriwether Hotel, which was what used to be here before the Foundation, apparently.

"I keep hearing about the springs, but I haven't seen them yet," I said. Then, realizing he could take that to mean I wanted to, added hastily, "I just came over to get something to eat. I'll have to make some time another day to—"

"They're just down the hill. On the far side of the quadrangle. Tell you what—"

"I really have to get back, Mr. O'Connor—"

"I'll have Miss Chaworth show them to you. Veronica! Would you come over here, please?"

Slim and pretty in a gray uniform with a Red Cross patch. "Veronica, a young hero, Jack Kennedy."

"It was involuntary," I said. "They sank my boat."

"Miss Chaworth, could you show the Lieutenant around?"

"I'd be happy to."

I dragged my eyes away, but it wasn't easy. "Look, I'd really like to, but I have to be back. The President's probably up and around, and I need to be there. Maybe later, okay?"

"Nice meeting you, Lieutenant."

"Mr. O'Connor, Miss Chaworth. See you, Merriman." I disposed of the last spoonfuls of ice cream and wiped my mouth and left.

▬

When I got back to the cottage the President's cousins were sitting in the living room. Laura Delano and Margaret Suckley looked primped and cool; I felt disheveled and smelly. Damn it, I'd meant to ask about laundry at the Foundation. Where did FDR get his shirts done?

The President was on the terrace again. This time the awnings had been unrolled, and the shade was welcome. He had the card table out and was sitting at it in a big leather chair. Reilly was perched on the balustrade, in the same position Hassett had been in that morning. He was wearing a straw hat. Roosevelt glanced up as I came out, but went silently back to what he was doing. Pasting stamps in a book, but having a tough time with the tweezers.

A stamp left his fingers and fluttered to the floor. I got up and retrieved it for him. He smiled and said, "Thank you." But he didn't try again. Instead he left it there, put his hands on the arms of the chair and sighed, looking out at the woods.

"Franklin, would you like some tea?"

He didn't answer. His cousin stood in the doorway, looking at him anxiously. She glanced at me, then at Reilly. Mike looked grave.

"Franklin?"

He glanced up then, and his smile was sweet and almost childlike. He made a motion to me to move his chair and said, in a weak, almost inaudible voice, "Thank you, Aunt Polly. I would . . . I would like some tea."

CHAPTER 30

Friday, April 6: Fort Benning, Georgia

The most glamorous woman in the world slammed the door of the noncommissioned officer's club so hard glass shattered. She buttoned her coat over a red-piped yellow jacket and black skirt as she struggled down the steps into the street, panting with rage. As she pulled on black gloves passing soldiers did double takes at her legs, triple takes at the face under the wide-brimmed yellow hat. She didn't look at them, though she knew, with that part of her that always knew exactly how she looked to others, that they were gawking.

The son of a bitch, she thought furiously, hands shaking so she could hardly button the gloves. After all she'd done for him. A sergeant from some hick town no one had ever heard of. She'd driven across the country to surprise him—and what did she get? She had offers every day on the sound stages. She heard hopeful murmurs now from the men straggling after her. *They* might treat her with respect.

She'd said it as a joke. Said she'd been thinking about what he said when he was in California, and that maybe he was right, maybe they should get married. Now. Today. And he'd turned white. No, yellow! Said he wasn't sure, maybe after the war!

Okay, screw him! She was through. She walked faster, blocky red heels tapping concrete. A wolf whistle. She almost gave them the finger. But that wouldn't be smart. They were her public. But to hell with them. All of them.

She was thinking this when she saw the dog. She stopped dead and looked at it, then at the building it was cocking a leg in front of—the base veterinary—then at the huge blue convertible in the commanding officer's parking space. And last, at the man in a gray overcoat who stood patiently holding its leash.

"Bill?" she said.

Hassett lifted his head from contemplating the way of a Scottie with a bush. He stared at her blankly, as if his thoughts had been far away, for several seconds before recognition lit. "Miss Wolfe?"

"I thought that was you! How are you, little Fala?"

"You two didn't get along very well last year," said Hassett, a smile touching lips that had looked pretty grim when she walked up.

"I liked him fine. Till he ran downstairs with my panties in his teeth."

Hassett blushed and the soldiers snickered. They formed a circle around them now. It was growing at its edges as others came running.

"How are you, Lauren?"

"In the pink, Bill. You?"

"All right."

"What exactly are you—I mean, what brings you here?"

"Taking him to the vet. What are *you* doing here?"

"Visiting a friend."

"At Fort Benning?"

"Yes. But it turned out we weren't as close as I thought." She lowered her voice. "You're here. Fala's here. That means someone we know is in Warm Springs. Even though the newspaper today said he was in Hyde Park."

"Wartime security, Lauren."

"Word's going to travel fast."

"He has that effect," said Hassett sadly, looking down at the dog. Fala sniffed at her nylons. Some of the soldiers offered to join the dog.

She smiled sweetly at her public. How young they looked! "Come on, boys. Do you mind me and my press agent having a private conference?"

"That your dog, Red?"

"Looks like Fala." The soldiers laughed.

"If you'll excuse me, I have to meet a plane," said Hassett, reining the dog toward the car. "Nice seeing you."

She looked around at the soldiers. Then went around to the passenger side. She gave them a little leg as she got in, but they still looked disappointed. As they drifted away Hassett frowned across the seat.

"Can you drop me outside the gate? My car's out there. It's too far to walk in this den of wolves."

Hassett said "Sure," and started the engine, looking relieved.

The President's man eyed his watch during the drive. She wondered who was on this plane he was meeting. He dropped her at the lot, and, to her surprise, turned back in through the gate again. She stood beside the Packard, searching her purse for keys. Remembering how excited she'd been at the prospect of a wedding, she got hot all over again. Men were such shits. Some other thought floated at the back of her mind, but she didn't want to think about it. "Shits," she said aloud, got in, and started the car. Then stopped, gloves on the wheel. Where was she going? Not back to L.A. She was still on strike. Levinsohn was still not budging. Where could she go now?

Suddenly she knew.

She spotted the blue convertible again out on the airstrip, parked near a twin-engine airplane. Now the top was up. Hassett stood next to it as Army men handed leather sacks out of the fuselage. There were four more soldiers in helmets and khakis sitting on motorcycles. They glared at the Packard as she pulled up, and a guard unslung his carbine. Then their eyes widened.

"Holy shit! It's Lauren Wolfe!"

"Hello, boys, it's nice to see you," she said, fast, because that way they didn't have time to think of the next thing to say, which with most men came out all too predictable. She motioned Hassett over. As he put his foot on the running board she said, "I'm coming to Warm Springs with you, Bill."

"No, Lauren. That wouldn't be right."

"Why not? What's the matter?"

"Nothing's the matter."

A face showed at the window of the Ford. Somebody small. "Who's that?"

"A visitor for the President, if you *must* know."

"That's my Bill. So he *is* seeing people."

"Only this person."

"Come on, Deacon. I'm much better looking, I can tell that from here. Didn't I make myself agreeable last time?"

"You were very entertaining. We all enjoyed having you—"

"He enjoyed it a great deal, didn't he?"

"He certainly did. As did all the guests, and the patients, and the staff. But this time—"

"Bill, I'm at loose ends. I'm coming along and you may as well get used to the idea."

"No, you're not," said Hassett. "And that's final." He made a start-your-engines gesture at the troops and they kicked their Harleys into earshattering life.

She got back into her car, slammed the door, and looked after the big Ford. The circle around her was slowly closing in. She put on a smile, but she wasn't thinking of them. She was thinking of an older man. He couldn't walk, or even stand. But she'd spent the most exciting night of her life with him.

Only Hassett said he wasn't seeing anyone. That she flat *couldn't come.*

She started the Packard and pulled out after the other car, giving the servicemen a cheery wave bye-bye as she left them behind.

At her first screen test, they'd said that she was unphotogenic. She couldn't project. A too-tall, awkward, sexless bitch. That hair her shade didn't come across in black and white. If there was one thing she couldn't stand—never, from the day she'd tried out for the third-grade play—it was being told there was something she couldn't do.

This morning when the President rolled out he was fully dressed, in blue trousers and a crimson Harvard tie, hair brushed neatly back. The purple bags under his eyes were almost gone. The vacation was working, I thought. I took the wheelchair over from Prettyman. "How are you this morning, sir?"

FDR raised his eyebrows and drawled, "Well, Johnny, I remember a story about the fellah who came to a little town up in the Tennessee hills and asked directions to another town. They told him to take a shortcut over the mountains. He hiked up and down hills all day and at nightfall, he found himself back in the same town again. 'Well,' he said, 'At least I am holding my own.'"

I chuckled and wheeled him outside. It was just cool enough to be comfortable, and the sun threw a thousand dappled images of itself through the tall Georgia pines to dance and shimmer on the sun deck. Grace was there, she'd come over early. They chatted while I went in to tell Daisy they were ready for breakfast.

"Johnny-Kay, draw up a chair, enough here for three."

"I don't want to take your breakfast, sir."

"Nonsense. Help me out with these eggs."

"Isn't this a beautiful day, Mr. President."

"You can say that again, Duchess. You know, let's work a little, then it might be time for that drive we've been planning. If someone could mention it to Mike—"

"I'll tell him, sir."

"Thanks, Johnny. I think it would be grand, if it gets as warm as I think it will."

"Good morning, Mr. President." Brown, maps and message board tucked under his gold-crusted arm. FDR waved him in casually.

The big news today was that the USSR had unexpectedly "denounced" its neutrality pact with Japan a week early, saying it had "lost its meaning." The President nodded at this, but didn't seem as jubilant as I expected. Meanwhile the Marines in Okinawa gained five miles on Ishikawa Isthmus, while Army forces advanced a mile and a half against stiffening resistance. FDR asked for casualties and looked both troubled and relieved when he heard one hundred seventy-five killed and eight hundred wounded. U.S. bombers hit Jap shipping in Hong Kong. In Germany, the British Second Army was forty miles from Bremen. The U.S. Ninth reached the Weser and there were reports the stream had been crossed. The Third Army captured Muehlhausen on its way to Leipzig. Five thousand planes were active over the Reich. The Russians continued their gains, reached Vienna's city limits, and cut the railway to Linz.

"Anything else from the Russians?"

"No sir. The Oder front is silent . . . the only other thing we have is an appreciation from General Eisenhower that says he'll probably have to declare V-E day rather than have any sort of clear-cut surrender. He anticipates a long period of guerrilla warfare."

"I'll yield to his judgment. Is that all? Very good. Thanks, Brownie."

Brown hesitated. "Yes?" said FDR. "Something else?"

"What did you plan to do about the note to Stalin, sir?"

"I think I made myself plain in the last cable," said the President, his voice going cool. "He seems to think I'm lying to him, or being played for a fool by my staff. Of course we're accepting German surrenders. But that's all they are, capitulations of military forces in the field. There's no separate agreement of the kind he alleges. Frankly, I can't avoid a feeling of bitterness toward his subordinates, whoever they are, for such vile misrepresentations of our actions. And that's exactly what I told him. The next move's up to him."

"And Poland?"

FDR spread his hands. "I've thought about it for days. I've done all I can do about Poland. And the other liberated countries in the East. I very much fear that they will be a problem only time will solve. Our only other choice is more war. That would make Georgie Patton happy, wouldn't it?"

"If the forces are in place, sir—"

"No," said the President sharply. "I will not commit us to another war. I simply will not consider it. Congress would not agree and the country will not support it. But Marshal Stalin will have a rude surprise the instant the war is over. I've directed that Lend-Lease be canceled the day Japan surrenders."

"Does Admiral Leahy know that, sir?"

"Not yet. It's a secret directive via the budget people. The Russians will need money to rebuild after the war. If meanwhile we can reassure them, get them to see that the UN assures their security without buffer zones and satellite states. . . ." He let the sentence trail off and turned in his chair. "At any rate, there it is. Thank you, Brownie. Grace!"

"Yes sir."

"Let's do the books first, I've put that off long enough. Johnny, would you mind asking Arthur to bring the box out?"

"The box" was books, about a hundred of them. Grace had packed them for the train; FDR planned to sort them out, throw some away and autograph others, deciding which would go to the new Presidential Library at Hyde Park, which to the Hilltop Cottage with him when he retired, and which to his children.

"Where do you want this, sir?" said Prettyman, bent double as he dragged the wooden crate out onto the sun deck. Fala jumped up, staring at the box as if it were a live thing growling and rumbling out to threaten us.

"Put the coffin close to the chair here."

Prettyman looked startled. "The what, sir?"

"The coffin, Arthur. Put it close to my chair here, so I can reach the contents."

Grace and I glanced at each other.

After FDR had gone through the books, I helped Prettyman box them up again. Then I went in again for the card table and set it up at the western edge of the semicircular deck, where the sun was warmest.

Tully worked with the President for about an hour, going over the correspondence she'd prepared since yesterday's session. I stood by, but after a while felt ignored. They had their heads close, going over some detail of legislation.

I made sure he had everything he needed at hand, then quietly stepped inside. Dishes clashed from the kitchen. Daisy and Lizzie were washing up. Esperancilla was on the floor wiping up a spill. He glanced up; our eyes met; his head bobbed in a grinning bow. Prettyman was sitting at the kitchen table, a mess of eggs and coffee in front of him. I nodded to them all and went out onto the front entrance.

The sun was bright in the driveway, reflecting from white gravel. I stood there for a few minutes, soaking it up.

On impulse, I went around the corner of the cottage and down the gravel path that descended the hill. Pebbles clattered from under my shoes, rolling down ahead of me. The path curved as it descended, hugging the side of the house and then the semicircular foundation of the sun deck.

It was cooler down here in the shadow of the pines. The marines I passed gave me inspection glances as they presented arms, and I started to salute back before remembering I was uncovered. So I just nodded to them too. Most were older guys, my age, but one was pimple-faced, thin, a kid's face, like Jackie Coogan's. Then I saw the white wound-scars on the back of his neck. And his eyes. The eyes were much older than the face.

A stocky figure turned as I got to the lowest guard shack. "Lieutenant."

"Major Dickinson. Everything jake, sir?"

"Copacetic as hell. Taking a stroll?"

"The President's working. I'm stretching my legs."

We heard his guffaw then, above us. I looked up at the curved terrace. From this side it was about a twelve-foot sheer wall. You could do it with a ladder, though.

"I understand you were on the train when they found the bomb," the major said, examining me.

"Yeah."

"Reilly says, no idea who put it there."

"Not that we can figure."

"Somebody who was on the train, though."

"Not necessarily," I told him. "They don't—I mean, they didn't count the luggage as it came aboard. So anybody at the White House could have put that suitcase out and Crim would have gotten it out to the train."

"I put on double guards," said Dickinson.

"How many men in your detachment, Major?"

"Sixty. All veterans."

"Yeah, I noticed the wound stripes. Somebody told me you've got a camp around here someplace."

He pointed. "About a mile in that direction, down in the ravine. Come over sometime, we'll feed you something good."

"What's your call on the security here?" I asked him.

"I always thought, pretty tight. Except that we never worried about air raids. The cottage, it's hard to spot in the woods, and you can't tell it from the others in the area. There's a lot of foliage, and the pines are good camouflage year round."

"How about a group assault?"

"We could stop anything short of light armor. We've got BARs, .30s and .50s. The terrain'd be real rugged to assault across." He patted his jaw. "What I worry about more is fire. The woods get real dry, and pine needles burn like crazy. You see how it comes right up to the house. We do a drill every week."

"What do you do with him, in case of a fire?"

"Reilly takes him out the door, into the car. We fight the fire and maintain perimeter security."

"We need to be real alert the next few days," I said.

"Why do you say that?"

"Just a feeling," I said. I didn't think Reilly had told him anything special was up. I wasn't going to either, but I wanted these guys on their toes, just in case.

When I went back up to the sun deck FDR had lit his first Camel and was joking with Tully. I felt relieved just at the sight of him. He looked better every day. Then I remembered: I thought that yesterday morning, too. He seemed normal in the morning, but in the afternoon . . . his body was there, his smile too. But his mind seemed to be somewhere else.

He glanced at his watch. "Ten already. The Deacon should be back pretty soon."

We heard motorcycles then, and fell silent. They growled and boomed weirdly up through the woods, echoing from the hills. Then they faded.

"That's something I always wanted to do," said FDR. "Ride one of those things."

Hassett came in a few minutes later. Long followed him, carrying two sacks of mail. "Deacon, you look upset," said the President, rolling himself back from the card table.

"Sir, you won't believe who spotted me at Fort Benning. I was standing there with Fala—"

"He got his shots?"

"Yes sir, all taken care of. He doesn't need to see the vet again till September. And we dropped President Osmeña at the guest cottage. He'll rest up today and spend tomorrow with you. But you won't believe who spotted me."

"Lauren Wolfe."

Hassett stared. Roosevelt's guffaw boomed out over the treetops. "Look at him! Just look at him! Come on now, Deacon, it wasn't mindreading. You were crazy about her last time. Who else would put you into a spin like this?"

"You're right, sir, but I don't think it's funny. Is Mr. Reilly around?"

FDR leaned back in his chair. "Mike!"

Reilly appeared instantly at the french doors. "Yes, Mr. President?"

"Mike, we've got a bit of a problem. Or at least Bill thinks we do—I'm not so sure." He leaned back again, eyes twinkling, and felt inside his jacket. I was ready with a light.

"What's the trouble, Mr. Hassett?"

Hassett told him he'd run into Wolfe that morning, that she'd taken it into her head to come to Warm Springs and see FDR again, and that he'd told her the President was not receiving.

Roosevelt shook his head. "That was your mistake. You should know better, Deacon—never say 'can't' to a woman. And especially not to her."

"She followed us in her car. I had the escort pull her over, but I have no doubt at all she's checking in at the hotel downtown this very moment. Now, sir, I—"

FDR interrupted, smiling. "Is it really so terrible?"

"Sir, people can't just invite themselves to see you. Mike?"

"He's right, Mr. President. Absolutely."

"She's a sport," said FDR, flourishing the cigarette. "She's done a lot for the war effort. The bond tours. And the party she gave was the most popular event at the convention. Just a moment. Let me—all right, here it comes." He squared his shoulders, flirted imaginary hair off his shoulders, and poised his cigarette. " 'You remember me, don't you, Mr. Stewart? I was just a little girl who didn't know how to kiss, didn't know how to walk, didn't know how to act. You laughed and sent me back to do some growin' up. How do you like what you see?' " He threw back his head and roared. I had to laugh, and Hassett and Reilly couldn't keep straight faces either.

"Well, Mr. President—"

Hassett: "She's not what I call a restful influence."

"She's fun. We could use her around here," FDR said wistfully, and we looked at each other. Reilly sighed.

"All right, sir," said Hassett. Then, to me, "She was alone. No publicity people. She'll need an escort . . . Lieutenant, would you mind? I don't imagine she'll be too hard to find."

———

She wasn't. I spotted the crowd as soon as I passed the station. I parked the roadster in front of the feed store and pushed through into the hotel lobby. She was standing at the desk, talking to Ruth Stevens. As tall as I expected, and nobody could miss the long flaming hair, wide mouth, broad forehead tapering to a strong chin. The Queen of the Screen, Shoulders, Red, Wolfe the Magnificent! The slightly slanted eyes were a pale and startling green, deeper than emeralds. No question, this was a stunning woman. But then something odd happened. The closer I got the less beautiful she looked. Her eyebrows were thin and her neck was too long and her nose was sort of humped. Up close her face looked strange. Not exotic, the way it came across on screen, just—strange. As I came up I caught her voice, fast and imperious, vibrating like a drill. Ruth said, "Of course we want to help you, Miss Wolfe. Oh, I loved you in *Bad Girl!* But you know, we only have twenty-two private rooms. And they're all occupied—"

"Good morning, Miss Cavanaugh," I said. That was the rich girl she'd played in *Rio,* the one who was charged with manslaughter and had to flee the country, only to get mixed up with some Nazi spies in Brazil.

"Well. Hello, Cassius," she snapped, looking through me as if I were glass. I noticed she squinted.

"You've got me typed," I said. "I can't sleep, I'm not sleek-headed, and I think too much. But I don't think I'm dangerous."

Her up-from-under look came back and fastened on me. "Who are *you?*"

"John Kennedy. The President sent me out to see if you needed any help."

"Listen to those A's! Boston Irish."

"You're from around there too, aren't you?"

"Not too far away. . . . That's nice of him to send you, but the first thing I need is a place a human being can sleep. Is my car all right out there?"

"I think so. This is a good hotel. Miss Stevens will help you."

"We'll have a room ready in an hour or two," Stevens said again. "You can leave your car there. No one will bother it."

"Don't give her my room," I said. "Unless I get to stay."

"Let's go," Wolfe told me, ignoring my crack. Authority? Leahy could take lessons. I fell in behind her as she clop-clopped out the lobby, beaming at the awed locals. I pointed out the Willys and got the door for her. She settled in, sighing as little girls with autograph books broke from the sidewalks. Looking at her profile I realized she was older than you thought at first, too. But none of it—the decisiveness, the gawkiness, the weariness that etched her forehead as she leaned back—meant she didn't look damn good. I groped for the ignition while checking out her legs.

"Let's *go,* or we'll never get out of here," she said, not looking at me. I backed out, narrowly missing a determined-looking farmer staring down into a Brownie. Wolfe adjusted her hat at the last minute, spoiling his shot. I gunned downhill past the station.

"You were pretty rough on Ruth," I said.

"What? What did you say?"

"You heard me. And I can't believe you just invited yourself to visit FDR."

"I don't believe I know who the hell you are to be telling me anything, mister lieutenant."

"You know Navy rank."

"I probably know more about the Navy than you do, mister mick beanpole. And the Army and Air Corps too. Why don't you just shut up and take me to your master?"

"I'm taking you, I'm taking you. What were you doing in Fort Benning?"

"Carrying a torch for the wrong guy. What are *you* doing this far from the front?"

———

Reilly and Tully were standing at the entranceway when I pulled in. "Ready to search me, Mike?" she said as she jumped out of the roadster.

"Hi, Lauren. You wish," he said, grinning.

"Hello, Grace. Is he here? Can I see him?"

"Hello, Miss Wolfe. Go right on in, he's expecting you."

We followed her in, but stopped to watch the entrance.

Because she didn't just *walk* in. She posed in the entranceway, and we, behind her, watched the faces turn and focus and light up. Then she was motion, swinging in, every line expressing joy and vivacity. She went right to the President as FDR rolled himself back from his table and stretched up his arms.

"Red!" he roared. "The beautiful star of the silver screen! Where have you been keeping yourself?"

To my surprise she was blushing, a deep color that suffused her face and shoulders. And hugging him, auburn hair falling across his chest. "And here *he* is. The greatest man in America."

"You mean, here *we* are, the two greatest *actors* in America." FDR patted her hand as she pulled up a chair. "The Deacon tells me you spotted him and decided to favor us with your presence."

"I shouldn't be here, interrupting you—"

"I'm very glad you came; it's grand to have you here. I only wish we could offer you your cottage again, but we had a previous booking at Doctor Roosevelt's Summer Sanatorium. President Osmeña. You'll meet him tomorrow, I believe. Well! Cigarette? A little drinkie?" FDR called out to Prettyman to bring martini fixings. I got up to light Wolfe's cigarette, then another for FDR.

"Lauren, you know Grace, and Mike Reilly, and Bill, and our new face, Johnny Kennedy."

"Actually, I go by Jack, sir."

"You may have heard of his father. Joe—"

"Oh, the RKO Kennedy," she said, looking at me again but without much interest. "You're his son? He's got a big family, doesn't he?"

"Sit down, sit down, Lauren. You make me nervous, striding around like that," said FDR. He sipped his martini, glancing at the desk. He'd been working with a magnifying glass when we came in, and now he rolled himself back toward it. "Or come over here and keep me company. Would you like to see a new stamp before it's issued?"

She bent over him, rubbing his shoulders. "Of course. Is this it?"

"I'm trying to decide if I like it. What do you think? A simple stamp without engraving. On the top line, '3 cents 3,' on the bottom line 'United States Postage,' and in the middle 'April 25, 1945.' "

"It's elegant. Simple but elegant. That's for—"

"The opening session of the United Nations Organization. I'll unveil it there."

"You've decided to go, sir?" Hassett asked him.

"Yes, I've decided to attend the opening."

"Oh, my," said Grace. "We don't have anyone working on a speech for that, do we, Mr. Hassett? Do you have someone doing a speech?"

"Oh, I shan't speak then, Duchess. Perhaps I may put in a few words at the final festivities. But I think I had better be in there head-to-head with Molotov and Eden, till we're sure everything is arranged."

"San Francisco's not that far from Hollywood."

"That sounds delightful . . . Lauren, remember last time, you told that great story about breaking your ankle the night before you were due to go on Broadway, *All's Well That Ends Well*, I think it was—"

"The *Merry Wives*. Oh, please. Some other time." She was blushing again. She must blush pretty easily, I thought. Maybe it went with being a redhead. Either that or she had a hell of a soft spot for old Frankie D.

Meanwhile Hassett had been going through the mail. He laid a stack of it in front of FDR and uncapped a Parker. The President pulled one toward him. Then glanced up and smiled at Wolfe. "Here's where I make a law," he said, and signed it.

"That's all?"

"Yes, easy, wasn't it? Now Bill can take over." Hassett knew his part in the little ceremony. He took the document up carefully and laid it out for the ink to dry. Pretty soon the mantel, the tops of the bookcases, even the floor was covered by what FDR jovially called "Hassett's Laundry."

———

Laura and Margaret came over. After greeting Wolfe they settled down out on the sun deck while FDR went in for his nap. I sat around listening to them yammer for a while, then got up. I felt antsy. I strolled back and forth on the drive, looked into the garage—the Ford was up on jacks, and two dogfaces were changing the tires—then went down and checked the pathway behind the cottage again.

Stood looking down into the green gloom of the woods. The pine needles looked dry and deep. Insect-clatter and birdsong ebbed out of it, but the brilliant noon sunlight seemed to stop a few feet in, turned to some different kind of light, a mysterious underwater glow.

The green-boarded sentry box looked more like a privy than anything else. I said to the marine inside, "I'm going down there, Sergeant."

"No can do, sir."

"I can't enter your perimeter without your permission, I know that. But I can leave it."

"I still wouldn't do it, Lieutenant," he said. When enlisted men call you by your rank instead of "sir" they think it's some kind of subtle insult.

"Why not?"

"It's heavy brush down there. When you get to the bottom of the ravine there are these kind of like bowls. You can't see ten feet. The Lieutenant would get lost. Then he'd stumble out maybe at one of the other guard posts and get hisself shot."

"I won't go all the way down."

He shrugged and went back to scanning the green sea below him.

I took a few steps in, pinestraw crackling under my shoes, then turned and looked back uphill. Already I couldn't see the cottage. I went ten or fifteen yards farther. The hill steepened, plunging downward into a world of green. I felt as if I were swimming, hovering above a green, shadowy abyss. The air was close and hot. Sweat popped up under my khakis. Something fastened itself hungrily to my neck and I slapped it off. All I could hear was the buzzing of flies and the distant baying of a dog.

I decided that was enough investigation and climbed back out, calling to the marine before I emerged into view again. He watched me pass silently, sucking a tooth; then spat and turned his face away, staring down with grim concentration into the woods.

———

By the time FDR came out again Daisy and Lizzie had fried chicken and biscuits and deviled eggs and pecan pie and gallon jars of tea packed. Their excited chatter echoed in the front rooms; Lauren had gone into the kitchen to help with the potato salad. I stood back as Esperancilla and Prettyman carried the wicker hampers out to the blue Ford, the black Secret Service car, and the roadster. Reilly informed me the Willys and Wolfe were all mine, at least till we got to Dowdell's Knob.

Reilly and Prettyman carried FDR out. He waved, but didn't say anything. His head lolled back on the seat when they had him in the Ford. Tully and his maiden-aunt cousins got in with him. Long stepped up on the running board, clinging to the windshield and the door. The black car started up and rolled off past the bump gate and sentry houses. The Ford drove off too.

Wolfe came back and got in. Not a word to me, naturally. Why waste her breath on a peon? I slapped my pockets, unsure for a moment if I still had the keys. I did, the little roadster's engine snorted, and we followed the others down the drive, gravel snapping under our tires like .22 shorts.

I thought we'd be going back down to the highway, but I was wrong; we stayed on what looked like a private road. It writhed through the woods, dipping, then rising again. We were following a ridge line, but the growth was too thick to see anything. I caught Long's head moving, sweeping the tree line. Yeah, great place for an ambush. I saw now why they didn't announce picnics till the last minute.

"So how does he look to you?" I asked her as we bumped and dipped like a PT in a heavy seaway.

She'd leaned back and closed her eyes, and answered without opening them. "He looks fine. He's lost weight, but that's good. Makes him look younger."

"Maybe so . . . how'd you get hooked up with him, anyway? Did you know him in New York?"

"No. It's a long story. I guess it started when I was shooting a picture called *The Archangel Mortimer.* It was about an angel that visits the White House to give the president advice, only you never know whether the angel is real or if the president's crazy. Well, this was in 1933, right before the inauguration, and Leo, Mr. Levinsohn, decides he wants to run the script past somebody from Roosevelt's organization. So as not to get in Dutch with the new administration, I guess. And they called somebody up, and it turned out Roosevelt said he didn't care, to do the movie any way they wanted. Can you imagine that? So that piqued my curiosity about him.

"I've been a supporter for a long time, you see. Hollywood's funny—all the writers are socialists and all the stars are stuffy Republicans. Under the scandals and the wild parties, they think they've made it, they don't see why everyone else can't suffer in silence. I remember how scared everybody was in '33, and I'll never forget—we had all taken pay cuts, we were afraid of being fired, revolution, dictatorship, we didn't know what—and five or six of us were sitting around backstage listening to him on the radio. I remember Victor Saville, Sid Franklin, Walt Reisch, some other people. Suddenly Garbo walks in. The men got up, but she told them to sit down, she just wanted to listen.

"That was when I heard him speak for the first time. 'The only thing we have to feah . . . is feah itself.' It sent chills up my spine. I looked around and those hardened people, some of them had tears in their eyes. And suddenly I knew it might take a while, but that the Depression had ended, just with those words.

"I finally called Steve Early at the White House, said I was a hopeless fan, how could I meet him. And he said that he spent Thanksgivings down here and arranged for the people at the Institute to invite me. The studio loved it, it was great PR." She smoothed her hair, mouth moody. "But it wasn't the kind of dinner I thought it would be. I felt so . . . guilty. I don't like sick people. They make me nervous."

"I know how you feel."

"Do you? I was embarrassed. I could run and walk, even if I can't dance; none of the others at that table could do any of these things, and they were just looking at me with . . . awe . . . then they carried *him* in . . . and suddenly it was *all right.* The little girls in braces singing. . . . It was hard not to cry. But he was so gay. So full of vitality and courage he made everyone happy. Even me. And it's not an act."

"That's hard to believe," I said.

She opened her eyes at that. "Why? What do you mean?"

"I grew up around pols, Miss Wolfe. Irish, but the same line of goods."

"Lauren, please. I'm an actress, Jack. I know when someone's projecting. He's real."

I looked over at her. She had a kerchief over her hair, but curls had crept free and were whipping in the breeze. I remembered her in *The Dying of the Light,* the self-centered tennis star who learns she has only a year to live.

"I think you're in love with him. Or is he some kind of father figure?"

"I've been in love with a lot of men. Put them all together, shake and pour, and they don't equal half of him. Father figure? I never knew mine. It doesn't take Dr. Freud to see that. So what?"

"So nothing, but don't count me as a worshipper at his shrine. You're here alone?"

"Yes, and going to stay that way, so wipe that smirk off your face. What are you trying to say? You're his aide but you don't admire him?"

"What for? As far as I can see, he's just another slippery logroller. He spent us halfway out of the Depression, but it took the war to jump-start things."

"While Hoover wrung his hands and did nothing."

"He didn't spend the country into debt. He didn't buy votes with relief money. What about this tax withholding they started in '43? Now the government takes your pay before you even get it."

"That's just temporary, a wartime measure."

"Maybe, but now everything's controlled and regulated and taxed. We've lost freedom, the one thing that made America great—"

"Yes, it's all so fine if you've got a full belly and a roof over your head. If you don't, it's just the freedom to starve. Why shouldn't the government help the less privileged? Who else will? The financiers—like your father? Don't make me laugh. When they were in charge they ran the country to fill their wallets. And put sixteen million people out of work. If *he* hadn't taken over we'd have had a revolution that'd make the Civil War look like a—like a picnic in the country."

"Are you joking? He doesn't have the faintest idea of economics. He's never run a business. He talked about building fifty thousand airplanes, and just shrugged when Dad asked him where the money would come from—"

"They got built, didn't they? Could your dear father have done that? He'd have rolled over and played dead for Adolf Hitler."

"If you don't care how much you borrow you can do anything—till it's time to pay up. And that's another thing. My father wanted peace. He didn't treat my Dad well at all—"

"Oh, yes, that. From what I hear, your precious fah-thah didn't get half what he deserved. But let's talk about you. That's most men's favorite subject, isn't it? Grace told me all about you after you went outside. I didn't realize you were a hero."

"It was involuntary. They sank my boat."

"How charmingly deprecatory. How Errol Flynn. Men are such spoiled little boys. . . . But I love your accent. Say something for me?"

"Anything."

"Parker parked the car in Harvard Square."

I repeated it and she squealed. "That's exactly how I used to talk, and how they laughed! It took me six months of hard work to lose it. Dear old Massachusetts . . . did you know Leo Levinsohn is from there too?"

"I know he used to live in Brookline. But you sound English. Sort of."

"Stage English. An actress picks them all up. Jus' call me Tangiah Doughty."

"Ole Virginny. So it's all learned?"

"Part of the shtick, like makeup. I've done lots of Southern girls. Englishwomen. I do a great Cockney. Accent's not that hard. And deep down we're all the same."

"Women?" I said, looking up above the trees, to where I thought I'd seen movement. Yeah. There it was again. A light plane, tracking our progress. I hoped it was a friendly.

"People. There are only two kinds, you know."

"Which are?"

"Winners and losers."

"You've got a reputation for not taking back seats. Not to anybody. Garbo, Laughton, Bankhead—"

She tossed a sarcastic laugh. "I stand up for what I believe in. That intimidates some people. If that makes me a bitch, too fucking bad. It made me a star, too. What about you? You're not professional Navy. What are you committed to?"

"I've thought of writing."

"Really? What are you working on?"

"Nothing right now. I'm—"

"Why aren't you writing?"

"What?"

"If you want to be a writer, why aren't you writing? Or making notes? Are you at least keeping a diary?"

"Well, no. But I—"

"I see. You're one of those people who want to be writers, or artists, or actors, but who don't want to make the effort. Oh, I understand. It's so much easier that way, isn't it? Especially when your father's rich enough that you'll never have to worry?"

"I don't think that's fair," I said.

"What's wrong with your teeth?"

"What?"

"You keep flicking your teeth with your fingernail. Do I make you nervous?"

"No," I lied.

"Why are there so many troops along here? Every time we pass a side road, there's a truck and a roadblock. It wasn't like this last year when I was here. Something's wrong, isn't it?"

This time I just didn't bother to answer. Whatever I said would come flying back at my head. The cars ahead were slowing, so I did too, but I screwed up somehow on the screwy fucking gearshift; I came within a hair of colliding with the Secret Service car. They gave me a dirty look and I lifted my middle finger from the wheel. We pulled off the road into a dirt parking area.

"Oh, this is such a beautiful place," said Wolfe. She got out and walked away, leaving me sitting there steaming.

——

When I finally went down I found everyone sitting on a ledge of rock that jutted out from the hillside. Beyond it was nothing but air and about a million square miles of Georgia. On the far side of the valley, at least thirty miles away, the hills rose again in a hazy blue rampart. In between the country rolled, mile on mile of forest and scattered patches of farmland and here and then a mercury glint of water. The girls—Margaret, Grace, Laura, Daisy Suckley, and Lauren—were sitting on blankets spread on the rock. The smell of fried chicken buttered the breeze. FDR was sitting in the Ford, parked about thirty feet from the edge. Reilly had jammed rocks under the tires. A fire crackled in a stone grill set at the very edge of the cliff. I strolled over and looked down on patrolling hawks.

I went to the hamper, made up a plate, and took it over to the car. FDR was leaning back, hat tipped over his eyes. He looked relaxed in white shirt and old fedora. The sun fell full on his face. I studied it for a few seconds, then cleared my throat.

"They left you all alone, Mr. President? How about some chicken?"

FDR blinked and lifted his hand for shade. "That you, Johnny?"

"Yes sir."

"They're over there talking girl talk. I don't mind. . . . Grand view, isn't it? It never fails to—to sort of—well, there's a peace here. Don't you feel it? In the old days we used to say, when we got hopeless patients, we ought to bring them out here and let them look out at the valley. Just like we're doing now. If they can look at this and not be inspired, then we'll know they're hopeless . . . but not before."

I agreed it was swell and he went on, pointing out various stands of timber below us and telling me when they'd been planted and how much they would be worth in ten years. It all looked the same to me.

"Over in that direction—that's my land. We've got two thousand acres. It was wasteland when I bought it. Now we grow grapes, pole beans, soybeans. Georgia white peaches, the best thing you've ever eaten. Smell like a delicious perfume. We've got six hundred acres of mountain land wired for cattle. And not one acre in cotton."

"What's wrong with cotton?"

"It destroys the land," Roosevelt said. "Cotton was the ruination of the South. The ruin of the soil and the cause of the Civil War. But it was the only cash crop they had.

"You know, I think about the proudest thing I've ever done was set up some reasonable use of land. The farmers couldn't do it alone. They were under the lash of production. Each man had to produce as much as he could, or starve, no matter how bad his soil was or how fast farming destroyed it, and the more he produced, the lower prices fell. Now he gets a fair price and the land's protected too."

"And people are being paid to do nothing," I said.

"I've heard that before, Johnny, and t'ain't exactly so. In the first place, I've never believed anyone should receive money without working for it. Doles are bad government, and they demoralize the people who get them. That was the idea of the CCC: to provide honest work for men who needed it.

"And in the second place, we *are* getting something for our money. Look at the Dust Bowl. They had to disc-harrow till the soil was so fine the least wind would pick it up. The time wasn't far off when all the topsoil would be gone and all the farmers too.

"The Resettlement Administration took people off the unproductive land and turned it into forests and parks. Then the Farm Security Administration took over. Now the farmer can practice crop rotation, contour plowing, and let the land rest between crops. And we'll have topsoil to last for hundreds of years to come, and parks, and timber for homes. Everybody gains—everybody—in the long run. Isn't that worth a few million a year? I think so."

He stopped then and laughed. "Sorry, I didn't mean to start orating. But we were talking about politics a couple of days ago, weren't we?"

"You're saying that it's not just maneuvering and backroom deals," I said.

"It's the grandest game there is, but you can't always win. I've had lots of flops. So what? You step back to the plate and try something else. That's the essential of . . . the essence of faith, in my opinion."

I stood beside the car, unwilling to disagree any more, but not buying any of it either.

"Actually, the reason I'm telling you this is I don't . . . I don't think the work's over. It's actually just started. Most folks still can't afford a doctor. Don't get much of an education, unless they're born as you and I were, part of a privileged elite. Did you know three out of four farms in this country still don't have electricity? And Eleanor's right, we've got to lift up the colored somehow. I never had the political horsepower to do it. Don't pick a fight you have no chance of winning! But this war's going to change a lot of things, Johnny-Kay.

Maybe we can cut loose the old-line Democrats who've held us back and forge a truly liberal party."

"And when everyone's living on a government handout, then what?"

"It's not a 'handout' to help the unfortunate, Johnny. We take care of our children in our families. We don't consider that a handout, do we?"

"Grown men aren't children, Mr. President. That's the difference."

He sighed then. "You're your father's boy, I can see that."

I noticed then he still had his hand up, and suddenly felt shabby arguing with him. "Is the sun bothering you, sir? I can put the top up."

"No, no, I've been looking forward to this afternoon for a long time.

"You know, I've spent a lot of time in these open cars," he went on, patting the door. I looked down at the big tires of the Ford. "You can't beat a convertible for campaigning. Put your wife beside you and the local boss— governor, mayor, whatever. They appreciate the boost. And leave the top down. Even if it's raining. So everyone can tell their friends they saw you."

"I'll remember that, Mr. President," I said, and he couldn't have missed the sarcasm in my voice.

He tapped a cigarette out, ignoring or forgetting the plate I'd brought for him. When I leaned to light it I saw two others, all stacked with food, sitting on the seat next to him. When he had the butt drawing he sighed, and closed his eyes again. The hot high sunlight fell on his face, making him look, for just a moment, as if he'd reached a sort of timeless peace at last.

"Mr. President! Why don't you join us?"

"Come on, Franklin! It's so pleasant out here!"

He smiled faintly. "I was just getting comfortable," he murmured.

Reilly was already headed for us. I reached for the handle, made sure FDR wasn't leaning against it, and opened the door. Mike motioned me aside, but I did what I'd watched him do. First the legs. They felt weird, light and limp. I remembered a mummified body I'd seen as a kid at the Museum of Science. Touching them made me shiver, but I swung them out, pivoting FDR on the leather seat. "Take one side, Mike. I'll take the other."

Reilly grunted doubtfully, but reached in and got an arm around the President's shoulders. I got one hand under him and locked with Reilly's.

"Okay, up he comes."

He slid out, taking part of the weight with his arms on the dash and door; then it was all on us. Reilly was taking most of it, but I could barely keep him off the rocks. We staggered downhill doing a sort of fireman's carry. The girls looked away as we approached, chattering as if oblivious of us, pointing to something far down in the valley. Just then a stone shifted under my foot. I twisted, trying to keep the President from going down.

Suddenly everything went to shit as my back locked. It was like a lit sparkler crammed right up my ass all the way to the top of my head. Somebody was screaming. It was me. I grabbed my spine as I went down, and a heavy soft weight toppled over on me, crushing me down at the lip of the long fall to the treetops far below.

CHAPTER 31

U.S. Route 29, South of Charlotte, North Carolina

K rasov came awake slowly, cramped like a closed fist at the bottom of the hole in the ground. Before he opened his eyes he felt the sick starving emptiness like a cored-out cavity in his guts. He was desperately hungry. But he knew even as he lay motionless, holding his stomach, that there'd be no food that day. The Germans didn't even bother pretending to feed their Soviet prisoners of war. He moved his elbows slightly. Felt the walls of mud, smoothed by his body. At the far end of the camp the English and Americans had barracks, they had rations, heat, visits from the Red Cross. The Soviets had holes in the ground, surrounded by wire and machine guns. All through the winter. Around them the bare ground had been plucked clean of the last blade of grass. And above them, unreachable, unscalable, the sky . . .

Once the shadows that surrounded him had been soldiers. Defenders of the People's State.

Now they were starving skeletons, eager to kill for a crust of brown bread, a canteen-cup of watery soup.

Every night now, as the searchlights slid across the pockmarked, wired-in ground, he heard screams. Faint, weak cries, soon brought to an end by the sound of blows. In the morning those who'd been too weak to fight any longer lay mutilated on the bare stony soil, the last strips of muscle hacked from their legs and buttocks. Sometimes they were still alive. . . .

Ivan Krasov suddenly opened his eyes, not on the muddy sides of a dugout in an East Prussian POW camp, but on the headliner of an American sedan. He was cramped awkwardly in the back seat. His neck hurt, and he massaged it for several minutes after he sat up, the blue eyes blank and staring as the dream-terror slowly ebbed. Leaving only the gnawing hunger. He peered uncertainly out into the bushes that screened the car from the morning light. Then reached for the pack of cigarettes and shook one out.

He'd been traveling since getting the call from Fence in New York. On the road all that time without a bed or a bath. He drove the cream-and-chocolate laundry truck through the evening into the first night. But his back crawled every time a car passed or he drove through a town and saw people looking at him. It was too conspicuous, people would remember it and the Hahn & Hurja logo . . . at some point someone would start to wonder about the dead men at LaFontaine's, would connect them to Smalls's death, and look for him at the cleaning plant. The American police were slack, but eventually someone would make the connection. And by now the company would have reported the truck stolen. Finally, when it ran out of fuel, he abandoned it in a ravine in New Jersey. Tramped on for a few hours, hitchhiking.

Then one of his rides had dropped him in front of a country church. Among the gaggle of cars parked on the grass, he found five with the keys left in them. He'd picked a '36 Chevy just because it had the most gas in the tank. That was the problem, traveling cross-country in wartime. Fuel, and money . . . and ration coupons.

He'd gone back, moving crouched among the Model As and dust-stained rusty Essexes and Stars in case someone came out of the white-painted doors and down the walk between the gravestones, and from glove compartments and sun visors came up with three Bs and Cs that looked negotiable. Each coupon was worth five gallons. Then backed the sedan out quietly, bumping over the rutted grass.

Southward. Along curving two-lane roads, through New Jersey, Pennsylvania, Maryland. Through Washington again, seething as he reflected on the wasted days, then resigned as mile after mile took him south. Near Richmond he'd run out of money again and had to rob a filling station. Keysville. Danville. Greensboro. He kept his speed down, a gas-conserving, cop-deflecting thirty-five. Small town after small town, doing most of his driving at night, blinking into the oncoming glare of headlights for hour after hour till his wheels crunched on gravel and he realized he was nodding off. Then it was time to pull off and hunt for a safe place to sleep.

Now he felt conspicuous again. The Chevy had New Jersey plates. He might have been seen coming out of the filling station. It was time for a trade-in.

Rubbing his eyes, he tried to remember where he was now. Somewhere south of Charlotte. Last night he'd turned off Route 29, finding first a side road, then a dirt lane that disappeared back into woods. An abandoned house had loomed up in the dusk, boards weathered silver, windows empty, trees growing up through the roof. As the light faded he'd cranked the windows up against the air-raid whine of mosquitos, eaten his last wedge of bread, and curled into the leather.

Now, as he slid into the front seat, he remembered he was almost out of gas. He had no more ration stamps and no more money.

According to the map, he had another two hundred seventy miles to Atlanta, then seventy miles beyond that to Warm Springs.

———

He sweated the gas gauge all the way into the next town.

Belmont, North Carolina. The Belmont Hosiery Mill Welcomes You. He left the highway at a crossroads and headed into town past textile and sock

factories. Paused as the crossing gates dipped to bar his way and a Southern
Railroad slow freight rumble-clattered past. Then put the sedan in second and
cruised on again. On side streets, glimpses of old, rambling homes with vast
porches, set back amid flowering trees the shape of shellbursts and the colors of
flame and lavender. He turned off South Main past the business district. Made a
couple of random turns, eyes drifting from house to house along quiet side
streets. Along Central Avenue short driveways were lined with azaleas and
tulips, bordered with alert daisies. Jasmine breathed through the open window
of the slow-moving car. Only occasionally did he see cars, and some, when he
slowed to check them out, were up on blocks. In storage for the duration, till
some husband or son returned.

The trouble was, even when an auto looked as if it was in running condition,
he couldn't just park and walk up the driveway to see if the keys were in it. Or
slide under the dash to short out the ignition.

He was peering off to the side, looking into an open garage, when he heard a
thud and the wheel jumped in his hands.

His first impulse was to smash down the accelerator. But even as the motor
roared, he eased up on it. His eyes searched the little square rearview.

Caught the crumpled body, the lifted arm.

He slammed on the brakes and the Chevrolet bucked and stalled to a halt.
He shifted into reverse, backed, stamped the brake again, shifted to neutral and
set the parking brake. He bent, slid the automatic from the glove compartment,
and tucked it under his jacket. Then jerked the door open and leapt out.

The girl was eleven or twelve, in bobby sox and saddle shoes. A pink
button-in-front sweater had the arms tied loosely over a flowered blouse. The
blouse was torn and abraded, with flecks of tar and gravel sticking to it. Thin
pale legs stuck out from under a tweed skirt. A few feet away the front wheel of
the Columbia spun with a clicking sound. The heavy red steel-tubing frame and
the rear rim and the wire-mesh basket were buckled where the wheels of the
Chevy had passed over them. He knelt beside her, caught her fearful, white-eyed
look.

"You okay, kid? I didn't see you."

"I don't know . . . it hurts."

"Where does it hurt?"

She didn't answer, retreating to some private world. A trickle of bright
blood ran suddenly down from the corner of her mouth. He glanced around,
noting the still-empty street, the neat painted wooden mailboxes.

"What's your name?"

"Jodie. Jodie Widgen."

"Are you from around here, Jodie? Which one's your house?"

"There . . . around the corner. The green one with the magnolia in front.
Number twenty-three."

Krasov bent. He got his arms under her and lifted. She smelled like bubble
gum and sweat. One leg stuck out, the other dangled. The sweater sagged away.
One shoe fell off but he let it go, getting her up, close to his chest. She was lighter
than he expected. She caught her breath as he jostled her. A broken rib, he
thought. That bright blood most likely meant it had punctured a lung.

"Twenty-three. Your mom home?"

"Yeah. Mom's there. She sent me for an egg." She was breathing fast now, freckles coming out dark as her skin bleached. "But they didn't have any at Armstrong-Lewis. . . . Oh. It really hurts. My chest, and—and in my leg."

He looked where she pointed, at the house on the corner. Two stories, with green-painted shingles and white trim. A huge twisted tree with broad leaves and white flowers spread shade over the front yard.

And to the side, parked, a green Nash two-door. Not new, the paint was weathered, but he could see tread on the tires. And it wasn't on blocks.

"Don't worry," he said. "It won't hurt much longer." He shifted her again in his arms, till her head was against his chest with his right arm under it. He curled his hand around her face, fingers probing for the handhold of bone under her jaw.

She didn't realize what he was doing until the last instant. He felt her tense. In another second she'd fight, or scream. But her head was already twisted by then, almost to the limit of its natural travel.

He pulled out and down, hard, and heard the crack.

Cradling the now-limp body in his arms, he went quickly up the walk. He squatted for a moment as he came abreast of the car, letting the girl's dangling feet rest on the gravel. Then hoisted her weight again, ran heavily up the porch steps, and kicked twice at the screen door, rattling it against the jamb.

———

The woman who answered wore a housedress and apron. As she stared at the girl in his arms her hand rose to her throat. Then, wordlessly, her eyes sought his.

"Found her on the street, ma'am," he said. "This your child? She said she lived here. Her bike's still out there. Saw a black car going around the corner. Must have been somebody hit her and drove off."

"Oh, my God. That's my Jodie, yes. Do you want to bring her in—"

"I don't think that's a good idea, ma'am. I think she needs to get to a hospital just as soon as we can get her there."

"Is she awake? She doesn't look—"

"Not now, but she was talking just a minute ago. Then she sort of passed out."

The woman pulled her hands down from her throat and said in a hoarse voice, "Put her in the car, I'll be right out."

Krasov carried the girl around to the side of the house and slid her into the back seat. Her head lolled and he reached in and straightened it.

The woman ran down the steps, almost falling, and threw her purse into the front. She reached back over the seat to touch the girl's forehead. Krasov held it steady. Then she turned and fumbled with the keys and thrust them into the ignition, her hands shaking.

But the car didn't start. The starter whined on and on. The engine fired, but faltered, didn't take hold.

"'Scuse me," said Krasov. The woman looked up at him with wild eyes. "It doesn't sound like it's gonna start."

"It's always started before."

"Sounds like you flooded it, this time."

"Oh, God. No. Not *now*—"

"Here. Take mine." He held out the keys. Jerked his thumb over his shoulder. To the sedan, still standing in the shady street.

"Oh, I couldn't—"

"This girl needs a doctor. You go ahead. Which hospital you takin' her to?"

"Gaston Memorial. Do you know where it is? Gastonia, off Cox Road?"

Krasov nodded as he opened the back door and slid the limp body out again. Carried it across the lawn. Behind him he heard the door come open. "I know where it is. You go on ahead," he told her again. "I'll get your car running an' meet you there. All right?"

"Thank you, mister, God bless you. I don't know what I—I've got to go—"

"You go on now. See you there." He stepped back and waved as the tires squalled.

When they were out of sight and quiet had returned to the street he lingered on the sidewalk, under the shadow of the broad glossy leaves. Looking up at the white waxy blossoms. So this was a magnolia. . . . He strolled up the drive again. Looked at the unhooked screen door, then decided against it. The car, that was what was important. He bent as he came abreast of the rear fender, grasped the protruding fold of cloth, and pulled the pink fluffy sweater, smudged with oily carbon now, out of where he'd rammed it into the tailpipe.

When he looked up a black woman was staring at him through the screen door. He couldn't tell if she'd seen it or not. Her face was expressionless, her eyes steady on his. He nodded but she didn't move a muscle. Just stood with arms folded, watching him through the rusty patched screen as he slid behind the wheel. The woman's purse was still on the seat. He set it on the floor on the passenger side. Put the clutch in, pumped the gas a couple of times, and started the car.

He pulled out quietly, steered around the smashed bicycle, and headed south.

———

Later that morning he stopped in Gaffney, parking behind a restaurant, out of sight of the highway. After lunch he changed the ten dollars he'd found in the purse into quarters and dimes. He found a phone booth and dialed the number Fence had given him. As he waited for the operator he reminded himself to keep it brief, keep it casual. He'd been lucky up to now, but he couldn't slip through forever.

"That will be seventy-five cents, please. Signal when through." He fed in coins and waited. She answered on the fifth ring.

"Hello."

"Hello."

"Where are you?"

"Getting there. In Gaffney."

A faint double click tapped against his ear. He stiffened. "What was that?"

"What?"

"I thought I heard something. And your voice sounds fainter."

"I didn't hear anything. You sound just the same. Where did you say you were?"

"Gaffney."

"Where's that?"

"North of Spartanburg, the map says. Things hold out, I could be there tomorrow." He leaned out of the booth to make sure no one was around. Then said, "Did you find out what I asked you to find out? How I can get to him?"

"Yes."

"How?"

The voice murmured in his ear, "Do you know anything about photography? Or, if you don't—can you learn?"

He listened carefully as she began to explain.

C H A P T E R 3 2

Saturday, April 7: The Little White House

The president of the Philippines smiled anxiously as Hassett ushered him in. Osmeña bowed to Roosevelt, who kept trying to make him sit down as Esperancilla, the houseboy, stood beaming from the kitchen door.

I stood stiffly behind FDR's chair, trying to keep the pain from showing on my face.

When they'd untangled us yesterday, ten feet from the edge of the cliff, I couldn't move. Reilly took care of the President first. Then he'd come back and stood over me as I lay gasping and clutching my back.

"You okay?"

"Shit, do I *look* okay? My fucking back went out."

"This happen often, Kennedy?"

"Once in a while. It always picks the—ah!—worst times to go out."

"A few feet closer and we'd have gone over. That what you had in mind?"

"Yeah, I'm a real kamikaze. You can tell by the slanted eyes."

"I don't have anybody to send back with you. I'll walkie-talkie for a jeep. I want you to see Bruenn the minute you get back."

"Sure, Mike." It was hard to argue with somebody who could walk when you couldn't. You just had to sort of agree, then finagle things your way later.

Halfway back the jeep jolted things back into place somehow. I could breathe again and even sit up. I was still wringing wet, though, when I staggered into the cottage.

Bruenn said there wasn't much he could do for me. He wasn't a back man. But there were plenty of specialists just down the hill. Some of the best in the country. He called over and got me an appointment later that morning.

I felt Reilly tense, and came back to the present. The little man had leaned forward from his chair to touch Roosevelt on the knee.

So this pudgy-faced little fella was Osmeña. A startling streak of gray in his patent-leather hair. The former vice president had escaped with MacArthur from Bataan, then taken over the government-in-exile when Quezon died.

Everyone had seen the photo of him wading ashore at Leyte behind Mac. He'd looked like a child beside the paunchy general with his mashed hat and corncob pipe.

"And are you well, Mr. President?"

"I'm well, Mr. President. Recovering from a bit of prostate trouble."

"My condolences," said FDR. "This is a historic occasion. I think it's the first time in history that this little town in Georgia has hosted two presidents simultaneously! What I thought we could do, Sergio, is to have our talk, then treat you to something special—a drive down to the cove. It's a beautiful spot. Then I'd like you to come back and have lunch with me—"

Osmeña's smile turned grim as he brushed aside FDR's honeyed words. "Mr. President, I have looked forward to this visit for weeks. It is very important to me and to all the people of my country. I appreciate your offer of a drive, but it is more important that we have a thorough discussion of the situation in the Philippines and how America will help us recover. Manila, which I left last month after its liberation, is three-quarters destroyed. The Japanese behaved bestially. You would not believe the stories our people tell, those who remained behind. I have sent you a memorandum to guide our discussions—"

"Yes—ah—let me see that, Bill," said FDR, barely stifling a sigh. He held it, nodding occasionally as Osmeña went on. I felt Reilly tense each time he leaned forward to make a point. Roosevelt had his serious face on now. He didn't interrupt anymore, or try to tell jokes.

Finally the little man winced and looked around. Said, apologetically, "I am sorry, but my operation—you understand. Is there somewhere—"

"Show President Osmeña into Eleanor's bathroom, please, José." The houseboy leaped forward, face lighting.

When he was out of earshot FDR gestured to Hassett. As the Vermonter bent he whispered, "Bill, get the correspondents over here, all right? I'm not up to six hours of this."

"Yes sir."

I caught up to him in the driveway. "Mr. Hassett, I've got a doctor's appointment. Okay if I take the roadster? I can stop by the comm office and have them get the word to the reporters—"

"Yes, of course, thank you," said Hassett gravely. "Tell them to be here at noon exactly. I heard what happened, John. I hope the doctors at the Foundation can help."

▬▬▬

The President, Hassett thought, knew how to set a stage. The secretary stood watching the reporters file past him into the living room. FDR and Osmeña sat side by side, FDR in his big leather and brass-studded chair, the smaller man in a swiveling chair that had been raised to put them both at the same level. The blinds were open and the sun haloed them with streaming light.

The journalists took the kitchen chairs facing them. There were only three at this conference, the nine hundred ninety-eighth of Franklin D. Roosevelt's presidency. We ought to celebrate the thousandth, Hassett mused. A party?

FDR loved parties. Though it wouldn't be a big one. He and Reilly had cut the press contingent down to the three pool reporters. Merriman Smith, UP. Harold Oliver, AP. And Alice Sobelski, INS. The Hearst press hated the President, but it was too influential to ignore. He looked away as Sobelski crossed her legs, disciplining his mind. Grace Tully took her seat by the fireplace, flipped open a steno pad, and looked up as Smith greeted the President.

FDR's booming voice made Hassett flinch. "Hello there, Merry-man. Come on, all of you, a bit closer, that's fine. . . . Good morning, gentlemen, Mrs. Sobelski. President Osmeña and I have been having a nice talk, and I thought you could come up and write a story for release when we get back to Washington. It may be in another week or ten days.

"The President and I talked about many things, and it so happened that while we were together this morning, the announcement came in about the fall of the Japanese cabinet. It is a piece of very good news. Outside of that, we have been talking about a great many things to do with the Philippines."

FDR fiddled as he talked, trying to fit a Camel into its holder. He missed twice, and Hassett tensed. Then the shaking fingers succeeded, Smith leaned with a light, and FDR sat back, talking around the cigarette. The mobile face passed from welcome to concern, and the tenor voice dropped an octave.

"President Osmeña is just back from the Philippines itself, and he tells me about the terrible destruction in Manila—about three-fourths of the city has been destroyed. We talked about—wait till I get this memorandum, just to use as background—first was the military campaign and the possibility of intensifying it. There are still a great many Japs in pockets in a number of places all through the islands. We have not been to Mindanao, have we? Eventually, we will get to Mindanao where President Osmeña says he has some very good guerrillas fighting . . . then we talked about more current problems, after the islands are cleared of the Japanese. We are absolutely unchanged in our policy of two years ago, for immediate Filipino independence."

He went on about relief, communications, then about rebuilding bridges and the Cathedral of St. Dominic. Listen to him, Hassett thought affectionately. He's bringing the New Deal to the Philippines. But then, to his unease, FDR began talking about security in the western Pacific.

"It seems obvious that we will be more or less responsible for security in all the Pacific waters. As you take a look at the different places captured by us, from Guadalcanal, the north coast of New Guinea, and then the Marianas and other islands gradually to the southern Philippines, and then into Luzon and north to Iwo Jima, it seems obvious the only danger is from Japanese forces; and they must be prevented, in the same way Germany is prevented, from setting up a military force which would start off again on a campaign of aggression.

"So this means the main bases have to be taken away from them. They have to be policed internally and externally. It is necessary to throw them out of their mandated ports, which they immediately violated almost as soon as they were mandated, by fortifying these islands."

Hassett looked at Osmeña, but the little man was sitting back at his ease, smiling faintly. FDR spread his hands like a magician distracting his audience. Smoke hung in twisted veils in the sun-shot air.

"We talked about what bases will be necessary, not for us but for the world, to prevent anything being built up again by the Japanese, and at the same time give us a chance to operate in those waters. The Filipinos and ourselves would in propinquity maintain adequate naval and air bases to take care of that section of the Pacific.

"Then we talked about the permanent setting up of a Philippine government . . . it all depends on how soon the Japanese are cleared in the islands. This autumn, we hope, which would be prior to the date of July 1946, set by the Congress in 1934, as approved by the Filipinos under the Constitution of 1935. Now, what else was there? Other things—important things, but detailed really, such as the scrip."

"Mr. President, on the question of the Japanese mandate that you say will be taken away from them, who will be the controlling government in these mandates? The United States?"

Hassett held his breath, but FDR steered neatly around that live mine. "I would say the United Nations."

Oliver asked a couple of technical questions, on tariffs and harbor control. FDR waved them both off as premature.

Mrs. Sobelski said, "Mr. President, you mentioned the collapse of the Japanese cabinet. Do you think there's any connection between that and the Russian renunciation of the nonaggression pact with Japan?"

"I would get into what you call the speculative field if I tried to answer that one. I'm not what you would call a prognosticator."

Hassett joined the chuckles. Merriman directed the next question to the so-far-silent Filipino. "President Osmeña, are you going to San Francisco?"

"I am returning to Manila. We have a delegation going, however."

Oliver said in his gentle voice, "Sir, I realize this is a press conference primarily on Philippine affairs, and I'm going to cover it that way. But I wonder if we will have a chance to talk with you on other subjects, such as Poland?"

FDR said, "I think you will see me several times before I go. Some of you boys simply cannot get your facts straight. It would really be fun if I went on the air one day and simply read the things which have appeared in the papers."

His voice trailed off at the end and Grace Tully said, from beside the fireplace, "I am sorry, could you repeat that?" and he raised his voice and said it again.

Oliver said, "There certainly have been as many different interpretations as I have ever seen on anything. For example, there's a rumor that the London Poles—the Poles that went to Warsaw last month, at the invitation of the Russians, to form the new government—the rumor is that they've all been arrested."

"That has not come out in any paper," said FDR.

"No sir, it may be unsupported. We see a lot of that in the news business."

"In the political business too," said Roosevelt. The reporters chuckled. "By the way, that is all off the record," he added.

"What about the three vote situation?" Mrs. Sobelski asked him.

"Well, that came about as—Stalin said to me—and this is the essence of it—'You know there are two parts of Russia that have been completely devastated. One is the Ukraine, and the other is White Russia. We think it would be grand to give them a vote in the Assembly. In these sections millions have been killed, and we think it would be very heartening—and help to build them up—if we could get them a vote in the Assembly.' He asked me what I thought. I said to Stalin, 'I think it would be all right—I don't know how the Assembly will vote.' He said, 'Would you favor it?' I said, 'Yes, largely on sentimental grounds.' He said, 'That would be the Soviet Union, plus White Russia, plus the Ukraine.'

"Then I said, 'By the way, if the Conference in San Francisco should give you three votes—I do not know what would happen if I don't put in a plea for three votes in the States' . . . but it is not really of any great importance. I told Stettinius to forget it. I am not awfully keen for three votes. It is the little fellow who needs the vote in the Assembly."

"They don't decide anything, do they?"

"No," said FDR.

Hassett caught his glance and moved forward, saying, "Thank you, gentlemen, Mrs. Sobelski." They got up at once and said thanks. As they filed out Smith took him by the sleeve and drew him outside.

"What is it?" Hassett said, blinking in the sudden glare.

"Bill, he looks lousy. What's wrong?" Smith ripped out in his harsh, fast way.

"He's all right," Hassett said, and felt guilty, because it was a lie. He tried to rephrase it. "His doctors say he's fine. A little bronchitis. He'll come back. See the tan he's getting?"

"He does have a little tan," said Oliver.

"He'll bounce back. It's being cooped up in Washington all winter that makes him so pale."

"When will we see him again?" said Mrs. Sobelski.

"I'll call you, let you know. This is not exactly hardship duty for you folks, is it? Have you got everything you need?"

"I guess," said Smith. "Well, you know where to find us."

Hassett waved as they climbed into the car, but at heart he felt sick. He'd had a concupiscent fantasy looking at Mrs. Sobelski's legs. He'd lied—in the line of duty, true—but that was no defense. He had to go to confession. He couldn't face Communion with those sins on his soul.

And tomorrow was Easter Sunday.

———

I took it easy as I drove down toward the Foundation. The road was dirt with red-clay edges. Why didn't they pave them? You'd think the CCC would have jumped at the chance. I turned left, left again, then right. But I guess it should have been three lefts because I found myself at the bottom of the hill looking up at the buildings from the back.

Near the springs. I scoped them out as I pulled the roadster into a turn that spewed red dust. I'd visited Bath, in England. This looked like the same arrangement: built-over natural springs feeding pools and swimming areas. A big glass greenhouse sparkled in the sun. There were open pools too, and I could see rails along the sides. A few people were playing what looked like water polo.

I was startled to see kids jump out of the other pool and run around, chasing each other. Then noticed a slide too, and understood. One pool for normal people, the rest for the polios. The air was cool enough that only a few kids were out, though.

I drove up the hill and parked at Georgia Hall and went in looking for the doc Bruenn had set me up with.

People were sitting in the colonnade listening to the radio. The "Make-Believe Ballroom" or some daytime music program. I passed two of them maneuvering their wheelchairs around each other. Poor geeks, they thought they were dancing. I didn't want to stare, but wherever you looked there were more, shuffling along on crutches, playing checkers with legs caged in braces, rolling along in chairs. Some had twisted necks, others listed to one side, some had withered, useless-looking arms, some had faces that had . . . melted. . . . I walked quickly along, trying not to limp, though God knows nobody would have looked twice in this crowd. Finally I saw a nurse and asked her where the Medical Building was.

"Lieutenant Kennedy. We've been expecting you."

Dr. Hubbard introduced himself as an orthopedic specialist. He got me undressed and on a table, asking questions while he pushed and probed. I gritted my teeth when he hit pay dirt.

"This operation you mentioned, I take it it's been less than fully successful."

"Doc, I'll raise you and say it was a complete failure. How about you? Any experimental serums you want to try?"

"I don't think we want to attempt any operations," said Hubbard thoughtfully. I followed his gaze out the window. It was a softball game. Only the two teams seemed to have different rules. Catching my look he said softly, "The polios have the ABs—the able-bodied, that's what they call us—tie our legs together and get on crutches. It makes for an interesting game. And builds understanding, I think."

Before I could say anything the curtain slid back. I had just enough time to yank my trousers over my cheeks.

"This is Miz Helena Mahoney. Our chief physiotherapist."

She was big, with gray hair piled high. Arms like a washerwoman and a no-nonsense-from-you-young-man expression. "Who's this, Doctor? One of our Navy wounded?"

"Not exactly." He explained as Mahoney gave me a once-over, prodding here and there as if I were a questionable side of beef. When he got to the part about Dad she frowned.

"Kennedy. Oh, yes. He was here in '32, during the President's first campaign. I remember . . . there were some newspapermen, and Missy was with them."

"Mexican hats," said Hubbard.

"Yes, but he didn't wear one. Roosevelt and the newspapermen wore the hats, remember? Kennedy was the tall one with the glasses. I walked into Meriwether Inn and there he was. He looked like a country fellow to me. Red face and a red head, like he'd just come off the farm." She cranked her heavy gaze up to my face. "You don't look much like him, young man."

"I've been sick."

"Your father got rather angry at Mr. Roosevelt afterward, didn't he? We always felt it was because he wanted to run for president and Roosevelt wouldn't step aside for him."

"Helena, really—"

"S'okay, Doc," I said. "But look, how about my back? Can you do anything?"

"Perhaps he could benefit from hydrotherapy," Hubbard told Mahoney. "He's got swelling and discomfort. It should afford symptomatic relief and might take some of the strain off the affected vertebrae."

"I'm not getting in any of those pools," I said.

"For heaven's sake, why not?"

"I'm just not getting in. I don't see it myself, how you can work with *them.*"

"With whom?"

"The cripples. The—polios."

Mahoney looked appalled. "Oh, Mr. Kennedy. Are there still people who. . . . They're not contagious. You can't get polio at Warm Springs any more than you can get scarlet fever from somebody who's deaf because they had it years ago." She put a big hand on my back. "The doctors swim in the pools. Now, no more nonsense. Get your shirt back on and come with me."

This pool was indoors and smaller than the ones down the hill. The water steamed and rippled under incandescent lights. A colored man issued me swim trunks. I lay down on a submerged table that elevated my head. The water felt good, warm and more buoyant than it should be. Like hot sea water.

Mahoney came out in a gray horror of a bathing-dress, slid in and went to work. I tried to relax. It wasn't easy with those big hands taking me apart.

She worked grimly and silently till I said, "I got a guy I want you to arm-wrestle. A guy named Reilly."

"I know Mike."

Maybe if I got her talking she'd go easier. "How long have you been here?"

"Since the beginning, Mr. Kennedy. Mr. Roosevelt brought me and Dr. Hubbard down from New York when he started the Foundation."

"When was that?"

"Nineteen and twenty-seven. This used to be a summer resort. First they used the old Meriwether Inn for the patients, but it was wood and three stories high, and if there was a fire, of course they couldn't have gotten out. And many of them couldn't quit smoking, even though they had intercostal trouble. . . . So they built this hall, and the other new buildings." She found something that when she pressed on it made me holler, and gave it a good thorough thrashing. "You don't smoke, do you, young man?"

"No. No! I swear!"

"Once people heard there was a place for polios . . . Mr. Pless called Mr.

Roosevelt one night and said, 'There are two people come in on the train, and they can't walk, what you want me to do with 'em?' So he got a cottage fixed up, but they just kept coming.

"And we got bigger. Every summer we had five or six or ten coming in a night. The Edsel Fords gave the glass house over the big pool. A family in California gave the ambulance. Mrs. Georgia Wilkins gave the land for the chapel. Somebody gave the chapel, another gave the bell. The physios don't get paid much but they got together and gave the service—"

"Physios?"

"The physiotherapists. You've seen them around."

"Yeah, I have."

"Don't get any ideas, Mr. Kennedy. Those are nice girls, from good families."

"Good girls date."

"They won't date sailors. They won't date *you.*"

"Ouch! Not so rough!"

She said grimly from above me, "We don't coddle people, Mr. Kennedy. Our patients learn to do things for themselves as fast as possible. They can't stay here forever. They've got to go back and live in the world."

"Some of them look like they'd be better off dead."

It was crude, I knew that before it was out of my mouth, but it was honest. What good was life if you couldn't move? Couldn't walk? Hell, you wouldn't see me out rolling around twisted up like a Coney Island pretzel. I waited for her to push me off the table and body-slam me under.

But she didn't get mad. Just said, "You'd have thought that about Hugh Hawley. Remember him?"

"Uh, no."

"Didn't I see you eating ice cream here the other day? That was him behind the counter."

"Oh."

"You can see how he had bad polio in both arms and both legs. His wife had left him, and Hugh was stuck in one room. This was in upstate New York. Somebody told Mrs R about him. When she saw him she told her people, get him ready, he's going to Warm Springs tomorrow.

"They couldn't keep him on a seat, he'd just roll off. So by the time he got to us the railroad people had put him in an empty coffin they had in the baggage car. When we took him off the train he looked like a little bird that had fallen out of the nest. But we helped him, and he worked and worked and after a while got well enough to open the shop. He does laundry and dry cleaning and all that too—"

"Laundry? Great—"

"And now he's into photography, developing pictures. Now what would have happened to him, staying up in that room?"

"I guess nothing good," I said. "How about your most famous graduate? Did you work with him?"

"Yes. We did muscle tests and I prescribed a regimen. I have never seen a more determined patient. I remember one day particularly. We had been in the pool all morning, and I asked him what he hoped to achieve from therapy. He said, 'I want to walk without crutches. I want to walk into a room without scaring everybody half to death. I'll stand easily enough in front of people so that they'll forget I'm a cripple.'"

"But he never did," I said.

"Well, no. The quadriceps and other leg muscles simply did not respond. But in a way he came close. He came down and stayed for three weeks with his son Elliott, before he ran for governor. He was trying to work out a way of walking with somebody's arm and a cane. And braces, of course—he couldn't stand without them. I warned Elliott, 'Don't forget, if he loses his balance, he'll go down like a tree.' And FDR said, 'Don't scare us, Helena.' And finally he got so he could do it."

"This place means a lot to him, I can see that," I said. "It's great that he got the government going on it."

She gave me a funny look. "This isn't a federal institution."

"State?"

"Private. Mr. Roosevelt spent two-thirds of his fortune to buy it. Then he and Mr. O'Connor set it up as a nonprofit organization. No one is turned away. They'll say at the office, we have an unpaid bill for something, what are we going to do? And they send it to Hyde Park. And he pays."

I didn't say anything, because it didn't figure. The people I knew didn't give money away. Not unless they got something for it, like publicity, or votes, which generally translated into more money, so it all paid off in the end.

She worked on me for a while before she murmured, "Your father . . ."

"What about him?"

"I didn't like the man. I'm sorry, but I really didn't. Why is he like that?"

"Like what?"

"He didn't look at anyone here. It was as if he couldn't bear to look at anyone who wasn't able to walk."

"Dad doesn't like sick people," I said.

"Well, as I said, they aren't sick now. They'd just been sitting in corners because nobody knew what to do with them. Those who'd lived in hospitals could hardly do anything for themselves. They felt helpless. Often they were terribly, terribly angry. It was especially difficult for the adolescents; and so many polio victims are in their teens.

"Then they came down here and saw people like themselves driving cars, going to school, having boyfriends and girlfriends. It's just fantastic what they've done, but they had to find out they could do it. And it's all due to Mr. Roosevelt."

"Yeah, he's a real humanitarian," I said.

She didn't talk then for a while, just kept working deeper and deeper into my back. At first it hurt. Then the hurting dropped away and a warmth seeped in where her fingers had torn holes. I started to feel sleepy.

"There, you're done." Water sloshed as she pulled herself out of the pool, like a leopard seal, big and solid and gray. I slid backward off the table, swam a length, then got out. To my surprise my back felt better.

"I'll write up an exercise plan." She tossed me a towel. "Pick it up tomorrow from Dr. Hubbard's office. Or no, tomorrow's Sunday—come in Monday around this time. I think we can help you."

"Thanks," I said. And stood looking after her, thinking as I toweled off.

CHAPTER 33

Easter Sunday, April 8: Warm Springs

She sat in the last row, fidgeting with her hymnbook as the organ prelude ebbed away into a light-filled silence.

The little chapel was simple but attractive. And SRO, she thought. Not only were the pews full, but the wide aisle was parked so full of wheelchairs only a narrow passage remained. White-painted pine pews for those who sat, and an open area before them, crowded with wheelchairs and stretchers. Three pulpits and one altar, a simple gold cross, vases of Easter lilies. The cream walls were trimmed with mauve. Light streamed through the arched windows, warming a maroon tile floor.

No one had noticed her yet. The people next to her were strangers; one had a cane propped in front of him; neither had looked when she'd slipped in. The large hat and heavy veil helped too.

A wheelchair rolled past, and she turned her head with the others.

It was *him,* in a gray suit and blue tie, his uncovered head nodding slightly. She caught her breath at the gray empty face. Daisy and Margaret were with him. They stopped at the two empty pews. The women slid in first and settled, fluttering, like lavender and gray moths. Reilly helped the President in after them. Then he and the other Secret Service men slid in one seat back. She noticed that the pew behind *them* was filled with uniforms, as were the seats in front of the President. He was walled in by protective flesh.

The minister stepped forward, and she bent her head for the invocation. A clatter; an officer bent, groped, then handed FDR his glasses and a hymnbook. The President inclined his head and leaned forward as the rest of the congregation, those who could, knelt.

She'd spent yesterday evening at the cottage, but it hadn't been a late night. Hassett had explained gravely that the President turned in early now. Hell, she could see he was tired. He was still gay, still charming, but now it looked like an effort.

That was one thing she could do for him: take the burden of entertainment off his shoulders. She'd kept them laughing with Hollywood stories. Told them what the people they saw on the screen were really like—Miriam Hopkins, Charles Laughton, Errol Flynn, for God's sake. She wished she could tell them the really juicy stuff.

God! How innocent they all were, around him! And he was the same way. The most powerful man in the world! But she understood them now. Self-assured, anointed by the right family and the right manners and the right schools. The kind of people who'd intimidated her once, though not anymore. It wasn't fair, she thought. It took you so long to learn. And by the time you did you were thirty-seven, next door to forty. Almost too far along to do anything about it.

But not quite.

"Please join me in Hymn 168."

—

The epistle was Colossians 3:1–3, "If ye then be risen with Christ, seek those things which are above, where Christ sitteth on the right hand of God. Set your affection on things above, not on things on the earth. For ye are dead, and your life is hid with Christ in God." A man in a wheelchair sang "Open the Gates," and together, a little ragged, the congregation sang "The Strife Is O'er, the Battle Done."

This morning she'd slept late. Then, when she drove in from town, found the grounds covered with children in wheelchairs. An Easter egg hunt. She'd parked by the colonnade and walked briskly past them, ready to be pleasant, but so intent were the children on the treasures in the grass they'd not even looked at her.

She smiled now, thinking about it. Would she ever have a child? It didn't look like it. Not after two marriages and the recent run of so-called lovers. Either they were arrogant bastards or such milquetoasts they couldn't stand up to a real woman in bed or anywhere else . . .

She suddenly realized people around her were getting up, reaching for purses and hats. Then a little murmur of surprise started next to her and rippled outward.

She smiled sweetly around, collected her purse, and swept out grandly.

At least it started out that way. Only all the wheelchairs were leaving at the same time, like cars after a ball game was over. A steel footrest caught her stocking. The telltale rrrrip seemed to echo under the lofty rafters. The boy in the chair struggled to speak, but paled as he realized who she was.

She suppressed a swear word, keeping the smile pasted on and patting his arm even as women whispered around her. She'd have to go back to the hotel. An ordinary woman could soldier on, but *she* couldn't go anywhere with a laddered stocking.

She stopped outside and shaded her eyes in the bright morning, searching the lawn, the faces. She'd thought she might see the kid, the lieutenant—Kennedy—he'd had a little spark in his eyes when they'd argued, on the way to the picnic. Then she realized he wouldn't have been at this service. What was she thinking of? He'd be at a Catholic church, somewhere else. If he went at all.

I put my cap on and helped an old lady down the steps. She was Italian, or Polish, I couldn't tell. Grace Tully was with me, but I didn't see Hassett. It hadn't been easy even finding a Catholic service in south Georgia. Two people I asked in the hotel lobby just stared at me, as if I'd asked for the nearest mosque.

Then Ruth had said there was a call for me. It was Grace asking if I wanted to go with her to mass, in Manchester. We got to Elizabeth Seton five minutes after the service started.

I always tried to make church every Sunday. What the hell, it made Mom happy. Come to think of it, I owed her a letter. Maybe I could get to it this afternoon if Hassett didn't need me.

I stood outside after the old lady thanked me. Nobody else gave me a second look. There hadn't even been any girls worth looking at.

Finally Tully came out, making the sign of the cross. I said, "How about a soda, Grace? Or coffee, or something?"

"That would be nice, but every place will be closed. Except maybe the Foundation . . . let's go there. They'll be done with the Episcopal service at noon."

When we went through the gates I saw the cars on the lawn outside the church. The blue Ford was there too. I parked away from the crowd and we walked over. People stood around, chatting in their Sunday finery. FDR was sitting in his wheelchair, wearing his old fedora, talking to a short man I recognized as Basil O'Connor, the man I'd met at the soda fountain. "How are things with the Red Cross these days, Doc?" FDR was asking him as I came up.

"Hectic, but good. I'm planning a cross-country train trip next week."

"And the Foundation?"

"We raised ten million in the March of Dimes this year. Left half in the communities for individual care. The rest came to Warm Springs."

"Research?"

"Half a million," O'Connor said. "Warm Springs itself is in good shape. We'll treat six hundred fifty patients this year. Not including the amputees and wounded we're getting from the military hospitals."

FDR shook his head. "Doc, I want to apologize."

"What for?"

"Look what I've got you into."

"All I ever wanted—"

"I know. To be a lawyer." Roosevelt leaned forward in his chair and tapped his knee. "There's this to be said for your life, though. Most men just go down the middle of the street, doing their chosen work. You've done that with the law. But you've worked the sides too—helping take care of the other fellow who's had some trouble. It's not a bad way to make the journey, and I take back that apology. Hello, Johnny!"

I looked around, but Grace had gone off in the crowd. "Hello, Mr. President," I said.

"Do you know 'Doc' O'Connor?"

"Yessir, we've met."

FDR fumbled inside his jacket. I lit his cigarette. He and O'Connor and a man I didn't know started talking about the pools. I drifted off, wondering what I was going to do with myself today. Stick around the cottage? I'd better check with Hassett. Funny, I'd pegged him as a pious guy, and he hadn't been at mass. Nor was he here. Grace didn't know where he was. Then I saw Reilly, standing with his back against a brick wall. It was laid with gaps between the bricks, so that ivy twisted through. He waved out a match as I came up and flicked it at my feet. "Kennedy."

"You seen Bill?"

"The Deacon's not feeling well this morning. I think he twisted his ankle or something."

"He say what he wanted me to do?"

"No."

"What's the drill, Sundays?"

"Same's usual in the afternoons," said Reilly, exhaling smoke. He kept his eyes on FDR, though two of his men were standing behind the President's chair. "Just got a call from the FBI," he muttered.

"Yeah?"

"About the bomb. They completed the analysis."

I waited. Reilly said, low but still casual, so that anyone watching us would have thought we were talking about the sermon, "Interesting stuff. They say it's Soviet."

"Russian?"

"Yeah. The main charge was an ammonium derivative of trinitrophenol. The French call it explosive D. They and the Reds are the only ones who make the stuff. A tetryl booster. The detonator was a clock mechanism. When they took it apart they found Cyrillic lettering on the parts."

"Christ, *Russian?* That doesn't make sense."

"Well, that's what the FBI bomb boys say it is," said Reilly, and his face was a study in nonchalance as he tipped his hat to a passing girl on crutches.

"What about the stuff in the bottle? The shit that knocked me out and killed Jerry Hunley?"

"They don't know anything about that," Reilly said softly.

I thought about that for a while, but the more I ground my brain against it the less sense it made. Stalin didn't have any reason to bump off FDR. Hell, they were supposed to be buddies. Reilly leaned against the bricks, smoking and watching the people disperse. A bird started singing right above us, in the ivy.

"Have you told *him* about it?"

"About the bomb?"

"Everything you just told me."

"Yeah."

"What'd he say?"

"Nothing."

"Nothing, Mike? Not anything? I mean, literally?"

"Just looked at me with his head cocked to one side, the way he does. Then started telling a story. Either he's not afraid or he just doesn't care."

"He can't *not care*. Not if the Communists are trying to kill him."

"I wouldn't bet on that. I wasn't there when Zangara tried for him in Miami. But Hunley was, and he told me about it. He was talking to the American Legion from an open car, sitting on the back. After the speech Pushcart Tony, Mayor Cermak, goes up to shake his hand. All of a sudden this crazy bricklayer jumps up on the bandstand and lets go. Five shots from a .32. Cermak takes Roosevelt's bullet. Roosevelt holds him in the back seat all the way to the hospital. Keeps telling him to keep quiet, it won't hurt if he keeps quiet. Now, normally after a guy's been shot at, you'll see a shock reaction. His face goes white, his hands shake, his voice gets a quaver in it. Doesn't mean he's yellow, just that he's a little shaken up. But Jerry said FDR showed no reaction at all."

"I don't buy it," I said. "He's got to worry—"

"Yeah?"

"Nothing," I said, but I was remembering what FDR had been telling me at the picnic. About how he liked to ride in open cars. Still. . . . "No, wait, hell, I'll say it: That's a load of bull. I get shaky when I think about that goddamn bomb. Don't you? Come clean, Mike."

"I don't look at it that way, you got to know. The Sacred Service, we train different from regular cops. When they take fire, they look for cover. We shoot back standing up. To take the bullets, so they don't hit *him.*"

"That doesn't scare you?"

"Like I said, I don't look at it that way. I figure it's more important to the country that Franklin D. Roosevelt's safe than that Michael F. Reilly gets to enjoy old age. And if some asshole wants to punch FDR's ticket bad enough, he's gonna do it. All it takes is the willingness to trade his life for the President's."

"So you think *he* figures like that? That if they're going to get him, they're going to get him?"

"There's a lot of loonies out there, that's for sure. But I don't think it's fatalism. I think—this may sound strange—I think it's faith."

"Sure it is," I said.

FDR was saying goodbye to O'Connor. The driver started the Ford. Reilly shoved himself lazily away from the bricks, and for the first time since I'd come up, looked at me. Then he stiffened.

Before I could move he had me slammed back against the wall. Branches stuck through the open spaces and he was grinding me back against them. "What the—"

"Shut up! You little son of a bitch. You son of a bitch! How long have you been—"

"Only since I—"

The buttons tore on my khaki blouse as he pulled the revolver out. He looked at it unbelievingly.

"God damn! My back—"

"Fuck your back! Where'd you get this?"

"It's my issue sidearm. Give it back."

"Like hell!"

"I told you, it's Navy issue!"

"I don't give a fragrant shit if Jesus Christ Himself issued it to you! You shit! I wanted you out of here long ago. Only he said no, he liked you around. Now you turn up with a gun!"

"Jesus, Mike, I was trying to help protect him—"

"Bullshit." Reilly looked like *he* was in shock, pale and using words I'd never heard out of him. "I ought to break your fucking neck. I mean it! Christ! What if—God *damn* it."

"So *you* wanted me out," I said slowly.

"From the start! Now maybe they'll see it my way. I'm wiring Leahy today. If the Navy won't recall you I'm putting you under arrest. Your father makes a stink, I'll let Congress decide. And you can kiss your political ass good-bye."

"Damn it, I don't care about politics. All I want to do is help keep him safe. Mike, please—"

"Save it, Kennedy. And don't bother reporting to the cottage anymore. You're through."

When he left I just stood there. I'd just stuck the gun in my jacket pocket, thinking I'd take care of it before I got to the cottage. Just like I'd been doing. Then I'd gone by the chapel, and seen people coming out, and went over without thinking of it. And now he had it. I felt naked now. Ever since Abrams died, when I'd realized Leahy was on to something, that somebody was really trying to kill FDR, I'd felt vulnerable without a gun.

I was standing there, feeling sorry for myself. And mad, just browned off in general. When I got a funny feeling. As if somebody was watching me. I turned my head slowly, but saw nothing but brick, and beyond it greenery. I could smell something, though. Something like perfume.

———

She stood in the little enclosed garden, her ear cocked by the glossy green cascades of ivy. But no one spoke on the other side. Had they left? Could she leave now?

And how about what she'd just heard?

She'd been sitting quietly, alone on the worn wooden bench. It was a private spot beside the chapel, a bower she'd discovered when she looked for somewhere to adjust her stocking. A place to meditate, pray, or just sit and think. Which is what she'd been doing when she heard the murmurs on the far side of the wall. At first she'd tried to ignore the conversation. Then, when she'd heard *his* name, well, of course she'd gotten up and moved a little closer.

She made up her mind and touched her hat and walked quickly out into the sunlight.

The Irish lieutenant was leaning against the bricks, looking casual except for flushed cheeks. His hands were in his pockets and his military cap tucked under his arm. His sandy-red hair stuck up in a cowlick. He looked like an angry little boy.

"Hello," she said, smiling.

"Well. Look who's here."

"Yes, it's me. Did I see you in church?" She took out a cigarette, held it poised in her fingertips. He looked toward the road, and his face tightened as a black car rolled by. Then he lit it for her.

"No. Actually, I just got here."

She tilted her head back and exhaled slowly, glancing around. The closest ears were a little girl's, fifty yards away. She was in a wheelchair, trying to reach something in the crotch of a tree.

Wolfe murmured, "It's no use pretending, Lieutenant. I heard it all."

"I told you, the name's Jack. Don't you remember our intimate little drive? That ended with me dropping the Commander in Chief on his can?"

"Never mind that. I want to know more about what you were talking about a minute ago. Did I really hear what I thought I heard?"

"I don't know. What did you thought you heard?"

"You and that Secret Service man—"

"I don't know what you're talking about."

"You and Reilly. God damn it, don't play stupider than you are! Am I to understand that there was a *bomb* aboard his train? Is that what you were talking about? And that somebody's still trying to kill him?"

Kennedy gnawed his lip. She closed in grimly and fastened her hand on his arm. From the lawn it might have been a friendly conversation. "Don't try to freeze me out, buster. Or it'll be in a hundred papers tomorrow. Who should it be, I wonder? Ilka Chase? Hedda Hopper? Elsa Maxwell? I saw all that fresh beef in there today, sitting two deep around him. Is that what it's all about? Some sort of . . . assassination attempt?"

"Take it easy, Lauren. You overheard something you weren't supposed to. Now forget you heard it. It's a matter of national security. Don't take it personally. But I just can't talk about it."

"You just did. Out in the open, where anybody could have heard you. You're lucky it was me behind that wall. What if it'd been one of those newspapermen? Or a spy?"

"A spy, in Warm Springs?"

"Why the hell not? And don't give me this smug 'national security' line, little man. I've done more for the war effort than you have. One of my *Bad Girl* posters went for two hundred grand in war bonds. What have you done to win the war? Aside from getting run over by a Nip PT boat?"

"That's a low one, Lauren. It was a destroyer."

"Excuse me, I'm sure. But get me mad and I fight dirty. Are you going to spill it? Or am I going to go look for a telephone? Because one way or another, I'm dealing myself in."

Kennedy didn't answer her for a couple of seconds. He was thinking, and at the same time—he couldn't help it—checking her out. She was dressed for church. A white bow blouse and a green skirt, a light hat with a veil, a silver pin at her throat. The outfit was elegant, but she was old enough that the effect was spinsterish. Up close her face wasn't beautiful at all. Her nose was too large, he'd noticed that before, but now he saw that there was something strange about everything in her face. On the screen it looked exotic, but up close it was almost malformed, as if the bones were put together differently from everyone else's. She looked like she should be fragile, but her hips and shoulders were wider than they looked on the screen.

And she was always *moving.* She fidgeted. She wriggled. She fiddled with the cigarette, tossing her cocked arm away between nervous puffs which she did not inhale, simply sucked into the wide mouth and then expelled. The green eyes were in constant motion, widening as she spoke. The long, awkward neck. . . . When you looked at her piece by piece, she wasn't that attractive. But when you put them all together, she was irresistible. Maybe, he thought, it was the allure of danger.

Because eyeball-to-eyeball with her you realized that if you didn't come up to her mark she'd roll over you like a Sherman tank. Maybe only a guy like FDR could have handled it. Or maybe it would turn out the same way it had for him and Eleanor. He had the feeling that if he blinked she'd have him declawed and fixed, poodle-clipped and begging for bonbons.

"What's wrong with your face?" he said.

She flinched, but gave him a level look back. "Do you want the studio version, or the truth?"

"Wait. I remember now. The auto accident."

"The auto accident. Yes."

"Is that the truth?"

"If getting your face broken in a car door is an accident."

"Jesus. Who?"

"My mother." She looked away. "I was ten. I must have been difficult that day. She put my head in the door and slammed it. Five or six times . . . who knows? I might not have made it in pictures without that. But this face, they remember."

"Jesus," he said again.

"That's where the bitchiness comes from, I guess. I reach right down to that. And when I have to feel vulnerable . . . that's not too far down, either." She took a deep breath. "Maybe that's another reason why I had to meet *him.* To see how he handled a raw deal."

"You've got it bad for him, don't you?" he asked her.

Wolfe gave him a long, hard examination. "Maybe I do. So what? He's got everything *I* ever looked for in a man. Everything they left out of all the weak-kneed, limp-brained, self-absorbed twits I keep coming up with."

"That solves our problem, then."

"What?"

"If they do get him, we don't have to worry. Just wait three days and he'll rise again."

"I don't think it's funny. If there's any danger, I'm going to be between it and him. How about it? Last chance before I rip the lid off." She reached up and flicked a crushed ivy leaf off his uniform.

Kennedy thought: Hell. Maybe she's right. She wasn't around when Abrams died. Or when the bomb got into Number One. She wasn't a suspect, which was more than he could say for anybody else in the inner circle. And she was one smart, pushy, determined broad.

"Have you got a gun?"

"A what? Oh, that's right. He took yours away. No. I'm afraid of guns. We don't need one, anyway."

"You weren't afraid of them in *Eye of the Storm.*"

"I was when it started. It was all I could do to hold it in my hand. I was shaking. But Stevens made us do thirty takes on that scene. He wanted to get the splash right, but it wouldn't come out the way he wanted it. I kept shooting Victor Mature and he kept falling backward into the lagoon. Then they'd fish him out and get him another captain's uniform and we'd do it all over again. I got used to them, but I still don't like them. I'm glad he took yours. Where did you get it?"

"It's my service revolver. I've been carrying it since I got to Warm Springs. About a week now."

"And this is the first time he noticed?"

"I forgot and left it in my pocket. He spotted that right away."

"Where did you keep it before?"

"In my hat, hooked in with a coathanger. It was heavy, but nobody ever searches there."

"Well, I think he did the right thing."

"Yeah, except that now, if somebody tries for FDR, we have to hold him back with our bare hands."

She held him off at arm's length, and a little smile tilted her mouth. She drawled, "So I've convinced you?"

"Halfway."

"What do I have to do to get the other half?"

"Well—look. Maybe it can work. But promise me one thing. Don't let it out of the box, that you know. Don't tell Reilly. Or Hassett. Or anybody. They're already sore at me. Let's keep it between us."

"All right, Jack. I'll play Mata Hari to your Philo Vance. Is there anything else I ought to know? Such as, is there anybody you suspect? Or Reilly suspects?"

"I don't really suspect anybody. As far as what he thinks—who knows? He doesn't exactly confide in me."

"Nobody? Really?"

"Well, I had some doubts about Bruenn—he's FDR's doctor, I don't know if you've met him. But he doesn't seem like the mad bomber type. He's a Republican, not a Commie."

"That's something else I didn't follow. What Mike was saying about the bomb . . . I didn't understand that technical stuff, but he was saying it was what, made in the Soviet Union? Did I hear that right?"

"That's what the FBI said."

"But that doesn't make sense. They're on our side."

"Maybe they're starting the next one early."

"They were antifascists long before we were. Some of my best friends are

Reds. They'd never consider—no, it's ridiculous. Someone's got his signals crossed."

"Yeah, they're real high-minded. Like when Adolf and Joe carved up Poland together." Then he remembered the drop-dead date Leahy had given him. "Anyway, let's not argue about that. If we can protect him for a few more days, we're home free."

"Then put 'er there, partner."

Solemnly, they shook hands.

C H A P T E R 3 4

Monday, April 9: The Little White House

The sun sliced itself apart coming through the green blinds and lay in strips across the pine floor. The french doors were open, and the woods-smells blew in through them. The wind felt warmer than yesterday, but cooler, I suspected, than it would tomorrow. Spring was at hand.

FDR sat in his armchair beside the fireplace. The flames had died; only a faint glow lingered under the ashes. But I could feel the heat against my cheek, still radiating from the rough-cemented Georgia fieldstone. In the kitchen Lizzie and Daisy were singing. Grace Tully swept in and out, looking preoccupied. Hassett sat in FDR's spare wheelchair, shoeless foot propped up, looking at a rare-book catalogue. He'd turned his ankle Sunday hurrying up the path to check on the President before Mass. Now the lanky Vermonter was nearly as immobile as the Boss, who had a field day ragging him.

"Here's a copy of Amasa Delano's travels. Interested in that, Mr. President?"

"How is it described?"

" 'A narrative of Captain Amasa Delano's voyages and travels, including three circuits of the terraquaeous globe. One volume octavo, calfbound, condition good, thirteen dollars.' "

FDR pondered over his stamp collection. "I don't think so, Deacon. Amasa was one of the Maine Delanos. A distant cousin of Grandfather Warren. You recall, the one who gave me that sea chest and the other things I showed you at Hyde Park. But Grandpa never met him, and—I really don't think so."

"How about this: *A History of the Rebellion and the Civil Wars in England.*"

"It seems to me I—I know I have a couple of histories of that period—"

"This one's by Edward Hyde."

"The first earl of Clarendon."

"For whom Hyde Park was named."

"Actually it was his grandson. Score one for Professor Roosevelt. What saith the catalogue?"

" 'Scarce edition, three volumes in six, 1705 to 1720. Seventeen dollars and fifty cents.' "

"I don't think so. I know I am a pack rat, Bill, but I don't think any book is worth seventeen fifty."

"He's feeling the pinch of poverty this morning, Jack," Hassett muttered to me. FDR squinted at us but didn't say anything. I noticed that his hands were steadier today. He'd been at it for an hour and hadn't dropped a stamp. He even lit a cigarette himself.

When Long brought the mail in I helped Hassett sort, since he couldn't leave the chair. I handed the newspapers to FDR. He shook the *Star* open and ran his eye down the front page. Just then a phone rang. There were three of them on the shelves near the fireplace. "The top one," Roosevelt said. I picked it up and said, guardedly, "Hello?"

A male voice. "General Marshall for the President."

"He's here. Just a moment—Mr. President, General Marshall."

"Is the—is the machine on?"

"The scrambler? Yes, sir."

He took the phone and threw his head back, looking across the room. "Hello, General? How are you? Our boys seem to be doing wonderfully, according to this morning's headlines."

I heard the front door open. Voices murmured. Then Wolfe appeared in the hall. She was dressed for Walden Pond today, slacks with the cuffs rolled up, a sweater, walking shoes. She smiled at Hassett and me as Roosevelt, listening intently, stared into the fire. Then he spoke, loud and confident:

"She's giving you the business, eh? Well, better you than me . . . what do you think of that treasure cache Third Army found? In the salt mine? No, that's spoils of war, my boy . . . grand . . . what did you have for me, General?"

Wolfe crossed the room on tiptoe and put her hand on Hassett's arm. "How are you, Bill? How's the ankle?"

"Fine, Lauren. I should be back on my feet tomorrow."

FDR boomed, "What does that mean? Explain that to me in English, will you? . . . Well, Leahy's an ordnance expert, and he tells me it won't work. Oh. Who? How about Oppie? When's the test? . . . perhaps I will; let me know the exact date when we're closer. . . . Tell Groves if it's a fizzle I'm going to have Congress send him the bill, all right?"

"Where's Mike?" Lauren asked me. I pointed toward the sun deck.

"Yes . . . yes . . . I guess we'll see. Who? Invite *them* to the test? I think not. In fact, in Europe—I want to get teams in early and sweep up all the Germans who've worked on this. I don't want Stalin getting hold of them. All right? Well, thanks for phoning, General, I know how much you dislike this infernal instrument."

FDR hung up. He rubbed his hands over his cheeks for a moment, then sighed. "General Marshall," he said to Lauren. "Have you met him? He's got a dalmatian named Fleet. The stupidest animal I have ever seen on four legs. When the war started George donated him to the K-9 Corps. They starred him in a training film. George was so embarrassed when I screened it for him. Fleet was the dog who did everything wrong." He laughed so hard the panes rattled in the windows.

———

I stayed around till after lunch, then checked out with Hassett when the President turned in. Lauren offered me a ride, but I wasn't sure how long I'd be.

The Willys was low on gas, but it was enough to get me down to the Foundation and back. I stopped by the hotel to collect my laundry. The room was pretty messy and I had to root around for a while to find it all. I'd have to have a word with Oliver. I was good enough to share with him, he ought to keep things picked up a little. I stripped off the shirt I was wearing and put on my last clean one.

I was headed out the lobby when Ruth Stevens called to me. I went back to the desk. "Yes?"

"Telegram for you, Lieutenant Kennedy."

I don't like telegrams. I get a feeling of disaster when I see that yellow envelope. I ripped it open. Disaster, all right. It was from Dad.

TIMILTY REPORTS CONDITIONS RIGHT FOR RUN THIS NOVEMBER BY VETERAN HERO NOTED AUTHOR STOP YOU MUST SWALLOW BITTERNESS OVER JOE AND TAKE UP THE CUDGELS STOP FAMILY WILL RALLY BEHIND YOU STOP YOUR HERO HAS SHOWN THAT DESPITE MEDICAL PROBLEMS A DETERMINED MAN CAN RENDER SIGNIFICANT PUBLIC SERVICE STOP HAVE MADE GIFTS TO LOCAL CHARITIES IN YOUR NAME LUNCHED WITH GOVERNOR TOBIN AND THE WAY IS CLEAR STOP TRIED TO REACH YOU BY PHONE AT HOTEL NO RESPONSE STOP INFORM PRESIDENT WILL ARRIVE WARM SPRINGS EVENING TRAIN 12 APRIL DISCUSS YOUR FUTURE

I looked up to see Stevens waiting. She said, not looking at me, "I hope it's not—"

"Nobody died," I said.

"That's good. These days, when you get one—"

"They don't send those by telegram," I said. "They send a guy around to tell you news like that. Or a priest."

The switchboard buzzed. She listened, dialed, swapped a plug. "Have you heard about the barbecue?"

"Barbecue?"

"Well, you know yesterday I was talking to Mr. Smith, the reporter, and he asked me if I'd make him a nice big pot of Brunswick stew. And I said, 'Honey, I just bought me a three-hundred-pound pig, let's have a whole-hog barbecue.' I hadn't really, it was just bragging like. But Mr. Allcorn was there in the Pine Room, and he said that was a fine idea and we could have it at his country place over to Pine Mountain. I'm going to ask Mr. Hassett if the President would like to come. Maybe we'll have it Wednesday or Thursday? I bet you don't get barbecue in Boston."

I wasn't really listening. I crumpled up the flimsy yellow telegram paper, leaned over the desk, and two-pointed it into the trash.

No, nobody'd died . . . but I felt like somebody had. Someone I might have become. Damn it! It was over. Now Dad was going to take control again. Steering me. Telling me what to say and what to do, all in the name of The Family. But in the end, only really for himself. I realized Stevens was watching me. "I don't know," I said. "Maybe. I'll let you know. But thanks."

———

When I checked in at Hubbard's office he wasn't there. Neither was Mahoney. The receptionist said she was in Atlanta, but should be back on the evening train. I told her, already hearing the note of defeat in my voice: "She said she'd leave a treatment plan for me."

"Mr. Kennedy? Here it is."

"But if she's not here, how do I—"

"Do you know the way to the indoor pool? Miss Chaworth will be there. Show her the plan. She'll give you any necessary directions."

"Okay."

There were people in the pool this time, kids, mostly, shouting and splashing. Their happy yells bounced off the glass ceiling. I walked down to the shallow end. "Hi," I said.

Just seeing her made me feel better. She was in up to her waist, working on a girl patient on a treatment table. I averted my eyes from pale, wasted legs. Chaworth had on a gray swimsuit with a Red Cross emblem. A whistle on a silver chain nestled where my eyes settled. Slim, but with swimming muscle in her arms and shoulders. A curl of dark hair twisted from beneath her swimming cap. Dreamy-looking eyes and a neck I yearned to sink my teeth into. She looked blank, so I gave her the grin as I said, "I'm Jack Kennedy. Mr. O'Connor introduced us a couple days ago. I've been having some back trouble. Helena Mahoney left this treatment plan."

"I'm the only physiotherapist here, Mr. Kennedy. And I'm with Emily right now." She kept working as she spoke, drawing up the girl's legs again and again, encouraging her to lift. She rolled her over gently in the water and I caught a glimpse of deep brown eyes. I looked away.

"Call me Jack. Veronica, right? How about this—I'll get changed, and you can do me when you're finished with her."

"I have another patient scheduled then. But Emily has some exercises she should do on her own . . . all right, go ahead, get in."

I went back into the changing room. The same colored man gave me what looked like the same pair of trunks. When I stared he said, "Them's same ones as you had Saturday, General. Only they been washed."

"Thanks," I said. If he was looking for a tip, he was out of luck, though. I threw my shit into a locker and pulled them on. God, why did they have a mirror here? I looked like an anatomy class skeleton.

Chaworth was at the side of the pool reading my plan when I came out. She told me we'd start with a light massage. I said that sounded good and dove in and came up and swam back to her. The water was *hot.*

"Please don't dive again, Mr. Kennedy. It's against the rules. Other people can't always get out of the way."

"Sorry."

"Lie down here. Face down. Arms up, please." I complied and felt strong legs slide around me. Then her thighs clamped down.

"Your skin tone, Mr. Kennedy. I noticed it . . ."

"I'm a half-breed. Sioux."

"Oh, are you?" Her hands stopped. "I didn't—"

"Just joking. Touch of malaria. A lot of guys have it who've been in the tropics."

She leaned into my back again, smoothing out the long muscles on either side of my spine. Her hands were smaller than Mahoney's but just as strong. I closed my eyes. The moist heat made sweat prickle on my scalp. "That's right, someone told me you served in the Pacific. Most of our wounded are from Europe. You're with the President, aren't you? A bodyguard."

"An aide. How about you?"

"You know what I do."

"Yeah, but how about your personal life? Got a boyfriend?"

"We don't date, Mr. Kennedy."

"Call me Jack. Are you putting me on? I can't believe it. How old are you? I guess twenty."

"Twenty-one." She sounded as if she was smiling. It was uphill work, but maybe I was climbing. She leaned over and I had a vision of peeling gray, wet fabric down and licking the freckles off those muscular shoulders.

"Does this hurt too much?"

"Go ahead. Hurt me."

"You're a naughty sort of fella, aren't you, Mr. Kennedy? Are you one of those wolves?"

"*Jack.* No, I just want to enjoy life for a change. You know, we used to dream about American girls. We'd see women in grass skirts with their . . . chests hanging down, but what we wanted was Susie or Edie or Veronica. Some of us didn't really have a girl, but we all knew one we'd have liked to know better."

"How old are you, Mr. Kennedy? Twenty-five, I'd guess."

"Close." Twenty-seven, she might think that was too old.

"But you've been back a while, haven't you?"

"Yeah, stateside duty . . . the White House . . . you know. Not much chance to get out. Want to catch a movie with me tonight?"

"We don't go out."

"What is this, a nunnery? News flash: it's 1945. Women have the vote, you know. They ferry bombers across the Atlantic."

"Mr. *Kennedy*," she whispered, glancing around.

"Jack. Look, I'm serious. I've never met anyone like you before. I'd like—you like to swim?"

"Of course, but—"

"Me too. Let's go for a moonlight swim. Just you and me. Is this pool open at night?"

"No. Of course not! Mr. Kennedy, you don't really think—"

"Then down the hill, how about that? At the open pool. I'll meet you there. Nine sharp. We'll do a few laps, then talk. What do you say?"

"I really don't think Miz Mahoney would approve of that sort of thing, Mr. Kennedy."

"How about this. We don't *tell* Miz Mahoney. Call it a top secret assignment to boost Navy morale. Just sneak out and meet me down there at—what did I say?"

"Nine."

"Nine. Great. We'll get to know each other."

"I don't think so. I won't be there, Mr. Kennedy."

"Jack, okay? Well, I will. Waiting in the moonlight. I'll bring a blanket, so we can . . . talk. Think about it. Nine sharp."

She gave me a look and turned away, calling to the crippled girl, who let go the edge of the pool and dog-paddled toward us.

I got out and toweled off, then padded into the changing room. The old guy was leaning on a mop, like that joke about the CCC guy with his arm in a sling. They ask him what happened, and he says he was leaning on a shovel and termites ate through it and he broke his arm when he fell.

"Hey," I said. "You ever clean up down at the main pool? Down at the springs?"

"Yassah."

"What time do they close?"

"Right after supper, sah."

"That's at five?"

"Five o'clock, sah."

"Are they lighted?"

"Lighted? No sah, General, they ain't lighted. What for you want to know? Anything I can help you with?"

"No thanks," I said.

I stopped by the soda fountain on the way out and gave the guy there, Hawley, my shirts and a bag of net laundry. His hands didn't move, just lay on the counter. He grabbed the bag with a steel pincer thing that closed when he turned his wrist. There was something wrong with his mouth, too. I couldn't make out what he said, so I just said uh-huh and backed away. He clicked the steel clamp at me like a giant lobster.

I don't know. If I was him, I think I'd have stayed shut up in that room. Where nobody could tell you what to do—or make you into something you didn't want to be.

———

Wolfe sat relaxed in the big leather chair, smoking one of *his* cigarettes. God, she thought, these are harsh. Can he really inhale these? Maybe the holder cooled the smoke? She'd used them in boudoir scenes, as props.

But *he* used it as a prop too. To divert attention. And as a trademark, like a character actor. His old hat. His cape. The glasses that made him look trustworthy. She hadn't seen it at first. He did it so well. But now he was tired, and the effort showed through, like a threadbare costume.

She thought about what she'd overheard at the chapel yesterday. And what Kennedy had told her. Reilly was outside on the sun deck. She could see him through the blinds, standing like one of those stone temple dogs, looking down at the woods. He was always there. Never more than a few feet from FDR. If he got any closer, she thought, he'd be sleeping with him.

What would it be like? Living with him? She doubted if there'd be anything sexual. But that wasn't what she thought about when she was with him. It was on a higher plane. Kennedy sneered at it, called it hero worship. Well, why the hell not! There weren't that many heroes. She'd seen a few up close. If it hadn't been for the war they'd have been Edward G. Robinson gunsels. Or else they were second-rate Jimmy Stewarts, gawky hometown boys muttering aw shucks as they toggled away the bombs on Jap battleships. No, there weren't very many real heroes.

There weren't even very many real men. In two marriages and a generous helping of side dishes, she'd run into mainly two kinds. The weak ones, who didn't speak up or threaten her. But they didn't satisfy, either. They wanted a mother or a slave master, not a woman. The other kind were even worse. So wrapped up in themselves that washing a dish demeaned their manhood. The conquerors, who couldn't keep their worn-out flies buttoned. Oh, she was sick of them.

But the problem went deeper than that.

Her eyes drifted around the room. Quiet, unpretentious, rustic. There was nothing presidential about it. She'd like to have a cabin like this. Somewhere unspoiled, where she could be Amy Weilbacher again. No more masks, no more crowds, no more acting the role of the glamourous, sexy Lauren Wolfe . . .

Reilly at the window, shading his eyes to look in. She gave him a smile and waved the cigarette. Should she try him? Start a conversation, gradually bring up the things she'd noticed—the increased security, the lack of fun, the rings of marines around what had changed from a cottage to an armed compound? Deciding, she swung herself out of the chair.

It was bright outside and warm. No, *hot*. She'd dress lighter tomorrow. Reilly turned, a little too fast, as she came out. "Afternoon, Miss Wolfe."

"Oh, don't be formal, Mike. You were calling me Lauren by the time I left, last visit."

"Sorry—Lauren." He shrugged as if uncomfortable, and she noticed that his jacket was unbuttoned. She crossed to the balcony and looked down.

"You have a lot of guards out these days."

Reilly didn't answer. She swung across the sun deck, trailing smoke, and got the expression right. Then suddenly spun to face him. "Mike—is something wrong?"

"Something's always wrong as far as I'm concerned."

"But this is such a remote, beautiful place . . . I can't imagine anything bad happening here. Can you?"

"Ford's Theater was nice too."

"My, we're cheerful today."

"Sorry."

"You're pretty rough on young Mr. Kennedy. Couldn't you ease up a little on him?"

"I don't trust him, that's why. If the President hadn't asked for him this morning, he wouldn't even be here. What are you putting in for him for? He a friend of yours?"

"Not particularly." She noticed only now that Reilly was looking at her rather closely. To gain time to think she searched her purse for cigarettes. He took the pack out of her hand and put two in his mouth, lit them both, and gave her one.

"In memory of Cass Cavanaugh. A little weepy for me, but Roby loved it."

"Roby?"

"My wife."

"I didn't know you were married."

"She succumbed to my Irish charm in '35."

"And you're happy?"

"Yep."

"I'm so glad." She took a quick drag and lifted her jaw, blowing smoke into the sky. The wind took it back into the cottage, through the french doors, and since she couldn't think of anything else clever or interesting to say, she followed it back inside.

———

She was standing by her car, wondering whether to stay or go, when Kennedy drove up in the roadster. He pulled in beside her, but rolled too far and banged the fender into a tree. "I'm glad I wasn't standing there," she told him.

"It's this damn hand brake. I keep hitting the floor with my foot, and by the time I remember, it's too late."

He didn't get out, though, just sat there. He looked different than he had that morning. His shoulders were slumped and his smile was thinner. "Are you all right?" she asked him.

"Yeah."

On impulse she swung the door open and got in beside him. "Let's drive."

"Where?"

"Just down the road. I want to talk. I just thought of something."

"What?"

"Start the car."

When they were crackling over the gravel she threw her arm across the back of his seat. "I've done some thinking."

"That right?"

"About what we were talking about. We can't just stand around and wait. That's what Reilly's for. Here's what I thought. If the bomb was Russian, then we have to find a Russian, right?"

"There aren't any here."

"Then somebody who sympathizes with them. Or works for them . . . don't be an ass, you know what I mean! If we could find them we'd have our hands on the assassin."

"Sounds like the plot to a B picture."

"Life is a B picture, Lieutenant."

"Well, I don't think it's that simple. Anyway, how would you find out? Whether somebody sympathizes with the Russians?"

"I'll set up a talk, out in town. Or down at the Foundation. About "Our Soviet Allies." Or, "Our Soviet 'Allies.'" With quote marks. We'll announce it and see who shows up."

He pulled his eyes from the road. "That's the lamest idea I've ever heard. You think a professional assassin's going to come out of hiding to go to a lecture? Anyway, everybody in town will come anyway. Just because it's you."

"Thanks—I think. Well, have you got a better idea?"

"No. Actually I don't think I'm going to be around much longer. Reilly's asked Leahy to recall me. He'll probably just send me my discharge papers here instead. I'll catch the train to Palm Beach and that'll be it. Unless my dad gets here first."

"He's coming?"

"Thursday." He told her about the telegram.

"And you don't get along with the old man, right? Is that the right reading on that line?"

"Something like that."

"But since you're afraid of losing your bone china place setting at the family trough, you're going to do what he says. Let him come here and take you by the ear and lead you away to your fate. Some war hero."

"Cut it *out,* Lauren. I never set myself up as a hero. That was him, building my image. He's a great believer in image. He wants me to go into politics. In fact, he's got my hat in the ring for Massachusetts this fall."

"Jesus. And you're leaving with him? Is that it? I thought you wanted to protect FDR."

"Some people think I'm the danger."

"Reilly. And I can see why. Wearing a gun around the President without telling him."

"I told him why."

"Do you want me to talk to him?"

"Forget it. I just want out."

"You're quitting?"

He tapped his fingernail against his teeth and didn't look at her. "Yeah. I'm quitting."

"Going back to Mommy and Daddy?"

"Knock it off, Lauren. Just knock it off. You going to dinner?"

"I've got an invitation."

"Here?"

"That's right. Here where I can do some good. Turn around."

He gave a casual glance over his shoulder and pulled the Willys into a U-turn. A horn blared, brakes squealed, and pebbles roared as a sedan tore past, barely missing them, rocking as it pulled back onto the road. "Jesus!" she said. "Did you see him? Did you know he was behind us?"

"Take it easy, he missed us . . . so now if somebody barges in with a tommy gun, you can burn him with your cigarette. I'm going down to the Foundation."

"Wait! What about my idea?"

"It's your idea, all right. Good luck with it."

She didn't know what had changed, but the sparks were gone. He acted like something, some spring or gear, had broken inside.

"Jack, why don't you just tell him to go to hell?"

Kennedy pulled into the driveway, slowed, watching the sentry, then gave it gas and bumped the gate open. "Who?" he said.

"Your father, for God's sake! Sometimes that's the only thing that works. When I walked out in the middle of *Boadicea,* ten thousand extras standing around with spears in their hands, that made Cecil sit up—"

"I don't want to talk about it any more, all right?"

"You're afraid of him. Aren't you? He has some kind of organ-grinder's handle and all he has to do is turn it, and you dance. What is it, I wonder?"

He got out and opened her door. Stood there, looking away, his face taut and wooden. For a moment she felt sorry for him. Then she thought: If he hasn't got the balls to stand up to his father, that's his tough luck. I can't do it for him. He's a Hamlet. An indecisive Hamlet . . .

"Thanks for the drive."

"Don't mention it," Kennedy said. She looked after him as he backed into a turn and drove away.

———

When I left Wolfe at the Little White House I felt like driving. Driving east till I hit ocean and not stopping even then. Only I couldn't. No coupons. Plus Reilly had told me to leave the Willys in the garage that night; it was due for an oil change. I felt like doing something crazy, though. Dad was coming here. To "discuss my future" with Roosevelt.

I could read between the bold print lines. He was going to call in FDR's promise of political support for Joe Jr. after the war. And pin it to me like an oversized suit for the fall election.

I couldn't go far, but I drove as fast and recklessly as I dared. Slamming the little Willys along clay roads. Negro children and squawking chickens fled as I tore past. I leaned on the horn passing beat-up farm trucks and once, coming over a rise, almost hit a hay cart. That sobered me a little. I checked my watch and decided it was time to be a good boy. Time to go back.

———

I turned the roadster over to the Secret Service guys—they did the servicing on the President's vehicles—and walked down to the Foundation.

The dining hall was full when I got there. Lines of steam tables and a steady stream of wheelchair traffic. I got a tray and filled it without looking at the food. I carried it out and looked over the cripples. Finally I saw a block of gray uniforms and went over.

"Mind if I join you?"

"Hi, Lieutenant."

It was Chaworth, looking hot and tired. I pulled out a chair, smiling at who I assumed were the other physio girls. She introduced me: Janet, Mamie, Nola, Suzanne, Sylvia. I said hi. The girls were easy to talk to, especially when the subject was movies.

"Have you heard, Lauren Wolfe is here again?"

"Yeah. I just dropped her off."

"Oh my *God!* You drove her? You talked to her? What's she like? She's soooo . . . wonderful. I couldn't stop crying in *Morocco,* at the end, when they're waiting for the plane to take him away. Don't you think?"

"She's something, all right," I said.

I kept trying to catch Chaworth's eye. It wasn't easy, but I got a half-smile. Would she meet me tonight? I couldn't tell.

One of the others asked me, "Are you coming to our bash tonight?"

"Bash?"

"We're having a celebration at the cottage. It's Sylvia's birthday."

"Sure, I guess . . . what cottage did you say?"

"The physio cottage. You know where the chapel is? The next street over. The big white house with like stone arches in front of the porch."

"You, uh, want me to bring anything? Booze, or anything?"

They giggled, staring at me. Chaworth said, "Oh, we're not allowed to drink. Helena would kill us. We've got Cokes and cake and ice cream."

"Do you want me to come?" I asked her, staring right at her.

"Sure, why not?" She didn't look as if she cared one way or another, but I was starting to catch on. Hard to get was fine with me, as long as she came across in the end. And if she didn't, Sylvia kept giving me eyelash flutters. Maybe a party was what I needed. Take my mind off my troubles.

I was feeling tired, though, so after dinner I went back to the hotel. Oliver wasn't in. I took a long bath and unpacked the one set of civvies I'd brought from Palm Beach. Tan slacks and a sport shirt and saddle shoes. I hadn't worn them since 1940. The guy in the mirror was a stranger now. I didn't have a sport jacket, but Oliver's fit me.

It was a pleasant walk through the evening, across the tracks, then along the road. I passed an old Negro leading a donkey, and a boy riding a Victory bike. That was all the traffic, in this fourth year of gas and rubber rationing. The good part was you got to walk on the pavement, not the dirt. I hate to show up with dirty shoes.

When I got to the physio cottage it was nearly dark. A two-story, white clapboard sprawler with red trim, and a big porch fronted and arched with white-painted fieldstone. I knocked and waited, listening to Bing's casual voice drawling out "Montmartre Rose."

Veronica opened the door. "Hi."

"Hi. Here I am."

"I'm glad you came."

"Are you? I wasn't sure."

"You were sure," she said. She looked me up and down. "You look different out of uniform."

"Better?"

"Different. Come on in. We're about to cut the cake."

Three or four callow-looking guys were drinking Cokes in the living room. Nola was sitting with one of them. The other girls were circulating. It all looked pretty clean-cut. Nobody was even smoking. Veronica introduced me around, then gave me a tour of the house. The first floor, anyway. A kitchen in back. Pantry. Steep stairs led upward from the central hall. "What's up there?" I said, knowing the answer.

"Where we live. Showers and bedrooms."

"Want to show me? I'm thinking of a career in interior design, after the war."

"Oh, we can't go up there. I mean, you can't."

"But I'd like to see where you live."

"Miz Mahoney wouldn't like that. Sylvia, remember the lieutenant we met at supper? He's here for some cake and ice cream. Doesn't he look different now?"

"He looks even cuter."

"Yeah, well," I said, and gave her a kiss. "Happy Birthday, Sylvia."

"Oh my," she said. "Where did you come from? Are you my present?"

That worked. Veronica snagged my hand as soon as I had my plate and yanked me back into the sitting room.

Somebody had taken Crosby off and put on "Night and Day." We got a corner of one of the sofas and ate ice cream while Swoonatra sang. I talked to the other guys. The older one was Army, a tanker, with a reconstructed arm he was learning to use again. The others were male physios.

Somebody turned the lights off after a while and I concentrated on Veronica. She didn't mind tangling tonsils but when I started exploring she fended my hands off. I joked about getting another back massage upstairs, but she said we couldn't go up.

"Jim and Mamie just did."

"I don't think so. I think they're out back sneaking a smoke."

"Oh my God. What will Miz Mahoney think?"

"I know what you'd like. Would you like to see some pictures?"

"Pictures of what?"

"Pictures of us. And other stuff. The first girls to come here started it."

She pulled the chain on the lamp beside us. It didn't seem to bother the writhing couple on the other sofa. He had his hand under her blouse and they were breathing hard. When I saw the album I almost walked out. I decided to giver her ten more minutes, then it was Sylvia's turn at bat.

"This is Mary Hudson, she was the first physio. This is when it started . . . in 1926 I think. This was the old hotel that was here then. They used to have stagecoaches coming in to White Sulphur from Columbus. And a stagecoach from here would go over there to pick up people when this was a summer resort. But after it turned into the Foundation things didn't work like that anymore.

"This is Miss Mahoney. She came down from New York with Dr. Hubbard—"

"Yeah, she told me about that."

"Oh, she did? Wait a minute—let me up, I have to change the record—do you like Martha Tilton? Now this was at Thanksgiving. Every Thanksgiving is Founder's Day, and Mr. Roosevelt comes down, unless of course there's a war. These children, they drew to see who would sit with him at the head table.

"This is the indoor pool. Mr. and Mrs. Ford came down for the dedication.

The physios did an Aquacade thing, like at the World's Fair, they swam under this bridge and made a letter R in front of where Roosevelt was sitting."

"This is really fascinating," I said.

"These people are sitting on the front porch of the inn . . . This is the inside of what used to be the playhouse. And here's the Little White House being built."

The next page had a big picture of the house we were in. Girls stood in front in matching calf-length dresses. Veronica said, "They started wearing them because when people first came here they'd already spent so much time in hospitals, who wanted to see a uniform."

"How many girls are there here now?"

"Eleven. Some of them are over on night duty and we're two short."

"And there's probably a house mother—"

"Oh, we don't need one. If you knew Miss Mahoney . . . she lives down on the other side, but what she doesn't already know she'll find out pretty quick."

"You'd be surprised," I said.

"I know you think I'm Elsie Dinsmore, but it's not like we have a lot of free time to date and that. We work in the mornings, and then there's rest hour, and walking. We play badminton and tennis and of course we swim every day after work. Do you play bridge?"

"Only if someone holds a large-caliber handgun to my head."

She kept plowing through the album. "This doctor was from Atlanta. Dr. Hoke. He's the one that did the fused foot so they would stand on it instead of it wobbling. This is Mr. Roosevelt . . . this is me giving exercises to the patients in the pool."

"You ever work with him?"

"With Mr. Roosevelt? Sure. One of the ladies I showed you was his physio the longest time. It don't make any difference, though, you do the same thing for him you do for any other polio.

"We had a cocktail party here for him once. Here at the cottage. And all the Secret Service men were outside, he was the only man here, and he was very cute about that. I had—the only cocktail napkins we had had little elephants on them. And I said, he'll like this. So when we gave him his drink he saw them, and he said, 'I have a story to tell you about that. When I went in the White House somebody gave me an elephant. And it was this big and this high. And it stood on my desk for a long time and I finally had to send it out to have it cleaned. And when it came back it was this big and that high.' And he said, 'That went on for quite a while, till I had to send it out again. And it keeps getting smaller and smaller. And one of these days that elephant is going to disappear.' "

I wasn't listening. I was rubbing right on the old Chili Williams polka dot spot, and maybe getting somewhere at last.

"This is Mr. Roosevelt at the indoor pool. And this was on a picnic—"

"Hey, that's my dad," I said. He was grinning, sitting with Roosevelt on a blanket at Dowdell's Knob. FDR's legs stuck out, clamped in black steel.

"Is it? See that man behind him? He took out polio insurance and a month later had polio. Lucky thing, he's on a nice pension for the rest of his life. Now there's us physios all loaded in Will Moore's car. And there are the patients in the pony cart."

At last, the end. I reached for the lamp as she flipped past several as-yet-empty pages and closed the book. But not before I caught a glimpse of something. "What are those?"

"What?"

"Those pictures in the back."

"Nothing. Just some pictures of the girls."

"Lemme see."

"No, I said." But she let me flip back again.

They were nudes. She let me look in silence. "What *are* these?" I said again.

"Silhouettes."

"They're what?"

"Artistic photos. You know, where you put the light behind you and you can't see anything but the outlines. That's me, there."

I hated to tell her, but I could see everything. "Wow," I said. "Who developed these? Wait, I bet I know. Good old Hugh . . . Look, how about we go upstairs now. You can show me how you take these—these silhouettes."

"I told you, we can't."

"Why not?"

"The girls live up there. What if somebody's in the shower and comes out?"

"I won't look."

The couple on the other couch moaned. "Why don't you show me your room," I whispered. "It'd be . . . quieter."

The staircase was narrow and dark. She made me take my shoes off, and I carried them in my hand. Bedrooms and a communal shower opened off the upstairs hall. I caught a glimpse of black and white tile, panties hanging to dry. There was a trapdoor at the top of the stairs, leading apparently out through the side of the house. "What's this?" I whispered.

"Fire escape. There's a steel chute we go down. Like a slide, and it comes out down by the kitchen."

"I get it. Which room's yours?"

"Right here." The door creaked open. "It's kind of messy."

Another long kiss and I started unbuttoning things. She whispered, "Jack, don't, we shouldn't," but held up her arms so I could get her blouse off. A second later I rolled off her and unbuckled my belt.

"What are you doing?"

"I've got a bad back. Remember?"

"Yeah, and?"

"How about if you get on top. You know, like when you were working on me before, in the pool. Only I'll be face up now. Okay?"

She stepped out of her panties and planted her knees firmly on either side of me. Her thigh muscles felt like chiselled marble. "Like this?"

"Yeah. Yeah! Just let me pull these down."

Just then a startled squeal came from downstairs. "*Miz Mahoney!*"

Chaworth went stiff above me, and I heard a muffled squeak. Then she was rolling away, gasping, "Oh, oh, no." I reacted without thinking, grabbing my shirt and shoes, but couldn't find the jacket. There wasn't time to look and I sure wasn't going to turn the light on, not with her shoving me out into the hall and whispering, "Get out. *Get out!* I told you you couldn't come up here—"

Heavy footsteps lifted themselves slowly up the stairs. Buckling my belt, I snatched open the door to the showers, thinking stall, curtain, maybe a place to hide. But it was just a big open tiled room with nozzles. By now the footsteps were halfway to the second floor.

I stuck my feet in one shoe after the other, hop-scotching down the hallway, and found the trapdoor by feel just as a huge square figure loomed up. "You there! Stop! I want your name, young man—"

The trapdoor swung up and I lunged in headfirst, banging my shoulder on the frame. It was black inside and slick underneath. I kicked her hand off my foot and let go the edge. The door banged shut, cutting her voice off, and I started sliding down, gathering speed. It was like a ride at the state fair. It grabbed me and spun me around about three times, going faster and faster through the rattling sheet-metal dark, then straightened and spat me out like a bad taste. I bounced to a belly landing like a shot-up B-17, cursing as gravel bit my outflung palms.

I scrambled up as soon as I had my breath back. Screams came from inside the house. The windows were lighting up one by one like startled eyes. The kitchen window slid up and the tanker climbed out, hung for a second by what I hoped was his good arm, and dropped into the shrubbery.

I squatted in the dark, pissed off as hell once I was sure I was in one piece. This was getting to be a habit. Like the apartment in Logan Circle, when I'd actually been in the saddle when Royce barged in. What now? Would Mahoney call the cops? There had to be some kind of security, with all the rich folks on the grounds and all the poor ones outside. I wasn't worried, but it might pay to put some distance between me and the cottage.

I eased into the backyard, then faded into the woods, remembering belatedly that Oliver's jacket was still in Veronica's room. Well, couldn't be helped . . . the woods were cleared but unlit between the cottages and I had to grope from tree to tree before I came out in another backyard. I wasn't sure where I was but I got a star fix and kept heading east. Fortunately there weren't any dogs. A few minutes later I came out in front of the chapel and turned onto Oak Road, the one leading out of the Foundation. Then stopped again, trying to decide whether to give it half an hour and go back, see if Mahoney had left and Veronica wanted to pick up where we'd left off, or just say the hell with it and get some sleep.

I was standing there on the road when I heard the purr of a motor. I opened my eyes wide and looked into the black walls of the pines.

It was coming up from the state highway. Pretty late for visitors, I thought. I heard it shift gears as it climbed.

The headlights burst suddenly around the curve. I looked away, cupping my hand over my eyes to spare my night vision. As it approached I could see the pines around me, the dirt road under my feet, every clod thrown into high relief by the merciless glare. But I couldn't see the car itself, couldn't see anything behind the light as I stepped aside, off the road, into the edge of the woods.

Then they went off, suddenly, and the motor dropped to an idle. It coasted on toward me, the tires whispering and crunching over the clay and pine needles. Then came the soft squeal of the brake, everything close and intimate and somehow threatening in the warm lonely dark.

"Hey," I said.

As my eyes recovered I made out the silhouette of a car, then, framed by the window, the shadow of the driver. He sat motionless, as if waiting for me to approach. I couldn't tell if he was black or white. "Hey," I said again, louder. I didn't want to startle him, but I didn't understand what he was doing, sitting there with his lights off.

———

Sitting behind the wheel of the Nash, Krasov rubbed his chin with his free hand, feeling the bristle of a week's beard. After the incident at Belmont he'd decided to grow some concealment. Concealment . . . the night woods close around him felt reassuring. He'd pulled up this road to take a leak; the dirt track looked deserted, but now he sat for a few seconds before he got out, enjoying the night air.

Sometimes he imagined that people were following him. A large gray sedan that he could swear he'd glimpsed before, outside Hartwell, had fallen in behind him as he drove slowly through Winder. He'd sweated for five miles before pulling off and watching it go by. But the two men in it had never looked his way. He'd thought of changing cars again. But he was so close now, he was in Georgia, he didn't want to have to stop again and take the risks a swap always involved. So he'd taken to driving at night.

And now he was in Warm Springs. He'd finally caught up. Now to find the mysterious woman he'd talked to but never yet met.

He felt in the back seat for the squared-off bulk of the big camera. He'd bought it and a used suitcase and a well-used suit from a pawn shop in downtown Atlanta. She'd been quite specific as to what he needed. It was a reasonable plan. It sounded like it might work. But he had to make contact with her first. Discuss the details, how it would be done, how he would escape afterward. Get himself hired. Then find a room in some nearby town, someplace he could lie low till it was time.

Now he looked in the rearview and saw nothing, no lights coming up from the highway. He opened the door and got out, stretching. Then reached down and unbuttoned his fly.

As water rattled on the dust he looked up at the stars. He remembered all the other roads he'd stood on in his life. As a child, back in Ohio. As a teenager, in Russia. As a man, in a Europe riven by war. A war he was still fighting. It seemed that his life had been consumed by war, the titanic convulsions of political parties and states that would decide the fate of humanity for centuries to come.

And despite his lack of uniform, he was still in battle.

He had to accept, at times he almost forgot, that his apparent escape from the catastrophe was only an illusion. He might not survive this last action. He didn't want to throw his life away. But assassination was a dangerous act. His quarry would be surrounded by guards and military. As much as he might plan, as careful as he might be, there would be tremendous risk.

He was thinking this, buttoning his fly when the shadow stepped out of the pines and said, "Hey."

—————

"Who's that?" the man by the car snarled.

"Take it easy. Take it easy! Sorry if I startled you."

The shadow seemed to regard me, then to relax. It opened the door and I heard the click-slam as it closed. Then its head and shoulders leaned out.

"Say, Mac. You happen to know where the reporters live?"

I stood stock-still in the road, under the stars. "The reporters?"

"Yeah."

"You're kind of off the beam, friend. This is the road to the Foundation. I think they're at the hotel. I know Oliver is. Which one you looking for?"

"The hotel. I'll try there. Where's it at?"

"Turn around and head back to 41. Hang a right, go down to the crossroads. It's not far. The train station? It's right across from it."

"Thanks."

"No trouble at all," I said. The figure waited for a moment, black against the faint shining of the dash lights. I saw something bulky in the back seat, luggage or boxes, something with a square outline.

Suddenly I remembered something. I checked my watch, but couldn't see a thing. "You know what time it is?" I asked him.

The shadow lifted its arm and studied it briefly. "Quarter to nine."

"Thanks."

Then I heard the clash of shifting gears. The lights came on again, and suddenly curious eyes glowed from the woods. A cat, or a raccoon. The car crunched off, turned around at a wider spot in the road, and went past me, the note of the engine gradually fading as it moved away down into the valley.

A quarter to nine, I thought. Would Veronica remember about the pool? Would she join me there? I figured my chances as even. I glanced around, getting my bearings.

The Foundation grounds were deserted, empty. I could see lights on in the medical buildings, but they seemed far away as I circled the hill. The air was cool now. It smelled of pine and woods. Occasionally unseen things rustled away in the grass ahead of me. Rabbits, I guessed. I kept looking up at the stars, hoping I was headed in the right direction.

—————

As I came out above the pool the moon was rising above the mountain. Kate Smith, where are you, I thought. I listened to the faraway growl of a plane. One dim light reflected off the water. I crouched and waited, alert for a guard or a night watchman. But no one stirred. As the plane's motor faded a dog barked far off. He was answered by one, then another; then the whole valley throbbed to a far-spread chorus, greeting the moon as it drifted up above the pines.

There was no fence, but the door to the glassed-in pool was locked. I went around it, still moving cautiously. The outdoor pool was smaller, but still huge. The moon rippled faintly under the water. Steam reached up with white fingers.

I pulled my shoes off in the shadows. Then, after a short hesitation, the rest of my clothes. I couldn't tell how deep it was, or what was under the surface, so I didn't dive. Instead I swung myself over, held the side for a moment, then let go.

The warm, buoyant water received me silently. The steam shrouded me in the darkness. I took a few strokes, then turned on my back and floated, watching the moon as it slowly climbed.

Gradually my anticipation died away. I no longer cared if she was coming or not. This was all that existed, the stars, the moon, and this warm amniotic water that buoyed me up.

Gradually I recalled another night I'd drifted like this, looking up at the sky—dark, then, and overcast—and waiting.

Waiting to die.

Two thousand gallons of 100-octane gas makes a hell of a fireball. Once it died down it took a while for the fire to burn itself out. The flames licked hungrily on the water, on the bow too.

We'd hung on to 109's wreckage for a while, waiting for the Nip tin can that had just run us over to come back and polish us off.

When it didn't, we started trying to get everybody back together, the guys still on the wreck and the ones who'd gone into the water. We had to swim out and look for them. Marney and Kirksey, we never did find. They were both in the starboard turret, right where the Jap knifed into us. They probably died instantly, ground under by the destroyer's bow or torn apart by her racing screws. Anyway we never found a trace.

After the fire burned down it took three hours, swimming and calling in the dark, to get everybody who was left alive back to what was left of 109. She was still floating, though we didn't know for how long. We stayed with her all through the night, but toward morning I could see she was sinking. Taking her time, but she was going down.

When the sun came up we were in a hell of a jam. Lennie Thom, my exec, figured the Japs could see us from their lookout posts on Kolombangara, and their outpost at Gizo was even closer. All they had to do was send out a launch with a couple guys with burp guns and that would be it. We had to decamp. Unfortunately, we didn't have a life raft. I'd told the guys we didn't have room for it once we mounted the 37 mm.

So around noon we all got on a couple planks and started swimming. We towed the wounded. It took us four hours to cross Blackett Strait to the little atoll we'd picked out as probably not Jap-occupied.

I took a deep breath, remembering how I'd felt when we dragged up on the beach. Sick. I couldn't forgive myself. The guys never said a word. But they didn't have to. I knew.

As soon as we had everybody ashore, the wounded more or less comfortable, I told them I was going out into the strait and try to flag down a PT. They knew we'd been hit. They'd be out looking for us. But they wouldn't know where we were. The guys were pretty exhausted by then, from swimming and not having water or food. Johnston and McMahon were badly burned. I figured I had to get somebody's attention or we were all up a tree in a serious way. So I took the one battle lantern we had, my revolver, and a life belt and got back into the water . . .

Which was a lot like this. There hadn't been any stars. But the water had been just as warm.

I was scared as hell. I mean, we'd seen sharks already, I didn't know what the currents were, and I had to swim two or three miles just to get out into Ferguson Strait, where our boats patrolled, but I felt surprised, even now, that I'd ever come back. I remembered groping along the reefs. There were places I could walk, then the bottom would drop away and I'd have to swim. Every so often I'd lurch against coral and feel it sting, faint at first, then like iodine as the saltwater hit the cut. All I could hear was the waves, and the wind, and once or twice during the night the hum of engines. I couldn't tell if it was a boat or a plane, ours or the Japs', but when I heard them I'd stop and float and look. Once I saw flares way off in the distance. But I never saw anything worth signaling to. The water was warm, but as the night wore on it got cold. I couldn't tell if it was a current from somewhere or whether I was just losing heat. Anyway my teeth were chattering and I was shuddering, and finally I couldn't keep on. I was exhausted. I had to stop and rest, letting the life belt hold me up.

It was on the way back, toward morning, that I remember giving up.

It wasn't anything dramatic. I'd just been swimming all night long after being adrift for a day and a night before that. My legs had gone numb, and then my arms. I figured the current was sweeping me away from the island. I'd untied my shoes from my belt and let them drop, even though I knew I'd need them if I got back. The coral would slice hell out of bare feet. But I didn't care anymore.

Because I just knew, accepted, that John F. Kennedy wasn't going to make it back. Because he didn't deserve to.

For a while I think I stopped swimming. Just drifted in the warm blackness, letting whatever was going to happen go on and happen. I was through fighting. If I hadn't had the kapok on I'd have gone down.

For a while there I seemed to float away, as if it wasn't me there at all. As if I'd already died, and what was left bobbing at the intersection of Ferguson and Blackett Straits was just another used body shucked away and left behind in a war that had already left too many bodies to count, all over the world.

Then after some black time I didn't remember at all, daylight came, and a little strength with it. When I lifted my head and blinked through salt-crusted lids I saw I wasn't that far from one of the smaller islands. I started swimming again, and after a couple of hours crawled up on the white sand, through the sweetrotting piles of naqi naqi leaves, and made it to the base of a scrubby, bent coconut tree.

Where I fell asleep. So fast asleep that I was finally able to forget what had torn me apart since the instant of the collision. What had driven me out into the strait again, leaving my men behind, even though they'd tried to stop me. That had driven me out to sea, not caring, and even halfway welcoming, that I'd probably never come back.

⸻

My thoughts were interrupted by a nearly inaudible splash at the far end of the pool.

I turned over quietly and squinted through the silent wraiths of twisting steam. At water level it came up almost opaque in the moonlight. I couldn't see farther than a few feet, though if I looked straight up I could see a million light-years. Weird . . . but yeah, there was another splash, closer. There was definitely somebody in here with me. I glanced around the poolside, the bathhouses. We were alone.

I thrust myself into a breaststroke, gliding stealthily through the heated water. She'd remembered. Kind of late, but maybe she couldn't get away before now. Warm water rushed along my naked body like a long caress.

A round wet shadow took shape from the mingling mists. We met and curled into a dolphin kiss. My hands ran over muscular shoulders. Her hair was wet under my hand. It was like a dream, but this wasn't a dream. She was naked. She didn't say a word, but her trembling hands slid over my face, my chest.

We came up against the side of the pool, and something bumped my legs under the water. I flinched—part of me was still back in Blackett Strait. But it wasn't a shark, or coral, it was one of the submerged tables. We rolled over onto it, nibbling each other's lips. My hands ran over her breasts, firm but smaller than I'd imagined. The steam eddied between us and the moon glittered off rocking waves. I caught a gleam of moon on eyeball, unearthly dark.

I leaned back, waiting for her to wrap those marble-hard thighs around me. But she didn't move. Her tongue was hot and busy. My heart was pounding like the engine room of a carrier. My fingers slipped into something softer than silk and warmer than the pool. At the same time my knee slipped. I started to slide off the table and kicked a couple of times to get myself back up on it. As I kicked my toes brushed something limp and . . . lifeless.

I jerked my fingers out, evaded her checking hand and explored downward. She flinched but I heard nothing beyond that hushed intake of breath. She lay motionless, no longer resisting, looking up with the immense craters of melted shadow that were her eyes.

"You're not Chaworth. Who the hell are you?"

But I knew. I knew the instant my fingers touched her legs.

Touched wasted, flaccid thighs I could close my fingers around.

"It's me. Emily. Emily Aldrich. Don't you remember? I was with Veronica in the pool this afternoon, and you told her—"

Yeah. I remembered, though at the time I hadn't spoken to her, hadn't much noticed her; had been too busy eyeing Chaworth's bazooms through wet cotton. This was the patient she'd been working on when I came in.

"You overheard us. I told her to meet me here. And you decided to—"

"Uh huh." Her hasty whisper tumbled out. "Don't be mad. Please. I fell in love with you."

"You *what?*"

"I didn't mean anything wrong . . . I just think you're the cutest boy I ever saw. The cutest man, I mean. And I know about servicemen and girls. I mean . . . I saw *Destination Tokyo* and *Flying Fortress* and *Fighting Seabees.* And *The Clock,* where Judy Garland meets Robert Walker at Pennsylvania Station and he only has twenty-four hours and—and all of them."

"Shit!"

"When I saw you there at the pool, you were so handsome. Then one of the girls told me you were a *real* hero. So I thought . . . if she didn't come, maybe . . . and I waited and waited and she didn't. Was it stupid of me? Are you mad? I'm sorry. I'll go. You'll have to help me get out, though, I can't get back in the chair by myself—"

"You came down that hill in a chair?"

"There's a path. You can make it if you go slow. Then I let myself into the water. But I can't get out again."

She lifted her face, till I could almost make out her expression in the dim glow from inside the covered pool, gleaming out through the glass walls.

She said quietly, again, "Veronica didn't come."

"No."

"Well. Don't you want to—with me?"

Right then I couldn't think of anything that appealed less. Her shoulders and arms and breasts, her lips, felt like anybody else's. But now my skin crawled at what had been so desirable a moment before. I knew what Mahoney had said was true, that she wasn't sick any longer. But that didn't matter.

"You don't want to do this. Emily? It's going to hurt. You might get pregnant."

"The girls say if you do it right after you fall off the roof, you can't make a baby. And I've hurt a lot worse, I bet." Her voice held a fierce triumph. "If you're thinking, She's too young, I'm not. I'm seventeen."

You son of a bitch, I told myself. You don't want to put the blocks to this girl. But I didn't want to turn her down either.

"Look at the moon. Isn't it beautiful? Hugh says someday we'll fly there in rockets."

"He does, huh? Maybe in a thousand years."

"I was pretty sure Veronica wouldn't come. She's got a boyfriend. One of the doctors. I saw them kissing. Are you awfully mad at me?"

"No."

"I really enjoyed kissing you. Do you want to do that some more?"

Her lips were warm and soft, and her hands moved along my back. Despite everything, I felt a shiver worm its way downward.

I kissed her again, and the steam rose to shroud us, and the dogs bayed far away as the moon rose silently overhead. She received me with her head back, lips parted.

It must not have hurt too much after all.

———

We lay together in the warm moving water, my arm under her head. "So, was that what you thought it would be like?" I asked her.

"Sort of. And sort of different, too . . . did you like it?"

"Yeah."

"You didn't have to. It was nice of you."

"No, it was great. I wanted to. Emily."

"Am I your girl now?"

"Well, sort of. I guess."

"I don't even know your name. I don't need to. But I'll always be your girl."

I rubbed my hand over my eyes surreptitiously. "This steam. We're gonna look like stewed prunes tomorrow."

"I don't care. I'll always remember you." She reached her arm up to the moon. "Whenever I see the moon, I'll think of you. Will you remember me?"

"Yeah. I will."

"Tell me a secret."

"Huh?" I said.

"A secret. I've always wondered . . . everybody has something they've never told anybody. So if you do, it means you and that person, the one you tell it to, there's something you share that nobody else in the whole world shares. You know what I mean?"

"Sort of. I guess. What's your secret?"

"You first."

"No, you first."

"Okay. *This* is my secret. What we did tonight. Do you know what it's like, being crippled? You can't go anywhere without help. You can't say anything mean, or cross, or swear. Because you've always got to be brave. And I'm not. Not always. And other people, the way they look at you, then look away . . . I'll probably never do anything like this again, ever. But I'll always remember it. That's my secret. What's yours?"

"You really want me to tell you a secret?"

"Not just 'a secret.' It has to be something you've never told. Something you'll never tell anybody else, long as you live."

I rolled back and looked at the stars. They seemed so near. Just as they'd seemed far away, that night in Blackett Strait . . .

I said in a hoarse, choked whisper, "Two men died, because of me."

She sighed.

"You want something I've never told anybody. That you'll never tell anybody . . . well, that's it.

"It was in the Pacific. I was in a PT boat. A Jap ship came through our picket line. We should have got him. Stopped him. At least, tried. Instead I"—I took another deep breath, feeling like something huge and jagged was tearing its way slowly out of my chest—"I turned away."

"You—you what? You ran away?"

"Not exactly. See, at night, as soon as you detect a target, you turn toward him, increase speed, and line up. Then you fire when he's in range.

"I could see him coming two miles away. He was hauling ass, throwing up a bow wave higher than my mast. It glowed, like a green headlight. He wasn't firing or anything. I think I spotted him before he saw me. I should have turned toward him, head-to-head, and let him have it. The torpedoes need four hundred yards' run to arm. I don't know if they'd have had it by the time they got there. They were old and slow, and he was coming at me at thirty, thirty-five knots. But I should have tried.

"Instead, I lost it. I hauled the wheel over away from him and kicked her in the ass. And he ran right over me and two of my men never came up and I lost my boat without ever firing a shot."

I exhaled, looking up at the stars. I don't know why I told her. Only that I'd carried it long enough. "And that's my secret. I'll never tell anybody else. How can I? They gave me a medal and wrote an article about me. My brother was a real hero, but he's dead. I'm alive. But I'll have to lie about it for the rest of my life."

My voice trailed off. I waited, staring at the shadow next to me. Waiting for her to shove me away, tear me apart with a word. But the next thing I knew she was holding me. Hugging my head between her breasts, and saying, "It's all right. It's all right." And I was crying. I didn't understand it. Any of it. But somehow, though I knew it wasn't all right and would never be, for a little while it didn't hurt quite as much.

CHAPTER 35

Tuesday, April 10: The Hotel Warm Springs

W hen she woke the sun was so bright she lay for a dreamy time not opening her eyes, just bathing in the scarlet radiance. Then sat up all at once and looked around the room. She felt energetic and cheerful, though she'd worked late . . . she glanced at the bureau. At the heavy book, with its old-fashioned embossed covers. She'd found it downstairs in the rack of mysteries Ruth kept for guests.

It might be the key.

Standing at the window, she pulled on a chiffon robe as she looked down through the budding branches at the old man sitting on the station house steps. He didn't seem to have anything to do but sit there and every so often lift a cup and spit into it.

Only then did she remember her fizzled romance. She glanced at the clock. It happened a little later every day. Pretty soon she'd be over it. And be ready to try again.

Only she wasn't sure how many more tries she had left. She could feel herself going sour and hard, like an orange left out too long. Sometimes now she could see it on the screen, how in some scenes her mouth went tight and ugly.

Sometimes she thought love was just God's joke on women.

She took her time over her makeup, examining every pore and tiny wrinkle in the wavery stare of the old mirror, hating her face even as she pampered it.

Her heart was still young. But outside, she was getting old. She'd already moved from ingenue to sex goddess. There weren't many roles after forty but hags and bitches. Or queens. She'd already done Boadicea. Davis had done Carlota and Elizabeth. Who was left? Victoria? Wonderful.

She drew her eyebrows next, hand sure as an artist's. If only she could bludgeon Leo into letting her direct. All she needed was experience behind the camera. Why couldn't a woman direct? Look at Lois Weber, forgotten now, but she'd been box office in the silent days. Or that Nazi bitch, Reifenstahl. A few years of that, picking her own roles, hoarding capital, then she could produce.

Another possibility was going back to the stage. You could last in theater as long as your memory held out. There were no closeups on stage.

She finished her mouth and brushed her hair and stood in front of her closet, lighting a cigarette. It would be a hot day. Finally she decided on a light peasant-style skirt and a ruffled, low-neck, sleeveless blouse. Strap heels. She needed a big floppy hat in off-white. Maybe she could find one across the street; she'd seen hats in the window there.

She hesitated at the door. A white corner showed just under it. She bent and picked it up. No name. She ripped it open, scanned it, then tossed it on the bed. The little girls with their autographs, the salesmen with their love notes. Her public.

Maybe she owed it to them, to keep on? She loved acting, once had never wanted to do anything else. But where were Clara Bow, Lillian Gish, Mary Pickford now? She was at the peak of her career. The only direction left was down.

Clamping a vivacious smile over the fear, she swept out into the hallway.

———

When she came out onto the second floor landing the other guests were at breakfast. She smelled coffee and ham and hot bread. She'd have to watch herself. They were intent on eating and she found a seat before they realized she was there. The Kennedy boy looked terrible, saffron-yellow, haggard. She helped herself to a modest plateful as a little man with a mustache said, "Come on, Jack. Give us a bone. A scrap. My editor called this morning and asked if I was still alive. You see FDR every day. Give us something harmless, we'll embroider it, and he'll call us in and rake us over the coals. How about it?" Kennedy mumbled something into his coffee.

Ruth Stevens came up the stairs, carrying a chiffonnier of eggs. "Good morning, Miz Wolfe. Hope you slept well."

"I did, Ruth, thank you."

"There was a call for you came in last night. Real late, so I didn't want to wake you. A Mr. Selznick—"

"He's my agent, yes—"

"—He wanted you to call him back today." Wolfe nodded as Stevens went on, "Have you heard about the barbecue? All you gentlemen, Miz Sobelski, Miz Wolfe, have y'all heard? Well, you know Mr. Smith here asked me if I'd make him a nice big pot of stew—"

"That ain't exactly what I said, Stevie—"

"—And I said, Honey, I just bought me a three-hundred-pound pig, let's have a whole-hog barbecue. And Frank was there and he said that was a fine idea and we could have it at his place over to Pine Mountain. So we called up Mr. Hassett, and he said the President would probably come over for a plateful if we had some of that brunswick stew he likes. So now I've really got myself into a jam. I'm going to need a lot of hungry folks to eat three hundred pounds of brunswick stew and barbecue."

Lauren said, "Why, that sounds like such fun. Count me in. When is it?"

"Well, first I thought Wednesday, but Mr. Hassett said the President had to write a speech that day. So we figured on Thursday, if this nice weather holds. Sometime in the afternoon."

"Great," somebody muttered. It was Kennedy.

"What on *earth* is the matter with you?" Lauren hissed.

"That's when Dad's getting here. Thursday."

"Stop thinking of yourself all the time. A little fun could be just what he needs."

"Dad?"

"No! FDR!"

A man she didn't know asked for the jam, just, she was sure, to be able to say he'd spoken to Lauren Wolfe at breakfast. "We need to talk," she told Kennedy. "Are you almost done?"

He hung back at her door, and she had to pull him in by the sleeve. What a bag of bones he was. A Mickey Rooney smile, kind of cute, but that wasn't enough to interest her.

"Sit." She pointed.

"I've got to get down to the cottage—"

"I said, *sit*. Are you all right? You look like you've been strained through a condom."

He looked shocked. "Uh, I feel kind of punk. Maybe I'm getting the flu or something."

"You'd better get some rest. Anyway, look at this."

She handed it to him. It was a carbon copy; she'd done them the night before, clattering away at Ruth's desk after everyone else had gone to bed.

Kennedy read it. Then looked up, frowning. "What the hell is this?"

SELECTIONS FROM SHAKESPEARE
In Modern Dress
Read by Miss Lauren Wolfe
Wednesday, April 11
8:30 P.M. Community Center—All are Welcome

"Remember my idea? The Russian lecture? I admit, that was rather lame. But yesterday it gave birth to a rather better plan. Could you—?"

She poised a cigarette. Kennedy groped in his pocket, looking resigned, and leaned forward and lit it. She took a puff, tossed her hair back, and went on, narrowing her eyes in the smoke. "I was thinking about it, you see, and for some reason I kept thinking of Hamlet. Someone I met reminded me of him. Do you remember how he tested what the ghost told him? How he decided his uncle had murdered his father?"

"The play within a play?"

"You remember it—"

" 'The play's the thing,/Wherein I'll catch the conscience of the king,' and so forth? I can't say I remember it all, but—"

She got up. Balanced the cigarette in an ashtray. Stood looking at the wall for a moment, then turned, and suddenly he leaned forward, catching his breath.

"There is a play to-night before the king;
One scene of it comes near the circumstance
Which I have told thee of my father's death:
I prithee, when thou seest that act a-foot,
Even with the very comment of thy soul
Observe my uncle: if his occulted guilt
Do not itself unkennel in one speech,
It is a damned ghost that we have seen. . . .
Give him heedful note:
For I mine eyes will rivet to his face;
And, after, we will both our judgements join
In censure of his seeming."

When she stopped he sat stunned. Instead of an upstairs hotel room in small-town Georgia, he'd been in Elsinore. Horatio had been standing next to her, and the gloomy castle round, where every hanging concealed an ear. She danced the edge of overacting, vibrating with anticipation, vengeance, hesitation, and a nervous, hectic dread, until your hands quivered, wondering if she'd fall from the high wire.

"Well? What do you think?"

"You're—not bad. Do you really know Shakespeare that well? To pull things out like that?"

"I've done my share. I was Titania in *Midsummer Night's Dream.* Shared an Oscar for that in 1937. And Miranda in *The Tempest* on Broadway, and Kate in *The Taming of the Shrew.* But why fib, I swotted up that passage last night. Why? Why are you frowning?"

He got up and looked out the window, and she saw sweat glint on his forehead, though it was cool in the room. "I don't know. Maybe I'm still not in the picture. The idea is what? That you perform that scene, and—"

"Not right off the bat, no." She pulled a book off the bureau, a heavy thick one, and he saw it was interleaved with scraps of paper. "We'll start with something light—from *Tempest* or *Merry Wives.* Then get darker. Lady Macbeth's speech in Act One, seven, maybe—that might do."

"Julius Caesar."

"That leaps to mind, but I rather think we've got to accentuate the assassin's agony, his premeditation, over the act itself."

"Why?"

"Because that will reflect what's going on in our quarry's mind. Look. We know that if there's a would-be assassin here, he's part of *his* inner circle. In other words—an American. No American could consider killing the President without terrible inner conflict. There's surely a motive, cash or blackmail or madness, but even a madman can be horrified at what he's about to do. If he's got any conscience, I don't think he can watch his act prefigured on stage without some kind of reaction. Not necessarily a violent one, like Claudius's. But some emotional response—paling, looking around—whatever one person is doing that the others aren't."

"It sounds—operatic."

She strode rapidly back and forth, trailing smoke. "Well, you said my other idea was a B movie. I guess that's progress."

"It takes getting used to. So this handbill—"

"Take it to the Little White House. That's your job. Ruth will get it to FDR's local chums. The tricky thing will be keeping the general public out."

"Yeah, what about them? As soon as they hear you're giving a reading, they'll pack the place."

"That's why we're not advertising it."

"And if the assassin doesn't come?"

"Then we've all simply had what *he* calls 'a grand time.' "

"Yeah, how about him? It won't be real tasteful if he's there."

"*He* doesn't stay up that late now."

He looked at the sheet again. "Tomorrow night. Is that enough time for you to—?"

"Sure. It's not that long a program, and I already have a lot of the lines—as you see. Also, Ruth tells me there's an amateur group that can help out, so it won't be a one-woman show. Now, the important thing is that you—or Reilly, can he come? Will you ask him? Maybe not—then you'll have to observe. I'll watch, but it's hard to see the audience when the broads are on you. The lights. I'll want you on stage for part of this—"

"Now, wait a minute—"

"I can't read to the air. I'll need a foil."

"Is that all I am to you, Lauren?"

"My dear Jack, of course you know I'm head over heels about you. Why else would I go to the trouble of concocting all this, just to get you into my bedchamber? Oh, don't shrink back like a divinity student. I'm joking. I'll need you to read, but for the climactic scene, I'll want you where you can observe the audience."

"Uh huh. What about them? Aren't they going to be kind of upset at all this murder stuff too?"

"I really don't think so. 'We that have free souls, it touches us not. Let the galled jade wince, our withers are unwrung.' And I told you, it won't be all murder—just the last portion. They won't notice a thing. Trust me."

———

When I let myself into the cottage Admiral Brown was standing in front of the fireplace looking at his briefing map. "Good morning, sir," I said.

"Good morning. Where were you? Hassett wants you."

"Sorry, sir, I was delayed."

"You seem to be delayed often, Lieutenant."

"Yes sir, that seems to be true," I told him. We looked at each other without much warmth. Finally he shook his head and turned away, tucking his clipboard under his arm.

Hassett and Tully came in from the sun deck. I could see the ladies out there already, Daisy and Polly. Grace looked tired. Hassett leaned on a cane, favoring his ankle, but walking. The first thing he said to me was, "Heard about the bar-becue?"

"Yes sir. Ruth told me about it. Is the Boss going?"

"Depends on how he feels. Doctor Bruenn's in there with him now."

I tensed. "Is he all right?"

"Oh, yes. In fact, I think he's looking definitely better. Don't you?"

"I think so too, sir. Look, talking about the barbecue—there's something else coming up you might be interested in."

I showed them the handbill. Tully and Hassett were definitely interested, Brown less so, but they all said they'd probably be there, more to see Lauren than to hear the Bard. "What about the troops?" Brown asked me. "Are they invited?"

"I don't think there's room, sir. She asked me to hold this to Little White House staff only. Grace, can you tell Hacky and Dorothy?"

The bedroom door opened and we all turned as FDR rolled out, looking alert and chipper. Bruenn was behind him, smiling. "And so I told him, 'General, you want me to approve these drawings? Go to that window there and tell me if the Navy and Munitions Buildings are still there.' 'Of course they are,' he said. 'They've been there since the war.' And I said, 'That's just what I mean, General. They were not "temporary." Now you go back to your office. Design me some buildings that are guaranteed to fall down around your ears in seven years. Wood, not concrete and steel, and the uglier the better. Then I'll ini-tial your plans with pleasure. But remember, not a second longer than seven years!' "

"Good morning, Mr. President."

"Hello, Cardinal, Brownie, Johnny-Kay. I was just telling the Doc about why—why we have such ugly temporary buildings all over the Mall. What a perfectly grand morning! What's the news?"

Bruenn left before I could tell him about the reading. I'd have to call him; he was definitely one I wanted there.

As Brown began briefing I helped Prettyman get the President into the leather armchair where he spent most of the day. I caught the highlights: We were one hundred thirty miles from Berlin, and one hundred fifty miles from linking up with the Red Army, raising the possibility, Brown said, of cutting Germany in two. The Russians had captured Vienna. On the other hand, progress on Okinawa was slow, with heavy resistance. The casualties, Brown said gravely, were high.

That took the gaiety out of the President, who had been picking at his breakfast tray. He stared out the window, blinking in the sunlight. Today he had on a chalkstripe gray suit and a rather startling tie, red with large white freeform spots, that looked like it would be more at home on a racetrack tout. He did look better, though. His face wasn't gray anymore, his lips weren't blue, and the tremor in his hands had almost disappeared. And he wasn't dead weight. He'd helped swing himself to the armchair.

"What day's this, Brownie?"

"The tenth, sir."

FDR brightened again. "Deacon! Don't we have visitors today?"

"Visitors, sir?"

"From South Carolina."

"Oh. Yes sir."

"Mike . . . Mike! Oh, there you are. We'll be taking a drive around two."

"Yes sir. Where to?"

"We're going to meet some people," said Hassett, in a meaningful voice.

FDR turned to Tully. "So we'd better buckle down, hadn't we? Today I'd like to look over what we have on San Francisco. See what Hiss has set up, and see if—see if we can improve on it."

Hassett cleared his throat. "The Jefferson Day speech, sir. It's only five days away."

"The UN today, Jefferson tomorrow. That satisfy you, you slave driver?— Hello Aunty! Margaret! Please come in. We ordered up another beautiful day for you."

———

Roosevelt worked hard through the morning, huddled with Tully over the procedural plans for the new United Nations Organization. It would meet for the first time on the 25th, two weeks away. State had sent up a lot of blue-bound folders with the draft arrangements. Hassett tried to tell him that was detail, he shouldn't concern himself with it, but he simply smiled and asked for the next publication. He read them with his massive head tilted back, pince-nez poised, mouth slightly open. At first I thought he was skimming them, but when he put them down and started dictating changes I realized he remembered every clause.

The rest of us more or less sat around and watched. The ladies came in for iced tea, then picked up their books and crocheting. Reilly prowled like a restless cat from sun deck to driveway to sitting room. I kept expecting Wolfe, but she didn't show. Memorizing her lines, I suppose.

When he turned in after lunch for his nap I went back into the kitchen and told Prettyman and Lizzie and Daisy Bonner and Joe about Lauren's reading. They looked at me with eyes like lead, and for a second I didn't understand. "What is it?" I asked them. "You're all off by then, aren't you?"

"Lord, Lieutenant, you are from Boston, aren't you?" said Bonner.

"She means, there ain't room for us in that meeting hall, Lieutenant," said Prettyman. He waited, and when I still didn't register added, "We are in Georgia now, Mr. Kennedy. Unless they got a colored section in back, and I don't think they does, we ain't going to be welcome."

"I'm sure Miss Wolfe won't mind—"

"It ain't Miz Wolfe's hall," said the cook. "An' it sure ain't her town. Honey, I wish I could, I see all her movies. But we do thank you for thinking of us, Lieutenant." She got up and adjusted her apron. "Now, I got me some cleaning to do, if you'll excuse me."

———

The President, as excited as a boy going to the circus, had himself lifted into the convertible at two. I climbed in beside him and, after a short wait, we rolled after the Secret Service out of the gate and down the hill and out onto the state highway.

It was really a beautiful day. Hot and sunny with little clouds high up. The country road was twisty, and there weren't many other cars on it as we held a wartime thirty-five miles an hour down Route 41 to Manchester and on through woods and fields of wildflowers and farming hamlets and crossroads general stores. FDR was enjoying himself, waving at folks on the sidewalks and along the road, calling out, "Howdy, neighbor!" and sometimes their names. They stared after us as if they couldn't believe their eyes.

Once, as I looked back, I saw an old Negro woman shading her eyes after us. As I watched she looked stealthily around, then bent swiftly and patted the road where his tires had passed.

Then we came up a rise and saw a black car parked ahead, a Cadillac with the top up. "There she is," FDR said. "See her? There she is. Johnny, do you mind?"

I got out and held the door as two women, both veiled, picked their way over the clay road. The tall one got in back with him. I saw them exchange a kiss as I got into the black car with Long and Reilly. "Who the hey was that?" I asked them.

"Friends of the President."

"It looks like it. Were they really—?"

"You didn't see that," said Long, giving me a look like a riveting gun. "Understand?"

Reilly grunted, "Name's Lucy Rutherfurd. Lives in South Carolina. The other one's a painter. Shoumatoff."

"Russian?"

"Yeah, but she checks out. Emigre family. They hate the Communists more than you or I ever will."

"Does she have relatives there?" I asked him. He didn't answer, just looked at me, then back at the road.

"What's the deal with you and Wolfe?" he asked instead.

"There's no 'deal.'"

"I keep my eyes open. Come on, give."

"I'm helping her with the reading. That's all."

"I didn't know you were interested in the thee-a-tur," said Long.

"You want to pick up some young, fresh poon, there's no better place, Dewey."

"You might have something there," he said. After which we rode in silence, watching the big blue convertible ahead of us, and the heads snuggled close together.

The first thing she had to do after Kennedy left was return Myron's call. She did it with her feet up on the ottoman. When she got through his secretary asked her to hold, he was washing his hands, she'd call him right out.

"Lauren, darling. Where are you now?"

"A little town in Georgia, Myron. Called Warm Springs."

"Really? Is anyone else we know there?"

She started to answer, then remembered she wasn't supposed to say. "Oh, I don't know, I haven't been up to the cottage. I don't think so. I just thought I'd find a quiet place to relax while Leo sweats what I'm going to do."

"Uh, yeah."

"How is it going? Has he snapped yet?"

"Uh, I'm afraid I have bad news."

"What is it?"

"You're off *Hearts and Hands*."

"Off?"

"He's reshooting all your scenes. They started yesterday. You're gone, there won't even be a credit."

"What? Who's playing my role? Who's playing Melissa?"

"Irene Dunne."

"That little . . . that little *scab* . . . and she took it? She stabbed me in the back?"

"Lauren, she has no choice. She's under contract too."

"But that's what this whole thing is about! Whether they can treat us like field hands! Do I have to fight it all alone?"

"Lauren, listen. I talked to Leo yesterday. He's still willing to renegotiate. Another fifty thousand a film."

"Do I have script approval?"

"He won't budge on that. None of the studio heads will compromise on that, Lauren."

"Do I get to direct?"

"He didn't say."

"And you didn't ask? Whose side are you on?"

"Yours, Lauren, you know that. But what's so terrible about being a star? That's what I don't understand. We make much more acting than you ever could directing—"

"Oh, I get it. I get it now! So that's why you didn't ask. Because your precious percentage would suffer!"

"No, Lauren, no, you've completely misinterpreted my position in all this. Listen, darling—"

She slammed the receiver down, then picked it up again instantly. Said to Ruth, on the switchboard, "Miss Stevens? Listen to me. I will not take another call from Los Angeles. Do you understand? I just will not be here."

"But I couldn't tell them that, Miz Wolfe. Not if you're really—"

"All right, all right. I'll make it easy for you. I'm going out."

———

Still steaming, she swung along the street to the community center, a small Doric building on the main street. She let herself in and gradually her rage ebbed as she investigated it. The stage was small. She guessed the capacity at a hundred. Lighting would be a problem.

She mentioned it to Mayor Allcorn when she cornered him to get permission. He thought there might be lights at the high school and promised to get them set up by tomorrow night.

"Now, about these tickets," he said, looking at her over his coffee. They were sitting in the Pine Room, at the hotel.

"There aren't any tickets, Mr. Allcorn. It will be by invitation only."

"Fine. I have some friends—"

"I'd love to have you and your wife, and naturally Ruth. But the seating's so limited. I'd intended this for those close to the President. And a few people from the Foundation—again, those who know him."

Allcorn pointed out that the community center was supposed to be used for the town as a whole. She countered by saying that if she couldn't do it there, she'd hold the reading in Manchester. They compromised on his wife, Ruth, his sister and her husband, and two friends.

She smiled, got up, pulled on her gloves, thanked him, and went across the street to buy a hat.

She spent the rest of the day in her room, memorizing lines and blocking. The phone sat silent as a sphinx, and she had to resist calling down to ask if anyone was trying to get through. It didn't matter, she had to think. After an early dinner she stopped by the desk and asked Ruth to put her through to the Little White House. When she picked up her room phone Louise Hackmeister was on the line.

"Hello, Hacky. Is Mike there?"

"Hold on a second, Miss Wolfe."

"Reilly."

"Hello, Mike? I was wondering, is this a good time to come over?"

"Lauren? Yeah, I'd say so."

"Do you need anything from town?"

"Naw, we're fine. See you in a little while."

———

The woods seemed to lean over her as she drove up the hill. She felt nervous looking out into the rustling blackness. Somebody could be hidden there looking right at her and she'd never know. When floodlights illuminated the striped crossing-guard and the waiting marines, she felt relieved.

They took their sweet time looking in the back seat, checking the Packard's trunk, looking her over thoroughly at the same time. She kept smiling, and when the officer handed her back her driver's license said, "You must be Major Dickinson. Is that right? I wonder if you'd do me a favor. Take this sheet. For you and your men here—the ones who guard the President. Tomorrow at eight." She returned his salute with a wave and put her bumper against the gate and pushed it open and drove through.

When she let herself in a fire was roaring in the sitting room. Popcorn was rattling in a tin skillet in the kitchen, mixing with laughter and the tinkle of glasses. She paused in the foyer, looking in.

He was in the center, in his big chair, in an old pullover sweater and bow tie, his hair combed back and the firelight flickering on a bemused, happy look she'd never seen before. A woman sat across from him, sandy-haired and stately. The other was shorter and dumpier, gray-haired, and sat fidgeting with an empty highball glass. Miss Suckley crocheted, Miss Delano held a book. Bill Hassett leaned his chair in a corner. Kennedy stood by the drink cart, arms folded. He looked bored and tired. She craned around, but couldn't see Reilly.

"Looking for me?"

She swung. He'd come out of the bedroom behind her—Eleanor's bedroom, though as far as she knew Eleanor never came here. "Hello."

"Go on in, Lauren. Oh, I heard about your little benefit."

"It's not a benefit. Just a reading."

"Hell of a swell thing to do."

"Well—thank you."

"Why are you doing it?"

She thought this one through. Reilly didn't know she'd overheard his conversation with Kennedy Sunday. Unless Kennedy had told him. On the other hand, he was perfectly capable of figuring out she knew *something.*

"Just to keep busy. I can't bear idleness for long. Can you? Are you coming?"

"No. I don't think the Boss will make it, either."

"I understand." She smiled up at him, knowing he was waiting to see if she was disappointed, then turned and went in.

"Lauren! I was telling Lucy you were here and she said she so wished you'd come over, she'd love to meet you. And here you are."

She smiled as FDR introduced her around. The tall woman was Mrs. Winthrop Rutherfurd, an old acquaintance now living in Aiken, South Carolina. Her companion was Madame Elizabeth Shoumatoff, a portrait painter.

"Miss Wolfe, are you here on vacation, or business?" Mrs. Shoumatoff asked her.

"I'd call it a vacation." Wolfe looked at her steadily, thinking: a Russian. Elderly, yes. A woman. But only five feet from the President. She didn't see a purse, or anywhere else she could hide a weapon, but she decided to sit right next to her all the same. "I've done five A films in a row and I told the studio I needed a few days off. I understand you do portraits?"

"Yes. I've portrayed the President before—"

"I've decided to give Mopsy another chance," said FDR, holding up a finger to Kennedy and pointing to Wolfe. "She—wait till I tell her what the Deacon said. You'll love this. Mopsy, Bill thinks your first portrait of me was too pretty. He says it's a 'picture of the president with a capon.'"

"With a *cape on,*" said Hassett, but FDR was already roaring.

"'With a capon'! Don't you just love it? I thought it was rather flattering myself. It made me look all of thirty-five."

"I can make this next one more—realistic," said Shoumatoff stiffly. "I will begin tomorrow, but I will need photographs. I do a sketch here and establish color values. Then finish completed portrait in my studio. I will have a photographer here Thursday."

"I thought he was coming with you," said Hassett.

"He was, but my regular photographer had an accident. Fortunately I was able to secure a replacement."

"You look very well now, Franklin," said Mrs. Rutherfurd gently.

FDR looked pleased. "I *do* feel better. This is what I needed—to sleep twelve hours out of twenty-four, sit in the sun, let the world go hang. The interesting thing is that it never does. Another week and I will be ready to get back. We have the Jefferson Day speech, and then it's off to San Francisco."

Kennedy, beside her, with a glass. She took it, shook out a cigarette and let him light it, listening as Mrs. Rutherfurd said, "And what is to happen there, Franklin?"

"We'll set up an organization to ensure we never have to go through a war again. That's what I hope to accomplish, my dear."

"And what must we do to ensure that, Franklin?"

"Well, we'll all have to give up some of our precious sovereignty. Some of our separateness . . . you know, Eleanor said once it amused her when any group of people thought that because they'd been privileged for a generation or two, they were set apart in any way from the men or women who had to scratch and scrape to keep the wolf from the door. It was only luck and a little veneer of gentility. And before long the wheel would turn and they or their children would have to begin again.

"Well, that holds true for nations too. We are just going to have to learn how to share."

"You have spent yourself too much, Franklin. I hope you will give yourself a long rest when this horrible war is finally over."

"I'm going to retire," said Roosevelt. He looked around at them. "I'm serious. From the presidency, that is. But someone is going to have to act as chairman. We're thinking of calling the position Secretary General."

"Surely you're joking, Franklin. You need rest, not more work."

He didn't argue, just turned to Wolfe. "Lauren, it's so good to have you here. Tell us that wonderful story about how you kissed Clark Gable so hard you broke his dentures."

She did, and everyone laughed, and Miss Suckley asked rather timidly what it was like, to kiss him. She thought about it for a moment. "I have to say . . . he's the most exciting man I've ever kissed. My knees literally buckled when he held me. I'd never marry him, I really don't particularly like him—but the physical attraction—oh, my!" she fanned herself with her hand, laughing.

"Do you ever—well, I suppose you have to kiss men you don't like—"

"It's my job, dear. That's how I think of it."

"It's not that different in politics," said Hassett. "Having to kiss people you don't like, I mean."

Wolfe chuckled with the others as she stubbed out her cigarette, but with a tinge of bitterness. Watching the firelight play across their entranced, envious faces, she wondered for a crazy moment if she should tell them what it was really like behind the glamor. Maybe they'd enjoy hearing about the leading man who'd killed a pedestrian, driving drunk down Sunset Boulevard, and how studio management had persuaded a cinematographer to confess and go to prison in his place, "for the good of the studio." The sex goddess who hardly bothered to disguise her lesbian affairs. The discreet brothels kept for visiting clients, with each girl selected to resemble a famous star. The prizewinning director whose arrests for soliciting boys never made the papers. The quiet arrangement that assured America's most beloved kid star a steady supply of speed and heroin. The dirty little deals the studio chiefs had made with Hitler and Mussolini, censoring their own writers and directors to keep raking in millions from European distribution rights. For one mad moment . . . then she looked again at those sweet naive faces and knew she couldn't. Give them what they want, wasn't that Tinseltown's motto? That was what they wanted, to hear that Clark Gable's kisses made her knees weak.

"Mr. President, there's something I wanted to ask you. When I was here before, you said that after the war the New Deal would return—"

"And it will, child."

"Then I hope part of it will be the Federal Theater. That was a wonderful idea! I get so tired of the narcissism, profiteering, the politicking I have to go through to produce one hour of art. Imagine a theater where playwrights and composers and actors could concentrate on it!"

FDR said, "We had to drop a lot of things, Lauren. But when peace comes, so will change. I've never—some people can never understand that you have to wait, even for the best things, until the right time comes—1946, 1947 will be the right time. If we can resurrect a national theater—will you head it?"

"Me?" She was so astonished she could hardly speak.

"Why not? You'd be perfect for it. Frances has done a wonderful job at Labor. Why shouldn't you be in charge of a new theater?"

It was so incredible an idea she literally could not think. "I—I'd really have to sleep on that, Mr. President."

"That's all right. Take your time." He smiled. "We'll talk about it after the war."

━━━

I didn't say much that night. I was the sap who gets the drinks and lights the cigs and laughs on cue. That was okay. I wasn't up to sparkling conversation. I felt bad. Weak. And my stomach was cramping like hell.

Whatever it was, malaria or swamp rot or whatever, it was back.

So I wasn't listening to everything he said that night. But I noticed something I hadn't before. There was a subtle condescension in his nicknames, his chaffing, his ribbing. And a subtle subservience in all of them. It looked like a family, or a circle of friends. But it was really a court. Even the mysterious woman who called him Franklin, whose hand rested on his arm. I didn't know who she was, some modern Pompadour or de Genlis or whatever her name was, but there was more than friendship there. She was the closest to an equal. But she was not an equal either.

For some reason I thought of what I'd felt on 109: the loneliness of command. I knew some of the decisions FDR had had to make. He didn't avoid them, but he didn't run to meet them, either. Some he made instantly, and never looked back; others he put off, delayed, waffled, till some mysterious sense told him the time was right. And it seemed that none of this crushing weight worried him.

But it *had* to. War had aged and finally destroyed Lincoln and Wilson. *He* just didn't tell anyone about it. He never let anyone see that he was afraid or in doubt. And so they thought he was some sort of hero.

I thought suddenly: Maybe there aren't any heroes. Maybe there are only men.

—

Near the end of the evening the President started reminiscing about Woodrow Wilson. The glasses were empty, the fire was coals, and his voice came out of the near-darkness by his chair, where he and the tall woman sat with their hands locked.

"I remember—this is a ways back, but when I was in the Navy I went to the Peace Conference with the President. I can't say I had a major role. I was the junkman, trying to sell all the equipment we had left over there. Got rid of a radio station for four million, which I believe was rather a coup. . . . At any rate I came back on the *George Washington* with him, and one day, to my great delight, I was summoned to his cabin. He had some questions for me on the subject of the Covenant. And I remember he said to me then, 'The United States must go into the League, or it will break the heart of the world. She is the only nation that is disinterested and all trust.' But it broke his heart instead."

"That was very sad, when he died," said Hassett.

"His mistake was standing on principle. I saw that in him the first time I met him, in the fall of '11. The Senate was narrow-minded in rejecting the League, but Wilson was not without blame. He used to say, 'It is only once in a generation that a people can be lifted above material things. That is why conservative government is in the saddle two-thirds of the time.' He should have listened to his own advice. But he wouldn't compromise on Article Ten. And that is why we lost the League."

"And got another war."

"Well, perhaps. Actually I rather think that is more where unconditional surrender comes in. If the Allies had insisted on it in 1918, I don't think Germany would have nursed this stab-in-the-back myth Hitler uses so effectively. This time it must be perfectly plain that they lost the war on their own, and we have to make sure they never forget it."

He paused, as if listening, then went on. "The world's going to change after this war. And go on changing. We need a world body to manage change in a peaceful way. The UN won't be the ladder to heaven. It will have to be amended, just as our Constitution had to change when we moved from horse-and-buggy days to the automobile. But if it assures peace, and—and through the educational and scientific organizations, moves the whole world upward, just as the New Deal moved the forgotten people of America—"

He stopped, looking into the fire. His mouth hung open, then slowly closed.

He seemed surprised to discover Mrs. Rutherfurd's hand in his. The silence stretched out.

Hassett rose. "It's getting rather late," he murmured. Mrs. Rutherfurd rose at once, tall and dignified. She bent over FDR and kissed the top of his head. "Good night, dear one," she whispered.

He roused himself. "Good night, Lucy . . . good night to you all." I looked after him as Prettyman wheeled him off. The circle was silent after he left, and a little while later we all went off to bed.

CHAPTER 36

Wednesday, April 11: The Little White House

O ut," said Reilly, jerking a thumb toward the guard shack.
I climbed slowly out of the Willys and held up my arms for the pat-down. Then followed him down the path.

Inside the white-painted shack were a worn chair and a built-in desk. Many bored people with pocketknives had sat at it. "You're late again," Reilly said.

"I don't feel well."

"That so? Maybe this'll perk you up. Just came through." He handed me the Navy Department telegram as I sank into the chair.

When I looked up again he said, "I'll expect you out of here on the Monday morning train. *Mister* Kennedy."

"What do you get out of busting my balls, Mike? I'm just trying to do my job—"

"You kill me. You little malingerer! The Boss wants some Hah-vud glamour boy to keep him company? Fine, we put up with you. But now he's got Lauren and Lucy you're a fifth wheel. Don't kid yourself, nobody here's going to miss you."

"I'm not a malingerer," I said weakly. It wasn't the greatest comeback, but I couldn't muster the strength to give him a fat lip.

He didn't answer and I sat irresolute as a trapped fly buzzed in circles above my head.

Effective at 0700 Monday, I was a civilian again. The President of the United States thanked me for my record of service to my country. I could wear my uniform to my place of residence or of initial induction. Information on my eligibility for a disability pension and other veterans' programs would be sent to my home of record.

So that was it. I didn't feel like going through the drill, calling Leahy, begging to be extended on active duty. The important thing was that FDR was still alive despite two tries on him. Maybe I'd helped bring him through those, even if nobody else thought so.

"I want my revolver back."

"Forget it. I'll turn it in for you. I don't want any more trouble out of you, hear? And stop whining!"

I dragged myself slowly back up the walk, returned the pimply-faced marine's casual salute, and let myself into the Little White House.

FDR was on the sun deck with Tully. The card table was half in the sunlight and half in the shade. On it was a dictionary, a thesaurus, and the wire mail basket. Grace sat in a rustic chair, holding a steno pad. She had on a sky-blue short sleeved dress and white high-heeled sandals. The President wore the blue suit and the red tie. A handkerchief shared his breast pocket with a fountain pen. His shoulders were hunched. He looked determined, but weary. Fala lay at his feet. The dog's eyes flicked up as I came in; his tail twitched and sagged to the deck again. Tully held up the finished mail. "Lieutenant, could you take this in for me?"

When I came out again she was laying a thin sheaf of papers in front of FDR. He adjusted his glasses, picked them up, and sighed. "What a God-eternally-damned stinker," he said irritably. Tully waited patiently, pad propped on her crossed legs.

Hassett came out. FDR glanced up with what looked like relief. "Yes, Deacon?"

"Had a call from Major Dickinson, down at the camp. He invited you to have dinner with the men Sunday, if you'll be in."

"I shall, and I accept with pleasure. But we've got to make some plans for San Francisco soon, Bill. When are we going to sit down and do that?"

"Sir, I don't think you're in any condition to—"

"Deacon, I've decided. I'm *going* to open that conference, come hell or high water. Now about the itinerary—where's Dewey?"

Hassett went in and came out again with Long. FDR tilted his head back, dictating to the treetops as the transportation officer scribbled. "We'll leave for Washington on the eighteenth. I believe that is a Friday. There is a state dinner scheduled for the Regent of Iraq. He will sleep over the night of the nineteenth. On the twentieth, I'll leave for San Francisco via the B & O to Chicago. I don't have any preferences as to the route after that, just pick the fastest way, but I—I don't want to go through the Royal Gorge because I have already seen it twice. Is that clear? Mike, what is it?"

"Sir, I looked at that itinerary, and I recommend we park at the Army reservation in Oakland."

"I don't want to stay over. I want to get there at noon, make the welcoming speech, and leave by six. We'll go from there to Los Angeles, where Betsy, my daughter-in-law that is, will leave the train. I want to be ready to start back to Washington by six P.M. on the twenty-sixth. Oh, and Eleanor will be going with me. Is all that clear?"

"I have that, Mr. President," said Long, but he looked doubtful.

Roosevelt cocked his head at me. "Johnny, you look rather like Robert Louis Stevenson at Vailima. Are you in a dispute with some germs?"

"I don't feel well, no sir."

"Pity you just missed the doc. Why don't you take the afternoon off? I remember when—all right, Grace, all *right*. Deacon, who *wrote* this so-called speech?"

"Someone on the national committee, I believe."

"I guess that explains it, but I can't—can't Sammy—"

"Sir, Mr. Rosenman is still in London. I'll be glad to take another look at it—"

"Never mind. I bow to the inevitable. I am going to have to take this fertilizer and make roses out of it."

I watched them work for a while, then wandered over to the balcony. The woods looked dead and still. I remembered other woods, other jungles. How you could stand on the beach and the boom of the surf shook the world, yet a hundred yards in it was as if the sea had never existed, that nothing existed but the deep green dripping silence. Then the crack of far-off rifles, the screams of the cockatoos . . . and the tiny sirens of mosquitoes. Waiting among the white orchids was malaria, breakbone fever, blackwater fever, filariasis, cerebral malaria. If we'd learned one thing from the Pacific war, I thought, it was never to send Americans to fight in the jungle again.

Behind me FDR was dictating. "Today comma as we move against the terrible scourge of war dash as we go forward toward the greatest contribution that any generation of human beings can make in this world dash—"

My legs felt weak and I sat down on the railing.

Dad would arrive tomorrow. I wasn't looking forward to being in the room when he and FDR met to decide my future. Hell! But the only alternative was to chuck it all, tell Dad I wasn't going to be a politician, didn't want the allowance, and didn't consider myself part of the Family anymore.

Then start looking for a job. But what? I didn't want to be in business. I didn't have a graduate degree, so teaching was out. And okay, call me spoiled, but I couldn't see myself dragging through some state college on the GI Bill. Writing? You didn't make a living writing. Not the kind of living I considered living.

That left journalism. I knew some publishers. But without Dad, would they give a shit about me? When you've got a famous father people envy you, they think you've got it easy. It helps, sure. But it makes you wonder if you're any good yourself. The only time I'd ever been on my own, really, was in the Pacific.

And look how that had ended up.

"—The contribution of lasting peace comma, I ask you to—to keep up your faith. I measure the, uh—what does it say?—the sound comma solid achievement that can be made at this time by the straightedge of your own confidence and resolve. Period."

I felt shitty. Depressed. I thought about going to bed early, then remembered: Lauren's reading was tonight. I didn't expect much from it. But she had to do something once she'd overheard us talking; had to take over somehow. What a dame. Not my type, but a capital W Woman.

"And to you comma, and to all Americans who dedicate themselves with us to the making of an abiding peace—comma there—I say, colon: The only limit to our realization of tomorrow will be our doubts of today, period. Let us—hm."

So the rest of the week was: the play tonight; Thursday, Ruth's barbecue; Friday, Saturday; Sunday, church again and lunch at the marine camp. Then a wake up and I'd be plain Jack Kennedy, unemployed. There were a lot of people who said when the war ended the Depression would come back. I didn't know if I could take hardship. With Dad I'd always have the trust fund, the sure thing. I gritted my teeth as my stomach cramped.

Looking down then, looking down into the woods, I realized something about myself. However much I daydreamed about it, I'd never tell Dad off. I'd never try to make it on my own. All this other stuff—playing around, chasing tail, even going back into uniform—it was just to postpone admitting that.

The President was still laboring away at the last sentence. "Let us—Let us move forward. No—Let us move forward with strong and active faith. Period, full stop. Have you got all that, Duchess? Will you read that back?"

Tully read in a soft monotone, "Today, as we move against the terrible scourge of war—as we go forward toward the greatest contribution that any generation of human beings can make in this world—the contribution of lasting peace, I ask you to keep up your faith. I measure the sound, solid achievement that can be made at this time by the straight edge of your own confidence and your resolve. And to you, and to all Americans who dedicate themselves with us to the making of an abiding peace, I say: The only limit to our realization of tomorrow will be our doubts of today. Let us move forward with strong and active faith."

"That's better, but I still hear some extra words in there. We'll do another draft tomorrow."

Tully flipped the pad closed as FDR wheeled himself back and yelled, "Mike! Is Lucy here yet?"

"They just pulled in, sir, I think they're in the powder room."

Mrs. Shoumatoff came out, saw the President, locked her hands, and looked heavenward. "Oh, Mr. President, Miss Tully. I am so happy! I spent the entire night lying awake, thinking and praying for guidance. I am so anxious to get a good pose. And I think it has finally come to me."

The Rutherfurd woman appeared at the french doors; FDR's head swung toward her; his eyes brightened. I set a chair for her close to him.

Shoumatoff kept talking, moving around and framing him with her hands. They ignored me, and finally I decided to take his advice, about the afternoon off that is.

Hassett looked at me quizzically. "You *do* look terrible. Are you sure you can make it down to the Foundation?"

"I thought I'd see Bruenn."

"That's where he is. Swimming, I believe. He and Hacky and the reporters seem to be spending most of their time at the pool. You can phone down if you like, make sure he's there—"

"I'll drive, sir," I said. I didn't want to go into the Foundation. There were three females in there I didn't, for various and different reasons, want to run into. But I could check the pool. Then maybe get my head down for a couple of hours before the performance.

That evening, Mike Reilly watched as FDR and Henry Morgenthau shook hands. Roosevelt's boyhood friend, now Secretary of the Treasury, had called that afternoon. FDR had invited him for dinner, eagerness in his voice, and had even had himself rolled out into the driveway to wait for him.

In the kitchen Daisy was making noodles and veal. She told Lizzie to warm up the waffle iron. "Waffles, girl?" said McDuffie. Daisy frowned. "Since Mr. Morgenthau done give him the waffle iron, he probably like to see the President eating waffles from it." Lizzie said, "They won't much like waffles for dinner, uh uh." Daisy told her to dress them up with whipped cream and cocoa sauce and they would like them fine for dessert.

In the sitting room, Morgenthau's heart sank as he watched the President trying to mix cocktails. FDR seemed confused and awkward at first. But after two martinis he started to sparkle. Morgenthau kept trying to steer the conversation around to Germany, what was going to happen after the war. He wanted the Ruhr wrecked and leveled. He wanted Germany broken into smaller states. Roosevelt said, "You know I'm with you, Henry, a hundred percent." But he wouldn't discuss specifics. He slid around them and kept going back to the Hudson Valley, where they'd grown up. After a while he sent Prettyman to get the ladies.

While they ate Roosevelt kept talking about people they'd both known as children. He asked him if he remembered when the river used to freeze solid and they'd gone iceboating on it. Morgenthau said he remembered how they'd nearly killed themselves.

After dinner they talked a little longer, then FDR rolled slowly toward the door. Reilly opened it. When they were outside Roosevelt looked up at his old friend.

"Good night, Henry," he said. "I feel a little stronger. Tomorrow we're having a grand barbecue. Did they tell you? I hope you'll come. I don't like to say good night so early, but I need the sleep."

"I understand, sir."

Getting into his limousine, Morgenthau wondered what was really going to happen in Europe. If the Allies didn't destroy Germany's war-making capacity, another twenty years and they could be fighting World War Three. And now FDR didn't want to talk about it. For some reason he remembered when the President had said to him, "Never let your left hand know what your right hand is doing, Henry."

"Which hand am I, Mr. President?" he'd asked, only half-joking.

"My right, Henry, but I keep my left under the table."

The Secretary of the Treasury sat unmoving for a long moment of fear. His old friend was ill. What would happen if they lost him? He was the only one who knew what all the hands were doing. He shook his head, then leaned forward to the driver's turned ear. "Home," he said.

I stood at the corner of the little stage, looking out at the front row. I was in uniform, more because my roles called for it than because I wanted to wear it. I searched the faces as the guests murmured and fanned themselves. The hall was cooler than outside, and the doors in the back were open, but with a hundred people crammed together on folding chairs from the local mortuary the temperature was rising fast.

Good, I thought. Anything that added to the tension helped.

I scanned the front rows again. We'd filled them first by the simple expedient of telling the people we wanted in them that the curtain rose at eight, while the general public was told eight-thirty. Waiting in the front row now were Hassett, Tully, Dorothy Brady, Louise Hackmeister, Margaret Suckley, and Laura Delano. Mrs. Shoumatoff and Lucy Rutherfurd had come in late, but they were there. Admiral Brown, sitting with George Fox, looked bored already. Major Greer and Major Dickinson sat with them too, phalanxing the uniforms.

Behind them the reporters perched together: Allie, Harold Oliver, Merriman Smith. They jotted busily; this was newsworthy. Beside Allie was Dr. Bruenn, then Dr. Hubbard, Basil O'Connor, and the Great Stone Face, Helena Mahoney. She'd given me a glare as she settled in her seat. I'd smiled back.

Back one more row were the local dignitaries. Stevens and the grizzled railroad agent. The sheriff, and five or six others, friends of the President since the twenties. Allcorn's seat was empty. The mayor was fidgeting backstage, getting ready to kick things off.

There was Dewey Long. I suddenly remembered he was the only man, aside from Reilly, who'd been at the White House, on the train, and was now here. Long! Could it be Long? Behind him was a small sea of locals in Sunday clothes, buzzing excitedly as they settled into the chairs.

Far in the back was a scattering of dark faces. So they *had* let them in, after Wolfe had laid down the law. *Her* law. Esperancilla, Daisy Bonner, Lizzie McDuffie's round face. I didn't see Prettyman but that didn't surprise me. I'd never seen the valet leave the President.

Three minutes. I drifted over to the light and reexamined my playbill. Wolfe had made it up. It didn't have lines; just the scene order and who played whom. There were five scenes, each from a different play. Some were familiar. Others would be new to the audience. The supporting actors, local hams she'd dug up from a Little Theater group in Manchester, were reading from their own marked copies of Shakespeare. I fingered the heavy hotel copy I'd use. Apparently she didn't need a script at all.

———

I don't *believe* I have the willies, Wolfe thought. I don't believe that here in the backwoods, with a hundred people out there, I've got butterflies in my stomach.

But she did. Funny, how you forgot there was an audience when you made movies. You played to your leading man, ignoring the camera. And after a few years you forgot there was an audience there, after the lenses and the mikes were packed away. So that when you faced one again, whispering and rustling, *waiting* out there in the dark, suddenly back rushed the same fear that had made you pee your sixteen-year-old pants waiting for the curtain to rise on the high school play . . .

But she was a pro. How many years had she been at this? How many thousands of lines had she memorized? She felt more comfortable now on a sound stage, being someone else, than she did walking down the street, being herself. So she acted someone she'd made up, this character called Lauren Wolfe.

It was easier that way.

The titters rose and then quieted, and suddenly Allcorn's voice, Rotarian-hearty, boomed out on the other side of the curtain. He began by introducing the other players, amateurs from the local group. Then he was introducing her. Listing her stage plays, her films, her Academy Award, her War Bond tours.

Then he was done and she swallowed in a dry throat and pointed at the wide-eyed kid on the curtain. The lights came up and her nervousness dropped away as she stepped forward.

■■■

I found myself a stool back of the curtain and waited out the first scene, since I wasn't in it. I felt better after a four-hour nap, but I had the feeling I'd better conserve my strength. If this was what I'd had before, it was going to get worse before it got better.

The curtain went up on Lauren, in a businesslike but close-fitting suit, confronting the other players, who were smoking and talking and flirting with each other. She cleared her throat sharply and the audience giggled. The amateurs, old people and high school kids and a couple of faggotty-looking 4-Fs, glanced up as if startled.

"Speak the speech, I pray you, as I pronounced it to you, trippingly on the tongue; but if you mouth it, as many of your players do, I had as lief the town-crier spoke my lines."

Lauren went on, briefing the players briskly on their shared art. The magazines all said she was a holy terror on the set. I could believe it. I could see the audience from where I sat, but not well enough; later on I'd have to get down there with them. She'd left me out of the last two scenes.

"O, there be players that I have seen play,—and heard others praise, and that highly,—not to speak it profanely, that, neither having the accent of Christians nor the gait of Christian, pagan, nor man, have so strutted and bellow'd, that I have thought some of nature's journeymen had made them, and not made them well, they imitated humanity so abominably." The audience tittered.

A fat old man stepped forward and bowed. "I hope we have reform'd that indifferently with us, madam."

"O, reform it altogether. And let those that play your clowns speak no more than is set down for them: for there be of them that will themselves laugh, to set on some quantity of barren spectators to laugh too; though, in the mean time, some necessary question of the play be then to be consider'd; that's villainous, and shows a most pitiful ambition in the fool that uses it. Go, make you ready."

The players exited, muttering, and the lights dimmed. Time for Uncle Jack. I straightened my tie, put my cap on, and strolled out. Wolfe gave me a steely warning glare. Those perfect lips could look grim. She'd taken off the jacket and dropped her hair to her shoulders, and somehow dropped twenty years at the same time. Yes, damn it, she was wearing penny loafers and bobby sox! The lights came up and I hastily found my place. Took a breath, and pitched my voice to carry.

"But, soft! what light through yonder window breaks?

"It is the east, and Juliet is the sun!"

The audience was silent, rapt. I gave it all I had, yearning up to her as she stood gazing out, triumphant, indifferent.

━━━

"Ay, me," said Lauren, to the audience, searching their faces.

So far, so good. The lighting was off-cue, but good enough. The audience seemed to be hooked. It was working.

"And sails upon the bosom of the air," Kennedy finished, below her.

She underplayed "O, Romeo, Romeo," then gave it more steam in the "Tis but thy name" speech. Kennedy came in on cue, his voice weak, but he had some stage business the audience liked; some sort of military routine, straightening his tie, pushing his hat back. As long as he didn't start hamming it up. The next scene, fine, that would be the comic relief.

━━━

"Sleep dwell upon thine eyes, peace in thy breast!" I said. From my kneeling position I lifted my hands as if in prayer. "Would I were sleep and peace, so sweet to rest! Hence will I to my ghostly father's cell, His help to crave, and my dear hap to tell." And held it, arms stretched up to her, as the lights faded.

The crash of applause startled me so much I flinched and dropped my cover. It rolled around the stage and I chased it, but even that didn't stop the clapping. I made an awkward bow and exited, grinning like a fool. When I got offstage I collapsed back onto my stool, sweating.

━━━

Hassett, still clapping, turned and said to Brown, "He may not be a wonder as an officer, but he does well as an actor, don't you think?" The admiral grunted. Hassett faced front again, swallowing. He was getting a little nervous.

━━━

To her surprise and pleasure the Manchester players had done the *Shrew* in '43 and remembered their lines. The prize was the fat man with the beard, the one who'd bowed in the Hamlet scene. The lights came up to the two of them alone on stage, she a Southern belle in flowered dress, floppy hat, and sandals, he an aging fop in a too-small bowler. The people in the rear of the hall howled before he opened his mouth.

"Good morrow, Kate; for that's your name, I hear."

"Well have you heard, but something hard of hearing; They call me Katharine that do talk of me."

The scene was witty, fast-paced badinage; she made sure everyone got the bawdy parts. The audience gasped, then roared. She caught a glimpse of three uniformed men; they were smiling broadly. Good!

"What, with my tongue in your tail? nay, come again, Good Kate; I am a gentleman."

"That I'll try." She gave him a resounding stage slap. He spun around and fell and kicked his heels. My God, who'd he studied under, Mack Sennett? He was stealing the scene. He was bringing the house down. And she didn't mind a bit.

To her surprise, she was enjoying herself.

———

When the curtain fell on Baptista, Gremio, and Tranio I was in front of the stage again, standing against the wall. If I stood out of the footlights I could see all the way to the back. People were crammed in even as far as the lobby, standing, craning over each other to see the stage. Not an empty seat in the house. No, there was one—beside Grace Tully. I searched my mind frantically. Who had been sitting there? How had he gotten out without my seeing him? Shit, if this thing worked, and I *lost* the assassin anyway, after all this—

Now things turned gloomy. Lauren had picked out Act One, Scene Seven, the somber castle of Macbeth. The curtain rose on torches, guttering on an otherwise unlit stage. The procession entered, slow march, passing from left to right. Then a tall, bent man I hadn't seen before entered. He wore a dark cape that looked familiar. His sonorous, gloomy voice filled the hall. My jaw dropped. It was Hassett.

> "If it were done—when 'tis done—then 'twere well
> It were done quickly: If th' assassination
> Could trammel up the consequence, and catch,
> With his surcease, success; that but this blow
> Might be the be-all and the end-all here,
> But here, upon this bank and shoal of time,
> We'ld jump the life to come. But in these cases
> We still have judgement here; that we but teach
> Bloody instructions, which, being taught, return
> To plague th' inventor: this even-handed justice
> Commends th' ingredients of our poison'd chalice
> To our own lips. He's here in double trust;
> First, as I am his kinsman and his subject,
> Strong both against the deed; then, as his host,

Who should against his murderer shut the door,
Not bear the knife myself. Besides, this Duncan
Hath borne his faculties so meek, hath been
So clear in his great office, that his virtues
Will plead like angels, trumpet-tongued, against
The deep damnation of his taking-off;
And pity, like a naked new-born babe,
Striding the blast, or heaven's cherubin, horsed
Upon the sightless couriers of the air,
Shall blow the horrid deed in every eye,
That tears shall drown the wind,—I have no spur
To prick the sides of my intent, but only
Vaulting ambition, which o'erleaps itself
And falls on th' other."

Hassett's Macbeth was horrifying enough, in his paralyzed hesitation before the terrible deed. But the hall, which had grown deathly still, stirred with a collective shudder as a figure in dark garments slowly materialized behind him. It was Lauren, but shriveled, crouching, two score years older. Her eyes glittered in the bloody light. The Deacon heard her and turned. "How now! what news?"

"He has almost supt: why have you left the chamber?"

"Hath he askt for me?"

"Know you not he has?"

"We will proceed no further in this business," Hassett announced.

I recoiled, hearing the scorn and fury in Wolfe's voice. The loathing as she called him coward and beast and hissed that she'd smash her own baby's brains out, if she'd sworn an oath like this, rather than break it. The audience sat frozen, without cough or whisper.

"If we should fail?" Hassett whispered.

"We fail!" Lauren hissed. "But screw your courage to the sticking-place, And we'll not fail."

They discussed the bloody deed, how to kill the king and how to blame his guards. Finally she brought the wavering Macbeth around.

"I am settled, and bend up
Each corporal agent to this terrible feat.
Away, and mock the time with fairest show:
False face must hide what the false heart doth know."

The curtain fell, and as the lights came up I scanned faces swiftly. Bruenn sat hunched forward. Long looked entertained, but detached. Was that an assassin's smile on Brown's lips? He levered himself to his feet, and I tensed; then realized he was letting Hassett return to his seat. People leaned to congratulate him. He looked embarrassed.

The buzzing rose, then faded again as a sharp rap came from the stage. The curtain rose on two men, entering behind another, seated. No, one of them was Lauren. I opened my book, feeling tension cramp my back. If this was going to work, it would work in the next few minutes. Or not at all.

> *Enter the* TWO MURDERERS.
> FIRST MURDERER: Ho! Who's here?
> SIR ROBERT BRAKENBURY: What wouldst thou, fellow? and how camest thou hither?
> FIRST MURDERER: I would speak with Clarence, and I came hither on my legs.
> BRAKENBURY: What, so brief?
> SECOND MURDERER: 'Tis better, sir, than to be tedious.—Let him see our commission and talk no more.

It was the scene in *Richard III* where the two assassins debate divine judgment, payment, conscience, and duty as they prepare to kill the king's brother on Richard's order. It is a long scene and the tension built, the way Lauren played it, till it made me want to scream.

> "How darkly and how deadly dost thou speak!
> Your eyes do menace me; why look you pale?
> Who sent you hither? Wherefore do you come?"
> "To, to, to—"
> "To murder me?"
> "Ay, ay."

The audience murmured in shocked horror, and I felt my flesh creep. Oh, Lauren, I thought.

Clarence was the fat old man, but he wasn't comic now. He sat hunched forward on the bed, as if he couldn't rise. He adjusted his pince-nez, looking up at his murderers. Then, to my horror, he screwed a cigarette into a long holder.

The audience whispered uneasily as the deadly dialogue between the helpless man and his executioners swung to and fro. As the first murderer wavered. As Clarence pleaded for his life.

> "My friend, I spy some pity in thy looks;
> O, if thine eye be not a flatterer,
> Come thou on my side, and entreat for me:
> A begging prince what beggar pities not?"
> (SECOND MURDERER) "Look behind you, my lord."

In Shakespeare, Clarence is run through, then drowned in the butt of malmsey. This time, instead of a sword the inexorable First Murderer pulled a pistol from his pocket. The sudden crack made the audience gasp. Clarence slumped forward.

As blue smoke rose Lauren was left on the stage, wringing her hands. "A bloody deed, and desperately dispatcht! How fain, like Pilate, would I wash my hands / Of this most grievous guilty murder done!"

The First Murderer came back, hands empty but a great red stain across his shirt. I was staring at it when someone moved, out in the audience. Only one person. I stood up, frantically searching over the heads.

A back, moving away.

"How now! what mean'st thou, that thou help'st me not?"

I started to shove through the standees, but they resisted, rapt with the play. I couldn't make headway. So I fought my way back again to the stage. Found the side exit in the dark and plunged through it, the door closing behind me on "Take thou the fee, and tell him what I say—"

Into the cool night air. I ran, knowing I had only one chance to catch whoever was leaving. He had to push his way through too, to reach the exit. Perhaps I could catch him out front. If I couldn't—

There he was, a shadow in the moonlight, walking away down the dimmed-out street. Footsteps echoed from dark storefronts. I ran now, my feet thudding on the pavement. The footsteps hurried, seemed about to break into a run; then stopped.

Allie Sobelski turned and faced me, her cheeks so pale in the moonlight.

"What is it? What's wrong, Jack?"

"You left. Why did you leave?"

"I felt faint."

"Why? Why are you in on this? What have they got on you?"

"I don't know what you mean, Jack. Please let me go."

"Like hell I will. I'm turning you in, Allie. You felt faint! That's a good one."

"It's the truth."

"Now tell me it's a coincidence. That you jumped up and left just when he was shot."

"I didn't leave then. Actually I started to feel faint when Lauren said that—when she said that, about killing the baby."

"What?"

She looked up and down the empty street, then leaned closer. "I wasn't going to tell you till—afterward. But—maybe now is as good a time as then. Jack, I'm pregnant."

I stared at her. "It's yours," she added, rubbing her cheeks. "I haven't been with Jan for over a year. He hasn't been home, and I . . . I've been good . . . except for that one time with you. Oh, how am I going to tell him? It's yours, Jack."

"But we didn't—"

"We did enough. You know we did. What are we going to do? No, wait. You don't have to answer right now. I know it's a shock. I haven't made any decisions."

"Pregnant," I said.

She patted my arm, smiling sadly. "Your face is so . . . I'm sorry. I thought about not telling you. Then I thought, maybe he'll be happy. You seemed to like me, back in California. But that . . . oh, shit. We'll talk about it tomorrow. Okay?"

Her heels clattered in the empty street.

I stared after her, unable to think. Unable to say a word or stir a step, till I turned and stumbled back toward the lights, the open door, the chattering, still-excited playgoers spilling out into the silent street.

CHAPTER 37

Thursday, April 12: Warm Springs

I didn't get much sleep that night, between wondering what would happen when Dad got here, and what I was going to do about Allie. My back started to hurt again. When dawn came I was still awake. On the other hand, I was up early enough to force breakfast down and get to the Little White House on time for a change.

Reilly patted me down, expression blank, as I held my hands above my head. He looked in my cap too. I didn't say anything, just took it back and went into the sitting room. Nobody else was up yet, so I just waited, reading the spines of the books on the shelves—mysteries, mostly—and staring out at the woods. It looked like another hot day.

Admiral Brown came in at nine and took the sofa, propping his clipboard on the cushions. I showed him my orders. He said quietly that he'd write up my detachment fitness report. It wouldn't say anything adverse, and maybe he could get the Commander in Chief to sign it. It would make a nice keepsake. I was surprised; he didn't gloat or act pleased he was finally getting rid of me.

Fala barked from the bedroom. A few minutes later Roosevelt wheeled himself out. He looked chipper, except for the oysters under his eyes. His face looked fuller too. He was in the dark gray suit, and the crimson Harvard tie he often wore. And a vest, which I'd never seen before. Bruenn lounged out after him, jingling change in his khakis.

"Good morning, good morning. How's the war going, Admiral? Johnny, how are you?"

We said good morning, said he looked well. Roosevelt said he felt grand, better every day. He'd have breakfast outside, but would be working in the sitting room today; Shoumatoff preferred to paint indoors. Prettyman and I got the card table out and set it and the armchair in front of the fireplace.

Hassett arrived while we were on the sun deck. The air was already warm. FDR kept pointing out various robins and finches, playing ornithologist. They made quite a racket. The woods stirred in the morning wind. The first thing Hassett said was, "Mr. President, the mail is going to be late today."

FDR looked up from eggs and toast and bacon. "That so? What's the holdup?"

"Fog in Washington. No outgoing flights. Steve Early called around seven. He put it on the train to Atlanta. I'll have Dewey drive up for it."

"When do you expect it?"

"I'd plan for around noon, Mr. President."

FDR nodded and rolled his chair back from the table. I caught his glance and went in and got his Camels. He lit one eagerly and leaned back, inhaling with an expression of bliss. Hassett had told me he was supposed to be down to six, but as far as I could see he was still killing a pack a day. The smoke drifted out over the woods, swirling and dissipating at the edges, but holding together till it passed from sight.

The President's secretary said, "Are you getting ready to leave, John? Is there anything we can do for you?"

This was the first time, as far as I knew, that anyone had told FDR I was leaving. I'm not sure what I expected, but he didn't seem to mind. Maybe he didn't even hear. Anyway he didn't say anything. I told Hassett no thanks, and complimented him again on his performance as Macbeth the night before. He hemmed and hawed and even, I swear, turned red. "Is Lauren coming over this morning?" I asked him.

"I really can't say. Perhaps. The other ladies should be here soon, for the sitting."

"I'm sorry I missed the show last night, Cardinal," said Roosevelt. "I don't know why she scheduled it so late. Maybe I'll ask you two to do the scene over again this morning, command performance, just for our little audience here."

"Oh, no, Mr. President. Please," said Hassett, going so shy he had to escape into the driveway and walk around for a while.

Brown set his coffee down and started his briefing. I perched on the balustrade and listened as FDR had another cup.

Germany was crumpling like an empty popcorn bag at a matinee. This morning the Second Armored was sixty-three miles from Berlin, after making fifty miles yesterday. The Canadian, British, and French armies were moving forward rapidly on their respective fronts. The British press reported a rumor that Hitler was dead, Himmler had taken over, but Eisenhower reported there didn't seem to be any basis to it. Two thousand Allied planes bombed rail yards and airfields in central Germany. The RAF sank the *Admiral Scheer* at Kiel. The Eighth and Fifth Armies reported progress in Italy.

In the Pacific things looked less rosy, Brown said. Jap resistance was stiffening on Okinawa. The advance was stalled and losses were climbing. There were reports that a Nip hospital ship, the *Awa Maru*, had been sunk by one of our submarines.

As he finished we heard voices from back in the house. A clatter, and the blinds swayed. Peering in, I caught the round figure of Lizzie McDuffie, armed with a duster. FDR said, "Thank you, Brownie," then rolled his chair toward the french doors. "Lizzie!" he called.

McDuffie appeared, looking apprehensive.

"Lizzie, you've been having a grand time in there."

"Oh, my, I'm sorry, Mr. President. Did I disturb you—"

"No, no, but I heard you arguing. Was that Joe? What in the world are you two arguing about?"

The maid looked embarrassed. "Well," she said, "do you believe in reincarnation?"

"In what!"

"Reincarnation."

Roosevelt sat up, looking around at us, letting us in on it. Brown smiled indulgently. He swiveled back to McDuffie. 'Well, tell me, Lizzie: Do *you* believe in reincarnation?"

"Oh, I don't know as I do or not. But that's what Joe wanted. I told him I don't know. But if there was such a thing"—she slapped the duster against her apron, looking out over the woods and smiling dreamily—"If there was, I want to be a canary bird."

FDR looked blank. Then he roared, rearing back till the springs squeaked in protest. "A *canary* bird! Don't you love it? Don't you just *love* it?"

"I do," said Wolfe, behind her.

———

Lauren clicked past her, crossed the deck and bent to skim FDR's cheek with her lips. He smelled of cologne and cigarettes and coffee.

She straightened and swept her smile around at the others: Hassett, a naval officer she didn't know, Kennedy. It lingered on Kennedy, dimming. She still didn't understand why he'd disappeared last night at the climax of the play. Then come back saying he'd seen nothing out of the ordinary, no one had seemed disturbed, all their efforts had gone for nothing.

She strolled to the balustrade and looked down at the soldiers. One youngster noticed her, and his eyes widened. She gave him a little wave and turned back, poised a cigarette for someone to light. "Good morning, all! What a beautiful day to be alive—whether one is a human being, or a—canary bird."

"Lord, Miz Wolfe, you do look fine today. Maybe I will change my mind, and come back as you."

"I rather think your first choice was wiser."

"You don't seem happy this morning, child. Anything I can do?"

"No, Mr. President. It's just that this wonderful interlude can't last forever."

"What's the next treat? You know we screen your films at the White House as soon as they come out."

"I'm afraid I can't say right now. There's a little struggle going on between me and the studio, you see."

"I'm sure everything will work itself out. I frankly can't imagine how they could refuse you anything, Lauren."

"You're too kind, Mr. President."

"You was wonderful in that Alabama movie, Miz Wolfe," said McDuffie wistfully. She was still hovering, occasionally taking a swipe with the duster.

"'That Alabama movie' . . . Oh. *The Forsaken Hills?*"

"I don't believe I saw that," said FDR. "Give us a bit, Lauren. I was trying to persuade Bill here to perform for us before you arrived. He was taken with stage fright, but perhaps you'll oblige us."

"You wouldn't like it very much. Jussie was a horrible person."

"Wasn't she the girl who tormented that poor lawyer? John Gilbert, wasn't it?"

She looked questioningly at Hassett. "I saw it twice," he muttered. "You were so good it made me hate you. I was surprised, when you came here, that you didn't speak like that at all. Isn't that funny?"

She puffed, exhaled, swung her arm away. She always felt so theatrical with normal people. They didn't move like actors, or talk, or even smoke like actors. What must it be like not to inhabit a role, just to be yourself? She couldn't remember a time when she'd felt that way.

"I suppose that's a compliment. At least I'll take it as one. I hired a girl from Selma for eight weeks. She never stopped talking, and I listened to every word. The big scene is where I try to get Peter Hurl to sleep with me. And of course he's too high-minded."

McDuffie said, hovering by the french doors, "That's where you says they's certain things a woman got to have—"

Wolfe found Jussie inside herself. She turned suddenly and saw their eyes startle. She knew her face had gone white, malevolent and tortured. Her voice had changed too, gone debased and rotten, charged with hatred so pure it was like an electric shock.

"Ah'm not sure you understand me even yet, Mister Hurl. Maybe you're not capable of understanding me. I—love you? . . . Yes, it was possible once. Once, long ago, when we both were—whole. But now . . .

"You see, there are certain things a woman needs in a man. It's not enough to be worshiped. I can't be happy with a name, a ring, a kiss—a pretense. Do you understand me? That's why ah went with the major. Because you're not a man. You're a thing, Mister Hurl, just a puppet on your crutches—only half a man—a poor, useless, unhappy *cripple*—"

She stopped dead, and the last word hung in the air. Hassett looked horrified. She lowered her arms, appalled. What had she done? She didn't dare look in FDR's direction.

But he was clapping. "Wonderful. Grand! Isn't she incredible, everyone?"

She muttered something and groped for a chair, feeling like creeping away under a door. FDR lifted his chin sharply. "You know, Lauren," he began.

"Yes sir." She waited miserably for the rebuke.

"You have something very wonderful. That fire. It's much rarer than ordinary beauty. You see what pleasure you give Lizzie and Bill, and Johnny, and myself. You are very lucky to have found a craft you love. And the wonderful thing is, you are still so young. I shall be looking forward to seeing you when you're seventy. By then you should really be something."

It was incredible. As if he'd guessed what she was thinking, what she'd feared, and had fled across a continent to deny and escape. As if he knew the whole thing, what she was fighting for with Levinsohn and all the rest; with all the others who thought if a woman wasn't beautiful, sexy, young, she was worthless. As if he knew it all and was telling her: You don't have to be afraid. You will prevail. And inexplicably she believed him. Looking at him, gaunt but still jaunty in his chair, cigarette cocked upward, she knew it was so . . . because he had done it. Prevailed against something far harsher than she would ever have to fight.

And a weight that had lain on her heart for years was suddenly lighter.

She said softly, "There aren't very many parts in films for seventy-year-old women, Mr. President."

"Then you may have to write them yourself. Or is it the studio that's your stumbling block?"

"You might say that. You could say that."

"Then you'll have to show them the way. We all have to battle for what we believe in, Lauren. Fight and scheme and compromise until we get a better world. But isn't it a *grand* game?"

"A grand game? . . . why, I suppose it is," she said wonderingly.

He smiled again, then swiveled his chair and said casually to Kennedy, "Johnny, how about some coffee for Lauren?"

"Thank you," she whispered. "I'd like that very much."

▬

The ladies arrived a little later. Sharp-faced, busy Laura Delano. Miss Suckley, quieter, carrying a bag with her eternal crocheting. And Mrs. Rutherfurd, tall and stately, with a half-smile that made me think of La Gioconda. They settled on the sofa, and FDR signaled me to wheel him inside.

A hollow clatter came from the front hall around eleven. I went out and found Mrs. Shoumatoff struggling with an easel. She haughtily permitted me to relieve her of it. Behind her was a husky man in a short blond beard and a brown suit worn shiny. Horn-rimmed glasses splinted with adhesive tape made his eyes small and deep-set. He had a tripod too, and a big portrait camera. I noticed his heavy brogans, which looked odd with the suit.

Reilly was behind him. I pointed at the guy and made a patting motion; he nodded. "He's clean," he muttered as he brushed by.

"Come right ahead, come right ahead, Mopsy," Roosevelt boomed from the sitting room.

The photog said, "There's another bag in the car. How 'bout a hand, Mac?"

"I'm not the Philip Morris redcap, pal. You'll have to get it yourself."

He didn't respond, just kept going after Shoumatoff. He was a husky boy, and for a second I wondered why he wasn't in the service. Then thought: hell, look at all the 4-Fs in the major leagues. Like Ed Mackay. Along with the fifteen-year-olds and the one-armed infielders. It would be nice to watch a real game again, when the war was over.

When I went back in Shoumatoff was setting up near the windows. FDR was sitting in his big leather chair, right where the light streamed in. I guess portrait artists needed light the same way photographers did. Speaking of photogs, I didn't see the blond guy around. He must have gone back to the car.

Just then tires crackled outside. A few seconds later Long came in, the leather mailbag under his arm. "Heavy load today, sir," he said to Hassett.

"Bring it over here, Dewey."

"Mr. President, why don't we leave it till after the sitting?"

"No, let's get to it, Deacon. Mopsy's not quite ready for us yet."

As Hassett started sorting out the red tags FDR waved Long over. They discussed the schedule again for the San Francisco trip. Finally the President said, "Yes, that sounds fine. Start setting it up with the railroads," and Long left. Roosevelt shot his cuffs and looked through his pince-nez at the first document Hassett placed in front of him. "What's this?"

"State Department letter, sir. It's the message replying to Stalin you wanted."

FDR read it, rubbing his forehead absently. "I wanted it polite," he said. "The last one he sent was polite, I wanted to send back something cordial. But I don't know. 'Thank you for your frank explanation of the Soviet point of view of the Berne incident, which now appears to have faded into the past without having accomplished any useful purpose. There must not, in any event, be mutual mistrust, and minor misunderstandings of this nature should not arise in the future. I feel sure that when our armies make contact in Germany and join in a fully coordinated offensive the Nazi armies will disintegrate.' What does that mean to you?"

"I'm not certain."

"It's a typical State letter. It says nothing at all."

"I'm glad I didn't write it, Mr. President."

"Deacon, that wasn't a complaint. To pleasantly say nothing is the essence of diplomacy." He initialed it and held it up. "Send it."

Hassett waved it a couple of times and set it aside to dry. Next he fanned out appointment letters. FDR signed them rapidly, murmuring something I didn't catch. The signed documents went on the mantelpiece and around him on the floor.

"Senate bill 298. Commodity Credit Corporation."

FDR looked it over, eyebrows raised, lips parted. The poised pen vibrated. He glanced at Mrs. Rutherfurd and smiled. "Here's where I make a law," he said.

"You make it look so easy, Franklin."

"I am ready to begin," Shoumatoff announced imperiously from behind the easel.

"Sure all this paper won't bother you? Bill's waiting for his laundry to dry," said Roosevelt, with a chuckle.

"Sir, will you need me for the next hour? Major Greer and I should check on the arrangements for this afternoon—"

"Yes, of course, Deacon. It's a wonderful day for a barbecue. We're going to have a grand time. Tell me again what our schedule is."

"Ruth's been up there since dawn, getting things ready. The barbecue starts at four for our staff, sir, and the others the mayor invited. Mike will bring you over to the mountain at four-thirty."

"Bun Wright, will he be fiddling?"

"Yes sir, he'll be there."

"Wait till you see him clog dance, Lucy. And remember, I don't want to be set apart or anything—"

"Just another seat at the table, sir. I'll check on that. Major Greer will have the comm team set up so in case anything breaks you'll be in touch—"

"Grand. Oh, and before I forget, remind Frank Walker I want the first sheet of UN stamps, when I get to San Francisco. He can have photographers there if he likes."

"Yes sir." Hassett made a note, then pulled the rest of the red-tags out of the pouch. He arranged them in front of Roosevelt, glanced at Shoumatoff; she nodded.

Bill left, and the artist took over. First she had Prettyman and me move Roosevelt's chair. She measured his nose and head, then ordered Prettyman to fetch the cape. She draped it over FDR's shoulders, stood back, made him turn this way and that. He obeyed without objection, but he was beginning to look tired.

She started sketching. I watched her for a while, then picked up the *Times* from the pouch. I'd already heard all the war news I wanted, so I leafed to the sports page, still thinking about baseball for some reason, and read how good Bevans and Roser were doing pitching for the Yankees. Yeah, the war must be about over—Old Golds were putting aluminum foil back into their packaging.

The photographer came in from the front hall, and I looked up. "Where have you been?" Shoumatoff asked him sharply. He shrugged, tossing his hat on the sofa arm next to Mrs. Rutherfurd. For an instant something about him seemed familiar. But I didn't know any bearded photographers. He unbuttoned his jacket, looking at the President, as Reilly ran his hands up and down him again. "Do you feel like working now?" Shoumatoff asked him sarcastically.

"Yeah. What did you want now, lady?"

"I will need several photos, in various poses. I will use them as references, so they must be sharply focused. Just let me rearrange that cape." She hovered around FDR, who raised his eyebrows at Lucy Rutherfurd. She smiled back sweetly.

FDR pulled a folder of his stamps from the bookcase and began to go through them. I watched as he idly stuffed several into an envelope marked "To give away." Then he did an odd thing. He took his wallet out of his jacket and thumbed through it. He took out a worn card, held it for a moment, then flipped it into the wastebasket beside him. It had looked just like a draft card.

"Mr. President, what are you doing? Stop doing that. Turn your head back, the way it was. Lift your chin a little. Pick up a report. I would like you to read a report. Look serious, please."

Miss Delano moved around the room, taking the flower vases into the kitchen one by one to refill them with water. Miss Suckley's fingers worked busily at her crocheting. Then came a muffled clack as the photographer, hidden beneath a black cloth, opened the back of the camera.

The Tokarev fell into Krasov's hand, the steel cold from the night it had spent in the trunk. There was more than enough room for it inside the big portrait camera. Only one of the guards had thought to check there, and when he put his hand on it he'd spoken up; said if the plates were exposed he'd have to go back to Atlanta for more. And the man had taken away his hand, nodded, waved him on in.

He smiled, hidden under the black cloth. Then the smile faded.

It was time to finish what he'd come so far to do. To join those few men who had altered the course of history with a dagger or a bullet. Brutus. John Wilkes Booth. Gavrilo Prinzip. Yes, Prinzip had started a war too, a war that had destroyed empires. He would be the new Prinzip. For out of his act would come the utter destruction of the Soviet Union and the liberation of Europe.

He flipped the cloth off his head with his left hand, leaving his right still concealed, and looked over his glasses—secondhand, twenty cents, and impossible to see through—at the President. He'd seen Roosevelt before, in the basement of the White House. But never this close. Never without a screen of burly men around him. Fence had been right. Things were laxer here. The only guards in sight were the Navy man, by the fireplace, and the big Secret Service agent leaning against the wall by the front lobby.

All he had to do now was wait.

"Mr. Belinkov!"

It took him a second to react to the name he'd given her when he called, asking if she needed a photographer. "Yeah?"

"Will you take this pose or not? I have asked you twice. Just like this, with the light falling against his cheekbones. Take it now, please, before he moves!"

"Yes ma'am." He ducked under the cloth, pretended to focus—since there was no ground glass in place, it was a mime—and groped for the rubber bulb. The shutter went ka-*chunk.*

Shoumatoff wasn't easy to get along with. She was émigré aristocracy, her Russian so larded with French he had trouble understanding her at times. It had been tough to come up with a story for her. He had to make it clear he was Russian, but it had to be a history she couldn't check on. Finally he'd told her a variation of the truth, that his family had moved to this country in the twenties, then back to Russia; he and his mother had returned in 1938. Only his father hadn't, and they hadn't heard from him since. Shoumatoff had swallowed it. The Bolsheviki, she intoned magisterially, had no doubt imprisoned his unfortunate father.

That put the last link in place. What she would tell them would make his Soviet connections perfectly clear, after the event.

The murder weapon itself, of course, would be the final and conclusive piece of evidence.

He glanced at the clock again and eased the hammer back to cock. Slowly and silently. That was it, he was ready. The Tokarev didn't have a safety.

"Mr. Belinkov! Are you *listening* to me, young man? Are you *deaf?* Take this pose. Just as he is, with the cape thrown back."

"Yes ma'am." He ducked under again, pretended to focus, and snapped the shutter. Ka-chunk.

He extracted his head again, squinting out over the glasses through the french windows. He felt a nudge of concern. They were open, but he didn't smell anything yet.

Then, in the distance, he heard a shout. He smiled and took his glasses off with his left hand, leaving his right under the cloth. He took a deep breath, focusing his whole attention on the chest of the haggard old man who sat, pretending to read a sheaf of papers, ten feet away.

Then the phone rang.

—

By now I knew which phone was which from the sound of the bell. I reached across behind FDR's table and picked up on the local line, on the lowest shelf. "Little White House," I said, looking past the President's motionless, slightly bent back to the blank lens of the camera. The man behind it was taking off his glasses. As he did, he looked familiar again, just for a moment; then he didn't.

Weird, I thought, and said into the phone, "Hello?"

"This is the operator at the Foundation. Is there a John Kennedy there?"

"Speaking," I said.

Across the room Reilly shoved himself away from the wall. He was frowning. "Say, mister," he said.

"Yeah?"

"You took what, three shots so far?"

"Something like that."

Reilly said, "Maybe I don't get how you're doing this—but how come you don't change the plates after you take a picture?"

In my ear the tinny distant voice said, "Mr. Kennedy, I'm calling for Hugh. You know, who runs the dry-cleaning service?"

"Yeah, Hugh. I know who you mean."

"He said to tell you that your shirts were ready."

I stood frozen as the chain of association completed itself in my head. Like a chain of lightning, running down from the sky again and again to the same point. Lighting everything up so stark and blazing that you suddenly saw all kinds of things around you that you never had before.

Shirts.

Laundry.

Laundry.

Suddenly I knew where I'd seen the blond, round-faced man before.

Only he hadn't had a beard then. Or glasses. He hadn't been a photographer.

He'd been in the basement of the White House, pushing a laundry cart.

We stared at each other across the distance of ten feet. Nothing between us but the big old-fashioned camera, and the President. And I saw the blue, slightly protuberant eyes change, and know, and saw that he saw that I knew too.

At the same moment, as the voice in my ear said, "Hello? Are you there? *Hello?*" someone outside yelled, "Fire!"

The paralyzed, suspended instant of knowledge and horror broke. I whipped around, the phone still in my hand, and yelled, as loud as I could, "Reilly!" But Mike was already lunging forward, one hand going inside his jacket as the other reached out.

———

The man in the uniform had recognized him. He saw that in his face, and in the sudden whiteness of his fingers on the telephone handset. The other, in the blue blazer, was already moving toward him. Something had gone wrong. In a moment they'd call for help.

The man in uniform turned his head. "Reilly!" he screamed suddenly.

Now, Krasov thought. He whipped the black cloth away, like a stage magician, to expose and clear the automatic in his right hand. Dropping it to eye level, he stepped back and around the camera and sighted at the bright red splotch of Roosevelt's tie.

He was squeezing the trigger when something black and heavy hit him on the arm, knocking it down. His wrist went numb and he almost lost the gun, but got it again before it left his hand.

He raised it again and finished the trigger-pull just as the big man reached him. As the automatic cracked like thunder inside the room, someone started to scream.

———

Reilly felt the shot as a heavy, numbing blow. He staggered. His leading arm, which he'd stretched out like a basketball player guarding an opponent, flailed down. But he was still standing. His other hand was still groping for the revolver in his shoulder holster. He was eyeball-to-eyeball with the photographer, who looked at him coolly over the sights. Then his eyes dropped, fixing on the open black hole pointed at his chest.

Right where he wanted it.

"Down, Mr. President!" he shouted hoarsely, but felt with horror his strength draining away. He had to keep standing. Had to keep himself between the gun and the President. But he couldn't seem to help it, that somehow he just couldn't seem to keep his legs under him anymore.

———

I picked up the next telephone, intending to throw it too, but it was screwed down. I could see the gun. It looked huge. Reilly stood like a wall between it and Roosevelt. There was something strange about the way he stood, though. Why didn't he lunge? Go for the gun? It seemed to me that everything was happening very slowly. I stood helplessly tugging at the bolted-down phone.

Then Reilly collapsed, going down like a dynamited building. All the women were screaming. I felt like screaming myself, but my throat was locked. Smoke was a blue tint to the air.

The blond man with the round, faintly smiling, cherubic face stepped casually around the Secret Service chief toward the President.

———

Krasov knew he had a couple of seconds, no more. There'd be other agents outside. The cry of "Fire!" might have distracted them, but the shot would bring them back.

But he couldn't resist the incredible realization that whatever happened to him afterward, he had already triumphed. He'd failed three times before. But *this* time everything had worked as he planned it. How arrogant they were! How rich, how well fed, how confident of their safety and power! But *he* had outthought them, tricked them, penetrated all the layers of protection, smashed through the last line of defense.

Now he faced the President across six feet of pine floor. FDR sat openmouthed in his chair. The thin boy in uniform stood behind him, pulling futilely at one of the telephones. A telephone, that was what had knocked his arm down . . . made him miss the first shot. Roosevelt's hands moved across the card table as if seeking something, then gripped its edge and pushed it violently away. It toppled, spilling stamps and documents across the floor. But the heavy chair didn't move an inch.

Krasov felt quite calm. He had shot many men before, first at the orders of Chekists in leather jackets, then at the orders of officers in Nazi field gray and SS black. He had no hatred for the one before him. But History demanded that he die. That through his death liberty might come to a suffering people, and freedom to an empire of cruelty and terror.

He centered the front sight in the notch, placed them on the red tie, and pulled the trigger. The screaming filled his ears like sirens.

Someone burst in through the front lobby, someone big. Krasov spun instantly and fired twice, fast, a burst. The man reeled back into the wall and went down, and photographs and prints smashed down after his outstretched hands and glass and wood shattered across the floor.

It was time to leave. He was no martyr. He'd planned his escape as carefully as the rest, and now it was time to leave. The smell of smoke filled his head. Gunpowder smoke and, behind it, the smell of burning leaves. He aimed the gun, which was shaking now, at each of the people left in the room. They shrank back. For a long instant no one moved.

He fired again at the slumped-forward man in the chair, knowing this shot missed, the gun was shaking too badly now, but it didn't matter. It was finished. He opened his hand and the pistol fell from it to the floor. It hit the carpet and spun to rest, showing the five-pointed Soviet star molded into the black plastic grips. Could not be better. Could not be better. Leave it here. Now *go*.

He turned, his body feeling huge and numb and heavy, and ran with stumbling leaden feet out into the sunlight.

———

Lauren had gone to stone, half-risen from her seat, when the gun pointed at her. But when the man dropped it and disappeared into the light she was up and bending over FDR. She couldn't see any wound, but dark blood soaked the front of his shirt and the gray suit coat. She looked toward the open doors to see Kennedy silhouetted in them now, leaning over the balcony, looking down.

———

The sun deck was empty. I ran to the balcony and craned over. Glass glinted in the grass. His glasses. He must have swung himself over, hung by his arms, and let go. A six-foot drop.

Smoke was blowing out of the woods, swirling around the trees, drifting out of the pine boughs like fog. It smelled cheerful, homelike, like burning leaves in the Massachusetts fall. Below me rifles stood propped against the shacks, but the shelters were empty. Except for one. I could see a guard in there, but when I shouted he didn't answer. Maybe he couldn't hear me. Others were shouting and screaming behind me in the cottage, and out in the woods, too, where the smoke was coming from. Upwind of us.

Far too late, I realized how brilliant it was and how carefully he'd planned it. He'd set a smoldering fire upwind of the cottage, then come back and taken his position behind the camera. I still didn't know where the gun came from. Reilly had searched him twice. But he'd had it, and he'd simply waited, pretending to take photographs, until the sentries noticed the fire and sounded the alarm. Everyone knew how FDR worried about fire. The marines and Secret Service had been drilled on what to do. He'd arranged for a distraction and waited till his escape route was clear. Only at the last moment had Reilly and I caught on. Almost in time to stop him . . .

Almost.

Now he was out there, in the smoke, getting away.

All this went through my head in about half a second. I considered dropping from the sun deck, as he had, but all I had to do was wrench my back and I'd be out of action. I spun and ran back into the cottage.

———

It frightened Prettyman, how heavy the President was. Heavy and limp. He needed help. The Wolfe woman. He told her, "Get his legs, miss. We need to get him into the bedroom. Has anybody called the doctor? Miss Suckley, Miss Delano, somebody please call the doctor."

The massive balding head he knew so well lolled back as he maneuvered the upper body through the door. Thank God he'd made the bed. Oh, what was he thinking of? The President was shot. Why did all this seem so familiar, as if he'd lived it all before? Then he remembered the book he'd read in school, about Abraham Lincoln. He felt sweat gush suddenly on his back. Oh, God, let him not die. All the good Presidents died. He felt icy numb with horror, as though he were trapped inside a glacier, looking out.

The tall woman came hesitantly into the bedroom and sank into a chair. Prettyman arranged the President's arms and slipped another pillow under his head. He said to the faces in the doorway, "Have you called the doctor, for God's sake?"

"We called him. He was down at the pool. He's coming right away."

"Let's get his shirt off," said the Wolfe woman loudly. It wasn't a suggestion, it was an order. Grateful to her for taking over, he bent obediently to help, fingers fumbling on the blood-sodden cotton. He unknotted the red tie, crossed the room and hung it up, aware that it was ruined but unable to stop himself. In the center of the bloody undershirt was a small black puncture mark. Then his horror, already too intense to bear, doubled.

The President opened his eyes and looked up at them.

The leather chair sat empty beside the pushed-over card table. The air still smelled of burnt powder, and it was getting hazy from the smoke outside. Someone was crying in the bedroom. I halted, looking in, but I couldn't help in there. The phone was ringing again. I started for it, then felt a hand on my shoe.

Reilly, his arm outstretched. I bent and took the snubnosed .38. "Get the son of a bitch, Jack," he grunted.

I said, "I'll try," and ran for the lobby.

When I stepped outside everything looked oddly quiet. The blue sedan was parked out front. So was Shoumatoff's car, to my surprise. Brown lay on the driveway, where, judging by the trail of blood, he'd crawled after being hit. He'd cinched his uniform belt tight around his thigh. No marines in sight, and no Secret Service. They must all be down in the ravine, fighting the fire. Smoke blew across the driveway, growing thicker by the minute.

I stood irresolute. *Get the son of a bitch.* I was willing to try, but how? I had no way of tracking him. I had no idea where he was headed.

Suddenly I heard an unearthly howl behind me.

Fala, every hair on end, crashed into the screen door from inside. It tore, he lunged again and kicked, it came free and he was through. His paws kicked up gravel. He rounded the cottage, barking furiously, plunged past the guardhouses and disappeared into the woods.

"Holy shit," I muttered. I shifted the gun to my right hand and ran after him. Down the slope, uniform shoes skidding on the grass, and across the path. Past the guardhouse with the sentry inside. It was the pimply-faced kid. He leaned back against the inside of his box, eyes empty. One hand draped over the bayonet that pinned him to the wood.

I didn't see his rifle anywhere around.

Heart thudding, brogans crashing into leaves and needles, Krasov blundered heavily through the smoky woods. A chaos of Russian and German and English thundered through his brain. The rifle was heavy, swinging in one hand. The young marine had tried to stop him. He'd called "Halt," then aimed. But by then Krasov was inside his guard.

The smoke drove toward him between the trees, thick and woolly, like choking brown-stained cotton. The soft ground clutched at his heavy shoes. Patches of it were black and smoking, still burning-hot beneath the surface ash. As he crashed through bushes he searched his coat pocket for the compass. The needle swung crazily and he had to stop to let it steady. Then he lunged off again, correcting to the left. He'd set not one but two fires, a hundred yards apart. There should be a clear lane between them. Leading out.

Hoarse shouts and cries ahead, and a figure loomed out of the blue-brown pall. A marine flailed a branch with leaves attached at orange flames that twisted desperately to escape. Then the smoke curtain shifted and rolled toward him, over him, so thick he couldn't see, couldn't even breathe. He sucked a deep, whooping breath and held it and blundered into the wall. Heat seared his cheek. He veered away from it and a few meters on came out into clear air again, hacking and coughing.

So far, though, everything was jake. He knew where he was and nobody else did. All he had to do was keep going.

Then he tensed. The hair rose on the back of his neck.

Behind and above him, faint behind the crackle of flames and the shouting, rose the high wild barking of a dog.

——

I plunged downward, revolver held out and away in case I fell. My leather soles skidded and slid through dry leaves and pine needles. The ground was dry as hell. Sparks and burning leaves sailed blazing above me like comets. Flames curled hungrily up where embers had landed and caught in advance of the main fire.

The ravine was much deeper than I'd expected, and the drop so steep that at last my feet shot out from under me. I just sat and slid downward. Ahead of me, barking and whining echoed from the trees. I skidded to a stop in a patch of clear air, but when I looked up smoke sealed me off a few feet above my head. It was thick and getting thicker, a whitish-yellow, greasy, roiling ceiling that dimmed the sun to a reddish glow and made my eyes sting and my nose water.

The barking was getting fainter. Damn it, I thought, wait for me. I scrambled up and lunged into a run, panting, sawing at the air with my arms.

A line of men loomed up between the trees, beating at the ground with branches, stamping at flames with their boots. They called hoarse warnings, coughing and spitting. Yelled, waving me back. I didn't answer, just kept running. For a second I debated telling them what was going on, that the President had been shot and the assassin was somewhere down here. Then I realized what a snafu that would be, twenty marines taking potshots at each other, and at me, in the smoke. A night battle in Blackett Strait would be nothing to it.

Maybe I could catch him myself. With a little four-legged help.

Someone ahead, crouched, looking at a smoking patch of ground . . . I gasped and jerked the revolver up, but it was only a bush. Shit, the fire was closing in. The bush caught suddenly, all at once, blazing up from the roots into a huge crackling torch. I backed away, shielding my face with my arm, and staggered around it. My skin felt like it was melting. My eyes and nose were running with snot and tears. This seemed to be the dead bottom of the ravine.

To either side, for the short distance I could see, the forest floor sloped up. I hesitated, nearly blind, coughing, wondering which way to go.

Ahead, and closer, the barking burst out again. I stumbled back into a run, but now my legs were lead. My shoe soles seared my feet. Flame roared from all sides, a hollow drumming roar like a tropical downpour on the steel roof of a Quonset hut.

Fala took shape out of the rolling smoke, outlined in fire, paws planted wide in the smoldering floor of the forest. He was crouched between two roaring masses of flame, watching them creep together. His singed black fur smoked. He growled and coughed, searching the opacity between the pines. As I crashed up he turned his head, then lunged forward again just as the flames merged. I slowed, sucked a sobbing breath, and plunged after him into the wavering brown curtain of smoke and hot gas above a solid wall of flame.

I hoped Scotties had good instincts. Mine were telling me to turn around and get the hell out of there.

Now he was barking frenziedly ahead. No, to my left. Heat roasted my eyeballs. I couldn't see. The underbrush was heavier here, and it was all on fire. Sparks stung my hands and face like angry wasps. I closed my eyes and stumbled blindly forward.

———

When the dog started again, Krasov looked up from the compass. The land sloped up now. That was where he had to go. Up, then down, then up again to the road. He hadn't expected the fire to spread so fast, or get this far. The ground was drier than he'd thought, and the wind lighter. It was spreading upwind almost as fast as it was down.

The barking came again, low and growling, close behind him. He fumbled with the rifle—it was American, unfamiliar—and got the handle back and another cartridge fed into the chamber. He held his fire till he saw the shadow in the smoke.

———

A bullet cracked into a tree to my left. The boom of the shot was penned by the ravine, hard to distinguish from its own echoes. But I thought it came from ahead. Shit! Up till then I'd hoped he hadn't taken the dead kid's rifle.

Clear air, very suddenly, and an uphill slope. As I burst out of the smoke I saw him. Fifty yards ahead and climbing, a smudged face back-turned between the smoldering rough boles of the pines. I didn't see Fala at all.

A flash, and another crack. I swear something brushed my ear. I hit the deck, but it was on fire. I yelled and scrambled up, hands blistering, and almost dropped the .38. The rifle boomed again and dirt and pine needles blasted up a yard away, spraying me with sparks. I swung the revolver up and squeezed one off in his direction, blindly, just to make the rounds stop coming.

Then stood waiting to get shot, smoke and hot air sawing in and out of my desperately pumping lungs. I felt dizzy, like the top of my head was lifting off, like I was about to pass out.

A furious crashing shook the bushes, the tops of the small trees ahead and above me. He hadn't stuck around to take that last shot, the one that would have had me. He was fighting his way upward, through the brush.

I panted, bent over, and suddenly someone in my head informed me that maybe it was time to think this over. I was outgunned. A short-barreled pistol like Reilly's, you had to get within arm's length of a guy to hit him, unless you were a crack shot. Mike probably was, but I'm no Tom Mix. And an M-1 wasn't something you wanted to dick around with. I'd seen Jap bodies cut in two with .30 slugs. If it hit you in the shoulder it'd blow your arm off. This was like a face-off between a PT boat and a destroyer. I could turn around and head back. Or better yet, just stay here, and wait, and let him escape. Nobody would know. I'd just say I lost him in the smoke. It was almost the truth. Nobody could blame me for that.

Except myself.

Something desperate and vicious rose up in me. I wasn't going to let this son of a bitch escape. And I wasn't going to turn away again. From anything, or anyone. Ever again.

I hoisted myself out of my crouch and ran stumbling and weaving uphill, praying desperately for air.

———

When the shot came back, not close but showing him that the thin man had a gun, Krasov decided not to hang around. He couldn't be far from the road now. This was the end of the ravine. He just hoped it was the right ravine. If it was, then at the top of this rise was a narrow dirt road, wide enough for one car. They'd checked it out together the night he arrived.

He spun and stumbled uphill, planting his heavy brogans sideways in the yielding, tumbling rot of leaves and soil. He slipped and fell, but got up again immediately, though he wanted to lie there and rest and breathe. He couldn't afford to rest. The other was just below him, crashing through the brush like a clumsy shadow. Could he be discouraged? He swung the rifle up and pumped two more rounds into the smoke, where the noise came from. It stopped, then started again.

He was almost to the top. Blue sky glowed through the treetops. The top of a telephone pole! His heart thudded, shaking his chest, but he kept lifting his legs, dragging his unimaginably heavy body upward foot by foot.

"Hold it!"

He spun around, raising the rifle. The Navy man stood ten yards downhill, aiming a pistol. Before Krasov could react, he fired. But the shot snapped over his head and whined off.

He grinned tightly, centering the peep sight.

The dog burst out of the bushes, snapping at his crotch. He yelled, startled, and brought the rifle-butt down on it. He missed and slammed his own thigh. The dog lunged again, growling and snarling, and he screamed as its burrowing teeth pierced cloth to flesh.

Behind him the crashing steps stopped. Ivan Krasov heard the click of the hammer going back. But he never heard the shot that shattered his skull.

———

I fell to my hands and knees, wheezing and crying. Mucus stranded into the leaves. It was black with soot. Beside me Fala growled and snapped. I didn't want to look at what he was doing. I bent forward and let breakfast come back up onto the pine needles.

I was wiping my mouth with my sleeve when I heard a horn honk above me, up at the top of the slope. I listened and, yeah, there was a motor running up there. A car, idling.

I wiped my mouth again, and got up and scrambled up the last few yards to the top of the rise.

———

In the President's bedroom, Bruenn pulled his bag open hastily and set out clamps and stats and bandages on a clean white towel Prettyman brought from the bathroom. "Clear these people out of here," he said tightly. "Call the Foundation again. We're going to need a surgeon. And an ambulance. We've got three badly wounded men."

The faces vanished from the door, all except for Wolfe. She stood for a moment, then asked, "Is he going to make it, doctor?"

Bruenn lifted FDR's eyelids. He seemed to be fading in and out of consciousness. Pallor told him there was major blood loss, even if you ignored the pool in the bed. The skin felt clammy. He tore the shirt farther down, searching for another entry wound. No, it looked like one bullet.

He sat irresolute for a second, watching the blood pump out and run down FDR's ribcage. That meant a major vessel had been nicked or pierced. He listened; no suck-click, so no tension pneumothorax.

Okay, now what? The Medical Corps said that when you had more casualties than medical personnel, you triaged. You didn't treat the ones that wouldn't make it. On the other hand, this wasn't a battlefield situation. This was the President.

But based on the location of the wound, and on FDR's age and general condition, he really didn't think operating would do anything more than kill him more quickly.

He took a deep breath and decided to stop blood loss first. As he cut the gauze and fastened it in place Roosevelt's breathing grew labored. Prettyman came back and hovered. He was crying. "He going to be better, isn't he, Doc?"

"That's in God's hands," Bruenn said. He debated whether there was anything more he could do. With FDR's heart, it wouldn't take him long to die. He might come out of it briefly before the end, or he might not. If he did, there was no reason for him to suffer. He found a morphine Syrette and injected it and noted the time.

"Will you stay with him, Chief?"

"I'll be right here, sir."

"Call me if he wakes up."

Prettyman said he would. Bruenn went into the sitting room, carrying his bag, and started on Reilly. The Secret Service man was conscious, white with pain. He didn't say anything as Bruenn probed the wound. Just stared out through the french windows, sweat trickling down his face.

———

She sat tensely in the coupe, all the windows rolled down, wondering if she should hit the horn again. The shots worried her. They sounded awfully close. Maybe she should leave. But Ivan, Johnny, needed her, to help him escape. The Party needed her. She'd never done much for the Party, though she'd been a member for years. Ever since she'd realized what sort of man her father was. Not just a capitalist but an arms maker, a profiteer from war, a monster who coined gold from human blood. She'd confronted him with it, horrified, and he'd just—laughed.

So that after that she'd known there was only one road for her to take.

To her surprise they hadn't asked for much. They hadn't asked her to denounce her family, or fight in Spain, or even do union work, although she'd been perfectly willing. Only that she penetrate the Hearst organization, for higher pay than she'd ever gotten at *Amerasia.* Not much of a sacrifice.

And then they had. She didn't quite understand it, even now. She'd thought Roosevelt was a progressive ally. Shoulder to shoulder with the working class in the struggle against the fascist beasts. But she'd been around long enough to know how fast the Party line could change. As it had in June of 1941, when Hitler went from ally to enemy overnight. This time she was in the vanguard, that was all.

A hot breath of smoke from the ravine recalled her to her danger. The shouting seemed closer. She took a deep lungful, in case the smoke got worse, and pressed the pedal, racing the engine. If he didn't get here in four more minutes she was leaving. The Party didn't ask you to sacrifice yourself needlessly. If he'd been caught, it was her duty to escape and pass the news upward along the secret chain that had, at its very top, the great leader of the masses in their struggle for world revolution.

Or, if she couldn't escape . . . to make sure that none of *them,* the old enemies turned friends who had inexplicably but inescapably been deemed new enemies again, would be able to make her reveal her links upward into the next cell.

"Allie."

She flinched and looked up from the gearshift. It wasn't Krasov. It was Jack Kennedy, face blackened, nose running, shoes smoking. A gun dangled from his hand.

"Why, Jack. What brings you out here?"

"Alice," he said again. He came out onto the road and put his hand on the door. He looked dazed, as if he couldn't believe what he saw. "Well, well."

"Have you . . . did you see another man out there, in the woods?"

"Yeah."

"Where is he?"

"I shot him."

She nodded slowly. There was only one more thing to know, then. Something *they* would ask her instantly. "And what about *him?* Is he dead?"

"Who?"

"The President."

"Oh." He stared at her for another second, then motioned with the revolver. "I don't know. Get out of the car."

"I'm not getting cut, Jack. What do you want? Do you want a ride?"

"Knock it off, Allie. I'm not in the mood." He released the door and staggered around the back, toward the driver's side. She glimpsed him in the rearview. "Move over. I'm driving."

She wasn't a fool. She wasn't going with him, to be judged by one of their bourgeois courts. There were people who'd hide her, change her identity, protect her.

She waited till he was right behind her. Then she bent forward, making herself small, and let the clutch up and stamped on the gas.

▬

That should have warned me, the snarl of the engine before the DeSoto slammed into gear. But I was slow, sick and exhausted and still in shock. The car shot forward, out from under my hand. Only with a flying lunge did I manage to grab the bumper.

The revolver jumped out of my fingers as the car pulled me off my feet. I slammed down to my knees, and my back went rigid with a blinding familiar pain. The coupe, gathering speed down the dirt road, dragged me over grass and dirt, faster and faster. The road tore at my uniform. I heard the motor ease off as we skidded around a curve, then roar again. My knees felt like they were being held against a bench grinder. I had to let go. Once she got to pavement she'd kick it up to fifty or sixty. If I let go then I'd tumble. Break arms and legs, or my head. Trees flashed past in a green blur. The road was an ochre streak. My hands were cramped tight as vises. But I had to let go *now*—

The brakes went on, worn-out wartime linings shrieking, and the tires skidded, locked, spewing up red dry dust. The coupe slid to a stop. I let go and lay wheezing on the rutted ground for a stunned second.

I don't know what warned me. My back was telling me I couldn't move. Usually I listened. But somehow, this time, I got my fingers dug deep enough into the red clay to roll myself over.

So that the wartime recapped tires just missed my head, as the coupe shifted into reverse and backed over me.

When I blinked up from between the front wheels Collier was gazing down at me thoughtfully. A pump shotgun was cradled in one arm. The big black-and-white squad car was parked across the road, blocking it. "Afternoon, young miss," he said to Allie. "Hey there, Lieutenant. Made any headway on that dog killer?"

"I was about to ask you the same thing, Sheriff."

"Looks like somebody here got some things to explain to me. Like, what in hell is going on. What all that shooting's about. Or is this just a Yankee version of a hayride?"

"Let's do it up at the cottage," I said, getting up slowly. *Very* slowly, my back reminded me. Once on my feet I bent cautiously to check things out. The knees of my uniform trousers were bloody holes. If it had been a gravel road . . .

"Yeah?" Collier prompted.

"Up at the cottage. Watch her, Sheriff. She may be armed. The President's been shot, and she was in on it."

Alice said angrily, "Yes, he's been shot. And *he*'s one of the assassins! I was driving to find help. He was trying to stop me."

"By hanging onto your bumper? Sheriff, you *saw* her trying to kill me. If I hadn't rolled out of the way—"

Collier's eyes searched from one of us to the other. He hoisted the shotgun, reached inside the cruiser, and tossed an antique set of black iron cuffs into Allie's DeSoto. "Put 'em on," he said. "Both of you, left hand to right. Then we'll go on up and ask Mike what all this is about."

──────

"Where's Hassett?" Reilly grunted around the massive absentness in his gut. It hurt, too. But he had to know.

He'd failed. Blown it. He'd taken one of the President's bullets. But others had found their mark.

"Here, Mike." The Vermonter bent over him, long face squeezed white. He felt his hand gripped.

"Take me in there."

Hassett, bless him, didn't argue. Just said to Dewey Long, "Put him in the wheelchair. Roll him in. Hurry up."

In the bedroom Prettyman and Wolfe were standing over the President. With the first glance Reilly saw he was still alive, and he felt relieved. Then he saw that his lips and hands were blue. "Doc?" Reilly said.

"He's slipping away," whispered Bruenn.

"Mr. President," said Hassett. "Mr. President! Can you hear me?"

Roosevelt opened his eyes. The lips barely moved, but they could all hear, in the hush, "Hello, Deacon."

──────

Collier pulled into a Little White House drive crowded with vehicles. The Foundation ambulance. Jeeps. Automobiles. Ho-ly cow, he thought. What I got myself into now. "County sheriff," he roared at the marine who trotted over, cheeks pale beneath their coating of smoke-smut. "What's going on here, boy?"

"Don't know, sir. My orders are to seal off the—"

"Seal off the area. Nobody goes in or out. Got that?" Collier swung heavily out and jerked the back door open. Kennedy crawled out, dragging Sobelski behind him by the cuffs. "Inside," the sheriff said, stationing himself behind them with the shotgun.

The bedroom was small and dark, paneled with unfinished pine. On the wall were a barometer and two or three ship prints. The desk and swiveling office chair were cut low, for a man in a wheelchair. A sea chest. A bed table and lamp. On the bare floor, a hooked rug with his name embroidered in it.

And the short, plain wooden single bed that the President lay on.

"What happened, Mike?" FDR whispered. "They . . . get you, too?"

"An—assassination attempt, Mr. President."

"Who?" It was barely a breath.

"I'm not sure, sir. At present it appears"—he glanced at Kennedy, who'd just come in with the Sobelski woman. He glimpsed Sheriff Collier behind them. "—It appears to me to have been a Soviet agent."

"Soviet?"

"I should say, Russian. Mrs. Shoumatoff says he's Russian."

"Was," Kennedy said. He leaned forward. He looked terrible, scorched and bloody. "He *was.* I got him, Mike. He's dead." He nodded at Sobelski, who stared down at Roosevelt with hatred. *"She* was in a car, waiting for him."

"Is that true? Who were you working for?" Reilly asked her. She raised her head sharply, but didn't answer.

"Mike, I've got morphine here."

"Hold the dope for now, Doc, thanks." He turned back to FDR. "I guess that's all we have at present, then, Mr. President. There may be more involved. We've sealed off the area and we . . . we're continuing the investigation."

". . . You all right?"

"I'll live. What are your orders, sir?"

Roosevelt's faded eyes searched the ceiling. "Deacon?" he whispered.

Hassett leaned in. "Here I am, Mr. President. I haven't called anyone in Washington yet. But I'll have to soon."

Roosevelt kept looking up at the ceiling, so fixedly that Lauren glanced up there too. But she didn't see anything. He murmured something half-formed.

"Sir?" said Hassett, leaning over him.

The eyelids fluttered closed, and the stertorous breathing resumed. Bruenn shoved them aside, leaned with a stethoscope.

"What did he say, Bill?"

"I thought he said—'secret.' "

"His heart's weakening," said Bruenn.

Wolfe turned on him. "Aren't you a doctor? If it's weakening, do something about it!"

"I can administer stimulants. But it won't really help. I gave him something to lessen his pain. That's really all I can recommend."

Hassett asked him, "Will he regain consciousness?"

"He may be conscious now. Mr. President. Blink if you can hear me."

FDR's eyes slowly opened. "Secret," he whispered again, loud enough, this time, for them to hear him.

"What is it you want, Mr. President? I'll call Mrs. Roosevelt—"

"Lucy—"

"I'm here, Franklin. Franklin, I'm here."

Kennedy moved Reilly back to let Mrs. Rutherfurd next to the bed. She and Roosevelt held hands and looked steadily at each other. They didn't say a thing, but the blue lips formed a smile. "It was grand, Lucy," he said faintly.

"You'll have to leave, Mrs. Rutherfurd," Reilly said. "Soon."

"I understand. Believe me." She stood, and there was something regal in the way she held herself, sorrowing but unafraid. "I'll be in the next room, Franklin. I'll be waiting. Remember that. I'll be waiting."

When she was gone Roosevelt rested for a little while. Then he turned his eyes to us. "Listen," came the whisper.

"Yes, Mr. President."

"First of all. Don't tell Eleanor that Lucy . . ."

"All right, sir. We understand. *She* wasn't here."

"—Hard on her. Too hard."

"We'll make sure she leaves before anyone's notified. Don't talk now. Save your strength."

The President's eyes opened wide. He struggled to sit up. Bruenn got an arm under him and another pillow. "Listen," he whispered again, an agonized, barely interpretable hissing. "Got to get along with Uncle Joe. Convinced he . . . can't be behind it."

"Sir, the murder weapon was Soviet—"

"Convinced, I said. Know what's going on, Mike. Dastardly. . . . Got to save the United Nations. If it does . . . sacrifice worthwhile. Only hope for peace. Even if I'm wrong . . . Stalin won't live forever. Too important. Prevent another war. No more boys will die."

Hassett said, sounding horrified, "Sir, are you asking us to deny that—to pretend that—"

"Yes, Mike. Bill. The quietus."

His fingers fluttered, started to rise, then fell back. The massive head rolled away from them till all they could see was the sparse graying hair and the scalp beneath. "Not sorry," the whisper faded "—been so sick—the bomb. Don't want to decide. But . . . invade . . . can't decide. Maybe better . . . could have done better . . ."

Kennedy said, his voice hoarse with smoke, "You'll be immortal, Mr. President. Like Lincoln."

"No," he whispered. "I'll be forgotten. Had . . . grand time of it. But I think after all I may have been a little too—"

His mouth stayed open, but the light behind the eyes went out. He kept breathing, though, for a little while. Hassett took his hand then, and held it until the breathing stopped.

——

Hassett sat with the cool limp hand in his, not feeling the air still oozing in and out of his own lungs. It was as if the whole world had stopped breathing when *he* had.

He thought: He never finished his last sentence. The man who loved so to talk.

Sitting there, he watched death take the man he'd loved. The man he'd never felt he really understood.

Maybe no one ever had, the Deacon thought. Though so many had assumed they did. They'd called him so many things. Politician, scion of the rich, friend of the poor. "The Fox." Crafty and two-faced, the traitor to his class.

And courageous and farsighted, the man who saved the country from disaster and revolution and the world from Hitlerism. Maybe that was how they'd remember him. As a man who cared, and who was not afraid.

And perhaps, perhaps—would they say this of him one day, generations from now?—the man who drew a blueprint to liberate the future from the threat and scourge of war.

———

I stood frozen for a while when it was over. We didn't look at each other. Only at the unmoving man in the bed.

Then, gradually, we drifted out. Prettyman and Bruenn stayed. The rest of us found chairs around the sitting room and sat in a drained silence.

Franklin D. Roosevelt was dead.

"Should we do it?" Hassett said at last. He sounded doubtful. "What he said? About—keeping it secret."

Reilly grunted, "That's what he wanted. What he *ordered.*"

"But does it make sense? He might not have been thinking clearly."

"Bill, he knew exactly what he was saying. A Soviet agent killed FDR? If this gets out, Patton and MacArthur will have us in a shooting war with the Russkis inside of a day."

Hassett said, and his voice was angry for the first time I'd heard: "You're saying we let Stalin get away with it?"

"No. Not exactly. If it *was* Stalin. I'm saying we tell whoever—the vice president—Truman should know. After he takes over. It's his call, what we do then. But till then, we follow the Chief's last order."

"Can we do it? Keep it secret? He's dead, he's *dead*. What do we say?"

"Natural causes," said Reilly.

"Doc?" They both looked at Bruenn, who had come quietly out in the middle of the discussion.

Bruenn looked shaken, absorbed in his own thoughts. "What?" he said.

"Can you go along with that?"

"With what? Saying he died naturally? Well—maybe. If it was closed coffin. But that would look suspicious."

"If he'd died naturally, what would he have died of?" Reilly bored in. "Heart attack?"

"No. His heart was weak, but he was receiving proper treatment."

"Well, we don't want to make you look bad, Doc. Stroke?"

"A stroke would have done it. It would be sudden."

"Would it be credible?"

Bruenn took a deep breath and let it out. "With his medical history—sure. I've been afraid of one for months. Mike, listen. I have to get you on your back. I need to get you down to the Foundation and prepped for surgery."

"In a minute. First I want to make sure we're together on this." He searched our faces. "Okay. What were his last words?"

Wolfe said, "I have a terrific headache."

We swung to look at her. "What?" said Reilly.

"Adelle Birmingham's last words in *The Dying of the Light*. 'I have a terrific headache.'"

"Everyone understand that?" Hassett said. He seemed to be coming out of his shock. "I'll go over it again. Mrs. Shoumatoff was sketching him. He was sitting at the card table. He put his hand to his head. He said, 'I—have—a—terrific—headache.' Then he slumped over and we called Doc Bruenn. Doc, you take it from there."

"I can—fabricate the subsequent history," said Bruenn tightly. "To Admiral McIntire, and to the press. Mr. Hassett, you or Mike will have to help me instruct the—undertakers."

"Everyone understand?" said Reilly, turning his head painfully to glare at each of us in turn.

"Hold on," the sheriff, Collier, said. His forehead gleamed with sweat. "Hold on a minute, now. What about the fire? The shots? People at the Foundation heard those. Hell, you could hear that in town. What about that?"

"Pine trees exploding," said Reilly.

The sheriff rubbed his lip as he considered it. "Won't wash."

I said, "One of the marines dropped his rifle in the brush. The fire cooked the cartridges off."

"The dead kid?"

"Accident. One of the stray rounds hit him."

Collier brightened. "Better. And the brush fire—"

"Just a brush fire."

"Exactly. That's right."

"Mike?"

"That's right, Sheriff."

"Okay . . . I can probably put that over, if you think—if you think the country needs me to, Mr. Hassett."

"It's not me," said Hassett. "It's what *he* ordered."

Sobelski said, from the sofa, "You've forgotten one thing."

Reilly turned his head again. He couldn't quite see her, so I nudged his chair around a bit. "What's that?" he asked her.

"Me." She got up, hoisting herself without using her hands. The cuffs jingled. She stood, and even bruised—she'd resisted arrest, resisted the cuffs—she looked straight. Proud. As if she'd done something noble by giving up the President to his murderer.

"What about you?"

"I'm not going to keep quiet. I'm a member of the press. I demand a telephone. I demand the right to file a story."

We stared at her incredulously. "You're not filing any stories," Hassett snapped. "From what Jack tells us, you were an accessory."

Collier said, "That's right. You're under arrest, miss. You're not going anywhere."

I said, "Wait. Okay, she's under arrest. And we're going to—what? Put her on trial? Imprison her? We'll never keep it secret that way. We can't arrest her. But we can't let her walk, either."

"You're saying, what?" Reilly grunted. A sheen of sweat coated his face. "Kill her? I'm not going to. Are you?"

I hesitated. "No," I said at last.

"That's my Jack," Allie said.

Reilly squeezed his eyes shut, then opened them. Bruenn got up suddenly and started preparing a needle. Reilly ignored him. "So, what do we do with her?"

Wolfe stood up. She swung across the room and stopped, staring down at the floor. At something we'd all forgotten, lying next to the knocked-over card table.

The Soviet automatic. We watched as she bent and picked it up. "Is it loaded?" she asked, turning it over gingerly. I remembered she hated guns. Nobody answered her. "Move," she said to Allie.

I expected Alice to resist. Scream. Demand a trial, a lawyer. To my surprise, she didn't react at all at first. Then she gave me a white smile out of a white face.

She got up, gracefully, and smoothed her skirt. Then she went across the carpet, and stood in front of the french doors, looking out. They were closed, but the smell of burning was still leaking in somehow. I didn't see any smoke outside, though. The fire fighters must be just about done. I wondered, out of a suddenly empty brain, whether the flames had gotten to the body in the woods.

Then she flung the doors open, with a gesture of finality and freedom, as if they were the doors to a cell. She and Wolfe went out onto the terrace. The rest of us looked nowhere, or at the floor. Hassett's hands went to his mouth.

The crack of a shot, the echo clattering away through the trees.

When I went out Allie was standing beside the balustrade. Her hands clutched her throat. As she turned slowly toward me the beautiful face was distorted. Her eyes mirrored incredible hatred, incredible terror, and incredible pain.

Then she crumpled at Lauren's feet.

When Bruenn looked up he shook his head.

"Okay, that's that," Reilly snapped from the doors. Then, to Long, "Get a blanket. Cover her. Collier, you'll have to figure out what to do with the body. With the one in the woods, too. Better hustle, before the jarheads fall over it. Move!"

He fumbled for the wheels, and managed to shove himself a couple of inches before he gave up and sank back. Bruenn seized his arm then. Reilly sagged as the needle went in. He panted for a few seconds, till the drug softened his face.

After Bruenn wheeled him out, Hassett stood in front of the fireplace. He muttered, maybe to me, maybe just to himself, "But how did they get inside? Get so close? This was a conspiracy. We should have had some warning. Someone must have known. Somewhere."

I said, "Maybe. But maybe we'll never know."

We looked out the french doors, where Lauren was still standing, out to where the birds were singing. Fala squirmed in through the torn screen door, panting, and trotted through into the bedroom. We heard a low whine, then silence.

And after a while Hassett sighed and said, "Okay, Jack. Hand me the phone."

THE
AFTERIMAGE

Berlin

The hatchet-faced, clubfooted little man in the black leather coat and high-peaked hat limped up the stairs of his residence, glancing warily up at the stars. Clear weather, Dr. Joseph Goebbels thought with dread. In this sixth year of war, only overcast skies could bring surcease from the Royal Air Force by night and the U.S. Eighth Air Force by day.

Tonight would be doubly bad. Cloudless and moonlit.

Berlin was still burning from the daylight raid. The Hotel Adlon was in flames. Goebbels, the Gauleiter of Berlin, was the only German leader who toured bombed-out cities and visited the ever-nearing battle fronts. As Propaganda Minister, he still gave bitter victory-or-Bolshevism speeches, still conducted the weekly conference that coordinated the media throughout the ever-smaller Reich. Tonight he was in a foul mood. His tour of Kuestrin today had convinced him Army Group Vistula had no chance of holding when the long-awaited Red offensive came.

His butler received his coat, but seemed to have something to say. "Herr Reichsminister—"

"What is it?"

"The news—have you heard it? Roosevelt is dead."

He halted on the carpet, transfixed, feeling for just a moment a weakness, a dizziness. "How have you heard this?"

"The BBC. A flash. It just came over the air."

Goebbels stared at the man, who was smiling tentatively but also with fear; listening to the Allied radio was grounds for harsh punishment, even death. Could it be true? He'd given up hope long ago. Allowed himself to sink into bitterness and doubt. And now, at the final extremity—this. Could it still be possible? All, all still possible? He felt the wings of the Angel of History rustling above his head. For a moment it resisted comprehension. Then, like pins in a lock, the consequences fell successively into place in his brain, just as he had thought them out months before.

He glanced at his watch. In a few minutes Hitler would convene the midnight military situation briefing. He limped past the servant and picked up the telephone. His personal switchboard operator connected him to the Führerhauptquartier within seconds. He waited for an entire, dragging minute while someone went to notify Adolf Hitler that Herr Doctor Goebbels was on the line with an important call.

"Yes?" The familiar voice was hoarse, lead-heavy, dragging.

He spoke rapidly. "My Führer, I have something of the utmost consequence to report!"

"Yes, yes. What is it?"

"I must report in person. I ask you this: postpone your briefing until I arrive. I have wonderful news! It is the turning of the tide!"

"Oh?" The dull voice took on an inflection of interest. "I will give the necessary orders. We will wait—but not too long."

"Heil Hitler!"

The telephone rattled down at the far end, hurting his ear. He slammed his down too and snapped to his adjutant, "The car. To the FHQ, immediately, now. And bring the book. No, not that, the Carlyle! At once, hurry!" As he turned for the door he remembered one more thing he ought to bring and sent the butler scurrying back.

The heavy Mercedes ground through darkened streets toward the Wilhelmstrasse. Over shattered, melted asphalt. Torn-up streetcar rails. Past immense craters where gas mains and electric cables had been blown to the surface. The car's heater brought him the dead smell of burning, brick-dust, raw sewage, and scorched and rotting flesh. As the limousine bumped along, stopping occasionally while his escort went ahead on foot to check the condition of the pavement, he switched on the reading light and opened the book.

Thomas Carlyle's *History of Frederick the Great.* The passage where the encircled king of Prussia, trapped in his ruined palace in Breslau, had been saved from defeat by the coalition of his enemies by the death of his sworn foe, the Czarina Elizabeth of Russia. She had been succeeded by her nephew Peter III, a friend of Frederick's. The reversal of alliances that followed had saved Frederick and Prussia and ended the Seven Years' War.

He switched off the light and sat thinking, not looking out as they bumped past the bombed-out facade of the Propaganda Ministry.

The Mercedes slid to a stop in front of the dark, blown-empty windows of the New Reich Chancellery. The bunker itself was under the old chancellery, but the entrance was in the new one. There were three checkpoints. This was the first, as you entered the immense damaged building that had once housed the government. Damaged, but the chandeliers still burned brightly overhead, fed by emergency generators, and the scarlet carpet was still spotless. He followed it down a long passage, at the end of which the stairs began, descending to what he always thought of as the lair of the Minotaur. Tall SS guards, with sub-machine guns slung over their chests, checked his identification and that of his adjutant. They took the brown-paper-wrapped package into the next room for X-ray examination.

Waiting, the Reichsminister remembered the days when he'd been received by liveried footmen in the gleaming halls of porphyry and marble above. Then he smiled. Those days might come again.

The sergeant came out, returned their identification and the cylindrical package, and waved them on. A second set of guards checked them again at the entrance to a long tunnel lit with strings of bulbs, like a mine shaft. At the end of this was a sharp corner, then a narrow flight of concrete stairs leading down. At the bottom was the entrance to the upper bunker and the third checkpoint. Here the Propaganda Minister turned over his pistol. No one approached the Führer armed.

Through the upper bunker and a long narrow dining hall. This was uncarpeted. The smell of wurst and boiled potatoes came from the kitchens. Goebbels recalled he had missed dinner. He did not, however, turn aside. His news was too important. Another door, then a steep curved stair-case leading downward again. The iron steps echoed hollowly under their boots.

At the bottom two more SS sentries stood guard at a door like that of a bank vault. It rumbled open to admit him to the central hallway.

Of the Führer's bunker. Brightly lit but low-ceilinged, red-carpeted but with unplastered, unpainted concrete walls. He wrinkled his nose at the smell. The bunker was thirty feet below Berlin's sewer systems. To the Doctor's knowledge, the Leader had not seen the sun or moon since the middle of January. As he limped rapidly toward the apartments the hum of a diesel generator grew, then faded.

He stood waiting in his blue-paneled study, surrounded by his generals. His hands were locked behind him. The glassy blue-gray eyes examined his minister as he extended his arm in salute. Goebbels was no longer shocked by the bent posture, the gray hair, or the tremor that made Adolf Hitler lock his hands behind him. He accepted that the man he had followed to the apex of power was aging, perhaps dying. Now Hitler extended a limp hand to be shaken, but limited his greeting to a curt "Well?"

"My Führer, I congratulate you. Roosevelt is dead! The leader of the enemy's conspiracy has been crushed by Fate. This is the miracle we have been waiting for. An uncanny historical parallel! It is written in the stars. It is the turning point! My Führer, I salute you and Germany, whom you have brought through a terrible ordeal by your faith and will!"

Hitler did not respond, only stood, bent slightly forward, as if awaiting more. Goebbels looked around, his gaze jumping from face to face. The assembled generals: Jodl, Krebs, Heinrici, Keitel, Burgdorf, Buhle. Admiral Dönitz. Himmler like a deadly shop-clerk, his tiny mustache an echo of the Führer's. Bormann's ratlike smirk. He cleared his throat. "Don't you understand? The arch-criminal is dead. The ring is broken!"

The generals glanced at one another, faces unreadable as concrete walls. Goebbels waited. Their reactions did not matter. Only *his* mattered.

Without a word, the Führer turned to face Anton Graff's immense portrait of Frederick the Great. He had moved it with him from headquarters to headquarters since Munich in 1934. It was the only picture in the room. In utter silence, he studied the stern face of the soldier-king.

"So. The cripple has croaked."

"Yes, my Führer! We received the bulletin at eleven P.M."

"You are right. This is a most remarkable turn of events. It changes the entire complexion of the world situation. The U.S. Army and the Red Army may soon be exchanging artillery barrages over the roof of the Reich Chancellery."

"Yes, my Führer!"

"I predicted it again and again to those whose faith was wavering. The split was inevitable. The West cannot afford to lose Germany to Bolshevism. It is the mysterious hand of divine Providence."

He paused, eyes lifted as if seeking inspiration; and no other stirred or spoke. "We thought all was lost in 1918, but the true miracle, the resurgence of the German national spirit, was yet to occur. The generals predicted disaster in the Rhineland, in Czechoslovakia, in Poland, in Russia. Again and again, only my own faith brought victory! Now the tide will turn again. Stalin has only starving slave-soldiers left. One blow from the combined armies of Britain, America, and Germany, and Bolshevism will crack into a thousand fragments."

Goebbels stood smiling as his master paced from one end of the fifteen-by-ten concrete-walled room to the other. For a moment he wondered if he should confess his own role in the "miracle." Then decided on modesty, at least until the results were plain.

Hitler was in full flood now, and for forty-five minutes no one else spoke or moved. He passed from recounting his struggle for power, to how his plans had been sabotaged by the General Staff. Powerful, ruthless generals, men of blood and iron, cowered at the spittle-laden lash. Hitler raged that they were defeatist, lying traitors. Horse-breeding, incompetent Junker *Schwein.* Worst of all, they were cowards. Like Von Paulus, surrendering when it was the duty of a soldier to close ranks and fight to the last bullet. "Imagine surrendering to the Bolsheviks, when with one shot of a pistol he could have achieved national immortality! That is the way a general should die," he shouted.

When the splenetic river of oratory slowed at last Goebbels nodded to his adjutant. The colonel unwrapped the bottle with a flourish, and the Reichsminister lifted his hand and turned it palm upward in a graceful gesture of presentation. "My Führer, I know that you do not indulge. But perhaps you will allow less lofty men a moment of rejoicing that the bloody-handed man responsible for world war has fallen. Champagne!"

Hitler nodded curtly. His eyes still glowed, and he stared at the situation map. As the generals gathered around the table, as the adjutant filled their glasses, he adjusted his green spectacles. His hands trembled with eagerness as he imagined rivers of blood, darkened skies, countries aflame, fire, killing, death, death! The Slavs would suffer the bloodiest defeat of all history before Berlin.

Ignoring the others, he began to plan where he would direct the powerful blows of the combined panzer armies of Guderian and Patton when the fateful telegram begging for his leadership came from the West.

—

An hour later Dr. Goebbels emerged from the rubble-filled stairwell. It felt to him like emerging from a mass grave. He stood at the top, breathing the night air with claustrophobic relief. It was the middle of the night. The moon glowed like a focused searchlight above the shattered skeleton of the Reichskanzlerei. He pulled on one leather glove, finger by finger, and then the other. Then he frowned. Something was out of place. Something was missing. Then he realized what it was.

He heard no drone of engines from the sky. No bark of flak batteries from the Zoo fortifications, a mile away. No crisscross of searchlight beams pinning the RAF heavy bombers. In fact all was silent. There were no aircraft in the sky at all! Had the split already taken place? Were the Anglo-Americans at this moment winging their way toward Moscow? He lifted his hands in the darkness, exulting.

A moment later the sky cracked open. Bombs came thundering down all around him, the terrifying instantaneous flashes of high explosive outlining the shattered walls of once-great buildings. The earth shook as scythes of metal reaped the hissing air. Covering his head with his arms, the little man fell cowering to the ground.

—

On the Road West from Warm Springs, Georgia

As the bottle-green Packard hummed toward the setting sun she found her vision dimmed, now and again, by tears. Then by rage. She pounded the wheel in hopeless anger. She'd been there! She had seen the pine needles clinging to the photographer's heavy brogans, and she hadn't said a word! Hadn't thought to wonder what a photographer had been doing, prowling around the woods!

No, she hadn't spoken, and now she'd regret it till the day she died. She didn't regret killing the bitch. She still couldn't believe it, she'd never been that angry before. But she had. When none of *them* had been man enough to. . . . But Sobelski, Fents, whatever her name was, she'd paid. And it had hurt. She hadn't faked that last expression. As if all the torture in the world could be compressed into a bullet in the throat. She had to remember that, that expression. It was effective as hell.

But gradually, as the miles went by, as the endless road unwound rivers and railroad crossings and hamlet after red-clay hamlet in front of her, rage and regret dwindled to a hopeless and inconsolable ache of loss. Not just for herself, but for the country. He was gone, the one who'd cared truly for everybody. Who had once said he welcomed the hatred of those who owned America, because he wanted it to be said that in him they had met their match and their master.

It was so hard to believe that it didn't seem as if it could be true.

She had her own answer now, because of him. She might love again. But it would never disappoint her now, because she knew it would never be her great love. Her greatest love was already there, had been in her heart since the day she'd looked out over the faces from the little stage in her grammar school, and she'd been eight, and had known that someday she'd be an Actress.

And maybe Leo Levinsohn was right, and she would age, and her face would no longer be beautiful. Maybe she would be a horror, and the audience would gasp when she loomed up on the screen. But she would still be an actress, a great actress, and that would never change.

And maybe the system would not collapse before her righteous wrath. Maybe she'd have to compromise, and work, and sweat and connive and plot to get what she wanted. But someday she *would* direct. Someday she *would* produce. And when that day came she'd be beholden to no one, and it would be original and fresh, innovative work no one but she could ever have thought of or made.

It would be a grand game.

Thanks, she said to wherever his spirit had gone. Maybe to these black children playing in the dust. To the old people who watched her spin by, rocking on their porches, knowing now they'd never have to starve, or beg, or lose their land. No, it would always be here, somewhere under the hard bright sky that overarched all America and all Americans.

Lauren, you are such a sentimentalist, she thought. You really are. She cocked up her wrist, glanced at her watch, and smiled through her tears as she shifted up to fourth.

———

Washington, D.C., 4936 Thirtieth Place NW

The short, heavy man sat naked in a darkened room, on an elevated toilet set round with layer on layer of oriental rugs. The door was open, so that he could gaze out at the antiques and classical statues that cluttered the living room, at the window that overlooked Rock Creek Park. He held a glass of Jack Daniels Black Label, no ice. He was alone. He lived alone, except for a housekeeper who slept in the basement.

He was musing on power. What it was. How to guard it. And what would happen to those who threatened his possession of it.

He was not truly an ambitious man. He had never coveted the trappings of public office, though he enjoyed publicity, being recognized. But that was secondary. He was only human, after all! Behind the natty suits and chummy photos with singers, stars, politicians, Mob figures, he was content to be what he really was: the guardian of the American way.

For America was in danger.

He scowled as he thought of them, carrying their knapsacks of lies and subversive propaganda. Throwing acid into the eyes of America while they debauched the land he loved. It was a fifth column, more heinous and more insidious than the Nazis, who after all were not the real enemy. Karpis, and Dillinger, and Barker—they made the headlines. But they weren't the real enemy either. Even the Japanese-Americans weren't. He'd stood up for them when Roosevelt wanted to move them inland, but he'd been overruled.

At least *they* were clean. The real enemy was harder to detect. *He* knew them, though. Their dirty minds and dirty bodies. They were mongrels. Disease carriers. Boring from within, less a party than a malignant disease, creeping and infecting . . .

He got up and flushed and went to the sink and washed his hands three times with the special soap. Then wandered out into the living room, the deep-piled carpets yielding under his bare feet. He stood at the window, looking down. Though it was not yet fully dark, the night boys were on duty, parked at both ends of the street.

They denied freedom, denied God Himself as they stealthily undermined the ramparts that were the lifeline of the country's true greatness. They were the ones who'd designed tourist cabins, where married couples might sleep on mattresses that had been used hours before by prostitutes or worse.

The frightening thing was how close they'd come already to power. Even the President's wife! *She* had attacked *him*. Called him a Gestapo agent. Oh, it made sense. The first step in the destruction of a nation was to undermine its law enforcement agencies. That the FBI was feared by the forces of darkness was proved by the unceasing chorus of hate and vilification directed against it by the Reds, their mouthpieces and fellow travelers. The radicals, the false liberals, the crypto-communists throughout the country would like nothing better than to smear and destroy J. Edgar Hoover.

For beyond this war would lie another, then another. But *he* would not fall or weaken. He would stand guard, and use the power God and Congress and president after president had granted him to keep America clean and bright, as she had shone since Valley Forge.

He moved through the cluttered maze of antiques and statues and keepsakes like a restless shadow. Regular police methods were useless against such a foe. Only a national police could maintain control. Now, with the nation aroused by a Communist assassination of the President, he would direct this nobody Truman, this failed haberdasher. With wartime centralization the tools were ready to hand. All they lacked was a strong hand to grasp them.

A threat like this could not be fought by gentlemanly methods. He would tell the truth about these human rats, their diseased, filthy women, the slimy shysters and politicians who cooperated with them to profit from the degeneration of America. If anyone presumed to interfere, he had films, photographs, files, recordings. Reports of homosexual arrests. Details of connections with organized crime. Records of child molestation hearings.

Now his last and greatest enemy had been defeated. Donovan was finished. He was waiting in London for FDR's approval of his central intelligence system. Bypassing the FBI! Dictating to *him!* Well, he'd wait a long time now. And as soon as the word spread that the Reds had killed the President—he had plenty of evidence, recordings, photographs, linking *her* to the Communists—*she* would be swept out too, with her colored, diseased lovers, and all the fellow travelers and compromisers.

Talking to the German had been quite enlightening. The SS colonel, Heudeber. This time, others had accomplished his ends. He'd simply had to—watch. Wait. Monitor the situation. And do nothing, beyond assuring those who doubted that FDR was safe, untouchable, unassailable. But he'd learned. If anyone threatened him, placed obstructions in his way from now on, he had learned.

Even presidents could be dealt with.

He stood by the telephone, waiting for the call. Finally it came. "Mr. Hoover? This is Special Agent Candler, from Atlanta. Sir, we've just gotten word that the President is dead, in Warm Springs."

"Dead? The President?"

"Yes, sir."

"I want a full investigation. Call in your agents and get them out to Warm Springs. I want a full report as soon as possible."

He hung up and called the office next. "Crime Records," the voice said, alert, awake, intelligent, manly, clean.

"This is the Director," he said, a smile on his bulldog lips. "Bring me all the files on Harry S Truman."

The Washington *Evening Star,* Fourth Extra, Thursday, April 12, 1945

PRESIDENT DEAD
Brain Hemorrhage Fatal
to Roosevelt at Warm Springs

The White House announced late today that President Roosevelt had died of cerebral hemorrhage. Death occurred at 4:35 P.M. (Eastern War Time) in his summer cottage at Warm Springs, Ga. He was 63.

The White House statement said:

"Vice President Truman has been notified. He was called to the White House and informed by Mrs. Roosevelt. The Secretary of State has been advised. A cabinet meeting has been called.

"The four Roosevelt boys in the service have been sent a message by their mother, which said that the President slept away this afternoon. He did his job to the end, as he would want to do.

" 'Bless you all and all our love,' added Mrs. Roosevelt. She signed the funeral message Mother.

"Funeral services will be held Saturday afternoon in the east room of the White House. Interment will be at Hyde Park Sunday afternoon. No detailed arrangements or exact times have been decided upon as yet. . . ."

Cabinet Members Assemble

Cabinet members began assembling at 6 p.m. for an emergency meeting.

The news of the President's death was announced to the press at Warm Springs by Secretary William D. Hassett.

"It is my sad duty," he told the reporters, "to announce the President died at 3:35 p.m. (central time) of a cerebral hemorrhage."

Mr. Hassett urged the reporters to rush to their telephones immediately as a simultaneous announcement was being made at the White House in Washington.

Comdr. Howard Bruenn, naval doctor, was taking care of the President in the absence of Admiral McIntire, Navy Surgeon General. Dr. Bruenn said he saw Mr. Roosevelt this morning and that he was in excellent spirits at 9:30 a.m.

Mr. Roosevelt died in the bedroom in his little white bungalow atop Pine Mountain, where he had been going for 20 years to take the after-treatments for infantile paralysis with which he was stricken in 1921.

Long before his presidency, Mr. Roosevelt helped found the Warm Springs Foundation for polio victims. In recent months he had taken a deep interest in expanding it for servicemen afflicted with the disease.

Only two persons were believed to be in the cottage at the time of his death. They were Miss Laura Delano and Miss Margaret Suckley. They frequently had kept house for him on many of his recent visits . . .

President Stricken Suddenly While Sitting for Portrait
by the Associated Press
WARM SPRINGS, Ga., April 12.—President Roosevelt's death came a little more than two hours after he had suddenly complained of a severe ache in the back of his head while an artist was making a sketch of him.

Announcement that the President had died of a massive cerebral hemorrhage was made by Comdr. Howard Bruenn, naval physician, shortly after White House Secretary William D. Hassett called a hurried news conference. Comdr. Bruenn said Mr. Roosevelt died of a massive cerebral hemorrhage.

The Nation's only fourth-term Chief Executive died in the little white house on top of Pine Mountain, where he had come for a three-week rest.

Comdr. Bruenn said he saw the President this morning and that he was in excellent spirits at 9:30 a.m.

"At 1 o'clock," Comdr. Bruenn added, "he was sitting in a chair while sketches were being made of him. He suddenly complained of a very severe occipital headache (back of the head).

"Within a very few minutes he lost consciousness. He was seen by me at 1:30 p.m., 15 minutes after the episode had started.

"He did not regain consciousness and he died at 3:35 p.m."

. . . In response to a question, Comdr. Bruenn said the President died without pain.

News of the President's death spread quickly and caused deep grief among the 125 infantile paralysis patients at the foundation here.

Mayor Frank W. Allcorn of Warm Springs was giving a barbecue at his mountain cabin this afternoon for the President and about 50 other guests. Mayor Allcorn was awaiting the President's arrival when reporters got word through the Army Signal Corps telephone and summer White House telephone communication to rush to the foundation.

Warm Springs

The rails sloped downward out of the station for the first quarter-mile toward Atlanta. When the train began moving there was no jolt or hiss, just a noiseless smooth-as-oil glide. I hadn't slept all night. But I didn't feel tired now. Just kind of empty.

"Will you look at that," said Dad, beside me.

Through the windows I looked out on the people. They lined the rails on either side, standing far up the sides of the hills. White and black, not separated, but together in grief. Some waved handkerchiefs slowly in farewell. But most just stood, watching with an un-self-conscious sadness I'd never seen before.

That morning's hastily arranged cortege had been impressive less for its pomp, the trucked-in troops, the muffled throb of drums, than for the way people reacted as it passed. The black man playing "Going Home" on the accordion. The children sitting on their fathers' shoulders, somber as if their own grandfather had died. The patients in their chairs in front of Georgia Hall, crying unashamedly as the hearse rolled by.

Now, two cars ahead of us, the coffin sat in the quickly stripped presidential Pullman. The faded flag from the Little White House flagpole covered it. A hastily carpentered pine bier hoisted it high enough to be visible through the big windows. At its four corners stood a sailor, an airman, a soldier, and a marine.

Dad shifted beside me. He hadn't said much since he arrived last night. And I'd been too busy to talk to him, helping with the arrangements. This was really the first time we'd had just to sit down together.

"Yeah, Dad?"

"You have to realize something, Jack."

"What's that?"

"We may have had our disagreements. The President and I. But deep down we were always on the same side. We respected each other."

I didn't answer him. I didn't think it was true, for one thing.

Dad had wanted the presidency and tried every way he knew to undercut FDR and get the nomination. Not because he had a platform, or some great vision for the country. He wanted it for what it represented. Like some kind of exclusive golf club, which, when you made it no one could deny you were one of the elite.

But that wasn't what the men and women outside were mourning.

"Too bad it had to happen just now. His endorsement would have helped a lot in the Eleventh District. But maybe we can get this new fella, Truman, to give us a letter of support."

"It's not going to happen that way," I told him.

"What's that?" he said, and I heard the threat.

"I said, forget it, Dad. I'm not running for Congress at the crack of your fucking whip. I'm not doing what you say, just because you give the order, ever again."

"You ungrateful bastard. Okay, make your own way, if you can. Bobby— Bobby will do as he's told. From now on, you're no son of mine."

I didn't answer him. I kept looking out at the passing faces. Nearly every one was crying. They looked stricken, bereft. Abandoned and afraid.

He'd said that was what politics was for, to make a difference for your fellow men. I guess, judging by these people, he had.

"If I go into public service, Dad, it's got to be different. It's got to be for the people nobody else can help. To change the rules so it's a little easier for them to win."

Dad didn't answer me. He sat silent, frowning, as if I was speaking a foreign language.

"I can't do it because of what's in it for me. It's got to be, what I can do for the country. If I ever go into politics, I'm warning you, that's going to be how I do things. Not your way. Mine."

He looked at me with something in his eyes that wasn't fear, and wasn't respect. But it wasn't contempt, either. I didn't know quite what it was.

"So you'll run?"

"I just might. Yeah. I just might."

"You'll do me a favor and take my money? Use my connections?"

"You haven't been listening, Dad. I won't be doing you a favor. That's the point. You won't be using me. I'll be using you."

Dad leaned his head back and thought about that for a long time as the train gathered speed, his eyes closed to slits behind the round glasses.

___

Manchester, Georgia

From the *Manchester Mercury,* page 3:

Unidentified Negroes

```
The Sheriff's office reported that in the morning of
April 14 the bodies of two individuals of the Negro
race were found off the road between Woodbury and Gay.
One was that of a male. The other was that of a female.
Both bodies were partially burned. The faces were in
unidentifiable condition. There are no suspects at
present, according to Sheriff Collier. He says it is
possible that the bodies were brought in from outside
the county. Any citizen having information as to the
identity of these individuals or the manner of their
death should call his office in Manchester.
```

___

Washington, D.C.

Colonel Hans Dieter Heudeber looked up from his watercolors as the officer rattled the lock open and rolled the bars back. They looked at each other, then the other's eyes slid aside.

"It's time," the officer said.

Heudeber sat for a moment contemplating the picture. It was Picardy, done from memory; a pasture he'd seen perhaps a hundred times when he was stationed there. When he'd started it he could see the scene plainly. Could recall the colors, the way the wind had felt on his cheek; it was permanent, concrete, as solidly in his memory as if he were there instead of in this cell. But when he dipped his brush and began to set it down it seemed to waver. The colors dissolved and ran. They grew muddy and confused, like the water into which he dipped his brush again and again to clean it, flipping to a fresh sheet to try again.

Looking at the picture, he saw that it was hopeless. He had skill, but not an ounce of talent.

Talent had been given to others. To Jews, alcoholics, homosexuals, drug addicts. To Gypsies and the insane. To a Dutch madman who saw God blazing in the whirling heavens and the hot hearts of sunflowers.

"Want a drink?" the guard asked. He placed a flask in front of him on the table. Heudeber started to shake his head. Then thought, Why not? He uncapped it and took a long swallow.

Vodka. The taste brought back the Russian front, burning villages, sharing out captured spirit in tin cups while the tanks moved on ahead.

"Time to go," the officer said again, when he lowered the flask. He shuddered and handed it back. Looked around the cell—nothing to take with him, was there? No. The Bible lay on his bunk unopened.

In the corridor the guard touched his shoulder to turn him to the right. Two more men fell in behind them. One wore a U.S. Army uniform. The other, the gray suit and polished shoes that told Heudeber FBI. The Army had constituted the secret court that had tried him and judged him and condemned him to death. But he knew that the gray men had decided what sentence that court would pronounce.

He smiled grimly to himself. They still weren't convinced. So they were staging this charade. Just as the Gestapo sometimes did, to frighten their prisoners into confessing. Well, whatever they thought, he didn't have anything more to tell them. He had told them all he knew.

Down a long corridor. Now they entered a part of the building he had not yet seen. They passed other cells, but when he glanced in he saw to his surprise that they were empty. Magazines lay on the bunks. Turds floated in the pails. But no eyes met his. They must have been evacuated to another part of the building. Since being taken into custody, he had not seen or spoken to another human being, except the men in gray. Even the clergyman had been FBI.

The lights were very bright.

Ahead, at the end of the corridor, he saw it. The District of Columbia's red oak electric chair.

And suddenly he understood, just from the looks on their faces, that this was not a charade.

But . . . *it didn't matter.* He hadn't really wanted to live since a hot summer afternoon in the Ukraine. He thought of his brothers as hands hastily adjusted the straps to fit a one-armed man. We died for nothing, he thought. We were mad! We lost one war, and out of arrogance, and greed, and obedience to a fatal maniac, made another. Now we have lost that one, too. And more. We have forfeited our souls to the demon.

Perhaps, though, he'd made a modest atonement. Prevented one useless death. They didn't answer when he asked if they'd caught Krasov. Maybe they hadn't. But knowing he was at large, having his description, knowing his intended target and the identity of his co-conspirator—the gray men certainly had prevented him from getting anywhere near President Roosevelt.

Could there really be a God? Could He really forgive?

Even though he didn't want to live, he was still afraid to die. Here, at the very end, as they fitted the black hood close over his eyes, wedged the electrode into his mouth, he wanted desperately to believe. But he couldn't. It was as if he no longer had a soul to pray with. As if it already belonged to someone else, someone who waited now in the darkness, smiling, beckoning him on.

The first high-voltage surge galvanized every muscle of his body into rigid contraction against the leather straps. Unable to move or speak, larynx and lungs paralyzed, he suffered in silence for four and a half minutes as the lower-voltage, high-amperage second current cooked first his muscles, then his internal organs, and finally, last of all, his brain. A thin white ribbon of smoke eddied toward the ceiling, hovering above the slumped, motionless figure in the chair; then thinned, faded, and vanished as if it, and he, had never been.